P9-DEV-760

Love and the Silver Lining

TAMMY L. GRAY

BETHANYHOUSE

a division of Baker Publishing Group
Minneapolis, Minnesota

© 2021 by Tammy L. Gray

Published by Bethany House Publishers
11400 Hampshire Avenue South
Bloomington, Minnesota 55438
www.bethanyhouse.com

Bethany House Publishers is a division of
Baker Publishing Group, Grand Rapids, Michigan

Library of Congress Cataloging-in-Publication Data
Names: Gray, Tammy L., author.
Title: Love and the silver lining / Tammy L. Gray.
Description: Minneapolis, Minnesota : Bethany House, a division of Baker
    Publishing Group, [2021] | Series: State of grace
Identifiers: LCCN 2021004783 | ISBN 9780764235917 (paperback) | ISBN
    9780764239182 (casebound) | ISBN 9781493431519 (ebook)
Classification: LCC PS3607.R39685 L68 2021 | DDC 813/.6—dc23
LC record available at https://lccn.loc.gov/2021004783

Scripture quotations are from THE HOLY BIBLE, NEW INTERNATIONAL VERSION®, NIV® Copyright © 1973, 1978, 1984, 2011 by Biblica, Inc.® Used by permission. All rights reserved worldwide.

Cover design by Susan Zucker

Author is represented by Jessica Kirkland, Kirkland Media Management.

21 22 23 24 25 26 27   7 6 5 4 3 2 1

To my remarkable son, Christian

You are a treasure to me, and the only person I know who loves dogs nearly as much as Darcy does.

This one's for you.

ONE

MIDLOTHIAN, TEXAS

I'm supposed to be on an airplane, flying to Central America to teach children to speak English. Instead, I'm sitting on the couch and nursing my third pint of Rocky Road ice cream, watching a Telemundo soap opera in Spanish.

As if the woman on-screen understands my devastation, she cries out and slaps her now ex-boyfriend, who's cheated twice in the last six episodes. I wish my own heartbreak could be resolved with a hand slap. But I don't get the luxury of blaming a person. Only rotten circumstances.

"You tell him, girl!" I say as ice cream dribbles down my chin onto my wrinkled T-shirt. I grab for a towel, but I must have dropped it somewhere between my third trip to the freezer and my pity party on the couch. I check under the coffee table and spot it five feet away, right on the threshold where my living room carpet meets the kitchen tile.

"Piper." My three-year-old Maltipoo pops her nose in the air from the spot beside me, her ears keen to hear my next command. From that angle, she could be mistaken for a

5

teddy bear, which is why her breed has been lauded one of the cutest in the world. And my gal is especially beautiful with her soft array of caramel-and-white fur, a little button nose, and a forever puppy face to match her 8.2 pounds. "Piper, fetch."

She jumps off the couch, her head swiveling to look for our usual play toy—a stuffed mouse she fell in love with at the pet store.

"Fetch the towel." I point to the crumpled blue cloth and give her the hand signal to retrieve it. She's a smart gal, so it only takes two round trips to the kitchen to find what I'm pointing at. "Good girl!"

She hops back on the couch and drops the dangling cloth on my lap. I reward her with lots of neck scratches and a few tasty chin licks before I wipe away the rest with the towel she brought me. If only people were as predictable as dogs. In fact, I would venture to bet that if the nonprofit mission organization I chose to partner with were run by animals, they would have told me months ago that the Guatemalan school was in financial crisis and not to spend every free moment I've had for the past year desperately raising money to fund my teaching salary.

"*Ugh* . . . Why?" I scream at the ceiling nearly as loudly as the woman did on my TV. It's not the first time I've yelled at God since getting the heartbreaking news three days ago that my one-year mission trip was canceled, and I doubt it will be the last time. That is unless I quit speaking to Him altogether, which is not off the list of possibilities.

I slam my head into one of my throw pillows, replaying the phone conversation again and again.

"*I'm so sorry, Darcy,*" she had said. "*If there was anything we could do, we would have. They raised our taxes again, and it crippled us.*"

"Rest assured all your money will be refunded."

"We're heartbroken, too, but when God closes one door, He usually has another opportunity just waiting for you."

Then she cried. My sponsor—the woman who walked me through every application, background check, and financial deposit—sobbed on the phone with me for five minutes while I sat there numb and unmoving.

Even now, days later, it still doesn't feel real to me.

After two years of preparation, one year of brow-beating savings and fundraising, quitting my job, ending the lease on my apartment, and giving half of my worldly possessions to charity, I have nothing except humiliation and a Facebook post with 143 comments. If I see another prayer emoji, I may just smash my computer against the wall.

Piper snuggles under the pillow covering my face and licks at my neck until I sit back up. She knows I'm upset, has sensed it since the moment I ended the worst call of my life, and she hasn't left my side since. I guess I should be grateful, especially considering I've had my phone on *do not disturb* for forty-eight hours now, so contact with the outside world has been nonexistent.

The screen flashes to a commercial, and I take the opportunity to stretch and use the bathroom. A mistake, considering the reflection in the mirror is as scary outside as the turmoil inside. My hair is matted, and my eyes are dark and puffy from too much TV and not enough sleep. I attempt to make some positive progress and gargle mouthwash. Yeah, it's no toothbrush, but it's all I have the energy for.

I flip off the light switch and shuffle back to my couch, now also my bed since I put my mattress in storage a week ago. That day was a celebration, every box a step closer to achieving my goal. We ate pizza, toasted with Dr Pepper and cinnamon cookies. I thought packing day was the first real movement toward the incredible journey God had planned. Who knew it would be the beginning, middle, and final leap off the cliff of disappointment?

The last commercial fades away and my favorite character is back in her living room, tears flowing down her face. She screams she will have vengeance and I believe her, especially when they zoom in close and show the determination in her gorgeous dark-chocolate eyes. I pick up my soupy ice cream container and spoon melting heap after melting heap of sugar into my mouth until my doorbell dings three times with persistence.

Ugh. I should have put that contraption on *do not disturb*, as well.

"Go away!" I yell, though it's likely muffled, since I'm trying to keep the ice cream from running down my chin again. Only one person would show up at my apartment unannounced, and I don't want to see him right now. Cameron Lee has been my best friend for nearly thirty years, and I have no doubt he will be there for the next thirty. But he's a lousy liar, and I know he's secretly thrilled I'm no longer moving away. "I told you I needed time."

"Well, your time is officially up," he yells back through the door.

I ignore him. It's rude, I know, but one has that luxury after getting the most devasting news of her life. The way I figure it, I can't be held responsible for any decisions made for at least four more days.

"Darcy." He pounds again.

I ignore him again.

Then it gets quiet, and right when I'm about to sink back

into my misery, the lock clicks and my front door swings open.

Crap. I forgot I gave him a spare key.

Cameron strides through my front door like a Spanish soap star, complete with the superhero determination and charming good looks, which he is fully aware of and uses to his advantage as needed. Luckily, I've never been swayed much by his sparkling blue eyes or rich brown hair that lies perfectly angled over his forehead.

"Holy cow." He waves a hand in front of his nose. "Your apartment smells like depression and stale milk."

And then there's that. The honesty that comes when you've known someone since sharing a crib and having your diapers changed at the same time. "What exactly does depression smell like?"

"Something rank." He shuts the door and flips on the ceiling fan. "It's a million degrees in here. Why isn't your A/C on?"

"I've been practicing getting used to the heat, since the school I was going to only had swamp coolers." I shrug, apathy and resentment rolling through each word. "I guess I succeeded."

He pauses halfway through the living room, the tough love, bang-on-the-door guy morphing into a soft mush of pity. "Ah, Darc, I'm . . ."

I shake my head, not wanting to hear the word *sorry* ever again. It's too insignificant for what I'm feeling.

Cameron continues past me toward the hallway, where the thermostat's located. A click and then cold air rushes through my ceiling vent and down the wall behind me. Piper feels it, too, and snuggles underneath one of my throw pillows to stay warm. Not sure her choice of shelter is the best decision.

That pillow has more snot and tears in it than stuffing at this point.

My best friend appears in front of me and squats down so we're eye to eye. "You can't stay like this, Darcy. It's not healthy." When I turn away, he pushes aside my trash collection on the coffee table and sits so he's not having to maintain his balance. "Listen. It's time to pick yourself up, brush off this turn of circumstances, and return to the real world." He picks blanket fuzz from my unwashed hair and attempts to smile. "Who knows, maybe all of this will be for the best." Did I mention the dimples? He has two of them, deep and prominent on each side of his winning rock-star smile.

Yeah, even those don't work.

"You think me living out my worst-case scenario is for the best?" I cross my arms and sink deeper into the cushions. "Gee, thanks. Love the support. Really."

"I'm just saying that maybe you're missing the bigger picture here." He shifts closer. "Sometimes it takes having your perfectly planned life detonate right in front of you to discover what you really want. Trust me, I've been there."

I press my lips together because I don't want to admit he may have a point. Along with fundraising until I bled green, I've spent the last four months trying to support my friend through the hardest decision he's ever had to make—leaving the steady yet stagnant praise-team band he's been a part of for six years to join a secular rock band on the cusp of fame and fortune.

"Before I decided to leave it all and go on tour with Black Carousel, do you remember what you said to me?"

"Not really. I said a lot of things, most of which you didn't listen to."

He ignores my sarcasm. "You said that sometimes the answer to prayer is NO. And like it or not, we have to accept that answer." He spreads his arms. "This is your NO. And I'm sorry it happened, and I'm sorry you're so wrecked by it, but it's not going to change, no matter how many pints of ice cream you consume."

I look at the ceiling to keep the tears in my eyes from spilling over. I'm not typically a crier, and yet I feel like that's all I've done this past year. First with my parents' divorce, and now with the annihilation of my dream. "You don't understand."

"That's just it, Darcy. I do understand. I understand more than any person in your life right now." He cups my neck and pulls me forward until I have no choice but to use his T-shirt as a tissue. Sobs come fast and hard, but Cameron doesn't release me or pull away.

I guess there's one positive result of my chaos: at least I get to remain in the same country as my best friend. I'd call Cameron the brother I never had, except I do have a brother, and honestly, it hasn't been all that pleasant. If not burping, farting, or poking fun at my greatest insecurities, Dexter was tormenting me with his body odor and loud music. Cameron, on the other hand, has had my back since we toddled around at our church's Mother's Day Out program.

I finally come up for air, and Cam offers me my crusted blue towel. I wipe my eyes and nose before tossing it in my lap. "I think I ruined your shirt," I say, pointing at the massive wet circle in the middle of his chest.

He shrugs one shoulder. "No biggie. I have a drawer full."

"But that's your favorite," I insist, and finally he catches the joke.

Relief works through his eyes and relaxes his brow. "You

can't claim a shirt is my favorite simply because you bought it for me."

"I can too, especially if I scrimped and saved for two weeks to afford it."

"It was twenty dollars at Target."

"Which is a lot of money for a broke teenager." I smile through the mist in my eyes, and he squeezes my hand. "And look, it's lasted you twelve years. How can it not be your favorite?"

He nods. "You're right. It is my favorite."

I turn toward my little dog snuggled in the corner of the couch. "See, Piper. Give a guy some tears and they always cave."

Cameron snorts and stands, taking my pile of trash with him. "So, not to turn on the waterworks again, but have you made any headway with the landlord?" He disappears into the kitchen.

I groan and fall back into my new favorite slumped position. "Nope. It's like the old saying: 'I don't care where you go, but you can't stay here.' And my new apartment isn't available until September." Thank goodness for online applications or I wouldn't even have that.

I hear the snap of the trash lid, the refrigerator open and close, and then Cameron returns with two bottles of water.

He hands me one. "Does that mean you're definitely moving in with your mom?"

"Are you trying to make me cry again?"

He chuckles and joins me on the couch this time instead of the hard wooden coffee table. Probably a good thing, since it's older than I am. "Actually, I have been trying to come up with viable options to get you out of it, and I think I may have one."

I feel a spark of energy. "Do tell."

"Move in with us. I already cleared it with the guys."

The spark fizzles right away. "I thought you said 'viable options.' Living in that tiny three-bedroom apartment, tripping over you, Brian, and Darrel is ludicrous. Where would I even sleep?"

"I'll get a mattress to put on my floor, and you can have the bathroom. Brian's gone most of the time anyway, so I can use his."

The fact that I'm actually considering this idea instead of staying with my mom is proof that I've somersaulted into the Valley of Humiliation. Any minute now, Apollyon will begin slinging his arrows at me.

"Just promise you'll consider it." He falls back and mirrors my defeated position. "I need an ally in that apartment."

"The tension between y'all is that bad, huh?"

"It's been unbearable since I got back into town." Cameron's roommates are part of the praise-team band he quit to join Black Carousel in February. The tour they went on was only a small stateside three-month trip, but by the time he came home, resentment had ruined seven years of friendship. "And hey, it would only be until September. Then I could move in with you and we'd be roommates just like we envisioned as kids."

Oh, to have the luxury of being a kid again. When dreams and hopes and wishes don't die through the line of an 1,800-mile-away phone call.

"I guess we did have some epic sleepovers." Water-balloon fights, bike riding until dusk, Star Wars marathons. And then I turned eleven and my dad said no more. That was when Cam and I made a pact that when we became adults, we'd get our own place and stay up all night playing video games and eating junk food.

We turn our heads to face each other, and Cameron takes my hand. "I'll only say I'm sorry once for feeling this way, because truthfully I'm not sorry, which probably makes me the worst friend on the planet. But I'm relieved you didn't go. I need you here."

As young as I can remember, it's always been Cameron and Darcy, Darcy and Cameron. I suppose in a world riddled with failure and disappointment, that one security is worth its weight in gold.

TWO

I remember a time when I enjoyed going home. When my mom was my best friend and my dad was still my hero and the standard for all the men in my life. Now it's something I dread. Not just because there's been nonstop drama since the day my parents said the word *divorce*, but also because they've transformed into people I don't recognize.

We were a family that went to church on Sundays and prayed around the dinner table. We'd share our highs and lows for the day, listen to my dad as he'd give some funny anecdote from work while my mom would smile and shake her head because he likely said something inappropriate. My dad has always been the social one: handsome, funny, hardworking. A dreamer, some would say, mostly because he was always hatching some entrepreneurial plan to skyrocket his net worth. We'd be driving and he'd point to a house three times bigger than ours and say, *"One day we're going to own a home like this on the lake, and your mom and I will spend our evenings fishing until dusk."* He did eventually strike it rich, but instead of buying a lake house, he bought two new suits, a convertible, and an apartment in Dallas. But I'm pretty sure Mom got the fishing poles in the divorce, so there's that.

I trudge up the front steps of my childhood home and try to forget that my dad's car will never again be parked in the garage. Mom's called me four times in the last two days, and I'm not really in the mood for a guilt trip. One hour to fulfill my daughterly duty and then I can get back to my own depression.

"Mom," I call out as I open the front door. The house is clean, impeccably so. I shouldn't be surprised. My dad was the slob in the family.

"In the back, hun."

Her voice is coming from the master bedroom. The same room that once held a king-size bed my brother and I would jump on to snuggle with them on Saturday mornings. I can barely look at the smaller, more feminine bed frame that's there now.

I continue my path, down the hall, past my old room that was long ago turned into an office, and into the bedroom suite my parents added on when they first bought the property.

Mom's in front of the mirror applying eyeliner in just a bra and tight jeans. There was a time she wouldn't dare be so exposed, but the married weight was another thing that went away with my dad. She's now thinner than I am.

"Perfect timing. I need your opinion on my outfit." She drops the stick and blinks to dry her makeup. Then she's back in her closet pulling a silky tank top from a hanger. She slides it on, fluffs her blond hair, which is two inches past her shoulders, and does a pirouette. "Well, how do I look?"

Sad. Broken. But that's not the answer I'm allowed to give. "Beautiful, Mom. What's the occasion?"

"I have a date tonight." She smiles wide like it's a new thing. It's not. Mom's been actively dating since Dad carted his last suitcase to the car. I think it's her payback for my dad's infidelity. A way to show him she's still desirable.

I lean against the doorframe and try not to show my disapproval. "Is this another one you met online?"

"No, actually. A friend from work set us up. He's recently divorced, too, and is supposed to be tall and handsome."

Great. Divorced—check. Attractive—check. Whatever happened to all those lectures I got growing up about wise dating and finding a guy who loves the Lord first and me second? It's like all the rules and values changed simply because she is no longer married. How is that right?

"Anyway, I'm nervous for some reason." She presses her palms to her cheeks and sighs. "I think this could really be something."

I can't hold in my snort. "How? You haven't even met him yet."

"Trust me, dear. When you get to be my age, a man who has a steady job and isn't addicted to smut on his computer is a rare find."

Ah . . . another qualification. Not a loser—check.

If I'd held to the same standards, I'd be married with children already.

"Well, have a good time." There's not a whole lot of feeling in my voice, but that's not new either. This scenario is just one more thing I'm stuck with now that I'm not moving. My brother gets to live hours away in Oklahoma City with his wife. He's had exactly four interactions with our mom and dad since they broke the news, whereas I've had to be parent, girlfriend, and shopping buddy. And let me tell you, there isn't much worse than going to Victoria's Secret with

17

my mom, knowing the items she's buying are not for my dad.

Mom flips off the bathroom lights and settles into one of the chairs by the French doors to slip on her heels. "And how are you doing? Any more thoughts about my offer to live here?"

I'd rather camp in a tent in the Amazon rain forest . . . and I loathe spiders. "I have. There's another option I'm considering, as well."

"Really? What's that?"

"Possibly living with some friends."

"Oh. Yeah, I guess that would be nice." Her voice holds a hint of hurt, but thankfully she doesn't say so. "Anyone I know?"

I'm not eager to share, but then again, Mom's recent choices pretty much guarantee I won't get a lecture on propriety. "Yes, actually. It's Cameron."

Instead of a warning on all the dangers of living with a guy, I get a smug smile. "Well, that's quite a turn of events. I was beginning to think the two of you would never take that leap."

"And we still haven't. Cam and I are strictly platonic."

"For now," she says in a singsong, overly romantic voice. "But you two aren't kids anymore. Moving in together is not the same as a Friday night sleepover."

I bite my lip because she just summed up the pressing worry that's been haunting me since Cameron threw his offer in the ring: could we take this risk and still remain friends?

The two of us are such different people that I've often wondered if we would be close friends if we'd met as adults. I'm a realist, the first to call a spade a spade. Cameron will turn a spade into a heart and then try to convince me it's always been that way. It's irritating but it's also him, so I don't stay mad for very long. In twenty-nine years, there's been only one fight that's threatened to sever our bond, and I still blame our parents for it.

When we turned sixteen, our parents began to see our friendship as more, so much so that every time we hung out, they'd start to talk about weddings and how cute our kids would be. Cameron, being the dreamer that he is, bought into the madness and went so far as to ask me out our senior year of high school. *"We're perfect for each other,"* he'd said. *"It's so easy with us, and isn't friendship the foundation of every good relationship?"*

But I didn't want just an easy friendship. I wanted passion and flutters in my stomach. I wanted the challenge of learning something new about the person I was going to marry. I wanted more than I knew I'd ever get with Cameron. I told him as much, and he didn't speak to me for a month. Then one day he called, and we never discussed the issue again.

Truth is, even back then I wanted what I thought my parents had, and now I wonder if maybe I've been the one to confuse reality with fantasy because I still want what I remember being so perfect. And deep down, I know he does, too.

"Nothing is set in stone," I say, indecision being my new best friend. "I still have eight days until I have to move out, and who knows what may come up between now and then."

"Okay, well, just know you always have a place here. You've taken the news of this trip so hard, I've been worried about you."

Despite her tone of concern, I doubt it's true. Mom hasn't been a mom in months. Seven to be exact. Sometimes I don't know who I resent more for it. Her or my dad for making all this happen. "Well, no need to worry. I'm fine. Other opportunities will come."

"Or maybe this is God's way of telling you it's not your future."

I grit my teeth to keep from rolling my eyes. The last thing I want to hear from my mom is a sermon about patience and trust. She's shown neither.

"Darcy, like it or not, it's a mess out there, and you're going to be thirty soon. If not Cameron, then find someone else. I worry that if you continue to wait, there won't be any good guys left."

"Yeah, because getting married at twenty-two worked out so well for you." The harsh words come out before I can stop them, and I immediately wish I'd shown more self-control the minute my mom recoils. She's vulnerable, and I hit the tenderest nerve. "I'm sorry, Mom. I shouldn't have said that." It's not technically her fault my parents split up; Dad's the one who bailed, but deep down I'm still mad at her for giving up. Or maybe for moving on, I don't know, but it's there between us every time we interact.

She takes a deep breath and looks up at me. "I got thirty-five wonderful years and two beautiful children out of my marriage. You can't judge the journey simply by how it ends."

My throat burns because it's the nicest thing she's said about my father in months. And even though I've been too angry to speak to him since the divorce, her words make me miss him so much my chest aches.

She gets to her feet and walks toward me. "I know this has been hard for you, Darcy."

I swallow because it's all I can do to keep from crying. I know I'm an adult and shouldn't care as much as I do about the split, but I want my family back. Not this broken version of a mom and dad.

Her hands cup my cheeks, and she lightly kisses my forehead. "The worst of it is over. And in time, you'll see how all these disappointments work out."

I wish I shared her optimism, but I don't. I had it all figured out. Saved every penny for a year, beat the pavement to get support. Studied Spanish until I went cross-eyed. "It's just not fair," I say, more to myself than to her.

"No, it's not." My mom smiles the way only moms can when they've lived so much more life than we have. "But life rarely is." She clears her throat and drops her hands. "Anyway, I better get going. Michael is meeting me at the restaurant in fifteen minutes."

Ugh. I now hate the name Michael.

She grabs her purse from the bed and blows me a kiss. "Lock up when you leave, okay?"

"I will."

After one more check in the dresser mirror, she rushes out in a flurry of perfume and determination. I plop down on the chair she just vacated and close my eyes. Glimpses of the woman I've known my whole life are all I get now. Moments of authenticity before pain and bitterness bring her back to reality. I don't want to be that. I don't want to spend the next year being angry at God for allowing this to happen. I just want some kind of clarity as to why He gave me a path and then jerked it away before I could even step onto it.

What was the point?

As usual, I hear no grand answer. Just silence. I'm almost getting used to it.

I pull my phone from my pocket and text the one person I know will understand.

> **Me**
> What are you up to tonight?

> **Cam**
> Nothing really. You?

> **Me**
> Giving fashion advice to my mom before her 100th first date.

> **Cam**
> Yuck. Wanna come over?

> **Me**
> Be there in 5 minutes.

I stand, slip my phone back in my pocket, and catch a glimpse of my reflection in the mirror. Rarely do I see my mom when I look back. She's tall, while I'm fairly short. She keeps steady highlights in her hair, while mine is the same maple-brown it's been since birth. And my eyes are my dad's—a blue-green mix that have always been my favorite feature. Today, though, I see her in my eyes. The sadness, the defeat, the utter lack of any kind of positive future.

I've asked "why" too many times to ask again, so I simply walk away and count today as one more day I've managed to survive.

THREE

My refund check comes on Monday for every penny I sent in—six months' worth of salary. I should be relieved, especially since my bank account is quickly approaching zero, but mostly it's just the final confirmation that my trip was canceled. Cameron's right. No amount of ice cream is going to change that very real fact.

Only about a third of the money was my personal savings. The rest represented hours of PowerPoint slides and pitches to mission teams in churches all over Ellis County. The same teams that will eventually get all their money returned. Just not today.

Today I'm going to pretend that my life isn't completely spiraling out of control.

I park my truck along the curb and make sure to lock the doors before heading up the sidewalk. Bryson's one-bedroom rental is in what most would consider a rougher part of Midlothian. Public drinking and violence are common at the park down the street from his house, and every time I've come there's been at least one house with eviction furniture thrown on the lawn.

Cam says Bryson picked the location because he knew no one would complain about the noise coming from the house, and I guess he was right because it's been Black Carousel's practice space for the past three years. I don't normally watch them rehearse, or even perform for that matter, but today especially I'm finding it very difficult to be alone.

I finish my trek up Bryson's front steps and ring the doorbell. Cameron's car isn't here, nor is Jay's or Harrison's, but I don't really want to hang out in my car either.

"It's open," I hear through the chipping wood door and turn the handle.

Inside, Bryson pushes a large leather couch to the back wall. It's on sliders, as is the other furniture shoved into the corner.

It's remarkable how even doing such a menial task, Bryson can still carry himself with the cool confidence of a rock star. Even more remarkable is how little he's changed since high school. His clothes have adapted to the most current fashion, and the material gets heavier or lighter depending on the season, but every stitch is still a midnight-black.

He finishes his task and runs a hand through his wild, untamed hair. Also black. Bryson is Greek by heritage, though he's never known the father who gave him both his looks and his last name Katsaros. Maybe that's why he's spent a lifetime creating an image that screams *Back off*. The only thing mildly warm about his appearance is the one trait he can't change—his eyes. They're an intricate hazel and shine like polished granite. They're also the only thing I still recognize in the boy I've known since elementary school.

Finally, he turns, though his surprise makes it clear I'm not the one he thought he was inviting in. "Darcy?" He shakes his head like he needs a second to process I'm really here. "How have you been?"

"Wallowing, actually." That gets a rare genuine smile from him and makes my cheeks warm for some reason. "Can I help you with anything?"

He looks around. "Um, sure. You can grab the lamps and put them in the kitchen."

"Okay."

An awkward air of silence hangs around as I move to the end table. Bryson and I have an odd relationship. There's shared history and moments of friendship, but there's also this wall he projects. One that makes it impossible to be much more than acquaintances.

I unplug the lamp from the outlet. "I heard the tour went well."

"Yeah, it did. Lots of exposure, though I am happy to be home. The road gets weary after a while." He stops and tugs on the back of his neck, projecting the same uncomfortableness that we always seem to feel when alone together. Not that it's happened much. We shared many of the same friends growing up, yet Bryson always hung on the fringe of our group.

"Cameron's already geared up to go on the next one. He thinks Oklahoma could be another good market."

Bryson doesn't say anything, but his small grunt implies plenty. His and Cameron's is another relationship that's very hard to decipher. At times they seem like lifelong buddies; then other times there's such an edge of competition that it's hard to be in the same room with them. The only constant is the magic they make onstage together. Somehow, when the lights are on and guitars are pressed into their hands, they connect. The rest of the time is a crapshoot.

I set the lamps and other breakable items in the small alley kitchen, and by the time I return, the living room looks more like a recording studio than a home. Harrison's drums sit back in the corner, while electric cords and amps fill the perimeter. Cameron has also arrived.

"I saw your truck outside." He meets me halfway into the living room. "What are you doing here?"

"Looking for you." Instinctively, I exhale, feeling better simply because he's here. "My refund check came in today. And I was just sitting there, staring at the envelope and the boxes, and I don't know, I suddenly felt completely trapped." I look past him to Bryson, who watches our exchange until our eyes meet, and then he busies himself with some other plug. "I can go if you want me to. I didn't mean to crash your practice."

"No, of course not." He pulls me in for a much-needed hug, and I tuck my head into his shoulder. "Stay as long as you want to, though I can't promise it won't be rough. We're learning a new song."

I ease out of his embrace just as Harrison and Jay walk into the house.

"Hey, look at this. We have a new Alison," Jay says, winking at me. "I love cute groupies."

"Not funny." The edge in Bryson's voice is understandable. Alison and he didn't exactly part on the best of terms. So bad, in fact, that she moved two hours away and unfriended all of us on social media.

"Let's go, Cam," Harrison says before slamming his sticks against the drums. "I have a date tonight, and I'm not canceling again."

Cam hesitates to leave me. "You sure you're okay?"

"I'm fine." I push him toward his bandmates. "I'll probably just stay for a few minutes and then slip out."

"Whatever you need to do." He nods and joins Black Carousel in the center of their makeshift stage while I find a seat in the back corner and try to become invisible.

Life is ironic. While some things stay so familiar, like Bryson's black clothes and Jay's always inappropriate comments, other things completely turn upside down. Six months ago, Alison and Bryson were dating, Mason was the lead guitarist instead of Cameron, and I looked on the future of our group with wide-eyed hopefulness.

Bryson starts with a song I know, so I guess they're going to warm up before they get to the new stuff. His voice is edgy and dark, his eyes fixated on some invisible person in the crowd. This is usually when most girls would swoon. Bryson has that bad-boy allure. Sharp features, a smile that's more a smirk than anything authentic, and intense eyes that promise behind the persona there's a depth he'll never let you near. He is handsome, no one could deny that fact, but I miss the kid he used to be.

We were in the third grade when Bryson showed up in our Sunday school class with tears in his eyes. Mason was the first to talk to him, of course; he's always been the most inclusive. Within minutes they were laughing. Mason waved us over, and our little group of four became five. After that, we saw him every Sunday without fail. He didn't go to our school. Bryson lived in Mansfield, but his mom and stepdad would drive to Midlothian on Sunday mornings just to come to Grace Community. Back then he was sweet, shy, and always the first to make someone feel cared for; he even picked a dandelion for me the weekend after my hamster died and told me he was sorry I was so sad. I felt super special, until Cameron called it a weed and jerked it out of my hand. I think it might have hurt Bryson's feelings because he never gave me another one.

27

A wave of sadness hits, and not just for the changes in Bryson over the years, but for all of us. For Cameron, who quit inspirational music despite it being his first love. For Alison, who pushed friendship into more and got her heart broken. For Mason, who hasn't spoken to any of us since Bryson fired him from the band. And for me, sitting here, lost and afraid, clinging to bits and pieces of the past since my future is only a long road of unknowns.

I don't even make it through the end of the song before I feel the pressure in my chest that warns a breakdown is coming soon. It's one thing to cry and blubber in front of Cameron, but I'm not about to shed a tear in front of the rest of the band.

I disappear into the kitchen and out the back door. It's a small yard with only a waist-high chain link fence, but Bryson has made it somewhat of an outdoor space. Along an extended porch, there's a couch swing, two rocking chairs, and a metal fire pit. He definitely won't need that anytime soon. The temperature today is supposed to reach ninety-two degrees.

Carefully, I sit in the swing, not totally sure if it will hold me, and kick my feet back and forth. Time seems to pass slowly, seconds ticking like minutes, but that also seems to be my new normal—finding ways to kill time. I readjust and try to pull my shorts down on my thighs. Even in the shade, my legs are sticking to the lacquered wooden swing. Sweat trickles down my back, but I stay put . . . ten minutes, then twenty.

The backdoor screen squeaks as it opens and closes again. From my shadowed spot in the corner, I see my new guest faster than he sees me. Bryson stands with his hands on his hips, his shoulders slumped, his head lowered as if watching the trail of ants I noticed earlier.

It's an odd stance for him and makes my chest twinge with both compassion and curiosity. Bryson isn't the kind of guy who shows emotion. At least not that I've ever seen.

He lifts his head and blows out two long, intentional breaths, then lets out a frustrated growl.

"Practice not going so well?" I keep my voice nonchalant and direct, a default of mine when I'm not quite sure how to gauge a situation.

Bryson turns at the sound of my voice. "If Jay missing two lead-ins and Harrison fumbling through the beat is not going well, then yes, practice is abysmal." He rolls his shoulders and stretches his neck. "Cam's been on a tear writing music again, and he doesn't exactly know how to write songs for the common musician."

Cameron's a musical prodigy. He can play every instrument I know the name of and some I don't. But like most musicians, his creativity is directly linked to his state of mind, which has been jumbled for a while now. He spent months artistically blocked, writing and trashing every song or idea out of his head. But something changed when he got back from the tour. A dam broke and a flood of music has poured out ever since.

The swing catches and moans as Bryson sits, but it only takes a few seconds before our feet move in unison, pushing us lazily back and forth.

"We thought you left."

I assume the "we" includes Cameron, which is probably why he's not out here checking on me. "I was going to, but the backyard was closer."

"I'm guessing your escape act wasn't due to our tempo issues. You doing okay? I mean with everything that's happened?" This question is more tentative, like he knows it's potentially the unraveling string on a sweater.

"Oh yes, I'm fantastic. My future got blown to smithereens, but yes, I'm doing just fine."

Bryson turns to look at me, and I avert my eyes to focus on the skin around my cuticles. "Well, at least this setback hasn't ruined your ability to use sarcasm."

I shake my head. "This isn't a setback. It's a bolted coffin."

"Come on. All you have to do is find another school and you're back where you started."

"Where I started?" I look up, unsure if I feel more appalled or irritated at his lack of understanding. "I'm not doing this again."

When he gives me an eyebrow that basically screams *quitter*, the pressure I've barely been keeping at bay comes tumbling out in a massive verbal deluge. "Imagine asking a girl to marry you, and then, while you're all in love, you plan the wedding. Spend all the time and money picking out flowers and tuxes and invitations. You count the days on your calendar, so thrilled you will get to spend the next year with your bride. And then the day comes, and you stand at the altar waiting for that moment when all the planning and worry and stress becomes worth it. Only she doesn't come. Instead, she leaves you standing at the altar with a note that says, 'Sorry, but don't worry, there's more fish in the sea.'" I take a deep breath. "Now, tell me, how likely are you to go track down that girl and ask her to marry you all over again?" I stare into his eyes, daring him to argue with my logic.

Yet somehow he finds a way. "I can't answer that. Your analogy is flawed."

"It is not flawed; it's perfect."

"Hardly."

"Why?" I demand, my annoyance growing stronger the closer he gets to laughing.

"Because I'm never getting married."

"Shut up. You know what I mean." I close my eyes and seriously consider wringing his neck. "God said no. End of story. Now I just have to figure out what the heck I do with the next ten years of my life."

"Ten years? Maybe you should just start with ten days." He bumps my shoulder with his. "Overachiever."

I laugh even though I don't want to. There are times when Bryson's worldview is nice to latch on to. He keeps his circle small, his mind focused. People come in and out, but he never attaches. "Honestly, Bryson, I'd be happy just figuring out the next five days."

"What happens then?"

"Well, let's see. On Saturday, I will be officially kicked out of my current apartment, and since my new apartment isn't available until September, I'm left with two temporary living options. Move home and watch my mom date a bunch of men who aren't my dad, or move in with Cameron and share an apartment with three guys who are barely cordial to each other right now." I run frustrated fingers through my hair. "Believe it or not, Cam's offer is the lesser of the two evils."

He rolls his shoulders, and I notice how tense his body has become. It's probably the heat. He has to be catching on fire in those clothes, but I long ago quit teasing him about dressing like he's going to a funeral every day of the week. "Wow. You and Cam living together."

I don't know why hearing Bryson say it makes me feel guilty, but I do all of a sudden. "It's not like we'd be *living* together. It'd be more like a platonic slumber party."

"For three months?"

"Yep."

He pulls on his shirt, oscillating it to get some relief from

31

the heat. "In that case, you could always move in with Zoe. She has a nice two-bedroom apartment with nothing in that second room but an old treadmill she doesn't use." He tosses the suggestion so nonchalantly that I'm not sure he recognizes the depth of what he's offering.

"Are you serious? Because I have to be honest, my sense of humor is really limited right now. And if this is just some sick way of making fun—"

"Darcy," he says, cutting me off. "I know I'm not always the most sensitive person in the room, but I would never minimize what you're going through. I do know a little of what it feels like to be homeless."

I nod, feeling bad that I assumed the worse. It's a well-known fact that Bryson moved in with Cameron our senior year of high school to get away from his stepdad. The details are vague, and Cam has never shared the *why*, not even with me, but I do know that event has shaped Bryson's life. At least I assume as much, since that's when the black wardrobe started.

He stands, and though Bryson moves with an air of easy living, I can't seem to shake the idea that he's upset. "I'll ask her if you're interested."

Of course I'm interested, but the stars would have to align and my luck hasn't exactly been leprechaun status lately. "You're welcome to try, but I doubt she'd even consider it. Zoe and I have never really bonded." Even though Zoe is six years younger and we only interacted in youth group one year, it was a very painful year. I'm work boots and no makeup. She's gel polish and perfume. To say we clashed is an understatement.

"You leave my little sister to me." His eyes grow serious, and I'm mesmerized by the intensity that consumes them in a split second. "If you want this, I'll make it happen. Or . . ." And then his demeanor shifts just as quickly back to the apathetic, couldn't-give-a-flip attitude I've come to expect. "You can move in with Cam and plan the next ten years of your life. It's your call."

My call. My decision. What a change from the compressing black hole I've been falling through for a week now.

I hesitate for a second because I know this choice is opening a world of uncertainty, especially with someone like Zoe, but I also know that moving in with Cameron is not something I'm ready to do. It's too big a risk when his friendship is the only absolute in my life. "Call her and ask," I finally answer. "If she says no, then I'm no worse off than I am now."

His mouth turns up into a barely perceivable smile. "Consider it done."

FOUR

*A*s Mafia-like and convincing as Bryson's promise was to me, I'm still surprised when Zoe calls me the very next day to schedule a tour of the apartment. A feat that seemed way harder than it should be for a twenty-three-year-old, but as she put it, "My new marketing career keeps me so busy, it's impossible to swing any free time."

But after a ten-minute list of all she'd accomplished in her first year out of college, and then another five minutes of fumbling through a myriad of scheduling conflicts, we finally settled on noon Thursday.

My first thought when I pull through the gates of her apartment complex is that I misread the directions. My second thought is that Zoe's marketing job must be paying better than average.

Bryson's toss off about a spare room did not prepare me for the opulence that is to be my new home. Rock balconies with dormers jut out from slate-gray buildings, giving them a very high-end Craftsman feel. The bottom floor apartments have garages, while others have reserved carports, not that it's necessary. There's a ton of area parking, and with the security gate, I doubt this place gets too many unintended guests. Not like my old apartment, which had a tight twenty-car parking lot that often filled to the point I had to park along the street.

I follow the curve of the drive, scoping out all the amenities a place like this would offer. Chairs and large beige umbrellas dot the decking around a huge serpentine pool, the water clear and glistening in the sun. No one is utilizing the area, which I find surprising considering it is full-blown summer in Texas. It makes me wonder what type of residents live here. Probably ones like Zoe, who implied she had little time for such frivolous activities.

Building 7 is easy to find. It's right next to the pool, clubhouse, dog park, and fitness center. Zoe lives on the second floor, apartment 723. I park the car, ease from the driver's side, and force myself to take the stairs versus explore the complex. For a year now, I've eliminated all luxuries from my life, a way to prepare my mind and heart for living in a Central American country. Now I'm so overwhelmed by them that I totally understand why other nations think all Americans are rich.

I pause at the top of the landing. Each side of the long walkway has a small personal alcove and fancy wood door with etched silver numbers. I walk forward, looking to the left and right for Zoe's. Hers is halfway down, left-hand side. There's a stunning summer wreath on the door, a welcome mat in cursive, and two potted plants to greet me. Another reminder of how different Zoe and I are from each other. My idea of decorating is making sure there's no residual pet hair on the furniture. Although now that my dog-grooming days are over, or hopefully so, maybe it's time to collect some nicer things.

I ring the doorbell and remind myself that no matter how

difficult Zoe is, living with her is only temporary and by far the best option on my pathetic list.

She opens the door with her phone crushed between her ear and shoulder. "Yes, and I'll take care of it first thing tomorrow morning." She waves me in with a perfectly polished hand adorned with two silver rings and rushes back to an open laptop on her kitchen counter. "Two hundred. Not a problem."

Left alone by the door, I take a second to assess my new surroundings, which could only be described as modern. No, ultramodern. Everything is white. The leather couches, the lacquered furniture, the area rug, even the wood flooring has a whitewashed finish. What isn't white is furry, mirrored, or dangling with crystals. And worse, nothing looks even the slightest bit used.

"Sorry about that," Zoe says from behind me. "I swear that office would shut down if I took a day off." She comes to my side and claps her hands together. "Well, this is it. Two bedrooms, two baths, thirteen hundred square feet. We have a balcony that overlooks the pool just through those French doors, and the area is super safe. Want to see the spare room?" She smiles, and though it's hardly genuine, it makes her entire face glow.

Zoe as a preteen was pretty, but Zoe the adult is the kind of beautiful that turns heads in a crowded room. Her hair is long, blond, and full of trendy waves. She has Bryson's eyes, only bigger. Same color, though, and with it that same combination of complexity and intrigue. Her skin is lighter than his, giving her that delicate porcelain appearance. Her nose slopes slightly, and her mouth has a bow shape that makes her more old Hollywood glamour than the average pretty girl. If any person could fit the décor in this space, it's her. Whereas I'm more like that old piece of antique furniture your aunt gives you that's too much of an heirloom to throw away so you stick it in the corner where no one can see it.

"Yes, that would be great. Thanks," I say and follow her to a little hall.

"My bedroom suite is at the end. Your bathroom is here." She pauses by a door in the hall, leans in, and flips on the light. "Sorry it's not private, but no one really comes over except my boyfriend, and he'll use mine."

I peek in. It's simple. Two sinks, a shower and toilet. Plenty of storage, not that I need it. My makeup routine is mascara and lip gloss, and that's only if I'm meeting friends somewhere. "This will work just fine. Thank you."

She turns off the light and walks two more steps before opening another door, this time on the right side. "Here you go."

The room is medium-sized, probably a hundred and fifty square feet. Not bad for a second bedroom. There's a four-paned window that lets in a lot of light and a chandelier-type ceiling fan dripping with more silver crystals. The treadmill Bryson was referring to is still against the back wall, along with a set of small dumbbells.

"This is really perfect, Zoe. You sure you don't mind me putting you out like this?"

"Not at all. I haven't used this room in ages. The treadmill was my mom's genius idea," she snorts sarcastically. "But come on. What's the point of working out if you can't go to the gym in cute leggings and pick up boys?"

"No idea," I say, even though I've never worn fitness leggings or tried to pick up boys.

"But that's Mom. She's always trying to . . . and I quote, make me stronger." She rolls her eyes. "Talk about compensating. Anyway . . ." She checks her watch. "I need to head back. I'll get the spare key for you." Then she's gone in a flash of perfume.

A whirling sickness grows in my lower belly. This wasn't what my life was supposed to look like this summer. I was supposed to be sharing a room with another missionary teacher, not bunking with Bryson's half sister. I look at the raised ceiling and wonder again what I did wrong to deserve such disappointment. "Where are you? Why did you do this to me?" I ask under my breath.

I've been a Christian my whole life and never have I wavered or doubted. Until now. First my family is destroyed and now my future, too. I swallow down the hurt and blink away the sorrow so I can return to the kitchen with at least a little dignity intact.

Zoe's waiting by the counter, laptop packed up in a bag slung over her arm. She holds out a single key for me. "Here you go. I'm not home much, so move in whenever you need to."

"Thank you." I stare at the key as it passes from her hand to mine and realize in our lightning-fast tour she never once addressed logistics. "Bryson didn't mention rent or utilities." I'd already calculated what my max might be and hope her answer doesn't exceed it. My plan is to live off the savings I've recovered from the trip until I can figure out what I want to do with my life. "How much do I owe you?"

"Nothing." She waves her hand again like it's the silliest question in the world. "Just don't mess with my things or try and steal my boyfriend and we'll be good."

"Zoe, I need to give you something. My being here is a complete inconvenience to you. Not to mention, I could be totally psycho. You've hardly asked me any questions."

She opens the door and passes the threshold, examining

38

me the way I've been examining her all day. "It took a lot for my brother to call. If he's willing to do this for you, then I'm pretty certain you're not the next Single White Female stalker." She closes the door, then pops it back open. "Make yourself at home, roomie."

The door clicks shut and I'm left alone, still dissecting Zoe's words. She said *willing to do this.* As in something in the future. What exactly did Bryson agree to, and why in the world would he even bother? It's completely out of character for him.

I push aside the questions and tell myself it doesn't matter. Every time I begin to think Bryson still has that sweet little boy inside, I'm painfully reminded he doesn't. If he did, he wouldn't have fired his best friend, and he certainly wouldn't have dumped Alison.

Lost in the silence, I take a moment to peruse the apartment alone. The fridge is empty minus three salad kits and some kind of bottled fruit and vegetable drink. What a shock it's going to be when I stuff my ice cream, Dr Pepper, and lunch meat next to whatever paleo diet thing she must have going.

The kitchen drawers are all pristine and organized, every single one. I keep going, checking the living room and bathroom for some kind of proof that my new roommate isn't completely OCD.

I meander to the laundry room, though it's bigger than any laundry room I've ever had. My old apartment's consisted of a stackable washer/dryer combo with a flimsy accordion door. This one has side-by-side appliances and a folding counter. Underneath, there's a deep two-foot drawer I can't help but open. To my delight, it's stuffed to the top with junk. I don't know why this makes Zoe feel more human, but it does. I move aside the hammer and screwdriver, lift the duct tape, and freeze when I spot an old faded journal I immediately recognize. It's identical to one I have at the bottom of one of the boxes taped up in my storage unit. Grace Community gave them to all incoming seventh graders when we joined the youth group, and I'm pretty sure the tradition continues to this day.

I gingerly lift it from the drawer, having no intention of invading her privacy, but the pull of something so concrete and familiar in my life is too tempting to resist. Most kids look back on adolescence and hate that period in their life, but not me. I miss it. I miss the youth group and how our family would intentionally make Sunday a rest day. We'd play games or watch movies. Even after my brother left and it was just me, Sunday nights were still my favorite.

Unlike mine, the leather on Zoe's journal is worn and well used. I think mine might have had two pages filled out before I realized that writing down my feelings was not exactly part of my personality code. I press the book to my chest, memories of good times and laughter filling my heart. A tear falls, then another. Not for my trip this time but for the greater loss that I still haven't quite accepted.

Mom and I still do Sunday night dinners, every week without fail, but they're painful now. A shadow of what it was intended to be.

I move to tuck the journal back in its hiding place when a page slips from the cover and floats to the tile floor. Black words stand out on crisp white paper, scratched and messy, like someone didn't just want to get the words out but wanted to hurt the pristine sheet in the process.

"Forever invisible. Forever forgotten. Forever unseen."

Horrified that I've stumbled upon something so intimate,

I snatch it from the floor, slide it back in the journal, and return everything where it was before my invasion. I don't know when Zoe wrote those words or even if she did, but they certainly don't match the self-assured, time-deficient businesswoman who gave me a tour just ten minutes ago.

I push the drawer shut and return to the kitchen. The last thing I need is to press my nose into someone else's pain. Especially when I'm still trying to cure mine.

FIVE

When I was little, my fourth grade Sunday school teacher told us that God puts people in our lives for a reason. She had us make links out of construction paper and bond them to each other with Elmer's glue until we ran out of paper. Rows and rows of purple, blue, and red weaved between chairs and table legs to give us a visual on how God's kingdom is uniquely tied together. I clearly remember picking up one section and telling Cameron that he and I were linked by forces beyond the universe, so he really didn't have a choice but to be my best friend. Somehow I knew, even back then, he would be in my life through every storm.

"Well, that's the last box. You ready to go?" Cameron stands next to the driver's door of his brother's truck, watching me. He called in reinforcements this morning. The entire Lee clan, including his brother-in-law, came out to move my couches to the storage unit, sort through the mess for my bedroom set, then haul it right back to my apartment to load the last of the boxes. And to top it off, his sister and cousin stayed behind to clean my entire place while I was en route.

I'd scheduled three hours for this nightmare, and it took

less than two. They offered to meet me at Zoe's for the unloading, but it just felt like too much imposition.

"Please tell your family again how much I appreciate their help. Especially your mom for taking Piper for me today." This move is traumatic enough. Adding a spastic Maltipoo, running up and down the steps in a frenzy, would have done me in.

"I think you sufficiently thanked them with the massive amount of breakfast burritos you provided."

"I hope so." My throat swells as I take one last glimpse of my apartment. Now that the task is finished, I have nothing left to distract me from the cold reality sinking in.

Cam puts his arm around my shoulder for the first time all day. While he's come through as he always does, he hasn't been happy about my choice not to move in with him. "They wanted to be here for you," he says as if he can sense my growing sorrow. "You're part of our family. You know that, right?"

I swallow back rising tears and lay my head on his shoulder. The term *family* doesn't mean what it used to, at least not to me. Not one member of mine was here, and I doubt any of them care that today is the hardest day I've had since getting that miserable call two weeks ago. I've lived in this building seven years, nearly a quarter of my life, and I was supposed to leave in victory, not in defeat.

"Anything you want to do, remember? We're going to turn in your keys and consider it freedom." His pep talk comes with another gesture that's been missing all morning. His smile.

"Can I assume this means you're not mad at me anymore?"

"I was never mad at you." Cam squeezes my arm before dropping his hand. I shouldn't have said anything. His voice has returned to the blank monotone it's been all morning. "It's Bryson I'm not so pleased with."

"Don't get all moody again." I push his torso, but he hardly moves. "I'm the one who complained about my options. Bryson was just being helpful."

An annoyed hiss escapes through Cameron's teeth. "I wish he'd minded his own business like he usually does."

I return his jab with a steely glare.

"What? I'm bummed, okay? You and I have barely seen each other in months, and now, when we finally get this opportunity to hang out daily, you turn it down. I just can't figure out why."

Sadly, I can't explain why, only that I knew it wasn't right for us. "It wasn't just you, remember, it was also moving in with Brian and Darrel. Not to mention the fact that we'd be sharing that closet you call a bedroom. You'd be miserable, Cam, and sick of me in two days."

"I'd never get sick of you."

His voice turns more serious than I'm comfortable with, so I reach out and tickle his side. "Fine, then I'd be sick of you in two days. I can only comment on a new song so many times."

He swings his arm around my neck and pulls me in for a knuckle rub. "You drive me crazy, you know that?"

I push him off, laughing. "That's my job." I pinch his cheeks. "To keep you humble. Goodness knows, no one else does."

My attempt at easing the tension works, and we each head to our vehicles. My little single-cab Chevy truck is packed tight with boxes, while Cam's brother's F-250 is hauling my bedroom set. I chuckle a little when I think of the contrast. Distressed oak furniture against Zoe's wonderland of white.

Oh my, what a pairing this is going to be.

The drive to Zoe's apartment takes fifteen minutes through traffic and at least twenty stop signs. Gone are the days when Cam and I could pop over to each other's place in less than five minutes. A thirty-minute round trip is going to take some more planning, and by his annoyance this morning, I imagine will include a lot more complaining.

He slams his driver's door the same time I step out of my truck. "This is fancy." He glances up and then around the complex. "And far away."

"I know. But hey, they have a pool." My attempt at optimism falls on deaf ears.

"It's not too late to change your mind. We're still loaded."

I don't bother answering, especially since I know it's not a real suggestion, and walk toward the stairwell.

Bryson's midnight-black truck is waiting on the far end of the building with a dolly in the back. It's the same one he's had since our junior year when his stepdad bought it brand-new off the lot, and I imagine he'll drive that machine until the day it dies. Paint's chipping on the fenders, the engine's been rebuilt, and the passenger seat has a tear in the leather. When he added a lift kit about five years ago and a rumbling muffler, Cam and I joked that if there was ever a vehicle that mirrored its owner in appearance and personality, it would certainly be Bryson's black beast.

I look at the stairs and then at the two trucks. "What should we start with? My furniture or boxes?"

"Furniture." Cameron pulls down the tailgate and hops into the back. "And don't think I'm not racking up hundreds of you-owe-me points, because there should be a law against stairs on each end."

"Dude, are you seriously complaining already?" Bryson calls out.

I look up and catch him descending from the landing. He's in all black again. Joggers instead of jeans this time, and his T-shirt has the sleeves cut off. A tattooed ring of barbwire encircles his left arm. It's faded some since high school but still gives that *I'm untouchable* vibe.

"Already?" Cam retorts. "Where have you been for the last two hours?"

"Fixing my hair," he says with far too much arrogance. Cam ignores him and starts unlatching the tie-downs. Bryson's expression changes when he finishes his descent and stands in front of me. "How are you feeling this morning? I know today can't be easy."

I hesitate. "No, it's not." This isn't the Bryson I'm used to engaging with. His voice holds too much concern, and his eyes keep watching me as if he can somehow see all the upheaval swirling inside. "But that's life, right? No need to complain about what you can't change."

"I don't know. There's something to be said for verbal processing."

"Really?" My voice is half surprise, half teasing. Never in our history has Bryson been one to talk about anything, let alone his feelings. "And how would you know?"

He smirks. "I read it in a magazine somewhere."

We stand there for a brief second, both seemingly unsure of what else to say. Already this conversation is well out of the norm for us.

Bryson clears his throat. "Well, we better get to work. Rehearsal starts at three."

Yes, rehearsal. The one thing Bryson lives and dies by. And I guess I can't totally blame him. Bryson wears many hats in the band: lead singer, manager, and bookkeeper. He's also the only band member to go in full time. Jay, Harrison, and Cam all still keep part-time jobs. I guess in the grand scheme of things, he has the most to lose if Black Carousel doesn't reach its full potential.

Bryson jogs to his black beast and lifts the dolly out of his tailgate while Cam pulls at the bed frame until it's hanging over the edge of the truck. "Do you know where all of this is going?" He wipes his wet brow with the bottom of his T-shirt, and I know he's completely miserable out here.

"Yeah. I've already taken measurements and have a layout in my head."

"There really wasn't any hesitation, was there?" He sets his hands on his hips and sighs. "Why didn't you just tell me you didn't want to move in? We could have figured out something better than Zoe's apartment all the way across town."

"Cameron."

"Forget it." He turns away and pulls the metal slat out farther. "It is what it is."

And I know my best friend well enough to back off and let him stew. Which he does in monumental fashion.

The next hour is proof that heavy furniture, summer heat, and a flight of stairs are a recipe for drama. Bryson and Cameron argue about everything. Which way to go through the door, how to hold the mattress going up the steps, what blasted music to listen to. Ugh. I was half tempted to send them both home and do all the heavy lifting myself.

Thankfully, when one only has a bedroom to furnish, unloading doesn't take long.

"Last box," Cam says and drops it on my bare mattress.

47

He's soaked in sweat, as is Bryson, who disappeared into his sister's bathroom a few minutes ago.

"Want me to make some lemonade?" I offer tentatively. The most I've gotten out of him are grunts and one-word answers since our tiff outside, so I'm surprised when he attempts a smile.

"Thanks, but I need to get Caleb's truck back to him." He starts to run his fingers through his hair, then thinks better of it. "And obviously shower before rehearsal."

"Okay, I'll walk you out."

We walk in unison to the front door, but each step feels like acid on my feet. This awkwardness isn't us. We don't fight. We hardly ever argue.

"Hey, Cam," I call out when he crosses the threshold. "Maybe after practice we could go get ice cream?"

This time the smile comes with dimples, so I know it's genuine. "Haven't you eaten enough ice cream to dry out every dairy cow in the metroplex?"

Relief spreads through my whirling stomach as I fake outrage. "You cope in your way, I'll cope in mine. And Rocky Road is not just ice cream; it's heaven's perfect treat."

He cinches his eyebrows. "It's marshmallows and chocolate."

I spread my arms and wait for more fodder because he pretty much just validated my point.

He must realize it, too. "Fine. You win. I'll call when we're finished."

"Sounds good."

I shut the door, relieved he's no longer angry, but also relieved he's gone. Despite all the reasons I love Cam, and there are many, his ability to make every situation about him is not one of them.

I move through the stark apartment, wishing Zoe would allow some color in the room besides metallic gray. It's making my skin itch and aggravating all the frustrations I've kept buried for the past hour.

The balcony is the quickest escape I can find. The doors swing open effortlessly, the sheer curtains billowing as if they enjoy the oppressive heat from outside. I don't care that they remain open or that I'm releasing a room full of air conditioning. I just want to close my eyes and go back in time to warn my younger, naïve self to abandon all her worthless dreams.

"Cam take off?"

I turn around, my mood still sour. "Yeah, just a couple minutes ago."

"Good. He was getting on my nerves." Bryson leans against the doorframe, freshly showered. His hair has that towel-dried look and is far wavier than he usually wears it. He's changed his shirt, as well. "Do you want me to show you around the complex? They have a pretty cool dog park."

I shake my head because what I really want right now is to be alone in my misery. "I've seen it."

He pauses like he's not sure if he should stay or leave.

I give him the out we're both looking for. "Well, thanks for your help. I'm going to unpack and get settled."

He runs a hand through his already-messy hair and sighs. "I know you said you didn't want to talk, but I'm here if you need to. This is a lot of change in a short period of time."

"Yeah, well, I'm good at change," I lie.

His eyebrows peak. "Since when?"

"Since now, okay?"

"Are you sure, because from where I stand, you look ready to implode. In fact, a lesser person would already be to the moon with the amount of pent-up tension you have rolling around in there."

Words, dry as chalk, lie on my tongue. He doesn't know what he's asking. The enormity of what's lodged in my chest, crawling up into my throat. Hurt, frustration, anger, sadness, fear, and the list goes on. If I dare to let one shred of what I'm feeling escape, it will be a flood of unending chaos. I swallow, forcing calm into my voice. "While I appreciate this whole attempt at counseling, I'm fine."

"You are?"

"Yes."

He steps closer. "Then why do you look one breath away from crying?"

"Stop it," I growl, because he's right. I *am* one second away from bursting into tears and I refuse to do that in front of him. "Saying yes to this apartment was not an open invitation into my life. You helped me, and I genuinely appreciate it, but you and I are much better off sticking to what you do best— mindless banter and zero expectations."

His head rears back as if I've slapped him. "Where is all this hostility coming from?"

"Where do you think? Or did you not notice the absence of two people who should absolutely be here. Except they aren't here, or even speaking to us . . . because of you." My thoughts whirl while my biting words slice across the space between us. "You have this ability to cut people out of your life when you're done with them, and I really don't feel like being the next person on your list who thinks for one second you might care."

Hurt flashes, and then just as quickly, the cold, unfeeling hardness I'm used to seeing from Bryson returns. "First off." His voice lowers, the tone now matching mine in both curtness and accusation. "I didn't cut Mason out. I told him from the beginning he wasn't permanent. His choosing not to hear me or strive to get better is his fault. And second off, Alison and my relationship was complicated in ways I can't explain to you. But don't think for a second I didn't care for her."

A tight silence follows while a balmy breeze dances across the balcony. He studies me, his eyes as dark and deep as a raging sea. I look away, unable and unwilling to battle with him on the subject.

"You know what? Forget it. There's no point in even trying to explain when you've already played judge, juror, and condemner without my participation." He retreats into the apartment and walks right back out onto the balcony seconds later, a disgusted smirk twisting his lips. "A housewarming gift." He tosses me a small red package that looks like a five-year-old wrapped it. "Feel free to chuck it into the trash."

This time when he storms away, all that follows is the slamming of the front door.

Regret comes an instant later. I hold the little box, knowing I should go after him and apologize. Sure, those were all thoughts I'd had for months now, but I didn't have to attack him with them simply because I was feeling shaken.

I slowly tear open the wrapping and lift the box lid. Inside is a new pendant for Piper's collar. It has her name and Zoe's address engraved in a plastic pink bone. I squeeze the gift in my hand and dash toward the door, but by the time I make it to the stairwell, his truck is already squealing out of the parking lot. Guilt and shame make their dive in the cesspool of my emotional baggage, ripping at my chest all the way down.

My mom used to say that hurting people hurt people. Unfortunately, that statement is very, very true.

SIX

I'm still feeling like gum on the bottom of my shoe when Cam calls three hours later. And by the sound of his tone and general aggravation, I have a feeling he needs the ice cream as much as I do.

We agree to meet at Marcie's Parlor, a local ice cream spot halfway between his apartment and Zoe's. The inside tables are all packed, and the line is at least six deep.

I pull out a white metal chair from one of the tables outside and drop my phone on the tabletop as I sit. There's a striped canvas awning over the seating area and entry door, which blocks the worst of the sun, but it's still hot and sticky. I don't mind. In fact, the heat is about all I have left to hold on to when I look at where I was supposed to be.

My phone buzzes against the iron slats, obnoxiously pulling me from my introspection. It's my mom, and since this is call number three in the past hour, my conscience forces me to answer it.

"Hey, what's up?" I stretch out my legs and try to settle comfortably in the hard chair.

"Oh good, you're available. I was all ready to leave a voicemail." Her voice sounds giddy, almost breathy in its excitement. "Did today go well?"

I'm surprised that she remembered, especially considering we spent approximately five minutes on my move and the rest of Sunday night dinner talking about her *"amazing date"* with Michael. *Gag.*

"It went fine. I'm all moved in." Turns out unpacking one small bedroom only kills about an hour and a half of time. I'm going to need a new hobby, or maybe I should consider getting a job after all.

"That's wonderful, hun," she gushes with far greater a reaction than my response warranted. "So, you'll be at dinner tomorrow night?"

Ah . . . now it makes sense. Sunday night dinner is Mom's leash around my neck. Her way to stick it to Dad that he may have gotten the good TV in the divorce, but she got their only daughter.

Cam's car turns the corner and parks three spaces down from where I'm sitting. I wave and then refocus on my mom.

"I haven't missed one yet, have I?" My answer is dry, but I swear we have this conversation on repeat.

"I know. I know. I just wanted to confirm because this one is special."

My heart flutters, and that little girl in me who still hopes and dreams for her parents' reconciliation wrestles awake. "Why?"

"Well, sweetheart . . ." She pauses, and I can tell she's trying to choose her words carefully. "I invited Michael."

The flutters stop and drop like a sinking weight into the pit of my stomach. Cam must see it on my face when he walks up because he sits down next to me without saying a word.

"Now, I know you've made it clear you don't want to meet

any of the men I date, and I respect that, but Michael is different." Her voice takes on a dreamy quality. "This time is different."

I cover the mouthpiece with my hand, and whisper to Cameron, "Can you go with me to dinner tomorrow?"

He shrugs, then nods his head.

"Darcy, are you still there?"

"I'm here." I sigh. "I'm not sure what you want me to say."

"Just say you'll come and give him a chance."

A chance at what? To be my new daddy? To show me how life as I know it is now over?

"Yeah, Mom, I'll try. I'd like to bring Cam, though, if that's okay?"

She chuckles, and I seriously want to throw my cellphone across the parking lot. "Of course. He's practically my son-in-law anyway."

I ignore her comment, just as I have for ten years now. "Okay, well, I'll see you tomorrow, then."

"Thank you, Darcy. This means so much to me."

"I know, Mom. I'll talk to you later."

I hang up, stunned with disbelief, trying to find my voice. Sunday night dinner is sacred. It's family only, always has been. My parents didn't even let Dexter's wife come until they were engaged. "Mom's bringing Michael to Sunday night dinner."

"Oh, that's different."

And this is why I love Cameron. One sentence and he knows exactly why I'm upset.

"She's never introduced me to any of them before. Not intentionally, at least." There was the one time when I happened to be at her house when a guy showed up, but I left without so much as a hello. "And then, bam, she drops him

54

on me like it's no big deal, like we've always invited strangers to family night dinner. She didn't even hesitate when I asked if you could come. Not that I wanted her to, but still, she's *never* let you before."

"She must really like him."

I stick out my tongue like I swallowed something sour, but that's exactly how those words taste. "They've known each other a week," I argue. "And now I'm required to make nice with this guy like he's not some intruder in my life? My parents have only been divorced for a few months. How can she suddenly be so okay? I can't even walk into that house without wanting to choke."

"Have you told her any of this?"

"No, of course not. She still seems too fragile." I close my eyes and try to get the rising sickness in my stomach to settle. "I was supposed to be gone when all this went down." I look at Cam, those relentless tears finding their way back to my eyes. "Do you have any idea how many times that promise kept me going when the fundraising got so miserable?" I swallow back a sob. "I was supposed to be gone."

"I know you were." Cameron leans forward, slides his hand across the table, and squeezes mine.

I cling to him, the steadiest person in my life. The one who's never let me down, who's been my rock and support through the worst seven months of my life.

We sit a few more minutes in silence while he holds my hand. I think of Bryson's comment about my pent-up tension and realize he's right. Somehow I'm going to have to find an outlet for all this emotion.

"I don't want to think about this anymore. I need something positive to talk about." I release Cam's hand, giving him the freedom to stretch and go back to a more comfortable position in his chair. "How did rehearsal go?"

Cam snorts. "That is not the right question if you're looking for positive."

"Why? I thought you said Jay and Harrison finally picked up the song?"

"They did. It was Bryson who couldn't keep a beat or concentrate on anything, for that matter." Cam runs his hand through his hair, then pats it back down so it's not sticking straight up in the air. "I didn't think Bry was seeing anyone, but maybe he is. The guy only gets this way when there's a girl involved."

My pulse quickens, but I convince myself our argument couldn't possibly be the cause. Bryson doesn't care about anyone's opinion of him, especially not mine. "What do you mean?"

"Well, do you remember meeting Trina?"

I roll through memories until I land on her. Bryson had brought her to dinner with all of us a few years ago. Alison had hated her, of course, because Trina was—as most of his girlfriends are—extremely beautiful. But I remember thinking she was also surprisingly intelligent and very kind-hearted. "Yeah. She was probably the highest-quality girlfriend he's ever introduced us to."

"Exactly. And days after that dinner, he went into meltdown mode. Just like this. He broke up with her a week later."

"I remember. Though I never understood why."

"Same reason he bailed on Alison the first week we were on tour. The minute Bryson starts to feel trapped, he implodes. My guess is he needs to hurry up and break it off with whomever it is this time. Especially since we have a gig in two weeks and we kind of need our lead singer to sound better than a bloated fish." He slaps his palms on his shorts and stands. "I'm dying out here. Can we go inside? You did promise me ice cream after all."

He comes around the table, takes my hand, and pulls me until I'm folded in his arms and he's hugging me with the force of a bear. "Sorry I was a jerk this morning. I have all this stuff going on in my head right now and I let it spill over into our world."

Relief unwinds the tension in my shoulders. "It's okay."

"It's not okay, and I'm going to try hard to be more understanding through this transition." He pulls back but keeps his hands around my upper arms. "It's you and me. Always."

My throat turns scratchy. "Even if it means horribly uncomfortable dinners with my mom and her new boyfriend?"

He slides hair from my cheek and smiles. "Even then."

"Thank you. You're the best friend a girl could ask for."

"Yeah," he sighs, like it's a hardship, and pulls on the door to the ice cream shop. "I know."

After ten minutes of waiting in the driveway for Cam on Sunday night, I'm ready to take back all my comments about him being a great best friend.

> **Me**
> Where are you??? Been waiting forever.

> **Cam**
> Sorry. Practice is going long. Still struggling.
> Can you manage without me for a little while?

> **Me**
> Are you serious?

He sends me a prayer emoji. I send back the red-faced, ready-to-explode one.

Cam
I'll be 20 minutes tops.

But Cameron's promises are worthless when they're spun around music. An hour is a minute in that world, so I know, even when I send an *OK* in response, that I'm stuck navigating the bulk of tonight all on my own.

I begrudgingly exit my car and scowl at Michael's Escalade in the driveway. My mom has a two-car garage, and he could have parked to the right or left to give me space to pull in beside him, but no. He parked right in the middle, so I'm left parking along the curb like a guest.

The air is hot and sticky outside and it seems to settle against my lungs, choking me, or maybe it's just the dread I can't seem to shake no matter how many pep talks I've given myself today. I knock on the door and wait instead of walking in. This house doesn't feel like my own anymore, tonight more than ever.

Mom opens the door, still laughing until she spots me on the other side of the threshold. "Hey, sweetie. You didn't have to knock."

"I wasn't sure . . ." I trail off because this already feels miserably awkward.

Her expression softens. "You don't have to be so nervous. Just be yourself and he'll love you."

I clamp my lips together and attempt to smile. I couldn't give a flip whether Michael likes me or not. As far as I'm concerned, I'm here because I was raised to respect my mother and father, even when I completely disagree with their choices. No other reason.

"Cameron still coming?"

"Yeah. He's at practice and running late."

"Okay, good. I have enough chicken for an army." She closes the door behind me, and the smell of garlic and butter fills my nostrils.

I look at my mom, incredulous, and my heart squeezes to a cold knot. "You made scampi?" Chicken scampi was my father's favorite dish. The one she would cook for him on every birthday and special occasion.

"Yes. Is that okay? I thought you loved that meal."

"I do, but . . ." How can she be so oblivious? "Never mind. Scampi is great."

"Okay, whew." Mom's chest deflates with way too much relief. She's nervous, too. "Michael is really important to me. I really want you to like him."

"I know. And I'm going to try, Mom. For you."

"That's all I'm asking for." She wraps an arm around my stiffened shoulder and guides me into the dining room. "Michael, this is my daughter, Darcy."

The man in question turns and offers me a smile as broad as his build. "Darcy, so nice to meet you." He takes one stride forward, which would be two for most men, and stretches out his hand. "Your mom has told me so much about you."

"Likewise" is all I can say as he crushes my poor fingers in his own.

The man is Goliath. So much so he has to duck under the chandelier to walk over to me. He also has streaks of gray running through his sandy-blond hair and is wearing jeans that haven't been in style in ten years and a button-up plaid shirt.

Mom wraps her arm around his elbow and smiles up . . . way up at him. "Michael is a dog lover, too," she croons at him, even though I'm the one she's addressing. "He has two boxers that are the sweetest things."

"And hyper," he adds with the same adoring tenor. "I bet you could give me some tips."

"Definitely. Darcy trains dogs for a living. Right, hun?" She smiles brightly in my direction.

I shrug one shoulder. "Not really. Or at least I haven't in a very long time." Sure, my certification is in dog training and it's always been a passion of mine, but I've spent the last two years grooming overprivileged pups to raise money, so to label me one feels like a lie. "I'm currently unemployed." If Mom's trying to impress him, she's going to do it without me.

Mom's brow furrows the way it used to when I was misbehaving as a kid. "Don't sell yourself short, honey." She turns back to Michael and shoots him the exact opposite expression. "Darcy is extremely talented with animals. She's always had a gift, even as a child."

"Thanks," I say in little less than a grumble.

A pulsing silence rears up between us. An inevitable lull in the conversation taking root.

I fiddle with the hem of my shorts. This is so much harder than I thought it would be. If Dad were here, he'd crack a joke or tell a story in a way that would make everyone feel like they'd known him forever. Michael just stands there, lanky and bony and far less interesting than the man my mother loved for over thirty years. Is this one more way to stick it to my father? Pick someone who's the complete opposite?

Michael clears his throat. "Your mom told me you, um, had a mission trip fall through recently. I imagine that was very difficult." He actually sounds like he cares. I guess he's in impress mode, as well. "Any chance of a different location?"

"No. I've retired from missionary work." I walk along the now-empty walls in the room. There used to be a family photo in the spot above our gas fireplace. They'd had it professionally done to look like a painting. We were all dressed in blue. Dad and Dexter in a shirt and tie. Mom and I in stiff dresses. We smiled, posed, argued, then smiled some more. Finally, the photographer gave up and told us to take a break. He secretly got us when we weren't paying attention. Dad had made some comment about burning his shirt, and both us kids cheered and said we wanted to do the same. The photo was of all of us laughing. And my favorite part was that Dad wasn't looking at the camera or even at us kids. He was staring lovingly at my mom.

A buzzer shrills from the kitchen, and we both turn toward the lady of the house, who quickly apologizes. "I'll be right back. Just a few more minutes and dinner will be ready. Darcy?" Her eyes turn pleading because, let's face it, I'm not exactly winning at the small talk right now. "Can you keep Michael company for me?"

"Yes, ma'am," I say automatically.

She hesitates, but finally the buzzer wins and she leaves the two of us to awkwardly stare at each other.

Mom always wanted an open floor plan. One that allowed her to participate in conversation from the kitchen, but when house renovations began, it came down to a five-figure kitchen expansion or a three-thousand-dollar man cave. Unfortunately, frugality won, which is why Michael and I are stuck here in painful silence.

"So . . ." He draws the word out like he's trying to come up with anything we could possibly talk about. "I have a daughter close to your age. She lives in Ohio now with her husband." Michael sits in the chair he vacated earlier and takes a sip of his water.

"That's nice," I say as politely as I can and lean up against the bare wall. Sitting feels too much like acceptance at this point.

"I keep waiting for that call with news of a grandbaby, but it hasn't happened yet." He clears his throat again, checks behind him to see if Mom is ever coming back, then turns around to smile uncomfortably at me. "What about you? Any plans for a family?"

"Right now, I'd settle for my own apartment. Kids are way off."

He nods. "Yeah, my daughter says the same. Career and all that."

"Yep." *Oh, my word, this is agony.*

He must feel it, too, because he gets up from the table with far too much nervous energy. "Well, I should probably see what's taking your mom so long."

Yes, because it's been all of two minutes. Then again, it feels like a lifetime already.

"Good idea."

And then he's gone like the Road Runner in a Bugs Bunny cartoon.

I pull out my phone and text in hyperspeed.

> **Me**
> I've changed my mind. You are definitely not the best friend a girl could ask for.

> **Cam:**
> It can't be that bad.

> **Me:**
> It is that bad! Like pouring buckets of hot-molten-lava-on-my-skin kind of bad.

Cam:
10 more minutes.

Me:
Cameron Joseph Lee. If you do not get over here right now, I'll call Cassie and tell her that you were the one who told your parents about her secret boyfriend in high school.

Cam:
You wouldn't dare.

Cam's baby sister was grounded for three months and missed her junior prom because he ratted her out. She may be twenty-four now, but she'd still kill him.

Me:
Try me.

Cam:
Fine. Leaving now.

And for the first time all night, I feel a little bit of relief.

SEVEN

*I*t turns out that the internet is a fabulous way
to waste time. In merely two days, I've planned
my dream vacation, which totals close to a year's
wages, played every solitaire game possible including the
really boring ones, and watched a dozen old episodes of *Dog
Whisperer* on YouTube.

Maybe taking the summer off from life wasn't the best
idea I've ever had. If I don't find something to do, and soon,
I'm going to officially die of boredom.

The options, few that they are, filter through my mind.
Cameron's dad offered me a data-entry position at his company once. Knowing him, the offer would still be open. I
picture myself getting dressed up, chatting mindlessly with
co-workers twenty years my senior, and sitting in front of a
computer all day, then immediately scratch that one off the
list of possibilities.

Which pretty much leaves me with Laurette. She's called
twice and offered me my old job back. I suppose I could say
yes. Go back to what I know and do well and forget that I
ever had plans to be more. I close my eyes and groan at the
thought. It wasn't that I hated it at Pampered Pups, I didn't

all the time, but it was never meant to be forever. And returning now feels like an enormous step backwards.

Piper hops up onto Zoe's stiff leather couch, then turns and turns hoping to find a comfortable spot. Eventually, she learns the sad truth that things are not always what they appear and hops off, disappointed.

"Yep, I know. They look comfortable, but they aren't." I readjust my position, trying to keep my right leg from going numb. "Don't worry, I understand if comfort trumps companionship."

Piper trots to her doggie bed in the corner and settles with a tiny chew toy. She, not unlike myself, is still trying to find her place in the new apartment. Zoe tolerates us both, but I can't say there's been any love connection on either side.

I return to my endless clicking, my lids getting heavier and heavier.

"Zoe, let's go!"

I jolt awake the minute Bryson comes barreling through the front door, obviously on a mission to find his baby sister.

"Come on. I'm already late. That idiot mechanic made me wait forty-five minutes just to tell me the stupid part wouldn't be in till Friday."

Piper, the vicious thing she is, pathetically growls from her corner but makes no move to defend her territory.

Bryson pauses, stares at my little dog, who's wearing her adorable pink tag, and then finally turns to see me on the couch.

I wave, unsure which one of us is more surprised to see the other.

"Oh." His brows pull together in a scowl. "I'm sorry. I should have knocked."

"It's fine. You belong here more than I do."

"All the same, I'll keep my distance, at least for the next couple of months." Any question about how we left things is fully answered with that one statement. He and I may never have been besties, but we've also never had such immense discomfort between us either. He's still upset from the other day, and I can't really blame him. I want to apologize, need to apologize, yet doing so with a guy like Bryson is new territory for me and I don't quite know how to begin.

"Zoe's not here," I say instead.

"Great." He pulls his phone from his back pocket and dials while walking toward the kitchen. "Where are you? You said one o'clock. It's one-ten." His shoulders tense as he turns his back to me. "What do you mean you can't get away. I just talked to you thirty minutes ago." Another long, furious pause. "Yeah, I know, which is why I had the guy drop me off here. If you couldn't do it, you should have just said so. I promised Charlie I'd be there before two, and now I'm stranded. . . . No, I can't just get an Uber. He lives twenty minutes outside of town!" He shoves his free hand through his hair. "Well, that's just lovely. Thanks. Nice to know I can always count on you." He presses his phone hard enough to know his last sentence was dripping with frustration and sarcasm.

I watch silently as he grips the counter, takes two deep breaths, and then shoves off. The refrigerator door gets his next dose of annoyance. He tugs it open, pulls out an armload of Zoe's fancy organic bergamot juice drinks, and slams the door shut.

I can tell what he's about to do even before he turns the first bottle upside down over the sink. "Those are fifteen dollars a bottle."

He smiles sardonically at me from across the bar counter-top. "I know."

I carefully set my laptop down next to me and unfold my legs. "Well, considering I'll probably get blamed for drinking those, could you maybe stop at just one?" I walk to the other side of the bar and slide between the two stools. "Or leave her a note exonerating me?"

His eyes narrow, more laced in humor, though, than bitterness. "I don't know. Sounds like two birds, one stone."

Yep. He's still mad at me.

"Or you could let me give you the ride you obviously need, and we can call it even?" I bite the corner of my lip and raise my brows, hopeful an apology will be that simple. With Cam, it usually is, but Bryson is a much more complicated person. At least to me.

He turns the bottle upright and puts the cap back on, even though it's empty. "Sure you want to do that? My evilness may just rub off on you."

"I never said you were evil."

"No, that's right, what you said was far less insulting. What was I again? Oh yeah, a self-serving narcissist who drops people the minute they're no longer useful."

Ouch. Okay, I was pretty rough on him the other day.

"You're right. I was out of line. I'm sorry."

He crosses his arms and studies me. "Sorry because you didn't mean it?"

I could lie, but that's not really my style. "Sorry because I was cruel with how I said it, and you're right, I didn't give you an opportunity to give your perspective."

"No, you did not." He glances at his phone to check the time. "But lucky for you, I'm in a bind, so you have a twenty-minute drive to apologize."

"So now you're doing me a favor?"

"Groveling is acceptable, too." He grins, and despite the fact that it's Bryson and I know I should be wary, I can't help but grin back. He's devilishly charming when he tries to be, which isn't very often. "Are you driving or am I?"

Since I have no idea where I'm going, I grab my keys from the hook by the door and toss them to him. "Consider this my apology. And for the record, I don't grovel."

~

If I didn't feel completely sure that Bryson was harmless and not a deranged serial killer, I'd be starting to worry. We've been in the truck twelve minutes and are now halfway between this-is-where-you-bury-the-body and yes-there-are-places-in-America-with-no-cellphone-service.

"Wishing you had asked more questions?"

"Something like that." I create a sunshade with my hand and try to find any traces of human existence in the acres and acres of farmland. "Where are we going anyway?"

"A little community called Griffith. I have a friend who lives out here, and he's had a rough go of it lately. He's got a big decision to make, and I didn't want him to have to do it alone." His answer surprises me, and he must sense as much because his jaw ripples with tension. "Wow, you really do think I'm a horrible person."

"I don't think you're horrible. Your explanation just took me off guard for a second."

"Which part? That I actually have a friend, or that I'm going to help him?"

I stare down at my fingers because I don't know what else to say. In some ways, yes, I've always seen Bryson as the black sheep in our little group. If someone was insensitive or hurtful, it was him. If someone got in trouble, it was him. If someone was the first to take a risk or rebel, it was him. Always.

"Listen, it's obvious that you have some pent-up resentment over Alison and Mason, so let's just get it all out in the open now." He glances at me and then back to the road. "What do you want to know?"

Once again, I'm taken aback—not by his bluntness, that's common with him. More by his openness. Bryson's the kind of guy you hang out with for twenty years without actually ever knowing him.

"Okay . . ." I pause, taking the time to compose a reasoned answer free of yesterday's accusation. "Alison was in love with you. I knew that. Everyone knew that, and I know deep down you knew it, too."

"I did."

"Then why date her? Why risk your friendship that way?"

"Because I was selfish." He studies the road, his hands squeezing and twisting the steering wheel. "We had just gotten the final dates for the tour, had gigs lined up for months. It was a rush, the biggest thing I'd ever accomplished, and I didn't want to do it alone." He shifts uncomfortably in his seat, clearly hesitant to share the rest with me. But true to his offer, he continues, and I find my respect for him growing. "I knew within a few days that I'd made a mistake, but I thought maybe if I just tried harder, it could work. But then . . ." He trails off like he can't bring himself to say everything he was feeling during that time. "I wanted to love her the way she loved me. I just didn't. And I knew the longer I pretended, the worse it would be, so I ended things. And now she hates me, and so do you, I guess, but I still know I made the right call."

He waits for my response like he needs me to exonerate

him or something. And maybe on the Alison thing I can do that, but I'm not sure I'll ever fully trust him. At least not the hardened version he's become.

"I don't hate you, Bryson. I just don't like seeing the people I care about get hurt."

"I don't like seeing them get hurt either." He stares at me, his eyes restless. "If you're wondering if I regret it, the answer is yes."

And really, what else can I ask for? He made a mistake and he's owning it.

"Do you regret firing Mason?"

Bryson pulls in a deep, slow breath, and I search for the same remorse he had with Alison, but it isn't there. "No, I don't. He wasn't good enough."

"But he started the band with you."

"No. I started the band. Mason was simply the first addition."

"And that doesn't deserve some measure of loyalty?"

"He got loyalty," he returns sharply, his voice turning indignant. "For five years I let him play, despite being completely stagnant."

"You could have warned him."

"Trust me, I did. Multiple times." His jaw twitches. "When Black Carousel came into being, we were equally average. But I killed myself to get better, worked two jobs to pay for lessons, sunk every extra penny I had into better equipment, and Mason, he just stayed the same. I told him year after year that he had to commit all the way, but either he didn't care enough or he just didn't have the talent. Personally, I think it was a little of both. And I wasn't going to sit back and let his inadequacy destroy my future, especially when Cameron was ripe and ready to take his place."

The cab falls into an uncomfortable silence, neither of us speaking; there's just the sound of cool air pumping from the air-conditioning vents and the rumble of my old V8 engine.

"Mason's leaving was inevitable," he finally says with complete surety. "He wasn't good enough. And like it or not, you know it's true."

As much as I want to argue, I can't because Bryson's right. I'd witnessed the difference myself. Cameron had begged me to come out and watch his first performance, so I pulled a hundred dollars out of my precious savings, drove two hours to a popular college bar in Waco, and watched Cameron step onstage for the first time as an official Black Carousel band member. They killed it that night. It wasn't just a great performance; they'd blown the roof off.

"Thanks for explaining. You didn't have to, but I'm glad you did."

"So we're good?"

"Not quite," I say with an air of jest so he knows I'm kidding. "I have more questions."

"That wasn't enough?" He groans. "What is it with women and their need to make men suffer?"

"How am I making you suffer?"

"I'm trapped in this truck, sharing feelings and regrets. You may as well be pulling out my fingernails."

I can't help but chuckle. "It's the last one, I promise."

"Fine. Let's get it over with."

"Okay." I rub my hands together just to make him nervous. "Why did you go out of your way to help me? I know convincing Zoe couldn't have been easy."

He snorts like I have no idea exactly how hard. "I helped you, Darcy, because contrary to what others in this truck may believe, I do consider us friends."

"We are friends." And I mean it, probably more than I have since we were kids. "And thank you. The dog tag was a really thoughtful gesture."

"You're welcome." His expression softens when he glances from the road to me again. "I wanted you to feel at home, even if it is just temporary."

"Well, I do. Sort of. Zoe's a bit of a puzzle, but she's not there much so it's kind of like living alone."

"Better than an apartment with three guys and a mattress?"

I laugh at the absurdity that I even considered moving in with Cam as an option. "Yes, much better."

"Good." Bryson slows, and I spot the first house I've seen for miles.

"Is this it?"

"Yep."

"Wow, it's . . . beautiful." The words come out in a loud whisper as we ease down the drive flanked by small oak trees on each side like a tunnel welcoming us home. "What a change from all the flat farmland."

"Yeah. It's a gem for sure. There's over sixty cedar trees on this property and two large tanks."

"Tanks?"

Bryson smirks at my ignorance. "You'd probably call them ponds. Tank is terminology we use for a livestock watering hole."

"Oh, okay."

The trees clear, offering a full view of all the buildings on the property. The main house, though quaint, is a beautiful one-story brick structure with the Texas star etched into the porch overhang.

Bryson follows the road to the right and parks between the detached garage and a massive tractor parked on the side. He stares out the windshield, his eyes clouded in thought. "You should have seen this place a couple years ago before Charlie's wife got sick. Sue Ann was a master gardener, and there would always be some kind of seasonal flower to welcome you in."

I don't miss the use of the word *was* or the sadness in Bryson's voice.

He cuts the engine and twists in his seat to face me. "Not to sound inhospitable, but you should probably stay in the truck or hang outside. It's been a pretty terrible year for Charlie, and he's not the best version of himself right now."

"I'll hang outside. It will be a nice change from my pity cocoon." I hear a faint sound of barking in the distance. "Does he have dogs?"

"Five of them. Each worse than the other." Bryson rubs his neck as if just asking about them brings a new measure of stress. "When Sue Ann adopted them, she thought she was heading toward remission."

"What happened?"

"She spent a year on chemo, and the tumors shrank miraculously to the point that her doctors felt they could get the rest through surgery. She never woke up." His voice catches. "That was three months ago. Since then, Charlie's barely been able to care for himself, let alone five unruly animals."

Hearing his grief lace through every word squeezes the air from my chest. "I'm so sorry, Bryson, I can't imagine."

"That's life," he says curtly. "Something always pops up to punch you in the face. I just hate that I was on tour when it happened. Charlie shouldn't have been alone. Not after everything . . ." The ache of what he doesn't say swells in my throat, but I remain silent as he reaches for the door. "Ready?"

It's more than just a question. It's the endcap on his sharing of feelings. I shouldn't feel so disappointed. Bryson's given me more today than he ever has before. If anything, I should be grateful we finally aired our grievances. Now we can go back to what we've always been.

I grip the door handle and pull. "Yeah. I'm ready."

EIGHT

*A*s soon as we exit the truck, the barking turns from faint to obnoxiously loud. The noise seems to be coming from two sources, each located around back and out of my line of sight. Based on tone and depth, I'm guessing they're both large breeds, and one is not happy at all to hear strangers descending.

"Here." Bryson tosses me a small bottle of bug spray. "I only got the tractor to about half the property last week, so some spots are still pretty high."

He mows too?

I carefully spray my shins and tennis shoes. "How did you and Charlie meet?"

"At Grace Community, actually. After things blew up with my stepdad, Mr. Lee thought it would be a good idea for me to talk to someone. It wasn't really my thing, but I was crashing at his house, so I couldn't exactly say no."

I chuckle because Cameron's dad is a lot like him. Persistent. "You probably wouldn't have been able to say no even if you weren't crashing there."

"True." He takes the bug spray from my outstretched hand and tosses it back into the tractor. "Lucky for me, Charlie was

way cooler than some therapist. We mostly just hung out and
worked on the land together. This place was my refuge for
many years." He pauses and sets his hands on his hips. "Now
it's my turn to be there for him."

"I'm sure he appreciates it."

"I doubt it," he snorts. "But I'm the only one as stubborn
and bullheaded as he is, so he's stuck with me. For better or
worse." Bryson unlatches a small wood gate and holds it open
for me. "Last chance to take shelter in the truck."

"Nah. I want to meet his dogs."

"You are an odd woman."

"I know." I step through the gate and start the trek down
the brick pathway. "But it's part of my charm." I glance back
to see if he agrees, and he must because he's smiling, a rare
thing for Bryson, and I feel pretty good that I've managed to
provoke one several times today.

The path takes us around the house and into a giant
backyard with a canopy of oak trees. An old barn stands just
thirty feet away next to a huge windmill so preserved and
picturesque, it makes the entire farm feel like an old western
backdrop. Remnants of carefully tilled gardens sit on different corners, though each now is more filled with weeds than
vegetables or flowers. "There's too much beauty to take in at
once," I say in awe. "Every time I turn my head, I see something new."

Bryson nods, but it's sad, and I decide not to gawk anymore. This place now hurts to come to. That much is written
all over his face.

We continue toward the dog kennels. There are three of
them all spaced a good ten feet apart. Each one is made of
hog fencing and large enough to be comfortable, although
they seem more like temporary housing than permanent.

Two of the dogs are visible. The first, a massive yellow Lab mix whose frenzied gait lends more to excitement than fear. He rushes to the gate, jumps against the fence, and spastically barks. Then he runs in a quick circle around the pen again.

"Did Sue Ann plan on keeping them?" I ask loudly enough to be heard over the other dog's manic barking, which has only increased in severity. It surprises me, especially since I can now clearly make out his breed. It's a blue Great Dane, and from his size and markings, he's very likely pure.

"No. She would adopt them, try and rehabilitate the bad behavior, and then find permanent homes." He points to the kennel on the right. "That's Louie. She only got him a week before the surgery, and he's either barking or hiding. It goes on for hours."

I turn toward his cage, and Louie backs away, hair straight up on his neck. The initial warning type of bark transitions into a panicked shrill. He's terrified. More than terrified; he's convinced I'm here to hurt him. Charlie's wife was more than just a dog lover. I haven't seen dog behavior this extreme since volunteering for the animal rescue society. "Poor thing. He must be exhausted."

Bryson huffs. "Poor Charlie. He has to listen to it twenty-four hours a day." He points to the middle kennel. "That's Sam. She's been here four months. Super sweet, but she's in rough shape physically. When Sue Ann got her, she had some kind of skin disorder and her hair was falling out in patches. It's cured now and a lot of the hair has grown back, but Sue Ann died before she could properly groom her."

I look for Sam, but she must be hiding in her doghouse. I don't blame her. Louie's barking is already starting to give me a headache. "And the excited one over here?" I point to the Lab, who has not stopped running since we walked up.

"That's Bentley. He's a nightmare. Try to feed him and he jumps all over you. Try to pet him and he gnaws at your hand. He's knocked Charlie off his feet twice. I bought those continual feeding and watering stations so he wouldn't have to come out here every day. It's helped a little."

I hear the weariness in his voice, and a newfound admiration settles in. "You're a really good guy, Bryson."

He smirks. "I'll try not to be offended by the surprise in your voice. Then again, considering how we started the day, this is progress."

I huff and push his arm until he teeters. "You're going to punish me forever for my outburst, aren't you?"

"Nah. I just like teasing you."

I roll my eyes, but I have to admit, it's nice to be treated like a normal human again. Between my parents' divorce and my fundraising efforts, the last several months have been the hardest, most stressful ones in my life. And unfortunately, that's not a combination that lends to being any fun. In fact, I can count on one hand the number of times I've truly laughed in months. "You said five, right? Where are the other two?"

"Inside. One is so depressed she hardly gets up to do her business, and the other is so aggressive she has to be crated. Thankfully, she's a terrier so she doesn't cause much damage."

"What is Charlie going to do with them?"

Bryson shrugs. "I don't know, but that's what he called me here to talk about. Sue Ann loved these dogs, and he wants to honor her. But he can't sustain the upkeep. It's too much." He takes a breath like he's been avoiding what he has to do and now has no choice but to face it. "Well, I better get inside. You good?"

"Yeah. I'll be fine."

"It might be a while." His grimace implies apology, but I don't need one. It feels good to be outside after so many days cooped up.

"Take as much time as you need. I'll be busy exploring."

"You sure?"

"Yes. Go." I push him toward the house and finally he acquiesces and disappears through the back door.

I head toward the middle cage, still curious about the dog that has yet to make a sound. Louie darts back to his doghouse and hides, though the barking never stops. "It's okay, big guy. I'm not going to bother you." Louie doesn't care. He still feels the need to yell at me.

I squat down in front of the middle gate as a bushy nose peeks out from the doghouse. "Hey, Sam, can you come see me?"

A head follows, then the body of a golden retriever mix.

"Oh my, you are a mess." Hair is completely matted on the underbelly, with patches missing from both front legs and on the neck. She takes a hesitant step forward and quickly lifts her leg, moving in a more three-legged hop. Bryson didn't mention any injury.

There's no lock on the gate, and while this probably isn't recommended for a novice, I know enough about dogs to take some risks. I carefully unhook the hinge and slide inside the kennel with her. She only makes it a couple of feet before giving up and waiting in a sit position with her paw raised.

I approach carefully. Bryson said she was sweet, but you never know how a dog is going to react to a stranger. "Hey, girl. Is your paw hurt?" I keep my voice smooth and careful, showing her I'm no threat. She whimpers and tries to walk again, only to quit after two agonizing steps.

"Don't worry. I'll come to you." I get within arm's length and her mangled tail wags excitedly.

Kneeling, I begin at her neck and start checking her fur and skin for any residual damage. There's still some healing spots and scar tissue, but no new sores.

Her response is immediate and heartbreaking. She howls and pushes her nose into my neck like a big doggy hug.

"There, there, sweet girl. It's all going to be okay."

A great grooming, along with some tender loving care, and she'd be a wonderful pet for anyone.

I pick up her front right paw, and she whimpers, tugging slightly. Inside a massive amount of fur, three sharp burs are nestled into her foot. The pads are swollen and raw where she's tried to bite at the pain. And based on the amount of hair around each bur, they've been in there for a while. "Poor Sammy girl. No wonder it hurts to walk." I attempt to pull at the first one and quickly pull my hand back. "Ouch." Two dots of blood form on my index finger.

Thankfully, I'm the type who likes to stay prepared.

Running as quickly as I can while not completely freaking Louie out, I make the trek back to the passenger side door of my truck. In the glove compartment is a first-aid kit, along with one of Piper's many dog brushes. I grab them both and my Leatherman and head back to Sam, who hasn't moved from her spot.

"Okay, now this will hurt a little but not nearly as much as keeping those wretched things in there." I turn her paw over and she yelps, high-pitched and pathetic. Her back legs press into the ground while she attempts to jerk her injured leg from my grip. I readjust my hold and slowly begin clipping at the hair until I can see how deep the burs have settled. Two are surface, but one is pretty severe.

I set down her paw, and Sam begins licking and biting at the spot while I search through my first-aid kit for any kind of ointment. The best I can find is some petroleum jelly. It's not ideal, but as long as I get it off and she doesn't swallow any, it should be fine. I squeeze the tube slightly and carefully massage it into her swollen pad. It seems to lessen the pain some because her chest relaxes and she stops gnawing at my hand. I flip open the pliers on my tool and tug at the first bur. It comes out quickly and easily but also exposes the infection that's begun around her foot.

The second bur takes a little more finesse yet also comes out smoothly. The last bur is implanted in her foot, and the skin is so red and raw that I feel it will be too painful to simply try to pull it out. I hold her paw with one hand and search my kit with the other. There's some antibiotic cream with a numbing agent in it. Again, not ideal, but leaving this thing in there isn't an option either.

Careful with every motion, I take the process excruciatingly slow, alternating between easing out the bur and rubbing the cream into each newly exposed piece of flesh. Sam whines at first, but as the pain increases, her barks and growls are nearly as loud as Louie's. I firm up my grip on her foot, even though she's actively fighting me now. "We're almost done, I promise."

It feels like hours have passed when the bur finally comes completely free of the skin, grabbing on to overgrown fur as I pull. I cut away more hair until victory is achieved.

"We did it." I sigh, exhaustion coating the words. Sweat trickles down my forehead and through my shirt. My knees and thighs ache from planting them into the ground, but the sacrifice was worth it. "Can you walk for me?" I stand and pull a little on her collar.

She takes a tentative step, feels the relief, and hobbles forward. She still has a limp, but with a few days of cleaning and treatment, she should be good as gold.

We walk over to her water station. After removing the three-gallon jug, I dip her foot inside the bowl to wash away any dirt still lodged in her paw. She licks at my hand while I'm cleaning, letting me know she's not super comfortable with what's happening.

"Almost done, sweet girl, I promise." I use my T-shirt to wipe her paw dry and inspect the pads again. I don't have a wrap, so I opt not to put more antibiotic cream on her foot today. "I'll come see you tomorrow and get you completely squared away." I scratch her bushy neck, and she plants a sloppy wet kiss on my cheek. Yeah, Sam is definitely a best friend waiting to happen.

I spend the rest of the time in her kennel pulling at weeds and shaking out the mat in her doghouse. She follows me everywhere despite her obvious soreness. The devil bur plant is growing along the outside of her cage and is way too vicious to uproot with bare hands. It's also too thick to cut with any of the tools on my Leatherman. The barn I noticed earlier has a hose attached on the outside. I'm guessing that's where Charlie keeps his tools and dog supplies.

Sam whimpers when I exit the gate, her water station jug in hand.

"Don't worry. I'm just going to spray this out and get you some fresh water." And maybe find some garden shears and gloves to take down the plant.

I'm halfway done with refilling the water when Bryson emerges from the back of the house. It's only then that I check the time and realize it's been nearly an hour since he went inside. It's also then I realize this is the first time in weeks I haven't counted the seconds hoping the day would end soon. In fact, nothing, not even my umpteen pints of ice cream, has made me feel as invigorated and satisfied as this last hour has.

"I came to check on you," A flash of surprise brightens his face and he laughs. "And it's a good thing I did." He eyes me from my sweaty red face, down my wet T-shirt, to the scratched skin on my knees. "What on earth have you been doing out here?"

I toss the running hose where it won't soak my tennis shoes and walk over to turn off the spicket. "Sam had burs in her foot. I cleaned them out, but we need to get rid of the bur weeds along the edge of her cage." I wipe another round of sweat from my forehead and rest my hands on my hips.

Bryson stares at me, mouth open, eyes wide. "She let you touch her?"

"Yeah. She's super sweet, just like you said."

"I know she is, but she's never let me touch her." He glances over at Sam, who's waiting patiently at the gate for me. "I tried last week and she nipped at my hand."

"Weird. She came right to me. Maybe I remind her of Sue Ann."

"Maybe." He stares at her again, and this time I sense a regret that wasn't there before. It bothers me, sending a jolt of protectiveness I can't ignore.

"What did Charlie decide?" I ask, even though the pit in my stomach tells me I won't like the answer.

"He's going to surrender them to animal services tomorrow."

"What? No! I thought he couldn't part with them. I thought they reminded him of Sue Ann."

"They do." He turns sharply, his tone laced with stress and

defeat, "But what other choice does he have? They aren't adoptable in this state, and he's doing more harm to them and to himself by keeping them."

Adrenaline pulses through my limbs, conviction and passion I haven't felt in months filling my chest. "I'll do it."

"Darcy."

"No, really. I can do it." I step closer, my voice coming close to a plea. "I'm a certified trainer, and yeah, I'm a little rusty, but I know how to read animals. It's one of the few things I'm really very good at."

He jams his hands through his hair and latches them behind his head. "It was an agonizing decision, but Charlie finally made it. I can't go back in there and tell him not to do it."

"He's grieving, Bryson. And I know the death of a dream is not even in the same stratosphere as the death of a wife, but you don't think rationally when you're in the midst of trauma like he is. Let me take care of them and work with them. And afterwards, if he still wants to get rid of them, then at least they have a fighting chance to be adopted."

He's wavering; I can feel it. "How are you even going to have the time to do this?"

"Are you kidding me? All I have is time. So much in fact that I'm haunted by it. Please. If not for them, then for me." I look out at Sam, hopefully trusting me to return, and feel more certain than ever that this is the path to healing my still-broken heart. "I need some kind of purpose in my life, Bryson." The words choke me, and I take hold of his hand and squeeze it to my chest. "Will you please just ask?"

"Fine," he growls, and I leap into his arms in a thank-you hug that nearly knocks us both to the ground.

Strong arms latch around my waist, keeping us securely

planted. I expect him to release me as soon as we're steady again, but he doesn't. Instead, his grip pulls me closer and his breath teases the skin on my neck.

Electricity that feels completely different from the earlier adrenaline tingles down my spine and into my fingertips. I back away, embarrassed not only by my boldness but also my reaction to his touch, and put some distance between us.

His eyes lock with mine, and it's a look I can't define because I've never felt such intensity from one stare. It touches deep in my bones, makes every inch on my skin flush with confusing heat.

"Thank you," I whisper.

He jerks his gaze away, first to the ground and then toward Charlie's house. "I'll be right back." Without looking at me again, he heads to the back door, his strides long and deliberate.

I busy myself with finishing the task at hand, needing some kind of distraction before he returns. There's a scooper as well as a pair of shears in the barn. I take the water jug and flip it over into Sam's station, then return for the tools.

Bryson's gone another fifteen minutes, and I'm grateful. It gives me time to rationalize. Time to convince myself that whatever strange feeling that hug provoked, it was directly related to my overwhelming need to help these five animals. Nothing more.

When he finally appears again, Sam's kennel is clean and free from plant hazards. I meet Bryson at the gate, trying my best to read his body language. It's impossible.

"Well?"

Bryson sighs like I've lost my mind, and excitement simmers beneath my skin. "He'll give you until the end of July. Not a day longer."

"Yes!" I leap but am careful not to touch him this time.

"There's a caveat. He wants them all adopted in that timeline. He has some of Sue Ann's contacts and mentioned different adoption dog fairs that happen on the weekends. And he wants to see progress. Meaning he expects there to be fewer dogs here over time. If not, he's going to reconsider."

I nod, willing to agree to anything at this point. "No problem. A little TLC and I could have Sam placed this weekend."

"Are you sure, Darcy?" His eyes hold a warning I don't miss. "This isn't the kind of thing you can change your mind about."

"Have you ever known me to quit something?"

He shakes his head. "No."

"I won't let you down. I promise." The word burrows inside, takes root, becomes more than simply a promise, but a surety beyond any explanation. I was meant to save these dogs. Every single one of them.

fter Bryson delivered the good news, he took me inside to meet the other two dogs and Charlie, who said approximately two words to me before disappearing into his bedroom.

Bryson apologized for him, but I know it's not personal. After all, it wasn't that long ago that I refused to open the door for my best friend or answer phone calls. There's a bit of security in isolation, like if you can pretend the world doesn't exist, you won't have to face your present reality.

I scribble another note on the page in front of me, using Zoe's coffee table as my new workspace. I have my plan all laid out for each dog. The easiest one is Sam. I spoke to Sue Ann's contact at the rescue foundation today and got their adoption-fair schedule, which basically runs every Saturday during the summer. They primarily stay within Ellis and Tarrant Counties so none of the fairs are too far away.

Ms. Elledge put me down on their list and then went into great detail about what an amazing woman Sue Ann was and how much they miss both her and Charlie. She's also going to see if she can find any additional history on the dogs Sue Ann adopted so I know exactly what I'm dealing with.

Done with four of the five plans, I tear a new page out of my notebook and move on to Louie. He's the one who stumps me the most. He's not aggressive, yet I wouldn't put it past him to lash out in fear. He hides the minute you come too close to his cage yet barks until his throat gets too hoarse to continue. In the two hours we were there, Louie only stayed quiet for the fifteen minutes I was inside the house. Getting him to trust me enough to even begin making progress is going to be the real challenge, especially in six weeks' time.

"Knock knock."

"Hey!" I wave Cameron in from the couch and bite my pen. Louie will definitely have to be the last one placed. He'll need to see me care for him safely for a while.

"No Zoe tonight?" Cameron shuts the door behind him. He brought his guitar and our ongoing list of summer movie rentals.

"Nope." I set down my notebook and shift over to give him room.

The minute Cam sits, Piper is up in his lap giving him a slew of kisses. She adores him, even though he mostly tolerates her. "How's life with a roommate? Things going okay between the two of you?"

"Yeah. She's hardly ever here, so we pretty much do our own thing. It feels a lot like living alone, actually."

"I guess that's better than catfights and hair pulling, which was a real possibility. This is Zoe we're talking about."

I chuckle. "She's not that bad. I mean, what little I've interacted with her doesn't seem that bad."

"I'll take your word for it," he says dryly as he sets Piper on the floor. Normally, she'd hop right back up, but she seems to have gotten her fill of affection and trots back to her doggie bed in the corner. "So what's all this?" He picks up one of my pages, studies it like it's illegible, and sets it back on the coffee table.

"I'm finalizing my strategy for Charlie's dogs."

His perplexed expression tells me my answer did nothing to explain.

"Charlie's a friend of Bryson's, which is crazy because he's seventy years old. Oh, your dad knows him, by the way. Bryson said he connected them after he moved in with you guys." I shuffle my papers into a pile. "Anyway, we went out to his farm today, and Charlie has these five incredible dogs that he was going to surrender to animal control, which we all know means they'll be euthanized. Especially these dogs. They're all in really bad shape." I take a breath as my story comes out more like a run-on sentence. "I don't know what happened: I just found myself volunteering to get them adopted. Well, begging was more like it, because Charlie's mind was made up, but somehow Bryson convinced him to let me find them homes." I fall back on the couch. "Pretty insane, huh?"

"Very insane." Cameron stares at me, and I can't tell if he's still confused or just trying to filter through all the data. "I had no idea Bryson had friends, especially ones who are senior adults."

"I know, right! But I'm excited. This feels . . . good. And nothing else has."

"That's great, Darcy." He squeezes my thigh in his usual supportive manner. "I'm glad you have something to keep you busy. Your TV and internet habits were getting a bit concerning." He winks at me, and I push his arm away, fighting a smile. He pushes me back, and luckily we've grown up a little since high school so it stops there. "Exactly how did all this come about? I mean, I've never known you and Bryson to hang out before."

"It's kind of crazy, actually." I cross my legs in a pretzel and tell him the entire story from the moment Bryson stormed into Zoe's apartment until the last twenty minutes when he had me drive home so I could get a feel of the area. Cameron listens without a word, his fingers periodically picking at the guitar strings. Music is so ingrained in him that half the time he doesn't even realize he's playing.

"Now I have a month and a half to place these dogs, and from what I saw today, it's going to take a miracle to pull it off." I look down at my stack of notes and feel the enormity of failure. "I can't explain it, but I can't *not* do this. They need me, and after all the disappointment lately, it feels really good to be needed."

He pauses, somehow bothered by that last comment. "Of course you're needed. I wouldn't have made it through this past year without you. I mean, it's great that you have the dogs to focus on and not all the disappointment, but don't think for a second that they're the only ones who value you being here." There's too much desperation in his voice not to catch my attention, and it's the first time I really notice the stress in his forehead and the darkness under his eyes.

"Cam, is everything okay?"

"It's fine." He shakes his head. "I already promised myself I wasn't going to unload all my problems on you again."

"You're not unloading. We're friends. That's what we do. Goodness knows, you have a lot of *I-owe-you*s piled up from my one million phone calls during the divorce." I squeeze his hand. "Talk to me."

"Honestly, I don't even know exactly what it is." He sets down his guitar and glances around Zoe's immaculate apartment. "I feel like I'm running on a treadmill, or worse, moving backwards." He stands, his movements agitated. "When I left the praise band, I made myself a promise. I was going all in, no excuses, no limits. And if we didn't get signed by my thirtieth birthday, then I would be done, with no regrets because I knew I'd laid it all on the line. Darcy, these next eight months with Black Carousel are it for me. If we're not signed by March, I'm done. I won't spend the rest of my life chasing a fantasy." He blows out a shaky breath. "Before, when you were leaving, it all made perfect sense. You'd pursue your dream; I'd pursue mine. But now that you stayed, I need you to know there is an end date to my obsession. I want a family one day. I want a wife and kids. I promise you; I won't feel this unsatisfied for the rest of my life."

"I know you won't." I stand and walk to his side. His shoulders slump. Spent. Weariness all that's left in his expression. My heart tugs in my chest. He's sacrificed everything for this shot. To watch it slip through his fingers would be devastating. "But more importantly, I know it's going to happen, Cam. All of your dreams. The music, the stage, the screaming fans, your name as a headliner. It's all going to work out."

He shakes his head as if to ward off any more unrealized promises. "I'm not so sure anymore. I feel like I'm watching my life slip through my fingers. You included. Which I know sounds ridiculous since you're here and we're us, but I can't help but have this sense that I'm going to lose you."

"That's absurd. We've been best friends our entire life. Nothing is going to change that. I won't let it."

An anguished smile pulls at his lips. "Sorry, it's been a tough week. Bryson won't even discuss another tour, and rehearsals have been horribly inconsistent. Plus, we both know I'm not at my best when things feel uncertain."

"Hey, if you need something to take your mind off things,

you could always help me with the dogs." It's a rhetorical offer. We both know that while Cam respects my love for furry beasts, he does not share in the joy.

"As appealing as that sounds . . . between work and rehearsal, I'm lucky to even get a night like this." He rolls his shoulders like he's trying to pull himself out of the mood he's in and sits down, his guitar immediately finding its way into his lap. "At least one good thing has come from all this turmoil; I have another new song."

I try not to cringe. "Good for you. That's four now, huh?"

"Six, and they just keep pouring out of me. You'll really like the one I wrote yesterday."

That I seriously doubt. I haven't liked any of the songs Cameron's played for me lately.

"I'm going to go make some popcorn. Wanna pull up the next movie? They're all in my watch list."

"Yeah, sure." He grabs the remote to access my online video library while I make my way to the kitchen.

I feel bad for avoiding the song conversation, especially when music is usually a great tool to pull him out of his head. Ten minutes of playing and singing, even though I'm pretty much the worst singer in the world, and we end up laughing away all our problems.

But music, like so many other things these days, no longer has its healing powers. Cameron's songs have grown increasingly dark, and the last one was so heavy, I wanted to mourn for the innocence he used to have.

> A man bleeding never stands
> On his knees he begs, watching them all, knowing,
>   waiting
> Who will see, who will fight, who will break?

I shake away the words that have haunted me since hearing them and focus on the popping sound coming from the microwave. In twenty-nine years, I've never felt uncomfortable around my best friend. But lately, I don't know. It's like we're both treading water, desperately fighting for breath, and neither of us has the strength to pull the other to shore.

The popping slows to that critical point, and I quickly open the door to avoid burning.

"Go ahead and make two," Cam calls from the living room. "I'm starving." He smiles at me from across the room, and it eases some of my fear that he's right and we are slipping away from each other.

We've both suffered great defeats this year. And I'm living proof that, good or bad, it changes a person. We just have to find our new normal, together, now that all the dust has settled.

I dump the first batch in a large bowl and start the microwave again. "Wanna order some pizza, too?"

Cam jumps from the couch. "Darlin', you read my mind!"

I chuckle at his impression of a Southern belle as the rest of my concern melts away. We'll get through this. We have to.

TEN

y Friday, Sam's coat has been completely transformed. It's taken hours of work, but I was able to salvage eighty percent of her fur. She seems to instinctively know she looks good even without the benefit of a mirror. She's strutting around with her head held high. And it hasn't escaped my notice that Bentley has been pacing much more often along the fence that runs parallel to hers.

I set down his food bowl. "Sorry, old boy, but she's way out of your league."

Bentley takes his usual running leap and tries to knock me to the ground. I grab his collar, force him down despite his hundred-pound girth.

"No," I say forcefully, annoyed that I now have mud smeared on my shirt. "We do not jump." This guy is going to need some serious one-on-one leash training. I've tried several tactics this week and none of them has been successful. "Just you wait, mister. As soon as Sam finds a home, you and I are going to start bonding. And my definition of what that looks like is very different from yours."

His tongue hangs from his mouth, his slobber coming out in streams as he tries to lunge at my face again.

Exhausted and ready for a shower, I give up on his bad manners for today and ease out of the kennel.

It's time to go inside, though it's that final task I dread the most. Charlie spends most of his day in the recliner, aimlessly staring at the TV. He's acknowledged me once, but only to tell me I need to get that blasted dog to stop barking. I told him I was working on it, though truthfully, Louie has only gotten worse. He used to stop barking when I went inside the house. Now it continues until . . . well, I don't know when because it never stops the entire time I'm at the farm.

I knock on the back door as a warning and slowly open it. The rooms are dark as usual, and I can hear the hum of a news channel in the background. Penny and Macey are the two indoor dogs. Penny is a purebred Jack Russell terrier, while Macey is a hodgepodge with so many different markings, I've only been able to narrow the breeds down to Red Heeler, pit bull, and possibly some Ridgeback in there as well. Ironically, it's Penny who's had to be crated because she viciously attacks Macey every time she's let out of her cage. From what I've been told, despite having a fifty-pound advantage, Macey simply cowers and takes the beating.

"Charlie?" I call out carefully. "It's Darcy. I'm going to feed and exercise the dogs real quick, okay?" I hear a grunt coming from the living room, which is my signal to go ahead but also to mind my own business.

Macey's dog bed is in the living room with Charlie, and I swear she moves as little as he does. It's like they're both steeped in the same depression, even though they stay on opposite ends of the room.

I follow my daily path through the kitchen first, no longer noticing its beauty like I did the first day—high ceilings, a huge wood-topped island that has to be eight feet long. The cabinets are a distressed white, while the countertops are black granite. Despite being an old farmhouse, the interior is elegant and welcoming. Or at least I see how it could have been that way at one time. The dining room is similarly special with a long, distressed farm table and buffet. At one point, I imagine there were people filling each chair. It makes me sad for Charlie all over again. Surely, he also sees the ghosts of what once was here.

Neither Macey nor Charlie acknowledges me when I step into the living room, not that I had much expectation otherwise. Macey hates it when I come because I force her to get up, walk at least two loops around the barn, and do her business. She, like Charlie, would rather sit here and waste away until they share Sue Ann's fate.

I clip the leash to Macey's collar and get her to reluctantly stand. "Um, Charlie, I just wanted to let you know that I'll be taking Sam to the dog fair tomorrow morning. Just in case . . ." I let my words trail off, unsure if I should finish advising him to say goodbye.

Charlie lifts his hand and rubs it over his face like he's waking up from a long dream. His untamed white beard reaches the collar of the same red robe he wore yesterday. "I saw her last night. She looks real good."

I wait to see if there's more, but there isn't. His hand falls back to his side, his head transfixed on the bright TV screen. I tug on Macey's leash, and she slowly moves along the hardwood floor.

It wasn't a real conversation by any means, but today definitely feels a little like progress. In my world right now, that's a lot to celebrate.

96

It's five-thirty by the time I get back to the apartment, and I'm gross enough to want to douse myself in hydrogen peroxide. My shirt is covered with hair, my boots caked with a layer of thick, black Texas mud.

The private alcove has become my transition space. I unlace my shoes, shake out my shirt, and brush as much dirt off my jeans as possible. When I feel sure I won't trail filth inside Zoe's apartment, I pull out my keys and opt to leave the boots until I can get back out here and clean them.

I slide in my key, surprised to find that I didn't need it at all. Not only is the door unlocked, but Zoe is sitting on the couch, legs curled in front of her, a book in her hands. She looks cute enough to be in a TV commercial, even with her hair pulled into a messy bun. More shocking is that Piper is snuggled next to her while Zoe mindlessly scratches her back.

I close the door, and both of them jerk up and turn to look at me.

"Oh, hey." She sets her book in her lap and smiles. "I made dinner if you're hungry?"

I should probably not look so surprised, but not only has Zoe been a relative phantom in this place, but I've seen no evidence that cooking has ever occurred here.

"Um, yeah. Famished." It's only then that my Benedict Arnold of a dog hops off the couch and comes to greet me, though barely long enough to count. She hasn't been super thrilled with the smells I've been bringing home with me. It was the same when I worked for Pampered Pups. My dog barely spoke to me until I showered. "I just need to change real quick." I walk carefully to the laundry room and shed the rest of my soiled clothes. I've learned to keep at least two spare outfits in here lately so I'm not streaking across the living room in my undergarments. I slide on a fresh

T-shirt and a pair of athletic shorts and head back to the front room. "Sorry. I was way too disgusting to get anywhere near food."

I continue into the kitchen to find a plate already waiting with a warming lid on top. After washing my hands, I carefully remove the plastic cover and see a visual masterpiece that could be photographed in a food magazine. On a bed of rice lie thinly cut strips of meat in a teepee formation, cooked perfectly medium, and layered on top of that are four asparagus spears. I look over the bar at Zoe. "This is really impressive. I didn't know you cooked."

She sets her book on the coffee table and eases off the couch. "It's a hobby I picked up a couple years ago. I tend to do it more often when I'm alone and bored." Her tone reveals hurt, like being alone isn't necessarily her idea. "Nate's doing boys' night tonight, which basically means he's going to show up here at two in the morning completely hammered." She rolls her eyes, but I get the impression that despite her annoyance, she doesn't plan to turn him away. "What do you have going on tonight?"

"A long shower and a very early bedtime." When she gives me a horror-filled expression, I add, "I have to be up at six tomorrow morning."

She slides onto a barstool and sets her elbows up on the counter. "On a Saturday, why?"

"I have to pick up Sam for the dog fair, and unfortunately, Charlie's farm and the park we're setting up at are in opposite directions. Plus, I want to make sure I have time to groom her again before people start coming."

"Makes sense. Those adoption fairs are kind of like a farmers' market but for dogs, right? People weave between station after station and pick out the best-looking option?" She glances at my untouched plate. "You should eat that before it gets cold."

"I don't know if it's that impersonal. I mean, most people who come to these things are looking for a lifelong companion." I scoop up a forkful and put it in my mouth after making my point. The rice is a little dry, and the meat could use more salt, but overall I'd say Zoe definitely has a future as a chef.

"So, the appearance doesn't matter at all?"

I sense I'm being baited yet answer honestly. "No, it matters. That's why I've spent all week painstakingly brushing out Sam's coat. She'll definitely stand out tomorrow."

"And what about you? Do you have a come-check-out-my-dog outfit picked out?"

I set down my fork, even though I want to keep eating. "It really doesn't matter what I wear."

Zoe's perfectly plucked eyebrow soars to the ceiling. "I beg to differ. You aren't just selling . . . her name is Sam, right?"

I nod, though I don't care for her terminology.

"I thought so." She pauses as if trying to remember exactly where she left off. "You're not just selling Sam, the product. You're selling a feeling. A promise of fun, comfort, companionship. They're going to judge both of you for that feeling."

"Sam isn't a product. And I'm not 'selling' anything." I return to my plate and finish off the last of the meat medallions.

"Well, technically, you're asking the adoptive family to pay for food, vet bills, and grooming for the next ten-plus years. That's a big financial commitment."

I hadn't ever looked at it that way.

"So . . ." She claps her hands together, and I have a sinking suspicion I've somehow solved her boredom problem. "This is what we're going to do. Tonight we are going to find you the perfect outfit for tomorrow. Then I'm going to show you how to add a little volume and curl to that hair of yours so you won't have to pull it up into a ponytail."

Maybe Cam was right about the catfights after all. "I appreciate the offer, Zoe, but I can dress myself."

Determination sparks in her eyes. "So you're willing to risk Sam's future on your pride? Because here's what half those people are going to see when they come up to you. A beautiful dog being held by a girl who looks frumpy, tired, and depressed. But then next to you is this sharp-looking guy with trendy jeans, a crisp, clean button-up, and an adorable dog who makes him look like a magazine model. Which one would you want to be?"

I'm too stunned to speak. Too offended to even know how to answer her question. "I don't look frumpy and depressed." Okay, I'll admit I've been a little lazy with the hair brushing lately, and half my stuff is buried in storage so my clothing choices have been pretty limited, but I'm not *that* far from where I used to be.

"Have you looked in the mirror once since you've moved in with me?" When I don't answer, she continues, "You're an incredibly striking girl. You always have been. I sort of hated you for it growing up. But lately, your outside"—she motions with her hand up and down—"looks like a walking ad for Prozac."

I bite my lip and look down at my plate, suddenly wishing I hadn't eaten that last bite. It's rolling in my stomach now, along with a sudden shot of anxiety. It never occurred to me that I was wearing my feelings so blatantly.

"You've been through trauma, Darcy, I get that. Trust me. But at some point, you're going to have to pick up the pieces and move forward." Zoe must sense that she's hit a nerve because her tone softens a little. "A bit of physical updating might just be the spark you need."

I think of Sam and how her confidence soared with each tangle we freed. How brush after brush was healing to her brokenness. It's wild how our life can be reflected through an animal. "You really think it will help Sam's chances if I—" I can hardly get the words to come out of my mouth—"dress up a little?"

"Without a doubt." Zoe's victory smile is wide and excited. "Trust me, this is what I do for a living. When we're done, you're going to be so irresistible that not only is Sam getting adopted within the first hour, but I bet you'll have at least two date offers, as well."

"Random dates with strangers is the last thing I want." That is reserved solely for my mom, although the Michael guy is still around, which I find a bit unnerving. "But I will concede that my current wardrobe is lacking."

"Lacking? Darcy, those jeans you wore the other day were the same ones you wore to youth camp when I was a seventh grader."

"How do you know?"

"Because you sat on a blue highlighter, and it stained the denim right below your left back pocket. That blue stain is still there, next to the fraying pocket that is only halfway attached to your pants."

Oh my word. She's right. And maybe it's the end of a long week or just the fact that I'm standing in Zoe's kitchen, getting a lecture about clothing, but I suddenly find myself laughing.

The disease catches on and Zoe joins in. Even Piper responds with a melody of barks.

When we finally ease to a stop, Zoe jumps off the barstool

and pulls her wallet from her purse. "Now go shower. We have a lot to do in a very short amount of time." She slides a gold plastic card from one of the credit card slots and waves it in the air. "And don't worry. If there's one thing I'm an expert at, it's retail therapy."

ELEVEN

*J*ames McKnight Park in Mansfield is a beautiful treed area with lots of walking trails and baseball fields. It was a bit chaotic when we first showed up, mostly because I hadn't ever done one of these before. It took me fifteen minutes to find my point of contact, all while navigating a lawn chair strapped to my back, a rolling cooler in my left hand, and a very curious dog in my right. Keeping Sam close by my side and away from a tidal wave of unruly foster dogs was a feat in itself.

However, once I was sufficiently schooled on the paperwork and adoption criteria, the lady in charge showed me my reserved area and scurried off to help the next novice. By eight, everyone was settled, and by nine, the radio station along with six bounce houses were set up and ready for action.

Sam and I are near the half-mile marker and well shaded from the summer sun. It's not the prime location, since most of the families haven't left the play area, but it's not Siberia either. And since I've chosen optimism today, I'm going to appreciate the fact that my location will cut out being bombarded by curious onlookers who have no interest in adopting a pet.

I squat down and run a brush once more through Sam's silky fur. I added fish oil to her diet this week, and it's already having a huge impact on her coloring and skin quality. When satisfied she looks as beautiful as possible, I stand and tug at the denim skirt Zoe talked me into buying.

Overall, the outfit isn't too impractical, though the skirt is on the edge. Luckily it reaches to my knees, so I can still bend without showing unmentionables. The top is a lightweight button-up that ties at the waist. It's simple, fur-resistant, and actually really comfortable. The shoes were a bit of an argument, but we settled on slip-on Vans in a dark gray. They aren't the well-worn, comfy tennis shoes I bought last year, but far better than the two-inch open-toe sandals she suggested.

Surprisingly, the night was kind of entertaining, even though shopping is at the bottom of my fun list. In some ways, Zoe reminds me of Bryson, and in others, she's the polar opposite. They share the same charisma, especially when passionate about a topic, but Zoe has a layer of insecurity I've never seen in Bryson. Then again, the guy's been on his own since he was seventeen, and I seriously doubt he's ever once used his daddy's credit card.

Zoe, on the other hand, is a spending machine. Shoes, a leather purse, a pair of sunglasses that cost more than my entire outfit. When I mentioned the growing tab, she laughed it off, saying, "Daddy likes paying for my things. It makes him feel like we're bonding." I didn't say a word, but I imagine there are mountains of self-help books written specifically on the dangers of that kind of daddy-daughter relationship. Then again, my own relationship with my father is therapist worthy right now, so who am I to judge.

Sam and I wait as another ten minutes drag by without any guests, and Sam chooses to lie down on the grass and stretch out. I'm close to wanting to do the same when I spot a tall guy dressed in all black walking toward us. I know in a millisecond it's Bryson. Who else wears combat boots in June?

He looks my direction, squints, then glances back down at the paper in his hand. Then he spins around and seems to count the spaces leading up to mine again. This time I wave, and even though he has to see me, I swear the man hesitates before coming closer.

Sam jumps to her feet, tail wagging.

"Sorry, girl. This one isn't in the market for a new puppy." In fact, Bryson isn't in the market for much more than a hit record, so I have no idea why he's here.

"Wow," he says the minute we're within earshot of each other. "You two look like you belong on the cover of *American Canine*." His gaze trails from the top of my head down to my no-show socks. "How is there not a line in front of you?"

I shrug off his compliment but can't help the way his words cause my stomach to dip. "You know what they say about location. And the magazine-cover thing is Zoe's doing." I pick up a wavy lock of hair. "Down to the blisters I now have from her curling wand."

"Tell me you didn't fall for the 'you need to sell the product' line."

I open my mouth and close it again. "How did you . . . ?"

"She gave me the same pitch last week."

I cross my arms. "Did she call you a walking advertisement for Prozac?"

A smile plays behind his eyes. "Not that I remember, but then again, I block out half of what Zoe says." He squats down in front of Sam and scratches the thick fur on her neck.

"Her hair feels like silk. Charlie was right. You've worked a miracle with her."

Warmth fills my arms at his praise. "Charlie said that?"

He glances up at me. "He did. He also gave me the address and told me to get out here and help you."

Now I know he's lying. "Nice try. What did he really say?"

"Something I probably shouldn't repeat since it wasn't PG. Turns out you were right. Giving up the dogs in theory sounded good, but he's hurting especially bad today." Bryson stands back up. "I figured if I could tell him a little about the family that adopted her, it might ease the sting a little."

"That's if I can get a family over here to meet her."

"You will. Just let the excitement of the bounce houses wear off a little." He scoots next to me in the shade, and I can hear his relief as the air cools at least ten degrees. His shirt is tight and likely Dri-Fit, but it's still black, and in the Texas sun, that's enough to roast a person.

"So, what did Zoe want to change about your style?"

He turns his head to look at me. "She thinks the all-black thing has run its course and that we should update our image now that Cameron's in the band and we actually have a real shot at making it."

It's funny how Zoe's honesty feels a lot less biting when not directed at me. "She has a point."

He sighs like he knows I'm right. "It's a tough thing to reshape your identity, no matter how important the reason. I guess I haven't felt ready to do it."

"I understand. My entire adult life I've been known as the missionary girl. I'm still struggling with what I am now that it's gone."

"Well, to the five dogs on Charlie's property, you're a savior. Not bad for an identity, at least for a little while."

Our gazes meet and my cheeks flush from the sincerity in them. "Thanks."

He clears his throat as if embarrassed and glances back to the crowd. "Hey, don't look now, but I spot a single dad with two kids coming your way."

"Really?" I follow his gaze, and sure enough, the trio is approaching, the older of the boys pulling on his frazzled dad's arm, fighting to get him to hurry. The younger one clings to the dad like a draping monkey, disheveling both his polo shirt and pressed khaki shorts. "Okay, Sam, this is it." I tug her collar and she sits, her back straight, her hair billowing out around her. I turn back to Bryson, but he's backed away almost to the edge of my assigned square. I wave at him to come forward, but he shakes his head. I guess I understand. He's pretty intimidating in his current attire.

The eager boy releases his dad's hand when they get within a few feet of us and comes rushing over, only to halt a few inches from Sam's nose. His hair is a tight buzz cut, and his matching Reebok shirt and shorts combo looks just slightly too small. I wonder if that's why Bryson assumed the guy was single or if it was the sheer exhaustion and panic written all over the poor man's face.

"Can I pet him?" the boy says in an excited squeal.

"Joshua," his dad scolds, walking as fast as he can while lugging a smaller boy on his hip. "What did I say about running up to dogs like that? You can scare them."

I squat down so I'm eye level with the little boy. "Your dad's right. You have to be really cautious with new animals." I scratch Sam's head. "Luckily, Sam here loves to be petted, although you should know she's a girl, not a boy."

The kid carefully touches her fur. "Isn't Sam a boy's name?"

"It's short for Samantha, I think."

"Hi, Sam, I'm Joshua, but my friends call me Josh, so my name is shorter, too. I think you and I are going to be great friends."

Sam must agree. Her tail wags to a spastic degree and she inches as close to him as I'll allow before starting a lick fest on the boy's throat.

Joshua laughs and laughs, going from hesitant touches to full-on hugging. "Can I have her, Dad? Pleaaasseee. She's the best dog ever."

Yeah, that poor guy is going home with this dog for sure.

Dad sets down the boy on his hip, who seems old enough to walk by himself, and presses two fingers to each temple. "Let's look around some more first. You may find one you like better."

I'm thinking not. Sam and Josh are now rolling in the grass together.

"I'm Darcy," I offer with an outstretched hand.

Dad shakes it, his eyes darting between me and Bryson in the corner.

"Sam really is a great dog. I've been working on leash obedience, and she's picked up on my cues really quickly. I'll be happy to show you some techniques if you're interested."

"Looks like I am whether I want to be or not," he grumbles. Joshua is now getting thoroughly soaked by Sam's tongue and loving every second of dousing. "How intense is the upkeep and shedding?"

Smart dad.

"I won't lie, you will need to brush her daily and add fish oil to her diet. But a little each day will prevent a great deal of long-term problems. You may want to get her professionally groomed each quarter just to thin out the hair and help with shedding, but we've found that kids who take responsibility for a pet at that age are more likely to apply that work ethic in other areas of their lives." I finish my speech with a tug on Sam's leash, and she hesitantly returns to my side.

Dad checks on his younger boy again and sees he's inched closer and closer to Bryson. The kid's nearly identical to his brother minus the four-inch height differential. Same buzz cut, matching outfit, similar inquisitive nature. "Jacob, come back here," the man calls out.

"That's my friend Bryson. He's only scary on the outside." I smile reassuringly and head-motion for Bryson to come join us. "We can keep an eye on Jacob if you want to see how Sam does on a leash with Joshua."

Behind us is an open field that would be a perfectly safe place for the two of them to practice.

Joshua pulls on his father's shorts. "Please, Dad. Come on. You promised."

Dad looks at his kid, then at Sam, who is rocking some seriously potent puppy eyes, and caves. "You're sure you don't mind?"

"Not at all."

He turns to Jacob, who's eye level with a squatting Bryson.

It takes me aback for a second, seeing him in such a parental position. Especially since he's now pulling out a small metal thing from his pocket and bringing it to his mouth. A beat later, harmonica music fills the void, and the little one laughs and claps and begs to try to play it for himself.

Dad returns his attention to me. "Okay, we'll just be a few minutes."

"No problem." I hand Sam's leash over to Dad. "Two tugs mean she needs to stay next to you on your left. One tug means to sit. If you give her slack, she knows she's free to explore, so only give her what you're comfortable with."

Joshua unsuccessfully attempts to pull the leash from his dad's grip. "Stop," his dad says firmly. "I'll let you try when there are less distractions around us."

I watch them leave, proud of how carefully Sam is behaving. People don't give dogs enough credit. I have no doubt that she feels the weight of this moment nearly as much as I do. I return my gaze to Bryson—who's wiping down the harmonica with one of my antibacterial wipes—and move closer to the duo.

"Okay, little guy, blow out and suck in."

Jacob carefully holds the instrument to his mouth and attempts to make sound come out of it. Nothing happens. Bryson adjusts the boy's hands and where the metal is placed against his lips. Two more attempts later, an ear-piercing shriek comes from the other end.

Bryson doesn't flinch like I do but continues to instruct and encourage the little boy. By the time his dad returns with Joshua on leash duty, Jacob can sustain a shaky sound for almost five seconds.

"Well, how did she do?" I ask the father-son duo, both of whom are smiling now.

"We're going to adopt her," Joshua says firmly. "Dad said so."

I wait for the decision-maker to concur, and he nods. I can't tell if he's totally on board at this point, but I can see that Sam's already charmed him a little.

The next fifteen minutes are spent filling out paperwork and giving a list of suggestions on upkeep and food. I give Sam one more big hug. "I knew you'd find a great family," I whisper in her ear. She nudges me with her head, and I have to blow out a shaky breath to avoid a barrage of tears.

Slowly, I stand and hand over the leash, forcing myself to let go.

"We'll take good care of her," their dad promises, and his compassionate words only make it that much harder to remain composed.

"Bye, Darcy!" Joshua yells, waving as he skips beside his new best friend. Dad holds the leash in one hand and Jacob's hand in the other, though I doubt the little boy has any intention of running off. He clutches the harmonica to his chest as if it's his most prized possession.

Bryson comes to stand next to me, and while he doesn't make any attempt to touch me, I still feel as if his proximity is an intentional offer of support. It breaks the little bit of control I have left as tears leak from the corners of my eyes.

"This is so stupid," I say, angrily swiping at my lashes. "I'm happy for her. It's what I wanted."

"I know." He sighs as if he hurts for what I'm going through. "Doesn't mean it's not hard letting go, even when it's the best thing."

I wipe the remaining moisture off my face. "You were really good with Jacob, by the way."

He shrugs. "I like kids."

"You do?" How is it that I learn something new about him every time we talk?

"Yeah. It's why I got my teaching certification." His brow lifts when I stare at him like my head just exploded. I think maybe it did. "I substitute a lot at the elementary school by my house."

"Don't you have to have a degree to do that?" Last I knew, Bryson made no attempt to go to college.

"Yes," he says in a tone that's more amused than offended. "And as of four years ago, I fall into that category."

My mind reels from this newest revelation. Bryson . . . teaching little kids. "What grade?"

"All of them. K through sixth. Wherever they need me."

"Wow. All this time I thought you were doing the band thing full-time."

Bryson snorts. "I'd be out on the streets if I relied on Black Carousel to pay my bills. Maybe one day we'll get there, but certainly not by booking a gig every few weeks."

I think back to how effortlessly Bryson engaged with Jacob. "Is that how you knew he would take so quickly to the harmonica?"

"Nah. That insight was unfortunately learned though the nuances of life." He averts his eyes, looking out at the bustling scene of gleeful children. "Music is a voice for the voiceless. Jacob said his mom went away, and I figured if his brother was getting a dog, why not give him something, as well."

"Divorce sucks," I say with a measure of heat.

"Yes, it does."

We stand there quietly for a few minutes, me contemplating how that one word has affected my adult life. Bryson contemplating . . . well, I don't know what. The two of us aren't close enough to surmise each other's thoughts. Although, for some reason, that fact bugs me today.

"I guess I should pack up." I look around the small area and realize there's really very little left to bring home. I sent the cooler full of dog food, toys, and grooming supplies with Sam's new family, so all that remains is my unopened folding chair.

Bryson leans down and swipes the small bag from the ground. "I'll walk you to your truck."

We move in tandem down the walking trail while I resist every urge to stop and cuddle with all the adorable animals.

"When did you realize you wanted to be a dog trainer?" he asks when we get through the thick of the chaos.

"College. Before that, I thought I wanted to be a veterinarian."

"Yes. That's right." Bryson laughs. "Remember when we'd play Treasure Island on the playground? You were always on the ship pretending to operate on sick parrots."

"And you were the pirate thief who was out to steal all the gold."

"Only because Cam would never let me play the hero," he grumbles.

"Gosh, that feels like forever ago." Memories come flooding back. "How many times did you walk the plank that summer?"

"At least a hundred."

Our laughter trails to silence as we reach the parking lot. My truck is two rows in and down to the very left.

I stop when we reach my driver's door. "Sometimes I wish I could wake up and do it all over again."

"Do what over again? Your childhood?" Bryson heaves the lawn chair over the side of the bed and lays it down.

"Maybe. I guess part of me wishes I'd made different choices."

"Like what?" He crosses his arms and leans his hip against the truck, his full attention narrowed on me.

I don't know why, but his question makes me squirm a little. Bryson is an intense person by nature, but there's something unnerving about his focusing on every word I say. Or maybe it's just that I've never shared something so personal with him before. Well, with anyone really, except maybe Cameron.

"I wish I hadn't spent so much time following all the rules. I wish I'd lived freer, like you."

He rears back as if slightly horrified by my comment. "You wish you had my life?"

"Not exactly your life. But in some ways, yes. I mean, when we were kids, you made being the thief look fun. And even now, you do what you want, when you want to. No apologies." I fall back against the truck and play with a piece of my hair. "I spent so long doing the 'right' things, making all the 'right' choices, and yet here I am: my parents' marriage imploded, my mission trip canceled, my apartment gone in a blink. I mean, what is the point of working and straining to hear God's will when in the end I'm just as lost as if I'd never tried in the first place?" I stare down at my shoes and kick at the gravel. Two steps forward, one step back. "Wouldn't it be easier if I just didn't care at all?"

"There's a lot of subtext with that question. Are you asking me if being a rebel worked in my favor, or are you mad that you couldn't bribe God with your good behavior?"

"I don't know what I'm asking or even what I'm saying." I kick the gravel some more. Watch as the dust rises and disappears into the air. "I just feel like a fool for playing by the rules my entire life with nothing to show for it. Maybe it's time to break out, do whatever I want to do, and stop waiting for some audible voice to make my decisions for me. Just look where I've ended up—confused and disappointed."

Bryson quietly digests my words, and the longer he doesn't say anything, the antsier I become.

"What are you thinking?" I finally demand.

"Honestly?"

"Yeah. I wouldn't have asked if I didn't want your opinion."

"Okay then. I think it's a slippery slope that you're on, and if you're not careful, you may end up doing something you regret." He walks over and opens my truck door for me. "You want to know what it's like to be a rebel? Well, Darcy, I truly hope you never have to find out."

I stare into his eyes and see there is so much he's not telling me. "That's not really an answer to my question."

"It's the best I've got." He jerks his head toward the door, a nonverbal command to get in the truck.

I comply even though I don't want to, which is my ongoing problem. Doing what I'm told, following orders. Well, maybe after this, I just won't do that anymore.

"I'll tell Charlie what a great kid Joshua is. You should feel proud of what you did here today."

My annoyance with Bryson's stubbornness fades slightly. "Thanks for coming. Sorry I unloaded on you."

"Don't worry about it." He smirks, and I'm thrown by how my stomach flips at the way it makes his eyes crinkle on the sides. "Next time we play Treasure Island, I'll save the parrots and you can be the thief."

"Promise?"

He doesn't answer but instead shuts my door and backs away with a small wave. I guess some things about Bryson will never change. There will always be that impenetrable layer of self-preservation. To hope for otherwise would only make me a bigger fool than I already am.

TWELVE

*T*he minute I walk in my apartment, I'm struck with another first for the century. Zoe is sitting on the couch, wearing a faded, oversized, wrinkled T-shirt and crying into a ball of tissues. And not only is her hair not styled to salon perfection, it doesn't look as if she bothered to brush it at all.

I quietly shut the door behind me. "Zoe, are you okay?"

She blows into her tissue and wipes at her fire-red nose. "Nate broke up with me." And then she starts crying again. "I knew something was up when he didn't come by last night, but I had no idea he wasn't happy." She drops her hands into her lap. "I did everything to make him happy. We went to the restaurants he preferred; I even watched his stupid sporting games." She grabs a new set of tissues and presses them to her eyes. "What is wrong with me?"

"Nothing," I quickly say, moving toward her. "Nate's an idiot." I don't exactly have a lot of experience in girl drama since our group was mostly guys, but I remember a very similar scene when Bryson broke up with Alison. And like then, my job as a friend is to list all the ways she is way better off without the scumbag, or whatever choice term she's using. Of

116

course, the Bryson who was Alison's ex-boyfriend is nothing like the Bryson I saw today.

"He's not an idiot. He was perfect for me. Successful, funny, cool. I should have tried harder to be what he wanted. I shouldn't have worked so much."

Zoe's obvious rose-colored glasses shake me out of the confusion that's haunted me since Bryson shut me away in my truck. Figuring out Bryson can come later. Right now, his poor sister needs a healthy dose of reality.

"No, Zoe, the perfect guy won't want you to be any different from who you are. The perfect guy will appreciate how generous and hardworking you are. And he won't be threatened by all your success."

"What success? I'm just a stupid assistant." She blows her nose. "Not even an assistant. An assistant to the assistant," she wails. "Everything I told you was a lie. Or wishful thinking, I guess. I don't get to make marketing decisions. I go for coffee runs and pick up ads from printers all over town. Nobody takes me seriously. Some even call me Workplace Barbie when they don't think I can hear them."

I press my lips together to avoid laughing.

"See, even you think that's all I am."

And now the guilt slides in, because that was exactly how I'd stereotyped her in my head. "I admit I may have thought that when we first interacted, but I don't anymore. And if they would take two seconds to talk to you and get past their own insecurities, they'd see how great you are, too."

Zoe shakes her head miserably. "It's been a year. I'm never going to change their minds."

"Then stop trying to. You're beautiful and blond. That doesn't make you stupid or give them the right to make you feel less for it. We can't spend our whole lives worrying about how some random person perceives us."

"I guess you're right. I mean, being called Barbie isn't the worst insult in the world. She is famous after all." Zoe sniffles and then seems to notice what I'm wearing for the first time. "You look really cute, by the way."

I chuckle because that's the first thing she's said that actually sounds like Zoe. "See, someone did listen to you, and look what you accomplished. Sam got adopted by the very first family that walked by our section."

"Really? You're not just saying that to make me feel better?"

"Nope. Your plan totally worked. Even Bryson said we looked like we could grace the cover of a canine magazine."

"Well, of course Bryson said that, he's had—" She stops herself abruptly. "I need chocolate. Nate had a thing about me eating sweets. He was all stressed out that I'd get fat."

Wow. This guy was a real winner. "Zoe, from everything you've described, I'd say Nate is lucky you gave him the time of day to begin with."

"He is lucky, isn't he?" She scoots her tissue into a big pile. "You should have seen his last girlfriend. Her teeth were like fangs, and she reeked of cheap perfume. I'm the hottest girl he's ever going to get."

Not really what I meant, but . . . baby steps. "You're far more than just a pretty face, Zoe. You cook, you're excellent at makeovers, and you've managed to charm Piper, and she's a very good judge of character."

At the mention of her name, Piper pokes her head up from underneath the mound of Kleenex. Zoe picks her up and nuzzles her with her nose. "Piper is pretty awesome."

Yes, and she unfortunately has way too much experience with tissues and tears.

"What do you say we order a slew of junk food and watch hours of cheesy romantic comedies?" I offer.

"I'd say heck yeah!" She sits and lifts her chin like there might actually be hope for the evening. "You know, I wasn't sure what to expect when Bryson asked me to let you move in, but I have to say, it's nothing like I anticipated. I mean, look at us. We're polar opposites."

"Agreed."

"Yet somehow, in just five minutes, you made me feel better than my mom has in twenty-three years." She picks up a book from the end table and shows it to me. "This was her idea of a pep talk."

I study the cover. The title *Take Control* runs from corner to corner in bright red. "Is this for work?"

"No. That might actually have been helpful. This gem is the fourth in a series of books she's given me on self-assurance, which is totally hypocritical coming from her, since she cares so much about what others think that she waxes her legs, even in winter. And who is she kidding about taking control? My dad controls her like a puppeteer." Zoe tosses the book onto the floor, a physical representation of her disgust for the subject. "I swore I'd never become her and that's exactly what I let Nate do."

I don't say a word. There's no need to when Zoe's seeing the truth likely for the very first time.

She shakes her head. "This probably seems really immature to you."

"It doesn't, actually. We all go through a time when we question who we are or where we're going. You're lucky you see it at twenty-three. If I had at your age, I wouldn't be crashing in your second bedroom, trying to figure out where it all went wrong."

"Well then, it sounds like junk food is exactly what we both need tonight." She stands, empowered. "You are going to rock your next dog-adoption fair, just like you did this one. And I'm going to rule my next relationship. Girl power." She offers me a fist bump I have no ability to ignore and return the gesture. "Oh, and before I forget, I have something for you." She eases around the coffee table and waves at me to follow her.

Zoe's bedroom wasn't part of the original tour, nor has she invited me into the space before now. The room's a mess, which is nice to see considering she keeps the rest of the apartment immaculate. Clothes hide half of the floor; her sheets and comforter are thrown to the side as if she intentionally left them disheveled. I take one step over the threshold, hoping this is what Zoe wanted. I hear her riffling through her walk-in closet but hesitate to enter her bathroom to get there.

Instead, I take advantage of the invitation and fully examine the space. There's a half-full water bottle on the nightstand next to the journal I found buried in the laundry room drawer. Any question as to whether or not those words I read were hers has been answered.

"Zoe?" I call and step closer to her bathroom.

"One sec. I'm almost done." Her voice is muffled but clear enough to stop me from following it.

I lean against the doorframe, noticing the artwork on her walls. They aren't pictures but letters artistically painted in different sizes and directions. The word is hard to make out at first, but soon I follow the pattern: *Forgive*.

Tears are drawn as droplets from the last *e* and fill the bottom of the frame with a pool of dark water. Five other art pieces cover her walls. I step closer to the next one, determined to find the hidden word in that one, as well.

"Okay, this should be it."

I jump back as Zoe emerges from her bathroom with an armload of clothes.

"What's all this?"

"Yours." She continues through her room and back into the hallway. "I paid attention when we went shopping, and you and I are practically the same size."

I have no choice but to follow her again since her destination is becoming apparent: my bedroom. "Zoe, I have clothes. You don't need to give me half your wardrobe."

She snorts. "Girl, this is not half. This is one tiny corner, and it's all stuff I'll never wear again." When she finally makes it to my bedroom, the pile is transported from her arms to the center of my bed. "It's mostly jeans, a few sundresses, and shirts that are casual without being dumpy. Basically, I stuck to your carefree style and simply elevated it a little."

"Zoe . . ."

She spins around and crosses her arms. "Look, if you wanted the clothes in your storage unit, you would have gotten them by now. But you haven't. And maybe you will, and maybe you won't, but in the meantime, you can have options."

I massage my temples, my head suddenly throbbing. Zoe isn't completely out of line. I haven't wanted to go into that storage unit, though it has nothing to do with hating my wardrobe and everything to do with hating how it represents my failure.

"Girl power, remember? Part of that is helping each other feel better. You need to stop hiding behind fraying clothes that are a decade old." When I don't say anything, her arms drop and her voice becomes a plea. "Just promise me you'll try them on. I only picked ones I thought would look really good on your body type."

I chuckle because there's no use arguing with her. Call Zoe what you will, but she certainly does make life a lot more interesting. "Fine. I'll wear the new clothes . . . when practical," I clarify. "If . . . you promise me you'll never change who you are for a guy again. That means no weird vegetable diets because some jerk is superficial enough to worry about your dress size." The more I think about Nate, the angrier I get. "Stay true to you. That's my bargain."

Zoe swallows, and I can tell she's fighting back tears. I expect her to argue or at a minimum defend her choices. Instead, she walks over and hugs me, tightly and with purpose.

I'm affectionate by nature, my whole family is, but I get a sense that neither Zoe nor Bryson had that luxury while growing up. This hug feels too wrapped in need to be something commonly received.

"It's all going to be okay," I say, rubbing her back the way my mom used to rub mine when I was little. "I know it doesn't feel like it, but it's all going to be okay."

They're the same words I've been telling myself for weeks now. Maybe one day I'll believe them, too.

THIRTEEN

Zoe's already gone when I wake up on Sunday morning. So are the awful vegetable drinks, which means she's hopefully sticking to our bargain. I found a six-pack of them in the trash when I poured my second cup of coffee.

Normally, I'd be getting ready at this time, eagerly anticipating morning worship at the church I grew up in, but something in me refuses to go today. Maybe my inner rebel is coming out after all.

Besides, I need to get out to Charlie's and start working with the other dogs. Sam was a win, but an easy one. The others are going to take far more time and discipline. Starting with Bentley. If I don't get his jumping under control, there's no way I can place him in a home with children. And this dog, more than any other, needs lots and lots of playtime.

The drive to Charlie's has become routine now, so much so that I no longer need Bryson's hand-drawn directions or the barely there bar on my phone. I don't even have to slam on my brakes anymore to make the turn into Charlie's sharp driveway, which is a good thing since I practically fishtailed the first time I took this route without Bryson's help.

Louie's barking penetrates through the windows the minute I cut the engine. The edge of fear in his bark means more to me now that I know his history. Ms. Elledge was able to find information on both Penny and Louie, but not the others. Penny's story is one I've heard too many times to count. A family bought a breed of dog they didn't do the research on and was later surprised to learn that dog behaved as nature intended. After crating and neglecting Penny for a year, they tried to surrender her to a no-kill shelter. By then, her temperament had become so fierce, the shelter declined and she ended up at the local pound. Sue Ann kept her number on file with the front desk for just such an occasion and picked Penny up the next day.

Louie is an entirely different story and especially heartbreaking. Ms. Elledge thinks he's two years old, but they don't know for sure. The first family who found him said he'd been dumped in the country and showed up on their property searching for food and water. She wrote that she suspected he was repeatedly abused prior to the dump. His fur was patchy, his paws were split, and he walked with a limp. The first family was scared of him, but their neighbor knew Great Danes were gentle giants and found him a home versus calling Animal Control. Unfortunately, that home had no training for Louie's erratic behavior. So for six months he'd been sent to one place after another, until a friend of a friend called Sue Ann for help. At that point, Louie had been in seven different homes, and despite knowing she was going into surgery, Sue Ann didn't have the heart to refuse him a stable environment.

It's weird. I never knew Charlie's wife, and yet I feel her loss every time I step foot onto this property.

Louie's barking is joined by Bentley's when I emerge from around the house. Bentley seems especially agitated today, but

I imagine it's because Sam is no longer next door. "Sorry, buddy, but I promise she found a great place to live, just like you will." I stop at his kennel and he leaps forward, his paws punishing the posts that are already bent. He waits for me to pet him, but I refuse. "Down," I say forcefully. He doesn't get down. Instead, he barks in my face, a way to prove he's still the alpha.

I leave him there and start getting the food bowls ready. I do Louie's first, mostly because I'm one to get the hard stuff out of the way. As he has since I took over his care, Louie darts to the side of his doghouse the minute I touch the latch on his gate. The space is only a few feet wide and butts up to the back corner, but the tight fit seems to give him an extra measure of security.

"Now, how are we going to get to know each other if you keep yelling at me?" I ask him in my most calm and tender voice. His bark gets more severe, but I expected as much.

Like Bentley, Louie's food and water are in gravity-controlled feeders. They should require filling at least every three days, but Louie barely eats enough to stay alive, so once again they don't need any filling. My stomach curls at the thought of him starving himself. Abused, abandoned, passed off again and again. Of course this poor dog is traumatized. Who wouldn't be?

"Alright, Louie, we're going to try something new today." This exercise isn't a cure, by any means, but it will show him I'm not a threat. And while I know in my heart he's not either, I prop the gate open just in case I need a quick escape.

Ever so slowly, I lower myself to the ground in a position my mom used to call crisscross applesauce. The barking escalates and he's added a growl in there, as well. An extra warning for me to stay away. "It's okay. I'm just going to sit right here. You and I have to learn to trust each other."

The barking continues with a quicker cadence. I can tell he's getting tired, so I just sit there and wait, taking the opportunity to examine him fully.

Louie's blue markings are nearly perfect, except for a white patch at his toes. His light-gray fur is thinner than I'd like to see, and his protruding rib cage confirms his poor eating. His elbows are marred with scar tissue, which is common for Danes but excessive on him. He likely spent many months on concrete without any bed. His head is nicely shaped, square with a thick jaw. Even with the continual barking, I can tell his jowls are huge.

"Something tells me you're a big slobberer, huh?" We used to get a lot of Great Danes in our salon, not for a grooming but to clip their nails and clean out their ears. Louie's head is bigger than any I've seen, and his size is pretty exceptional, too, especially since he won't stop growing for another few months. "I bet you're already thirty-four inches at the shoulder. What do you think?" I pause to see if he'll react in any way, but he continues to yelp, his voice growing hoarser.

"I'm not leaving until you calm down, so if I were you, I'd save all that energy for tomorrow, because we're going to be doing this exercise until you stop barking at me."

This close, the noise echoes in my head like a clanging gong, but I push through, knowing this dog has suffered far worse than I am in these seven minutes.

Louie finally drops his hindquarters in a tense seated position.

"Now, that's not so bad. Just stop shouting and I'll let you be all by yourself."

Another excruciating five minutes pass until finally there's a short pause between each bark. He slides his front paws forward and eventually drops to his elbows, his stomach flat on the ground. The pauses get longer and longer, and then finally Louie lays his head between his front paws and only lifts it to bark three more times before going silent. His torso is manically constricting in and out, so I know he's still agitated, but at least he can sense he's not in immediate danger.

I continue to sit, relishing the stillness. My back aches and my tailbone has gone numb, but it's all worth it. Louie is staring at me, examining me the same way I did him earlier. Louie's eyes are an especially vivid blue, and his ears, though clipped, were likely not trained as long as they should have been. The tip of the right one flops over periodically, giving him a much less intimidating profile.

"You're quite the beauty. It probably saved your life. People tend to keep the pretty pets."

He sighs like he agrees with me, and I can't help but smile. I know I can help him. I know it so clearly that it makes my stomach twist and my heart rate spike. Me and dogs; I don't know why God gave us a bond, but He did.

"Okay, buddy, I'm going to get up now. Nice and easy." I move my legs first and freeze when he growls. I give him a few seconds to calm again before pushing myself to my feet along the fence. Louie stands, too, and soon the barking starts back up.

I temper my frustration as I close his gate and force myself to focus on the small victory. He didn't bark for two minutes with me inside his kennel. It's minor, but it's something.

Bentley runs along his cage as I pass by him again, eagerly awaiting his turn. "I'll get to you, but I need to take care of the other two first." Plus, it's good for him to wait. He wants to be in charge, and there's no way I can properly direct his behavior if I let him win.

I do my usual courtesy knock and let myself in the back door. "Charlie, I'm here to feed the dogs."

The routine grunt doesn't come. Instead, a much younger, much more familiar voice answers. "Go right ahead."

Bryson's here? I glance out the window looking for his truck, but there's only a small Toyota Corolla in the driveway.

I quickly take care of Penny, who tries to nip at my hand while I unlatch her cage. She's unruly today as if she, too, can sense that another change has taken place. Turns out that Sam didn't just calm my anxiety but all theirs, as well.

After two running laps around the barn and a near catastrophe when Penny's leash slipped out of my grip and she hightailed it for Bentley's kennel, I get her back in her crate and vow to bring some toys with me next time. The only time Penny isn't snapping at something is when she has some loud and squishy object in her mouth. Go figure.

I wash my dirt-stained fingers in the kitchen sink and grab a paper towel from the holder. I dry my hands, wipe my face, and try to figure out why I suddenly feel butterflies in my stomach. Maybe it's Bryson's presence, or maybe it's just the idea of seeing Charlie now that Sam is gone. Yeah. I'm going with the Charlie theory. The other is too confusing to consider.

Both men are on the couch, hunched over and watching a small laptop. I pause when the voice I've listened to every Sunday for the past six years echoes from the speakers. Pastor Thomas.

Quietly, I move around the living room until I'm standing behind them, watching the same thing they are—a livestream video of today's worship service.

Guilt gnaws at my chest. Unlike Charlie, who's still in the throes of grief, I really have no excuse to skip except my own stubbornness.

Bryson turns around and acknowledges my presence with a small lift of his chin. It brings another wave of guilt because I can see the question in his expression. Why am I here when I should be there? Even worse, he knows the answer because I practically spelled out my rebellion in the parking lot yesterday.

I slip back around the couch and ignore how Bryson's gaze follows me across the room.

Macey's tail wags when I clip a leash onto her collar. She's peppier today, and I wonder if it's the result of Bryson being here, or maybe it's simply that Charlie is dressed in real clothes and not the robe and sweats he's been wearing all week.

I tug on her collar and guide her out of the room and into the backyard. Pastor Thomas is preaching on obedience this morning, and right now that's the last thing I want to hear.

FOURTEEN

By the time the back door screeches open and Bryson emerges from the house, I'm so frustrated with Bentley that I nearly scream.

"How's it going out here?"

"Terrible." As if he feels the need to show him what I mean, Bentley lunges toward Bryson, nearly pulling my arm out of its socket. "I can't get him to listen to me because he's too busy trying to go after all the things he's not able to chase while in the kennel." I get my footing, and now Bentley is the one who's running and running with no forward progress. "I need a smaller yard. One without trees and squirrels running everywhere." Bryson chuckles at my misery, and I throw him a hot glare I usually reserve for my brother. "It's not funny."

"I'm sorry," he says, pressing his lips together to stop the ongoing smile. "It's just rare to see you so frazzled. Especially with an animal in your grip."

"Bentley is no ordinary animal. He's a tank. A stubborn, bullheaded, will-not-listen-to-anything tank." I look down at my boots, which are covered with Bentley's muddy paw prints. Failure, once again. "I don't know, Bryson, maybe I was too confident. Maybe I can't—"

"There's no second-guessing now. You made a promise. To Charlie and to these dogs."

I look up at him, relieved he doesn't give me an out, but feel no less defeated. "Then what am I supposed to do? I can't train him here."

"We'll go to my place. Small backyard. No trees. And if he ruins something, it's no big deal because half my stuff needs an upgrade anyways."

I consider the offer. It could work, and at this point I'm willing to try anything. "Any idea how we're going to get this beast to stay in the back of my truck?"

"Let me look. Sue Ann had plenty of supplies. I'm just not exactly sure where she put them." He darts into the barn while I continue to wrestle with Bentley's leash. Minutes later, Bryson returns carrying a large metal crate that will easily hold a massive yellow Lab.

"And you said you never play the hero," I tease, following him.

"No, I said Cam never *let* me play the hero." He slides the crate into the bed of my truck and opens the latch on the crate's small door. "Two very different things."

I guide an eager Bentley over to the tailgate, and it takes no prodding for him to leap up into the cage. He's obviously done this sort of thing before and enjoyed it. I give him a treat all the same when he lies down and lock the crate up so there's no chance of his flying out the back.

"Why did you always let him win?" I'm curious because I've never considered Cam to be dominant, especially with Bryson.

"I don't know. I guess some things are worth the fight and others aren't." He pauses and rests his elbow on the truck. "Back then, there was so much turmoil at home. I didn't want any on the playground. And besides . . ." He pushes off and studies me with that superior smirk I'm starting to think is more defensive than arrogant. "Every good story needs a villain, and I'm an expert at playing one."

Guilt returns again but for a very different reason. I judged Zoe without truly knowing or understanding her. Every day I'm learning I've done the same thing with her brother . . . for years now. "If you say so." I toss my keys to Bryson and hop into the passenger seat. Maybe it's time to fix both of those mistakes.

The headway Bentley makes in Bryson's backyard is staggering. In only an hour, I managed to get him to sit, stay, and even take a pig ear without mauling me.

Now I get to bask in the glory of my progress while Bentley gnaws vapidly at his treat in the corner of the yard.

The screen door opens, and Bentley looks up once but then quickly returns to his mission.

"I thought you might be thirsty." Bryson holds two large glasses of iced tea, and I eagerly accept the gift.

"I am. Thank you."

He leans lazily against one of the overhang posts and watches the now-calm canine. "Wow. I don't think I've ever seen him not moving."

"Food is a very good motivator."

"True." He holds his sweating glass to his chest and leans his head against the post, his eyes closing. "It's nice out here today." It's so rare to see Bryson still that I can't help but watch him more than anything in the yard. The black is still there, covering his torso and legs, and today more than ever it feels like a shield instead of a part of him. Bryson's always

132

had a quiet strength about him, but lately it's the hidden
things I see more. The loneliness, the self-deprecation, and
that same quiet need his sister has that he never expresses.

"I heard you playing inside. Is that a new song?"

His eyes open as if he's forgotten I'm out here with him.
"Yeah. No lyrics yet, but I can't seem to get the melody out of
my head."

"I liked it." And I really did. It was soft and gentle, unlike
anything I've heard him play before. "I think Bentley did,
too. He seemed to behave a little better when the music was
going."

"Nice to know." Bryson shifts so his back is against the
post, and his eyes are now focused on me. "It's always a good
sign when a dog doesn't feel the need to howl in agony at one
of my songs."

"Play him Cameron's new one. I'm sure the reaction
would be very different." Bryson tenses the moment the last
word leaves my lips, and I want to kick myself. They aren't
just Cam's songs, they're Black Carousel's now, too. "Sorry. I
didn't mean to be insulting."

"Yes, you did," he says plainly. "Though I can't understand
why. I think it's the most honest thing he's ever written."

I shake my head, the lyrics coming back with horrible clarity. "Nothing in that song reminds me of Cameron."

"Then maybe you don't know him as well as you think you
do."

I stare up at Bryson. His head is blocking the sun, leaving
his features shadowed. It bugs me. I can't read the sudden
shift in his tone or his expression. "I know him. Maybe not
this new version that's popped up since you guys got back
from touring. But the real Cameron, I know."

Bryson sits, not on the swing next to me like before but

133

in the chair farthest away. He was like that in the truck, too. Distant, though more emotionally than physically. "Ever notice how no matter what we're talking about, Cam seems to slip into the conversation?"

I open my mouth to protest, then close it because he's right. "I guess he's always been the link between us, even though we've known each other for nearly as long."

Bryson sets down his drink and puts his elbows on his knees. "Let's try for the next ten minutes to talk about something that doesn't include your best friend."

"Okay." Though even as I agree, I feel my head swimming with confusion. Everything in my life is linked to Cam in one way or another. Everything except . . . "Zoe and Nate broke up yesterday."

"Nate?" He tilts his head like I'm confusing him. "I thought she was dating Sean or John or something like that."

"Nope. Nate. And why, I couldn't tell you because everything she described was disgusting."

"Sounds like every boyfriend she's ever had." He shakes his head. "My sister is notorious for picking losers. Then again, she has my stepdad for a father, so it makes sense." The spark of anger in his tone is hard to miss.

"Yeah, she mentioned her dad . . ." I hesitate because I'm not sure if our conversation was supposed to be confidential or not. Then again, Bryson lived it, so I wouldn't really be telling him something he doesn't already know. "She said he could be controlling."

"That's the understatement of the century," he grunts. "But money is money, and both my mom and Zoe let him rule with it. He pays for that apartment, you know, and her car and everything else she could possibly desire. I keep hoping at some point she'll wise up and get out from under his fist."

His voice rises with his conviction and lowers again when he looks at me. "Why is it that our parents can have such a profound effect on us even now?"

"If I knew the answer to that, I wouldn't be hiding out here, trying to kill enough time to avoid Sunday night dinner with my mom and her new boyfriend."

"You don't like him?"

"I don't just not like him." I look down at my fingers. "I hate him. Or maybe I hate the idea of him, I don't know. The two are impossible to separate right now." The same indignation I've been struggling with all day rears its ugly head again. "For months I've been the dutiful daughter, walking on eggshells, holding in all the things I wanted to say because my mom was too broken to hear them. And now, when I'm the one who needs support and guidance, all she wants to do is talk about her new love interest, who, by the way, is nothing like my dad." I tug my phone viciously from my pocket and hold up the screen. "Three texts in the last fifteen minutes. *Michael's grilling. What kind of steak do you want? Can you pick up A1 on your way over?*" I shove it back in my pocket. "She just assumes I'll go. Because that's what I've always done. Well, you know what? I'm sick and tired of doing what people expect me to do." My arms cross in staunch determination. "I'm not going. Not tonight, and maybe not ever again."

Bryson listens, not moving or saying a word, just like he did yesterday. And like then, I want to rip out his voice box and demand a response.

"If that's all you have to say, maybe we should go back to talking about Cameron." I don't mean to sound resentful when the words come out, but part of me is. Bryson keeps opening this door of honesty in me, and once I say all the horrible things I'm feeling, I can no longer deny they exist.

His brows pinch together. "Why does my quietness bother you so much?"

"Because I can't read you. I don't know if you're judging me, or if you agree with me, or if you understand at all."

"I understand. A little too much." He bolts up and returns to the spot by the post, as if all the things running through his head are forcing him to move. "I just feel inadequate to offer you any kind of advice, except to say don't do what I did when I was faced with the same crossroads."

"What did you do?"

"I cut them off."

"Completely?" As much as my mom frustrates me, I couldn't imagine not talking to her.

"Yep."

My heart squeezes for the boy I know still exists under all that armor. "Why?"

He crosses his arms against his chest. "How much has Cam told you about why I moved in with him our senior year?"

"Nothing really. It was a simple, 'Hey, by the way, Bryson lives here now,' and that was it."

Bryson chuckles. "You sound just like him."

"I've had a lot of practice." And once again my best friend springs up between us. Maybe it's becoming both of our defense mechanisms. Well, not today. "Why did you move out?"

"I didn't move out. He kicked me out." Bryson pauses, his eyes meeting mine. A vulnerability, totally out of character for him, leaks through his stare. It whittles into my chest, makes me want to leap from my spot on the swing and erase all the pain he's gone through. "We never got along. Ever. I hated him from the first day I met him, and that opinion did not change over time. The only thing that did change was my size

136

and my attitude, and once I couldn't be physically bullied, he moved on to controlling me through other means—money." His fist closes and opens again. "It worked for a while, especially when he showed up with that incredible truck on my seventeenth birthday."

I remember that weekend. Bryson drove up to the church like he owned the universe, and to most in our group, he did. I was the only one who refused to gush over something so insignificant, especially when it only seemed to rot away at his character. "What happened?"

"Not one particular thing." He shrugs. "It was more an awakening to the fact that I, too, had been bought off by this man I despised. This man who would shake hands with people at church and act like he was so strong in his faith. He'd hug my mom like she was his soulmate when people were around and then belittled everything she did at home. Insulting her. Mocking her. He was a fraud, our life a smoke screen dictated by what he wanted the world to think of us. And my playing the obedient stepson was all part of the image." Bryson tugs at the back of his neck. "It took four months of my calling him out on all his crap before he snapped.

"It was a random school night. Nothing special. He was badgering me about rinsing out my cereal bowl, and I made some snide comment about how it must be nice to have his wife bought and paid for so he didn't have to lift a finger. Just a stupid teenage comment that was really more insulting to my mom than to him, but it was the last straw. He exploded. Then I exploded. And just when I thought the guy was going to bury his fist into my face, he turned away and stormed out of the room." He pauses, and I'm sure he's picturing the moment in full color. I can see it in the set of his shoulders, in the way his stance has moved into a defensive position. "I thought we were done, but then he came rushing back through the living room with my guitar in his hand. He threw it on the lawn, along with everything he knew mattered to me at the time. He said if I couldn't respect him and his rules, then I could figure out how to live without them." Bryson's jaw clenches. "I had ten dollars in my wallet and a quarter tank of gas. He knew it, too. He wanted to see me beg him to stay." His eyes get dark, the anger pushing through. "To this day, I've never stepped foot into that house again. I picked up my things, loaded the truck, and never looked back."

Nausea rolls in my stomach. I knew the relationship between Bryson and his stepdad was strained, but this is way beyond normal conflict. I think back to Bryson's music, to the songs I've never understood or appreciated till now, because even though that event took place over a decade ago, his lyrics prove that rejected seventeen-year-old kid still haunts the man he's become.

He starts to speak again, to correlate the story to my situation, but I can't register anything about that now. I'm too busy standing, too busy closing the gap between us, until my arms are wrapped around him in a hug I know he needs as much as his sister did.

I press my check to his chest and squeeze, though he's made no effort to respond besides turning to stone next to me.

"What are you doing?" There's a hint of fear in his voice that makes me even more determined to shatter the wall he lives behind.

"Hugging you."

"Why?"

"Because that story breaks my heart. And I think it broke yours, too."

He tries to wrestle free. "It was twelve years ago. I've recovered."

I squeeze tighter. "Well, I haven't, and right now I need to be held, even if you don't."

My last words seem to break the remaining resistance. Bryson's hands slide to my waist and then land around my back. The surrender is immediate. I feel it in his muscles, his chest, even in the way he sighs like he's lost whatever fight he has left. For three blissful seconds, we stay there, holding each other in an innocent bond of friendship. And then, like it did the last time we dared to touch, a spark eliminates all chance of platonic denial.

Only this time, instead of letting go, Bryson's body takes the lead, his legs brushing against mine, his arms tightening like a ratchet moving me closer to him.

My nerve endings flare as awareness takes over every inch. His nose nuzzling my hair, his breath caressing my neck, his heartbeat matching mine in unfamiliar cadence.

"Do you feel better?" he whispers, his words offering me a way out while his body pulls me closer.

I should say yes and let go, but I don't want to. I want to inhale the scent of him, to wonder what his touch feels like on bare skin, to lift my head and feel our lips—

Two sharp paws slam into my hip, carrying the full force of a giant Lab. Gravity takes over as momentum pushes us sideways, forcing separation as we scramble not to fall. Bryson's successful. Me, not so much. My elbow bangs against an unsuspecting chair as my knee scrapes along the hard concrete. Bryson's last-minute attempt to catch me breaks the worst of the impact but doesn't stop the stinging pain of broken skin.

"No jump!" I growl, trying to find my footing despite the obnoxious animal standing over me.

Slobber rolls down Bentley's tongue and lands on my forearm. He's smiling at me like he did me a favor, and maybe he
did. Ten more seconds and who knows how much of a fool I
might have made of myself. "Stupid dog," I say, half laughing
as I use his collar to pull myself to my feet.

"You okay?" Bryson's not laughing. In fact, he looks ready
to strangle the poor dog at my side.

"I'm fine. More annoyed than hurt." I rub at the scratches
that are peppered with red droplets of blood. Minor injury considering I was completely upended. "Sorry. I about
took you with me." I drop my arm and force a casual smile.
"Thanks for, um, appeasing me. And for your advice. I think I
will go to dinner tonight."

He watches me carefully as if he knows I've just mini-
mized this moment between us. If it bothers him, I can't tell.
He already has a smirk in place. "That's the shortest-lived
rebellion I've ever witnessed."

"Who says it's over?" Bentley pushes his wet nose against
my thigh, and I instinctively reach down and scratch at his
neck. "Maybe I'm just pressing pause for a juicy piece of
steak." I smile up at Bryson, ignoring the way my pulse still
races or the way I catch just a hint of disappointment in his
eyes.

"You did say food was a good motivator to behave."

Before I can agree, Bentley barks twice as if to concur and
demand his prize. I squat down and rub his head affectionately.
"Nice try, ol' boy, but you and I still have a lot of work to do."

FIFTEEN

*I*t's not the steak that brings me here, as I claimed. It's not even Bryson's story or his obvious regrets about severing ties with his mom, though those did have an impact. No, I'm here because it's not easy to break a twenty-nine-year habit of surrendering to expectations.

I mash on the doorbell and wait for my mom's call to come in. It never comes. Instead, the door opens and I'm greeted by a man who has no business answering my childhood front door.

"Darcy, hey, perfect timing! I was just asking your mom how you like your steak cooked, and she was guessing medium-well." Michael's wearing a long black apron that says *Barbecue King* and holding an unopened Coke bottle he very likely just pulled from the fridge. My dad's fridge. My dad's grill, too.

"Medium," I say, though I'm still reeling from Michael opening the door as if he's the new man of the house.

"Great. I will make a note for the future." He says *future* like it's a foregone conclusion, and immediately my nerves bristle. I thought I could do this again, but now I'm not so

141

sure. Having Cameron as the buffer last week made a bigger difference than I realized. I wait for him to move so I can enter the house. Instead, he glances over my head and waves. "Hey, Mrs. Snyder. How's Henry doing?"

I turn around and gape as my notoriously grumpy neighbor, the very one who used to chase me and my brother from her yard with a broomstick, beams at the man in the doorway.

"So much better, Michael. Thank you for coming over so quickly."

Michael moves past me and down the driveway. "Anytime." He gives her a quick side hug. "And you tell him to stay off that ladder from now on. I'm just a few feet away, okay?"

A few feet? I nearly choke on the words. How much time is Michael spending here?

I leave the two of them to their lovefest and walk inside the house like a detective. A pair of reading glasses I don't recognize sit on the end table by Dad's recliner, along with a book my mom would never read. I consider going into Mom's room but realize I really don't want to know how serious they've gotten.

"Mom?" I call with a shaky voice as I check the kitchen and laundry room. I open the back door and find her on a lounge chair, sporting a very revealing swimsuit she would have never let me wear while growing up. Her hair is piled on her head, shades cover her eyes, and AirPods fill her ears.

"Mom." I practically have to shout before she finally reacts, sitting up with a jolt.

She gently pulls the white earbud out of her left ear. "Oh, hey, honey. Did you get the A1 sauce?"

I show her the bottle, still having no idea how to stomach Michael's new comfort level in my childhood home. Random dates were one thing, but this . . . this feels much too permanent.

Mom swings her legs over the chair so she's sitting. "You look upset, honey. Is something wrong?"

Before I find the courage to answer with the truth, the back door opens and closes.

"Well now, that was quite a blessing." Michael emerges holding a cookie sheet with three seasoned chunks of raw meat. "I was telling Mrs. Snyder about Dexter's recommendation on the ski resort in Utah. Her daughter lives up there and knows the owners. She promised to get us a family discount." He turns to me. "We're taking Dexter's family skiing this fall. You should join us."

My mouth literally hangs open. "You've been talking to my brother?"

Michael misreads my tone and chuckles like I'm somehow happy with the news. "Yeah, he gave me the third degree until we realized we have all the same hobbies."

"It was quite funny." My mom carefully makes her way over to Michael's side, and for some reason it feels like a choice. Him instead of me. "Dexter calls now more than he ever has. I think he likes Michael more than he likes me."

"Not possible," Michael adds in a sickeningly sweet tone.

Mom smiles up at him and rubs his back with her hand. "Do you need any help?"

"Not at all, beautiful. You relax and let me do the hard labor." He leans down and kisses her right in front of me, and it's the final break to my control.

I suddenly don't care that Bryson hasn't talked to his mom in twelve years. In fact, right now I welcome the idea. I look between my mom and her new boyfriend and feel complete clarity. No matter how nice he tries to be, or how many gourmet dishes he tries to make me, there is one thing he will never be able to do. He will never be able to replace my dad.

"I'm sorry, but I have to go," I say and set down the A1 bottle on the closest flat surface. I'm back in the house seconds later and halfway through the living room when I feel my mom's hand around my arm.

"Darcy, what is going on? Why are you leaving?"

I turn around, and gone are the shades covering her now very concerned eyes. "Sunday nights are supposed to be for family, Mom. *Family*. That's why I come every week. Not so I can play nice with your new boyfriend."

"But I thought you liked Michael."

I close my eyes because I have no idea how to express what I'm feeling, especially to her. "Aren't you the tiniest bit concerned about how fast this is moving? He's here every time I call; he's cooking, answering the door, making vacation plans with Dexter. He's rooted himself in your life, and you hardly know him."

"I know him better than I ever knew your father," she says unapologetically. "He's kind, considerate, and has never cheated."

Her words are a slap across the face, and I look away because it suddenly hurts to breathe.

A gentle touch lands on both of my arms. "Darcy, you have to let go of this fantasy that your dad is ever coming back. He's not, nor do I want him to. We don't love each other anymore."

"Do you love me?" The question catches in my throat.

"You know the answer to that."

Maybe I do, but it doesn't lessen the spear in my heart. I feel lost and alone, as if no one understands or cares how much it still hurts that Dad is gone. The family I'd known and counted on my entire life no longer exists.

"Come back outside. Spend some time with him, try having a real conversation, and then maybe you'll see why—"

"This isn't about Michael!" I yell for the first time since my parents sat me down and told me the news. "You're happy and I'm glad you are, but I'm not, okay? I'm not happy seeing another man sit in Daddy's chair or cook on his grill. It hurts me, every single time. And maybe I'm the one who's wrong here. Maybe I need to do the growing up, but I don't know how to do that. All I know is that I need my mom and dad, and I don't recognize either of you right now." Mom drops her hand, and I back away, hating that I'm hurting her but also knowing it's the only option for me right now. "I need time. Time to figure out how to cope with this new reality. And I can't do that while you're acting as if everything is rainbows and butterflies. I'm sorry, Mom, but I just can't."

"I knew you were angry with your father. I guess I didn't want to see that you were angry with me, too." Tears snag on her eyelashes.

I shake my head. "Mom . . . I'm angry at everything right now." It's the most honest I can be, and it's enough for her to nod and let me leave, even though I know she doesn't want to.

On the edge of completely breaking down, I flee from the house that's no longer mine and run to my old faithful truck, slamming the driver's door as hard as I can. The steering wheel gets my next dose of fury. I punch it, once, twice, four times until my knuckles burn from the contact.

The pain doesn't help.

I set my forehead on the steering wheel as those cursed tears that never stop flow down my cheeks once again. How, after twenty-nine years of life, am I in this place? What did I do to deserve this for my life? I've been good. Kind to people. I prayed, went to church, went out of my way to make people feel loved and welcome. "I did everything right," I cry out.

Once again, no answers are given. No explanations or comfort.

Instead, a new feeling creeps in, though to call it a feeling is a stretch. It's more like a void, a numbness that seeps into my limbs, climbing into the chambers of my heart.

Emptiness replaces the anger and the hurt, and somehow, the nothing feels a whole lot better.

SIXTEEN

*T*he next five days are an exercise in avoidance. Me avoiding my mom's cautious, are-you-ready-to-talk-yet texts, and Bryson apparently avoiding me, though I'm not sure why.

He's been cordial enough, still allowing me to use his backyard for Bentley's training. But the first day I came back, he hung outside for five minutes, hardly looked me in the eye, and then bolted. The second time, he simply texted that he'd left the gate open for me.

It's probably a good thing. My growing desire for his friendship is more than unnerving. I've longed to talk to him about my mom and what went down at dinner. I want his advice and maybe even help understanding how I suddenly feel nothing toward either of my parents. Crazier yet is that I haven't shared any of what happened with Cameron. Not that I've seen him much either. In fact, this past week has felt more isolating than any to date.

Maybe that's why I all but begged Cameron to call his brother to let me come over to socialize Bentley. Caleb has two American bulldogs who are the biggest babies in the world. They're indestructible, friendly, and the perfect test to see if Bentley can be placed in a family with other dogs.

I park along the curb and exit my poor truck, which has logged tons of miles these past couple of weeks. "Not too much longer, ol' girl," I say, patting her metal side. Each day is a ticking clock looming over my head, but if all goes well tonight, Bentley might actually be ready for the dog fair in the morning. He's already made more strides than I ever thought possible.

He barks excitedly as I unlatch the crate and clip the leash to his collar.

"Okay, come on out."

In pure Bentley fashion, he leaps from the cage, off the back of the truck, and lands gracefully on his feet. He tries to tug when he sees the grass, but I quickly remind him who's in charge now. Reluctantly he submits, and we walk in tandem to Caleb's front door.

I ring the doorbell and wait. A few seconds later, Cameron's brother answers, sporting the same dimples as the rest of the Lee clan. It's the only real similarity to my best friend, though. Caleb favors his mom in both build and facial features, whereas Cam is the spitting image of his dad and arguably the much more attractive brother. Not that Caleb isn't cute; all the Lees won the gene lottery. Caleb is just shorter, his skin and hair paler, and he's always been a self-professed nerd. A title he wears proudly in both style and personality.

"Hey, Darcy. Cam's running a little late. Come in." He moves aside to let us enter, but I shake my head.

"I think it's better if we introduce the dogs outside. I'll go through the gate, let Bentley get settled, then maybe we could do one at a time?"

He shrugs. "Whatever works is fine with me. I'll meet you

out back." He shuts the door, and I marvel at another very different trait from his brother. Caleb is as easy-tempered as they come. He never gets mad; I've never even heard him raise his voice. Cam, on the other hand, is an emotional roller coaster most of the time—the tortured artist to an infinite measure. Maybe that's why Caleb and Cam have always had a sort of love/hate relationship. Or maybe it's just a brother thing.

I reach over the fence and unlatch the wooden gate. Bentley tugs, barely containing his eagerness, but again I pull him back and force him to wait. As much as he's grown in the past several days, I still wish I had more time with him. Whoever decides to adopt him should strongly consider investing in more obedience training.

As soon as I have the gate securely shut behind us, I free Bentley of his leash. Caleb appears seconds later and examines the dog with a smirk.

"Lots of energy, that one," he says.

I join him on the porch. "You have no idea."

We stand side by side and watch as Bentley races through the backyard, sniffing and marking every available vertical post.

"Cam told me you're training dogs again. Any chance I can get you to work with my two fireballs?"

"No way." I laugh at the thought. "Those dogs are far too spoiled to change." I give him a sideways glance. "Plus, their owner is a complete pushover who will unravel all my good work."

"Yeah. It's true. I admit it."

Kelly, Caleb's wife, sneaks out the patio door, barely holding back her eager pets. "Jasper and Jupiter are ready to play. Is it safe yet?" She's blond like her husband and petite enough to shop in the juniors' section.

I give her a hug and shake my head at the two wet noses pressed against the glass. They may be spoiled rotten, but they sure are cute. And since Kelly and Caleb have yet to have kids, these two are unquestionably their surrogate children.

"Let's try Jasper first," I advise. "She's female, so it may go better." All the dogs are fixed, but the alpha thing is still alive and well, even when neutered.

We work together to hold back Jupiter while freeing Jasper, and after the poor guy howls his objections, Kelly goes back inside to keep him company, which doesn't surprise me. She's also one of the kindest, most selfless women I've ever met. But those are the type of people the Lees attract. Every one of Cam's in-laws are solid, faith-filled, and eager to serve. It's a high standard that's been set and probably the reason Cameron has never introduced any of his girlfriends to his family.

I carefully guide Jasper to Bentley and supervise while they sniff each other. Within seconds, they're prancing and playing together. Ironically, it's Jasper who won't stop jumping and mauling at Bentley's neck playfully. He even glances at me to help, and I intervene.

"See, now you know how it feels, don't you?" I tug Jasper off and get her to calm down before releasing her again. This time, she's much less spastic.

A few minutes later, we let Jupiter come out and play. He does a lot more sniffing, but in the end, the three of them settle into a nice rhythm together. In fact, it goes so well, I feel comfortable leaving them to play while I join Caleb on their outdoor sectional.

"Well, did that go how you expected?" he asks when I sit.

"Better, actually." I continue to watch the three dogs run back and forth along the fence. "He seems to improve when

I take him off the farm." I think of Bryson's backyard and immediately my mind catapults to our afternoon together and the rare moment of vulnerability he shared with me. "Hey, can I ask you a question?"

"Sure." Caleb twists so we can face each other easier.

"You were living at home when your family took Bryson in, right?"

He nods. "I wasn't around much, but yeah." Caleb spent his first two years at college living at home to save money. "Why?"

"What was he like when he got there? Cam's never talked about it."

Caleb raises an eyebrow. "Probably for a reason. It was a pretty bad situation."

"Bryson told me about his stepdad kicking him out."

Maybe it's the confirmation that Bryson already told me what transpired, but Caleb seems to take those words as permission to open up. "It was more than just being kicked out. Bryson lived out of his truck for a week before Dad learned about his situation and called his parents. His stepdad actually had the gall to tell Dad that Bryson was old enough to figure it out. The poor guy was dehydrated and starving by the time he showed up here."

My stomach turns inside out. "A week? Why did Bryson wait so long to tell someone?"

"Because that boy is more stubborn than a mule. He probably would have stayed living out of his truck indefinitely if Dad hadn't threatened to call the cops."

Disbelief rocks more of my preconceived notions. "All this time, I thought it was Cam who initiated the rescue."

Caleb shakes his head. "Nope. It was Dad. Cam agreed, of course, but you know how he is about sharing his stuff. You'd think the guy was an only child." Caleb cocks his head to the side, studying me. "Why the sudden interest?"

"I don't know," I say, still reeling from the knowledge that Bryson spent a week cold and alone. "I've spent some time with him these past couple of weeks, and I'm starting to realize he's not who I thought he was."

Caleb's expression morphs into that of a protective older brother. His reaction makes sense. I am practically his little sister. "Be careful, Darcy. The guy's not known for being gentle when it comes to breaking hearts."

My cheeks burn. "It's not like that between us. He's been a good friend, that's all. Especially lately."

The furrow in Caleb's brow tells me he doesn't believe a word I'm saying. "I really hope so because I've seen his patterns. And chances are, his 'friendship' has some kind of string attached."

I'm struck with a sudden need to defend Bryson. To somehow verbalize what I've seen in the man he's become. But before I can form an argument, Caleb rushes on.

"Trust me on this, Darcy. There's always a motive with him, and it's usually ninety percent self-serving. He manipulated Cam into quitting the praise band, and he'll manipulate you, too—it's what he does."

"You're not giving him enough credit."

"And I have no doubt you're giving him too much." His voice turns sad. "Bryson lost something in himself a long time ago. Just listen to his music. It's not for show. The blackness . . . it's part of who he is now."

A year ago, even a month ago, I would have agreed. But no one can love as deeply as I've seen him love Charlie and be empty. I know this firsthand, because right now I don't love anything . . . not even myself. But Caleb can be unyielding in his expectations. He doesn't understand brokenness, so he has no capacity to see that I've become more like Bryson than the person he grew up knowing. So instead of arguing a futile point, I fight for a smile that will dismiss his worries. "I appreciate the concern, Caleb, I really do, but it's unnecessary. I've known Bryson a long time. There are no blinders here."

"Nobody really knows Bryson. He makes sure of it." With that warning, Caleb leans forward, his eyes growing intently serious. "Some scars don't heal, Darcy. They just pass from that person to the next one he decides to damage. And in this case, there's more than just you to consider. I don't want to see either one of you get hurt."

"Who's getting hurt?"

I twist behind me to see Cam and Kelly approach with fresh glasses in their hands.

"No one, hopefully," Caleb says before I can answer. "What took you so long?"

"Rock 'n' roll, what else." Cam plays an air guitar, and Caleb rolls his eyes. The two of them argue less now that they don't live together, but Cam still likes to poke at his brother's calm-and-collected shell.

"Darcy, are you staying for dinner?" Kelly asks, joining her husband.

"Of course she is," Cam answers, plopping down next to me. "Aren't you?"

I check the dogs, who are doing just fine. "Sure, if it's not an imposition."

"Please. You're family." Cam pats my leg, and once again I notice the admonishment in Caleb's expression. Now I wish I'd never opened my big mouth. Older brothers. They're the same no matter what family they come from.

"How'd practice go?" I ask, though the answer is obvious in Cameron's good mood.

"Outstanding. We're so ready for tomorrow." He stops as if he just considered a horrible thought. "You're coming, right?" He twists toward his brother and sister-in-law. "Y'all too. We play at nine o'clock."

"Sorry, kiddo. I'm halfway to dreamland by then. Besides, you know I hate the bar scene."

"You've never even been in one." Cameron scowls. "And don't call me kiddo. I'm only two years younger than you are."

"In age, yes." Caleb stands, not needing to say any more because it's true. He's been married five years and has had the same steady, full-time job for twice that long. Cam, well, he still lives like a college student. "I think our fur babies are good." He takes his wife's hand and pulls her up. "Want some help with dinner?"

"Well now, that is an offer I won't turn down." She smiles sweetly at the two of us. "We'll call you when it's ready."

Cameron sulks until they disappear. "I hate it when he gets all judgmental like that. Not everyone has the same dream to be old and retired at forty."

"I'm sure he didn't mean to insult you. Caleb's all about order and routine and comfort. You're a risk taker and a dreamer. He has no idea how to relate to you."

Cam stretches his arm around the back of the couch. "You've managed to do it."

"That's because I'm awesome," I say, hoping it will get his good mood back. I much prefer Cameron when he's happy.

"True." He smiles and I'm relieved it worked. "You look good, by the way." He studies the clothes Zoe gave me. "Are those new?"

"Sort of." I don't bother to explain. "And thank you. I've been trying not to wear my depression like a coat."

"Well, it's working. Maybe this is a turning point for both of us." He lifts his glass in a toast, and I *clink* mine to his.

"Maybe." Except I'm currently not speaking to my mom or my dad, and Caleb thinks I'm crushing on Bryson, which I certainly am not. But yeah, I guess this is still an improvement over ice-cream slobber and stale breath.

"Oh, before I forget . . . I have a flyer for you." Cameron jumps off the couch, his eagerness as explosive as his movements. "Our photographer was incredible. Bryson was spot-on in his vision for us." He disappears into his brother's house, leaving me nothing to do except watch three frolicking animals and digest the information Caleb gave me. Bryson had been homeless a week. Seven days living out of his truck, acting toward the rest of the world like everything was normal. No wonder he cut those people out of his life. How they could do that to a kid is beyond my comprehension.

I turn around to check for Cam, irritated by the way my fingers itch to text Bryson and just talk with him. To try to understand why he's spent so much of his life pushing everyone away when he already has so few people in his world who truly care.

The back door opens, and Cam finally returns, tossing a handful of peanuts into his mouth while he walks. A brightly colored paper is gingerly held in his other hand.

"Is that the flyer?"

"Yep." He sits and offers me the smooth page with the headliner in the middle, Black Carousel on the top left, and a smaller duet on the top right. Below the band names are three times listed. "The updated picture turned out great." I run my thumb along the faces of Black Carousel. Bryson stands in front, dressed in his signature black T-shirt and jeans, accented by his black leather jacket. His hair is a mane of rebellious waves, his arms crossed and tense. My chest constricts when I study his face. Maybe because it feels like a contradiction that his expression can be so strikingly handsome and yet so hardened by life. What was he thinking about when the camera flashed? His stepfather? The night he was kicked out? Our moment in the backyard?

Flutters assault my stomach and I force my gaze to wander left, where Cameron stands in the photo, holding a violin by his side. The distraction works and the flutters dissipate one by one. I study this new rock-star version of my best friend. He's also in black jeans, but I'm grateful to see his shirt is a patterned button-up of dark and light grays. He's giving a slight grin, which shows just a hint of his left dimple, and though his type of handsome is totally different, Cameron definitely will get lots of female admiration from this shot. Jay and Harrison aren't nearly as attractive as this picture makes them out to be. Jay's blond hair is spiked high, and his wrists are adorned with multiple bracelets. Harrison holds drumsticks as usual. Tattoos cover most of his arms, and his head is shaved bald. Both guys are older than our group by five years, and I'm pretty sure Bryson found them through an ad. They've never hung out with us, besides the occasional post-performance drink.

I fold the flyer and put it in my back pocket. "It feels weird not to see Mason on here."

"I can't believe that's the only thing you noticed." Cameron stands and paces near the edge of the patio, defensiveness laced through every word.

"It wasn't the only thing I noticed. You all look amazing.

I just…" The backpedaling isn't working so I give up. "I'm sorry, Cam. I wasn't trying to make you feel bad."

"I know you weren't. It's my own guilt I'm dealing with." He sits back down and squeezes my knee, perhaps perceiving the harshness in his tone. "Our gig this weekend. It's big. Huge. Potentially life changing. And Mason won't be there."

"You miss him." I understand the feeling. I miss every part of our old life.

He sets his elbows on his knees and folds his hands together. "Yeah, I do. We had plans, you know? Dreams, and I feel like maybe I stole his."

I set my hand on his, my voice as reassuring as I can possibly make it. "Mason's tough. Knowing him, he's already moved on to his next big adventure." I think of my conversation with Bryson and his reason for firing their old friend. "Honestly, I don't think Mason ever understood or loved music the way you do. He liked being in the band because it was fun, and he got to be with his buddies, but he never took it seriously."

"I know. That's the only thing that makes me feel any better." Cam glances toward the sky. "I just feel this constant rumbling inside of me. Sometimes it fuels me and I'm good with the sacrifices I'm making. They feel worth it. Other times, all I can feel is the void of every person I've lost in the process. And worse, I don't know if God's preparing me for greatness or if I'm being punished. At this point, they feel exactly the same."

"You're not being punished for pursuing your dream," I say with absolute certainty. "Change is inevitable. And there's no way God gave you the talent He did just to see it fizzle away."

Cameron's entire body deflates, the tension leaking away. "Thanks. I needed to hear that."

"You're welcome. Besides, if anyone deserves to be punished right now . . . it's me." He looks my way, confusion
making his eyebrows vee. "I yelled at my mom and made her
cry."

The line creases deeper. "Whoa, back up. When did all
this happen?"

"Sunday. Michael was at dinner again, and they were kissing and making plans." I shiver. "It just all came out, everything I've been stuffing down."

"Why didn't you tell me?" Cameron's voice hitches like he
can't believe I didn't lead with that fact.

"Because I'm embarrassed that I don't feel bad about it. I
feel justified." The truth is, I resent my dad for leaving, but
even more, I resent my mom for never giving me a chance
to mourn. She made me her friend, her rock, her confidante
when I needed to be her daughter. "She's tried to call me, but
I can't talk to her right now. I'm too . . . numb, and I worry I'll
make it worse."

"I'm sorry, Darcy." He squeezes my shoulder affectionately.
"What can I do?"

That's just it. There's nothing he can do. Nothing anyone
can do. I take a deep breath and smile. "You can go back to
being happy Cam. The one who bounced in here all high on
music and potential fame."

"You got it." He winks at me, and I love that he knows
when not to push. "Okay." He slaps his hands together. "It's
time to start the negotiations."

"What negotiations?"

"The ones you're going to make me go through in order to
get you to stay and watch part of Firesight's performance."

When I start to shake my head, his voice turns more urgent. "Darcy, this band we're opening for is legit. They won't

be playing the bar scene for long, and if things go as I hope tomorrow night, this opening gig may very well extend into the future." His lips morph into a kiddish pout. "Please? I really want your opinion."

"You look like you're five when you do that."

He fights a smile. "So, is it working?" His pout gets more extreme, and I can't help but chuckle.

"No," I lie.

"Not even a little?"

I push his face away. "Fine, I'll stay for two songs and two songs only . . . on one condition."

"Our friendship is conditional now?"

"Apparently."

"What is it?"

"Just a teeny tiny small favor."

He scowls. "Last time I did you a favor, I ended up hauling furniture up and down stairs for three hours."

"It's nothing that hard," I assure him. "I need some help with Bentley tomorrow morning." Somehow, I know without asking that Bryson will not be dropping in this time. "I just need you to carry my stuff so I can focus on keeping Bentley from running toward everything that moves. You won't have to stay. I'm good once we get settled."

"What time are we talking?"

I hesitate to answer. "Eight-ish?"

He groans and slouches down in the couch. "Why are all your favors early on a Saturday morning?"

"Because I'm awesome."

"That answer doesn't work in this context."

I catch the dogs starting to fight over one of Jasper's toys and stand to intervene. "That answer works in any context."

He watches while I put space between the agitated animals

and confiscate the offending piece of plastic. "Are you going to miss him?"

"Bentley?"

He nods.

"A little." As big of a pain in the butt as he is, I do admire his gumption. If Bentley were human, no way would he have spent the last twenty-nine years trying to say and do everything right. I scratch his favorite spot behind his ear and consider Bryson's comment about trying to bribe God with my good behavior. Obviously it's not working, so what's the point? If my life is going to feel like punishment anyway, I might as well have a good reason why.

SEVENTEEN

*T*urns out that Zoe is not just good at retail therapy and makeovers, but she's also a NASCAR driver in three-inch heels. We're twenty minutes late leaving the apartment, which, yeah, is mostly my fault because I didn't get home from the dog fair until seven. But it was Zoe who insisted I shower and primp versus my usual throw-my-hair-in-a-ponytail routine.

Unlike my experience with Sam, this dog fair was a nail biter. Bentley got lots of attention, but he also made a lot of mistakes. Knocked down two little girls and made them cry, barked, tugged at the leash whenever another animal crossed our path, and got so excited once that he peed on a poor guy's shoe. By six, I was ready to pack it up and call the day a wash, but then a miracle arrived in cowboy boots and Wrangler jeans. An old rancher—not too much younger than Charlie—took one look at Bentley, asked how fast he could run, then signed the paperwork. "I'm looking for a cow dog with lots of spunk," he said. I warned him of Bentley's bad habits, but the guy assured me this wasn't his first unruly animal and, to my utter shock, had Bentley securely at his hip when he walked away.

I feel a little guilty that there were no tears during our goodbye. As much as I loved the stubborn ol' boy, I can't say I'm not relieved that he's gone.

"You'll never guess who called me last night," Zoe says, zooming into the right lane only to zig back into the left one after passing a car easily going sixty-five—the current speed limit, I might add. "Nate. Can you believe that? He's all apologetic, like I don't know he just got dumped by the girl he dumped me for."

I grip the dash to keep from being thrown into the door. "What did you say?"

"I said, 'Too bad, sucker, I've moved on.'" She grins at me, and I nearly yell at her to watch the road. "Liam is so much better than Nate. He's cuter, smarter, and I've had a crush on him for *months*." She slows when both lanes are blocked. "Anyway, he's supposed to be meeting me here tonight and"—she winks at me—"he has a friend."

"No thanks."

"You don't have to date the guy. Just keep him occupied so he doesn't feel like a third wheel." She gives me a sideways glance. "Who knows, you might just have a good time for once."

"You say that like I'm incapable of having fun."

"Aren't you?"

I scowl and don't bother to answer her question. There was a time before I made the decision to go overseas that it would have been easy to refute her implication. But now, I can't say. It's like a line has been drawn between the before and after, and everything before feels blurry. Resentment boils as I try to remember any time in the last year that hasn't felt burdensome and come up short.

"You know what, Zoe, you're right. Tonight, I'm not going

to think. I'm just going to do whatever feels . . ." I stop there because I don't know what I want to feel. Happy maybe? But that seems like a leap. Mostly, I just want to feel something else entirely. Something that isn't sadness or anger or depression or even this new overwhelming numbness. I want to be free of it all, even if it's just for a night. "Let's just say it'll be a new me."

Zoe hoots like a sorority girl on spring break. "It's about time!"

There's already a line to get in when we finally make it to the bar, and parking is nonexistent. Zoe circles the block once, then pulls into a hotel valet drive.

I eye the sign on their podium. "Parking is twenty-seven dollars a night."

"So," she says flippantly and checks her makeup one more time before the valet opens her door. "It's not like I'm paying for it."

She hands off her keys, and we walk the two blocks to the venue entrance.

"Where are all these people coming from?" I ask when we join the line. Black Carousel has never had this kind of following.

"It's Firesight that's drawing the crowd. Why do you think I'm here?"

"For your brother?"

"Hardly. Bryson hates me coming to these things. In his mind I'm forever sixteen."

We make it to the front, show our IDs, and pay the cover fee to get in.

I hear Bryson introduce himself and the band, pocket the

loose cash, then hurry inside. The treads of my Vans stick as I walk across the smooth floor, and I'm immediately grateful I won the shoe battle. If I'd worn the ones Zoe suggested, the only thing I'd get out of tonight would be a sprained ankle. It's bad enough that I caved on the sundress she insisted I wear.

As soon as we enter the crowded room, the vibration of Harrison's drums beat against my chest. They've started with their most popular song and by far the loudest and edgiest in the set. It's not my favorite, but the crowd seems to love it. Several girls are already lining the foot of the stage, their arms in the air and their hips swaying. I stare at them a little too long before Zoe nudges me.

"Jealous?" she asks in my ear.

"No." The idea is ludicrous. "The guys can do whatever they want."

"Even Cameron?"

"Especially Cam." I look for any space that isn't packed with people and come up short. The room is smaller than ex-pected, the stage barely ten feet from the massive bar at the center. Zoe pushes me that direction. The stools encircling the counter are all full, but there are pockets of space we can squeeze into. Zoe takes the lead and somehow manages not only to find us a corner but also to snag two stools.

"What do you want?" she asks, her credit card in hand.

"I don't know. I don't usually drink."

She turns back to the waiting bartender. "Two lemon drops. One of them easy on the alcohol." He takes her card, and she tells him to keep it open.

I lean my back on the bar in a spot no larger than twelve inches and watch my best friend hypnotize the room. He's electric tonight, his violin firing out sounds as if he were in competition with the devil. Bryson is equally thrilling, his charisma and dark sensuality making the crowd scream for more. I watch him closely, study each line in his brow, examine the way his lips form each word, then focus on his eyes, barely visible through half-closed eyelids. For a moment, I think maybe he sees me, too, only to scold myself for being so ridiculous. There's easily two hundred people here, and between the lights and the crowd, I'm lucky if I'm barely another face among many.

"Here." Zoe nudges my arm and offers me a glass that looks like a funnel of lemonade. The edge is coated in sugar, and a thin slice of lemon is hooked on the side.

"It looks more like artwork than alcohol."

"It also tastes like candy," she says, sipping on her own drink—the one that did not go light on the alcohol. When I hesitate, she scoots her stool closer so we can hear each other over the booming music. "Come on, Darcy. You said you were going to have fun tonight. You're at a bar. This is what you do."

Despite being nearly thirty, I've never really explored the bar scene like most of my friends did in college. Truth be told, I spent more time hanging out with Cameron on the weekends than ever taking the time to fit in with the girls on my floor. Maybe that's why I fast-tracked my general studies degree and came back home to pursue a certification in dog training. How crazy that years later, I'm here, having a drink with Bryson's little sister, watching Cameron sing about darkness and fear and sticking it to the man, whoever that is. I feel fairly certain our younger selves would not approve.

But instead of letting the guilt win, I bring my lemon cocktail to my lips and tell my annoying conscience that my younger self never envisioned being purposeless and a failure before thirty. She was also naïve and sheltered and believed in people and commitment. She hadn't experienced the disappointment this year has brought, and she has no right to judge me or Cameron for our chosen coping mechanisms.

"To no rules," I whisper to myself and take my first sip. Cold tartness fills my mouth, along with the sweet sugar. My eyes widen in surprise. It's not just good, it's really good.

"Like it?" It's a rhetorical question since I'm already taking another drink, this one much larger.

"Yeah. It's surprisingly yummy."

"Can't go wrong with a lemon drop." Zoe lifts the edge of her glass to her mouth and takes a drink, smooth and quick, as if she's done it a thousand times.

We both refocus on the band. They've moved on to a second song, one Bryson wrote his senior year of high school. Back then he'd perform it acoustically, just him, a microphone, and a guitar. Now there's two electric solos, a bridge that showcases Bryson and Cameron's harmony skills, and a tempo twice as fast as the original.

I've heard Black Carousel perform this song at least three times, yet the words hit me differently tonight. They aren't just a run of angry lyrics but a weaving of scar tissue that has yet to heal. Bryson leans into the microphone, belts out the climactic note that soars an octave higher than a man should be able to reach. The crowd explodes in cheers while my heart aches with indescribable compassion. Bryson's voice is roughened by agony and pain, and he's stuck in it. Just like I am.

The song ends, and Bryson flips his sweat-soaked hair back. He grins at the girls by his feet. Leans down and touches a line of fingers. Cameron sets down his violin and picks up his Fender. I can tell by the color in his cheeks and the joy in his eyes that he's loving every minute onstage. Music is his first and only love, and he's reveling in it.

"Cameron looks hot tonight. I don't remember him being so sexy." Zoe's voice turns smoky, and I nearly fall off my stool. "I bet he's a good kisser." She turns to me and bites her bottom lip. "He is, isn't he?"

"I have no idea," I say with horrified laughter. "Cam and I don't . . . We're just friends. Only friends."

She eyes me skeptically. "You mean you've never . . . in all this time . . . explored more?"

"No. Never." Well, unless you count one teeny tiny experiment when we were twelve, which I don't. And based on Zoe's tone, I'm sure she's not referring to an innocent peck on the lips by two kids. "Really. Totally platonic."

"Hmm. Interesting."

I don't like her tone or the way she's studying my face. "What's interesting?"

"Nothing." But there is unquestionably something. Zoe may use her stunning looks and silky blond hair to appear needy and brainless, but the girl is far more calculating than anyone gives her credit for. She raises her drink, finishing it off while I still have half of mine. She lifts her finger until she catches the bartender's eye, then twists back around. "It's funny, you know, how people surprise you."

I take another sip, unsure where this is going. "What do you mean?"

"I mean, you surprised me." She takes her second drink, and I don't miss how the bartender's fingers linger on the glass just a little longer than necessary. Zoe certainly can charm anyone. She smiles coyly and settles back into her stool. "I always thought you were this holier-than-thou, judgmental, stuck-up . . . well, you know. But now I actually think you're pretty cool."

I'm too shocked to do anything but chuckle. "Gosh. Tell me how you really feel."

"Sorry. Lemon drops bring out the honesty in me. It's the only drawback to this drink." She gulps down more, apparently not too concerned about it.

"If you felt that way, why did you let me live with you?"

"Bryson made me an offer I couldn't refuse." Her voice shifts, and just around the edges there's hurt. Not the kind of hurt I saw after the breakup with Nate, but a deeper kind. The kind that shapes futures and decisions and self-esteem.

"What did he offer?"

She hesitates as if she knows, even two truth-serum drinks later, that some secrets should not be revealed. Instead, she focuses on her brother. "I was just a little girl when he left. I came down from my room when I heard all the shouting and saw Bryson standing outside, his guitar and clothes at his feet. It's the only time in my life I've ever seen him look . . . afraid." She closes her eyes and breathes in the music. "It's hard to love two men who hate each other, but I do."

Her words sink down into my chest, much like the song they've shifted to onstage. This one's softer, not quite a ballad, but definitely more swaying than head banging. The houselights come up a little, making the room's vibe feel less like a concert and more intimate. My eyes trail back to Bryson, the heat in my checks doubling. His voice is so fluid, not silky like Cam's, but more like a dark espresso, layered with that hint of bitterness to make it special.

He shakes his hair from his face, and this time when he looks up, I know he sees me. Either that, or the guy has an incredible ability to make a girl feel as if she's the only person in the room. His eyes stay laser-focused on mine, his words raising goose bumps up and down my arms and legs. The lyrics are all about need. Needing peace, needing purpose, needing something you aren't allowed to have. His gaze shifts then, and now the first two rows get his attention.

I'm left gutted and, more than ever, I have to know what Zoe meant earlier. I touch her arm, my voice a plea. "Please, Zoe. If you consider me a friend at all, I need you to tell me what he offered."

She sighs like she knows she's going to regret telling me. "He agreed to come to Thanksgiving this year."

My mouth opens, the shock reverberating through my chest. "Why would he do that?"

"Why do you think?" She shakes her head. "Darcy. My brother gave up twelve years of silence . . . for you."

My face freezes, yet somehow I find a way to speak. "I don't understand."

"Please tell me you're not that naïve." She pauses, studies me. "Oh my gosh. You *are* that naïve." Zoe spots someone in the crowd and sits up straighter. "Word of advice. It's time to start paying attention . . . to both of them." She waves and then pats down her hair. "Liam's here. Remember, you promised to keep Tony occupied."

EIGHTEEN

*T*he minute Liam joins us at the bar, Zoe snaps into full flirtation mode. I never saw her interact with Nate, so I'm not sure if this behavior is typical for her, but I'm quickly learning why none of Zoe's relationships stick. The girl she's portraying is nothing like the person I know she is.

Even worse, I'm stuck entertaining Liam's talkative friend when I really just want to listen and try to make sense of the confusion in my head.

Tony leans in and shouts over the music, "They're good, aren't they?" He's the collared-shirt type with playful brown eyes and light hair styled just enough to look unintentional. Not nearly as striking as Liam, who's arguably prettier than Zoe, if that is possible.

"Yeah, they are. They're friends of mine." I glance at my roommate, who hasn't taken her eyes off Liam since he walked up. "The lead singer is Zoe's older brother."

"Really?" He surveys the stage, then turns back to me. "Cool. Maybe you can introduce me to them after their set." In truth, Tony isn't a bad guy. Just, I don't know, simple and a little too free with the hand grazes. I guess that's the drawback to having an extraordinary best friend. My standards have always been ridiculously high. Thankfully, I've had two more lemon-drop cocktails in the span of our conversation, and a warm sensation has replaced all the earlier shock waves. Well, most of them anyway.

Tony continues to talk, asking me where I'm from and what my hobbies are. He volunteers that he lives and works in downtown Dallas, running some kind of computer program for AT&T.

"What about you, Darcy? What keeps you busy during the week?"

I swallow the final drops from my glass, disappointed it's empty. "Dogs," I say simply.

He chuckles and takes the glass from my hand to set it on the counter. "And what does that entail?"

I turn toward him, accepting my fate that I'm stuck keeping Tony occupied. "I train them. Right now, I'm working with a group of foster dogs in hopes they can find permanent homes."

He inches in, his finger sliding down my forearm for not the first time. I subtly pull away, wondering when he's going to finally get the hint. "Wow. I never would have pictured you as an outdoorsy type. You're so tiny and feminine."

It's a good thing I don't have a drink because I know I would have spit it out on him. I place my hand on my mouth, holding in a burst of laughter. "Um, thanks." And now I understand why Zoe pretends. This environment isn't where you go looking for a long-lasting relationship. It's all about the persona you want to project. "The best things often come in little packages." Why not throw some clichés in there? He's not really interested in getting to know me anyway.

"True." Tony's smile grows bigger than it has all night. "How about another drink?"

I hesitate, but I guess something in my face says yes because Tony's already on his way back to the bartender. Part of me is relieved. It gives me a chance to properly dissect Zoe's words.

"For you," she had said, like some great love affair came and went, and I was too blind to participate. Which is ridiculous because, despite what implications Zoe made about my not paying attention, I know one thing for certain. Bryson has never not gone after something he wanted. It's part of what makes him, him. Not to mention that he's had multiple chances to make a move, and the only thing he's done lately is avoid me.

And now I'm frustrated with myself for letting Zoe detonate a bomb of self-doubt. The girl is an emotional wreck, and this wouldn't be the first time she's lied to me in order to maintain her image. If Bryson did agree to go to Thanksgiving, then I'm sure his reasons were way deeper than just me.

Black Carousel's seventh song ends with two drumbeats and a flash of stage lights.

"Thank you, Dallas! You've been fantastic tonight," Bryson yells into the microphone, every muscle in his arm flexing as he extends the microphone to let the crowd respond. And respond they do, cheering and screaming for one more song. Bryson pulls the microphone back, his adrenaline obviously racing through him and into the crowd. "Take it away, Lee!"

When his last name is called, Cameron moves the strings on his electric guitar like they're running from the law. It's overwhelming, the sound and energy he releases. I feel it, the crowd feels it, and I know Bryson and the band feel it, because when they come in on the beat, it's like witnessing magic in the making.

The noise becomes deafening until suddenly I feel lost in it all. The atmosphere, the crowd, the sheer perfection that is their performance tonight. The vibration rocks my bones, and I want to dance and jump as ridiculously as the girls down by the stage. Byson and Cam come together, backs touching as their guitars belt out a duet that could rival the greatest of classic rock icons. They turn, sing into the same microphone, their voices blending, Cam's high and smooth, Bryson's deep and edgy. They work as one, a rhythm only possible when two people know each other like they do. And even though their relationship is complex, you can't fake the kind of bonding that happens when two people share a childhood of laughter and now an adulthood of mutual dreams.

My heart fills with an impossible emotion for these two guys I've known forever. Though my future has died, their futures are just beginning, and it feels surprisingly euphoric to get to witness the birth.

Two hard beats of Harrison's drums and the lights onstage go black.

Tony appears like an apparition, and I'm surprisingly grateful when I see the shiny yellow drink coming my way. My throat is dry, and my heart is pounding like someone just scared me from the bushes. I take a gulp and then another one. The second one burns though, so I quickly stop my guzzling.

"Zoe and Liam took off," he says with a suggestive grin. "She wanted me to tell you thanks and that she owes you one. Whatever that means."

My eyes dart to the corner, where she and Liam have been sitting all night, and confirm Tony's words. She knew I was planning to ride home with Cameron, but still, she could have at least said goodbye. "She wasn't planning to drive, was she?"

"Nah. Liam's got her. He hasn't had a drink all night."

I consider the information and hope Liam is as good a guy as Zoe thinks he is. At least she knows him and isn't going home with a complete stranger.

"So, I was thinking . . ." Tony slides his arm around my waist, and I realize he's expecting the same result from our little encounter. I guess the warnings I heard my whole life about not letting guys buy me drinks are true. His touch has shifted from careful to aggressive. "My place isn't far from here, if you want to check it out. We have this private roof terrace on our building where you can see all the lights in Dallas."

"I'm sure it's lovely." Not that I have any intention of finding out. "But I need to go meet up with my friends." I try to move away from him, but his grip tightens.

An uncomfortable eeriness settles over me as I realize Tony isn't as nice a guy as I originally thought. Zoe was right about my naïveté. I'm not used to guys hitting on me in bars, nor am I skilled on how to get away from them once the moment becomes uncomfortable. "Really, I'm sure they're already wondering where I am." I somehow untangle from his hold, finally able to back up enough to make my pulse stop pounding in my ears. "It was nice to meet you," I lie, taking one more step back, only this time I collide with a hard body, one that not only doesn't move but seems to shift in closer. I jerk my head and freeze when I realize it's Bryson next to me, his eyes cold enough to commit a felony. Suddenly his arm is around my shoulder in an act of possession so overt that even I can't miss it, especially since he pulls me in so tight I nearly drop the drink in my hand.

Tony's surprise is no less obvious than my own, though he doesn't share my relief. "Oh, hey, man. You're with the band, right?" He takes a step away from us, and I can't blame the guy. Bryson is pulsing with bottled energy, the high from the stage visible in his flushed cheeks and wild eyes. Tony clears his throat. "You guys were really good."

Bryson doesn't say a word. Not one word. He just stares at Tony with me clamped to his side. A horrible tension fills the space between us, and I would feel bad for the guy if I didn't want him to disappear.

"Bryson, this is Tony. He works for AT&T." I have no idea why that's the one fact that flew from my mind, but it is.

Bryson looks down at me, and I see his mouth twitch in a barely-there smile. It fades the minute he looks back at Tony, and again he doesn't say a single word.

By now, my new admirer is at least four feet from the two of us and slowly backing away. "Darcy, it was a pleasure. Maybe I'll see you arou—"

"No, you won't." Bryson's words cut the air like a chainsaw, and Tony must feel the residual sting because he turns away without a goodbye.

Bryson's arm falls away. "You okay? You looked scared."

"I think cornered was more like it. I was probably overreacting." I swallow, trying my best to act unaffected. It's harder than it should be, mostly because my head suddenly feels like it's full of air and being tossed by the wind. I blink my eyes and try to shake away the odd sensation. That seems to work a little. "I'm sure Tony is harmless. His friend works with your sister." The same sister who told me Bryson broke twelve years of silence for me. The same one who said I wasn't paying attention. I stare at the way his damp shirt hangs over every muscle in his chest. Well, I'm certainly paying attention now.

Bryson snorts. "Trust me, the way he was looking at you was definitely not harmless. Guys like that make me sick. They know who to prey on. And you, Darcy, are an easy target."

"I am not."

"Really? Did he buy this for you?" He takes the glass from my hand, sniffs it, then takes a sip. Immediately his eyes widen and he coughs as if it went down the wrong pipe. "Please tell me you were smart enough not to drink this."

And now I'm offended. "I'm not a teenager, and I'm not driving." I steal back my glass. "And I don't need your permission to have a lemon drop . . . or four for that matter."

His eyes narrow, and I understand a little why Zoe might not have liked me when growing up. There's no fun in being judged. "Since when do you drink?"

"Since I decided I'm done playing by all the rules."

"And you think a stiff martini is going to solve all your problems?" His voice grows rougher. "I got news for you, it won't."

"And yet here you stand, the picture of mutiny, and every one of your dreams is about to come true." And now the anger is back, alive and well. "Why does everyone expect so much more from me?"

"Because you're better than this."

"Obviously, I'm not."

Before he can respond, a girl comes stumbling forward, her arms draping over the very chest I had admired before his words turned cutting. "Hey, you guys were amazing. Can I get your autograph?" She unbuttons her shirt down to the end of a long cleavage line and offers Bryson a sharpie.

He smiles sensually at her but writes his name on the inside of her wrist instead. "Thanks for coming." His arm finds its way around my shoulders again, and I realize this time he's not doing it for my benefit but his own.

She takes the hint and leaves, though I quickly realize she's not the only one who's noticed Bryson is now in the audience.

"Where's Zoe?" He eyes the group moving toward us. "We need to get backstage."

"She left with a guy from work."

"Of course she did." Bryson mashes his lips together and glances at the half-finished drink in my hand. "Who would have thought that she'd be the one influencing you." And then with lightning-fast speed, he snatches the glass from my fingers and sets it on the bar. "Let's go."

His grip securely around my wrist, Bryson pushes us through the crowd until we're in front of a closed black door blocked by a beefy bouncer in a tight black T-shirt.

"She's with me." Bryson waves his pass and opens the door without a pause. Beefy guy smiles, and I don't like the once-over I get or the way he lifts his chin at Bryson as if it's a secret high five.

"Is taking random girls backstage something you do often?"

Bryson stops and turns to look at me, his eyes dancing as if he can see the jealousy slithering up inside. "Are you calling yourself random?"

"No."

He steps closer, his voice dipping with arrogance. "Then why are you worried?"

"I'm not."

Bryson smirks but doesn't call me out on my lie. Instead, he leads me through the dark corridor until Cam and the rest of the band appear, each exuding the same buzzing high that's been springing from Bryson since he stepped offstage.

"Well, look at you, sexy mama." Jay whistles, turning everyone's head, including Cameron's. "Bare legs, flushed cheeks. Just my kind of fangirl."

"Save it, Casanova. She's way too smart for your golden tongue," Cameron says, pushing him aside affectionately. He eyes me with confusion. "Where'd you appear from? I was just about to come find you."

"Bryson got me backstage."

He lifts his chin toward his bandmate. "Thanks for looking out for my girl."

"Anytime." Bryson's voice is flat, and I don't miss the way he turns around right when Cam envelops me in a hug so tight I can hardly breathe.

"Did you feel it?" He nuzzles his nose into my neck and inhales like he's only just begun breathing again.

"I felt it." I may not be an expert in music like Cam, but I know when I've seen something supernatural. "You guys were perfect."

Cam swings me into the air. It lasts only a second, which is a good thing because he's come dangerously close to wearing regurgitated lemon on his shirt. When the room settles, I look for Bryson, but he's gone.

"I knew tonight was our shot. After all the sacrifices, the wasted time . . . it's finally going to happen." When he releases me, his eyes are blurry, and I'm suddenly hit with a trunkful of emotion I can't seem to control.

"I'm so happy for you, Cameron. Really."

Footsteps fall behind us, and we shift out of the way as three guys in leather huddle by the stage entrance. They each seem to have a pre-performance ritual. One's bouncing on his toes, another is cracking his neck, while the third is moving his mouth like he's going through the alphabet.

The neck cracker spots Cam when he's on crack number six and pauses. "Are you the guitarist who just did that solo up there?"

Cam stiffens beside me. "I am."

"Incredible sound, man. If you have some time after, we should hit some chords together."

My poor friend falls speechless. I subtly elbow him in the side.

"Yeah, maybe," he answers as if it's even in question.

The guy knows it, too. "And feel free to bring your girl-friend. It'll be a bunch of us."

"Thanks."

And since Cam spent most of the morning giving me this band's credentials, including their brand-new deal with Island Records, I know he just possibly got the "break" he's been waiting for.

We both remain completely still as the headliner the crowd is begging for fans out onstage. The lights go up, drums pump a beat through the air, and Cam looks at me in complete shock. "Did that just happen?"

I can't breathe. "Yes, that just happened."

He comes at me even more high on life than earlier. I give him the stiff arm, unwilling and truthfully unable to be spun around again.

"No spinning, please," I beg. "My head is already swirly from all the excitement."

"So you'll stay and hang out with us?"

I pat his hopeful cheek and shake my head. "Not a chance. I promised you two songs. That's it. Besides, do you really want to be worrying about me having a good time?"

He shrugs, disappointed, but we both know I'm right to decline.

We stand together and watch the manifestation of Cameron's dream. "That's us in six months," he whispers next to me, his envy strong enough to taste.

My stomach tumbles at the surety in his voice. As much as I've cheered him on, supported his dream, and encouraged him when his faith started to falter, this is honestly the first time I truly believe he's right.

NINETEEN

hen my obligatory two songs are over, I head out the backstage door and realize a little too late that it's the wrong exit. Instead of the beefy security guard and a roomful of half-inebriated people, there's a parking lot with ten reserved signs and a gate.

"Darcy?"

I look up just as Bryson closes the back of Jay's van.

"Bryson . . . hey."

"What are you doing out here?"

"I think I may have underestimated the power of lemons." I walk toward him, feeling a sway in my step that hasn't been there before. "How'd you end up with loading duty tonight?"

"I volunteered."

"Why?" Cam hates loading and unloading the equipment. In fact, sometimes I wonder if part of his desire to make it big comes from the idea that he'll have roadies to do all the heavy lifting for him.

"Because I'm tired and ready to go home. If I wait for them, I'll be here all night."

"Yeah, makes sense." I nod, but the act seems to teeter my already questionable equilibrium.

"Whoa." He cups my arm, keeping me steady. "Okay, Cinderella, the clock has definitely hit midnight for you."

"I know. I'm trying to get home," I slur, mashing my screen again. "But I can't get the stupid app to come up."

Bryson takes the phone from my hand. "Come on, you lush. I'll drive you." He guides me to the passenger side of his truck and helps me get inside.

I lean my head back against the headrest and try to close my eyes. Bad decision. The truck goes into a spinning carnival ride until I force my lids open again.

Bryson slams his door shut and turns to look at me with both amusement and a little pity in his eyes. "Where's Cameron?"

"He's watching Firemight or whatever their name is."

"And he just let you leave by yourself?"

"Nah. He offered to walk me out, but I assured him I was good." My head feels heavy and flops to the side. "He didn't know about the lemon drops. Though I don't think he'd be quite as rude about it as you were." I attempt to poke his arm but miss twice.

"I wouldn't be so sure of that."

I open my mouth to argue when different words fall out. "You've been avoiding me. Why?"

He sighs and slides his key into the ignition. "Let's just call it self-preservation and leave it at that." His answer doesn't make sense to me, but that could also be because my head is squishy.

I close my eyes again, thankful there's less spinning now. "Well . . . I missed seeing you. Just so you know."

Bryson's truck rumbles to a start, and it feels like only sec-

182

onds pass before I hear him ordering cheeseburgers from a drive-thru.

I sit up in the seat and look around at my surroundings. We're in Midlothian. Only a few miles from Zoe's apartment.

"Did I fall asleep?"

"Yep, and you sleep like the dead. I had to check your pulse twice." Bryson eases the truck forward and pays the attendant.

The smell of grease and French fries drifts through the truck window, and my stomach immediately growls in response. "You are now my favorite person in the world. That smells like heaven."

He snickers at me and reaches for the large paper bag the cashier is holding. "That's because you're drunk."

"I am not."

"Oh yes, you most definitely are. But this will help." He hands me the greasy treasure, and I immediately go for the nearest bag of fries.

"Oh my goodness. These taste soooo good." I shove another handful into my mouth. "Why have I never eaten here before?"

Bryson rolls up his window and puts the truck in drive. He's laughing at me, and I should be offended but I'm not. In fact, I feel like giggling myself.

"That AT&T guy tried to get me to go to his apartment," I say, unfolding the paper surrounding the most beautiful cheeseburger I've ever seen.

"I'm sure he did."

I ingest two delicious bites and wipe my mouth. "It's weird. I've never had a guy come on that strong before."

"Sure you have."

"No, really." I shake my head, grateful the worst of the

dizziness is gone. "I think it's the sundress. Tony said I looked tiny and feminine." Again the giggles come. "Imagine what he'd think if he saw the real me."

Bryson glances at me, then back to the road. "He'd think the same thing we all do. That you're just as gorgeous without all the frills as you are with them."

"Ah, that's sweet." I take another bite of my cheeseburger and wonder why his compliment makes me want to start crying.

"If I were a betting man, I'd say the only reason men aren't beating down your door is the fact that Cam stays permanently attached to your side. The two of you are pretty oblivious to the rest of the world."

"Please, Cam could get a master's degree in flirting. I swear he's had more girlfriends than I've had haircuts."

Bryson snorts out a laugh like I've said the most ridiculous thing tonight. "Name one that wasn't an exercise in passing time."

"I can name five."

He turns and raises his brows, waiting for me to continue.

"Okay, there's Cindy."

"Nope. She crushed on him for five months, so he gave her a few pity dates just to get her off his back."

"Fine. Lydia." I wait, knowing he won't have a rebuttal for that one. Lydia is Cameron's longest relationship to date.

"Boredom. She was there and available. Cam never had any real feelings for her."

"You're changing the rules. I said girlfriends, not soul-mates."

"And I said ones who weren't smoke screens." Bryson pulls the truck in front of our apartment and shoves the gear into park. "Try again."

I narrow my eyes at him, even though he's smirking. "Alright. January."

That wipes the grin right off his face. "Doesn't count."

"How so?"

"Because January was smokin' hot, and Cameron was blinded by it."

"You're just saying that because you hated her."

"I didn't hate her. I just didn't trust her. When you grow up in a family like mine, you get very good at spotting frauds."

"All the same, Cam's feelings for her—or at least the 'her' he thought she was—were very real. And I feel certain that if she hadn't lied, the two of them would still be together." I crumple the bag in my hand, my stomach now full and my smile nice and smug. "Now admit it. I win."

But Bryson doesn't continue our banter the way I expect him to. Instead, his expression turns hard, a deep line creasing his brow. "And that never bothered you? Seeing them together?"

My skin suddenly feels itchy. "No. Cam was happy. That's all that matters."

He shakes his head like I'm missing the point and shoves open his car door. "Let's get you inside."

The giddiness I felt for the last ten minutes falls to a pit in my stomach. I ease from the car, exhaustion and sadness wrapping me up like a blanket. Still, I trudge up the stairs and try not to feel completely humiliated by the fact Bryson has to help keep me steady.

He unlocks the door, and immediately Piper leaps at our feet, barking madly. I lean down and pick her up. My throat burns as I nuzzle her soft fur. At least she is too loyal to know what a colossal screw-up I am right now.

"I'll take her out for you," he offers.

I reluctantly hand her over and use the wall to stabilize my walk into the bedroom. Bryson was right. Slamming back martinis all night has accomplished nothing. I'm still here, stuck in this apartment, my professional life a complete disaster. My parents are still divorced, and my mom is probably sleeping next to Michael right now.

The bed whines when I drop down onto the mattress, my shoulders slumped, my arms hanging lifeless between my legs. And then the tears come. One at a time, rolling down my cheeks and onto the floor.

I feel Bryson settle next to me but can't seem to look at him. "I didn't set out to drink this much."

"No one ever does."

"I just thought if I tried something new and forbidden, then I wouldn't feel so cheated."

"How'd that work out for you?" I know he's trying to lighten the mood, but I can't seem to pull myself from the sorrow.

"I've spent my whole existence in this bubble with everything mapped out in perfect order. My parents sheltered me too much, and now that it's all gone, I feel like the ground won't stop moving."

Bryson's palm touches my back, moves up toward my shoulders, and squeezes. "They didn't shelter you; they shielded you, and that's not a bad thing. Boundaries are there for a reason. When I have kids, I'll do the same exact thing."

I chuckle through my sobs. "I thought you were never getting married."

"I'm being hypothetical." He studies my tear-soaked face, and compassion fills his normally stormy eyes. "You'll find your way through this." His voice shifts, its softness and layers of empathy reminding me that he isn't saying anything he hasn't already experienced himself.

"Thank you." My hand slides across the comforter and touches his. He startles at the contact but doesn't move. "For listening. And for taking care of me." I inch closer, my fingers trailing over his knuckles to the inside of his wrist.

"Darcy." His voice is full of a warning I don't want to hear right now. My hand trails up his forearm, the muscles underneath tensing with each lingering stroke.

I lift my gaze from his intoxicating skin and stare into the same eyes that captivated me when onstage. They blaze, a molten steel, and his gaze holds me like fire. My fingers continue their forbidden exploration. They're at his bicep now, my nails pushing against the hem of his tight sleeve. I scoot closer, the heat of his body surrounding me, filling this room, filling my head. He swallows and his breath comes out in quick hot waves. I glide my other hand closer until it lands lightly on his thigh.

If Bryson was tense before, he's now a solid rock of frustrated energy. He pulls his arm away first, then stands. "Time for bed."

"I don't want to go to bed." I want to go back to doing exactly what I was just doing.

"Maybe not. But I'm not interested in being another one of your experiments tonight."

Bitterness rises in my throat but there's no fighting the edge in his voice or the violent way he tosses aside the multiple shams that sit against the headboard. He folds back the sheets and waits, expectantly. I begrudgingly crawl over, kicking off my shoes in the process. He tucks me inside, sundress and all, and then walks out of my room without a word.

A hive of bees swarm in my chest and I nearly throw off the covers to follow him when he suddenly appears back in the doorway with a glass of water and a bottle of aspirin in his hands.

"Drink lots of fluids when you wake up and take two of these." He kneels so our faces are level, and slowly his tight, stubborn mouth relaxes. "Don't stay in this place too long, Darcy. You have so much more in you than this rebellion."

My insides jumble as though everything has been kicked and shaken. Strangely, he looks exactly how I feel. "Why did you do it?" I slide my hand through his, lace our fingers together. "Why did you make sure I lived here?"

He pauses as if trying to figure it out himself. "You needed options."

"No. If it were just that, you wouldn't have agreed to spend Thanksgiving with your family."

I can tell from his expression that he's surprised I know the truth. His shoulders are square, and his jaw holds the edge of a man busted. He sighs. "I did it because I'm selfish."

My voice feels weak. "How is that selfish?"

He detangles his hand and gently brushes a wisp of hair from my cheek. "The fact that you don't know the answer to that is exactly why I have no business being here right now." He stands, his body language suddenly cold and guarded. "Sweet dreams, Darcy. If we're lucky, you won't remember any of this in the morning." He then reaches his hand under my lampshade, and the room goes dark.

TWENTY

I made it out to the farm this morning, though how, I don't know. Throughout the entire drive, the sun scorched my eyes while my head pounded in a painful rhythm that mimicked the knocking of my aging truck engine. Twice, I had to fight the urge to pull my truck over to the side of the road and regurgitate the lemon drops that would undoubtedly taste worse coming up.

Bryson said if I was lucky, I wouldn't remember anything.

Well, I'm not lucky. I remember every humiliating moment from the last twenty-four hours, including the way I practically ripped his shirt off.

I grip the steering wheel, unable to move until the nausea subsides, and let my head rest against the warm leather. How did my life get so screwed up? I was going to be a missionary a month ago, and now I'm the girl who's not only skipped church more than I've gone but can't even find the words to pray. Or maybe I just don't want to pray. Because even though the initial trauma has subsided and my miserable attempt at rebellion has failed, I still feel this gut-wrenching anger I can't seem to get past. And worse, it all seems to be directed at the very entity I would normally go to for peace and comfort.

Sweat beads on my neck until I'm forced to move. My old truck has decent enough air conditioning when it's moving at a constant rate of speed, but not so much when it's simply idling in a driveway.

I push open the door and take my first shaky step onto the gravel. The sound is eerily quiet, and the nausea is immediately replaced by anxiety. Louie isn't barking. A phenomenon that has never occurred since the first day I met him.

Adrenaline takes over and I rush faster than I've moved all morning to the back of the house, only to find the dog in question is not only okay but standing in the middle of his kennel as if waiting for me.

"Now, aren't you full of surprises." Or maybe even Louie can sense that I'm teetering close to the breaking point.

I slide open the lock and take two careful steps inside, expecting at any second for him to scurry back to the corner and begin barking. He doesn't. Instead, he comes closer.

While Louie's erratic behavior has improved some in the past couple of weeks, never before has he gotten this close to me. I glance at Bentley's empty kennel on the left and wonder if his absence might be the very thing Louie needed to begin to trust.

I take two careful steps forward, watching the skittish Great Dane for any signs of distress. Normally I wouldn't let a dog I'm training set the tone, but I'm sensing Louie needs to be the one to take that first step in deciding if I'm really going to be his person or not.

With my arms at my sides, palms out, I wait. "Go ahead. Check me out. I can tell you want to."

He takes one step forward, then slides back and barks twice.

I don't move. "It's okay. Come on."

He tilts his head and watches me with those sad blue eyes. I can tell he wants to believe better times are coming; he's just too jaded to know what to look forward to.

"I understand, you know. My life hasn't exactly gone the way I planned it either." Though saying it out loud doesn't make me feel any better. "But you and I, we're overcomers. At least that's what I keep telling myself."

As if he understands my words, he tries again, making it within a foot of me before jumping back and barking so erratically one would think I'd lashed out.

"Now, how scary can I be? You outweigh me by at least thirty pounds," I say as soothingly as I can and wiggle my fingers a little. "And in case you haven't noticed, I'm not exactly in tip-top shape this morning."

My voice calms him, and this time he gets close enough that I feel his cold, wet nose on my palm. His ears perk up. I can tell he smells the dog treats I always bring with me.

He sniffs with purpose now, first against my hand, then his snout presses into my pocket. A bark comes, sudden and loud, and it's so unexpected I jump, which of course sends him flying back to the corner.

"I'm sorry. I'm sorry. You scared me." I reach into my pocket and pull one of the treats free. Kneeling on one knee, I extend my hand to him. To take the meaty morsel, he'll have to come closer, will have to believe I'm safe enough to touch my fingers again.

He does the inching forward, jumping back thing two more times before he's close enough to take the peace offering. His large wet nose brushes against my knuckle, and then his tongue gently swipes the treat from my fingers. I don't make him sit, don't give him any commands at all. This isn't about obedience; it's about trust. Trusting me to provide for him, trusting me not to harm him, trusting me inside his broken heart.

"That's a good boy, Louie."

When he's done swallowing, he comes back to my hand, sniffs my palm for more, and this time I'm ready when he barks at me.

"Sorry, that one was a freebie, but barking demands is not how we are going to communicate." I stand and reach into my pocket. Louie dances in front of me in a mix of fear and excitement. He barks again, this time with an agitated tone. "Oh, I know you want this treat, but you're not going to get it that way. I need you to sit."

He stares at me, obviously confused. He doesn't know the command, and unfortunately he won't let me close enough to show him, but I have a feeling the big guy is smart enough to figure it out.

"Can you sit?" I move closer and raise the treat up.

His head naturally follows, and the momentum causes his backside to dip. Not all the way to the ground but close enough.

"Very good." I give him the treat and feel the scrape of his teeth on my skin. We'll have to work on that, too.

He watches curiously as I refresh his food and water. I wonder if he can see my renewed strength or if he even understands how much this one victory has nourished my hurting soul.

When I'm done with all the housekeeping, I pull one more treat from my pocket. "Want to make it three for three today?"

He comes forward, only hopping back once.

"Sit," I say and hold the treat up high. This time when his head rises, his hindquarters go all the way to the ground. "Good boy!"

He takes the treat from my hand a third time, and as much as I want to reach out and touch his silky fur, I know it's too soon for contact. Today was a huge step forward. And considering how my luck has been going lately, I better stop while I'm ahead. "See you later, buddy. I need to get inside and take care of the other two. Penny's probably bashing against her cage by now."

I lock Louie's gate and head toward Charlie's back door. I'm two hours later than usual, which make me feel a double measure of guilt. I know Charlie handles the inside dogs when they need to go out, but I'd established a morning routine with them over the past couple of weeks that shouldn't have been broken. Not when Penny's my next training case and she's so far from ready.

I knock on the door, poke my head in, and right when I'm about to call out my usual I'm-walking-into-your-house greeting, I see Charlie standing in front of the stove, cooking eggs and bacon.

Awkwardness and shock cement me in place. "Oh, I'm sorry."

Charlie turns enough to glance at me and then back to his sizzling meat. "Don't be. Come inside."

I step through the doorway and gently close it behind me. "I'll grab Penny and get out of your way."

"No need. I just took her out a little while ago." He pulls the pan from the burner and turns the knob. "Have you eaten yet?"

My stomach growls at the invitation, and I wonder if the food will make me feel better or worse. Going off the cheeseburger last night, I'm hoping for better. "No, I haven't. I'm running a little behind this morning, on everything . . . it seems."

Charlie turns around and leans against the counter. "Bryson told me you may not make it by today. Something about a rough night?" His voice is teasing, but I'm mortified.

"I, um . . ." I have no response.

Charlie may have chuckled, but I can't tell since his beard is so shaggy it covers his lips. "Don't look so stricken. You're not the first person to overindulge in this room."

"I just can't believe he called you." I guess it's true that one bad night can erase a lifetime of responsibility.

"I wouldn't recommend feeding him to the wolves just yet. He didn't say why it was rough, but I've experienced enough hangovers to spot the signs. You look like you've been run over by a semi."

"I feel like I've been run over by one." There's really no point in downplaying the situation when he already knows what happened.

"Well, I have the cure. Grab a couple plates out of the cabinet and we'll get some food in that stomach."

I wash my hands and do as he asks, holding out the plates to Charlie so he can fill them up with eggs, bacon, and two slices of toast. He gestures to the small kitchen table in the corner, and I set both heaping plates down carefully. In minutes we have forks, orange juice, and uncomfortable silence as Charlie says a quick prayer for our food.

The silence continues as I take my first bite of scrambled eggs. "This is really good, thank you."

"You're welcome. I figured I owed you an apology for my continual grumpiness. Nothing says sorry like a plateful of food."

I smile around my bacon. "There's no need to apologize."

"You're a sweet kid for saying so, but I'm long past due telling you how much I appreciate what you've done for the dogs

. . . and for me." His voice goes soft, the grief still audible in every syllable. "Sue Ann would have really liked you."

"I would have liked her, too." Charlie goes back to his silent eating, but I sense there's more he wants to say. I swallow a crispy piece of bacon and hope I'm not crossing an invisible line. "How did you two meet?"

He glances at me, surprised by the question, but then I see it. The relief that follows. He just got permission to talk freely about the person he loves most in this world. "She was a cashier at Tractor Supply, and I went in every week. At that time, I was at the bottom of the barrel you could say. Partying, drinking, hating life and myself. But when I'd see her and her gorgeous, optimistic smile, it would get me through days of self-loathing. Eventually I learned her schedule, and then after two months I got up the nerve to ask her out." He stares off as if reliving the memory. "She said she'd go if I could last one whole month without a drink."

"I take it you succeeded."

He nods. "That day was the last time alcohol touched my lips. She pulled me out of all of it. Helped me find the Lord and all the pieces of myself I'd lost." He stares at the plate in front of him. "It's always tempting to find answers in a bottle, but they don't exist there."

My heart squeezes as shame presses in from his words. I fell into the same trap, only worse because my motivation wasn't grief or addiction. Mine was so much more selfish. I set aside my personal convictions just to prove a point that didn't need to be proven. And look what I have to show for it now—regret and embarrassment. "Is the drinking still a struggle for you?" I ask, mostly because I want to make sure my behavior and the aftermath of it didn't cause Charlie any harm.

He looks at me, his eyes full of sadness. "No. I wouldn't dishonor Sue Ann that way." Relief from his words eases away a little of the guilt. "But I haven't exactly been coping well." He shakes his head. "Turns out answers don't exist in front of a TV screen either, though I've certainly tried to find them the last few months."

"When my mission trip got canceled, I watched TV for eighteen hours straight. In Spanish."

That gets a chuckle out of him, and I'm surprised by how much it warms my chest to see him smile. "Bryson says I need to start returning to my old activities. I know she'd tell me the same thing."

"What were they?"

"Sue Ann and I were pretty active in the community center in town. She liked to dance, and they'd have instructors come once a month."

"That sounds like fun."

"Yeah, it was." He looks at his plate, sorrow crashing down again. "We'd also do archery together and take Macey for long walks each day. Archery stopped when the treatments started, but Sue Ann never missed her daily walks. Even on the worst days, when my poor wife could barely get around, there was something therapeutic about the click of the leash. Sometimes we'd only get as far as the driveway, but it helped her all the same."

I look toward the living room and catch a glimpse of Macey curled in her usual spot. She's getting thinner and thinner.

Charlie must notice where my attention has gone. "You're worried about her, aren't you?"

"I think it's odd that she didn't come over when bacon is on the menu."

"Yeah. I can't seem to get her to do much but lie there these days." He sets his fork down and sighs. "It's probably my fault. Macey was Sue Ann's baby. That dog went with her everywhere. To the store, the post office. She even tried to come with us to the hospital when Sue Ann had her treatments."

"Macey lost a lot when Sue Ann died. Sounds like she's grieving, too."

"We're quite a pair, aren't we?"

I finish off the food, amazed by how much better it makes me feel. "You could maybe take her when you resume some of your activities. Was there something she especially loved to do?"

Charlie leans back in his chair and contemplates my question. "Our neighbor has a dog about her size. They'd play together a lot. But, um, I wasn't the nicest to her when she tried to bring me food after the funeral." He scratches his long, shaggy hair. "But I suppose we could start there."

"I think Macey would really like that. And if you're looking to impress, you could always shave a little before going. Might help the apology if you didn't look like the Unabomber."

Charlie's eyes narrow, but there's a hint of amusement in them. I can almost picture the person he might have been before this tragedy. The guy who mentored an angry young boy. A guy who undoubtedly was instrumental in helping Bryson turn into the man he's become.

I stand and pick up both our plates, unsure if I should suggest the other thing that would help Macey's depression. I decide it's worth it. If Macey continues this way, I shudder to think of the consequences. "There's something else that might help her, but it may be difficult for you." I rinse the dishes and put them in the dishwasher. Charlie hasn't moved or said another word, so I have no idea if I should continue. I don't want to push too hard, not when he's finally getting up and getting dressed.

He stands and brings our empty glasses over. "Can't imagine anything more difficult than what I've already experienced."

I press my lips together to suppress the sudden desire to cry for his broken heart. "Well, if you're willing, I think Macey would greatly benefit from a piece of Sue Ann's clothing. An old shirt of hers, maybe? Something you could part with?"

Charlie grips the edge of the counter as if I've asked for the world. Maybe I have.

"It's just an idea. You don't have to."

"No. It's okay." He leaves the kitchen, and while he's gone, I busy myself in cleaning up the remnants of breakfast. When he still hasn't returned, I check on Penny's food and find my way into the living room, where Macey is curled tight into a ball.

I pet her soft fur. "I know you're sad, sweet girl, but I need you to try to eat, okay?"

"She likes popcorn."

I startle at Charlie's abrupt entrance but work to keep things light. "Butter or kettle corn?"

"Butter. Just like Sue Ann." He comes closer and hands me a dirt-stained white T-shirt. "I haven't been inside her closet since she died. I thought it might kill me to do so, but it was nice. The room still smells like her."

I take the material gently, knowing exactly what a sacrifice it is for him to offer it. "Thank you." Carefully, I press the cotton to Macey's nose. Immediately she jolts to a seated position, her head rearing up. She whines and nudges the shirt with her snout. I lay it at her feet and stand.

She presses her face against the soft cotton, then barks and rolls on top of it like an old companion. I look over at Charlie. His eyes glisten and it shreds a piece of my heart. I open my mouth to offer some kind of comfort or maybe just to thank him again for being so continuously unselfish. But I don't get the chance. Charlie's door is already closing, hiding him once again from the pressing grief that will never fully go away.

TWENTY-ONE

I once read that reliving positive memories from childhood can bring a small measure of peace to those struggling with anxiety, even years later. Tonight, I'm really hoping that theory is true.

I'm in the playground at Grace Community. The old one behind the gym. The one they long ago quit using when the new children's building was built.

What used to be a 1960s hallway with low ceilings and a constant mildew smell is now a 20,000-square-foot, two-story children's wonderland. One that's filled every Sunday. But I miss the days when I knew all the faces that passed me in the halls. I miss my dad making my brother and me sit with them instead of our friends. But most of all, I miss feeling safe like I always did when I came to this building. Cameron says I'm the worst when it comes to change. That people like me keep the world from progressing. Maybe he's right. Change has never been a friend of mine.

Even when I'm the one forcing it.

My phone reads 5:45 p.m., and Sunday night dinner starts at 6:00. This will be the first one I've ever intentionally missed, except for a handful while I was away at college. But even then I'd make it as often as I could. Never have I been in town and not gone. Never.

Each minute drags on like an hour: 5:47 . . . 5:48. If it could just get past the six o'clock mark, then maybe this wrenching in my gut would finally go away.

I set my phone facedown in my lap and continue my rhythmic swinging, racking my brain for any kind of distraction. Cam is working until eight tonight, and I've already exhausted all my other time wasters. The only things left are the two things I'm avoiding: apologizing to Bryson and answering my mom's umpteenth text today.

I kick at the dirt, my stomach taking a somersaulted leap at the thought of dialing Bryson's number. Then again, time is only going to make the humiliation worse, so I may as well do it now and put the final nail in the coffin marked "rebellion."

My thumb slides across the glass, and I take one stabilizing breath before pressing his number.

"Hey." The answer is short and more direct than I expect.

"Hey, I um . . ." I scramble to find any common ground that doesn't include the night before. "I wanted to talk to you about Charlie."

"Really?" His voice dips like he knows I'm stalling.

"Yeah. He made some progress today. I just thought you should know so you could go by there tomorrow. Make sure he actually gets out of the house like he said he might."

"I will, thanks." He's quiet for a second. "Is that all?"

"Yes . . . I mean, no." I squeeze my eyes shut, the embarrassment of the night before coming back in full color. "I'm sorry . . . about last night."

He sighs into the phone. "It's really okay." His voice is different now. As if he needed to know that I knew I'd treated him poorly. It's ironic. A few weeks ago, I accused Bryson of using people and yet I'm the one who did that very thing to him. "How are you feeling?"

"Better. And you should know that my little drinking experiment is over. I will be shelving the lemon drops for an indefinite period of time."

He chuckles. "Good."

I press my toes into the ground and push the swing backward.

"Darcy, you okay?"

"Yeah, just thinking, I guess."

"About?"

"Life, family, Sunday night dinners, or in my case, skipping Sunday night dinners since my last one did not go so well."

He's quiet, and I wonder again why all my secrets seem to spill out to him. "Could that be part of the reason you went a little heavy-handed last night?"

I shouldn't be surprised anymore by this new profound version of him, but I still am. "Probably."

The line goes silent, but it doesn't feel awkward or tense. It feels like he's giving me time to reason through my feelings. And maybe that's why I want to share them. Why even though I made the excuse that Cam was working, the truth is that he has never once not taken my call when I needed him, so it was never about availability. I didn't want Cam tonight. I wanted Bryson.

"Do you want to hear something ridiculous?" I ask, twisting the swing until the chains cross, then uncross.

"Sure."

"I've been sitting in front of Grace Community for an hour now. Just sitting here in that old playground where we'd tag each other and run around until our parents made us pack it up and go home." I bite my lip and feel a sting in my throat.

"My life is so screwed up right now that I've come to a point where the only thing I recognize anymore is an old swing set and our youth building." I shake away the looming sadness and think back to all the days and nights I'd spent here. "Do you ever miss high school?"

That gets a snort. "No."

"Really? I do sometimes."

I hear a dinging sound and then a car door slamming. "What is there to miss? On top of not having any control over our lives, we had to deal with acne and insecurity and school-work."

"True, but we also had youth group every Wednesday night to connect with friends and feel empowered about our future."

"I think you have a selective memory. If I recall, you hated high school even more than I did."

"I guess. Maybe I just miss feeling a part of something." I look at the structure in front of me. Inside is a full-sized basketball court, several Bible study classrooms, and an entire section of the building set aside for junior high and high schoolers. And thankfully, other than a new paint job to match the worship center, the building has stayed relatively untouched. "After all this time, this place still makes me feel safe. I'd love to go hang out in the Shop just one more time." The Shop was our nickname for the youth room back when I was in school.

"They have foosball and a pool table in there now. A stage, too, with a seventy-inch screen and about a thousand digital movies and games."

"What? We so got the shaft when we were kids." The best thing we had back then was a slanted Ping-Pong table and an old Xbox. A rumbling engine echoes through the air. "Oh, hold on. I think someone's coming." I stand from the swing and watch as Bryson's unmistakable black beast turns the corner.

He parks the truck and emerges, still holding the cellphone up to his ear. "I thought you might want some company on your trip down memory lane."

I end the call and take a shaky step toward the fence that separates us. Images of last night fill my mind. His strong arms holding me steady up the stairs, my fingers sliding over his skin, the way his body heat rose with every inch I explored. "You got here fast," I squeak out, mortified by my own thoughts.

"I was in the neighborhood. Wanna go inside?" His lips tilt up into an endearing smile. It's sexy and daring and adorable all at the same time.

"I don't think breaking and entering a church is the best way to prove I'm back on the straight and narrow."

"It's not breaking and entering when you have a key."

I look at him through suspicious eyes, knowing there has to be some kind of catch. "How do you have a key?"

"Are you kidding me? I'm beloved around here."

I snort out a laugh. Our youth pastor couldn't stand Bryson or the obnoxious chip on his shoulder. The feeling was mutual, and Bryson quit coming here the minute we graduated. I assumed he quit church altogether until I saw him watching the service online with Charlie. "Seriously, where did you get the key?"

"Mr. Berny gave it to me. Though he'd probably deny it if you asked him." Mr. Berny has been the church's custodian for almost twenty years now. "The night my stepdad kicked me out, I drove straight here. I figured if I had to sleep in my car, at least it would be somewhere I knew was well lit." He leads me between two of the buildings and down a hidden sidewalk. "Mr. Berny tapped on my window at five-thirty the next morning. He took one look at all my things stuffed in the back and told me to get up and use the bathrooms before anyone got here. I later found this key in my duffel bag." Bryson pulls silver metal from his back pocket. "For a week, I'd wait until all the staff went home, then let myself in to shower and crash on one of the Shop couches."

I feel relieved to know Bryson didn't spend a week in his truck, though it pierces my heart to imagine him sneaking inside the building just to use the bathroom.

He slides the key into the lock and pushes the door open. "Voilà!"

"You're telling me that they haven't changed the locks on this building in over a decade?"

"Nope. Only the security code." He mashes four buttons on the keypad by the door. "But I have friends in important places, so I know that, too."

Bryson closes the door behind us and turns on the lights down the hall and into the old youth room.

I walk ahead of him, eager, terrified, excited, and enter the room that consumed most of my teenage years. They've painted it all black. The walls, the floors, the stage. A collage of old records covers an entire wall, giving it a retro vibe I admittedly kind of like.

Bryson settles next to me and rests his forearm on the doorframe. "It's pretty cool, huh?"

"Of course *you'd* like it. It's your signature color."

He grins and slides into the room. "You're just jealous that a generation half my age wants to be like me." He winks, smug and arrogant, and darn if it doesn't make me swoon just

205

a little. He tosses the foosball into the air and catches it. "You up for a game?"

"Heck yeah. But a warning . . . I can be ruthless."

"Can you?"

"Yep. Cam found this old game store in college. They'd let you pay a cover and then play board games, pool, and foosball all night long." I take a spot on the other side of the table. "You have no idea how many free dinners I got that month."

Bryson's smile falters. "Only a month, huh?"

"Yeah. Cam's the worst at strategy and doesn't have the best attention span, so his desire to keep getting beat waned pretty fast." I drop the ball through the serve feed and quickly try to match Bryson's movements. "We later found this coffee shop that had open-mic nights. That became our go-to." I move my goalie a half inch too far to the right, and the ball rushes past into the goal. "Dang it." I look up and see Bryson smirking at me.

"You said the wager is dinner, right?"

"Not if you keep slamming in goals." I slide the ball in again, determined to talk less this time and pay more attention. I focus and spin, move, spin again, and barely get past his goalie for a score. "Yes!" I hop up and down, fully embracing my inner teen.

"You willing to wager dinner now?" There's challenge in his eyes, and I instinctively know it's about more than this simple game. Yet at the same time I find myself wanting to play along. Really just wanting to do anything that feels as good as I always seem to feel lately when Bryson's around.

"Now . . . you're on."

We go back and forth, each taking turns scoring on the other, until Bryson makes a play that challenges all rules of physics and scores.

"No way!" I scream, staring at the winning point sitting in my goal. "That was an impossible shot."

He lifts both arms above his head in victory. "The impossible is what I do."

I pick up the ball and throw it softly at his chest.

"Ouch." He rubs playfully at the spot. "Talk about a sore loser."

"Oh please. I didn't throw it that hard." I lean over and pick up the ball from the floor. "So what's next? Pool? Ping-Pong? You have to give me a chance to redeem myself."

"I think we need some music first." Bryson's mood has changed, much like mine has in the last twenty minutes. He's energetic, funny, and a version of himself I didn't even know existed. "What are you in the mood for?" He connects his Bluetooth to the sound system receiver and scrolls through his playlists. "I have just about every genre you could possibly want."

I glance at the stage, where an acoustic guitar sits ready for just this moment. "Why don't you play that song you've been working on? The one Bentley liked so much."

Insecurity is an odd look for Bryson, but it's etched all over his face with that request. As if I'm not just asking him to play a song, but inviting myself into his life, his hurts, and past that shield of armor he's carried so proudly since we were kids.

"I still don't have any lyrics."

"So? It's beautiful, even without all that."

He hesitates, then concedes, though his gait around the sound booth looks more like a man about to face a firing squad, not play for an eager fan.

I pull a chair close and watch as Bryson slides the guitar strap over his torso and sits on one of the stage stools. He checks the tuning and, when satisfied, begins his first strum.

Strings fill the room, enveloping me with the rich sound. He changes chords, speeds up, then slows again, all while humming in that dark, silky voice of his. Then he moves to a new part, one he hadn't written the last time I heard him play, and my heart seizes at the agony of the sound. It's not angry like so many of his other songs. It's pain, real and authentic. It's a place one only finds after the rage is gone.

He hits the side of the guitar, then strums, creating a tempo that's unique and hypnotic. And then it settles back into rich, lengthy chords. If peace were a song, this last part is what it would sound like. He slows as it ends, pulling me along, tearing away any defenses I may have left. And then the room goes silent.

Bryson runs a hand through his hair and smiles tentatively at me.

"That was . . . incredible." More than incredible. It's a completely new sound for him. "Have you written more like this one?"

He shrugs. "Ballads don't make rock stars."

I think back to the night before. The energy and spark and sheer violence that came pouring off that stage and know he's right. Still, it seems like a waste that his song may never be heard by anyone but me.

"What's it feel like?"

He sets the guitar back in its stand. "What do you mean?"

"To be onstage. To have the whole crowd screaming at you like they did."

"Want me to show you?" He stands and waves for me to come forward.

I glance around the room, confused. "How can you show me without people?"

"Come here and you'll see." There's that spark in his voice

208

again. That edge between daring me to step out of my comfort zone and a certainty that I won't.

I hop up onstage, more for myself than to prove something to him. "Okay. I'm here."

He smirks and gently clasps my arms, turning me until we both face the empty chairs throughout the room. My breath catches when I feel him press into my back. "Close your eyes."

I do as he says, trying to steel my rising pulse. Music begins playing around me, pouring from every hidden speaker, quietly at first and then louder, until I'm sure he's turned his phone all the way up. "Let everything else out of your head and feel the music."

Maybe it's the darkness my closed lids have created or the way his chest vibrates against my back, but Bryson suddenly turns into that captivating man onstage. Confident, demanding, and so incredibly hypnotic that I can barely breathe.

"Let the chords dance over your skin." The tip of his nose brushes against the side of my cheek. Intentional, unintentional, I don't know, but I melt into his body, our shared heat penetrating through the thin material of my shorts. His fingers skim my skin, and it's such a sensational tickling that I begin to wonder if it's the music making my body hum or just the tender way his body has melded into mine, like he wants to experience every sensation I'm feeling.

"Feed off the drums, the beat slamming against your chest." Bryson angles his head, his mouth so close to my earlobe that his lips graze the sensitive skin as he speaks. Pleasing goose bumps form along my neck as his breath dances against the surface. "Now picture the crowd. Imagine that pulse of energy that soars from them to us and fills the air with power so intoxicating, it drives out exhaustion, hunger, thirst, whatever, and makes you just want to play until your fingers bleed."

I suddenly feel the same way about Bryson's breath on my skin. I want more contact. Want his arms to wrap around me and his lips to graze my jawline.

And then he stops talking but doesn't let go. I breathe in when he does, out at the same time. I don't know how long we stay there, it can only be seconds, but I feel as if we're journeying to an alternate universe where Bryson and I together might actually make sense.

He backs away, and my body suddenly turns cold.

I spin around, feeling like I've somersaulted into a world I've never seen in real color. "Wow."

"I know. It's addicting . . ." He glances at the floor and back up again, this time with a smile that's soft enough to send an army of tingles down my spine. "It's like an escape from every part of the world, including my own head."

"Well, you're lucky. I've spent the last month trying to find something that can get me that kind of escape, and being inside the Shop tonight is the first time I've even come close."

"Why do you think that is?"

I fiddle with the microphone cord. "Because it reminds me of life before the divorce. Before my dad abandoned our family. Before my mom started dating. All of that." My voice thickens with the anger that always seems to come when I think of my father and the bomb he detonated in my life. "That probably sounds really dumb coming from someone my age."

"Not at all. I have a place just like that. On the hard weeks, I go out there more often than I care to admit." He glances at the walls, the ceiling, and the couch that looks very similar to the one we had when we were in high school, and then back at me. "It makes sense that Grace Community would bring you peace. You always did fit here."

He says it like he didn't, and I guess I can see why he would feel that way. Bryson has a way about him that makes you want to know the deepest parts and yet feel certain he'll never share them with you. It makes it easier not to try. I know. I didn't bother for most of our lives, but that's not the case anymore. "Is your place nearby?"

"Somewhat. Why?"

I shrug. "I don't have anywhere to be right now, and if you don't either, I thought maybe you could take me there."

Hesitation comes again, along with the same insecurity he showed when I asked him to play for me. "It's nothing special."

I doubt that. If it wasn't important, he wouldn't look so afraid. "If you're willing to show me, I'd really like to go."

He comes closer, but there's restraint in his movement. A stiffness in his stride. A holding back. "Why?"

"Because it's important to you, which makes it important to me." I glance down at his hand. The same one I held the night before. I look back up at him and wait to see if he'll open up or if he'll bolt like he did the last time we shared a moment of intimacy.

Of course, last time I was drunk, and he was being a gentleman. This time I'm one-hundred-percent sober.

"You should know something about me." His eyes burn into mine and I see a hundred questions behind them. "I don't easily let people in."

"Tell me something I don't already know." I smirk, trying to clear the heaviness that's fallen between us.

Bryson will have none of it. "I'm serious here." He rakes back his hair, hesitating. I know with that small movement he's struggling to give me what I'm asking. "I'm an all-or-nothing guy, Darcy. I can't exist on the surface. I'm not programmed that way."

"I understand."

"Do you? Because if we take this step. If *I* take this step with you, everything's going to change. There are some doors that don't close again once they're opened."

My heart does the same fluttering it seems to do more and more when in Bryson's presence. Heat creeps up my neck and flushes my face. I don't know what he's asking of me, but I know I want to say yes, especially if behind that door is the man I'm only just starting to really see.

TWENTY-TWO

When Bryson admitted to having a special place, I was certain it would be something related to music. Never would I have guessed that it would be a baseball complex.

Bryson parks his truck, and I pull in right next to him and cut the engine. The parking lot that can easily hold two hundred cars is empty, and the sun is beginning its slow descent to the horizon. I exit my truck and wait for Bryson to meet me on the sidewalk. He seems rooted in place, and I wonder if maybe I asked too much of him this time.

Finally, his door creaks open and his leg appears. He's obviously in no rush to start this tour, as it takes three times the normal length to completely emerge from the vehicle.

"You play baseball?"

He shifts on his feet, glancing down for a moment. "I did . . . a long time ago."

We walk side by side up the long sidewalk separating two different baseball fields. A concession shack waits at the end, its window covered in wood and locked tight. There are remnants of an active Saturday in and around the trash cans, but not a soul lingers now. It would feel eerie if not for Bryson next to me, and I find myself inching closer as we get deeper into the heart of the complex.

He still hasn't said anything, and I don't know if I'm supposed to fill the silence or let him think. The whole experience seems to be new for both of us.

"This is it," he says when we reach the farthest field. It's smaller than the others, the bases closer. He walks through the nearest dugout and onto the field, me close behind. "I played here when I was six." He takes a deep breath, inhaling the air around us. "Even now, the smell of the clay dirt and that touch of hot breeze on my neck brings me back to that spring." He glances my way and smiles. "It's the last time in my life that I remember feeling completely secure."

I picture him as a little boy in tiny cleats and a baseball cap, his dark curly hair poking out under the brim. "What position did you play?"

"Dirt digger." He laughs out of nowhere and grabs my hand. "Come on, I'll show you."

I have to jog to keep up with him, until we're standing on the right side of the field where the dirt gives way to a big stretch of grass that, upon closer inspection, is mostly weeds and the kind of stickers that will cling to your socks and never let go.

"This is what I'd do, every game." He squats down and runs his fingers through the hardened red soil.

"What happened if a ball came your way?"

"It never did. Kids from all over the field would descend on the ball like ants on a jelly bean. There wasn't any point in trying to be one of the many." He stands and slaps his hands together to brush off the dirt. "Honestly, I thought the game was pretty boring."

"If you didn't like playing, why is this your favorite place?"

"Same reason you like to sit in the playground at Grace Community. The field reminds me of before. Before my step-dad came around, before I was old enough to realize I was never going to have a father." He stares off toward the dugout and words fade into silence. I see the struggle, his search for the apathy he's always painted on his face. It's beyond his grasp now. "I had the best coach." His voice turns soft, nostalgic. "Coach Tucker, but we all called him Tuck."

I step closer and gently touch his back. "Tell me about him."

A tortured smile pulls at his lips. "He was kind and chubby. I remember because my mom has always been super thin, and when he'd pick me up, it'd feel completely different, like being held by pillows." He turns and my hand falls away. "He was in love with my mom, poor guy."

"She didn't love him back?"

He shakes his head. "Nope, but that didn't keep her from leading him on. She liked being adored, and he certainly adored her and me." His voice catches, and the same anger that flows through each of his songs wraps around every word. "Until Charlie, he was the only example of a father I'd ever known, and she shattered his heart."

"What happened?"

"She met my stepdad." He pauses, a deep breath filling his chest, his nostrils flaring. "And because she didn't want to ruin their budding relationship by having me tag along, she kept me a secret and used Tuck as a fill-in babysitter whenever she'd have a date. Only she didn't call it a date. Mom told Tuck she'd decided to go back to school, so he was very understanding whenever she needed to study."

I flinch at the cruelty. "That's terrible."

"She's a shrewd woman, my mom. And now that I know

my stepdad like I do, she was probably right to keep me a secret. He would never have willingly raised another man's child." I hear the disgust in his voice and feel equally sickened. "Meanwhile, Tuck and I got closer and closer. He even brought me to pick out the ring. We both thought we were one yes away from being a family."

I cross my arms against my chest, my heart squeezing as if it can already feel the heartbreak that's coming in this story.

"He asked her to marry him on a Friday night. By Sunday, Tuck was out of our lives and I was meeting the man who stole my mom away. A man who only stuck around because Mom was already pregnant with Zoe." Bryson sighs. "I guess in some ways, the two of us never had a chance. From the very beginning, we both resented the other's existence." His voice catches, and the pain in it makes me want to wrap my arms around him and kiss away all the hurts he's ever suffered.

But I tried that once, and his stiff rejection made it clear he didn't want my comfort or pity, at least not in that way. I think of the foosball game and how cathartic it was to detach from the sorrow, even if just for a few minutes. Maybe that's exactly what he needs right now.

"You know what I liked to do as a kid?" I step backward until I'm out of the dirt and on the grassy area. I find a spot somewhat free of pokey weeds and plop down like a toddler. "On summer days, I'd pick a comfy spot, spread out my arms, and use the clouds to tell a story." Slowly I lie back, ignoring the sharpness underneath me or the way my ponytail snags on the tiny plants. "See, there's a knight holding his sword high above his head."

I hear the crunch of Bryson's steps and then feel the heat of his body as he lies next to mine. I resist turning to look at him, too afraid of what the closeness might do to my already elevated nerves.

I point to the spot in the sky where the pink clouds form a blob with a long streak. "Do you see it?"

He chuckles. "Not even a little."

"What? It's right there." I point again, and this time he takes my hand and laces our fingers together. It feels important, like our worlds are uniting in this moment. I ignore the surge of adrenaline and continue. "And look, there is his castle." He pulls until I'm forced on my side, facing him. "You don't like this game?" I ask, my voice shaky.

"I didn't bring you out here so we could pretend to be kids again." He leans up on his elbow, his other hand still entangled in mine. "I brought you out here because I thought you wanted what I do . . . for us to finally be honest with each other."

"Okay . . ." I search his eyes, my voice as unsteady as my heart suddenly feels. "You go first."

"I find your confidence staggering." He releases my fingers, but only to reach out and pick two stickers out of my hair. "The way you go through life is so genuine. From your effortless ponytails to your casual clothes to the crazy things you do without a thought to who's watching. It's why last night bothered me so much. It was the first time you didn't feel like you." His hand falls slowly and lands on the soft skin inside my wrist. "I spent my entire life suffocating under the image my mom and stepdad had for our family. It didn't matter what was true, only what people saw." His touch continues down to my palm. "But with you, I never have to wonder what's real and what's not."

He pauses, and I know it's my turn to reciprocate, to give him back the honesty he just gave me.

"I truly admire the man you've become."

His brow creases. "You do?"

"Yeah. You've overcome so much. Even your story tonight. It wasn't laced with grief like you're still living in it." I search his eyes and know he's done the impossible. "It didn't make sense before, but I see it now. Your willingness to go to Thanksgiving, your song, even your advice to me the other day. You've forgiven them."

"Well, it's more a work in progress."

"I understand. Every time I think of my dad or pull up his contact on my phone or ignore his weekly attempts at reconciliation, all I feel is this gut-piercing rage that refuses to go away." He opens his mouth, but I quickly beat him to it. "Nope. I don't want to talk about him. Not right now." I inch closer. "I just wanted you to know that I recognize the battle you've faced, and even more, how you're winning."

His eyes darken the way they always seem to when emotion hits him. "Sue Ann's death was the turning point. That's when everything spun upside down, and all the stuff that seemed so important at the time became insignificant. Suddenly, relationships mattered, and the people I'd all but let go of became a pressing thorn of regret in my side."

I nod in understanding. "Grief can certainly make you question everything."

"And sometimes it's exactly what you need to finally go after what you've always wanted."

I think of the band and how hard Bryson worked to get Cameron to join. "Black Carousel," I say, disappointed for some reason.

"No, Darcy. For the first time in years, I couldn't care less about what happens to the band." His fingers blaze a trail up my arm, his eyes never leaving mine. "But I care a great deal about what happens to you." There's a pause as if he's deciding how honest he wants to be. "When you told me you were moving in with Cam, it made me so nauseous, I thought I might lose it, right there on the swing next to you. I tracked Zoe down that night and refused to leave until she said yes. I wasn't kidding when I said I was selfish, Darcy. I didn't want you living with another man. Even one you claim is only a friend."

My heart slams against my chest, the air between us crackling as if lightning were about to strike us both for daring to say these things out loud. "In the spirit of honesty . . . I *was* jealous last night when that girl came up to you, and then again when I thought about you bringing groupies backstage."

He grins, slow and sexy. "You have no reason to ever feel jealous."

I lick my lips since they've suddenly gone completely dry. "Why's that?"

His hand moves across my shoulder and cradles my head, his fingers burying deep into my mess of a ponytail. "Because . . . when I was nine years old, I met the most beautiful girl I'd ever seen in my life." He closes the last of the space between us, his breath a whisper against my cheek. "And twenty years later, I'm still completely mesmerized by her."

His touch is gentle at first, a soft brush of lips against mine. The type of kiss you give when unsure if the other person wants the same thing.

I don't let him wonder for long, responding with my own pressure, deeper and more demanding. Sparks sizzle in the air, and my pulse races as each inch between us becomes an inferno of emotion and desire.

He eases his body over mine, slow and gentle, his hand and forearm taking the full brunt of the ground. I knot my fingers in his hair, pull him closer until I'm trapped beneath his weight, my skin so charged with want that I finally understand why every romantic kiss in a movie comes with music and fireworks.

The kiss slows, Bryson taking us back to the original pace. His long, artistic fingers caress my temple as the space between us grows and grows until he hovers over me, waiting for a response.

My breath is suddenly trapped in my chest. What do you say after kissing a guy you've known for twenty years? That was great, thank you?

He studies me, his eyes traveling over every inch of my face, his gaze apprehensive.

I wiggle free until I can sit up, my throat closing around my sudden uncertainty.

Bryson notices the retreat, his mouth growing tighter as I put more space between us. "Are you okay?"

"Yeah." But even I'm not convinced it's true, especially since my legs feel wobbly as I stand. I check my pockets. My phone is missing, and my car key has almost freed itself from my pocket. I shove it down and look over the ground for my lime-green phone case.

"It's right here."

I spin around, my breath matching the erratic feelings I can't seem to compartmentalize. "Oh, thanks." But as I go to reach for the device, Bryson pulls it back and forces eye contact instead.

"What's going on in your head?"

I shouldn't be surprised by his directness. He's been exactly that since the moment he sat next to me on the swing and upended my personal life. I take the phone, my mind tumbling, and slide it in my pocket. "I'm nervous, I guess."

"Why?"

"Because I don't have any experience with this type of thing. And you're . . . well, you're you."

Silence vibrates between us as hurt spreads across his brow.

"And you're you," he says slowly, carefully. "The girl who's always been off-limits, the girl who never once noticed me until your life fell apart." The tremble of fear in his voice slays me. He reaches up and caresses my cheek. "That doesn't exactly leave me with a lot of security either."

I don't move. I'm not sure I'm even breathing. Zoe had been right. I'd missed everything. "I never knew you felt this way."

"Like I said, I don't let people in very easily."

I stare into his beautiful, waiting eyes, the enormity of his admission pressing against my chest. "I would never hurt you."

"I know you wouldn't on purpose." He presses his forehead into my neck, runs a trail of delightful kisses to my ear. "Which is why I'm willing to risk being vulnerable, if you are."

I sigh, closing my eyes, lost in the wonderful sensations he's creating. "Oh . . . I'm definitely willing."

"I'm very happy to hear that," he whispers, moving to the underside of my jaw.

I giggle at the way it tickles and pull away. "Easy, tiger. Too much of that and we'll be back on the ground."

Creases deepen around his eyes. "You don't hear me complaining."

"Well, my stomach might pretty soon." I back away, unable to stop the perpetual smile on my face. "Last I checked, there was a dinner wager."

He swings his arm around my shoulder and pulls me tight

against his side, leaning down to kiss me one more time before we start our trek back to the cars. "Yes, and if I recall, you lost, which means I get to pick the place."

I pause, realizing I have no idea what Bryson's favorite restaurant is or even what type of food he likes. The thought warms my insides even more than his kiss did. It's nice that there are still some mysteries there. Ones I'm truly looking forward to discovering.

TWENTY-THREE

*I*n all the years I've known Bryson, I've never once seen him be affectionate, not even with his girlfriends. Yet in the past five days we've spent together, he hasn't gone one minute without holding my hand or finding some way for the two of us to be touching.

Even now, while I'm wet with perspiration, trying to get Penny to listen, his fingers graze the tips of my pulled-back hair.

"What is the point of this again?" he asks, his hand sliding lazily across my back.

We're both standing outside of Bentley's old kennel, watching Penny trot around with a tennis ball in her mouth.

I sigh, frustrated, not with him but with Penny's stubbornness. "She needs a job. Something that makes her feel useful so that we can redirect her aggressive energy into something positive."

"I think she'd rather just chew on the ball." He leans his forearms on the top of the kennel, the wire bowing slightly under the weight. His tattoo peeks out when his shirtsleeve rides up, and without thinking I drag my fingertips across his skin.

"Why did you get this?"

"To tick off my stepfather."

I push his sleeve until it stays tightly around his shoulder. "I'm serious."

"So am I." He grunts a laugh, his hazel eyes teasing me. "And if you keep touching me like that, I'm going to have to break your 'no making out in front of Charlie' rule."

I glance toward the house and confirm he's not around. "Why won't you tell me what it means?"

His muscles tense, which is how I know he's not being totally honest. Bryson's tells have become clearer since that first day on the swing together. When he's angry or upset, he distances physically and uses sarcasm or arrogant comments to force even more separation. But when it's deeper, when he's hurt or threatened, his entire body locks up. It's as if he creates a cocoon around himself to protect from oncoming blows.

"It's okay if you don't want to talk about it."

"It's hard to admit weakness." His struggle for words cuts a hole through me. He lifts his arm and stares at the ring of barbwire that has no beginning or end. "I got it a month after he gave me my truck. A reminder that I sold out. That like my mom and sister, I let him own me."

"I thought you loved that truck."

"I hate that truck and everything it represents."

"Then why keep it all this time?" And not just keep it. In just the short time we've been close, I've seen how much energy and money he's poured into it, just to ensure it stays running.

"Because it's also the last thing I have that connects me to them." He stares off toward the driveway, where the truck in question sits. "How's that for screwed up?"

I scoot closer and softly press my lips to his marked skin. "You're not screwed up." I don't have the words to tell him how strong I think he is, or how much I love seeing the tenderness of the sweet little boy I knew peek through the hardened shell he's formed.

Bryson reaches out and touches my hand. His fingers slowly slide up my arm to my neck and his thumb traces a slow, lazy circle over my collarbone. Then it's an invasion of my personal space, every part of him connecting to every part of me. Hot embers burn in my chest. I inhale the scent of him, one I'm starting to crave more and more.

"You're so beautiful." His lips brush against my eyelids, his voice tender.

"I'm a sweaty mess." I duck my chin, wondering when this feeling of light-headedness that he seems to bring out in me will go away.

"You're beautiful," he says more emphatically this time. "You always have been, but lately it's gut-wrenching how much I want to be near you."

He bends over and his lips meet mine, soft, loving, and I shiver beneath their touch.

"You're trembling." A crease deepens between his brows. "Did I admit too much?"

"No." I gently finger the hair at his temples, reassuring him. "I'm just trying to reconcile who you are with who I've always known you to be. You're so different. Or, I don't know, maybe you're not and I'm just finally seeing who you always have been."

"I'm no saint, if that's what you're implying." He grins mischievously, and my knees turn to water. "But I am happy, Darcy. For maybe the first time in my entire life, I feel completely . . . content. That alone will change a person."

A growl comes from our feet, and I reluctantly look away from Bryson to see what Penny is complaining about. The ball she'd been gnawing on is a completely mangled mess at her feet.

I untangle my arms from his embrace and stare at the shredded green material on the ground. "If you think I'm just going to get you another one to destroy, you're delusional."

Bryson scowls at the stubborn terrier. "I think you're the one who's delusional. That dog is never going to listen to you. She's too far gone."

"Don't be a hater." I throw him a glare that makes him laugh instead of cower. "Penny's smart. She'll learn."

"If you say so. I for one am going back inside where it's air conditioned." He slides his hands around my cheeks and kisses me deeply before letting go. "Join me when you're done beating your head against the wall." He winks when I push him away, my grin practically schoolgirl silly. He walks backward, never taking his eyes off me, until finally he reaches the steps and disappears through Charlie's door.

I watch the empty space, longer than I should, before turning back to my task. Any residual giddiness fades the minute I see Penny lying down with a new ball in her mouth. "Okay, it's time to get serious." I unlatch the gate and join the little dog inside the kennel. "No more fooling around."

Immediately she growls, a warning that I better not try to take her toy away. Not to worry, I need her to *want* to do this. Forcing her is only going to spark more aggravation. Mimicking what I want her to do, I jog to the shallow barrel on the far side of the kennel, pick up one of the tennis balls, and jog back to the gate to drop it into the empty identical barrel. I hold up the treat. "Now it's your turn."

She drops the ball in her mouth, eager to get a bite, but I

pull it back. "Nope, come get the ball first." Once again, I jog toward the full barrel, this time with Penny at my heels. No surprise, she's got this part down. It's the letting go she's not so good at.

"Good girl." I give her a small reward and point to the waiting pile of tennis balls.

She grabs one in her mouth and we both jog back to the barrel. Like before, Penny runs around the metal pot but refuses to drop the ball inside.

I motion for her again, wave the treat, and coax her forward. Nothing. In fact, I think she's laughing at me. "Ugh!" I growl up at the sky and lace my hands behind my neck.

Penny's fur rises on her neck, and I know I need to calm down before I do more damage than good.

"Tell you what, let's take a break, and you can chew all you want." I pick up the end of her leash and tie it to the fence. The spaces between slats are small, but if she really wanted to escape, she could easily push herself between them.

I lock the gate behind me and head to the water hose. It's ninety-five and climbing, and I want nothing more than to douse myself with a bucketful of water. For now, though, I'll settle for a good hands-and-face washing.

A bark stops me mid-step. I turn toward the only dog capable of making that kind of noise. Louie's out of his doghouse and standing by the gate, staring at me.

"Well, look who finally decided to make an appearance." I glance at Charlie's house and then back to Louie. Makes sense that he waited until we were alone to appear. It's not that he doesn't like Bryson, but he certainly doesn't share my same level of trust.

I abandon my trek to the hose and let myself into Louie's cage. "You smell those treats, don't you?"

227

He dances around and then eagerly sits the second I fasten his gate. "Wow. Look at you, Mr. Smarty-Pants." I reward him with a chunky morsel, only having to remind him once to take it gently from my hands.

He finishes chewing and sits again, closer this time.

"You're going to have to do more than sit for a second one." I carefully reach out and wait to see if he pulls away. He remains still, his ears relaxed, so I inch close enough that my fingers graze the soft skin on his snout. "Good boy," I whisper, careful that nothing I do is jarring in any way. I run my hand along his head and down the back to his neck.

Louie whimpers and leans his head into my hand like my touch is the most remarkable feeling in the world. My throat aches as I move closer, using my other hand to scratch behind his ear and down to the white patch of hair on his chest.

His back paw moves like Thumper, matching my scratches. "Oh, you like that spot, don't you?" My voice is caught between a laugh and a cry.

I squat in front of him, and Louie pushes my head with his nose, a fight for dominance, as well as his own try at reciprocating the affection. I lift my chin, keeping my head higher than his, all while eagerly scratching down his side.

My back pocket belts out a song that makes Louie freeze and look around as if he's missed something.

"Easy, boy," I say, standing upright again. "It's just my phone." I pull out the device and sigh at the name on my screen. Cam's calling me again. It's the third time today, but it felt weird to answer it earlier when Bryson was standing over my shoulder. Louie sniffs the metal, the continuing vibration making him bark emphatically. "Hey," I half say, half laugh into the phone.

"Well, it's about time. I was beginning to think you were abducted."

Louie pushes his nose into my stomach, obviously wanting more scratches. I oblige with my free hand.

"Sorry. I've been busy this week with Penny."

"I think you love those dogs more than me."

"Well, they do obey . . . sort of. And believe it or not, I'm currently petting one not-so-freaked-out Great Dane."

"Louie let you touch him?"

"Yep. First time ever."

Cam's voice hitches. "See, now we have two reasons to celebrate."

"What's the other one?"

"Have you not listened to any of my voicemails?"

"No. I'm sorry." I sigh, guilt rolling in for some reason. The last five days have been such a beautiful cocoon of Bryson that I haven't even thought of Cameron.

"We got a second gig with Firesight, and this time their label is coming to watch and consider us for their new tour." His giddiness is palpable. "If we impress, we'll be opening for them in twenty cities across the U.S."

"Cam, that's . . ." I don't know what to say. I'm beyond happy for him, but it also means a second tour. One even longer than the last one. "How did all this happen so fast?" I glance at Charlie's house, the real question filtering through my mind. *Why didn't Bryson tell me?*

"You remember their guitarist, Jax, the one who commented on my solo? Well, we met up after their set and played till three in the morning, just messing around. Darcy, he's the first person I've ever met who sees the music the way I do. Oh, and his girlfriend is amazing. You'll love her, and she's thrilled there's another girl around. Promise me you'll come hang with us next time. The whole band is really down to earth."

I listen silently, methodically petting Louie's head. "Sounds like you two hit it off."

"More than that. Jax wants us, and he's convinced this tour, with our combined talent, will make us both household names. I told him we were in, but you know how that goes. Promises mean nothing in the music industry. Plus, Bryson has been so weird about the band lately. Refusing to set up another tour and turning down two gigs just because they were a couple of hours away. Honestly, I half expected him to say no." His clipped tone highlights his frustration but the edge fades quickly. "By some miracle, it all worked out. Just like Jax promised. The contract for the opening set was signed this morning. Which means you and I are going to dress up and splurge on a swanky steak restaurant in Dallas."

"Are we?" I work to sound as excited as he is. "And when exactly is this outing supposed to happen?"

"Tonight. I'll pick you up at seven." He sighs like he's still in shock. "It's so surreal. I'm three weeks away from all my dreams coming true."

"I'm really happy for you, Cameron."

"For us, Darcy. I wouldn't be here without you." His voice turns soft. "I'd all but given up. And I would have if you hadn't been there cheering me on, reminding me why I'm sacrificing so much. You're my rock."

"You're mine too."

He's quiet for a second. "I hope so. More than ever, I feel like we need to take advantage of this time. Like something big is about to happen."

"Sounds like it already has."

"Yeah, I guess you're right." He laughs like a man who won the lottery and doesn't quite believe it. "So, seven?"

"Seven. I'll see you then." We say our goodbyes, and I slide my phone back in my pocket, my mind in a daze.

Three weeks. And then what?

Insecurity flares where it's never been before. Bryson admitted to dating Alison because he was going on tour and didn't want to be alone. And yeah, he regretted it, but that doesn't mean he's not prone to making the same mistake again.

I immediately shake off thoughts of my former friend. Bryson isn't the same man he used to be. He's proven that fact over and over again.

But even as I work to calm the growing unrest, Caleb's warning comes back with haunting clarity.

"Nobody really knows Bryson. He makes sure of it."

I slam my foot against the concrete step to knock the dirt off, Penny squirming in my arms. I'm mad, and not just at the twenty failed minutes of training I attempted after Cam's phone call. I'm mad because Bryson willingly chose to keep a monumental secret from me. And while it's only been five days and this relationship thing is new to both of us, I can't help but see multiple red flags, especially after watching what secrets and lies did to a thirty-five-year marriage.

When did he find out? That's the biggest question on my mind. I mean, come on, contracts had been signed. This wasn't like a missed email.

When my shoes are no longer caked in clay, I push through the door and try to calm down. Penny's already agitated, and my bottled-up emotion isn't helping. I set her on the floor and wrap the leash twice around my hand to keep her close.

Bryson's head pops up when I enter the kitchen. "You

done?" He's sitting at the island bar, reading something on his phone. Probably research on all the cities they'll visit while on tour.

"Yeah. We're definitely done."

"Good. We're just about to walk Macey to the neighbor's. Charlie's changing now."

Penny gives one warning growl before shooting toward the island, where Macey sits next to Bryson's stool.

My hand jerks forward, but the leash snaps taut just in time to stop the assault. I grit my teeth to keep from screaming. "No," I say firmly and roll the material tighter around my hand, the stitching pressing into my skin. Penny slides backward instead of forward, hopping on her back two feet.

The empty stool next to Bryson topples over as Macey tries to escape, creating more aggravation and chaos. I glance at Bryson, who's watching Penny with the same contempt I've seen on Charlie's face multiple times. "Can you help, please?" I say with more accusation than is fair. "Take her into the living room or something?"

His eyes pierce mine, obviously catching the bite in my tone, but instead of coming back with any defense, Bryson gets up and pushes his stool out of the way to get to her. When she refuses to move, he squats down and heaves her fifty-plus pounds in his arms. "It's ridiculous a dog this size is scared of that rat," he grunts and hauls the terrified dog out of the room.

I lean down and pick up Penny, who still has yet to quit growling and barking. "What am I going to do with you?" One on one, she's actually not bad. Stubborn but certainly not crazy. But the minute another dog enters the mix, she becomes a poster child for neurotic behavior. "People don't really like to adopt dogs that attack. Just FYI."

Penny pokes my cheek with her tiny nose and licks my face.

I take her inside the laundry room and wrestle her back into her crate. She hates this thing now, and the more time we spend outside, the harder she fights when I put her back. "I know, girl. I want to let you out, too, but I can't if you don't get your aggression under control." She continues her manic barking until I shut the door, and then slowly it fades into acceptance.

"I don't trust that dog," Bryson says when he returns to the kitchen. "You okay now?"

"I'm fine." I slide onto the stool and rub my face, exhaustion and the crash of my earlier emotions settling like a blanket over my good mood. "I just need more patience and time."

"The fair is tomorrow." He takes the seat next to me and hesitates a second before squeezing my tense shoulders with his hand. I guess he's learned my tells, as well. He seems to sense my frustration. "Surely you're not thinking of taking her."

"I was, until just now." I rub my temples. There are only a few more fairs left this summer, and I really need to take advantage of every one. "I guess waiting one more week won't kill the timeline."

"No, it will not." He leans into me and kisses my shoulder. "Plus, that frees you up to spend the entire day with me."

I know his statement should make me feel warm inside, but it only reminds me that three weeks from now, he could be leaving. Not could . . . *will* be leaving. Firesight's manager is going to see exactly what all of us did last weekend: Bryson and Cameron are magic together.

"Hey." He leans his elbow on the counter, turning himself until I'm forced to look into his eyes. "What am I missing?"

"Nothing." I should just ask him, straight out, but talking about the possible tour is not something I plan to do in the middle of Charlie's kitchen, especially when I still have no idea exactly what I'm feeling.

Charlie emerges from his room, and it's a transformation I'm completely unprepared for. He's dressed in thin khakis and a blue collared shirt. His hair is still long but tamed and styled, and his beard is four inches shorter.

I leap from my stool, grateful for a distraction. "Wow! I wouldn't have recognized you."

His cheeks redden. "I figured it was time for some grooming."

"You look great. And check it out, Bryson, blue." I glance at him over my shoulder and force myself to smile. He's still watching me with far too much concern. "You've heard of it, right? It's a color that isn't black."

Bryson comes behind me, wraps his arms around my waist, and sets his chin on my shoulder. "I'll wear blue if you really want me to," he whispers, and all my negative thoughts begin to unravel. No one could be this good at pretending, could they? Then again, my parents hid their fractures for years, and I blissfully went through life never noticing the ground beneath me was near collapse.

I try again to relax or at least appear that way. "Don't tease me, Katsaros. I will hold you to that."

Charlie shakes his head at our open display of affection, but I see a hint of a smile appear. He turns and whistles, the sound cutting the air as if it came from a toy. Macey comes running at a speed I didn't know she possessed, slipping twice on the hardwood floor. "Well, lookie here. It still works, even after all this time." He squats down, and she showers him with kisses.

I shift my focus from the swirling questions in my head to the pair in front of me. At least one thing in my life makes total sense. This job. And even though I'm skipping the fair tomorrow, I still get a win. Because whether he knows it yet or not, Charlie just became the proud, permanent owner of an adorable, ridiculously skittish mutt.

TWENTY-FOUR

*C*harlie's closest neighbor lives nearly a quarter mile away and down a small country road that has become more gravel than asphalt. It's a beautiful walk, though, bathed in shade by large oak and cedar trees.

Macey tries to stop at nearly every tree, sniffing and digging as if this is the first time she's been out of captivity in months. I guess, in a way, she has been locked away. Charlie too. Grief can be a prison if left unattended without hope or progress.

We crest the final hill, and a row of fencing breaks to reveal a gorgeous two-story home painted white with bright green shutters.

Charlie must recognize my awestruck face. "Pretty amazing, isn't it?"

"I'll say. It's like a postcard."

"There's a ten-acre lake right over there." He points beyond the house, and I barely make out a patch of blue glistening in the sun. "Bryson can take you sometime. Best fishing for miles."

My stomach tumbles at the mention of his name. We've barely spoken the entire walk. "Sounds nice."

Charlie's body suddenly jerks forward, Macey nearly up-ending her owner in her quest to explore. I lunge to steady him the same time Bryson grabs at the leash.

"I'll take that," he says, unraveling the leather from Charlie's wrinkled hand. "She's too excited to behave right now."

Charlie watches his pet with sorrowful yet optimistic eyes. This walk really has been a step toward healing. I can see it in both of their faces.

We reach the front door, quicker than any of us intend to, but Macey has set the pace for the last hundred feet.

"Well, here goes nothing," Charlie says and rings the doorbell. "Word of warning. Sheila's the type to tell you how it is, and I have a feeling she has a few choice words for me. Most of them deserved, I'm afraid."

The door opens to reveal a slim older lady with white hair and tight jeans. She pushes out the screen door. "Well now, look who finally came over to grovel."

Sheila and Charlie share a look that tells me everything is going to be okay between the two of them. Forgiveness is expected between old friends, grace given without the need for apologies. It's the backbone of relationships. The very thing that sustains time and distance and, in this case, the death of someone they both loved dearly.

Charlie clears his throat. "I brought a peace offering." With that, Bryson eases his viselike grip on Macey's leash, and her tail is wagging so hard she practically wiggle-runs to Sheila. The older lady squats and meets the dog with equal excitement.

"There's my girl! I've missed you so much." She stands, her eyes glistening. "Well, come in. No need to stand here and let out all the A/C."

Charlie steps forward, and before he can make it past the

doorway, Sheila gives him a hug that nearly cracks my resolve not to cry. I think it does his, too, because he nods and quickly moves inside, Macey at his heels.

Bryson comes over and wraps his arm around my shoulder, the first real contact we've shared since leaving the house. "What do you want to do?"

"I think we should give them some time."

He nods. "Hey, Sheila, you mind if I take Darcy out to the lake for a while?"

"Not at all." She smiles warmly, and her perfect teeth are either dentures or she has the best dentist in the world. "And thanks for getting him over here. We've missed him." She doesn't linger, which I like. Maybe it's a farmer/rancher thing, but this no-nonsense, straightforward world is definitely something I could enjoy for a long time.

"Ready?" Bryson's hand fills mine, his fingers sliding in between my own as he steps closer.

I nod and let him guide us down a path, first made of flat stone, then as it passes through the final fence and turns into caliche. With each step, the lake gets closer and seems to go on without end. A wooden deck juts out at least ten feet into the water. It looks new and sturdy, as if it's only been here a few years.

He pauses when we reach the edge and turns so we're facing each other. "Now that we're alone again, want to tell me what's upsetting you?"

"Nothing's—"

"Yes, it is," Bryson says, cutting me off. "You've been different with me since you came in the house earlier."

I watch the water as tiny ripples form from unseen sources. "I've just got a lot on my mind right now."

"You're worried about Penny?"

"No, I mean, yes . . . a little, but that's not what's bothering me." I already know that Bryson isn't going to let me deflect, and truthfully I don't want to. I may not have a lot of experience with relationships, but I do know I don't want one where I can't be completely honest. I force myself to turn back to him, to watch his eyes when I admit what's had me in turmoil for the last thirty minutes. "I guess I'm trying to figure out why you didn't tell me about the concert and the tour."

He stiffens, which answers one of my questions. He was intentionally keeping it from me.

I swallow down the hurt. "I mean, it's an incredible opportunity. I would think you would be thrilled about the news."

"You talked to Cameron." A statement. Not a question. Bryson inhales deeply, the same way my mom did right before telling me she was ready to start dating. "Nothing's a guarantee, yet. There's still a lot of stars that need to align before anything definite is going to happen."

"You signed a contract, Bryson, and didn't say a word to me about it. That's concerning, especially considering your history with Alison." I let go of his hand and take my first step onto the treated wood. The deck creaks but doesn't move, so I take one more, then another, leaving Bryson at the shore. My stomach knots with each foot of distance I put between us. I don't want there to be tension, but I also can't help but wonder if I should have put more stock into Caleb's warnings.

When I reach the end of the deck, I sit and let my sneakered feet hang over the water. A shadow appears, and Bryson sits next to me, close enough that I consider scooting away to get some distance.

"You're right." He tugs on the back of his neck. "I should have told you. I'm sorry. I guess I didn't want anything to mess up what we've started."

"Unless . . . this was why we started in the first place. You did say the road gets lonely."

"Hey." He shifts to face me instead of the water and picks up my hand. "This isn't like before."

Maybe it is, maybe it isn't, but either way, I'm going to give him an out. Something Alison never did. "It's not too late, you know. We could stop this thing now and still retain some semblance of friendship."

He groans and stares at the cloudless sky. "This is my punishment. This is what I get for ever dating her."

I pull my feet up and sit crisscross to where our knees are touching. "I'm not trying to punish you."

"I know you're not, but for some reason you still doubt me."

I look down at my fingers because it's true. A part of me still expects Bryson to hurt me.

"Do you want to know why I broke up with Alison when I did?"

"You already told me. You didn't love her the way she loved you."

"Yeah, that's true, but I didn't tell you when I finally accepted that reality." He sets his hand on my knee, his fingertips rubbing the inside skin, oblivious to the fact that it's sending tingles up and down my leg. "It was our first performance with Cam at lead guitar, in Waco."

"I was there that night."

He grins as if I'm missing the point. "I know. Cam didn't say a word about you coming. He just kept looking out at the audience, agitated, until finally I guess he saw what he was looking for and settled. I had no idea it was you until I stepped up to the microphone and there you were, sitting front and center." He picks up my hand and kisses the inside of my wrist. "I knew you weren't there for me; you hadn't been to one concert of mine that Cam didn't drag you to, but still, I spent the entire night watching you and hoping you were watching me. Let me tell you, that's a pretty sickening feeling to have for a girl, especially one who's sitting next to your current girlfriend." He looks down, shame written in the slump of his shoulders. "That's when I knew I had to end things. Even I couldn't stomach looking myself in the mirror that night." He glances back up, the plea in his hazel eyes far too vulnerable to be lying. "Darcy, these feelings I have for you . . . they aren't new, and they aren't small." He leans in and presses his lips to my neck right at the edge of my T-shirt. "I've spent *years* wanting to kiss this very spot." Fire races down my arm as he scoots closer, his breath trailing to my ear. "You tuck your hair to one side when you're nervous. I used to watch your fingers run right along this line and have to get up from the table to keep from touching you."

I close my eyes, no longer aware of the lake or the deck or even the pressure of Bryson's confessed feelings. All I can feel is the pleasure of new beginnings. Dangerous beginnings. Beginnings that threaten the last bits of security I'm furiously clinging to.

"You're not a fill-in or a distraction. You're the one I could never have." His nose runs along my cheek, his breath tickling the skin. "And for the record, I am way too far gone to ever go back to how things used to be."

I can't argue. My skin burns with his touch. Burns in a way it shouldn't between friends.

His lips lightly brush against mine. "Do you need more convincing?"

Unable to stand his teasing any longer, I kiss him, hard and deep. Bryson immediately responds, gripping the back of my head, cradling my body until we somehow end up horizontal. I want to melt into the feel and taste and scent of him. My hands roam over his back, clawing at the hem of his shirt, eager to explore the muscles underneath.

Bryson immediately pulls back, his face flushed, his lids half closed the same way they are onstage. "We need to slow this down." He sits against the deck railing, his breath coming fast and labored, and runs his hands over his face.

I lie there, nearly as stunned as he is. I always knew I wanted passion in a relationship. I just never knew until now what that might actually feel like. I sit up on my elbows, my legs still stretched in front of me, and choke out a laugh. "Yeah, I'd say I'm thoroughly convinced."

He lowers his head, his elbows resting on his knees, and begins to laugh with me. It's a nice sound, light and inviting, a release of so many battered moments in our lives.

He stands and offers his hand. I grip it, the skin callused and warm, and let him pull me upright. He wraps his arms around me, clasping his hands together at my lower back. "What do you say to dinner at my place tonight? Believe it or not, I am good for more than dog wrangling and clandestine make-out sessions."

I duck my head into his shoulder, slightly mortified by how quickly I lost control. "I wish I could, but I promised dinner with Cam. We're celebrating your big break."

The tension comes slowly but seems to grow as he processes my words. "I haven't seen him since the concert." He backs up, and it forces me to look at him. Every muscle in his face is tight with restraint. "How'd he take the news of the two of us dating?"

I can tell by the way he asks that he already knows the answer. "I haven't exactly told him yet."

Bryson's jaw ripples with tension, and I hate how it reminds me of the face he makes whenever he talks about his mom. "Darcy, I'm pretty sure this secret trumps the concert one."

"It's not a secret. I'm just trying to be delicate."

"Why? It's not like you haven't dated before. Cam dealt with it then. He can deal with it now."

"I know, but it's different this time. He knows you. We all are interconnected. Plus . . ." I disentangle from his embrace, which only seems to add to his rigid posture. "Cam will worry about you hurting me." Just like his brother. They've both seen too many of Bryson's bad choices. "He's protective that way."

"No. He's territorial. He always has been when it comes to you. It's why everyone, including me, keeps waiting to see a shiny engagement ring on your finger."

His words hit a much too familiar nerve. "Stop it. He's my best friend. That's all."

"Then tell him." He crosses his arms in front of his chest, a mountain of challenge in his stance. "If I'm wrong, your *best friend* will be happy for you. If I'm right, then we need to have a very different conversation."

"You are wrong. And I will tell him. Just not tonight. Not when he's so happy." I step forward, feeling the need to apologize for some reason. "Please, Bryson. Cam's already lost so many people in his life this year, and true or not, he'll feel like he's losing me, too. He can't compartmentalize like you can. He feels everything, and I don't want to cause issues right when he needs to focus the most."

"Do you even realize how much energy you spend trying to keep Cam happy? If he worried about your happiness even a fraction as much, he would be thrilled you found someone

who cares for you as much as I do." He presses his lips together, a thing I'm learning he does when he has more to
say than he's willing to. "I'm not naïve, Darcy. I knew when
I leaped into this thing with you that Cam has been the
number-one guy in your life for years now. But I took the risk
because you somehow convinced me that your feelings for
him are platonic."

"And they are." I take Bryson's hands and enclose them
next to my chest. "He's our friend, not to mention a critical
part of Black Carousel's future." Bryson flinches at that
reminder. "I think it's only fair that we ease him into this
slowly."

"Fine. I'll let you set the timeline." He steps back, sighs,
and everything about his stance conveys impatience. "But I
want to make it one-hundred-percent clear that I'm uncomfortable." He doesn't say with what. Instead his expression
turns cold and scrutinizing, far too much like the man he
used to be. The hardened version. The one who's been hurt
and abandoned by every person he's ever cared about.

I want to believe it's just the secrets and the timing he
doesn't like, but a deeper part of me knows it's more. I lay my
head on his chest and hug him until he finally acquiesces and
hugs me back. I'll just have to do better at easing his doubts,
just as he did for me today. It's the only option I have. I've
given up so much this past year, and I won't, not for anyone,
give up my best friend, too.

TWENTY-FIVE

*C*ameron's promise of a swanky steakhouse in Dallas turns into piles of Mexican food on the patio of Trinity Groves, our new favorite dining spot right over the bridge to downtown. The Dallas skyline is gorgeous this time of night. It's right after dusk, and each building is coming alive with thousands of lights.

"I'm glad you changed your mind about the restaurant," I say around a bite of our shared fajitas. "This is much more us."

He leans back in his chair, his dimples forming as he watches me eat very indelicately. "Well, I decided paying rent was more important than impressing you."

"Please." I lightly kick his foot with mine. "You know I'm cheaper than you are."

He laces his hands behind his head. "Maybe so, but I still owe you a big juicy steak. In fact, you better cash it in soon, because once I'm filthy rich, I'm going to be way too important for anyone but my new celebrity friends."

"What?" I toss my balled-up napkin at his face. "Where is your loyalty?"

"I'm kidding." His grin turns warm, almost insecure. "Trust

245

me, there's no scenario where I see my future and you're not in it."

I swallow, oddly uncomfortable. "Good."

An awkward silence falls that has never been between us before. Cameron shifts in his seat, feeling it, too. Maybe he can sense a change is once again coming.

"Cam?" My heart pounds in my chest, a nervousness I didn't expect all but closing around my throat. "Can I ask you a question?" I hadn't planned to bring this up tonight, but the words suddenly spill out.

His brows form a vee. "Since when do you need that as a lead-in?"

"Well, it's kind of a personal one."

"So?"

I wring my hands in my lap. "How did you deal with your girlfriends when they would get jealous of the two of us?"

He stares at me and slowly settles back into his seat. "That's out of left field. Why do you want to know?"

I should have guessed he wouldn't take the question at face value. The downside of his knowing every one of my expressions. "Just curious."

He tilts his head. "Curious because . . . you're chronicling our life together? Or curious because you're seeing someone and he's not comfortable with our friendship?" There's an annoyance in his voice I recognize. It's the same one he gets every time I venture into the boyfriend conversation. He has yet to like any I've introduced him to.

"The second one."

He swallows like he didn't expect my answer to be yes. "Who's the lucky guy?"

"That's not important," I say, even though I know he would disagree.

Cam blows out a long exhale. "I knew you'd been distant this week. I guess it never crossed my mind you might have met someone."

"Sorry. We're kind of in that mushy want-to-spend-all-our-time-together stage."

"So, it's a new someone. When did you meet him? We've hung out every weekend except this past one." His eyes widen, and I can see his mind calculating time. "Was it at the concert?"

"He was there, yes. But that's not the point. The point is he has some concerns, and I don't know how to ease those."

"Concerns about me?"

I nod, wishing I had more practice with this type of thing.

Cameron's pause is long and heavy, as if he's still accepting my line of questioning. "Well . . . it's simple. It's not your job to ease his shortcomings or insecurities." Cameron leans his elbows on the table. "You tell him the same thing I've told every one of my girlfriends. Our friendship always comes first."

"That is not what you told January," I remind him. "In fact, I remember a serious heart-to-heart where you made it clear to me that we needed to, and I quote, *back off and consider her feelings.*'"

He shoots me a scowl because he knows I'm right. "Fine. Maybe I was a little enticed by her. But . . . I would have told her that if she'd tried to make me choose. Lucky for me, she was too busy lying about her entire existence to bother with jealousy." His sarcasm makes us both chuckle and thankfully eases the tension in our conversation. Cameron reaches out and squeezes my hand. "January is proof of what we both know is true. People come in and out of our lives, but every time we land right back here—with you and me.

No new relationship is going to change that. Don't even let him try."

"You're right." I squeeze his hand back and think of all the times Cameron has been there supporting me, caring for me, walking me through all the hardest moments in my life. Bryson doesn't understand it because he's never known the purity of a friendship on this level.

Cameron flashes a grin that is pure mischief. "So, when do I get to meet him?"

My stomach flips at the question. It's inevitable that my two worlds will collide; I just have to find a way to minimize the impact. "When I feel sure that you're not going to be rude to him."

"I'm never rude to them."

"Please, you interrogated Adam for an hour."

His mouth opens in feigned outrage. "That's because he wouldn't stop undressing you with his eyes. Right in front of me, I might add. That guy was a jerk. You're lucky I had your back."

Okay, yeah. Probably not the best example. "Fine. I concede Adam was a dud."

He smirks, knowing he's winning our little battle. "Now, back to my question. When do I get to meet him?"

"Soon."

"Give me a date."

I hesitate, but then throw out an option that ensures the least amount of collateral damage. "The night of your concert. We'll all go out afterward and celebrate."

"That's three weeks away."

"So?"

"So, considering your usual patterns, he'll be out of the picture by then and I never would have met him." Both dimples appear, and his voice turns teasing. "We both know you don't exactly have the longest attention span when it comes to men. Except me, of course."

I narrow my eyes but have no ability to counter without giving more information than I'm ready to share. Never have I been as close to someone as I am to Bryson, and the fact that I'm this worried about making the three of us work is proof that I fully expect this thing with him to go long term. "Trust me. He'll be there."

"If you say so." Though nothing in his voice implies he believes me.

"I do." I settle back in my chair, relieved to have the conversation over with. It's probably for the best that Cameron doesn't think the relationship is serious. If he did, he'd push, and I'd cave and then we'd be forced to have a much more uncomfortable conversation. It's odd. I've never really cared if Cam liked the guys I dated or even if he approved, but that was often because I already knew they weren't right for me. Bryson's different. He sees me. The changed me. The one who woke up one day and discovered her life was a lie. He sees the one thing Cameron has yet to accept—I'm never going to be the person I once was.

"Hey . . ." Cameron waves a hand in front of my face. "Where'd you go?"

"Nowhere."

"You've been staring off into space for over a minute."

"Sorry." I go back to eating and try to push away all thoughts of Bryson. "Tell me more about Jax and the band. How did the whole tour thing even come up?"

"We were talking about a few places we'd both played, and then I mentioned how I want to venture into Oklahoma and Louisiana. Jax said I should be looking much bigger, and that was it." He chews on his fingernail, his voice far too lifeless for his usual favorite conversation.

"That's it?" My brow furrows. "Never have you ever talked about music in two sentences or less. And that was before you had the opportunity to play with another musical genius." Cameron suddenly can't meet my eyes. "What's going on?"

"Nothing."

"Try again. And this time don't chew on your nail while you're talking. It's a dead giveaway you're not telling me the truth."

"Okay, fine." He bites his lip, a complete departure from his usual confidence. "I didn't just bring you here to celebrate or hear about the next unfortunate guy in your life. There's something I've been wanting to talk to you about."

If my stomach weren't in knots, I'd smack him for the "unfortunate guy" comment. "Okay?"

"It's, um, well . . . it's about your dad."

I drop my tortilla onto the plate and try to ignore the rising nausea. "I take it back; you were right not to say anything."

"That's just it. I've been *not saying anything* for weeks now. And I can't keep quiet any longer."

"Cameron, whatever it is, I don't care. I don't want to know. And I certainly don't want to ruin the night by talking about him." I look toward the Dallas skyline, pain pouring into the places I thought I had shored up. My dad's apartment is only fifteen minutes from here, yet he may as well be a continent away. "He left me for a shiny new life. I tried to fight it and I lost."

"Darcy." Cam's voice is etched in compassion. "He left your mom. Not you."

"It's the same thing."

"No, it's not. Your dad messed up, yes, but I know for a

fact that he's tried to contact you several times with no response."

I scowl at my best friend. "And how would you know that?"

"Because he calls me to check on you. He says you haven't
spoken to him since the divorce was final."

"He made his choice. There was nothing left to say. And I
really don't appreciate your feeding him information."

Cameron snakes a hand through his hair, his expression
suspiciously guilty. "It's not like that. Your dad wants to be
a part of your life, even if it's just through me right now."
He hesitates, probably weighing how angry I'm going to get.
Finally he sighs, resigned. "He asked me to bring you to his
birthday barbecue."

"Did he? And in what universe did he think I would agree
to go?"

"Well . . . he wasn't exactly planning on me asking you. I'm
kind of going rogue here." He scrunches his nose, realizing
how bad those words sound out loud. "He thought if I could
just get you there, even coerced, you might . . . talk to him."

Blood pumps in my ears. "You know, Cam, it's been years
since you and I have really fought, but maybe we're due."
Dad's backyard barbecues are legendary, down to the special rub he puts on the baby back ribs. A year ago, the party
was at our house with fifty of my parents' closest friends,
including the woman we later learned he was sleeping
with.

"Obviously, I didn't agree with his method"—Cam's attempt at soothing my growing temper fails, especially when
he adds—"but I do think you should consider going."

"Why?" I demand, my heart pounding with a ferocity I
didn't know I possessed. "He's not the man I grew up with.
This version is one I don't even recognize. So why should I

sacrifice for him when every decision he's made this year has been one-hundred-percent selfish?"

"True, and I have no doubt he'll not be getting Father of the Year anytime soon. But . . . you miss him. And despite what he's done, he's still your dad, and it's his birthday."

I turn away, emotions bouncing so quickly between fury and heartbreak that my hands tremble. "It's like he doesn't even care what he's lost. He just goes on like nothing's changed—new home, new woman, same old party."

"The guy I speak to on the phone seems very aware of what he's lost."

The tears I've refused to cry for that man come tumbling over, and I can't respond for fear I might choke on anything I attempt to say.

Cam rushes around the table and slides in next to me. "I'm sorry I brought it up. Forget his stupid party. I always thought his ribs were overrated, anyway."

I chuckle despite my emotional turmoil, and Cam pulls me into his arms. They're warm and familiar, yet tonight I feel a twinge of unease that's never existed before. It's innocent, the hug, I know that, but I can't help but picture the hurt in Bryson's eyes when I admitted to keeping our new relationship a secret.

I pull away. "My dad's a jerk, yes, but his ribs are excellent, and you know it."

"Yeah okay, they are." His smile is wrapped in pity when he wipes away my fallen tears. "I hate that I made you cry. I just couldn't keep it a secret any longer. It was killing me."

I look down, suddenly guilty and uncomfortable. Here he is apologizing and I'm doing the exact same thing—protecting him with a secret. "It's okay, Cam. I understand why you did it."

When he sees I'm not mad at him, he returns to his seat across the table. "What do you want me to tell him?"

I realize then what a terrible position my dad has put him in. It's unfair. Cameron already shoulders all my burdens. He shouldn't have to shoulder my dad's, as well. "Tell him to stop calling you." Cameron is opening his mouth to protest when I continue, "If I want to talk to him, I will be the one to initiate it. I'm really sorry he involved you."

"Can't fault the guy for trying." Cameron shrugs and winks at me from across the table. "If I lost you, you'd better believe I'd fight to get you back."

My body warms, his words reinforcing my need to be careful with his feelings. Cameron's my person. Now and always. "I know. I'd fight for you, too."

TWENTY-SIX

I knock on Bryson's door, a detour I hadn't planned on this morning, but since he hadn't returned any of the texts I sent after Cameron dropped me off last night, I figured he might need some reassurance. I know I do, anyway.

The door swings in, and I'm struck by the physical reaction I have to seeing him wearing a tank top and gym shorts. My gaze trails over the lean muscle and olive skin he rarely shows. His hair is disheveled, and his face all but screams his sleep was as restless as mine last night.

He leans his forearm against the doorframe and looks down at me, his smirk far too reminiscent of the arrogant rock star he used to pretend to be. "How was your date?"

"It wasn't a date."

"Got news, Darcy. When a guy picks you up and takes you out to dinner . . . it's a date."

"Not when the guy is my best friend."

"A designation you and I still do not agree on."

"Are we really back to that? What can I do to make you believe me?"

He shoves a hand through his hair. "Rewrite history, I guess."

"Well, I can't exactly do that." I stubbornly cross my arms and look up at him with the same challenging stare he's giving me. It doesn't work. Bryson remains a brick barrier, refusing to let me pass. I redistribute my weight from my left foot to my right, suddenly nervous. "Are you really not going to let me in?"

He must sense my growing insecurity because he presses his back against the door to give me passing room.

I step forward, my insides tumbling. He told me he was uncomfortable, but he never said going to dinner with Cam was a deal breaker. "I texted you when I got home. You never responded."

"That's because it came in at midnight. About two hours later than I thought it would." There's a chill I'm not used to from him, which makes the hair on my arms stand up. He shuts the door but doesn't move any closer to me. It feels bigger than a physical rejection; it feels like we're breaking up.

I swallow, trying to keep my voice steady. "Well, if you had answered my text, I would have informed you that I told Cameron last night I was seeing someone, and you were wrong. He didn't get upset at all."

"Really? And did that someone have a name?" I bite my lip, my nonresponse answering his question. He shakes his head. "Yeah, I thought so."

I lift my arms and let them drop back to my sides, completely out of options. "What do you want me to do?"

His eyes meet mine, sharp and angry. "I want you to tell him. Not hint. Not leaving out details. I want you to tell him it's me. And that we're serious about each other."

"I will. I promise you, I will . . . when it feels right."

255

He grunts a laugh completely devoid of humor. "It's never going to feel right. That's the problem." No matter how much Bryson's softer side comes out when we're together, there's always that hint of darkness hovering right near the surface. He must sense it, too, because he rolls his shoulders, a motion I've often seen him do when he's trying to relax. "Do you have any idea how hard this is for me?" He rubs his forehead like it suddenly hurts. "I've watched Cameron pine for you for years. I've had a front row seat to the long, lingering stares. Been the recipient of the passive-aggressive warnings to back off. And it's not just from high school. It's now. It's all the time. It's him calling you 'his girl' and hugging you like he needs you in order to breathe. And despite how much you try to justify those behaviors, I'm here to tell you . . . they're not normal. I've had many friends who were girls, but there were lines, boundaries. Always. You and Cameron have no lines."

"Then we'll draw some, okay?" I clutch the front of his shirt, lifting up on my toes to kiss the stubble on his jaw. "I just need a little more time. That's all I'm asking for. Let Black Carousel get through this concert and then we'll tell him together."

"Time is not going to change the outcome." He sighs and the misery in his eyes cuts through me. "If you don't want this, if you have any hesitation at all, I need you to tell me now."

"I want this." He turns his face away, and I cup his cheeks to bring his eyes back to mine. "Hey, I want this. But you're asking me to do really difficult things. And I'm willing to do them for you, but you have to give a little, too."

He finally crushes me against his wonderfully hard chest. "How am I supposed to argue when you look at me like that?" he growls into my hair. Suddenly, my back is pressed against the door, his forearms creating a cage around me. "Tell me I'm not fooling myself." His face, his lips are inches from mine and all I can feel is Bryson, his eyes strained, his voice dark and smooth and hypnotic. "Tell me anything that will make me forget the last twelve hours of wondering."

Anticipation roars inside me, but he doesn't come closer, doesn't lean down or close his eyes or even tease me with the tickle of his breath. I press my palms to the wood to keep them from touching every inch of his beautiful skin. It's the contrast that makes my stomach whirl when he stares at me this way. Soft and hard. Angry and broken. Scared and sure. I've never met anyone so complicated in my life, nor have I ever wanted to understand someone more.

"I missed you." I bite my lip, feeling just as foolish as he admitted to feeling. "More than what's normal. More than I've ever missed anyone. More than I know how to express without terrifying both of us."

If words could calm a storm, those seem to do it. His entire body collapses into me. Bryson slides his hand down the door until it cradles my head. The pad of his thumb glides gently against my cheek. "I . . . missed you, too." He leans closer, his breath hot against my closed eyelids, then moves downward until finally he gives me what I've been waiting for. The contact, the reassurance, the same glorious shock waves that always seem to come when he kisses me.

The jerk knows it, too. He's all but cocky when he finally grins down at me. "So, is it safe to assume you're free today?" The question feels like a test, and luckily it's one I can easily pass.

"Yes. And I already ran by the farm this morning, so gold star for me."

He pushes off the door, allowing us both to breathe a little. "It's only nine o'clock. What time did you get there?"

"Six-thirty. Thankfully, Charlie was already up."

"After getting home at midnight?" Concern deepens his brow. "Did you sleep at all?"

"Not really."

"How come?"

"Just stuff with my dad." I shrug because that's all I really want to say on the subject.

"What stuff?"

"It's nothing."

"If it were nothing, you wouldn't have lost sleep over it." He takes my hand and kisses the inside of my wrist, intimate and comfortable. Two things I always seem to feel with him. "Darcy... openness has to go both ways."

I have no ability to deny his request, even though I know talking will do nothing but add to the hurt. Ever since Cameron mentioned the stupid event, an unexpected yearning has swelled in me. Memories I had all but buried have tumbled loose and with them the pain I've worked so hard not to feel. "Dad wants me to go to his birthday barbecue. It's the same one he's hosted every single year of my life."

"When is it?"

"Not for a couple more weeks, but time won't change how I feel. He isn't the man I knew and loved. He's just this person now who wrecked my family."

"Tell me what happened." He fiddles with my fingertips, that rare flash of insecurity popping through. "I don't have experience with divorce, but I certainly understand growing up in a dysfunctional environment."

I smile at his attempt to empathize. "That's just it. My home wasn't dysfunctional. I had a wonderful childhood.

The kind where I would lie in bed and thank God for parents like mine. The kind people saw and wanted to have." My throat tightens, and I pull my hand away, needing to pace and breathe. "Do you know they didn't tell us until after Christmas even though they'd filed months before?"

Bryson shakes his head, quiet. His silence used to bother me, but now it's one of my favorite things about him. He listens without passing judgment, without lecturing or trying to convince me I'm wrong for feeling how I do.

"Dexter came down with his family for the holiday weekend, and it was smiles and hugs, even the required thank-you kiss when they gave each other their gifts. Dad got Mom a gold watch, and she got him Cowboys tickets." The words choke in the back of my throat. "They even talked as if they would go together." I slump down on the couch, my hands shaking. "They waited until the night before Dexter was set to leave to finally tell us the truth. His family was tucked in bed, and I was saying my goodbyes when Mom politely asked me to come into the living room. They sat us down, took each other's hand, and told us they were getting a divorce."

Bryson sits next to me but doesn't take my hand. I'm grateful. I want nothing between us to remind me of that horrible night.

"I couldn't breathe. I just sat there thinking this is a joke. A sick, twisted joke that was in terrible taste. But then Dad started crying, and Mom walked away and shut herself in the bedroom. And all I could think about was that stupid gold watch and the printed-out football tickets." A fierce ache grips my heart as I stare at him, this wonderful new man who truly cares, and admit the biggest shame in my life. "Bryson, your parents aren't the only ones who pretended life was perfect. If Christmas was any indication, mine had been lying to us for a very long time. Long enough that my mom firmly believes she knows Michael—a man who's been in her life a mere month—better than she ever knew my father. And now I'm stuck with the reality that my entire childhood, the basis of my beliefs and my choices, was all an illusion. I didn't just lose my dad and my mom that night; I lost every wonderful memory I had. They're tainted now because I can't distinguish between what was real and what wasn't." I glance down at my feet. "I've never even heard them fight. Not once. And now I resent them for it . . . I resent them for not fighting."

I feel the cushions give and Bryson's warm arms around me.

"Come here." He pulls me close, attempting to heal my pain with affection and care. I love the smell of him and the feel of safety his touch brings, but I don't feel better. I don't feel less angry or less bitter or less betrayed. In fact, if anything, I feel trapped. I want to run. To move and go until I exhaust myself of all the emotion clamoring to explode.

My head jerks up. "That's it. That's what she needs."

I scramble to my feet, leaving my confused boyfriend on the couch. "What who needs? Your mom?"

"No, Penny. She needs to run. She needs to exhaust herself, and then maybe I can finally start to socialize her a little. If she's worn out, she won't have the energy to fight me so hard." I jump and clap my hands together. "We need to go to a hardware store."

He stands and scratches his head like he still can't keep up. "A hardware store?"

"Yes, for supplies. Now go change." I push him toward his room. "I'm going to make a list."

"Darcy . . ." He halts the movement, and I'm nowhere strong enough to budge him. "I don't think immersing yourself in a new project is what you need right now. I'm here to listen, to help you get through this."

"I know you are, and . . ." I lift on my toes and kiss him with all the thanks I can show. "I appreciate it so much, but I want to do this. Now. Today. I don't want to spend another moment crying over my parents. I feel like that's all I've done for the past seven months."

He hesitates but then obeys, leaving me to rustle through his kitchen drawers to find something to write with. The rescue facility I volunteered at had an obstacle course with tubes and stairs and long bridges. I wouldn't be able to make anything that elaborate, but for a little dog like Penny, I could certainly figure out enough to keep her challenged during our training sessions.

I draw, turn the page sideways, and draw some more. The task works, and for a brief ten minutes, I gloriously forget about my dad calling Cameron. I forget that tomorrow is yet another Sunday night dinner I'll be missing. And I forget watching my mom throw a very expensive gold watch straight into the trash.

TWENTY-SEVEN

*O*kay, bring her out slowly," I call to Bryson, who's standing with Macey just on the other side of Charlie's back door.

It's been a week of nonstop obstacle training with Penny. She has the course down to perfection, weaving in and out like a circus animal, but the purpose behind the course has yet to be realized. Today we spent an hour running, twice as long as we have in the past. We're both exhausted, and hopefully spent enough that Penny will actually choose to be civil to her housemate.

The screen opens slowly, Macey eager to take the steps until she sees Penny by my side. I can't really blame her for the tentativeness. Penny's attacked her every time we've tried to socialize them.

"Come on, girl," Bryson coaches, and they descend together.

I keep Penny close by my leg. She sees the other dog but hasn't reacted yet, which is no small thing. Last time, I brought Penny forward and allowed her to be the pursuer— a monumental mistake. This time, I'm letting Macey approach.

Bryson watches me for guidance, and I nod for him to

keep going. They get to the grass, and Penny surprisingly remains silent at my feet.

"Good girl," I coo and give her a small reward that she gobbles down.

Macey's tongue hangs from her mouth, her breathing intensifying. She's nervous, poor thing.

"Keep coming, nice and slow."

Bryson does, but as soon as he crosses the four-foot-away mark, Penny stands and growls.

"No," I say. She glances at me, by now recognizing my authority. I reward her silence with another treat and motion for Bryson to continue.

Three feet . . . two feet . . .

Penny lunges, almost as if she's calculated exactly how much slack she had in the leash.

Bryson immediately pulls Macey back to safety, only Penny is now beside herself, pulling and barking and twisting to get away from me.

"Take Macey around front." I groan, feeling utterly defeated. "I'll put Penny up."

Bryson's expression is sympathetic, and I appreciate the fact that he doesn't say *I told you so.* No doubt he's thinking it.

Nothing I try seems to work with this dog. She hates all other animals. She even terrorizes the squirrels who happen past her. "We're running out of time, Penny. You have to get better." I can't stand thinking of the alternative, but I may be forced to.

Charlie loves Macey, and his tolerance for Penny's aggression is getting shorter by the day. Even Louie has started cowering when she's around. It's like her anger is spilling into every corner of her life, and the only option she's giving us is to fight back or give in. Lucky for her, I'm a fighter.

I wrestle her back into her cage, a task that's becoming as much of a battle as the socializing is, and then walk Macey around for a few minutes. She doesn't need much time from me anymore. Charlie takes her everywhere, and both seem to improve with each outing.

After we finish our walk, Macey trots to her dog bed and plops down. I watch her with satisfaction. At least I've had three victories here. It feels good to remember that when the other two are making me question my ability and resolve.

Bryson wraps his arms around my waist. "I have a surprise for you," he says, setting his chin on my shoulder. "Something that should help with your frustration."

"Yeah?" I perk up. "What is it?"

"You'll see." He pulls me by the hand, and I happily follow along.

Charlie's UTV is parked outside waiting for us. I didn't even notice him leave to go get it. "So the surprise is close?"

"Yep, just down the hill." Bryson walks me to the passenger side of the vehicle just like he does when we're out on a date to-gether. It's sweet and gentlemanly and so odd coming from him.

"Why are you so good to me?"

His brow furrows. "Should I not be?"

"No, I mean, yes, you should be. I just . . ." I don't finish because his mood always seems to dip when I bring up the past. He wants to forget it, move on, but our past is always attached. It follows us even when we've outgrown it. "Never mind. Thank you." I give him a quick peck on the lips and hop into the seat. The Gator has thankfully been parked in the shade, so the vinyl is only slightly hot.

I watch as he jogs to the driver's side, still wondering when this fairy tale with him is going to end. It's not fair; I know this, but it's one of the drawbacks of knowing him for so long. I remember his past relationships. I remember how he treated his girlfriends in public and even had insight, mostly through Alison, on how he treated them in private. Bryson wasn't a bad guy. He didn't cheat or yell or anything like that. He was just always a little . . . cold.

He weaves us around the barn and down the hill to where Charlie, along with five archery targets, waits. Each one is a different distance away from a long wooden shooting table, which must be the starting point.

"I get to shoot!" I squeal, too excited to hide my elation. I'd been hinting for weeks that I wanted to see the famed archery range, but Charlie had dismissed it, saying the area was run-down and overgrown.

I take in the freshly cut grass and new golden pieces of wood holding up each target. I can see this job was not a quick or easy one. "When did you have time to do this?"

"I didn't." He parks several yards back from where Charlie stands and leans his forearms on the steering wheel. "Charlie did it all. I had no idea until he asked me to help him distance out the targets yesterday. I guess he's been coming out here early in the morning and working."

I run a hand along my boyfriend's back, knowing how relieved he is to see the Charlie he grew up with returning. "This place holds a lot of memories for you, doesn't it?"

He nods, and I can tell by his silence that not all of them are good. Bryson has slayed many demons on this range. I think maybe that's why he brought me here. To give me an opportunity to slay a few of mine.

"Okay, let's do this," I say, wanting to take away the new slump in his shoulders. "I'm ready to hit lots of bull's-eyes."

Bryson laughs. "You'll be lucky if you hit the target at all. It took me a month to even hit the outer ring."

I hop from the doorless vehicle and spin. "Well, I'm way better than you, so get ready to be embarrassed."

He laughs again. "Is that right?"

"Yes."

"You're positive."

"Absolutely."

He moves in, his breath tickling my forehead. "Enough to wager on it again?"

I shiver at the sexiness of his voice. He can turn it off and on so quickly, like a snake charmer who knows exactly which musical notes are the most hypnotic. I glance up through my eyelashes and give him my own dose of charm. Bryson isn't the only one who's learned what buttons to push and when. "What did you have in mind?"

He opens his mouth, but before the challenge can spill out, my pocket vibrates and Cameron's ringtone blares into the bubble around us, fizzling every ounce of electricity.

Bryson sucks in a deep breath. "How many times is that today?"

I mouth *sorry* and back away, pulling my phone free in the process. "What now?" I say into the receiver with a hint of both laughter and scolding in my voice. It's not uncommon for us to talk daily, or even multiple times a day, but ever since our dinner out, Cameron's been unquestionably clingier.

"Which shirt should I buy? I texted you some options."

"Um . . . did you forget who you were calling?" I'm only half kidding.

"No, I didn't forget, and I need your help. I've been to five different stores and nothing is right. Come on, Darcy, just give me your opinion. I have to look perfect for this concert."

"Okay, hold on." I put him on speaker and look through the multiple pictures he sent. Some even of him in the dressing room mirror. "They all look the same."

"What? No, they don't. Look again."

"I am looking, and they are practically the same shirt. Just pick one. You can't go wrong."

"But which is your favorite?"

I sigh, exasperated. I can hardly stand picking out my own clothes for the day, let alone his. My eyes wander to Bryson, who's standing next to Charlie and testing the string on one of the bows. His black shirt is wet where it clings to his back and fades right into the dark gym shorts he threw on. "Get the one with the least amount of black in it," I say automatically.

"Okay, yeah. Good call. I don't want to look like Bryson's twin."

I hear him shuffling clothes and then the scrape of a hanger. "Can I go now?"

"Oh, sorry, yes. Thanks."

I slide the phone back in my pocket and skip down to where two of my favorite men are standing. "So, which one of you is going to be my teacher?"

Charlie backs away. "Not me. I've seen how you girls shoot. Sue Ann nearly maimed me the first time."

"That's because they like to assume they're better than their instructor," Bryson inserts.

I scowl at my boyfriend, though it's layered in the same kidding jest he had when he said it. Bryson lifts the smallest bow from the table and walks it over. He's smiling enough that I almost think I'm going to come away from the interruption without a comment, until he leans down to whisper in my ear, "Five times, Darcy. Five times in two hours. I thought you were going to draw some lines?" He isn't upset, more annoyed, which is his default each time Cam invades our time together.

"He's stressing over a stage outfit." I take the offered bow and tug slightly on the taut strings. "You should be glad that he cares so much."

"I'll be glad when he has his own girlfriend to call," he mumbles, watching how I'm handling the bow. "Not like that. You'll hurt yourself." Carefully taking the contraption from my hands, he settles behind me, his body flush against my back.

I feel a gentle nibble in the crease by my shoulder and pull away, giggling. "Hey! You're supposed to be teaching me, not trying to distract me."

"I can do both," he teases, and my cheeks flush with embarrassment.

"Stop. Charlie is standing right there." My scolding has no effect on the man whatsoever. He takes advantage of every opportunity to brush against my skin while he demonstrates how to shoot, and there are many, many chances for instruction because, as it turns out, I'm terrible at archery. Not just bad. The worst. My arrows not only don't make it to the target but they barely make it past my own feet.

The only saving grace is that Charlie thinks my lack of shooting skills is hilarious, and his laughter is so unexpected and welcome, I probably would have missed on purpose if I knew this would be the result.

Bryson, on the other hand, is a pro, and when he stands there, focused and confident, he's practically the picture of a Greek warrior annihilating the opposing side. I watch the way his muscles contract and release, the way his dark hair whips in the breeze, and the beautiful touch of sunlight on his tanned skin. My mouth goes dry and I'm hit with a twinge of insecurity. My feelings seem to multiply for him daily. And while I know he cares for me as much as he cares for anyone, I can't help but wonder if there's a limit to how far it goes.

Another shot slams directly into the bull's-eye, and I clap, long ago conceding my defeat. He glances behind and winks, waiting for my reaction. I fan myself and act starstruck, which he seems to love.

"One more, then it's your turn again." He pulls back, ready to take another shot, and blast it if my phone doesn't blare Cameron's song again. I was amused when he uploaded one of his singles as his own personal ringtone. Now it's a battle cry. Bryson's back goes rigid, and he misses the target for the first time all day.

I'm walking away with the phone pressed to my ear before he can give me what I'm sure is going to be a look of pure irritation. "You seriously have issues today," I say into the phone.

"I'm at the grocery store. What kind of pizza do you want for dinner—pepperoni or supreme?"

"Neither . . . I have plans tonight. I told you that."

"It's not fair. This is the first Saturday I've had off in weeks and you're off frolicking with your summer fling. Ditch him and come hang out with me."

I choose to ignore the fling comment. "I can't do that."

"Yes, you can. And besides, you owe me and I'm cashing in."

"How do I owe you?"

"I moved you in and out of two apartments, both with stairs. And I got up early on a Saturday to help you with Bentley, which, by the way, came with a glorious stain to my favorite pair of shorts." I hear the beep of the self-checkout. "I got you pepperoni."

"Cam . . ." I glance over at Bryson, who's in deep conversation with Charlie. "We'll hang out tomorrow. I promise."

"I work tomorrow and Monday. Seriously, Darcy, it's been a week. Tell him you need some time with your friends." His frustration has leaked past the banter, and I can tell he's getting upset with me.

"Fine. I'll agree to try, but I can't promise anything."

"Did I mention the world's most awkward Sunday night dinner you dragged me to?"

I sigh, beaten. "Okay . . . you win. I'll be there soon."

"Awesome! I got movie snacks, too."

I end the call and head back down the hill, dreading every step.

"All good?" Bryson asks, and his voice is relaxed like he's doing his best to sound casual about the entire thing.

I glance at Charlie and give a quick smile before taking Bryson's hand. "Can I talk to you for a second?"

He comes without hesitation, but I can feel his stress growing as we walk toward the UTV. I bite my lip, rehearsing the words in my head. If it weren't Cameron . . . if he weren't a guy, anyway, Bryson would understand. Friends always get a little uncomfortable when a new relationship shakes up the normal. I'd felt my own round of insecurity not too long ago myself when January had come into the picture.

We stop by the driver's side, and Bryson grips the vehicle's metal frame. "What's going on?"

I swallow. "I know we talked about grabbing dinner, but if it's okay, I really think I need to hang out with Cam tonight instead." I can feel the weight of Bryson's disbelief as he continues to stare at me wordlessly. "He's my best friend, and in two weeks you guys are leaving on tour and will be gone for months." He looks away from me and shakes his head. "I know you keep saying that nothing is for sure, but it could be. And if the three of us are ever going to find some kind of positive coexistence, Cam needs to know that I'm not abandoning him."

Bryson remains silent, maybe to see if I have more to say or maybe to digest what I've already given him. I kick the dirt at my feet and try to respect his need for quiet introspection. Finally, he turns back to me, his expression blank. "Is this another attempt to make Cam happy, or do you want to go over there and be with him?"

It's not a fair question; there are too many layers of context inside of it. I press my fingers to my temples and sigh. "I want my hanging out with Cameron to not be so complicated. That's what I want."

Bryson wraps a hand around the back of my head and gently kisses my forehead. "Have fun." And then he's gone, walking away with his hands in his pockets.

I watch him all the way to the shooting table, watch him pick up a bow, and watch as he once again hits the center of the target.

TWENTY-EIGHT

I'm restless. Restless and anxious, and my insides feel as if they've spent the last six days in a rotisserie oven. And maybe that's why I'm pulling into Bryson's driveway when I know the entire band will be here in an hour.

Despite Bryson's acceptance of my early departure last weekend, he was different the next day. Distant, guarded. It took two hours and the intentional act of putting my phone on silent the entire night to pull him out of his shell. But out of it he came, and if Bryson had lingering doubts about the two of us, he certainly hasn't shown any. It's as if time has become his enemy and he's determined to capitalize on every moment we have together.

I'm the one who can't seem to cope. There are too many things going on in my head. Too many decisions to be made and events to anticipate and parents to try to forget about. It's all pressing in on me, like my stay of execution is finished and I have to deal with all the turmoil right now, this very minute.

"Knock, knock," I call out, peeking around the corner into Bryson's living room.

"Hey, I wasn't expecting you to come by." Bryson smiles, soft and genuine, and lifts his guitar strap over his head.

"I hope it's okay that I didn't call first." I step inside the room that's already been transformed into the band's practice space.

"Of course it is. What's going on?"

"Nothing . . . I don't know." I take a breath, wishing for the umpteenth time that I didn't constantly feel as if I were getting off a roller coaster. "I guess I didn't want to go a day without seeing you."

He lays his guitar down carefully and comes to meet me in the middle of the room. "You guess, huh?"

Embarrassment singes my cheeks. "You know what I mean."

He chuckles and wraps his arms tight around me. "I do know what you mean. I kind of like seeing you, too."

I press my forehead against his chest to keep from turning into a melting pile of mush, but that's what it feels like lately whenever I'm around him.

"Full disclosure. Cameron's coming early to work on some harmonies." He kisses the top of my head and pulls back.

"Oh . . . okay." I'm disappointed. "I won't stay long, then."

A frown pulls at the corner of his mouth but he doesn't push the matter. I was hoping the elephant would disappear if I ignored it. Unfortunately, it's only gotten bigger. He backs up and squats down next to the microphone wiring, making whatever adjustments he needs to.

I follow him over and sit on the armrest of the couch he's pushed up against the wall. "I think I'm going to have to try something new with Penny today."

"And how many strategies will that make now?"

I scowl at the reminder of my continual failure with the

273

little dog. "Four, but the obstacle course wasn't a complete di-saster. She does love it." Not enough to stop attacking Macey or stop lunging at Louie's cage, which was the whole point, but at least I can sort of justify the three hundred dollars it cost me.

"You know what I think?" He glances up at me from his hunched position. "I think deep down you know you need to cancel your spot tomorrow, and this is just one more at-tempt to stay in denial. Penny's not ready to be adopted. And in some ways, she's worse. She nearly took off my hand the other day when I put her back in her crate."

"I know." I rub my forehead, out of ideas. "But Charlie gave me until the end of July, which means I have only two more weeks to work with Louie, and he still only comes out of his doghouse when I'm alone. I don't have the energy to work on his fear when Penny's there attacking every moving thing."

"Charlie's in a much different place than he was before." Bryson slides the amp over and turns it at an angle. "He'll give you more time. You don't have to rush this."

"It's not just about Charlie." I groan. "It's everything. The estrangement with my mom, worrying about Cam and his reaction to the two of us, the tour that could very well mean you're leaving. And to top it off, Dad's stupid birthday party tomorrow is dangling over my head like a cartoon boulder. I just need something I can control right now. I *need* a victory."

Bryson stands, and I hate that he's watching me with a grin on his face. Hate even more that I think it's one of his sexiest expressions.

"Why is this funny to you?"

"It's not." He strolls over, his smile growing. "I just love how everything you're feeling rolled out in one breath." He pulls me up to standing. "One might even think you came over here because you needed to talk to someone . . . and yeah, the fact that I was your first choice makes me very happy." He nuzzles the skin by my ear, and wonderful tingles run down my spine.

I lace my hands around his neck. "What can I say, Katsaros? You've hooked me and now I'm no good without you."

He laughs into my hair. "Do you realize you only call me by my last name when you're feeling unsure of yourself?"

"I do not."

"Yes, you do." He kisses the top of my head with such tender sweetness I want to wilt. "But you don't have to be nervous with me. This transparency is what I've been waiting for . . . what I've wanted between us all along." He hooks his arm around my waist and pulls me forward with a jerk. "Now kiss me goodbye, because if you keep biting your lip like that, I can promise I'm not letting you go anywhere."

The contact comes just as furiously, my hands gripping his shirt in an effort to bring him closer and closer, all the way to my beating heart.

These are my favorite kind of kisses with him. The passionate ones. The ones that make me feel boneless and electric all at the same time.

The release is slow as neither of us wants to let go, but we know we have to.

"I'll come over after we're done," he whispers, his mouth still centimeters from mine. "And we'll figure it all out together."

For the first time in days, I feel a small measure of relief. "Okay. Thank you."

"You're welcome." He lifts his head, but instead of releasing me, he freezes.

"What?" But it only takes my following his line of sight to see the cause. Cameron is standing in the living room.

Our gazes meet and there's a condemning darkness in his eyes I've never seen before.

Ice fills my belly.

"Tell me I'm not seeing this." His eyes flick from me to Bryson, then back to me. "Tell me I'm hallucinating and he isn't the guy you've been dating." My best friend shoves both of his hands through his hair like his head is about to explode. "Tell me now, Darcy, that the lead singer of *my* band is not your summer fling."

Bryson's body locks up like a steel machine the minute those words dart across the room, but I don't have time to worry about misconceptions. "Cameron . . ."

His curse is loud as he storms away, the front door slamming with a force that makes the lampshades rattle.

I try to disentangle myself, but Bryson's grip only gets tighter. "Let him go. He'll cool down, and the three of us will finally have the conversation that should have happened a while ago."

"I can't let him leave like this. You saw how upset he was."

"He's not the only one upset here." Bryson's hold releases, though I can tell he doesn't want to. "Is that really what you told him? That this thing between us is just a fling?"

"No. He assumed that's what it was."

"And you didn't correct him?"

"Why does it matter?"

"Because it does."

My gaze shifts to the closed front door, every second a guarantee that Cameron will be gone before I ever get outside. "I have to go after him."

"Fine, then I'm going with you." Bryson moves to follow me, but I halt his motion with my palm to his chest.

"Please, stay here. Things are bad enough without him feeling like we're ganging up on him." Bryson stares at my hand, lingering for a long, scrutinizing moment before he finally steps back. I know I'm not being fair, but I'm also not going to participate in a three-way screaming match. Fair or not, Bryson's presence will only make this entire nightmare worse.

I rush to the door, ignoring the hurt and insecurity I'm leaving behind. Bryson is different from Cam. He's stronger. More mature. We can fix us later.

"Cameron . . . wait. I'm so sorry. I never wanted you to find out this way." I catch him just outside the front door, almost as if he was waiting for me to follow. "We were going to tell you."

He turns around, fuming. "When?"

I blink, taken back by the rage in his voice. I expected hurt and even a little anger, but not this. "After the concert. Just like I told you."

"Yeah, nice touch, by the way, with the whole 'trust me, he'll be there' line." His voice is filled with a disgust that's never been directed at me. "How could you do this to me? He's my bandmate, Darcy! He's tied to every one of my dreams."

"I didn't do it on purpose. It just sort of happened."

"Nothing just happens with him! It was premeditated from the first moment he saw you walk through this door." He throws his arms into the air. "Have you forgotten who you're dealing with here? It's Bryson! *Bryson*, Darcy. You know what he's capable of." Cameron walks across the lawn and then back again, his hard steps punctuating his growing anger. "What happens when he tires of you, huh? How am I sup-posed to get up onstage and pretend I don't hate him when he breaks your heart?" He stops in front of me. "Because that's exactly what he's going to do!"

I stare at him, apology quickly turning to irritation. "He's different with me. He really cares—"

"Oh, bull." Cameron looks ready to vomit. "He's the same guy he's always been. He's using you, Darcy. And this is nothing more than one more way for him to prove that he can get whatever he wants."

"So what are you saying?" I ask through gritted teeth. "That I'm just some stupid girl who let him?"

He spreads his arms wide. "Apparently!"

The silence that falls between us is so heavy I feel like drowning under its weight. We both need to calm down. Both need to stop and talk about this rationally like we always do.

But Cameron is still incensed. His nostrils flare and his eyes narrow at the house he just stormed out of. "I knew something was up. He's been too cagey; his resentment obvious. I just didn't want to believe he'd try to push me out this close to us finally making it." He paces again, shaking his head, his hands drawn into fists. "January warned me. She nailed him in one interaction and told me he'd do this the minute I outshined him. The minute my influence superseded his, he'd find a way to get rid of me. I got us this contract." He slaps his hand against his chest. "I did, not him. And he couldn't handle it. He has to be the star . . . always." Cameron steps closer, his chest an imposing wall. His eyes glow like a beast. "Don't think for a second it's a coincidence you two got together after that concert. He knew I wouldn't leave without a fight. And this was his kill shot—you."

I stand there, stunned with disbelief, trying to find my voice.

"And what I can't understand. What my mind cannot wrap

around is the fact that you let him!" His hands tremble as he backs away. "What were you thinking? You watched what he did to Alison. You comforted her when she came home crying. Or did it not matter that in one thoughtless decision you put a knife in both of our backs?"

"Hey!" Anger and guilt punch through the strangle in my throat. "If you want to talk about you and me, then fine. But leave Alison out of it."

"I can't leave her out of it, and neither should you!" He viciously pulls his phone from his back pocket and tries to shove it in my hand. "Call her. Call her now and ask her what it was really like on tour with him. Ask her how cold he became the minute we left town. How he flinched at every touch and made excuses to get away from her. Ask her, because I'm sure there's more." When I refuse to take the device, he shoves it back in his jeans. "He knows how to play the part. How to suck you in and make you believe he's not completely broken. But he is, Darcy. He is. He's the kind of broken that brings a random girl to his bed the same night he sticks his devastated girlfriend on a bus home."

A chill seeps through my skin, and I cross my arms to ward off the shiver. "I don't believe you."

"Oh, it's true, every word." He steps forward, his tone ripe with sarcasm. "And unlike you, I don't make a practice of lying to the people I supposedly care about."

My eyes burn with misery. I hate every one of our words. Hate that this person in front of me feels like a stranger.

He studies me, the line of his jaw still tight with anger, but his brows pull together, plaintive, sympathetic. "What is going on with you? Because what I saw in there makes no sense. He is not the man you want. Not the man you've spent twenty-nine years waiting for. How could you, for any reason, settle for *him*?" He points to the closed front door, his voice rising once more. "A guy who is incapable of caring for anyone other than himself! A guy who will never be the kind of father and husband you need him to be, because he has no idea what love even looks like. Have you thought of any of that?"

Bile rises in my throat with each one of his cruel words. "Stop it."

"No, I won't stop it. Not until you see the truth." He grips my arms, and both our bodies shake under the intense surge of emotion. "Bryson is just like your father. In every way. He's selfish and cunning, and when he's done bleeding you dry, he'll walk away without a second thought."

"Let go of me," I cry, pushing him away. Angry tears blur my vision while my heart feels as if it might explode into a thousand pieces of shrapnel. "It isn't the same."

"It's exactly the same!" His voice lowers and comes at me like a blade. "Is that what this is, Darcy? Some sick Freudian transference? You couldn't get your father to stick around so you decide to find someone just like him to fill the void?"

The air freezes between us, his words dragging through me like a tangled line, ripping open all the wounds I thought I'd closed. "I can't believe you just said that to me." I push past him, but he grabs my arm and whirls me around.

"Somebody had to. Because I don't even know who you are anymore." His own furious tears pool in his eyes as we stand there, a churning fire between us.

I can't stand it. The pain is too great, the betrayal in his eyes too gut-wrenching to stomach. I jerk my arm from his grip and run to my old truck, the gears grinding as I peel out of the driveway.

The rules of the road make no impression on me. I blow

through stop signs, speed at a rate that would undoubtedly get me thrown in jail, and push my truck to its absolute limit before pulling into Charlie's driveway. The tears have long since dried until all that's left are Cameron's hateful words rolling through my head over and over again.

I slam my door and kick the tire. One, two, three more times until it physically hurts to kick it again. I set my hands on my hips, breathe in and out until I convince myself I'm calm enough to deal with the animals.

It's my job, after all, and isn't that what I've been preaching to Charlie for weeks? That Penny needs an outlet, that she needs to feel useful and important and not stuck in some cage she has absolutely no control over.

I storm through the yard, ignoring Louie even though he runs to the gate and wags his long tail spastically. "Not today," I mumble.

Charlie's gone and so is Macey, a very good thing right now.

Penny scratches incessantly at the crate when I open the laundry room door.

"I'm coming." I tear the leash from the wall, undo the latch, and click the metal to her collar before she can bolt away from me.

We do our usual walk around the barn, letting her do her business before the real work begins. With every step, I work to calm my nerves, work to silence the voice in my head that screams maybe Cameron is right. Maybe I did go for Bryson because he was different and dangerous. Maybe all of this is part of the swirling vortex that has become my pathetic life.

I tug Penny forward, irritated it's taking her so long today. Louie sees us coming and chases along the fence, agitated, just like he used to before, like he can sense the charged energy I'm emoting.

Penny growls and lunges for Louie, only I'm prepared for as much and drag her all the way to Bentley's old kennel, her paws digging in the dirt as she barks ferociously at the dog who's ten times heavier than she is.

"Get in there!" I yell and shove the fighting dog to the middle of the dirt floor before locking us both inside. "We're not doing this today, do you hear me?" The edge in my voice makes her retreat, and all the hair on her back rises in defense. "I'm sorry." I take a deep breath. "I'm calm, really."

But nothing feels calm anymore, especially not me.

Louie's barking turns erratic, and I take my eyes off Penny for one second to assure him I'm okay.

It's one second too long. The leash slips from my hand as Penny struggles through the kennel's hog squares and races free.

"No!" Blood pounds in my ears as I rush to the gate, my shaking fingers fumbling with the lock. "Open, please, please open!" Finally it does, and I make it to the yard at the same time Penny forces her way inside Louie's cage. I take off in a sprint as the horrific sound of two dogs battling for dominance assaults my ears.

Everything falls into movie-like slow motion. I can't get my feet to run fast enough. Can't reach the gate or stop the two dogs tangled on the ground, mouths open, biting, growling, hurting each other.

Fear and chaos claw from my gut to my windpipe. "Penny, no!" I scream. Her jaw is locked around the skin at Louie's neck. I'm paralyzed, helpless to stop the fight without putting myself at risk. "Louie, stop!" I scream louder, but it's useless.

He's left with no choice but to defend himself the way Macey never has.

An ear-piercing cry escapes Louie's mouth, and instinct trumps all sense. I rush between the dogs, forgoing all my training, and wrestle away paws and nails until I grab Penny in mid-attack.

Pain slices through my hand, but I don't stop until I have Penny against my chest and my uninjured palm clamped around her mouth so she can no longer hurt anyone.

Louie rushes inside his doghouse, whimpering. He lowers his head and licks at his paws. My body goes cold, my heart crushed by the reality that I did this. I never should have come here. Not like this.

"I'm so sorry," I say to the terrified Great Dane. "This is all my fault."

Still holding Penny tight to my chest, I free us from the kennel and rush to the back door. She's stopped fighting me now, which gives me a chance to check her over for damage. Blood soaks her sleek white fur, and panic rises until I ascertain that it's my blood, not hers, and that somehow Louie managed to defend himself without seriously hurting her, something he easily could have done if he wanted to.

I gently put her back in her cage and lock it up. It's the first time Penny doesn't fight me on it. For once, the crate feels like a safe place.

The floor trembles beneath my feet, the adrenaline drop so severe I reach for the wall as I slowly sink to the ground. Red handprints slide down the white paint, but it's all I can do to steady the drop. I work to breathe, the air catching in my throat like hot coals, burning my chest with every inhale. I scoot to the wall to find some sense of support. It helps. The tightness in my chest eases until once again I can exhale without pain.

Penny watches me through the slats in the door. Probably asking me the questions I keep asking myself. *Why did you come here? Why did you jeopardize so much?*

I lower my forehead to my knees, unable to answer either one.

TWENTY-NINE

*T*he bleeding down my arm doesn't allow me to stay in my hunched position for long. Slowly, I rise to my feet, checking to ensure my balance is once again steady. My right hand screams out in pain as I spread it fully to examine the extent of the damage. The cut is in the soft tissue between my thumb and index finger, and it's deep enough that stitches are a real possibility.

I stumble to the kitchen sink, my body still fighting off the shock of earlier, and hold my hand under a rush of water. Burning fire scorches my skin at the contact, but I force it steady under the stream, all while pumping soap in my other hand.

Because my luck is just that terrible today, the back door opens right when I begin scrubbing the wound and long before I can clean up the trail of blood that extends from the door to the laundry room. Not to mention the permanently crimson-stained T-shirt I'm wearing that is supposed to be a butter yellow.

Charlie takes no time in assessing my state. He hurries toward me and grabs a handful of paper towels. "I'm calling Animal Control tomorrow."

"It wasn't her fault. I was upset and angry, and I should never have come out here."

"I don't care if you drop-kicked her to the moon. I will not keep a dog that bites in my house."

"She didn't bite me on purpose. She got loose and went after Louie. This happened when I was breaking up the fight."

"That doesn't change my mind."

"Well, it should!" I holler and immediately wish I hadn't. Charlie watches me like a handful of lit firecrackers. "Sorry." I hunch over the sink, my forearms bearing my body weight since my hand is still dangling in the stainless-steel bowl. "It's just that you and Macey, well, you deal with your grief by mourning quietly. Penny is different. She's angry at her circumstances, but deep down, it's still grief. Surely you can understand that."

He gently takes my hand and examines the wound, forcing me to stand back up. "I don't think it's deep enough for stitches, but you should still go get it seen."

"I had a tetanus shot this past year when I was getting ready for my trip. As long as I keep it dry and dosed with antibiotic cream, the cut will be fine. This isn't the first time I've been bitten by an animal." Though it is the first one I've felt responsible for. I watch him, my voice turning to a plea. "Please, Charlie, if you send her away because of my stupidity, I'll never forgive myself."

He presses his lips together and sighs. "Fine. But no fair tomorrow. I cannot in good conscience give that dog to someone else until I know this is an isolated incident." He sets my towel-wrapped hand on the counter. "Don't move. I'll be back with some bandages."

I hold my arm to my chest and lean my backside against the sink. Through the window I can hear Louie's barking, loud and steady, just like it used to be a month ago.

"Stupid, stupid," I moan, realizing for maybe the first time that it wasn't just Penny's progress that took a hit today but Louie's, as well.

Charlie returns with a first-aid kit in hand and finishes tending to the wound. From his silence and the scowl on his face, I know he's not happy with me or with his animals.

"I'm sorry," I say again, like it will make any difference.

"You said you were upset. What happened?"

"I really don't want to talk about it."

He glances up from his task, his eyes hard. "And I don't want to be bandaging up a dog bite right now. But here I am."

Since it's obvious I'm not going to get out of this conversation, I give him the quick version. "I got into a fight with my best friend, and he said some pretty horrible things."

He cuts the medical tape and presses the end to my skin, finishing the job. "This the same best friend who's also in Black Carousel?" When my eyes show my surprise, he continues, "Bryson's talked to me a little about the situation. He wanted my advice."

"And?"

"It sounds like it doesn't matter anymore."

I shake my head. "No, I guess it doesn't."

"So, what did he say?"

I drop my chin, a surge of anger coming back so fierce I want to scream. "Nothing I want to repeat."

Charlie crosses his arms, continuing to assess my body language like I'm feeding the story without saying a word. "I recognize this anger. Bryson had it for years before he finally dealt with the root issue."

I grind my teeth, too afraid that if I speak, it will only come out in curses and screams.

He squeezes my shoulder cautiously, like a father with an

estranged child. "It's a slippery slope, letting these feelings fester. Kind of like Penny over there, you end up taking your anger out on everyone else instead of dealing with the one person who caused it."

I think of my parents and know Charlie's right. I've avoided and coped and stayed away, but I haven't dealt with any of my feelings toward them. I swallow down the ache and push off the sink, refusing to look at the man who just pegged my issues to an alarmingly accurate degree. "I'm going to go check on Louie and make sure he's not hurt."

I'm almost to the door when Charlie responds. "This may not seem as bad as trying to drink away your problems, but, Darcy—" I look at him, and his eyes hold the wisdom that comes with seventy years of life—"burying the anger is just as dangerous."

It's dark by the time I pull into Bryson's driveway again, yet it's taken me this long to get all the raging emotions under control. I stayed with Louie until he stopped barking, a chore that took nearly thirty minutes. I spent another thirty petting him until finally he seemed docile and relaxed. Then I drove. Nowhere at first, but then I ended up on I-35 heading north toward Dallas.

My dad lives in a two-bedroom, fifteen-hundred-square-foot, ridiculously expensive apartment near Richardson. I've been there once . . . the day he took me for a tour of the area, spouting on and on about the benefits of not having to commute anymore. It was the same week my parents signed legal documents ending thirty-five years of marriage, and the last time I've spoken to him.

When his exit came, I took the turnaround and headed right back south.

Charlie was right about the anger festering. I'd been feeding an untamed monster for far too long. Stuffing it down until I hit the breaking point. And now, like with Penny, the aftermath is a mess for me to clean up.

I ease out of my truck, unsure what to expect to find. Bryson was mad before I left. Who knows what I'm walking into now? I close my eyes and knock on the door. I'd come here earlier because I wanted reassurance. Funny, I stand here now, feeling the exact same way.

No answer comes, but I know he's home. His truck is in the driveway, and I can hear music through the door. I turn the knob and enter, uninvited.

The living room is still set up for practice, even though Bryson is the only one here, sitting on a folding chair and strumming chords with focused aggravation. I know he hears me come in, but he doesn't move, doesn't even stop to acknowledge my presence.

I take a tentative step forward, unfamiliar with the tightness in my chest. I've seen Bryson this detached before, but never with me, even before we were, well, whatever we've been until today. "Hey."

His eyes lock onto mine and it seems there's no air in the universe. His stare reveals nothing; cold, calm, dead. Time stretches impossibly. And right when I finally find the courage to say more than a fumbling hello, he looks down at his fingers, strums a chord, and then mashes his hand against the strings to stop the vibration. "I guess I should have locked the door."

There's another chair close by. I pull it near his and sit down. Maybe if we're at the same level, he won't feel so far away. "You're angry."

"Oh, I passed angry a while ago. About the same time my girlfriend drove off without a word to me." He strums again, a clear indication he doesn't want to continue our conversation.

"I'm sorry. Everything got so heated, things were said . . ." I swallow down the sickness in my stomach. "You're right, though. I shouldn't have left that way."

He snorts in agreement but still doesn't stop picking at his guitar strings.

I reach out to touch his hand. A mistake. His physical rejection of my touch is as sharp as his verbal ones have been. I sigh, frustrated, and put my hand back in my lap. "I wish you'd at least look at me."

That gets his attention. His head jerks up, his stare icy. "You know what I wish? I wish for once you cared about my feelings as much as you do Cam's." He aggressively tugs off his guitar and stands. "I wish my walls were thicker than a sheet of paper so I wouldn't have had to listen to a complete annihilation of my character. But mostly I wish you had said one thing, just *one*, to defend me out there."

His words wash over me, and I feel sick with myself. Sick with the viciousness of Cameron's words—with how little I did to stand up for Bryson. "I didn't realize you heard us."

"Cameron wasn't exactly whispering, was he." He shoves agitated fingers through his hair. "Do you believe him?" When I don't answer immediately, he turns his back to me and stares out the dark window. "Of course you do. I was a fool to think it would ever be otherwise."

"So you didn't take a girl to your room that night?"

He spins back around, his jaw tight. I can almost see the explanation blazing in his eyes, but he holds back. "Would you trust my word over his if I said no?"

"I'd like to think I would."

"Funny. I'd like to think you would, too, but I don't." He works his jaw back and forth like he's having an argument with himself. Finally, he says, "Yes, I did take a girl to my room. She was an old friend from high school who happened to be in town. She stayed thirty minutes. We reminisced a little and then I hugged her goodbye. Any more details you need?"

I look down at my fingers, relief slamming into me.

"I'm not that guy, Darcy. I never have been. Something you of all people should know, considering what didn't happen in your room the night of the concert."

"I know you're not." And I did know, yet the doubt Cameron planted is still creeping up inside.

"Then why are you still looking at me like that?"

"Like what?"

"Like you did the day I moved you into Zoe's. Like I'm some kind of parasite out to destroy the people you love."

I hesitate, desperately wishing I could just trust Bryson's motives. Yet, even my father, the one man I thought to be above all reproach, found a way to lie to me. "The girl in your room wasn't Cameron's only accusation. Did you . . ." My throat is suddenly sand, and I realize I don't want him to tell me. My heart can't handle another crushing blow. And yet, not knowing is a fate I can't live with. "Did you use our relationship to try to get him to leave the band?"

He takes a step back as if my words are a shot and not a question. "You're really asking me that?"

"I have to." My voice is faint and weak, part of me recognizing I'm being completely unfair.

"No, you don't. You should have enough faith in me to answer it all by yourself." He stares at me for a long time, saying nothing, waiting to see if I'll take the question back. When I don't, he finally answers. "Darcy, if I wanted him out, he'd be out. End of story." He shakes his head, his breath hitching in disbelief. "I have spent the summer pouring my heart out to you, opening up about things I *never* talk about, all to show you who I am. He spends five minutes spewing pure hatred, and I'm the one in question here?" Bryson dips his chin, his eyes locked on the floor. "You know what? Forget it. I won't defend myself to you, not when I've given you no reason to doubt me."

"You're right. You haven't. I'm sorry," I say, lowering my head into my hands. "I've screwed everything up so bad today. You. Penny." I rub my temples, the throb from earlier coming in sharp, penetrating jabs.

"What happened to your hand?"

I jerk my head up and examine the bandage he's only now seeing. "It was an accident. She didn't mean to bite me."

"Wow, even a dog has more loyalty from you than I do."

"I'm sorry," I say again, completely at a loss as to how to break through this new layer of uncertainty between us. I've been spoiled. Up until now, he's given me everything I've asked for—honesty, trust, affection, forgiveness. Now he stands in front of me, a shell of who he was only hours ago. "Bryson." Finally he meets my eyes. "I'm sorry. I didn't mean to hurt you."

For one moment, there's a flash of the guy I was only beginning to get to know. "It doesn't matter anymore."

"Yes, it does." I rise from my chair and try again to get close to him. "Tell me what to say so I can fix this between us."

"You can't fix it." His voice holds more heartbreak than anger, though it's clear there's both. "Your words are meaningless when your actions continue to reaffirm a truth I haven't wanted to accept. I watched you two out there, and you don't get that kind of passion between two people unless they love each other."

"Of course we love each other. We've been best friends for nearly thirty years!"

"That wasn't the reaction of a worried best friend. If it were, I could live with it and even respect it. That was the reaction of a man who just had his heart ripped out." He throws his arms out and growls, "When are you going to open your eyes? He's been in love with you since he was eighteen years old. And not the surface kind. The deep, longing kind that has enabled him to stuff down his feelings year after year on the sheer hope that one day you will love him back."

Now I want to pull out my hair. "Why does it always come back to this? I've told you repeatedly that I don't have romantic feelings for Cam."

"Call it whatever you want to, but there's still something there. He's the first one you run to when you're upset. He finds his way into every single conversation we have. He's here between us, Darcy, and has been since we were kids." He laces his fingers on top of his head and presses his lips together. "I won't be Tuck. I'm not going to sit here in denial, holding my heart in my hands, until one day you finally wake up and realize what all of us already know."

"So that's it? One misunderstanding and we're over."

"This isn't a misunderstanding." His voice turns cold. "You walked out on me—twice. For him."

We stand there, eyes locked on each other, at a complete impasse. "This is how you do it." A sob rises up my throat. "You cut people out of your life and then turn around and make them feel like it's their fault."

"I didn't want this."

"Well, neither did I." I turn away, blinking, trying to make sense of what's happening.

"Darcy." He says it like I'm physically hurting him. "What else can I do?"

"Anything but this." I rush back, cradle his face and drag him closer, our foreheads touching, our breaths mingling. "I'm sorry," I whisper, and the apology throbs the air between us.

His arms circle around my waist, holding me tight as if every second spent in this embrace will erase time. "Okay," he finally says, and my heart leaps back into place. His hold loosens and he looks at me, tired creases at the corners of his eyes. "I'll once again deny every one of my instincts and try to move forward with us . . . on one condition." He pauses, and I know whatever he's about to say is non-negotiable. "I won't share your heart with another man. If you and I have any chance of making it, your friendship with him has to change."

My stomach crawls into my throat and I pull free of his embrace. "Change how?"

His lips tighten because we both know he means *end*, not change.

I shake my head, refusing to hear what he's demanding. "You're asking too much."

"Maybe I am. But that's where I stand."

A million thoughts collide in my mind. A thousand emotions, all of them hinging on the hope that if he would just listen to me, he'd see he doesn't have to do this. I work to calm my nerves, but my voice still comes out shaky. "Bryson, it doesn't have to be so black and white. We can find a middle ground. I'll do better. I'll put up clearer boundaries this time."

His eyes darken. "You asked what you could do to fix it; I'm telling you."

"No, you're giving me an ultimatum."

"I'm giving you a choice," he snaps back before taking a breath to calm down. "The same one I made when I got you Zoe's apartment and again when I kissed you, and I'll keep choosing you over and over again. Because it's *easy*. Because you mean more than Black Carousel ever has." Hurt leaks through his voice, and I know it's because I can't tell him the same thing.

"But I would never ask you to give them up for me."

A reply stills on his lips as if I punched the air from his argument, then he angrily runs his hands through his hair. "Darcy, there is no reality where the three of us happily coexist. He. Is. In. Love. With. You." Bryson's words come out in tight, emphatic clips. "This means every moment you spend together is driven by an ulterior motive. One I cannot live with as your boyfriend." He drops his hands and looks straight at me, his voice growing rough. "Just look at the damage he did in one moment. I thought we had crossed a threshold together. That we were moving forward into a new place of trust and openness and mutual respect. Now, just hours later, you've questioned my morals and my integrity, all because he told you to."

"Bryson, I admit I messed up. I doubted you and I shouldn't have, but my trust issues run deeper than just Cameron."

"Maybe so, but I can't forget the things he said or the obvious influence it has on your feelings for me. It will haunt me every time you're together, and that will ruin us." He sighs, his sadness contagious, and an ache falls over me. "Do you want to know the real reason why I didn't tell you about the tour? Because I never once thought we'd make it that far. I've known this entire time that Cameron was going to lose his mind when he found out we were together. I've just been waiting for the blowup."

"If that's true, then why did you let me think it would work? Why even agree to wait?"

"Because you weren't ready to let go of him, and I wasn't ready to let go of you." He reaches up, his knuckles tracing the line of my jaw. "I guess I hoped that if you had enough time, then maybe when we got to this point, you'd actually choose me." The air hangs heavy between us, and for a second I see that seventeen-year-old boy, bracing himself for rejection, all while hoping it doesn't come. And then just as quickly, the tenderness recedes from his eyes. The boy disappears, hardened and ready for the inevitable truth. I can't do what he's asking me to, and he knows it. "But that isn't what's going to happen, is it?"

"Bryson . . ." I feel crippled with loss, unable to say what I need to in order to stop this insanity.

"You don't have to explain. This one's on me. I knew better." His expression betrays no emotion except the glisten in his eyes, but it's enough to hollow me out. He walks to his door and pulls it open. "It's late. You should go home."

There will be no kisses goodbye, no promises of next-day phone calls, no teasing laughter. If I walk out that door, it's over. But if I don't, I'm making a promise I can't live with. Not yet. Maybe not ever.

THIRTY

Saturday comes like a baseball bat against the face. My hand throbs, my heart aches, and since I'm skipping the adoption fair, I now have no real excuse for missing my father's barbecue.

I struggle to sit up in bed, the bright sun shining through my windows. I should have bought curtains. Dark ones. Ones that would respect a person's need to wallow in misery.

Wet doggy kisses assault my face while little paws prance on my chest. I guess the lack of curtains isn't my only issue.

"You win, Piper. I'm getting up." I slide my legs over the mattress as Piper leaps off the bed, on the bed, and off again. "My goodness. Okay. I get it. You need to go outside."

She bolts to the front door the minute my bedroom door is cracked and barks excitedly.

"I'm coming. I'm coming." There's a pretty good chance I look like the Bride of Frankenstein this morning, but my neighbors will just have to deal with it.

I tie my robe around my waist, and just when I'm about to reach the door, Zoe comes barreling inside, nearly sending Piper across the room. Good thing my little dog is quick.

"Liam broke up with me," she says, dropping her overnight

bag onto the floor. Besides traces of her in the laundry room and kitchen, Zoe's been a ghost since the couple got together. "He said I was 'too young' for him. Please." She rolls her eyes. "He eats dinner at five o'clock, watches the news for exactly one hour, and says alcohol gives him a headache. I'm too young? The guy is practically geriatric at twenty-seven." She crosses her arms and studies me. "You look terrible, by the way."

"Thanks," I say dryly and return to my task before poor Piper has an accident on Zoe's wood floors.

Zoe jumps in front of me and unhooks the leash by the door. "I'll take her. You . . . go shower or something."

I cross my arms, annoyed. "I'm not that bad."

She raises her eyebrows but doesn't say another word before disappearing out the door, Piper right at her heels.

I drag my feet across the room, wanting nothing more than to crawl right back into bed. I go to the bathroom instead. A huge mistake. The mirror is as honest as my roommate. My hair is ratted, and there are still traces of my blood on the tips. Dark circles mar the underside of my eyes, proof of how little sleep I've gotten the past few days.

I've come full circle, with nothing but broken relationships to show for the journey.

My body suddenly feeling heavy, I ease myself onto the closed toilet lid. Elbows on my knees, face in my hands, I sit and wait for some kind of clarity. But there is none. No answers. No way forward. No promise of something better.

"Where have you been?" I whisper to the One I haven't spoken to in what feels like forever. "Why have you left me?"

I feel a pressing on my chest and a warmth around my body as if He were right here, holding me. Sobs burn in my throat, but I can't rein them back anymore. The flood comes, deep and heart-wrenching. And I let it. Let out all the tears I'd been holding on to long before Cameron shoved a knife into my chest or Bryson locked me out of his life. These tears fall for the first man I ever loved. The one I can't seem to find the strength to forgive.

"Well now, that's much better," Zoe says when I emerge from my room forty-five minutes later. I've showered, dressed, even added some curl to my hair and a coat of mascara. I haven't seen my father in months, and as stupid as it sounds, I want him to be proud to look at me. "Where are you going all dressed up?"

"Actually, a better question is where are *we* going? I need some backup today."

Zoe's perfectly plucked eyebrows furrow. "My boyfriend just broke up with me. I'm entitled to a day of chocolate and really bad movies."

"Maybe, if this were an uncommon occurrence for you. But this is the second breakup since I've moved in, and let's be real here. The only thing you really like about Liam is how he looks."

"Yeah, I guess you're right." Zoe sighs and squeezes a pillow to her chest. "But I'm not agreeing to anything until I know what you have in mind. I've seen your definition of fun, and it's not normal."

Despite the heaviness of my terrible weekend so far, a smile finds its way to the surface. "It'll be fun. I promise. My dad is nothing if not entertaining." I walk to the refrigerator and grab the orange juice. "And worst case, you get a free lunch at a swanky apartment in Dallas."

"Will there be cute boys?"

"No, probably not." I set down the carton, annoyed. "We're not going to a bar, Zoe; it's a family barbecue. Believe it or not, life does exist outside of the male species."

"Gee, okay. I was just asking so I knew how to dress." She pops up from the couch. "Give me an hour."

"You have fifteen minutes!" I call down the hallway after her and again find myself wanting to chuckle. And cry. Or maybe do both.

I grab the leash and take Piper out one more time while I wait on my roommate. The weather is ideal today. Big puffy clouds in the sky, a slight breeze that shockingly doesn't feel like a blow dryer, and no humidity.

Piper sniffs along the edge of the grass, searching for that perfect spot. I wait, enjoying the serenity, until my phone buzzes in my pocket.

Immediately my mind goes to Cameron, and I'm shocked by the devastation I still feel. He hurt me on purpose. He wielded a power only someone that close has, lashing out and attacking every one of my insecurities.

The phone vibrates again. The second notice that I missed a text. I ease it from my shorts slowly, only to find the text is from my dad, letting me know how thrilled he is I decided to come and what parking lot to use.

Relief and disappointment hit in equal measure. Cam's silence puts us at a stalemate. Which also means I somehow hurt him to the same degree he hurt me. Though how, I still can't understand. Maybe I never will.

"Alright, chica, I'm ready," Zoe calls from the top of the stairs.

I tug on Piper's leash, and she comes quickly, beating me up the stairs without much effort. I grab my keys and the wallet that mostly stays locked in my truck and try not to talk myself out of today's adventure.

"So, if this is a family thing, why isn't Bryson going?" Zoe asks when we get strapped in.

I work to keep the surprise out of my tone while my stomach does a somersault that is less than pleasant. "Why would he?"

"Don't even try it. I know you two are dating. He's been eating all my food, and last week at lunch I started calling him the Joker because I couldn't get him to stop smiling."

I start the engine and try to ignore the nagging ache inside. She waits for me to confirm her theory, which I won't because it doesn't even matter anymore. I turn around, check the rear for any movement, then carefully back out of the parking lot.

"Breakups are the worst when you're around people in love. He's going to be absolutely impossible to deal with now." Her sigh is dramatic when she continues, obviously missing the fact that my silence means I have no interest in discussing this topic. "But I suppose his happiness is justified. He's had a thing for you since forever, even after you dissed him at homecoming."

Okay, that I can't ignore. "I didn't dis him at homecoming. Bryson didn't even go to our school."

"Duh. Which is why he had Mason put the rose in your locker for him. And let me tell you, that note was no easy undertaking either. He made me write it because his handwriting sucked so bad, and then he rejected my first four attempts."

"How do you even remember this? You were, what, ten or eleven?"

She shrugs. "It was right before Dad kicked him out. I remember everything from that time period."

I shift in my seat, my neck going tight. I don't want to think about that night or any of the other things Bryson confided in me over the last month. "I never got any rose, or a note, so I think you misunderstood."

"Trust me, I was a preteen. Bryson's love life was the only interesting thing going on." She kicks off her sandals and crosses her legs in the seat. "The rose was for you. And Mason put it in your locker. I read the text confirming it."

"Well, I never got it." I don't know why my words come out with such a bite, or why my skin suddenly feels itchy and uncomfortable. Maybe because Alison and Cameron were the only other people who knew my locker combination and neither of them ever said a word.

"Too bad. He had the whole thing planned out. Dinner, a rented limo, a rose cors—"

"We broke up, okay?" The truck's cab falls silent, and I squeeze the steering wheel. "So you can stop with whatever romantic notions you have going on in your head."

"You broke up?" The horror in her tone slices me. "Why?"

"A disagreement." My stomach rolls, and I wish I hadn't drunk the orange juice after all. It sits on the edge of my throat and makes my eyes burn. "One we couldn't get past."

She turns her head to look at me, and it's the first time I've ever seen judgment in her eyes. "And you lecture me on my relationship turnaround time?"

I click on the radio. I'm glad Zoe agreed to come along, but that doesn't mean we need to talk on the drive there.

THIRTY-ONE

*A*s he usually does, Dad packs out the place with birthday guests. The parking lot was full, so we had to park a block down on the street. Zoe walks closely by me, carrying the card I picked up on the way. It's one of those generic dad ones, the kind that says happy birthday without saying anything positive about the relationship. Inside, there's a fifty-dollar Visa card. Another generic gift, and so different from the personalized grilling apron I custom ordered for him last year.

"You look nervous," she says, and I lower the fingernail I've been chewing on.

"My dad and I haven't really been on the best of terms lately."

To my surprise, her voice turns soft. "Did you use to be close?"

I swallow down the lump in my throat. "Very."

"Well, here's the thing with dads. No matter how frustrated they get, or how much we disappoint them, we're still their little girls." She chuckles as if she knows this from personal experience and hands me the card. "I'm sure everything will work out just fine between the two of you."

I study the woman who continually surprises me. "Thanks for coming, Zoe. I really needed you here."

"You know me, I'm always up for a party." She shrugs off the gratitude with a wink that looks so much like her brother's it takes me two steps to recover. "Which one is your dad?"

I scan the area in front of us. As usual, he's standing by the grill, the apron I gave him tied around his waist, a bottle of beer in one hand and tongs in the other. "Right there." I point, missing him so much it nearly trips me up.

"Oh my. He's a silver fox." She bumps my shoulder with hers. "I thought you said no cute boys."

"Gross, Zoe." I make a vomit motion that has her laughing out loud. It's a nice sound and much needed, since I do feel like throwing up, though for a completely different reason.

"I'm kidding. But he is handsome for an old guy. You look a lot like him."

"Yeah. People tell me that all the time." Not just that I look like him, but also that he's handsome and charming. The life of the party, my dad. Too bad that's the best thing he'll be remembered for now. The other stuff—loving husband, respected father, faithful man of God—will never again be part of his legacy.

He sees me a few seconds later and excitedly puts down the items in his hands. My feet want to plant themselves in the grass, or run away, back to my truck, back to the stupid bathroom where I made the reckless mistake of deciding to come here.

"Hey, sweetheart!" Fatherly arms wrap around me in a hug that tries way too hard to make up for lost time. "I'm so glad you made it." He releases his grip, looks me over like he hasn't seen me in years, and hugs me tight once again.

I work to get my arms to move, to make them lift and attempt to return the affection.

He finally lets go, and I don't miss the sheen in his eyes. "How was the drive?" He looks past me like he's waiting for someone else. "No Cameron today?"

I shake my head, emotion stirring in my belly. "Nope. No Cameron." It takes clearing my throat to make the sickness go away. "Happy birthday." I awkwardly hand him the card, which he takes much the same way.

"You didn't have to get me anything."

"I know." He looks down like he isn't sure if he should open it now or wait. I help him make the decision. "Dad, this is Zoe. My roommate."

Zoe and Dad do what two charmers always do when meeting someone new. They sparkle and laugh and make small talk look easy. When they're done, Dad puts his arm around my shoulder. "Well, come on. Let's get you young ladies some food."

It's funny how one's perspective changes over time. I've never noticed how short my dad is before. He's just always been my dad. But after meeting Michael, and then spending the last month next to Bryson's six-foot frame, I realize my dad must only be five-foot-eight, and that's probably generous.

A crowd stands around the picnic table littered with plates of food, and Zoe stealthily points at the two shirtless guys to her right. They're young, probably not much older than Zoe is. I study more faces and realize the trend isn't limited to the boys. This party is much more reminiscent of a college blowout than the usual crowd at my dad's birthday parties.

"Where are all your friends?" I ask my dad when I don't recognize a single person in the crowd.

His responding smile feels practiced. "They'll be by. You know these parties are come-and-go."

No, actually they're usually come and stay until Mom kicks everyone out.

He turns away from my confused stare and gathers two empty platters into his arms. "Go mingle. I just need to get these filled up again and then we'll catch up."

I look for the usual gifts, most of them jokes, but still piled there and wrapped every year. There's nothing. Only my lone card, which Dad set down on his folding chair. There isn't even a cake.

Moreover, the crowd that seemed so huge minutes ago has now dwindled. Some of them moved from the serving table to various picnic spots around the lawn. Others appear to have taken their plates back into the apartment building. A few of the guys throw a Frisbee, more joining them after disposing of their trash. Zoe and I stand and watch as they form into teams, neither of us interested in eating right now.

"Hey!" The cute one she noticed earlier comes jogging over. "We're starting a game of ultimate Frisbee." His eyes fall on my roommate's long, slender legs and trail up to her eyes. "Wanna join us?"

"How do you know my dad?" I ask, partly out of curiosity, and partly because I don't like how he's looking at Zoe, even if she doesn't seem to mind at all.

He shrugs like he doesn't really. "I think he's on the first floor by the elevators. That's where the flyer was, at least."

"Flyer?"

"Yeah. Said free food and beer. We all figured it was an apartment thing, until we came out and saw it was just one old dude. But hey, if he's buying, I'm drinking. So . . . you two playing?"

Zoe brightens. "Absolutely. Darcy?"

I'm still reeling from the flyer comment. "No, go ahead."

They run off together, and it's only then that I see the real picture before me. The small, gated park is packed, but not with old friends who are here to celebrate another milestone in my father's life. It's packed with strangers, here only because they were promised a free lunch. I turn around and watch my dad with new eyes. He's all alone by the grill, clinging to a past life that no longer exists. I wonder if that's what Bryson sees when he looks at me. A person oblivious to the fact they're living in a memory.

I shove my hands into my pockets and walk back over to the pavilion, suddenly not so angry at the man in my line of sight.

"You decided not to play?" he asks when I sit on top of the picnic table.

"Nope. I figured I'd come keep you company for a while."

He lifts a rack of ribs onto a massive cutting board and gets to slicing it, the smell so familiar it almost feels like we've gone back in time. Dad at the grill. Me eagerly volunteering to be his sous chef.

I can tell I'm making him nervous. I guess that's understandable considering how we left things. Him trying to talk to me. Me slamming the car door shut and nearly running over his feet.

"How have you been?" My question is different from what I might have asked before. Filled with more pity and less accusation.

"Great. Just great." Again, he gives me the façade. A layer of lies that can't possibly be true. Not when his only friend at the party is me, and he basically had to coerce Cameron into convincing me to be here. "Business is booming. We're even considering opening another office in Austin."

Yeah, I guess maybe that would make things "great," especially when it's all he has now.

He glances at me, then back to his chopping task. "But I

want to hear about you. Cameron says your trip got canceled. I'm really sorry, sweetheart."

"It's water under the bridge now." And it is, especially in light of the fact that yesterday I lost my boyfriend and very likely permanently damaged my relationship with my best friend.

"I'm glad to hear it. We Malones are resilient people." He finishes his plating task and brings the platter to the now-abandoned picnic table. He actually looks around for something to do. Probably since this talk is as fun as listening to clawing on a chalkboard. After straightening all he can, he returns and sits down next to me. "This is a little weird, isn't it?" he finally admits.

"Yes. It is." I look down at my fingers and pick at a chipped nail.

"How's your, uh . . ." He clears his throat. "How's your mom doing?"

"She's the most resilient of us all, actually." I'm annoyed he's asking. Maybe that's why I give him back brutal honesty. "She met someone. His name is Michael and it's pretty serious, I think."

He presses his lips together, and I know it bothers him even though he says, "Good. I'm happy for her."

I shake my head, irritation rising in my throat. "Why did you do it?" He sighs, and I know he wishes I would go back to being that girl who worshiped him and never questioned his decisions. But that girl is gone, and the one she's become needs answers. "Was it just about the sex?"

"Darcy." His voice comes out in shocked indignation. "I will not discuss my personal life with you. It's wildly inappropriate."

"You didn't mind so much last year when your mistress sat down next to me, hoping to '*get to know me better*.'" His face turns a deep shade of red. Good. He should be ashamed. "Where is she, by the way?"

"Blair is no longer in the picture. And that's all I'm going to say on the subject."

"Fine. Then at least tell me why you didn't fight for Mom after the affair was over. Why did you give up?"

"Darcy . . ." Frustration colors every syllable, and he stands, his movements as agitated as his voice. "There are things you are simply too young to understand."

"No. You don't get to expect me to behave like an adult when it fits your and Mom's agenda and then turn around and treat me like a child when I dare to ask why." When he remains quiet and refuses to give me the answer I'm searching for, I look down at my fingers, tears threatening to come as fiercely as they did this morning. "Do you even regret blowing up our family?"

"Of course I have regrets." He presses my bowed head to his chest and kisses my hair like he used to when I was a child and scared of the dark. "I regret ignoring the little things until they became too big to handle. I regret that I made the problems worse instead of trying to solve them. I regret how much this has hurt both you and Dexter, even though he pretends like it doesn't matter. And yes, there are dark moments where I regret every step I took in losing your mom, just as I'm sure there are days she regrets every step she took in doing the same thing." His hand runs along the back of my hair, soothing me as only a father can. "But those are my regrets and my burdens. They are not yours to carry." He lifts my head, and the moisture in my eyes blurs his face. "Do you understand that?"

"It's not too late," I plead through my tears. "You two can still try to fix this. You can do all the things you didn't do before. Marriage counseling, or you can finally take that second honeymoon you always talked about."

"Sweetheart." He sighs again, and I know what he's going to say well before he says it. "Your mom and I are never getting back together. There's a point when the damage becomes irreparable, and we hit that milestone a long time ago. But I love you. And I really hope that one day we will find a way past all the hurt. Because I miss my little girl."

Overcome by emotion, I slide off the table and fall into the arms of my father. He holds me tight, just like he has every time I've been afraid or hurt or lonely. He's my dad, good or bad. I can't change his choices, but I can change mine.

I ease away and wipe my tears with the heel of my palm. "I'm still really disappointed in you."

He swallows and nods. "I know you are."

"But I'm willing to try and forgive you. Because hanging on to this bitterness isn't doing any of us any good." I squeeze his hand in mine and try not to cry again when I see my father's eyes fill.

"Thank you, sweetheart." He swallows again, working to get his emotions to settle. "We can start slow. Maybe a Sunday night once a month?"

I consider it for only a second before shaking my head no, and not just because Sunday nights are Mom's and she didn't do anything to deserve them getting snatched away. My answer is driven more by what my dad and I seem to be suffering from—an inability to let go.

"Why don't we try a Saturday night instead," I say when his chest deflates. "Maybe start some new traditions."

He blows out a long, relieved breath. "I'd like that very much."

THIRTY-TWO

*C*ameron's mom likes to scrapbook. She cuts out pictures, buys expensive, fancy stickers, and creates a chronicled record of each of her four children's journey through life. Cameron claimed to hate it as a kid, but he's fallen into the picture craze much like his mother. Only his snapshots and selfies aren't on 24x24 pages. Instead, they're kept in boxes, each one labeled by year and stuffed to the brim.

I have both collections sitting in front of me. His mom's beautiful book of memories she gave him last Christmas, and Cameron's 4x6 printouts that are as artistic as the amazing music he produces. I carefully turn page after page and marvel at the fact that even though I'm not in his family, my presence is captured on almost every single sheet. Cameron and me playing Sorry when we were only seven. Cameron and me at Hawaiian Falls Waterpark, soaked to the bone, our arms locked around each other's shoulders. Cameron and me in graduation gowns, both excited because we ended up choosing the same college.

I close the book and slide the picture boxes closer. There's less of me in here, but only because I quit letting him freely take my picture a long time ago. It's the rest of his life that's represented. Old bandmates, co-workers, past girlfriends. I pick up the one of him and January. It used to be framed and sitting on his dresser. Now that frame holds a picture of Cameron onstage. The one I took at his first Black Carousel concert.

One by one, I take in the memories, too many to count, some good and some horrible, but ours nonetheless. Maybe that's why I'm here. Why I've been sitting on Cameron's bed for the past two hours, waiting for him to come home.

It's another hour before he does, and by the time I hear the front door open, I have a spread of every girlfriend he's ever had across his blue-and-white-checkered comforter.

Cameron barrels into his room, drops his violin case onto the desk, and kicks off his shoes. He doesn't see me yet, and I don't say a word until he goes to lift his shirt over his head.

"You may not want to do that."

He freezes, his stomach exposed, and then slowly he lowers his shirt back down. "How did you get in here?"

I shrug, only slightly surprised that his voice holds an edge of irritation. "You're not the only one with a spare key."

He backs up until he hits the desk, then crosses his arms. He's still mad. I guess that's fair. I still am as well.

I eye the violin case. "You guys had practice today?"

"I'm not quitting, and he hasn't fired me, so yeah, if he calls it, I'm there. We're professionals, Darcy. There's no law that says we have to be friends to put on a good show." He glances at the door as if strongly weighing whether to bolt or not, and then back at me. "Why are you here?"

"We promised to fight for each other. This is me fighting." I pick up a picture from my last fundraiser. Cameron and I are posed in a high ten because I'd just hit my funding goal. "My dad said that there's a point where the damage in a relationship becomes irreparable. I won't let that be us."

We begin a game of silence we've only played one other time, and it was over something so stupid I don't even remember what it was. Finally I cave, mostly because I came here to talk, or maybe to yell, but either way I came because I refuse to let one argument shake a lifetime together.

"You hurt me. The things you said about my dad were cruel and unfair." My voice is shaky, but I have to get that out.

"I know." He pauses. "And I'm sorry I said it the way I did. I was angry and confused."

I don't miss that he doesn't take back the words, only his harshness. His feelings weren't contrived from shock; they were real, and for some reason, that fact makes them all the more painful.

"You lied to me, and if I'd left my house even five minutes later, you'd probably still be lying to me." He stares down at his feet. "There's always been one absolute between the two of us; we tell each other the truth, even when it means hard conversations or disagreements."

I swallow down the guilt. "In my defense, I never actually lied. I told you I was seeing someone, just not who."

He jerks his head up. "That's a technicality and you know it." He moves again, getting close to the same spastic pacing he had outside of Bryson's front door. "I've been racking my brain for two days now, trying to understand why you didn't talk to me first, especially knowing the kind of impact it would have on the band. And then it hit me . . ." He looks at me and the hurt written on his face makes my stomach sink. "You already knew. That's what bothers me the most. You walked into that relationship fully knowing I wouldn't be okay with the two of you together, and you didn't care."

I have no counterattack because, deep down, it's true. It's why I left Bryson out of stories I'd tell. Why I put off telling Cam the truth, even though Bryson warned me that time wouldn't make a difference. "He's not the terrible person you think he is."

"I don't care if he's a saint, he's terrible *for you*. For any girl, for that matter, but especially for you."

"Is that why you got so mad? Because you were protecting me?"

"Yes . . . but it's more than that. He threatens *us*—what we have together. Bryson doesn't just exist in someone's life. He invades it. I mean, look what's happened. You've only been together a little while and he's already changing you."

I set down the picture I've been holding and pick up one of Cameron and Lydia. He wants to make this about Bryson's flaws, but I won't go there again. "Why haven't any of your relationships lasted?"

"Don't change the subject."

"I'm not. I actually think it's related to why you got so angry. Why this relationship—my first serious one—bothers you so much." My heartbeat grows when Cameron's face changes from frustration to the same tingling fear that's coursing through me.

"What are you asking me?" He takes a step closer, blowing out an unsteady breath as if he, too, can't stop the pounding of his heart.

We hold each other's gaze. One second. Two. It goes into three. He knows what I'm asking. He can see the trepidation all over my face.

Cameron takes another unsteady step forward. "Once we go here, Darcy, there's no going back." It's a warning that the territory we're stepping into is riddled with land mines.

TAMMY L. GRAY

"I don't think we have a choice," I squeak out, my voice catching in my throat. "Not after what happened." Either Bryson is right, and I've been naïve and blind, or he's wrong and our breakup was pointless. Regardless, I'm not leaving this room until I know exactly how Cameron feels.

Without another word, Cam sits on the edge of the bed and examines my handiwork. There are nine girls, all ranging from a few dates to serious long-term possibilities. And in every single case, Cameron was the one who ended things. He pushes the photos into a pile and drops them in one of the boxes I'd emptied. He then takes the pictures of us and lays them out in the same order and formation. "They didn't last because none of them was you." He looks at me then, the truth in his eyes a sledgehammer to all the denial I've clung to since high school when he first told me we were soulmates. "You weren't ready before, and I get it, we were only eighteen, and you had your dreams and I had mine."

I suck in a breath as years of innocent friendship are wiped away, replaced by the truth that between us the whole time, there's been this secret hovering on the fringe. "That was forever ago. Why haven't you said anything?"

"Honestly, I've been too big of a coward to chance a second rejection." He gingerly takes my hand. "I guess I've been waiting for you to feel what I do. And sometimes I think you do, and then other times it seems like you come up with excuses to put distance between us." He scoots closer to me. "But I've always known, no matter how long it took for you to be ready, that it was okay, because one thing has never changed in all these years. You've always come back to me."

I stand because Cameron is too close, and I need to move. To process all he just told me. He watches me from the bed, tentative. I know the look. It is practically the same one Bryson gave me when he asked me to choose. And even though Cameron doesn't say those words, I know I have to. And the choice is no longer between Cameron, my best friend, or Bryson, my boyfriend. Now it's a forever decision, because you don't just date your best friend. You marry him.

Cam rises from the bed, slowly, as if he knows that every step toward me will shatter who we are now.

I want to run, but I can't leave, not after being the one to insist we talk. I press my back into the wall, the one next to his dresser that has only about five feet of space before the corner.

He moves closer, never taking his eyes from mine. "Do you remember when we were twelve and we locked ourselves in the closet?"

I nod, panic rising in my chest, a trapped feeling I haven't had since I got an MRI my junior year closing in on me. We wanted to know what it would be like to kiss someone, and it just made sense that we'd practice on each other.

"You were my first kiss, and I've always been so grateful we had that," he says softly, delicately, his feet inching closer and closer. "I've thought of this moment so many times. Imagined it. Played it out in my head." He's right in front of me now, and I don't know whether to bolt or to let us try and see if I feel even an ounce of what I do when Bryson's near me.

Cam touches my cheek, and it feels different from before. Just as I imagine every look or touch or conversation between us will now be changed. His other hand goes to my waist, and my heart beats more frantically than I ever thought it could without going into cardiac arrest.

"Darcy," he whispers, "I've waited a lifetime to do this again." His head tilts and lowers.

I feel his breath, but it's not until he closes his eyes that I know I can't. I press both palms to his chest. "Don't."

He's so close, he could ignore me and I'd have no way to stop the contact. But true to the man I know he is, he pulls away, though it seems to be the most painful thing I've ever asked him to do.

"This isn't right. And it isn't fair, not to any of us." I take a deep breath, my pulse finally calming to a normal rhythm. "I need time to figure out what I'm feeling."

"You've had eleven years," he snaps, his mouth tight, his eyes bright blue with both desire and frustration.

Matching indignation roars inside me. "No. You've had eleven years. I've had about eleven seconds, so forgive me if I need a moment to catch up."

Cameron shoves his hands into his hair and turns his back to me. "What does he have that I don't?"

"That's not a fair question."

He spins back around. "Sure it is. You kiss him. You lie to me to be with him. You ignore all the warning signs of an inevitably damaged relationship. And now, when we finally have a shot at something mind-blowing together, you choose him. So, what is it that makes Bryson so irresistible? I truly want to know."

"I didn't choose him. I chose my best friend." I don't tell Cam about the ultimatum because he isn't stupid, and he can figure out what I'm getting at. "But now you're changing all of our history and asking me to promise more than I can. It's just too much, too fast." My lower lip quivers and tears burn my eyes. "I'm not good with change. You know that."

"I'm sorry." He comes forward, not as a pursuer this time but as the friend I've always known, and pulls me into his arms. "I shouldn't have pushed so hard. I didn't realize you had . . . ended things."

"He didn't exactly give me another option."

"They rarely ever do." Cameron chuckles, and his chest vibrates against mine. "I know this has been hard for you, so it feels wrong to be this happy, but I am. Bryson will move on; he always does. And you and I can go back to being *us*." He runs his hand down my back. "If being with you means I have wait a little longer, then I will. I'll wait for you forever."

But as I stand there, in the middle of his room, hugging the man I assumed would be a part of every important event in my life, I realize that making him wait indefinitely is crueler than saying goodbye. Because either way, whether it's Bryson or Cam or some other guy down the line making me choose, the truth is still vividly clear: I've been like my father, clinging to a memory that no longer exists. Cameron, my partner in crime, my childhood best friend, my safety net . . . is gone. And the real question looms over me like a phantom waiting to attack.

Can I love him any other way?

THIRTY-THREE

*C*ameron has never been good at waiting, so it was no surprise when his patience wore out only twelve hours after our conversation. Monday, he was respectful, only texting a couple of times to say how happy he was we made up. Tuesday, he called twice and left messages. Wednesday, it was five calls and two texts asking me to confirm I'm not dead. I sent him a thumbs-up emoji.

Needless to say, I wasn't surprised when the phone calls started early today, nine o'clock to be exact, right when I was pulling into the farm. But since today is supposed to be all about Louie, I left the device in my truck, feeling only slightly guilty.

"Do you think I'm a bad person for not wanting to talk to him?" I ask the massive Great Dane, who's currently snuggling with me on a picnic blanket. Louie stretched out is way longer than I am, easily seven feet from toe to nose. His front paws push against my shoulders, and I turn him on his back, exposing his big white stomach.

We're working on trust today, and putting him in vulnerable situations is the first step in showing him that I'm not going to hurt him.

319

"I know he's going to want an answer and I don't have one, so is it better to talk to him only to tell him I need more time, or just make him wait?" I rub the thin, sensitive skin on his torso, and Louie makes a loud *rawh rawh* sound. It's his way of talking to me. "Yeah. You're probably right. I already know what I'm going to say; I'm just avoiding the inevitable. But in my defense, Black Carousel plays tomorrow, and I'd never forgive myself if something I did ruined Cameron's performance."

Louie makes another noise, and I swear he calls me a scaredy-cat. His wet nose presses against mine. I move my face just in time to avoid a big lick of his tongue.

I push his giant head away. "That's sweet and all, but no licks on the face, okay?"

It's bad enough that I'm covered with Louie's tiny dog hair, slobber, and dirt on my clothes, and my ponytail is lopsided and loose. The last thing I need is dried saliva on my face.

I move to a kneeling position while fixing my wayward hair. "Up, Louie." He hops up, nearly knocking me over. I steady us both and pull his collar until he's in front of me. "Now sit."

Louie's backside hits the blanket and he's quickly rewarded with a treat. When he's done chewing, I pick up his left paw and carefully slide my fingers between each one of his pads. It's a very sensitive area for a dog and takes a great deal of trust to let me explore.

Louie leans down and licks my fingers. A reminder that he's a little nervous.

"It's okay. You're doing so good."

A car door slams, and Louie jerks his paw away, the hair standing up on his neck. I scramble to my feet and frown when Louie backs up and barks. He wants to go to his doghouse. Wants to retreat to what's safe versus facing the fear head on. "I guess I'm not the only one who's a scaredy-cat," I tease, holding his collar and trying to reassure him with long strokes down his back.

I watch the trail from the driveway to Charlie's back door, waiting to see who the intruder is, though part of me already suspects. My heart dances in my chest as I wait, anticipation as visible on me as it is on the dog to my left.

Bryson finally appears, and all the self-convincing I'd worked on for six days now disappears like powder in a storm. He doesn't look at me or for me, though I know he must have seen my truck here. Instead, he goes straight to the back door and swings it open. Charlie's waiting for him in the doorway, and Bryson obviously doesn't like what he's being told because he backs up and lets the screen slam shut. He turns, shoves his hands into his pockets, and finally makes the eye contact I've been waiting for. Though, once it comes, I question my desire for it. Bryson's eyes are dull, emotionless, and the black he wears today seems to strangle all other color from his face.

Louie sneaks forward, barks, and jumps back. He can sense our tension, which isn't good.

"Do you want to help me with a little experiment?" I call out, ignoring the way my stomach flips at the idea of his being closer. Bryson walks toward me, reluctantly, and Louie barks again. "Easy, boy. He's not going to hurt you."

Bryson pauses a few feet from us. "What did you have in mind?" His tone is flat, heartbreakingly absent of the tender affection his voice usually holds. I search his face for even a tiny hint of feeling but nothing's there but complete indifference.

Whereas I have to clamp my fingers not to reach out and touch him. "Louie is working on trust, and he's done great with Charlie and me, but it'd be nice to see how he responds to you."

Bryson eyes me suspiciously, and I can't help but smile. "Don't worry, he won't bite you. Just start slow. Maybe try to touch his head."

He reaches out while I encourage Louie the whole time. Both boys are hesitant and nervous, but as soon as Bryson makes contact, they both seem to exhale. Louie steps into the touch while Bryson's mouth twitches just slightly upward. "He seems to like it."

Louie leans his 160-pound body against me, nearly knocking me over. "Yes, he's very affectionate . . . and very heavy." I push him off, hopeful that maybe this exercise will do more than bond man and beast, but also maybe ease the discomfort between the two of us.

Bryson pulls his hand away and shoves it back in his pocket. "Looks like you've made a lot of progress."

"I have, and not just with Louie." I command the big guy to lie down, and he quickly does, stretching out again on our blanket. "Let me show you how well Penny's doing." I can tell Bryson doesn't really want to follow me, but he does anyway. "After our . . . um, incident, Charlie put chicken wire all around Bentley's old cage so there was no way she could get out during training. But then it hit me that I've spent all this time trying to fix the symptoms, all the while ignoring the root of her aggression. She hates the crate. It's a cage to her. A cage she is constantly stuck in." Our eyes meet for a brief second, and I quickly look away. "So we started putting her out here in the morning and leaving her until bedtime without any demands or training, and overnight she transformed." I stop at the fencing and lean my forearms on the metal. "Yesterday, she put the tennis balls in the bucket all on her own."

I watch as Penny trots along the wide space, toys all around for her to choose from. "All this time, she knew what she was supposed to do; she just wanted to do it on her terms."

Bryson slides in next to me, but it feels unnatural. Like every step he takes is carefully constructed to hide whatever he might really be thinking. "Does that mean Charlie's going to let her go to the adoption fair?"

I swallow down my rising emotion. "Yep, this weekend, finally. I just have to disclose the bite, and we both agreed she can't be placed in a home with other dogs." Bryson glances at my hand, and I roll it forward and backward. I'm down to just a small Band-Aid now. "Mostly healed."

"Good." There's a hard punctuation, like he's trying his best to end the conversation.

I ignore the effort. "Are you nervous about the concert tomorrow?"

"Nope. It's just one more stage and one more performance."

I wish that were all it was, but we both know it could very well be the last concert they play as an unsigned band. "And things have been . . . okay?"

Bryson turns and his gaze chills me. He's still angry, but I welcome it. It's the first real emotion he's shown since walking up to me.

I brace myself for whatever fiery remark he decides to throw, but Charlie appears before he gets the chance.

"Hey, Darcy, you ready for more lessons?" He winks at me like he has no idea Bryson and I broke up, which I know for a fact he does. "I can't in good conscience let you finish out the summer without hitting a target."

I glance at Bryson, who used Charlie's arrival to steadily ease away from me. He doesn't outright uninvite me, but his body language certainly wants to. "Maybe later. I still have some exercises I want to run Louie through."

"Yeah, that's probably a good call." Bryson rolls his shoulders, struggling to relax. I give him credit for trying. The old Bryson would have ignored me completely. This one is at least attempting civility.

Charlie passes by us in a hurry but stops when Louie stands, excited to see him. "Hey there, you crazy giant." He rubs Louie's face like they've been touching forever and not just for a few days now. "You want to walk with me to get the Gator?"

"I can get it," Bryson offers, his eagerness to get away from me more than apparent.

"Nah. You guys chat." Charlie's brows lift, and we both know it's more an order than a suggestion. "I'm going to get my workout in for today. Oh, and, Darcy, remind me to talk to you later about a phone call I got this morning."

"Okay? We can talk about it now."

"Nope, this is a sit-down kind of conversation." He pats his thigh. "Come on, Louie. Let's leave these two knuckleheads alone." They walk away, Charlie in old mud boots and a hunting vest. Louie leaping as they trot, because he's just now learning that there's more to life than hiding in a ten-by-ten-foot cage.

"Do you know anything about the phone call?"

"Nope." Bryson leans his back against Penny's kennel, annoyance written all over the set of his shoulders. He looks as though he's trapped here with me, and I hate that he might feel this way. Sure, we have some things to overcome, but that doesn't erase all we've shared together.

"I went to see my dad this past weekend," I throw out, desperate for something to break past his shell. "It was hard, really hard to see him, but I'm glad—"

"Don't," he snaps, stone still, his jaw clenched tight.

I heave a deliberate sigh. He's being impossible. "Don't what? Try and talk to you?"

He pushes off the kennel and pulls on his neck. "This isn't talking. This is sharing, and I'm not doing that with you anymore."

My eyes sting, and I feel the loss of him so severely, I want to rip my hair out. "So we can't even be friends?"

"No, Darcy. We can't. That's not how I work." A frustrated breath hisses through his teeth. "There's only one person who gets to know me intimately, the person I plan to be with forever. I thought maybe that could be you, but now that's not going to happen. So no. We can't be friends, because unlike you, I don't see a line. I look at you and it's still all there, so honestly, being around you sucks for me. But that's life, and I'll deal with it. But do me a favor and stop, okay? Stop trying to create something new between us, because—" His voice breaks and he curses, turning toward the pasture. "Why won't that blasted dog stop barking?"

The sound comes slowly, my mind so wrapped up in Bryson's words that I'd shut out the world around us. Louie's bark isn't just loud and continuous; it's manic and higher pitched than I've ever heard from him. "Something's wrong." I listen closer, the hair on my arms rising. "Louie's panicked."

The frantic dog runs toward us and then rushes back to the same spot, his head leaning down, his eyes fixated on something in the grass. His barking grows louder and louder. "What is he looking at?"

"It could be a snake. Where's Charlie?" Bryson looks around, but he's nowhere to be seen.

We take a hesitant step closer, then another, until we both see a color that makes the world stop moving. Shock rips through me, and right on its heels, gutting fear. "Charlie!" I scream, his bright orange hunter's vest barely visible through the long grass. Bryson takes off in a full sprint, sliding to the ground the second he gets to Charlie's motionless body. Bryson jumps right into CPR, pressing on Charlie's chest in quick, rhythmic movements.

"Don't you do this!" I hear him yell. "Don't you leave me, too."

Sobs rack my chest, yet I fight them off. I have to think. *. . . 911. I have to call 911.* Though my entire body's trembling, I somehow find a way to function and take off running. Sweat pours down my forehead, my eyes stinging as I stumble across the path to my truck. I tug open the door, grab my phone so quickly it falls from my hand. I drop to the ground, retrieve it, and somehow punch in the number.

"911. What's your emergency?"

"My friend is unconscious. I don't know how long, minutes or seconds." I rattle off Charlie's address as fear crawls up my throat. We're in the middle of nowhere. Miles from any hospital. "Please, please hurry."

"We've contacted a volunteer fire department in Venus. They aren't far. Maybe five or ten minutes." Her words give some relief, but even that short amount of time could be fatal.

I stay on the line and run to the road, listening for sirens, my hands shaking as I watch each minute tick away on my phone. A lifetime passes before there's a distant echo. Flashes of red appear, and I wave my arms frantically so they don't waste any time finding us.

Two trucks barrel down the highway in a line, one big, one small, and slow when they see me. I take off running again after they turn, follow the kicked-up dust, and start down the long driveway.

"He's in the back field," I gasp when they exit the vehicles. "CPR. My friend. Is doing CPR. I don't know if it worked. He was unconscious." I lean over with my hands on my knees, not sure if my winded state is from exertion or shock. *Pull yourself together*, I scream inside my head. *You have to keep moving.*

I fight for control as the firefighters grab the medical supplies they need and follow me around the house. My heart pounds with every step we take, Bryson and Louie getting closer and closer, but with each clearer image, my hope turns into panic.

Bryson's hands pump frantically, his body ready to collapse from exhaustion. Sweat drips from his hair, his black shirt soaked completely through, and his hands are stark white as if they've lost all feeling. Maybe they have because the firemen have to fight to pull him off Charlie. As soon as they pry Bryson away, he lunges forward, trying to finish what he started.

I block his path, pushing my hands against his shoulders in opposite momentum. "Stop. They're EMTs. They're his only chance."

Bryson looks down at me, his eyes wild, his chest heaving, gasping for breath. And then he collapses to his knees, my arms barely making it around him to try to break the fall. "He can't die. He can't." His breath is labored, his words short. I see the terror in his eyes and my throat turns thick and achy.

"He's going be okay." I rub Bryson's arms, trying to get his shivering under control while the firemen pump oxygen into the mask around Charlie's nose and mouth and lift him from the ground onto a stretcher.

"I'm going!" Bryson yells, shoving me off him. "Don't try to stop me."

"I'm not. I promise. Just let me help you." I wrap my arm around his waist and pull him to his feet. He teeters, blinks through the haze of shock, but manages to take a step. Then another until he's strong enough to walk on his own. We reach the truck just as they lift Charlie inside.

"Can he ride with him?" I all but beg the older fireman who seems to be in command.

He attaches a radio to his belt and stands face to face with Bryson. A flashlight appears and it only takes two swipes across Bryson's eyes for the man to nod. "Yeah. He probably needs to."

The man helps Bryson into the back, his legs so shaky that he nearly falls out of the truck twice. When he's safely inside, I rush to the driver's side window. "Which hospital?"

"Baylor, Scott in Waxahachie."

I back away and watch the trucks leave, holding two of the most important people in my life. Sobs fight to come again, but I can't let them. I have to be strong right now. I have to get Louie put up, Macey brought to Sheila's, and I have to be there for Bryson.

Yet with each step, my legs grow weaker and weaker, until I find myself on my knees, the gravel crushing into my bare legs. My entire life I've been taught to pray. Pray when you're sad, pray when you're scared. Pray when all seems lost.

I did, for months, when my parents split up. Did it even more the first two days after my trip got canceled. And then my prayers became shouts until I stopped altogether because it felt like a lie. Nothing changed. Nothing went back to how it was supposed to be. Like Louie, I've been yelling and yelling, trying to get God to see how disappointed I am with this life He forced on me. How afraid I am to trust Him again. And He's been patiently waiting, pushing me past boundaries, asking me to be vulnerable, testing me with new challenges, all to help me see that His way is better and perfect and it's okay that it doesn't always make sense.

My chin lowers as my clenched hands rise to my forehead. "Save him, please," I cry, letting the tears come in long streams. "But if your will is not his life, then I beg you, give me strength I don't have. I can't do this anymore without you."

I find Bryson in a small waiting room on the cardiac floor after asking at least five nurses where to go. He's hunched over in his chair, elbows on his knees, head down. In the corner sits an older lady with a long string she methodically crochets into a scarf, but other than her, the area is eerily empty.

As I get closer, I can see the fallout from Bryson's quick response. There's a rip in his pants at his left knee, and his shirt has multiple white salt lines running across the back. The sweat has dried in his hair, leaving it in wild curls around his ears.

I ease down quietly into the chair next to his, and though he must see me or at least hear me, he doesn't move, doesn't nod, doesn't say anything. "How is he?" I ask tentatively. The nurses wouldn't give me any details, but considering we're in a surgical waiting room, I'm almost certain Charlie didn't die on the way here.

Bryson blows out a long, harrowing breath, and it feels like the first time he's breathed since I walked in. "It was a massive heart attack." The words come out stiff and robotic. "They took him straight to the OR and told me to wait here."

I rest my hand on his back, unable to listen to the hurt in his voice and not touch him. The cotton feels coarse against my palm and is still slightly damp. "Charlie is going to be okay." I rub in a large circle, offering whatever small measure of comfort I can. "He's far too stubborn not to be."

Bryson doesn't move except to get rigid under my touch. I don't care. He can hate it, fight it, resent me for it, but I know he needs this right now. I continue to rub his back, across his neck, down his arm until I'm practically hugging him. I feel his heartbeat, his breaths, his worries, his brokenness.

"I can't lose him." He trembles beneath my hand and I move in closer, squeezing him against me in an attempt to give him any strength I might have left.

"You won't." I don't know if that's true, but it's what I'm choosing to believe right now. And if the worst happens, I'll find better words to say then. But for now, he needs to believe in a miracle as much as I do.

We stay that way for long enough that my arm gets a cramp, and not once does Bryson look at me or at anything for that matter. Not until a nurse steps near his chair and looks down at her paperwork.

"Mr. Katsaros?"

I cringe at how she butchers the pronunciation, but Bryson couldn't care less.

"Right here," he says immediately and rises to his feet, forcing me to let go of my grip around him. "Is Charlie okay?"

"He's still in surgery," she says slightly apologetically. I glance at the stack of papers in her hands and realize she's not here to deliver news. "I have you down as Mr. Honza's emergency contact?"

"Yes, I am," he says confidently enough that it's obvious this news isn't a surprise to him like it is to me. I knew he and Charlie were close, but typically that kind of designation is for children or at least immediate family.

"If you wouldn't mind, I'd like to go over some information with you." She glances at me. "It won't take long." A nice way to say I can't go with them, but that's fine.

"No problem." I take Bryson's hand and squeeze it. His fingers are ice cold, and he makes no effort to return my hold. "I'll be here when you get back."

Bryson glances down at my hand around his, then back at the nurse. "Can you give us one second?" She nods and heads to the exit to wait for him. When she's clearly out of hearing range, Bryson eases his hand from mine. "Thank you for coming," he says gently, but not in a way that implies he wants me to stay. "I'll text you the minute I hear anything."

The words slice my already fractured heart. "Bryson, I'm not going anywhere. I want to be here for you. For Charlie."

He kneads his eyes with his fist as if he's reached the limit of what he can handle. "I know you do. And that's what makes you . . . you." He swallows, and for the first time since he walked the path to Charlie's backyard, I see the man I fell for. The soft, vulnerable, loving man who needs me right now.

"I can pick up your truck. Bring you some clean clothes." They're all small things, but in a crisis, it's the little things that become significant.

"It's really nice of you to offer, but right now, what I really need is to focus on Charlie." He blows out a shaky breath. "And I can't do that with you here. It's too hard to be near you and not be . . . us. The *us* we used to be." Hurt pours out of his eyes, and my stomach clenches. My being here is causing him more pain, not helping him.

"Okay." I'm worn out. Physically, mentally, and emotionally, but I dig for the strength it's going to take to walk away. "If that's really what you want."

"I gave up the hope of getting what I want a long time ago. This is what I need."

Bryson has asked me for only one thing—to choose him. I didn't do that before, and I won't make that mistake again.

I nod, holding back the plea I want to make to give me another chance. "If you change your mind, I'm just a phone call away."

"Thank you." He walks past me then, and I have no choice but to turn and watch him leave with a woman in blue scrubs who has no idea that Bryson is bleeding inside.

I've never quite understood heartbreak. I thought I did when my father left my mom, and again when my trip was canceled, but those were different. They were losses completely outside of my control. But as I watch Bryson disappear with the nurse through the glass double doors, that's when I know this pain in my chest is greater than all the others.

Bryson's leaving is my fault. I pushed him away because I was too afraid to let go and love him the way he needed me to. I did to him the very thing his mom did. I chose someone else, and regardless of what I do now, it doesn't matter. I lost him the minute I walked out his door.

THIRTY-FOUR

I'm in my truck, staring at my apartment building for five minutes before finally cutting the engine. Cameron called me twice while sitting here, and both times I let it go to voicemail. For as long as I can remember, he would be the first person I'd seek out when feeling like my world is ending, but not anymore. His admission changed things between us, just like it had when we were in high school. It took a month to get back to normal then; I have no idea how long it will take this time.

The air is hot and sticky when I open the door, and the heat elevates my already frazzled emotions. I need a shower and a time machine to make this horrific day go away. My pace to the stairs is slow, but it's the best I can do when feeling like a collapse is imminent.

"So, you are avoiding me."

I glance up the minute I hear his voice, and anxiety fires through my veins. Cameron's sitting on the stairs, waiting for me, and the expression on his face mirrors my balled-up and twisted insides. "I can't do this with you right now."

He stands and waits for me to get to the top step. "I'm not

leaving until we talk." Dark circles mar his eyes, and he fidgets the way he always does when nervous.

I push past him and head to my apartment. He follows down the hall, into the alcove, and through the door right behind me. I'm grateful for the blast of air conditioning that hits when we enter; maybe it will calm down the rising heat in my chest. Piper barks and runs to greet me for only a second before running back to the kitchen. Zoe's in there cooking, and Piper is obviously reaping the benefits.

"Hey, I tried to call you. Cameron's been by here twice. He's all messed up about some—" She quits talking when she steps into the living room, where both of us still stand by the now-closed door. "Oh, I see you found her."

"We need a minute." Cameron grabs my arm and pulls me toward the bedroom in a move that's far more Neanderthal than I appreciate. This isn't how we operate. We don't demand conversation and impose our wills on the other. He lets go the second we're inside and shuts the door with bottled aggression. "Why won't you talk to me?" he barks. "I've been out of my mind wondering what you're thinking or doing." He runs both hands through his hair and grabs the strands like he needs to pull them out. "I can't play onstage tomorrow feeling like this. You have to give me something."

"I can't." I cross my arms, trying to find the compassion I've always had for him, yet nothing but bitterness remains. I resent him. Resent him for loving me the wrong way. Resent him for convincing me that he was all I needed. Resent him because I chose him, and I shouldn't have.

"You can't what? Answer my phone call? Take two seconds to put my mind at ease?"

"No, because all of those require me telling you what you

don't want to hear." The words fly out harsher than I meant them to, and I rub my temples trying to make sense of this entire mess. "I'm sorry."

He stares at me, and it feels like my world is caving in. This was my worst nightmare. Hurting Cam. Losing my best friend. But I can't pretend something is possible when I know it's not. Maybe if I hadn't known Bryson, then I could have convinced myself that what Cameron and I share is enough, but I know now what love—true, romantic, spend-your-lives-together love—feels like. And it's not this.

"You're sorry?" He stares at the ceiling now as if that might change my words. "Well, I can't go back to just being your friend. Not anymore." He looks at me as though I'm to blame for putting us in this position. "You opened Pandora's box, and my feelings are not going back inside."

"I know that." I swallow down the ache. "I know things between us have to change now."

He shakes his head, bewildered. "Why? Just give me one good reason why you and I aren't perfect for each other?"

I duck my head because I can't verbalize it.

He rushes to me and cups my face, his eyes pleading into mine. "You love me, don't you?"

Tears assault my eyes. I can see how this ends even if he can't yet. "You know I do."

"And I love you," he says with a ferocity that tears my heart in half. "Don't you see? This is our moment. You were leaving, and by some miracle you stayed, and I don't think it's coincidence. I think it's providence that we are here together right now." He leans forward, touches his forehead to mine. "This is the beginning of our love story, Darcy. If you would just stop being afraid . . ."

"I'm not afraid, Cameron." I pull his hands away and put

more space between us. "That's just it. For the first time in years, I'm completely at peace with where God has me."

"Then help me understand why you won't even try. We are soulmates. You know it. I know it. Our families know it." He throws out his arms. "Even Bryson knows it! Why do you think he forced you to choose?"

"He didn't make me choose for him. He did it for me." I rub my eyes, only just now recognizing that truth. Bryson knew I was caged by fear. That's why he couldn't waver. Why he couldn't let me have both. "You and I don't thrive together, Cameron. Don't you see that? Every time one of us starts to move and try something new, the other one keeps us stuck right here."

His breath hitches like I've slapped him. "You feel stuck with me?"

"No. Not just me. I've done it to you, too. We live safe and we live trapped and I don't want to live that way anymore." He takes a step back, the hurt so dark in his eyes I swear they change colors. "You know I'm right. You've called me fifteen times in the past four days. You couldn't even play your concert tomorrow without seeing me. That is not healthy. *We* are not healthy, Cam."

"This isn't you talking. This is Bryson. You've been pushing me away since the minute you two became involved with each other."

"Bryson's not why I've pushed you away." Though I almost wish he were the reason, because then I wouldn't have to admit the darkest truth to myself or to my best friend. "I think I've known for a long time that you and I . . ." I shake my head, unable to speak the words out loud. How do you break up with your best friend? How do you say goodbye to the one person you thought would always be there?

336

His jaw tenses as he reads the anxiety I'm emoting. "What do you mean you've known? Known what?"

Tears lodge in my throat. I can't say it. Can't say what I've only just now accepted. But I have to, because if I don't, I'll cave to him. I always do. Bryson's right. I've spent so much time clinging to Cameron, I've ignored the fact that I'm terrified to take a step on my own.

He comes to me again, gentler this time, my hesitation giving him hope that I don't know how I feel when really I just don't know how to tell him. "This is you and me, Darcy. We don't have secrets between us. I love you. And whatever is stopping you from taking this step, you can talk to me about it. We'll get through it together." His gaze remains fixed on me and I ache with his want, ache with what I can't give him. "Tell me. What have you known?"

"How you feel. I just didn't want to accept it." His eyes soften, and I duck my head, unable to look at him and see the agony I'm about to unleash. "I think part of why I wanted that mission trip so bad was to see what life looked like without you. And to give you time to let go of me."

The air immediately turns cold between us, and even though I knew this reaction was coming, it still sickens me when Cameron shoves himself away. "You wanted to get away from me?"

"You and I have been entangled my entire life. So much so that I don't even make decisions without first considering the impact on you. I've been Cameron Lee's best friend for so long that somewhere along the way, I stopped knowing who I am without you." I look up, bracing myself for what's to come. "A year away was my chance to find me again."

He chuckles and it's a horrific sound. "You're telling me

that you went through all of that work of trying to be a missionary just to get me out of your life?"

"That's not what I said." I did want to be a missionary, at first. Then it became more about leaving than actually what I was going to do. God was right to stop me. My heart wasn't where it needed to be. "This isn't about you, Cameron. It's about me and what I've had to learn through all the pain this past year."

"So now I'm a lesson?" He takes two more steps away, as if he doesn't trust me not to plunge a spear into his chest. "A lesson in what? How to hurt people? How to betray a twenty-nine-year friendship? Bravo, Darcy. You learned it well."

"Cameron." I move toward him, but he raises his hand.

"I heard you. Loud and clear. You want to know what your life looks like without me in it?" He smiles but it's not sweet. It's quite possibly the nastiest look I've seen him give anyone. "Your wish is granted. You're about to find out." He leaves then, slamming both my door and the front door on his way out.

The sound hits me like a wrecking ball, the gut punch so severe I have to lean over to brace myself.

He's gone. It echoes in my head, in my trembling body.

My best friend is gone. And this time, there won't be a make-up call weeks or months later. I know the difference. This is the kind of break that stays permanent.

I collapse to my knees, the sobs coming so fast and hard that my room becomes a blob of color around me.

A soft knock comes at the door. "Darcy, are you okay? Do you want to talk about it?"

"Not now, Zoe," I manage to squeak out. As much as I appreciate her effort, she's not who I need. I need my mom. I need her caring touch and her unconditional love. But mostly, I need her to tell me it's all going to be okay.

I'm still a blubbering mess when I reach out and press my mom's doorbell. I don't even remember what time it is or when Mom usually gets home from work. I only hope that Michael's parked SUV means that she's here and hopefully still willing to talk.

The door opens after my second press to the ringer, and her mouth opens in surprise. "Darcy?" Her eyes trail my pathetic state—the bloodshot eyes, scuffed knees, disheveled hair—and she immediately pulls me into her arms. "Baby, what happened?"

I break down, sobbing into her embrace like a little girl. I hear Mom mumble something about getting the door and feel myself being slowly moved to a more private location. I recover enough to recognize I'm in the living room, close to the couch. Michael stands in the doorway, fidgeting, while Mom uses her palms to brush the tear-soaked hair from my eyes. "Are you hurt? Did someone do something to you?" She's gone to the worst conclusion, and I shake my head to ease her fears.

"No. Cam and I had a fight." My breath shakes as I try to talk through the tears. "He's gone. He hates me. Bryson hates me. Charlie's in surgery." I break down again as Mom eases me down onto the couch.

Michael clears his throat. "I'm going to . . . um, go somewhere else."

I lay my forehead in my hands and start to laugh. Michael is truly the most socially awkward person I've ever met.

Mom runs her hand along the back of my hair. "Do you want some water?"

I sit up, the hysteria finally under control. "No, thank you. I'm better now." It's amazing how just being here helps. How even though I'm nearly thirty and long past adolescence, her touch can still heal a million hurts.

"Do you want to talk about what happened?"

I fall back against the couch cushion and look toward the woman who raised me. "Cameron wanted more from our relationship. I couldn't give it to him." My chest seizes, my mind still struggling to accept his final words to me. "You don't look surprised," I add when my mom shows no visual reaction.

"You're my daughter, so I can read you pretty well, and Cameron, well, he kind of wears his heart on his sleeve."

I look at the ceiling and shake my head. "How did I miss it for so long?"

"We see what we want to see, especially when we love someone. You probably knew this would be the result if the issue ever got pressed."

As usual, my mom is right. "What do I do now?"

"Are you willing to go where he wants you to?" When I shake my head, she sighs apologetically. "Then you can't really do anything. When and if he's ever ready, he'll come back. Until then, it's only fair you give him the space he needs to fall out of love with you." She touches my cheek and brushes hair from my eyes. "Considering how amazing you are, that may take him some time."

It's in that moment I realize how very much I missed her these past several weeks. "I'm sorry I haven't called you back." She folds her hands in her lap and looks down. "I didn't know how to be happy for you and still be sad for me."

She nods like she understands. "I've thought a lot about

340

what you said the other day. I've even written you three ridiculously long emails that I didn't send, because you asked me to give you time, and Michael convinced me I needed to respect that request even though I didn't like it."

Score one for Michael. Dad would have made her push. And like it did with Cam, pushing would have only led to words that couldn't be taken back.

"I should have talked about how I was feeling earlier," I admit. "I shouldn't have waited until I was that angry to unload on you."

"Well, if I'm being honest, I didn't exactly want to hear it. I wanted to move on, to keep going and looking forward so I didn't have to deal with the whys and the hows." We smile at each other, both cut from the same cloth in that respect. "I've been unfair. I've expected you to comfort me like my friend, while still expecting the blind support of a little girl." Her words nearly bring the tears again, because for the first time she truly does seem to understand my struggle. "But you're an adult now, and it's only fair that you be given the courtesy of my listening instead of assuming." Her voice shakes from nerves. "I know that for you, our divorce was a shock. We've never wanted you kids to stress about the two of us, and I guess we got a little too good at hiding our issues." She takes a stabilizing breath, then releases it. "I don't know what's crossing the line for you. How much you want or need to know, but I'll give you whatever information you ask for . . . even if I don't necessarily want to."

I pull out my ponytail holder and pull my hair back into a fresh tail, tired of the strands sticking to my face. There are so many questions I've been too afraid to ask. Too afraid to get answers for. And some of those still linger in my mind.

Were there other women? Were there other men? How long had they been unhappy? Was our Partridge family growing up a lie or was it real? But none of those questions will change the outcome; they'd only change my feelings toward my mom and dad. And if this summer has taught me anything, it's taught me to let go. My parents' marriage and divorce is not my problem to solve. It's their journey and their choices. Not mine.

"Do you remember when I was a kid and you'd make your special night-night concoction for me when I was scared at bedtime?" I later learned it was tea, hot milk, and some honey, but it never tastes the same when I make it. "Could you make me some now?"

She sighs in relief as if she realizes exactly what I have decided, that I'm not going to live in the wreckage of what's lost anymore. "Only if afterward you promise to tell me who Bryson and Charlie are." Sadness descends on me like a heavy cloud, and my mom sees it right away. Her face turns pensive, ready for me to dump all my burdens onto her. "Unless you don't want to," she amends.

No, I need to, but not until I do this first. I scoot over and wrap my arms around her. "I love you, Mom."

She presses her cheek against mine. "I love you, too, sweetheart."

Bryson's text comes three hours later, long after my mom soothed away my pain and helped me reconcile my choices. We ended the night with a long hug goodbye and a promise to never again go so long without speaking.

I sit up in bed, preparing myself for what his text might tell me. I don't think it's possible to cry any more than I have in the last twenty-four hours, nor can I fathom a world without Charlie in it. Carefully, I swipe up to see the full message.

Charlie is out of surgery. Critical but stable.

I hold the phone to my chest and look up at the ceiling, the enormous relief enough to liquefy every muscle. "Thank you, Lord."

Answered prayers come in many different forms, most of which we don't recognize. This one, though, came exactly how I'd hoped.

THIRTY-FIVE

I'm beginning to see the cycle in my roommate's dating ritual. It starts with phone calls, and then her mood picks up and she practically dances through the apartment. Calls turn into dates, which turn into Zoe disappearing because she's a big fan of the overnight stay. Days or weeks later, she's back, her heart slightly bruised, until new calls start the process all over again.

We're in the giddy stage right now.

"How's Charlie doing?" she asks, plopping on the couch next to me, nail polish in one hand and her phone in the other.

"Better. He's still in ICU, so they won't let me see him yet since I'm not family. I'm going to try again tomorrow."

"That's good." She leans over and carefully puts a foam separator between her toes. "Got any big plans for tonight?"

"You mean besides watching TV and going to bed early? No." Which I have a feeling will be the new normal in my life. Cameron has been radio silent since he stormed out, and Bryson's truck was gone when I went to check on Louie this morning. I guess he called someone else to take him home from the hospital, someone he obviously prefers more than me right now. Probably Jay or Harrison. After all, the biggest break of their career is happening tonight.

Turns out there was one more option besides my choosing between a best friend and a boyfriend. Me . . . all alone.

I brush off the sadness, refusing to fall back into the depressive state I've been in most of the summer. Charlie is alive. Everything else in my life is inconsequential comparatively. "What about you?" Though based on the freshly shaved legs and bright polish, I'm sure her plans are not the same as mine.

"The hottie from your dad's party is taking me out." She winks. "Thanks, by the way."

I think back to the barbecue, trying to figure out the appeal. Sure, he was nice to look at shirtless, but he was also inconsiderate to my dad and definitely not the brightest bear in the clan. "That guy is a waste of your time."

Her head pops up, and she genuinely looks confused. "What do you mean?"

"All he talked about was biking and running and mountain climbing."

"So?"

"So . . . your idea of working out is shopping for the best booty-shaping leggings. You two have nothing in common."

Zoe snickers. "I guarantee he'll like the leggings as much as I do."

I groan. Sometimes it's like talking to a wall. "I'm being serious." I pull my right leg up onto the couch so I can fully turn and look at her. "You always know exactly what these guys want in a girl and try for however long you can stand it to be that person. But have you ever stopped to consider what *you* want in a partner?"

Her hand freezes mid-stroke of painting red on her second toe. "Not really."

"Well, maybe that's what we need to do first. Give me three things, besides their looks, that you would find attractive."

Zoe stays quiet, but I can tell she's at least trying to come up with an answer. I guess it makes sense that she doesn't know right away. She's probably never bothered to ask. "Cooking, I suppose. It would be nice if the guy liked to cook."

"Okay. That's something." Not quite as deep as I was hoping for, but a start. "What about the guy's character?"

"I don't know. I mean, I hope he's a good guy." She laughs, embarrassed. "What do you want? Like, what was it about Bryson that made you finally say yes?"

Pain seizes my chest, but it's a fair question and brings an easy answer. "He's loyal and dedicated. To Charlie and to you. He loves passionately, even though he's spent most of his life not being loved back. He has integrity. He says what he feels and doesn't play games." I blink back a new round of tears and look down at my fingers. "I liked that he challenged me and pushed me out of my comfort zone. And yeah, Bryson has always been easy on the eyes, but when he's soft and vulnerable, I think he's quite possibly the most beautiful man I've ever seen."

I stop, even though there are pages more I could give her. But to continue means I'll have to relive yesterday over again, because the image of him begging me to leave him alone is now what's lodged in my mind.

"Anyway . . ." I look back at Zoe and force a smile. She's abandoned her nail polish and is now listening with focused attention. I don't miss the opportunity. "The point is that you need to stop letting these guys choose you as if you're lucky to have them. Zoe, you are kind and generous and beautiful—in

346

here." I point to my heart. "You are special. You are a catch, and you need to start choosing someone of equal value to be a part of that. And trust me, it's not going to be some dim-witted jock who had to ask me my name three times."

"You're right," she says with conviction, and in a way I've never heard her express. "We both deserve to be with men who love and appreciate us." She gets up and texts something on her phone. "Done. Date's canceled."

Wow. She actually took my advice. "That's great, Zoe. Good for you."

"And now that I'm available again, we're going out."

I should have known there would be a catch. "I'm in no mood. Really. Yesterday was literally the worst day of my life. And considering the year I've had, that is saying a lot."

"Too bad. You owe me." She raises her brows, and it's clear I'm not getting out of this. "I went to your dad's party when I wanted to sulk, and now because of your little motivational speech there, I have nothing to do on a Friday night. So, get dressed. We're going out."

"Zoe, I don—"

"Wear a cute dress!" She's down the hall and gone before I can argue more.

I drop my head to my knees and put my hands over my neck like we used to do in tornado drills. When will I ever learn to keep my mouth shut?

I don't realize where she's taking me until the car is parked and we're standing outside the club. In bright letters, the sign reads *Firesight, Friday, 9:00 p.m.* Underneath, in a smaller font, is the name that's practically branded into my soul: *Black Carousel, Friday, 7:30 p.m.*

It's 7:55.

My feet are planted on the sidewalk. "I can't go in there."

"Yes, you can." She tugs on my arm, but I don't move. "And more than anything, you need to."

"No, I don't. This is the last place I should be." I shake my head. "Cameron despises me, and Bryson has made it clear he wants me to stay away."

"Do you really think that?" She sets her fists on her tiny, jeweled waistband and lectures like my seventh-grade teacher did when Cameron and I would text in her class. "After all you know about my brother now, do you really believe he meant it when he said he didn't want you there?"

"Yes, I do." I swallow down the panic of what she is asking me to do. "This is their shot, Zoe. There are managers in there. Record executives. If I distract them or mess this up in any way for them . . . I'd never forgive myself."

"This venue is huge and sold out. I only have tickets because Bryson sent them to me four days ago, which he has never done in the history of ever. So that alone tells you he wants the people he cares about to see him play tonight. The guys won't be able to see us. I promise. And we'll leave the minute you say so." When I still don't move, Zoe comes closer, her voice more a plea than a demand. "If this concert is really his big opportunity, then he deserves to have you in there supporting him. Even if you and I are the only ones who know you did."

I wet my lips and try to keep my legs from trembling. "You're right. He does deserve that." I take in a stabilizing breath. "Okay, I'll go in . . . for a few songs."

"Good, because I really didn't want to cause the kind of scene we'd make by me swinging you over my shoulder." I chuckle at the visual of her size-two frame even trying to do that. "I know my brother." Her tone turns serious. "Actions mean everything. And your being here will matter more than you'll ever know."

I glance up at her, and a rush of appreciation surges through me. "When did you get so wise?"

She rolls her eyes, but it's accompanied with a smile. "I have this really annoying roommate who must be rubbing off on me."

"Thank you."

"Whatever. You know I'm here for the cute boys." Her arm links through mine, and she guides me to the front door and to a very burly-looking man taking tickets.

He clicks her phone when she offers him her screen. "These are VIP. You have reserved seats down front." He grabs a flashlight from the table next to him. "I'll take you."

"No thanks," Zoe says easily and flips back her hair. He follows it, slightly mesmerized. "We like the back. That won't be a problem, will it?"

He shrugs and sets the flashlight back down. "Suit yourself, but it's standing room only." Arm out, he backs up until the door swings in and darkness faces us.

Zoe walks inside first, pulling me behind her. The place is crowded, the air sour with alcohol and adrenaline. We push through sweaty bodies dancing until we make it to the back, far enough that there's no way the band could possibly make out individual faces.

"Does this work?" Zoe yells in my ear.

My eyes zero in on Bryson, and everything in me melts. Zoe was right. I needed to be here. "Yeah. This is perfect."

"Good. Then I'm going to get us a drink." True to her nature, Zoe's gone a heartbeat later.

It takes only two songs for me to realize I've once again

come full circle. Here I am, standing next to a bar, a drink in hand, watching Bryson and Cameron light up the stage in front of me. Only this time, the drink is water and it's not my best friend up there. He's someone completely different. Wild, angry, and working the crowd to a frenzy.

"We love you, Dallas!" Cam rips open his buttoned shirt and spreads his arms, his chest exposed under the lights. The screams from a line of girls are deafening. They love him right back.

Zoe leans into me. "It's kind of weird. I feel like I'm watching my brother and Cameron become celebrities tonight."

"You are. I have no doubt Black Carousel will soon be a household name." Any fear I had of Bryson and Cameron surviving our little love triangle is gone now. They're perfect. Not one beat off, not one line dropped. And if I didn't know better, I would believe they loved each other like brothers up there.

Cameron once told me that the true art of performance is giving the crowd the illusion they want. Bryson and Cam are both proving their artistry tonight, and they deserve every great thing this next tour is going to give them.

Bryson shoves his hair out of his eyes and leans into the microphone. "We have something special for you. A song I wrote, and it's the first time it's ever been performed."

The crowd screams, and my breath freezes in my lungs. Bryson's song. He finished it.

He drags over a stool, much like the one he had onstage in the youth room, and trades out his electric guitar for an acoustic one.

Zoe watches the scene unfold with wide eyes. "What is he doing?"

"I don't know."

Black Carousel doesn't do ballads. Maybe that's why Cameron backs away, why Jay sets down his bass guitar, and Harrison holds his drumsticks in his lap.

Bryson swallows. "This song is for someone who's incredibly special to me. I hope you like it. It's called 'A Decade of Love.'" He begins slowly, his fingers plucking away at the melody I first heard in his backyard. But it isn't until the lyrics flow through the hushed room that I realize exactly what the song is about.

My throat burns as I try to hold back the emotion pummeling through every inch of my body. His beautiful, touching words fall over me as a powerful, rushing warmth invades my bloodstream. It's the first time I've seen *my* Bryson onstage. The sweet, loving man who in an incredibly short period of time changed my entire outlook on life. His voice aches of pain, taking each one of us through the journey he faced, the prison of the anger, the pain of overcoming his weaknesses, and the beauty of finding peace in the arms of the one person who saw who he could be from the very beginning.

It's an epic love song. The kind that catapults artists to the top of the charts.

Zoe turns to me, her eyes watery. "He wrote about you."

"No." I shake my head, nearly too overcome to speak. "That song isn't for me. It's for Charlie."

Bryson's voice fades as he ends the song, and silence lingers for a fraction of a second while we all recover. Then pandemonium strikes. The crowd is hungry for more, dying to get their hands on whatever force invaded the building just now.

I cover my ears, the sound deafening. Black Carousel begins gearing up for their final song, and then comes the headliner. But all of us know that nothing else tonight will top what just took place on that stage.

351

"It's time to go," I tell Zoe, my chest aching from the vibration and from the black hole that's taken residence inside.

"Okay. I just need to hit the ladies' room real fast."

I nod and point to the door. "I'll be outside." Desperate to escape before I fall apart, I push my way through the crowd. Hot bodies press and pull me until I finally reach the exit, my lungs gasping for any air, even the hot Texas air hovering over the concrete outside. I fall back against the brick building, my eyes swollen and my hands shaking as I pull out my phone.

I press on his name and wait for voicemail. It comes in two rings, smooth and fluid.

"Hey . . . it's me." I press the phone closer to my ear and turn away from the busy street. "I just wanted you to know that you were amazing tonight. Well, amazing now since you're still onstage." I wrestle to find the right words. "Your song was perfect. I know Charlie will be so honored by the things you wrote, and I know how hard that must have been to get up there and sing something so vulnerable." A tear falls, then another. "You were right about everything." I swallow because my voice begins to crack. "I was afraid to let go. Afraid of being disappointed again. Afraid to trust you with my future. Just . . . stupidly afraid. So thank you—thank you for showing me what it looks like to be brave." My voice breaks again, and this time I can't stop it. "I . . . I love you, Bry—"

The phone beeps before I can finish, but I said what I needed to. Now I can let him live out his dream with no regrets. He'll know he is loved, even if I ruined any chance of his loving me back.

THIRTY-SIX

I was up at dawn even though I didn't sleep well. My heart kept hoping I would hear something back from Bryson: a call, a text, some kind of acknowledgment at all, but there has been nothing. For all I know, he and Cameron are on a bus together, heading off to fame and fortune.

At least I can call the day productive, even if my mind has been teetering between accepting my reality and clinging to the fantasy that Bryson will come back. The dog fair was remarkable. Penny got adopted within the first twenty minutes by an elderly woman who had just lost her longtime companion—a white Jack Russell terrier who could have been a twin to Penny. I know this because she showed me at least fifteen pictures. The adoption probably would have happened in ten minutes, but I spent an equal amount of time detailing all of Penny's hang-ups. The lady assured me Penny would not be alone or crated and there were no other dogs to compete with. Plus, I have to give that little dog credit; she knows a good thing when she sees it and was on her absolute best behavior.

But as happy as I am that Penny found a home when only

353

weeks ago she was terrifyingly close to being euthanized, her quick adoption leaves me an entire Saturday alone to try to forget the aching mess that is my broken heart. Maybe that's why I'm back at Charlie's farm. Who would have thought that one large Great Dane would become my closest friend?

Louie trots around his cage when he sees me coming and howls a hello to me.

I open the kennel, give him room to come outside, and hug on him. Though I can only stand it for about a second.

"You smell awful," I moan, pushing him away. "Did you get into a fight with a skunk last night?"

Louie sits, his mouth hanging open, a proud, satisfied look on his cute doggie face. I'm guessing that's a yes. I don't think he got sprayed, the smell isn't that horrific, but he definitely picked up some residual scent.

"Okay. Let's get you bathed." I take him over to the hose and clip him to the door. Unlike Sam, Louie loves the water, so this task will not be nearly as daunting as it was that first week on the job.

My mouth quirks up when I think back to that original adoption fair and Bryson squatting down to show Jacob the harmonica. That was the day that changed our relationship. His façade was completely gone, and we got to see each other for probably the first time since we were kids.

"How could I have doubted him?" I ask the canine, who has no idea what I'm saying. So many of our decisions in life are based on baggage and perceptions we've obtained. Bryson had asked me to look past all of those and see the real him. Unfortunately, by the time I managed to do so, it was too late.

I let the cool water run over Louie's back, soaking his fur. He leans into me, leaving wet hairy marks on my shorts, but I don't care. He's showing his love for me and

I'm caring for him. That's the way it's supposed to be. I scrub the soap, giving him lots of scratches, and finally rinse him off. My attempt at towel drying only lasts about a minute before he escapes to the yard, running in quick, excited circles.

He ducks his head and rubs it in the grass, somersaulting to his back.

"Really?" I ask, wetter than he is. "I just cleaned you."

He continues to use the ground as a back scratcher while I work to clean up the mess we made. A faint buzz stops me as I'm rolling up the hose, and I sprint to the steps where I deposited my phone for safekeeping.

"Hello," I say, breathless, having no idea who's calling since the sun's reflection made my screen too dark to decipher. Though if my stomach has anything to say about it, I can assume the sudden butterflies are directly related to my hopes that Bryson is on the other line.

"Darcy?"

I try not to deflate at the female voice on the other end. "Yes, this is she."

"Hi, this is Miranda Elledge from the rescue society."

"Oh yes, hey." I press my cheek to my shoulder to hold the phone while I wipe my hands dry. "I was going to call later today and let you know Penny was adopted. That just leaves Macey, and I fully expect her to stay here with Charlie, and then Louie, and I'll probably hold off on taking him to the fair until the end of the summer." Truth is, he could probably go now, but I'm not sure I'm willing to give him up. My new apartment will allow two pets; I just need to get a waiver about his size.

"Yes, actually that is what I wanted to discuss with you. We found Louie's original owners."

355

My heart sputters, and I ease myself onto the concrete steps. "The ones who abandoned him?"

"No. The ones who bought him." She pauses, and I wipe my palms on my shorts. I'm sweating and it's not from the heat. "Do you remember when you asked me to look into his past so that you could best know how to work with him?"

I nod my head. "Yes."

"Well, I kept digging, mostly because I wanted the breeder to know that he sold a dog to the kind of owner who abuses and abandons animals. The breeder just got back to me yesterday after contacting her clients. Louie was stolen out of their backyard six months after they brought him home. After all this time, they thought he was gone for good."

"Wow. That's . . . wonderful." I practically choke on the word, which makes me a horrible person because I should be happy. "Are they wanting him back?"

"They're not sure. I explained what all he's gone through, and they're obviously a little hesitant. They have two kids: a nine-year-old girl and a six-year-old boy. They want to make sure he's safe first."

"Of course. What do you need me to do?"

"Well, if you aren't busy, could you meet me there today?"

"Today?" A pain presses against my chest as I internally plead with God not to take another thing from me. I glance at Louie, who's now sunbathing on his side, his legs stretched way out. "Um, yes." I swallow down the *No!* I want to scream. Despite my own needs, I have to do what's best for him. "I can bring him there this afternoon."

"Wonderful. I'll text you the address, and we'll plan for one o'clock."

I end the call, my hand numb. I was supposed to have more time, and yet somehow I know this is just another step

God is forcing me to take. To trust Him, even when nothing is how I want it to be.

The drive out to Louie's owners is a beautiful one. They live in Ennis, nestled in a small neighborhood with large homes and even larger lots. Across the street is a park with walking trails and exercise stations. A perfect place for Louie to run around, I surmise, trying to squelch the small part of me that still hopes he comes back to Charlie's with me today.

The GPS signals to turn left, and I reach for the passenger seat to pet Louie's head. He's great in the truck. Hops right in and sits like an adult in the seat. I roll down the window when we slow to fifteen miles an hour and let him hang his head outside.

"Almost there, big guy. Just three more houses."

But Louie is no longer listening to me. Hair stands on his back, but his tensing isn't fear like I'm used to. He's excited. So excited that he's trying to climb out the window in a space that barely fits his head.

I grab his collar and hold him back while parking the car, afraid he's going to break the glass. Louie barks frantically and follows me out the driver's door, practically pushing me over in his eagerness. I grab the leash and holler out commands, but it's no use. He knows this house, and if I had any question whether the memories are positive, his thrill of being home answers them.

Two children sit on the front steps, waiting, and make a run for us the minute we appear from around the truck. Louie stands on his back legs and surges headfirst, pulling me forward until I either bust my chin on the ground or accept the onward motion he's demanding.

A lady hurries from the house, calling her children's names. "Lilly, Jaxon, wait!"

Her commands are as effective as mine, and the two kids and their long-lost puppy reunite halfway up the paved walk. They hug his neck, the little girl in tears. Louie howls like he's crying right along with her.

"I knew you would come home, Zeus. I just knew it!" she cries, kissing his long snout. Louie licks her face and nearly pushes her over trying to lean into her tiny body.

"Zeus?" I ask, kneeling between Louie and the kids, just in case. Their mom reaches us about the same time. "Is that his name?"

"I homeschool, and we were studying Greek mythology. They were quite fascinated," she says, winded and understandably worried.

"We picked the name because Zeus was the grandest dog of all of them!" Lilly says in a cheer. She reaches out for his leash. "Can I take him inside?"

I look toward her mother and wait for confirmation.

She assesses him nervously. Her hesitation is fair. Louie has likely tripled in size since they last saw him. "What do you think? Is he trustworthy?"

"Louie . . . I mean, Zeus, has never shown any aggression. He was recently attacked by a small dog, and even then, he defended himself without hurting her. You can never say concretely with an animal, but I believe he's extraordinarily gentle."

She bites her lip, then seems to make a decision. "Jaxon, go get your dad and tell him to meet us in the backyard. Lilly, take Zeus through the gate."

The kids both say, "Yes, ma'am," which leaves me no choice but to turn him over.

"Can I have just a second with him?" I ask, tears already filling my eyes.

"Sure." Her voice is compassionate, and she guides Lilly away by the shoulders to give us some privacy.

I squat down in front of Louie and scratch his ears the way he loves. "Well, I guess this is goodbye for you and me." He nudges me with his cold nose, and I try to laugh through my tears. "All this time, you had a home just waiting for you. And I can tell, they are going to love you even more than I do." I wrap my arms around his big neck and hug him. "Fear has deprived us of so much. Let's make a pact that from now on, we embrace whatever path God has for us." I pull back and put out my hand, palm up. Louie lifts his paw into mine, and we shake on it. "Good boy." It feels impossible, but I find a way to stand and walk back over to the little girl and her mother. "Here you go. Take good care of him, okay?"

She nods very seriously. "Oh, I will. I know how to change his water and feed him, and Mom got us a new brush today to use on him."

"Sounds like he's in good hands." I smile, and this time I really mean it. Louie deserves a best friend; Lilly will make a fine one.

I show her how to properly hold the leash and tell her to keep him on her left side. She concentrates on every word of advice and does very well considering his massive size.

"I think you have a future dog trainer there," I tell her mom.

"Yes, she wants to be a veterinarian when she grows up."

I chuckle at God's sense of humor. Life. Full circle. Once again.

"Thank you for bringing him here and for taking such good care of him." She glances at the house and back again. "My kids were devastated when he disappeared. I still can't be-lieve we found him."

Silence falls, and the anxiety it brings forces me to fill it. "I'm not sure if he's still housebroken. He's only been kept outside."

"Okay."

"And if you have any issues at all, please call me. I'd be happy to come help train him for you or work on any behav-ioral issues." I pull out my phone. "If you give me your cell number, I'll text you my info."

We're in the middle of exchanging contacts when a black sedan pulls in behind my truck. A woman I assume is Mi-randa exits and waves at us. She's more polished than I ex-pect. Black pencil skirt, button-up blouse, and three-inch heels. Obviously, she isn't the one handling the animals.

"Well, I seem to be late to the party." She quickly shakes my hand, her grip far stronger than her thin figure implies. "Darcy, it's so nice to meet you. And, Linda, how are you feel-ing about everything?"

Linda sighs. "A little better now that I've seen him with the kids. He's certainly beautiful."

"The name Zeus fits him. He's grand, as your daughter put it, even by Great Dane standards." I turn to Miranda. She has a large hardback folder in her hand. "Do we need to fill out any paperwork?"

"No, we do not. Since the Walkers were Louie's original owners, this is a return, not an adoption. My favorite kind of case." Her smile is bright and warm despite her corporate vibe. "Do you have any questions for me?" Her offer is to Linda, not me, so I wait to see if there's more she wants to discuss.

"No. I should probably get out back and see what havoc

has started." She goes to leave but then turns back and wraps me in a tight hug. "You are an answer to prayer. One my kids have prayed every night for a year." Her eyes are as glassy as mine when she pulls away. "Thank you."

"It was my pleasure." And God's providence that brought us to this moment. Of that I have no doubt.

Miranda and I watch as Linda disappears inside. She turns to face me a beat later.

"Well, this turned out to be a great start to the day." She flips open her folder and pulls out a stapled stack of paper-work. "Here's hoping you can make it even better."

Confusion furrows my brow. Didn't she just say we didn't need to file anything?

"I'm sure Charlie spoke to you about our conversation a couple of days ago," she continues, also pulling out a pen.

"No, I'm sorry. He didn't." But this is probably what he was referring to before his heart attack. "Is everything okay?"

"I'm hoping it will be." She smiles again, bright and in-viting. Miranda must be the fundraising guru. She has an innate ability to make you want to say yes to whatever it is she needs. "We'd like to offer you a position with the founda-tion." She extends the stack she's holding to me, but I'm too stunned to take it.

"A job? Doing what?"

"It's all right here." She pushes the papers closer, and I fi-nally take them from her. "And ignore the date. I've been in a rush since Charlie's call. But don't worry, the final documents will all be correct."

I flip up the first page and read the job title: Foster Co-ordinator and Trainer. Underneath are more details like work hours, pay, benefits. All of which are more than I need. "I don't understand. Charlie's call?" I close the packet and look at her.

"Yes. He told us that he hasn't seen someone this talented with animals since Sue Ann." Her voice falters a little, and I can tell there's still grief there. "And that he wholeheartedly approved you for the position."

I'm nearly too blown away to speak. "Why would he need to approve anything?"

"Well, because our new facility is going to be built on Charlie's land." She pulls out a surveyor's map. I recognize the road. It's the same address as Charlie's. "Before Sue Ann died, she donated the funds for us to build indoor/outdoor kennels and a training course. She also leased two acres to us for one dollar a year for the next ten years."

Miranda hands me the plans. It's the two acres of land between Charlie's house and Sheila's covered in beautiful hardwood trees.

"We expect the facility to be up and running by early November. Assuming you agree to take the job." Her smile falters a little. "A stipulation in the lease was that Sue Ann and Charlie had to approve our hire. Sue Ann didn't want someone they didn't like so close to their home." Her voice turns soft. "Charlie has rejected every résumé we've sent."

I stare at her and back down at the plans. How is this even possible? It's not just a great paying job, but it's my dream job, and I'll be doing something I'm totally passionate about.

She gently touches my arm. "There's a lot of Louies out there waiting to be saved. Will you at least consider the offer?"

"I don't have to consider it." I drop my hands to my sides, still slightly in shock. "Yes. I absolutely would be honored to work for your foundation."

Miranda's face lights up. "Excellent!" She points to the business card clipped to my application. "Look over everything and come see me Monday morning at nine. I very much look forward to getting to know you." She briskly shakes my hand.

"Yes. Me too." All this time I thought God had forgotten me. That He had left me purposeless and broken. But He was here the whole time, and like Louie, I just had to find my way home.

THIRTY-SEVEN

On Sunday, Charlie calls, ornery as ever, and tells me I better come visit him before he's forced to break free of all the coddling the hospital staff are doing. I'm so thrilled to hear from him, I rush to Waxahachie, barely taking the time to brush my teeth and throw my hair in a ponytail.

The nurses point out his room, which is thankfully no longer in ICU, and I try to prepare myself for what I might see. My grandfather was in the hospital when I was fourteen, and in only two days, he seemed to age ten years.

Charlie, thankfully, looks better than I expect, though still pale and weak.

"It's about time," he says when I enter his room. "I was beginning to think you'd forgotten me."

"As I told you on the phone, they wouldn't let me in to see you. ICU policy." I set my keys down on the nightstand and lean over to hug him quickly and carefully, or so I thought. Instead, the minute I feel his arms wrap around me, I break down and hold on until the tears stop. "I'm so glad you're okay." I pull back and use hospital-grade tissues to wipe my eyes.

"Eh. This old ticker just needed an oil change. Nothing a few bypasses couldn't fix."

I chuckle at the way he downplays his brush with death. "Is that what they did?"

"Yep. Cut open my chest and then had the gall to force me to try to walk across the hall this morning."

"I'm sure they know what they're doing." I pull over a chair and sit next to his bed. "Are you in much pain?"

"I'll live," he says gruffly, which means he is. Considering Charlie's history with addiction, I can only assume he's limiting taking pain medicine. "Tell me how it went with Penny."

"Great. She got adopted, and Louie went home." His brow furrows, and I give him the details of my crazy day yesterday. "And thank you for the job. I don't even know what to say."

"Say you'll hike yourself down to my door and come visit me and Macey as often as you can."

I smile at the image, wishing it included the one person neither of us has mentioned. "Absolutely."

He sighs and looks at the ceiling. "I heard that dog saved my life. I guess I should be glad you talked me out of getting rid of him."

"Louie certainly helped, but Bryson saved your life. I've never seen anyone fight the way he did." My eyes fill, but I push back the tears. This isn't the time to cry for lost loves. It's the time to celebrate the gift of life. I squeeze his hand, the lyrics from Bryson's song echoing in my mind. "You should be really proud of the man he's become. You had an enormous amount to do with it."

Charlie smiles at me, and his own eyes get watery, a rare and beautiful thing for him.

"Have you, um, heard from him since the concert?" I know I shouldn't ask, but I can't stand not knowing.

"Yeah. The boy's head is so big he's practically floating in the air."

"They got the tour, then?"

Charlie's expression turns apologetic. "And a record deal. A pretty sweet one from what I understand."

"Wow." I suck in a breath, having no idea why his confirmation punched me in the gut. This isn't a surprise. I knew they were that good. I knew it that night. But knowing something and *knowing* something are two very different things.

The door in his room swings open, and we both turn our attention that way, expecting a nurse's intrusion.

My heart plummets into my stomach. "Bryson." His name slips out in a breathy whisper. He's wearing a blue shirt, and I don't know what's worse, the fact that he waited until we broke up to finally ditch the black, or that the enhanced color makes his skin golden and his eyes a stunning array of greens and browns.

"Oh, I forgot you were coming by." Charlie's singsong voice tells me he didn't forget in the slightest. "Well, since we're all here . . ."

Bryson scowls at the old man, though as usual there's a hint of humor underneath. "You couldn't let me do it my way, even this once."

Charlie shrugs. "Your way was taking too long."

I look between the two men and suddenly feel completely out of place. "I'll let you guys have some time together." After all, Bryson is leaving soon. I stand, scooting back the chair, and squeeze Charlie's hand before I go. "I'll come see you soon."

"You better."

I focus on the floor as I walk by, no longer able to stand the sight of Bryson so relaxed and . . . joyful. That's what hurts the most. Here I am, devastated, while he's the happiest I've ever seen him.

His hand gently wraps around my arm as I slide past him. "Can we talk?"

I dare to glance up at him, though it's nearly my undoing. "Um, sure." I continue into the hallway and walk toward the end where there's a small nook and at least the appearance of some privacy. He doesn't come right away, so I stand there trying to get my nerves to settle and my mind wrapped around saying goodbye for what feels like the fourth time. Only this moment feels permanent because there won't be accidental run-ins at the farm or concerts for me to crash.

He finally comes out of the room and looks the other direction before turning my way and seeing me. A smile comes a second later, and it's so reminiscent of the ones he used to give me that my stomach whirls with a sudden hope that maybe, just maybe . . . I watch as he approaches, his eyes never leaving mine and his smile growing with each step, and just when I'm sure my chest might explode from anticipation, he's in front of me, way too close for a man who has asked me to keep my distance.

"Bryson, I'm—"

His fingers tunnel through my hair as hot, eager lips swallow the words I'm attempting to say. I wrap my arms around his neck, ignoring the fact that we're in a hospital hallway and just one door over there's a steady beat of someone's heart monitor. His hand slips behind me, bringing me closer. I press in, the yearning of days without him burning, the fear I'd lost him dissolving.

The release comes slow, neither of us wanting to let go. He touches his forehead to mine. "I love you, too."

Relief courses through every electrified nerve. "You got my message."

"Yeah. I got your message." He pulls back and his smile melts into my skin. "Though I'd planned on telling you in a much more romantic setting. Obviously, Charlie had other ideas."

My cheeks warm, embarrassment catching up with me. "I'm glad. The last couple of days have been really hard . . . you know, wondering."

"I'm sorry." He brushes my hair away from my face. "I promise I wasn't avoiding you. There were just some things that needed to happen first."

And that's the cruelest reality of all. Our second chance comes on the eve of his new tour.

"When will you be leaving?" I ask, trying to sound happy for him.

He smirks at me, his brow lifting in that arrogant peak I've learned is all part of his charm. "Cameron, Jay, and Harrison are leaving tonight at seven. I, however, am staying right here."

I back away, struck by what he's saying. "What do you mean, you're staying? Charlie said you got a record deal."

"Black Carousel got a record deal. I'm just no longer a part of the band."

I can't process what he's telling me. "How? I mean, what label would sign a band that has no lead singer? It doesn't make sense."

"You and I both know Cameron was never meant to play backup to anyone. He'll carry the band without me just fine. And the label, well, they weren't happy about it, but money talks, and I made them an offer they couldn't refuse."

"What could you possibly have given them?"

"Not given them," he clarifies. "I sold the rights to my songs, all of them, with the caveat that Cameron sings lead. Including 'A Decade of Love.'"

My heart seizes in my chest. "No. You didn't. Bryson, that song is going to sell a million copies. It's a guaranteed hit."

"Let's hope so, because I'm banking on a really fat royalty check." He chuckles, and I cover my face with my hands. It's not possible. No one gives up this kind of opportunity. Bryson lifts my fingers away, and my eyes plead into his for this not to be true. "You seem very distraught over my staying. Call me crazy, but your voicemail sort of implied you wanted me to." And now he's teasing me.

"This isn't a joke, Bryson. I can't let you walk away from your dream."

"Black Carousel has never been my dream. Not even close." He takes my hand and sweetly kisses my knuckles. "Do you know why I picked that name? Because I was surrounded by darkness, stuck on a constant loop of anger and rebellion. It was me; it was my music. It was the only expression I had of my pain. Darcy, that's not who I am anymore."

I desperately want to believe him. "Are you sure? Because I don't want you to wake up one day and resent me for keeping you here." I won't replace my dependency on Cameron with a new one on Bryson. It isn't fair to anyone. "You don't have to stay for me. I'll wait. Gladly."

"And I love you for saying that." He leans down and kisses me, soft and gentle. "But do you really think I would even consider leaving with Charlie lying in a hospital bed only two days out from open-heart surgery?" I shake my head, and he rubs the pad of his thumb across my cheek. "'A Decade of Love' is my swan song. When I stepped onstage Friday night, I knew it was for the very last time." He winks at me.

"Getting the call that the love of my life loves me back, well, that was just a nice bonus."

I throw myself into his arms and laugh. A dazed laugh. I feel weightless and lightheaded from the shock of it all.

Bryson chuckles as he kisses my hair. "You going to be okay?"

I nod, my face pressed into his chest, and pull myself together. "Yes, for the first time in a long time, I think I'm going to be just fine."

Our arms stay wrapped around each other as we walk back down to Charlie's room, Bryson no more eager to let go than I am. "Best to tell him the good news slowly. I don't want his heart rate to spike all of a sudden. The guy's been a mess since I told him we broke up."

I squeeze his waist and glance up at him. "He's not the only one."

Tenderness fills his eyes. "Yeah, I didn't much care for it myself." We stop in the doorway, Bryson blocking my entrance. "Is your mom still doing Sunday night dinners?"

I nod, confused by the sudden shift in conversation. "Tonight was going to be my first one back, but I can postpone the reunion."

"Actually, I was thinking you could add a plus one. I mean . . ." He shrugs, and it's adorably insecure. "You've met Charlie and Zoe. Seems only fair I'd get to meet your family, too."

I don't miss his underlying request. Am I ready to give him everything this time? No holding back parts of my life. If we do this, we do it all the way. I lift on my tiptoes and kiss his cheek. "I'd love for you to meet my family. But be warned. They're sort of wacky right now."

"Yeah, well, whose isn't?"

As if on cue, Charlie grumbles from his bed. "Are you two going to stand there making out all day or come in here and talk to me?"

We both burst out laughing and walk inside to let Charlie know his little matchmaking scheme worked.

THIRTY-EIGHT

*S*unday night dinners have become more than a family ritual confined to two parents and two kids. They now include Bryson, Michael, often Zoe, and even Charlie has been coerced into joining us on occasion.

It's been three months since the first time Bryson walked into my childhood home, quickly overwhelmed by the lavish affection my mom is known for. Now he's the one who initiates hugs and starts fights with her over guests doing the dishes.

I lean back in the reclining chair by the pool. It's a beautiful October day, hot enough for shorts, yet cool enough that by evening we'll all need a light sweater.

Michael is by the grill, a new one he bought a couple of months ago. It's happened slowly, but I now see all the wonderful traits my mom saw so early on. He still isn't charming and is quite possibly one of the most awkward small-talk initiators in the universe, but he listens well. He truly cares about people and is completely selfless with his time and energy.

Bryson comes over with a platter full of marinated chicken and takes up the space next to the man I'm currently analyzing. "Liz says she needs a ten-minute heads-up for the asparagus."

"No problem." He uses tongs to place each piece of chicken on the hot grill. "How's the new class going? Any luck getting the grant you applied for?"

Bryson took a full-time position as the music director at the elementary school by his house, and I swear he's the most dedicated teacher I've ever met. In only a few months, he's revitalized the practically nonexistent music program, and if the grant comes through, he'll have instruments for all the kids.

"Not yet. We're hoping to hear something by Thanksgiving. Meanwhile, those recorders we got have been game changers. They love playing them."

"Oh, that's great news."

Bryson winks at me, because we both know exactly who supplied the recorders.

That's the other thing about Michael. He's very generous. If that's because he has money to toss around, I don't know. Michael never talks about business or income or status like my dad always did, but if a concern comes up in conversation, it's a guarantee that a few days later, an anonymous gift will find its way into the hands of those who need it. In this case, a shipment of a thousand brand-new recorders addressed in care of Bryson Katsaros. A gift Michael denies he had anything to do with, though I stumbled upon the receipt in one of Mom's drawers days afterward.

Michael closes the lid to the grill and says something to Bryson I can't hear but assume it's related to me, because Bryson quickly catches my eye and then looks away. He nods and takes Michael's place as chef.

I sit up, as it's obvious something is going on. Michael is walking my way and biting his nail.

"I was wondering if I could talk to you for a minute?" he asks, blocking the sun.

I stand, and his face comes out of the shadows. "Yeah, sure." We've come to the point in our relationship where there's mutual respect, but deep, private conversations haven't really been established yet.

"Could we go into the living room?"

I nod, feeling an even wider pit growing in my stomach. Michael takes the lead, holding the glass door open for me when we enter. I can hear Mom when we pass by the kitchen, stirring something on the stove and listening to her favorite music station.

Michael walks over to the love seat and pulls out a box from under the cushion.

I blow out a breath because it's the kind of box that holds diamond rings, often worn on a very important finger.

He sits nervously, and I join him, feeling exactly the same way. "I know you and I had a slower start, but I hope these past few months have let you see how much I truly do love your mother."

"Yes. I can tell you do." He adores her, dotes on her, listens to her, and jumps from his seat the minute she needs something. I reach out my hand. "Can I see it?" He gives me the box, and I open it slowly, knowing that doing so will once again change the life I've gotten used to. Inside is a ring that feels very much like Michael and my mom. It's a simple gold band with a traditional cut diamond in the center. No frills, no excess. I close the lid and hand it back to him. "She's going to love it."

"I know it's a lot to ask for your blessing, but I don't want to walk into a new marriage with any dissent. Relationships are hard enough without inviting fractures early on." He stuffs the box back in its hiding place, and I wonder how long it's been there. "So, if you want me to wait, I can."

I'm assuming, since it's down to me, that the others involved are on board. No surprise there. Dexter has loved Michael since the beginning, and based on Mom's replay of meeting Michael's daughter, he's not the only one who adores her. I take another deep breath before I answer. It's a lot of pressure, his question, yet I also respect him for it. He could have just as easily proposed without my input or agreement. And maybe that's why I don't hesitate.

"You have my blessing, Michael. Completely."

He exhales as if he's been holding his breath. "Thank you. I promise I'll love her more than my own life."

I smile at him. Somehow, I know that he will.

Michael stands, though I remain planted since I don't want to engage in some weird congratulatory hug. "I'm going to check on the chicken." He steps around my legs and past the couch.

"Hey, Michael." He pauses and turns back to me. "When are you going to ask her?"

His eyes get that dreamy lovestruck look. "Wednesday. On her birthday."

"Good choice."

He remains standing there until the air grows awkward and then excuses himself again.

I stand and walk to the mantel covered in family pictures that long ago quit showcasing my father. Soon Michael will be up here. Probably his daughter, as well. A whole new life. I stop in front of the 8x10 photo of Cameron and me that has to be at least ten years old. We're in the backyard, his arm slung over my shoulder, and we're laughing.

Hands sneak around my waist, and I lean back into Bryson, welcoming the warmth and security I feel in his arms.

He kisses my neck and squeezes me closer. "You okay?" He must have known before I did what was going down in here.

"Yeah. I think so. Michael's a good man."

"Yes, he is."

We stay there silent for more than a few minutes, and I love that we don't have to fill the room with words. Cameron's face stares out at me, his eyes squinted, his dimples deep. It's been three months since our fight in Zoe's apartment. Three months of pure silence. But even though we aren't speaking, I still think of him. Wonder if he's doing okay and if he's pleased with the life he's chosen. Mostly I wonder if there will ever be a day when we can be friends once again.

"What's on your mind?" Bryson asks like he knows. And maybe he does. My eyes haven't moved from staring at the picture of me and Cameron together.

"I'm just wondering if he's happy."

Bryson turns me around so we're facing each other. "Of course he is. He's living out his dream." He smiles at me tenderly, and I want to melt into the hardwood floor at my feet. "And I'm living out mine."

I lift my eyes to the man whose face I see in every picture of my future. "No regrets?"

"Not even one." Bryson wraps me in a hug and kisses my forehead. "You, me, a family one day. Kids jumping on Charlie's back and calling him Papa. Maybe even a big house like this one where we'll host our own Sunday night dinners, with I'm sure a dozen rambunctious dogs barking in the background." He chuckles, and happy tears spring to my eyes. "That is my dream, Darcy. Don't ever doubt it."

I place my palms on his cheeks and once again thank God for this amazing, loyal, kindhearted man whom I never would have known if I'd gotten everything I asked for.

Somehow, against all odds, my worst-case scenario has turned into a bright, wonderful future.

ACKNOWLEDGMENTS

I'm not sure if it was coincidence or providence that I wrote and edited this book during the height of the COVID-19 pandemic. In a flash, our world was completely upended, and fear gripped me in ways I never expected. The church my husband and I work at closed its doors for the first time ever and went strictly online, myself and my husband both got sick, his reaction especially hard and lingering for weeks, my children suddenly required virtual school assistance and dealt with their own anxiety about school closing, and I watched as too many of my dearest friends buried their loved ones. Worst-case scenario was suddenly alive and right in front of me. But like Darcy, it was in those hard moments when God did His greatest work on my heart.

I pray you saw the beauty in Darcy's story. How with each dog she saved, God was right there, saving and loving her in the exact same way. Thank you to all who read these words I poured my heart into. And I especially want to thank those who made this book, maybe even my most favorite one to date, possible:

To Raela Schoenherr and all the Bethany House editors and staff, thank you for your guidance and push for excellence. Darcy's story would have been significantly less without your feedback and direction.

To my former agent, Jessica Kirkland, thank you for helping me sort out the right place to start this story and for all you've done along the way. I know your time as an agent has ended, but I will forever be grateful you were once a part of my writing journey.

To my amazing writing partners—Connilyn Cossette, Christy Barritt, Nicole Deese, and Amy Matayo—thank you for walking through so many iterations of this story. And for the weekend-long phone conversations as I plotted and replotted and replotted again. You pushed me to trust my instincts and I'm so very grateful.

Finally, to the most important people in the world, my family. This one was hard on all of us. Thank you for allowing me to disappear for entire weekends as I struggled to get words on paper. To my husband especially, thank you for carrying the burden of life on those days when there was already so much on your very strong shoulders. You are my rock, my best friend, and I love you so very much.

Tammy L. Gray lives in the Dallas area with her family, and they love all things Texas. Her many modern and true-to-life contemporary romance novels include *Love and a Little White Lie* and the 2017 RITA Award–winning *My Hope Next Door*, showing her unending quest to write culturally relevant stories with relatable characters. When not taxiing her three kids to various school and sporting events, Tammy can be spotted crunching numbers as the financial administrator at her hometown church. Learn more at www.tammylgray.com.

Sign Up for Tammy's Newsletter

Keep up to date with Tammy's news on book releases and events by signing up for her email list at tammylgray.com.

More from Tammy L. Gray

After hitting rock bottom, January decides she has nothing to lose in working at her aunt's church—while hiding a lack of faith. A minor deception until she meets the church's guitarist and sparks fly. Can she avoid disaster—especially when a handsome landscape architect has an annoying ability to push her to deal with feelings she'd rather keep buried?

Love and a Little White Lie • State of Grace

You May Also Like . . .

When pediatric heart surgeon Sebastian Grant meets Leah Montgomery, his fast-spinning world comes to a sudden stop. And when Leah receives surprising news while assembling a family tree, he helps her comb through old hospital records to learn more. But will attaining their deepest desires require more sacrifices than they imagined?

Let It Be Me by Becky Wade
A Misty River Romance
beckywade.com

Molly McKenzie has made social media influencing a lucrative career, but nailing a TV show means proving she's as good in real life as she is online. So she volunteers with a youth program. Challenged at every turn by the program director, Silas, and the kids' struggles, she's surprised by her growing attachment. Has her perfect life been imperfectly built?

All That Really Matters by Nicole Deese
nicoledeese.com

Zara Mahoney was enjoying newlywed bliss until her life is upended by her estranged sister, Eve, and Zara must take custody of her children. Eve's struggles lead her to Tiff Bradley, who's determined to help despite the past hurts the relationship triggers. Can these women find the hope they—and those they love—desperately need?

The Way It Should Be by Christina Suzann Nelson
christinasuzannnelson.com

◊ BETHANYHOUSE

More from Bethany House

In 1929, a spark forms between Eliza, a talented watercolorist, and a young man whose family has a longstanding feud with hers over a missing treasure. Decades later, after inheriting Eliza's house and all its secrets from a mysterious patron, Lucy is determined to preserve the property, not only for history's sake, but also for her own.

Paint and Nectar by Ashley Clark
HEIRLOOM SECRETS
ashleyclarkbooks.com

In the midst of WWII, Jane Linder pours all of her dreams for a family into her career at the Toronto Children's Aid Society. Garrett Wilder has been hired to overhaul operations at the society and hopes to earn the vacant director's position. But when feelings begin to blossom and they come to a crossroads, can they discern the path to true happiness?

To Find Her Place by Susan Anne Mason
REDEMPTION'S LIGHT #2
susanannemason.net

Few are pleased Sophie Deiner has returned to her Amish community, but a sudden illness leaves her no choice. She befriends a group of migrant workers but is appalled by their living conditions. She soon finds her advocacy for change opposed by her ex, the farm foreman, and that her efforts only makes things worse. Has she chosen a fight she can't win?

A Patchwork Past by Leslie Gould
PLAIN PATTERNS #2
lesliegould.com

BETHANYHOUSE

EX LIBRIS

ON THE HIGHEST HILL

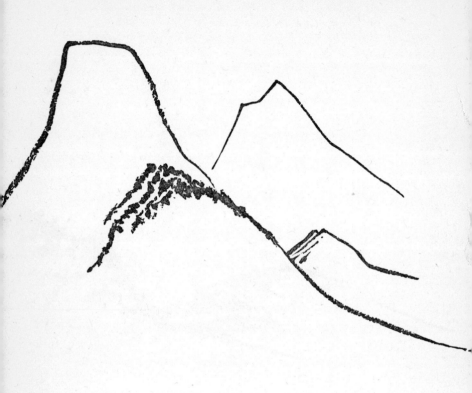

O N   T H E

HIGHEST HILL

RODERICK L. HAIG-BROWN

WILLIAM MORROW & CO., NEW YORK 1949

TO R. W. E.

For an idea and an unfaltering interest in it

PART ONE

THE ALDER FLAT

1

IT was very bright in the schoolroom. Fresh May sunshine washed down through the clear air and patterned the high windows across the desks and on the floor. Colin Ensley felt the brightness all through him, as he had felt it walking to school that morning and all day since then, clear in his eyes, fresh in his brain, vibrant in his body. Sitting awkwardly there, at the desk that was far too small for him, for once he did not feel awkward. Within an hour, his dreaming mind told him, he would be outside and with the brightness. But even that thought did not tear at him, as his thoughts so often did, and he was content to let it remain remote and vague. For the moment the intensity of the words he had set down on the page in front of him and the room's enclosing brilliance were enough.

In Colin's mind Mildred Hanson was part of the brightness, and the intensity of what he had written belonged closely to her. She was standing beside her desk, looking over her forty-odd pupils. She held an open book in her hand and had intended to switch the eighth grade section of the room away from the composition it was working on. But for once they were silent and busy, working not because they had to but because they wanted to. She had known she had reached them with her own enthusiasm earlier, when she had begun to talk of mountains; and they had followed her closely, clear around the world and back again, in search of mountains. She had spoken of the Rockies and the Andes, Himalayas, Urals, Caucasus, Alps, Pyrenees, then back over the Laurentian hills and the Rockies again to their own Pacific Coast Range, the tall snow peaks they could see from the schoolroom windows. For once even the dullest of them, even Tod Phalling and Jeff Burnside and Marge Elkhorn, had been stirred to reach into their own experience and find there an echo of the classroom words.

She wondered how long it would last. Colin Ensley was day-dreaming already, she saw. But he had written steadily for fifteen or twenty minutes and what he had written would have life in it. There would be clumsy grammatical errors, the pages would be untidy with his spidery scrawl and certainly there would be at least one blot. But there would also be several sentences of sharpest imagination, acutely felt, clearly and freely expressed.

It was Mildred Hanson's third year of teaching and she was confident and successful in a profession that had once seemed beyond her reach. She had been born in a small coal mining town, the sixth child of a family that later grew to twelve. Her parents were immigrants, steady, hardworking, unimaginative people, and their children left school at the earliest possible moment to go out and earn money. Only Mildred had varied the pattern; she also had gone away from home to work, but she had stayed on in school and in due time had qualified as a teacher.

Now she lived a disciplined, almost a dedicated life. She was

8

finding all the satisfactions she had expected in the intensity of working with children and she was free of the fears that nagged at many teachers—inspectors' visits, criticism from the principal, the attacks of aggressive parents, all were part of her chosen profession, to be absorbed into fuller understanding of it. And she felt no fear of the dull, deep-voiced, overgrown fifteen- and sixteen-year-olds, indefinitely stalled in her grade; she was scarcely aware of how completely her calm competence had killed their early attempts to break her discipline.

The children working intently and silently in the sunlit room marked the measure of her success. She glanced over them once more, closed the book in her hand and went quietly back to sit behind her desk. This, today, she thought, reached all of them. But why? Because they live with mountains? They live with logs and lumber, with salmon and salt water, with a dozen other, closer things, but nothing before has reached all of them and held them all quiet for so long. It should mean something. If they can be stirred once, even the dullest of them, they can be stirred again. The bright ones are so few. In three years, how many? Not ten. Perhaps ten who handled the work surely and of those, five who added something of their own to it.

In the ten there had been more girls than boys, probably because the pattern of the country still turned boys early from books to tools; in the five, more boys than girls, but one girl who stood out from them all. Margaret, Colin Ensley's sister, was two years older than he, a dark, handsome, responsible girl. Mildred Hanson had felt her strength and maturity even when she was in Grade 8 and had begun then to treat her more nearly as friend and equal than as pupil. This friendship between them had grown in the two years since Margaret had passed into high school and Mildred had learned that her first judgment of her friend was solidly based. Colin had none of Margaret's strength and sureness and even his intelligence was of a different quality; he was instinctive, emotional, casual, where Margaret was logical and tidy. Margaret's qualities were clear and orthodox, Colin's elusive and unpredictable. Yet—and Mildred resisted the thought as she had resisted it many times before—there was a power of

9

attraction in Colin that reached more deeply into her than the spoken, accepted affection of Margaret.

Mildred Hanson knew where this thought led her, because she had followed it before. It led by dangerous ways into a warm, safe haze of pleasure that was negation of every principle of her dedication. Today, because the sun was bright in the room, because the class was absorbed, because she was young and a woman, she disregarded the danger and let the dream take over her mind. His attraction was his awkwardness, his dependence, his simplicity. For all his clumsy size he was only a thirteen-year-old boy, a child still. Any woman might want to touch him, hold him in her arms, protect him. Then she felt her heart racing, felt the rush of blood through her body, speeding her breathing, parting her lips. It would be so safe—he wouldn't, couldn't possibly understand it. It could be done safely and stopped sharply at her own wish, short of his understanding. Safely, she thought, safely. The word held her by its repetition, twisted the dream and gave it shameful meaning. A boy who wouldn't understand, who was open to her because she was his teacher, who could be controlled because he was a boy, not a man. Safety! In the betrayal of her life's devotion for the pale echo of an experience. Now, with her blood quiet again and the haze drawn away from her dream, she knew there was no safety even in thought. The mood of the silent, sunlit room broke in her before it broke in the children, and she stood up.

While Mildred Hanson sat straight-backed behind her big desk, Colin sprawled at his small one. He was a very tall boy, big-boned, loose-jointed, with huge hands and feet. His face still had some boyish fullness and softness, but was fast becoming what the bones made it—high and narrow, with great dark eyes deeply shadowed between high cheekbones and the massive structure of his forehead. The nose was long and straight, though not excessively large, the mouth wide and easy, almost soft, the chin narrow and long.

Normally restless, Colin had moved little while Miss Hanson sat behind her desk. His mind was still with the brightness of day, inside and out, and with the elation of the swift words he had written on the page in front of him. He had never been in the mountains above timberline, but he had been born under the shadow of mountains, had lived his life within close sight of them and had listened often to the stories of hunters and woodsmen. He had only to close his eyes to have picture after picture vividly before him—gully and ridge and draw, shoulder and peak and face.

He had written easily, planting his wind-stunted trees in the rocky clefts, treading heather and moss, skirting snow-slides, climbing rock-slides, drinking from the clear pools in the torrents, hearing the solemn roar of the long, misty falls. No writing had ever poured from him so fast as these stored-up thoughts of the high mountains. He had stopped only when his imagination climbed beyond easy reach of words, and he scarcely knew that he had stopped; he had simply followed his thoughts into the mountains beyond reach or touch or need of pen and paper. Thought had climbed in him and with him, away from the room, from the valley, from the reality of the road home and suppertime and his father's return from work. It had become jumbled then, twisted and turned in upon itself, confused between its own brightness and the brilliance of the sunshine in the room.

Outside the window, the green of the alder leaves was so pale that it scarcely checked the sun; and the trunks of the trees were white instead of gray. Inside the room it was very quiet, and silver dust specks climbed in the light. Warm, safe, quiet, clean, yet exciting. Miss Hanson. Her eyes are very blue when she looks at you, bluer than the salt water on a day like this, and clearer blue; sometimes you can see them when you're only half awake in the morning, and see her pale white and gold behind them. It would be fine to do something for her, something big and important, and to kneel to give it to her. She would be cool and far away, but friendly, and she would smile. The sun is on her hair now, shining in the pale, clear gold of the thick braid around her head. Her neck is very white, like powder snow almost, but not cold. Her arms are the same, and you can see little blue veins in them, and when she moves in the sunlight a little gleam of gold hair. Would you feel that if you touched her, or only her smooth skin? Is it wrong to think like that? And to think about more of her than you can see? It's wrong to say it and laugh about it like some of the kids do, but not wrong to think about it your-

11

self—it can't be, because it's warm and sweet and good all through you. A person could do anything she says to, because she is blue and white and gold and beautiful. Maybe not write tidily when she says to or spell words right or even speak right. But big things, like climbing a mountain to find her in the snow and bring her down. There wouldn't be sunlight then. But she would be warm and easy to hold and she would smile. It wouldn't be hard to lift her. I can lift a hundred pounds so I don't know I'm lifting. Or I could swim after her if she was drowning. If the old man'd let me use his gun next fall I could shoot a buck for her; maybe she'd like that, maybe it could really happen. . . .

Her voice reached him, then. He knew dimly that she had spoken two or three times, but now the room was full of his name and the other children were laughing.

"Colin," she said again. "Will you please come back to earth and pay attention? Stand up and tell me what I've just said."

He scrambled up and stood awkwardly, silent.

"Well, what did I say?"

"You said to pay attention, Miss Hanson."

The class laughed again.

"Before that?" Her voice was cold and patient.

He searched his mind hopelessly. "I don't know, Miss."

"I said we've just got time to read over the compositions before the end of school. You've wasted a lot of that time for us, so you can stay behind and read yours after school. Sit down."

Colin sat down. His feet tangled in the legs of the desk and his knees bumped heavily against the wood, so that ink jolted out of the well and trickled down the sloping face.

COLIN sat at his desk while the other children went noisily out of the room. It was not the first time he had had to stay after school and he sat straight and still, his hands on the desk in front of him.

Miss Hanson was writing the next day's work on the board and he knew it would be five or ten minutes before she said anything to him at all. Some of the kids didn't like that silent wait; they said they'd rather be sent along to old Siddons and get the strap and have it over with. Colin didn't mind. It was uncomfortable

1 2

to have to sit straight and still for so long, but he liked being alone in the room with her and watching as she moved surely and smoothly in front of the blackboard.

She does send them up to Siddons once in a while, Colin thought, but not very often. She isn't mean, she's like Mother is and Johnny Harris and Johnny's old man, one of the warm people; you know how they're going to act, they don't get sore over nothing or tell you one thing one minute and another thing the next; if they do get sore there's a reason for it and you know it won't last.

He began to feel silly sitting there with his hands in front of him on the too small desk. He thought of coughing or moving his feet to make her notice him. But she spoke in time to keep him from that, without turning away from her writing.

"I suppose Margaret will be waiting for you?"

"I guess so, Miss Hanson."

She was writing on the board. "You know, Colin, you're just as smart as she is. Why don't you learn to be tidy and careful?"

Colin moved his feet uncomfortably. "Girls are different."

"No, they aren't." She turned around and he saw again how blue her eyes were. "There's nothing sissy about taking trouble. And keeping awake in class. It just takes determination." She sat down at her desk. "Bring your work up here."

He came up gladly and gave her the book, then stood beside her chair, a little behind her, his big hands hanging awkwardly in front of him. It was better not to have to read it aloud, he thought. Reading out loud from a book is not so bad, but when you've written it yourself the words sound silly and the other kids make cracks about it afterwards and you wish you hadn't put down so much.

Mildred Hanson read the untidy pages in front of her. She felt the wet moss underfoot, saw the fallen alder leaves at the edge of last year's snow-slide, heard the roar of the first fall storm across the peaks that closed the gully. "Why did you write of fall on a day like this?"

"I just thought of fall," he said. "Fall will come."

"Have you ever been in the mountains in the fall?"

"No," he said.

She turned a page and went on reading. He looked down at her and saw that her hair shone with the same pale gold even when the sun was not on it. He could see her shoulders clearly through her thin white blouse and the blouse was so clean and so fresh he wanted to touch it. His left hand moved a little, then she spoke again.

"Do you still think you'll be a bridgeman when you leave school, Colin?"

"I guess so," he said slowly.

She turned back to the beginning of the composition. Perhaps it's wrong to worry him about that again so soon, she thought. It's too much for him now. Yet he's got to stop and think about it. He's like all the others, rough and untidy and careless. He doesn't even keep his hands clean or brush his hair or look after his clothes properly. Yet he isn't like them. Things happen inside him and he can bring them out for the rest of us to see, like this composition.

What am I trying to do with him? Am I trying to kid myself that I'm the wise teacher who recognizes a Canadian Abe Lincoln or a beardless Walt Whitman in the little red schoolhouse? It isn't likely he'll ever be a statesman or a poet. The important thing is that he could be something and do something far bigger than the existing and job-serving and promoting that the best of these others will do. How do I know that? Just because he can be articulate on paper? Because something starts in him when I read good poetry? Woman's intuition—or a schoolmarm's hunch, maybe. It's a teacher's business to have hunches like that and do what she can about them.

Sometimes I feel about him as I suppose I'll feel about my own son. That's when I want to touch him and hold him, keep him near me as he is now. And that's why I may be wrong, why I may be lying to myself about him; because I let myself feel about him instead of thinking. If you give in to feeling it can grow and grow in you until those awful things happen, the things you read about between teachers and children. I've got to send him away, quickly, now.

"Colin," she said gently. "You must think hard about it. Try to want to go on and finish school."

"Yes, Miss Hanson." He was still watching her shoulders under the white blouse. His body was tense and his heart was pounding so that he could feel it all through his body. His hand moved again, towards her, just a little.

"Please try to want it, Colin. It's important—for me."

He touched her then. Just reached forward and set his big hand down on the white freshness of her blouse until he could feel the warmth of her shoulder against his palm. She felt the pressure, accepted it and held her body still under it. She moved her hand, as though to reach up and set it on his. Then all the intensity of her fear was with her again. He felt her body stiffen, then draw gently away from him. She turned slowly to face him and said only: "Why, Colin, you mustn't do that." But he saw the fear in her eyes and in the paleness of her face.

Colin's hand was at his side again and he looked away from her.

"You had better go now, Colin. We can talk about the rest of this tomorrow." She tried to hear her voice and thought it calm. "It's too nice an afternoon to waste indoors."

Colin heard the harshness of strain through the calm voice. He turned and found his clumsy way through the door, with tears of misery and confusion hot in his eyes.

Mildred sat on at her desk. She knew what she had done to him, but she knew also that it was useless to call him back, that there could be no explanation for him.

2

OUTSIDE the school building Colin did not hesitate. He crossed the yard and turned along the dusty road. As he walked he remembered the moment of fear he had seen in her eyes, tried to take the blame for it into himself and could not.

Surely it was a small thing, to touch her like that, even though she is a teacher. She even seemed to like it, just at first. Her shoulder felt warm where I touched it, smooth under her blouse and warm clear through me. I suppose that's sin, the sort of sin God might strike you dead for. A deadly sin. God and my father. God the Father. Father the God. My father is like God—Johnny Harris said so once, because my father has a big black beard. But my father isn't God. God is a spirit and couldn't have a beard.

Jeff Burnside and Tod Phalling were sitting at the side of the road, waiting for him. But he scarcely noticed them, even when they got up and began to walk with him, one on either side.

"How'd you make out?" Tod asked.

The question hardly reached Colin's mind, but he said: "O.K."

Jeff jostled into him from the other side. "Give us the angle, dope. What'd she keep you back for?"

"You heard her," Colin said. "For not paying attention."

"Yeah," Tod said. "What'd she do? Take your pants down and play with you?"

"Shut up," Colin said.

Tod stuck out a foot so that Colin tripped and stumbled. "Satchel-foot," Tod said. "What did she do?"

"Nothing," Colin said. He was scared but it was better to get beaten up than let them know anything.

"We know she's soft on you."

"That's right," Jeff said. "You may as well spill it."

"Nothing happened," Colin said. "You been kept back after school. You know nothing happens except more work."

"There's big sister," Jeff said. "Go tell her about it. We can wait."

Colin looked ahead along the road and saw Margaret standing there, waiting for him.

"Be seeing y', punk," Tod said.

They dropped behind as he walked on towards Margaret. They were scared of her, Colin knew, in much the same way and for much the same reasons as they were scared of Miss Hanson, but he hadn't expected them to give up that easily. Margaret had never backed down, even when she was much smaller; she never ran away or hid or did any of the other things girls usually did when boys acted tough. She simply stood her ground and made them feel cheap. Tod and Jeff had had their share of it and weren't looking for any more.

She was waiting quite calmly, her books under her arm, as though she had known he would need her. "What happened?" she asked. "I'd almost given you up."

"We got kept back."

She glanced at him suspiciously. "I've seen just about everybody else in your room go by."

"It was only me," Colin said.

Margaret laughed. "I'm beginning to think Mildred Hanson likes keeping you after school."

Colin turned on her fiercely. "Don't say those things."

She looked up in quick surprise. "I'm sorry," she said. "I didn't mean anything."

"It's O.K.," Colin said. "Skip it."

They walked on in silence. Margaret watched the dusty road ahead. That's what those other kids must have been saying to him, she thought. But it's not like Colin to get sore. Mildred keeps him back too often. She says he's good in class and his work is good, so she must do it just to help him. But it's not fair to make him more different from the others than he is already.

"What are you going to do between now and supper?" she asked him.

"I'm going back in the alders a way."

"I've got to stop at the store and pick up a lot of stuff. But I'll have time to milk and do chores if you want."

"Thanks," Colin said. "I'd like to go back there quite a ways."

"Don't be late for supper, that's all." She left him at the store.

It was still over a mile and a half to the Ensley farm, but Colin walked the distance without a pause, his loose, big-footed awkward stride carrying him far more efficiently than it seemed to. He was in a hurry to get to the alders—he realized now that he had meant to go there from the moment he closed the door of the classroom. And he was glad that Margaret was not coming with him. Nearly always he would have wanted her. But today he wanted to consider only himself, to be guided only by his own

1 7

desires in where he went, how fast he went, where he stopped and what he thought about.

He turned off the road a hundred yards short of the gate by the house and swung round the edge of the pasture, keeping well clear of the barn in case his mother or father should be out there and see him. He came to the creek, cached his lunch bucket in a fire-blackened stump and turned into the alders.

He left the hot spring day behind him at once and felt the difference clearly as he had known he would. The light was still bright and clear, but filtered by the green leaves high overhead and reflected without harshness from the clean gray trunks of the trees. Underfoot there was no dust, only moist dark leaves and soft black earth. The creek was running strongly but quietly between the clay banks, broken into light only where a tiny sandbar forced a ripple or a sodden black tree branch, buried deep in the soft bottom, stood against the current. It looped in unpredictable ways across the wide flat, now lost in a salmonberry thicket, now spreading to a skunk cabbage swamp where the ground was low, now weaving under rotting windfalls. But Colin knew its direction and knew the cattle trails and deer trails that followed it.

He had come there for safety, safety from people—from Tod and Jeff, from Mildred Hanson, from his father and mother, even from Margaret; from all people and from the eyes and voices of all people. He had not known this when he came and he scarcely recognized it as he found it; he felt only a sense of wonder that any place, on such a day, could be cool and quiet, empty of human life, in tune and tone with his need.

He had meant to stop in the open place under the maples, near the line fence, but instead he went on, over the sagging wires of the fence and into a part of the flat that was unfamiliar to him. The ground was a little higher and the creek banks were clearer and easier to follow. He walked smoothly, little conscious of the change, for thought was quick and urgent in him. Along the known trails, through the known part of the flat, the old thoughts had been with him. He had been the trapper, following his line through the snow; a tie-cutter, searching timber for his trade; an explorer, venturing where other men had not been, through dangerous ways to high achievement. Well-loved thoughts, these, tried companions of many days, kin to the thoughts of the Knights in the Round Table stories, men bold in quest and combat, gentle before their ladies, that had carried him again and again insensibly over the long morning miles to school.

Quite suddenly all these thoughts were dead and dull. They led nowhere, achieved nothing; they were part of evil. I must be bad all through, Colin told himself, if the best I can do is think fine things for myself. I'm bad in school, never the way Margaret is with all checks on her report card. I don't ever want to do the chores around home, except maybe split wood or go out and milk on a good morning. I tell lies. I think I hate my father sometimes and I talk back to Mother. I don't even know what I'm going to be when I grow up. The old man says I'm too awkward to be a bridgeman—he says I'd get killed inside of a week. But that's what he wants me to be. Miss Hanson thinks I ought to be something else, so does Margaret; but they don't say what except keep on with school and go to University. Fat Evans is going to be a telegrapher. Johnny Harris is going to drive truck. Jeff and Tod are going in the woods. I don't like Tod. I'd like to bust him one, right in the mush, every time he calls me punk or satchel-foot. Only I'm scared of him. He'd just hit me in the guts, like he did last time, and I'd crawl on the ground and be sick at my stomach again.

God could strike me dead for being no good, right here, by the creek where it's cool and soft. It would be quick, like a bullet in the heart, nothing a guy would feel at all. They'd all be sorry then because they wouldn't know what had happened. But then there wouldn't be any more sunlight and I couldn't see the creek again, or Margaret or Johnny Harris or Mother or Miss Hanson. I shouldn't even want to see her, but I do. It isn't bad, wanting to see her, not if you don't mean anything bad by it. I only wanted to touch her. There's nothing bad in that. I don't really mean those things I've thought about her—they're not like ordinary thinking, anyway; they're like the stories of the knights, not real but something that comes up in you so hard that it's all around you and close to you and seems real just for a little while. I won't let myself think those things any more. They're inside me right now, but I won't let them come forward. A person can't help what's inside him. He can't be watching all the time, either. Sometimes it comes up so fast nobody could shut it back, and once it's up there, with you, you want it too much to try to stop it any more. . . .

Colin noticed suddenly that he was near the end of the flat, and he stopped. For the first time since he had left the school he was fully aware of everything about him. The ground was dry and firm underfoot, even last year's leaves were dry. The creek was loud, rippling over a gravelly bed, and he could hear it in still louder sound as it poured down the mountainside. The alders were smaller, branched and more widely spaced, with a scattering of firs and hemlocks among them. Through gaps among the leaves ahead he could see the heavy dark green of the steep mountain slope climbing away from him. Because his eyes were fully at work again, seeing and feeling the brightness of the day that held on into the late afternoon, his mind felt free and healed. For the moment he was strong and sure.

There was a big maple tree beside the creek a little way ahead of him. He went to it and sat down on a root so that he could look into a deep pool below. Black water-striders moved across the surface from his shadow and he saw orange-tailed salmon fry holding in the current. A ruffed grouse drummed somewhere behind him. This must be a mile from the line fence, he thought. No, maybe half a mile. And it's a quarter of a mile from the barn to the line fence, less than a mile from our house to the mountains on this side. A man can climb up into Sales Gully in half a day from our place, Dad says, and that's four thousand feet, real mountain country, above timberline.

He tried to think seriously and calmly and usefully about himself, about being a logger or staying on in school to be something else. What did you get to be if you stayed on in school? A school-teacher, maybe, or a doctor or a lawyer. He watched the swoop and flash of a kingfisher farther along the creek. A logger could turn himself into a prospector or a trapper or a timber cruiser like Mr. Grant. That's better than a teacher or a lawyer; you've got to use your head plenty in a job like that too. But there was something more to be found, something none of them had found yet. He searched again for it, deep in himself, felt it but did not find it and his mind turned back from the search.

A grouse drummed again and Colin leaned back against the trunk of the tree to watch a blue jay on a limb above him. You could make it to Sales Gully and back in a day, he thought. This creek comes right out of there and a guy'd only have to follow it. . . .

MARGARET was glad to come to the farm gate. She liked the walk from school well enough, but hated carrying clumsy packages from the store. She looked in the mail-box, found some papers and a letter, and added them to her load. As she opened the gate she saw her mother coming towards her along the rutted, grass-grown road that led between wire fences to the house.

"You were quick, dear," Mrs. Ensley said. "Where's Colin?"

Margaret evaded the question about Colin. "Did the radio batteries come?"

"Nobody's come up with the freight yet. Did Colin stay to play ball after school?"

They were walking side by side, quite slowly, towards the house. Margaret thought: why does she worry about him so? "He's gone back in the alders, along the creek."

"He'll be brooding again," Mrs. Ensley said. "Brooding and dreaming. I never saw such a boy for brooding on things."

"Colin doesn't really brood, Mother. He thinks a lot and he's got a good imagination. You ought to be glad. He'll amount to something when he grows up."

"It doesn't seem healthy in a boy, to be off by himself so much, and he seems worse lately. I don't remember that my brothers were like that."

"There were plenty of them to keep each other busy," Margaret said. "Colin'll grow out of it."

They went into the house through the back door, which opened straight into the big kitchen. Margaret dropped her packages thankfully and Mrs. Ensley sat down. She was a woman in her forties, with graying hair and a strong, pleasant face, almost youthful in animation, but deeply lined in repose. She had the same high cheekbones that Margaret and Colin had, but her eyes were a dark and vivid blue. Even in relaxation her face and body suggested a power of quick, efficient, purposeful movement, yet she did not seem physically strong and the lines in her face were a deep weariness.

Margaret crossed the room to the stove as soon as she was rid of her packages.

Mrs. Ensley watched for a moment, then she said: "Will Colin be back in time to milk and do the chores?"

"No. I told him I'd do it."

Mrs. Ensley nodded. "Don't let his father know."

"Did they move out to the new bridge today?"

"He said they were going to, but it shouldn't make much difference to when he gets home. He says they can walk over the hill to camp and get there the same time as the rest of the crew."

"I told Colin not to be late for supper," Margaret said.

WHEN Colin came back to the edge of the alder flat and saw the open pasture ahead of him, he felt a sudden disappointment, although hunger had been hurrying him towards supper through the whole way out. It had been safe and calm in the alders, not confused in any way. Everything he had thought while sitting on the alder root had been fresh and important and exciting, free from any of the limitations that stifled good thoughts in the ordinary world.

Crossing the pasture towards the barn, he thought: now it will all start again. Margaret will say I'm late. Mother will want to know why I didn't come home for a sandwich after school. The old man will be home from the woods. It's not fair to think all that though. Mother's swell and they're all swell and I'm glad I'm coming home to supper. Sure it was good back in the alders, close under the mountain like that. I'll go back there one day when it's raining hard. And I'll go back there next winter in the snow, when the creek's frozen maybe.

Margaret was still in the barn, but she had finished milking. She had not heard him coming and he stood silently in the doorway, watching her, until she looked up and saw him. Then he laughed at the surprise and annoyance in her face.

"It's not funny," she said. "I thought you were never coming

22

and Mother said not to let Dad know I had milked for you. You always make it difficult for anybody to help you."

"I've been here a long time, watching you."

"You can't fool me. Pick up these pails and let's get back to the house. Dad's home already. Did you have a good time?"

"I'll take you back there next time I go. It's nowheres near as thick as you'd think and the creek's real pretty farther back. I went right over to the foot of the mountain."

They had come to the house and Colin turned away to separate the milk. Margaret went in. "Don't be long," she said.

Colin hurried because he was hungry, and he washed his hands and face at the outside pump in case his father was still using the sink. The kitchen woodbox had to be filled, he knew, but the wood was split ready for it and there would be enough in the box until after supper. He went quietly into the kitchen and sat down in his place at the table. Margaret was bringing the dishes from the stove. He could hear his father moving in the bedroom. Mrs. Ensley was mixing something but she turned and looked at him without stopping the movement.

"You'll be hungry now, Colin," she said. "You wouldn't come and see your old mother, even to get something to eat after school."

"I wasn't hungry," Colin said. "I ate all my lunch."

"And didn't bring your lunch bucket in."

"It's outside. I'll go get it after supper."

Mrs. Ensley came over to the table, set down a loaded dish, then ran her hand gently over Colin's black hair. It was the confident movement of a mother who knows she is loved. "Did you have a good time, son?" she asked. "That's the main thing."

"It was swell. Much better than I ever thought it would be."

"I want to hear about it. Not now. Your father's worried about something. But don't forget any of it."

Colin smiled at her. "I won't."

William Ensley came into the room as his wife moved away from the table. He was a fairly tall man—probably an inch or two under six feet—but so broad he seemed squat. He wore a heavy jet-black beard, spade-shaped and trimmed very square. His eyes were black under eyebrows almost as thick and black as

23

his beard. Thick black hair grew profusely on the backs of both hands. He seemed, and was, a man of great physical strength. Standing in the doorway of the kitchen, cleaned up after his day's work, wearing a good shirt of gray wool and heavy tweed pants, he seemed to have far more than mere physical power; he might have been John Brown or Daniel or Isaiah.

His wife said quietly: "Sit down, Will. Supper's all ready."

"So's Colin," Will Ensley said. "Ready and waiting." He turned his strong deep voice directly to Colin.

"You cleaned up, son?"

"Yes, Father," Colin said. "I did it outside after I was through separating."

"You don't have to remind him, Dad," Margaret said. "Colin never forgets that any more."

The four of them sat down at the table. Colin and Margaret sat straight-backed, their hands in their laps. Mrs. Ensley bent her head a little forward. Will Ensley held his head high, but his eyes were closed. "Almighty God," he said slowly, "Who hast seen fit to grant us of Thine abundance, bless this meal that is set before us. And of Thy mercy grant us strength to honor Thy Name through all adversity."

Colin listened, as he always did, to the rolling sound of his father's words rather than their sense. They were seldom exactly the same words—Will Ensley took pride in his power of extemporaneous prayer—but they usually carried the same implications of gratitude, humility and faith in bodily nourishment as a way to spiritual strength. Tonight there was a difference, not only in the words but in the solemn sound of them; they were spoken just a little more quietly than usual and with a shade of urgency beyond the normal duty of gratitude. Colin glanced towards his mother and saw that she had raised her eyes to her husband's face. She looked away again before Will Ensley opened his eyes, but Colin knew that she had noticed the difference too; it seemed to him that she had expected it.

They began to eat and Colin used his hunger. The Ensleys talked little at their meals—Will Ensley had made his growth on the silent meals of the New Brunswick logging camps, had brought the habit of silence west with him to the Pacific Coast

2 4

camps and even in his own house had not grown away from it. But tonight he seemed to want to talk. He asked first Colin, then Margaret about the day in school. He asked about the cows and chickens, wanted to know if Colin had played ball after school, even teased Margaret about the new long dress she was to wear at the high school dance. Martha Ensley waited and said little. After nearly twenty years she knew all the weaknesses, all the needs that were so well hidden behind the front of physical strength. Because she was what she was they had made and built her love for him, they were her eternal care and her religion within the simple, undemonstrative Christianity she devoutly lived.

She said at last: "You were right about the new bridge, Will. You got home just as soon."

"We didn't go out there," he said, and she knew she had led him to his trouble as he wanted to be led. "We aren't going to build that trestle—not for a while, anyway."

"Where will you be going, then?"

"I don't know. Some say there's a long shutdown coming. Some say the outfit's finished—bankrupt. That talk's been going around for weeks, but I never thought much of it till today."

"But you worked today."

"Sure, we worked," he said heavily. "On the mainline. There's some sills need replacing in the framed trestles."

"They wouldn't do that if they were finished would they?"

"It's good maintenance ahead of a long shutdown." He reached over and cut himself a slice of bread. "It isn't as if it hadn't happened already other places. Half the mills are down and there's no price for logs."

"It won't last," Martha Ensley said. "If they do shut down it will only be through fire season and that's happened often enough."

"There'll be work," Will Ensley said. "There's always work for a man that knows his trade. But it may not come so easy as it has."

3

SIX days a week William Ensley got out of bed at five o'clock, put on his working clothes, then ate a solid breakfast that Martha Ensley cooked for him. Breakfast over, he took his coat and his lunch pail and went out to wait at the farm gate for Mike Varchuk's car to pick him up.

The wait was something Ensley liked well enough, even in the dark and cold of a winter's morning. It settled his breakfast, brought him to terms with the day ahead. On a clear summer morning such as this, it did more than that. He was genuinely fond of the two big broad-leaf maples that stood one on either side of the gate; their permanence and solidity, here at the entrance to what he thought of as his "property," gave him an increased awareness of ownership, a keen sense of being an established citizen. He was not, he liked to remind himself, an improvident, transient logger, but a solid man, a skilled craftsman, trusted by the company he worked for, the head of a family and the owner of a substantial property. Occasionally, as he did on this morning, he liked to turn and look towards the barn. It was a good barn, square and strong, standing well out in the pasture from the house. He had built it, with the help of neighbors, eleven years before, and it reminded him that there were cows and chickens on his property. These were another sign of providence and solidity, a background detail, quite properly the care of Martha and the children, yet a credit to his own substance.

The sound of Mike Varchuk's old car as it came over the crest of the hill destroyed Will Ensley's appreciation of himself. Without quite realizing it, Ensley did not like automobiles any more than he liked cows and chickens. He had never owned one or learned to drive one and they did not fit at all with his conception of himself or of his world. He was never at ease with a machine, nor could he consider a machine as a tool, in the way he thought of his axes and augers and saws. Though he had worked close beside machines all his life, he felt that they were in some way obscene, against the will and purpose of God, and he shut himself off from them as far as possible. That Mike Varchuk should own a car was in itself a faint condemnation of cars in general. Mike was a foreigner—Ensley would not use the term "bohunk" even to himself, because he considered it degrading and un-Christian—who still spoke broken English. He was a loudmouthed man and a radical, one of the few loggers who regretted the wane of the I.W.W. and the O.B.U. Will Ensley might have been able to forgive all these things, but he could never forget that Varchuk was also an atheist and an indifferent worker.

The car stopped and Varchuk shouted a cheerful good morning over the noise of the engine. Ensley answered civilly and climbed to his place in the back seat. Varchuk ground the old car into gear and they started off to pick up the others who rode to work in the same car—John Meldrum, the pile-driver engineer, Tony Soretto, the section foreman, Earl Mayhew, the rigger. They were all family men, except Varchuk, all in their forties, steady and hardworking men who had settled near the outskirts of Blenkinstown to raise their families within reach of a company they liked to work for.

Will Ensley sat squarely upright in the back of the car, nursing his coat and lunch pail on his knee. He always sat the same way, stiffly and tidily, as though the car were much too fragile for the weight of his great body and the roughness of his working clothes. This morning he was hoping Varchuk wouldn't talk about the shutdown, but he knew that this was expecting too much, so he modified the hope a little—he hoped that Mike wouldn't talk until the others were in the car.

But Mike began to talk as soon as he had the car bumping along in high gear. He took one hand off the jolting wheel and turned almost clear around. "Looks like hard times come pretty quick now. This outfit fold up. Lots of men laid off. Wages go way down. Some people be pretty hongry before she's all over."

"I'll believe it when I see it," Ensley said. "The world's got to have logs."

"She come," Mike told him. "You see. All over the world and the poor people will starve and die some places. Maybe here."

They were almost at Earl Mayhew's gate, where the other three were waiting. Will Ensley waited till Varchuk had put on his brakes before he said: "No man needs to starve in this country."

The car stopped and the three men climbed in, wedging themselves into their usual places. As Ensley had hoped, the stopping and loading and starting broke the conversation. Mike was busy with his gears again and the others were settling themselves, stowing lunch pails and coats. Will Ensley withdrew into himself, his eyes on the stumps and salal brush and second-growth that lined the road. It was all going to start again—shutdowns and lay-offs, argument and trouble and conflict, breaking into a man's life, making him less than he was, forcing decisions upon him that had nothing to do with his skill or strength. It would be a time for men like Mike Varchuk, the talkers, the weak ones, the improvident ones, the godless ones. They were all saying the same things now, even John and Earl, leaning forward to be heard in the front seat.

"It won't last," John Meldrum said. "It's just the big guys getting squared to freeze out the little guys and make a clean-up."

"Sure," said Mike Varchuk. "Sure it's the big guys. So the working stiff is going to starve if he don't get wise."

"Nothing new about an outfit going broke," Earl said. "Another set-up always comes in sooner or later."

"In good times maybe soon enough," Mike said. "In bad times, maybe not soon enough so your kids got full bellies."

The slow thoughts swung heavily across Will Ensley's mind, a procession of black, distorted shadows, the suffocating stuff of all terrible dreams. That Varchuk is happy, saying the things he's saying. He isn't a man to say honest things, yet he believes these things he is saying and they aren't the things he usually says, nor said the way he usually says them. When men talk that way it means trouble, bad trouble. There wasn't any work after the war. It was only like that for a while, but it was bad while it lasted and there was trouble and they told you "no" and "nothing" when you went to ask for work. That couldn't happen again. There hasn't been a war. And it would be different now. They know Will Ensley now—everybody knows Will Ensley.

Varchuk was still talking and the others were arguing with him, but Ensley could tell they were worried. Just over fire season, they were saying, open up again in September. We can last till then and forget all about it. A man could get work some place else anyway—good riggers and good engineers don't grow on bushes. Will Ensley tightened the muscles of his great shoulders and looked down at the broad palms and thick fingers of his hands. "They just don't make broad-axe men any more," he heard the superintendent say. "Will here is the last of them all and we're lucky to have him." And that piece in the Vancouver paper: "Ensley's axe can square a timber truer than any sawmill and leave the faces as smooth as though they had been planed. He can build a house and furnish it with no other tool than his axe." Will Ensley looked out again at the stumps and salal brush and second-growth, the normal things that were all about him every day, and would be. He was slowly searching his mind for a phrase he had heard, a phrase he had taken for himself as he heard it, that belonged to his present need if he could only find it again. "Work finds a man. . . ." No. "A good man doesn't have to. . . ." Then it was suddenly clear and sound in his mind: "A man that's good never has to look for work. Work looks for him." Let them talk.

COLIN never woke to the slight stirrings about the house caused by his father's breakfast and departure for work. Usually it was necessary for Martha Ensley to waken him in time to milk, do the other chores and eat breakfast before leaving for school. This morning he was half-awake when she called, trying to explain to himself his reluctance to face the sunlit day that reached in through the window of the little room. Doing the chores would be easy and pleasant, with the cows quiet and sunlight outside the open door of the barn—probably Margaret would come out to help before he was through milking, because she loved such mornings as well as he. Walking to school would be good—especially good for some reason. What reason? He remembered three—the meadowlark near Mayhew's gate, the red-winged blackbirds in the swamp, the yellowlegs along the edge of Craig's Bay; he and Margaret had seen them yesterday, had talked about them and been sure that they would be there to be seen again.

But he was fully awake now and knew why he had not wanted

29

to face this day. Facing the day meant facing Mildred Hanson and Tod Phalling. He knew what would come from Phalling, almost certainly, and as he dressed he tried to recognize what he feared from Mildred Hanson. It wasn't anything really, he told himself. She couldn't be sure it wasn't an accident, likely she's forgotten all about it. She didn't say so much when you stop and think about it. Then his memory was suddenly sharp and clear again and he knew she would not have forgotten.

He scarcely saw the sunlight as he milked in the barn, and Margaret found him silent and gloomy when she came out to meet him. After breakfast when they were on the way to school, she tried to solve his mood. "Did something go wrong yesterday? Something more than being kept back?"

"No," he said.

"There's something wrong. Is it Tod Phalling and Jeff Burnside again?"

"I'm not scared of them," he said. But he knew he was, so scared that he didn't want to think about them and wished she'd stop reminding him. It isn't what they do to you so much as the way they suddenly turn into strangers, two different people altogether. And Jeff gets hold of your arms and Tod stands in front of you with his face all white and his shoulders hunched up. Then he asks you a question and hits you before you can answer, then asks another and hits you again. Everything they do when they get you like that is slow and quiet, but hard and mean. It's not like when other kids get mad and fight. It's so slow there's no getting mad to it at all and it scares you so you think your insides are going to run out and it goes on and on. "No," he said again. "I'm not scared of them."

"They're mean and dirty," she said. "Tod especially. And they're older than you—bigger than you really even though you are taller."

Colin said nothing. They were coming near the Mayhew's gate and he looked for the meadowlark on the fence post where they had seen it yesterday. He didn't want to see it now as he had when he was waking up, but he hoped it would be there because it would be something else to talk about. It was not there and Margaret said the thing he dreaded. "I'll wait and walk home with you."

"No," he said. "I'm playing in the ball game. You don't need to wait. They won't do anything." She doesn't know those guys. They don't give up that easy—Jeff might, but Tod wouldn't. He wouldn't care if he had to wait a week or till school closes or till it starts up again in the fall. She can't be around every place all the time. Once it's over they'll be O.K. and maybe I can make it tougher for them this time.

He heard the meadowlark then, in full song, as it flew up from the grass. They both stopped and watched its flight. Margaret said: "You told me we'd see it again today and you were right. You know, Colin, sometimes I'm proud of you." They started walking again and Colin said nothing; but something lifted inside him and he knew it would be there all day to help him. She hadn't meant to praise him because he had known the bird would be there.

MILDRED Hanson had faced the day with a concern at least as deep as Colin's, but she had at once a clearer understanding of what had happened and a more positive responsibility. In itself his touch had been nothing more than the lonely, yearning gesture of an adolescent boy. It had not been impertinent as Jeff Burnside's touch would have been or indecent as Tod Phalling's would have been. It would have been nothing and could have been passed as nothing had it not reached in upon her own dangerous thoughts and aroused all her fear of them. He saw that, she thought, and heard it in what I said. He will remember it for a long time and think that what he did was much more important than it was. I could have passed it off so easily—I didn't have to notice it at all. Anything would be better than what I did. There will be something between us now, something he doesn't understand, something to hurt him and make him suspicious. He's going to believe that he did something bad. He can never know that what happened came from inside me, not from him at all.

She was writing on the blackboard when Colin came into the room and did not see him go to his desk. Through the day Colin was silent and unresponsive, answering only when he had to. It has to be done slowly, she told herself, very slowly so that many, many little things are built up between him and that one thing I made so big.

Colin had been glad of the chance to get to his desk while her back was turned. He had anticipated the difficulty of looking into her face and wishing her good morning and had thought little beyond that. Now the difficulty was past and when she turned and looked over the class without singling him out he found himself wondering again whether she might not have forgotten.

At recess Tod Phalling spoke to him. "Going to play ball today, punk?"

"Sure," Colin said. "Why not?"

Tod laughed. "You're scared enough to wet your pants right now."

Back at his desk Colin knew what he should have done. Fighting in the school yard was always punished. But it would have been better to fight then, when Tod would have had to fight alone, even if it meant taking a licking from Tod first and the old man second. I haven't got the guts to think of anything like that until it's too late. Other guys do, but I haven't got the guts. . . . He felt the sweat hot all over his body and he was shaking.

The ball game was four innings only, but Colin played every minute of it with a concentration that let him forget what was ahead and even made him less clumsy than usual. He felt good at the end of it because his team had won, he had hit safely twice and fielded half a dozen chances well enough so that no one had yelled or laughed at him. Neither Tod nor Jeff had been playing and he lingered awhile over the break-up of the game. The security of the laughing, kidding, ball-throwing crowd made Tod Phalling seem unreal and distant. Why should he bother, Colin thought, he and Jeff have got more to do than waste an afternoon waiting for me. But the group of boys gradually broke up and he saw at last, as he had known all along, that there was no one there who would be going his way home. I should care, he told himself. They won't be waiting—not today; some other day perhaps, but not today. It's been too long.

He saw them as he came round the first bend beyond the school, waiting under the big maple tree beside the road. Jeff Burnside stood up when he saw Colin coming, but Tod stayed where he was. Colin made no move to turn aside, only walked on towards them, awkwardly, afraid, yet still not certain that what he dreaded would really happen. When he was still five or ten paces away Tod climbed lazily to his feet.

Tod hated Colin, but only with a tempered and intermittent hatred. He hated Colin because Colin was big and because he sensed in him a potential physical strength. He hated Colin for being untidy and awkward in appearance yet successful in school. He hated Colin because people who disliked Tod—which meant nearly every one in Blenkinstown—were fairly certain to like Colin. All these hatreds of Colin calmed into something approaching tolerance whenever he beat Colin, and he had learned years before that he could beat Colin into a crawling hulk with very little difficulty whenever he felt like it. Right now he felt like it. The multiple hatreds had been stirred into life by a precocious, muddled jealousy; Mildred Hanson's preference for Colin cut squarely into the cherished fantasy that made himself the recipient of her ultimate favors. So Tod now stood in Colin's way, legs apart and firmly planted, hands at his sides, fists clenched. Colin hesitated and stopped. Tod said: "So you weren't lying for once, punk."

Colin watched the pale eyes. The blood was throbbing in his body and his throat was tight. He tried to watch Jeff Burnside too, but knew he could not. He thought: why should this be me? I don't want to fight them, not even for what Tod did to me last time. Why should I be here, like this, and why should he hate me so his face goes pale like that?

Tod said: "You going to tell us now, punk?"

Colin looked down at his feet, then half-glanced over his shoulder at Jeff Burnside standing grinning behind him. "Tell you what?"

"Tell us what that chippy did with you yesterday."

The word reached into Colin's mind and slowly took on its full meaning. "You can't talk about her like that."

Tod thrust his pale face forward. "The hell I can't," he said. "Your mother's a chippy. So's your sister."

Colin jerked into awkward movement, felt Jeff grab his arms

from behind, felt Tod's fist in pain that shot up through his chest, half-choking him. But his slow strength responded, threw Burnside from him, crashed his own shoulder against Phalling, then let him stumble and fall full length in the gravel. They were on him in a moment, driving their knees into his back, twisting his arms. They rolled him over and Tod's hard fists hit him twice in the face. Tod laughed. "Quite the scrapper, ain't you, punk? Want to tell us about it now?"

"I've told you," Colin said. "I told you yesterday."

Tod climbed to his feet. "Let go his arm, Jeff," he said. "Let him up so's I can lick him good."

Colin rolled over, spat blood from his cut lips and began to get up. Tod kicked him.

Colin was crying. He heard himself say: "Let me alone, can't you?" But he got to his feet and lunged awkwardly at Tod. Tod sidestepped, hit him in the stomach, hit him in the face. Colin swung again, felt his right elbow smash solidly against something, saw Tod's startled face in front of him and struck at it with his left fist. Then he was held from behind again and Tod was standing in front of him, the red blood brilliant against his white face. "Why you awkward son of a bitch," Tod said slowly, and hit him. "You overgrown, under-balled bastard." Tod hit again, then brought his knee up hard into Colin's groin. Jeff Burnside let Colin slip to the ground.

Tod stood looking down at Colin. He raised his eyes and glanced up and down the deserted road. "I never did that to a guy before," he said. "Let's scram out of here."

4

COLIN was on his feet within two or three minutes of the time Tod left him. He felt sore and battered. His lips were cut and swollen, his cheeks were bruised and there was blood in his nostrils. His whole body ached and his head throbbed. But he was not as badly marked as he had been in previous encounters with Tod. When he came to a creek that crossed the road he turned into the brush and knelt beside a pool to wash the blood away from his face. Kneeling there he cried, because he had knelt in the same place before to do the same thing and it seemed to him suddenly that this could go on happening forever and he could do nothing to stop it and there was no one to help him. I haven't got any guts, he thought, I don't want to fight him and even if I did want to he's too quick and strong and there's always Jeff or somebody there to help him.

He rinsed the blood from his handkerchief, squeezed out the water and wiped his face again. A car passed on the road and he could see the dust from it, but it was quiet and cool where he was and he felt better. He remembered the surge of strength through him that had hurled Jeff away and jarred Tod. I did want to fight then, he thought. I might have got somewhere with it if there hadn't been two of them. Maybe I'll go on getting stronger until I can lick 'em both, easy. He held to the thought, keeping it hard in the front of his mind as he stood up and turned towards the road again. But deep in him he knew that he would never want to fight, that he would always be afraid of Tod's pale face and cold eyes. The old, often-used thought came back to him again, reducing his new strength but without renewing his unhappiness: if it could be quick, like a bullet in the heart, it would be good and quiet to die.

Tod Phalling kept away from Colin the next morning, but as they passed each other at noon he said almost kindly: "Feeling O.K., kid?"

Without looking at him, Colin said: "Sure." He wanted to say something more, something defiant, but he was afraid to.

"You sure caught me a dirty one in the mush," Tod said, and Colin looked at him then. He was smiling, his upper lip was swollen and a front tooth was broken. "No hard feelings," Tod said. "Jeff was sure scared when you passed out." He went away and Colin felt vaguely warmed and flattered. He fought against the feeling, remembering Tod's pale face thrust towards his and the hard, relentless fists, but he thought: it wouldn't be hard to like the guy, if he'd only stay that way.

THE problem of Tod resolved itself for Colin before the summer holidays. He disappeared suddenly, from the school and from Blenkinstown. For a week after his disappearance there were wild rumors of its reason—he had held up Joe's gas station, he had broken into the liquor store, he had tried to rape a girl, he had been caught stealing from mail-boxes. Whatever the crime, it exhausted the patience and influence of Tod's father; and Tod, it was learned much later, had been sent to the interior of the province to work under close supervision in an uncle's sawmill. It was several years before Colin saw him again.

Those early summer months seemed to solve other problems, too, for the Ensley family and for Colin. The Blenkin Lumber Company did not shut down, Will Ensley's crew moved out to the trestle on the new line and his job went on—at lowered wages, but it was still his job. Colin's school work improved and as the days went on he was less and less able to convince himself that he had ever seen the quick flash of fear in Mildred Hanson's wide, calm eyes. Mildred herself was largely responsible for this. She had tried at first to deny the problem by denying the attraction she felt for Colin. In time she convinced herself that this was unfair to him. He was different from the others, she admitted. He needed encouragement and affection as they did not and it was in her to give him these things. So she gave them, gradually, almost reluctantly, but with increasing conviction. She recognized his response and found a measure of absolution in it, though her dedication would not let her forget the moment of failure.

The school year had been a triumph for Margaret. Mr. Siddons, the principal, had driven out to explain to Will and Martha Ensley that she was the most brilliant pupil ever to pass through the school and that she must go on to the University in time. Will Ensley had been suspicious at first and reluctant to commit himself. Martha had seemed to agree with his doubts while cautiously and subtly resolving them. Mr. Siddons had said that he and Mildred Hanson would spend extra time with Margaret so that she would go to the University with every chance to get the most out of it. Will Ensley still did not commit himself, but he agreed to keep the matter in mind and see how things went in the next two years—a concession which meant, Martha well knew, that he would use the thing in bluster and argument and moralizing until he had grown used to it and fitted it to his own conceptions.

For Colin the end of the term was a release from the tension that was always on him when he had to come close to people outside his immediate family. He knew this tension only as a shadow that was over his days, growing stronger and darker when he had to speak in class or pass among the groups of boys in the schoolyard, deepening to utter confusion in the face of violence or intense competition or the jarring contempt of boys who found time to notice his physical clumsiness. He had learned that the shadow could often be made lighter by shutting himself away in his own thoughts, letting them carry him on and on until even the nearest and most jarring sounds were silent, and the pictures in his mind faded to a pleasant, quiet confusion of light. When he was with certain people, with his mother or Margaret, with a friend like Johnny Harris, the shadow withdrew altogether. When he was with his father the shadow was there; it could fade at times, almost to disappearance, or it could grow dark and heavy.

In spite of the shadow Colin was happy at school. His mind responded quickly to any phase of the work that went beyond the normal routines of learning. He had discovered already that there was pleasure and excitement and safety in reading. Mildred Hanson had been quick to notice this and lend him books that would lead him still farther beyond the narrow limits set by the Department of Education. She was opening up for him, as she had already for Margaret, the neglected splendors of Canadian history—the great journeys of McKenzie and Fraser and Hearne, the vision of men like Moberly, the westward thrust of settlement, slower, more orderly, more difficult but never less courageous than the same movement of the Americans. These were things to reach into a boy's soul and he was happy for them. He was happy also in things outside school hours. He liked to play ball, and he nearly always had a chance to because he had a strong throwing arm and was a good hitter; his lank awkwardness made him clumsy and slow as base runner and he was too erratic for the infield, but he could judge and handle long flies as safely as anyone in the school. The total of his virtues was far more than enough to carry him on any team he played for and adequately covered a lack of competitive spirit that would have betrayed him in a tougher league.

He liked also to be at the edge of a group of boys who were arguing or planning something, silent and unnoticed if possible, hoping that nothing would happen to turn attention upon him, but eager to listen and feel accepted. Nearly always he was accepted, and accepted on his own terms.

All these things lessened the shadow that was with Colin through his school days, but it had been too firmly planted at some earlier time to fade altogether, so the release of the summer holidays was something more for him than it was for most boys.

Summer meant many things to Colin. It meant fishing and swimming in the lake up beyond Mike Varchuk's place, with Johnny Harris and Dick Thompson. It meant picking blackberries in the old logging works with the blue grouse starting up from underfoot. It meant haymaking, when Earl Mayhew came to mow for them some early morning and later on to rake; Colin and Margaret would cock the hay from the windrows and Martha Ensley always came out to help when they had borrowed Earl's horse and wagon to haul to the barn. Summer meant hoeing the garden, which Colin did not mind because it let the long thoughts work in him. It meant going up to lie secretly in the hayloft with a book, it meant being alone when he wanted to, going alone to the big maples near the line fence in the alder flat, following the road to its end out beyond the lake, walking the other road out to the beach camp, to hide alone in the brush and watch the train come down with the logs.

It meant things Margaret would think of, books she would find for him, plans they would make together. He had an urgent plan of his own for this particular summer: he wanted to climb the mountain behind the alder flat. He had mentioned it once or twice since he had followed the creek back to the end of the flat, but he knew that Margaret had not really felt the idea with him— she had let it slide away out of their conversation very quickly and Margaret did not do that with any idea that really reached her.

Colin held to it, thought often of the ways it could be done and built pictures in his mind of what they would find as they worked far up from the valley.

There was one entirely new thing about this summer. Colin had known of it since the previous fall and had thought of it often because it meant for him a long advance towards manhood. Each year Will Ensley cut from the alder flat several cords of wood for the house. In previous years Colin had gone out to watch and had been allowed to help by cutting away limbs and brush and by piling the cordwood as his father cut it. He had helped again later in the year when they fed the cordwood to the circular saw that reduced it to stove-wood and when they piled the short lengths into the woodshed. From then on the daily chore of splitting and packing the wood to the kitchen had been entirely his care. In the previous fall, as they piled the last of the wood into the woodshed, Will Ensley had said: "Next year it's your job, son. You'll start it and you'll finish it. I'll help you with the gas saw, but that's all."

Colin said, "You mean I'll cut it in the bush, fall the trees and everything?"

"That's right," Will told him. "You're man enough to be learning now."

He did not mention the matter again until the evening of the third or fourth day after school closed. Then he called Colin out after supper, as he often did, to turn the grindstone for him. Tonight, Colin saw, he had only a double-bitted swamping axe instead of the great, heavy broad-axes he usually brought home.

"Turn slowly," Will said. "I only want to touch it a little." Colin took the handle and brought the even stone into smooth, easy movement. The axe sang against it in Will's huge hands, gathering a rippling film of water on the upper side of its edge. It was withdrawn, turned and it sang again. Colin had served a long, straining apprenticeship at this grindstone and he had learned to control it absolutely, to hold it always at the speed his father needed.

Will Ensley asked him: "How's your own axe?"

"Fine," Colin said. "I haven't used it since I last ground it."

Will straightened up and felt the edge of his axe with his thumb. "Bring it along. We're going out to the alders."

As they walked across the pasture together Will Ensley looked at Colin and smiled so that his strong teeth showed very white in the black of his beard. "Think you're going to be able to handle it, son?"

Colin thought he had never seen his father so happy about anything. "Sure," he said. "I'm a whole lot stronger than I was this time last year and I can chop better too."

"Think you can hit twice in the same place, maybe." Will Ensley was still smiling. In spite of his powerful conception of himself as head of the family, he seldom felt wholly at ease with his children. He had children because children made a family and because having a family was part of man's duty—he had accepted God's words to Noah: "Be fruitful, and multiply, and replenish the earth"; had Martha been a stronger woman the family would never have stopped at Colin and Margaret. But now that he had the children, they were a surprise to him. He found that he did not know quite what to expect from them or, usually, what to do with them. He worked steadily and brought home good wages so that they should be fed and clothed; he taught them the righteousness of God and was himself righteous before them and before God. He corrected them and disciplined them when it seemed necessary, he read their school reports carefully and approved their successes when he could understand them. But he had seldom been able to feel, as he felt now, wholly sure of the duty he was performing and of his ability to perform it. He had never before been able to feel, as he was feeling now, that in Colin was a repetition of his own boyhood.

As they came to the edge of the alders, he said: "I was a year younger than you when my father started me cutting cordwood."

"Was it alder?" Colin asked.

"No, mostly spruce. Some birch and poplar." They had stopped and Will Ensley was looking around him at the tall, gray-barked alders. "Nothing as big as these," he said. "Except the maples and a few pines, but the pine was mostly gone and we cut the maple into logs, not cordwood. This Pacific Coast is the greatest country in the world for growing trees, except nobody knows enough to take care of it. Log and burn, log and burn and move on, that's all they know."

Colin listened respectfully and with a strong sense of belonging where he was, with his father and in the woods. He looked at the huge, competent hands resting on the axe handle, at the wide black beard jutting forward as his father swung his head slowly to look at the trees. He's the finest axeman in B. C., my old man, Colin thought. Everybody knows that. And he knows everything there is to know about trees. I can't be the same as he is, I'll never be that strong, I'll never be able to learn like he did, from working in every province in Canada where they cut logs. But he can tell me and show me a lot of what he knows and I'm going to learn it.

Will Ensley slid the bright axe to his shoulder and walked across to a tree. He set one hand against the smooth trunk and looked at Colin. "Which way does this one go?" he asked.

Colin looked at the lean of the tree, looked along the ground, then back to the tree again. "Right here," he said and pointed along the line of the tree's lean.

Will Ensley shook his head. "No," he said. "Too many young trees along there. You'll want trees twenty years from now. No sense to breaking those down." He struck four short blows with his axe and there was an X on the side of the tree, clean-edged, deeply cut, perfectly proportioned. "Make your undercut on the mark. Drop her across the lean—there's nothing to hurt there and it'll let your tree down easier."

They went from tree to tree until Will had marked a dozen. "Those'll be enough," he said. "Till you see what you've got. And they'll square away this corner good."

They went back to the first tree and Will Ensley began to put in the undercut. He worked without a sign of effort, yet the bit of the axe drove deep and the hickory handle seemed to bend in the air and the heavy white chips flew out in bright arcs and fell fifteen or twenty feet away. It seemed to Colin that his father had struck not more than twenty or thirty times when the cut was finished—yet the tree was deeply notched, the lower side of the notch perfectly horizontal, the upper sloping to it at an angle of fifty or sixty degrees, the faces of both as smooth as though sliced by two cuts of a giant knife.

"Finish it off," Will said. And Colin went round to the back of the tree and tried to do as his father had done. The alder wood was soft and his sharp axe bit cleanly into it, but he hurried a little and drove his strokes harder than usual in the hope that the chips would fly far out as they had for his father.

"Not so fast," Will said. "And let the weight of the axe work for you." He thought: the boy's grown a lot and he's strong, going to be really strong. Takes after me. He'll have a weak back though—too tall for the big strength he'll have in his shoulders and chest. How does he come to be tall like that and with those great feet of his? I like to see a neat-built man, all in one piece and quick on his feet. The boy'd trip and break his neck on a bridge stringer, leave alone one of them little poles they spike between the bents. He don't get that from Martha nor me. Some say it's the coast climate, makes the kids grow tall and soft like the trees. I don't believe that, but it's a queer thing, just the same. Margaret's taller than her mother too, but she's neat on her feet, not like him.

He looked towards the top branches of the tree, saw them quiver to the axe stroke, and moved a little. The boy's strong, though, and he chops good, clean and good like a man that knows his trade, and he don't seem to tire none. The tree cracked sharply and the top began its slow swing in the line of the undercut. Colin had judged the cut well, leaving the tree strong on the side opposite its lean. The strength held it until it crashed forward and down, broke clear and lay perfectly at right angles to its lean.

"Good," said Will Ensley. "You showed that one who was boss. Could've drove a stake with it."

Colin felt a hot flush of pleasure in his face and for a moment he thought he was going to cry. Will Ensley reached forward and set a hand gently on Colin's shoulder. "You will be a strong man, son," he said. "And great strength is a gift of the Lord. You must learn to use it well."

PART TWO

THE FIRST VALLEY

5

IN spite of Colin's size and increasing strength, cutting the alder was a big job for a boy of his age and it ordered most of his summer holidays. He did not mind that at all. He was always happy when he was cutting it and when Johnny Harris came up to be with him and help he felt a vague resentment and tried to keep Johnny from doing very much. Johnny was a year older than Colin and his physical opposite—a short, thickly built boy, very neat and economical in his movements. He had a round, cheerful face with eyes that were strongly and inescapably blue and a rare, slow smile that showed short, even and very white teeth. Johnny talked little, at any time, but he always seemed at ease with himself and everyone around him. Probably because of this, Colin always felt at ease with him.

Johnny had already left school, to help out on his father's farm on the other side of Blenkinstown. He was used to working and liked working and whenever he came to see Colin and found him cutting alder, he would start in automatically to pile the cordwood or clear away limbs, anything that would keep his hands busy and speed the job along. After a very short while of this Colin would stop working himself and suggest that they do something else. Johnny would smile happily and agree, or else make a suggestion of his own, and they would go off to fish or swim or simply walk in search of anything at all. But once he said: "Look, Colin, why don't you let me help and get this darn job done with? Then we could go places any time."

The question embarrassed Colin. He had not admitted, even to himself, that cutting the alder was an ever-ready excuse to get away by himself and he did not want to admit to Johnny that he loved the work, the sharp, clean bite of the axe-strokes, the flight of white chips from the deepening cut, the scent of crushed leaves and stripped bark; or that he wanted the whole job to be his own achievement, from start to finish. He said: "You've got your own work to do at home. I don't have to hurry any with this job. Times like this, when you're free, we may as well go places and do things."

This was how it happened that Colin made his first attempt to climb the mountain with Johnny, not with Margaret. They started without plan or preparation, at about two o'clock one afternoon, simply turning away from the piles of cordwood and into the brush. They crossed the alder flat quickly and were climbing steeply as soon as they left it. Colin led the way, following the draw to which the creek had brought them.

Because he had seen the start of the slope from the flat and because he had made the climb so often in his mind, this first part seemed almost familiar to him. The draw was shallow at the start and they kept very close to the creek, crossing it from time to time to find easier going. The timber was mainly hemlock, but it was tall and straight and mature and little brush grew under

4 4

it. The draw grew deeper as they climbed and they worked away from the creek, keeping it always on the right of them, to the south. Then they came to a bench, where the creek spread in swampy ground and salmonberry bushes and devil's clubs grew thickly. On the far side of the bench they came to the first rock bluffs.

So far they had not stopped at all, but Colin hesitated at the foot of the bluffs. Johnny was breathing hard and his face was flushed. "Don't you ever get tired?" he said. "Let's take a spell."

"We started out so late I thought we ought to step on it," Colin said. They sat down on a slab of rock just below the bluff.

"You're not figuring to make it to the top, are you?" Johnny asked.

"I suppose not," Colin said slowly. "I hadn't figured much about it—just that we'd see how far we could get."

"We couldn't make it under a whole day," Johnny said. "Maybe not then."

"We can learn something about how it is today. Then we can take a day out sometime and do it right."

"Where'd you get the idea from anyway?" Johnny asked. "What do you reckon to find up there?"

"Nothing. I just want to see what it looks like." Colin searched himself for words to tell Johnny what he wanted of the mountain and why he wanted it, but he could find none that made sense. It was easy to see the mountain from Blenkinstown and it was not in any way a spectacular mountain. No one had even bothered to give it a name, so far as Colin knew. Its top was a rounded height rather than a peak, separated only slightly from the range that climbed back to divide Strathmore Valley, where the Blenkin Logging company operated, from the larger valley of the Wind River, to the north. The mountain was heavily timbered to within about a thousand feet of its top and from there on the timber thinned rapidly to bare gray rock that was snow-covered only in winter and early spring. Colin knew he wanted to come out to the scattered timber and the bare rock, to see and touch the lonely wind-torn trees that Mildred Hanson said grew in such places, to search the rock for the alpine plants she had described and to find the freedom of looking far out over Blenkinstown to

45

other mountains and other valleys. There was nothing in all that you could tell anyone about and he said: "I've always wanted to get up there. I think it would be different from down here. The air'd be different and you'd see things differently. Heck, I don't know why I want to get up there. I just do."

"That's O.K.," Johnny said. "My dad always says a man don't have to account for everything he wants to do. I guess I know how you feel."

They found a way up between the bluffs along the creek, climbing the damp and slippery rock slabs easily enough. Colin was happy because this was different from anything he had done before and the steepness of the climb gave him a sense of achievement. They came to another bench at the top of the bluffs and Johnny said: "I get a kick out of that. Suppose we'll find more like it farther up?"

"Should do," Colin told him. "Some a whole lot tougher, I guess. Everybody says mountains get steeper near the top."

But they climbed for another hour, following the creek through its timbered draw, skirting occasional bluffs and crossing several benches without finding any real difficulty. They turned then and made their swift way back to the routine of chores and supper, but Colin knew the day had been made important to him forever, because now he would certainly climb the mountain. It was far forward in him now, a real purpose, no longer a dream that might fade beyond recall at a moment's notice.

THE logging company was still running when school started in September. There were rumors of bankruptcy and shutdown, but Will Ensley worked steadily until an early snow came in November, forcing a shutdown that seemed likely to last over Christmas. The camps were still closed at the end of January, though the weather had been good and there was little snow in the woods.

Most of the married men who lived near Blenkinstown clung to hope of some kind through the early spring months; there were rumors again—a bunch of big shots coming up from town to look the place over; ten sets of fallers due on the Wednesday boat; a scow-load of steel had come in for the new line. But when Will Ensley and Earl Mayhew went up to the beach camp they found only old McPherson, the bookkeeper; he told them he knew nothing, nothing except he was drawing ninety bucks a month as caretaker. Mike Varchuk laughed when Earl Mayhew told him that. "She won't roll a wheel up there or put fire under a boiler, not till they get good and ready. They starve you out first, make you good and hungry. Then you go back and work for any wages they say, just to get full belly again. You see. She all happen before."

Mike Varchuk talked more than ever. Will Ensley still did not care for the things he said, but he found himself remembering them and trying to fit them in to what was happening. He could not make them fit, because he still believed in himself, believed in his strength and in his skill at his craft, and in the worth and importance of his craft. He believed that there was work to be done in the world; if a man could do the work he would be paid for it. The things Mike Varchuk said matched nothing in Will Ensley's experience and they were wicked, against God and against God's order. In spite of the easy laughter that Mike always found to go with them they were bitterness and weakness—the excuses, Will felt, of a man who was not a good worker.

Martha Ensley recognized the thing for what it was from the start. She was a child of a solid pioneer family and she had grown up to know her world as alternations of hardship and prosperity. The bitter periods were never far away, even in the highest prosperity; they could come suddenly, through fire or storm or sudden death, as well as by the slower, mysterious paralysis that crept periodically from the cities, out to farms and woods and even the salt water, cutting away the prices of logs and fish and beef cattle until there was no hire for men and no return for work. She was wise and experienced in meeting such times and she did her best to prepare for them when things were going well.

She warned Colin and Margaret of what might be ahead one day early in February. They had come in wet and cold from the walk from school and they were hungry and she had bread and jam and tea ready for them in the kitchen.

"You must be careful not to bother your father," she said. "He's worried and I'm afraid it's going to get worse."

4 7

"Some of the kids were saying the camps are going to open next week," Margaret said.

"They've been saying that since before Christmas," Colin told her.

"I don't suppose anyone really knows," Martha said. "But I've seen all this happen before and it's going to be very hard on your father. It's always hard on the men."

"What happens when nobody's working?" Margaret asked.

"Your father will find work," Martha said. "It won't be easy to find and there won't be the same steady wages he's been getting. All those things worry a man with a family."

Colin slumped a little farther down in his chair. There had been long shutdowns before, for fire season and for snow over Christmas, and he remembered his father's frowning silence and increasing irritability as the weeks wore on. They were stretched beyond that stage already and he was trying to picture what was ahead. "Won't we have enough money for things we have to have?" he asked. "Like food and clothes?" He felt a little ashamed because the idea seemed exciting, yet he knew his mother was worried.

"We'll manage," Martha said. "No one needs to starve in this country. But we'll have to make everything count."

"I could leave school and get a job," Margaret said.

Colin straightened in his chair. "So could I. Let me do it, Ma. She's much smarter in school than me."

Martha spoke sharply. "You can both of you put that sort of nonsense right out of your heads. As long as I have anything to do with it you'll stay in school and do your work properly. There may be a little more to do around here to keep things going, but the most important thing is to keep your father cheerful—do what he says and never complain in front of him." That's enough, she thought. They know him as well as I do. "Run along and do the chores. For all I know they'll be working again within a week and we shall have forgotten all about it."

"It's happening all over," Margaret said. "It can't be any worse for us than for other people." She stood up. "Come on, Colin."

Martha went to the window and watched them as they crossed the field towards the barn. They had taken the thing farther than she had meant them to, realized more of it than she was ready to admit to herself yet. But she was not altogether sorry. Her defenses were good. The farm would mean a lot—cows, chickens, fruit trees, garden—and the children could do much of the work. Will was the one who would suffer—Will's pride and power and faith in himself, Will's black strength, his black and exacting God. As she had before, Martha measured Will's God against her own, though without recognizing that they were different Gods. He gives us different kinds of strength, she thought, and if another kind of strength is better than Will's kind for a little while, he mustn't know it. That must be part of the other strength, to keep him from knowing.

6

IT seemed at first that Will Ensley was right in his belief that a skilled workman need never be without work. His ability was well known around Blenkinstown and several people asked him to do small jobs of hewing and building. They apologized because the jobs were small and the pay was low, but Will had never learned to measure himself in terms of wages and so long as the jobs were worthy of his axe he was contented enough. He was helped, too, by his confidence that the company would start work again; the small jobs merely filled in until that time and the low wages were at once a subsistence for his family and a service to his neighbors.

But as the months went on the jobs became fewer and smaller and once or twice the wages were no more than a promise to pay. In June Will went along to Earl Mayhew's house.

"I'm going to walk up to the beach camp," he told Earl. "Want to come along?"

The two men said very little as they walked. There was little that needed to be said. Each knew what he was going to look for, and each knew what was in the other's mind.

They reached the camp between rain showers and found it silent and empty in the June sunshine. There was no smoke from the stove-pipe over McPherson's cabin and they found the door locked when they tried it.

They turned and walked out along the wharf. There were logs in the water, two or three sections made up and ready for the tug. "Side Two stuff," Earl said. "The last we put in. Can't be much call for logs or they'd have taken them out."

The cables on the dumping rig were red with rust and there was rust on the casing of the blocks. Will looked down at the piles under the wharf. "The worms will be in 'em good," he said. "It's four years since we put in any new piles."

They turned and walked back along the track to the car-shop and the roundhouse. The big Baldwin and two Shay locomotives were inside, black and silent.

"Reminds me of a graveyard," Earl said. "A locomotive without steam up is the deadest thing there is—deader than a dead person."

"Must figure to use 'em again some time," Will said. "They put paint and grease on before they tied 'em up. Where's Number Three?"

They walked along a short spur line and found Number Three, a small Climax locomotive, painted gleaming black and with fresh gilt on the figure 3. The track had been seldom used at any time and the brush grew thickly to the edge of it. A strong shoot of salmonberry, green in the sunlight and still wet from the shower, curved gracefully right across the front of the little locomotive. Earl turned away. "Looks like she's going to be a tough one," he said.

Will knew that he meant the winter ahead.

FOR Colin and Margaret life was little different. Their father was at home more often but he kept away from the house during working hours, coming back only just in time to clean up for the evening meal. Martha worked harder than usual in her garden and was sometimes tired to exhaustion when they came home from school; but she seemed happier than she had ever seemed, quicker in her movements, surer and more purposeful in her planning. It was a gradual, almost imperceptible adjustment to the new conditions, as Martha intended it should be. She had begun to build the farm steadily, yet without spending money. She had bartered cream for setting eggs and doubled her flock of chickens. Colin and Margaret were raising calves and hoeing root crops. The fuel supply was sure and cost nothing except Colin's work. Everything that could be canned or stored or preserved was harvested in its season and set away for the winter.

Colin found his life fuller and more real to him and he was happier for it. He did his work easily at school, finding new satisfactions in it, but he did not grow out of carelessness or away from the long daydreams that crept into his mind with every lapse of attention. Mildred Hanson's calm competence had almost effaced memory of that air-built moment between them; Colin remembered it, but it became less and less believable to him. Sometimes, looking at her cool and inaccessible loveliness, he tried deliberately to recall the moment of courage that had let him touch her. He became instantly afraid then, and awed and unbelieving. He tried to crush the desire away from him by assessing its presumption and wickedness. The memory of her warmth and firmness under his hand would become strong and stirring and for a moment he could believe again that she had responded to his touch. Then memory would fade in disbelief. His mind would deny it because Mildred herself so plainly denied it in everything she was and did.

Mildred also denied her clear memory of what had happened, forcing it away from her with a control Colin did not possess. But she remembered the loneliness into which she had sent him and which must have been in him when he touched her. She saw it in him again, often, as he sat in class or walked about the schoolyard and always there was something in her, far deeper than any teacher's obligation or simple human pity, that longed to reach out and lift it from him. Because she did neither more nor less than any teacher would have done, she believed herself secure from the attraction she still felt for him.

Mildred spent several hours each week with Margaret, drawing her and rounding her beyond the narrow teaching limits of a small country school. Their friendship grew steadily and they often found themselves talking simply as friends rather than as pupil and teacher. Mildred welcomed this and worked quite deliberately towards it, not merely because she was fond of Margaret, but because she felt that Margaret could make more growth in it than she could in more orthodox study. They talked freely of music and painting and literature, drawing on Mildred's collection of books and the school's small library. They talked of religion, testing the differences between the Gods of Will and Martha and those of Mildred's Lutheran parents and friends. They talked of what was happening around them, of the broken stock markets, the innumerable remedies that innumerable prophets were proclaiming, of unemployment and strikes and misery, and of what was happening to Blenkinstown. Mildred's salary had been cut already, but she was not politically minded and she was not bitter. "It can't last here," she told Margaret. "Because the town depends on something essential. People have to have lumber. They can't live without stores and houses and bridges. They have to have new roofs and boxes to put things in, and paper to print news on."

Margaret laughed. "You talk like Father," she said. "He says over and over 'The world can't get by without logs and lumber.' I think maybe it can get by on a lot less than it's used to."

"What's happened to your father? I used to see him going past here every morning on his way to work."

"He and Mr. Mayhew have taken on some kind of contract," Margaret said. "They're cutting alder for a furniture factory. I don't think it's working out very well."

Mildred looked at her anxiously. "If it keeps on will you and Colin stop school?"

"Mother won't hear of it. Colin wants to go out and work, but that's silly—there isn't any work. And we both can help a lot at home, with the cows and chickens and garden."

"Colin might find a job somehow. He's growing very big and strong even though he is so dreamy and clumsy. You mustn't let him stop school."

"He isn't clumsy," Margaret said. "Not when you see him

working or in the woods. We tried to climb the mountain last week and he walks so much more quietly than I do that I'm ashamed. He doesn't slip on rocks like I do either. He seems to belong there."

Just for a moment Mildred hesitated, then she said: "He could be a great man. I don't know why I'm so sure, but I am. It's there in the way he speaks and looks, but much more in the way he thinks. He doesn't think like any other boy I've ever known."

"Colin?" Margaret spoke the name slowly. "He's so shy and gentle to be great. He's afraid of so many things and so many people. Great men are sure of themselves."

"Not always," Mildred said. "Great men have been weak and sick and blind, they've been half-mad by ordinary standards sometimes, shy and withdrawn and doubtful of themselves very often."

"They all wanted something very much though—to do something or be something. I don't think Colin does."

"A boy doesn't dream the way Colin does unless he wants something."

"Colin dreams all right," Margaret said. "But I don't think he dreams anything practical."

Mildred laughed. "Dreams aren't supposed to be practical, but practical things grow out of them."

"That takes something more than just being able to dream a dream," Margaret said. "Something Colin hasn't got."

"You're too close to him to see it. But I've seen it in some of the things he writes and in some of the things he does. It isn't anything you can name. It's a spark of some kind, it's being different in a special way."

Margaret tried again to think of greatness in Colin, but she could remember only slowness and untidiness and lack of purpose. She felt a sudden irritation because Mildred was so interested in him. "Everybody worries about Colin and makes allowances for him," she said. "I think it's time he did something for himself."

"He has to have a chance to grow into whatever he is," Mildred said. "That's what schools and teachers are for." She felt her deep conviction and it was in her quiet clear voice. "We have to watch them all and make them grow just as far as they can. It doesn't really matter whether I'm right or wrong about Colin. If

5 3

I think there's something special in him I have to help him find it."

"Won't he find it himself if it's there? Doesn't greatness always come out in the end?" Very gently her tone mocked Mildred's intensity.

Mildred hesitated. "No one can know that," she said at last. "I think most great men get help somewhere along the way. And we can't know about the ones who might have been great if they had had help at the right time. Think of the times when only rich people learned to read and write."

"If they had a bright boy in a poor family they made him a bishop's secretary or something. And he went on from there."

"A few maybe. But most of them used up their greatness herding pigs or dreaming dreams or in being good common soldiers for some baron." Mildred laughed. "At least that's what I like to think. I guess any teacher likes to think it. It's a long way from Colin, though. At least, he can read and write."

Margaret had been watching her closely as she spoke. She said: "You're terribly fond of him, aren't you? I mean more than just because he's bright in school?"

The direct simplicity of the question made Mildred flush. She knew that Margaret's mind had asked it, not her emotions, that it was simply a further shrewd point in her argument against Colin's potential greatness; but she knew also that anything she herself thought of Colin was colored by emotion, born of intuition even though nurtured on reason. "Yes," she admitted slowly. "I'm fond of him. He needs help so much. But I should still believe he could be great, even if I weren't fond of him. I get fond of lots of the children. No teacher can help that." That's the truth, she thought, looking into Margaret's dark eyes. It's the truth and it isn't the truth yet I don't really know why it shouldn't be. And I'm sure she can't know why it isn't. She can't know, she isn't old enough to know, and no sister could ever think it of her kid brother.

"I'm fond of him, too," Margaret said. "More than most sisters are of their brother, I think. Lots of people are fond of him. Perhaps that's part of what could make him a great man."

Mildred moved eagerly. "Yes," she said. "It is. It is part of it. All his gentleness is part of it. If you feel it too, it must be."

She hesitated a moment, then went on. "We aren't being fair though. He doesn't have to be great to make it important to help him. That's a stupid big word that doesn't mean much anyway. He just has to be what we both know he is."

7

BY the end of July Will Ensley knew that he and Earl Mayhew were going to make no money out of the alder contract, but they worked on until the job was finished in mid-August. Will said as they loaded the last log: "We won't get taken that way again. We've got to find something that'll make a few dollars next time —if," he added hopefully, "they don't open up soon as the bad fire weather's over."

"There's nothing that says they will," Earl said. "I'm going to get me a fall buck or two for the old lady to put up. They'll start to move down pretty soon now."

Will Ensley had never been a hunter, but Martha had the same thought as Earl—it was less thought than a simple reaction to the season of the year, and the times. Deer hunting had been a routine in her family, intensely pursued in the early fall, fluctuating vaguely through the rest of the year, but always a part of normal living. Her father had hunted and her brothers had hunted; and, though they found sport in the hunting, the family's meat supply had depended upon their success or failure more often than not. Unlike most other Blenkinstown boys of his age, Colin had never hunted, and he felt a sharp surprise when Martha said: "You'll have to shoot some deer this fall, Colin. Your father won't, but that's no reason you shouldn't."

Colin hesitated. "Father won't like it," he said. "And anyway I don't know how to hunt."

"Circumstances alter cases," Martha said grimly in one of her favorite phrases. "You can learn to hunt—Earl Mayhew will soon show you."

"He wouldn't want me along," Colin said.

"Nonsense," Martha said. "I've never yet seen the hunter who wasn't glad to help a boy out that way. When I was a girl every boy learned to hunt just as naturally as he learned to read and write—most of them learned it a good deal better. Your grandfather taught all my brothers to hunt as soon as they were old enough to hold a rifle—there weren't any butcher stores in those days."

Colin moved awkwardly from where he was sitting and crossed the room to the door. "I'll go ask Mr. Mayhew right now," he said. "I'd sure like to learn to hunt." He had thought past the learning and saw himself alone, a rifle over his arm, searching the timber, planning his hunt, finding his buck. It would not be hard. He knew that, because he had seen deer often and easily without thought of hunting them.

"You can use your father's rifle," Martha said and pointed to the Winchester hanging on the wall. "It shoots true even though it's never used."

EARL Mayhew was a good hunter but, like most loggers, a poor woodsman. Standing timber overawed him, even frightened him, and he kept as far as possible to the open logging slash, working the draws and swamps cleverly enough when he had to, but preferring the high grassy ridges even to these. He was pleased and flattered when Colin asked to go along with him.

"The boy'll be good company," he told his wife. "And he'll learn quick."

"I'm sorry for that boy," she said. "He might as well not have a father."

"Will's all right," Earl said uneasily. "Just different from the rest of us—kind of religious and set in his ideas, but he means well enough."

"He's a dark man," Joan Mayhew said. "And a hard man. I wouldn't want to be his child—or his wife. Not for a million dollars."

"He's a man you've got to respect. There's not a finer man at his trade any place. He's got a good house and he's raising a good family."

"He scares me," Joan said. "Him and his beard and his Bible. He scares the boy too and he'd scare Martha if he could, only she's too strong for him. Think of that boy coming to you to learn to hunt. He must be all of fifteen. Any natural father would have started him out years ago. You would have."

"We can't all be the same. Will's a good father—there never was a straighter-living man. If Colin grows up as good he won't come to any harm."

Joan glanced at him impatiently. She was a tall, big-boned woman of about thirty, with a decisive, practical face and the calm assurance that comes to a woman in love with a man less strong than herself. "How you all stick together," she said. "It doesn't matter about Will Ensley—I know he's your partner and I know he's straight. But be kind to that boy. He needs kindness."

The warning was unnecessary, for Earl was naturally a kind and gentle man. Colin hunted with him regularly through the fall months and they killed several deer. Joan Mayhew followed Colin's development with interest that turned at least as much upon Will Ensley as upon Colin. Even in November, after a year of shutdown, the men still half believed that the camp would open up again within weeks; but Joan, like Martha, had recognized the difficulty of the times almost at once and was fully aware of their threat to the security of her family. She sensed the weakness that was hidden under Will Ensley's strength and was almost instinctively afraid of her husband's close association with him. She was genuinely fond of Colin, but she felt that through Earl's interest in him she could reach out against Will.

One Saturday, late in November, she heard Earl come in from hunting with Colin. It was already dark and she had supper on the stove, so she did not go out to him; but she heard him drop a buck from his shoulders in the woodshed and knew that the hunt had been successful. She knew his every action from the sound of it, knew that he had hung the buck on the gambrel, knew that he had slipped his blood-stained coat away from him, taken off his caulked boots, put on the slippers that were waiting

5 7

there. She crossed the room and opened the door then. "It's good you got one," she said. "We need the meat. Supper's ready."

Earl came into the room, walking stiffly and blinking in the light of the gas-lamp. "We got two," he said. "I never saw anything like the way that kid can hunt." He took the kettle from the stove, went to the sink and began to wash.

"Where did you go?" Joan asked him.

"Up to the big burn and along the line of swamps to the Swan Meadow. It was a bad day to hunt too—frost every place in the shade. I wouldn't have bothered with it if it hadn't been the only day the kid's free to go out. Far as that goes I needn't have bothered—he shot them both."

"Colin did? He certainly learns fast. Did you hunt them up for him?"

Earl clamped a towel against his dripping face and laughed. "Let's eat," he said. He was still laughing when he sat down. "I can get my share of deer alongside most men," he said. "But that young Colin makes me look like a two-bit amateur."

Joan put their two plates on the table and sat down with him. "You rate pretty well in my book," she said. "It isn't often you come home without what you went for. But what's this wonderful thing Colin did?"

"I told you it was a tough day to hunt. Well, we didn't work at it much on the way out—just hiked on through to the meadow. Soon as we get there Colin stops and points down to a big buck track going away from the meadow. 'He ain't heading our way,' I told him. 'What we want is tracks going down towards the meadow.' 'You know,' Colin says, 'it's real warm in the sun when you get out of the wind.' Where we were standing was in shadow from that rocky hill on the south side of the meadow, so I said: 'If we keep right on the way we're going we'll come out into the sun again.' Colin didn't even seem to hear that. He said: 'You know, Earl, if I was that buck I'd go find me a sunny place out on the bluffs, sheltered from the wind, and lay there all day till feeding time in the evening.'"

Earl paused to eat, then went on with the story. "He told me he'd follow the track and for me to go round the other side of

5 8

the hill in case the buck heard him and tried to sneak off. I didn't think either of us'd stand much chance, but it seemed as good as anything else, so I started off round the hill like he said. I wasn't more than just round into the sun again when I heard him shoot. And when I got up to him, sure enough, there's a big four-point stretched out in the sun at the base of a bluff. He hadn't even got on to his feet when the kid shot him."

"I've heard you play hunches like that and have them pay off," Joan said.

"Sure I can get me a good hunch sometimes," Earl said. "But not follow a buck's track on a frosty day and shoot him when he still don't know I'm in the same country. Wait till you hear the other one though. It was down this end of the burn, where the big alder and willow thicket runs along the bottom of the draw. We'd gone up on the north side in the morning and were coming back along the south side, down wind from the thicket. Colin stops again for a buck track, going down towards the thicket this time. 'That was made last night,' he said. 'And we didn't cross any track coming out on the other side. I'm sure of that. Likely he's still in there.' So he starts down the trail to follow the track and I find a place up on this ridge where I can see both sides of the draw. Pretty soon there's a shot down in the thicket and I go down there and darned if he hasn't shot this buck too, right on his bed."

"How did he learn it all so fast? You haven't been out more than a dozen times all told."

"That's what gets me," Earl said. "I've noticed it in him before, but it seemed like today he just got his confidence to ask to do things his way. I asked him when we were cleaning the second buck how he learned to track like that. 'Track?' he says. 'It's just the same as hunting the cows when they go back in the alder bottom. Only easier. There's not so many tracks.' That's right enough, I guess, but it doesn't tell why an awkward-looking kid like that can go quiet enough to come up to a deer on its bed on a frosty day. Nor how he can shoot the way he does, just one clean shot in the neck each time. He's a natural hunter, that's all. But what I like about him, he hasn't got enough conceit even to know he's good."

"I'm glad," Joan said. "It ought to be good for him. He's a boy who needs something like that to bring him out."

Earl shook his head doubtfully. "It'll take more than that. Colin's the quiet kind. I never did see a kid take less pride in what he can do."

BECAUSE of the long shutdown, game seasons meant little that year in places like Blenkinstown. The coast country had gone back to hunting its meat and wise game wardens looked the other way, so long as the hunting was done in daylight and no one took more than his reasonable share. People needed meat and there was little money to buy it.

Colin hunted right through the winter, sometimes with Earl, sometimes alone. He liked hunting with Earl. Earl was kind and wise and always the same. Earl laughed easily at things that happened and talked of logging and the men he worked with as though life were all simple and pleasant and natural, as though no hard things really happened and people were never afraid of each other. He was never gloomy and depressed about the shutdown, as Will Ensley was, he was never distant and obsessed with things he would not share. When he was with Earl Colin felt that if he could only finish with school and go to work in the woods, life would have no more problems.

But though he liked being with Earl, Colin enjoyed the hunting most when he was alone, working through a thicket, following out a track, climbing along the open bluffs above the logging slash. And he never forgot that he wanted to hunt in the timber rather than in the open. Earl discouraged him at first. "There's far more deer in the logging works," he would say. "There's more feed for them there than there is in the green timber. Anyway, you'd just lose yourself in the timber." But as time went on and the effortless, unlearned quality of Colin's woodcraft became clear to him, Earl changed his mind. The next trip they made after the day at Swan Meadow he said: "I believe you're going to be one of those guys that really know how to hunt in the woods. Do you still want to try it?"

"Sure I do," Colin said. "It seems more natural that way, as though the deer'd be better up there."

"You could be right about that last," Earl said. "Most of the bucks down here are getting strong. They might be later up around the snow-line, especially if you pick out a spike or a real big one. Meet me back on the grade here by four o'clock, though. I don't want to have to worry about whether you're lost or not."

Colin turned and started on his way at once, half-afraid that Earl might change his mind. He crossed the half-mile of logging slash quickly and entered the timber without thought of hunting, climbing steadily until he could no longer see light through the trees behind him. He stopped then and stood still on the easy slope, looking about him. It was a day of cold rain, with a wind in the treetops that threatened to grow stronger. Everything, logs, moss, salal leaves, the fir and hemlock needles underfoot, was soaking wet. A creek rattled down a draw a few hundred feet away. The wind swept water in great drops from the crowns of the tall trees. But Colin thought only: it is quiet here. None of this is sound. It is part of the woods, part of being free and away from sounds; there is nothing here that I am afraid of.

He went on up the hill, hunting now, traveling in the swift silence that so amazed Earl Mayhew. Colin was not conscious that he traveled silently. Whether or not he was hunting he wanted to see without being seen, hear without being heard; this had grown in him from early childhood until he had strained his clumsiness into a wild animal's habit of breaking stride to avoid any stick or stone or hard object in his path. His eyes were quick about him as he walked and his ears were alert; in spite of his awkwardness he seemed able to pass among leaves without brushing against them, and the sum of his movement was smooth, swift, but little perceptible.

He came into scattered patches of thawing snow and saw fresh deer tracks. There were many tracks and he did not turn aside for them, but merely slowed his pace a little and began to watch more closely than ever. Earl had said it was difficult to see deer in the timber, but Colin had seen them there before and had a picture in his mind of what he was looking for. In a little while he had seen a two-point buck with a doe, then two more does, then another buck, and had passed them all without stirring them to flight. He was glad that Earl had said to wait for a spike or a big

61

buck. This is pure and clean, he thought, and it means something. Perhaps no one has ever stepped right here, where I'm stepping, in the whole history of the world, perhaps no one has ever seen these trees before, no one ever touched this rock till now. If I swing over a little way I shall come to the creek. People have seen that, but not the water I shall see flowing down it and not the ferns that I shall see hanging over it. Mother couldn't come here and Father never would. Margaret would and could, but only if I brought her. This is my own place, this whole hillside under the timber. No one else uses it or wants to use it. There is no one on it to stop me or turn me or tell me, no one to hear me, no one to see me. And the woods go back along the valleys and the hillsides, along the lakes until they run out in rock and snow and ice beyond timberline.

The big buck was feeding on the top of a little fallen cedar. Colin saw him and stopped, but made no move to raise his rifle. I could shoot him, he thought, and still go on, then come back for him later. But it wouldn't be the same. It makes so much noise. And there is the blood and the smell of him would be on me through the rest of the day. It wouldn't be the same. I don't want to shoot him, I don't want to hurt the silence, I don't want to see him dead and see his blood. I hate the blood. But I ought to want to shoot him. We have to have meat and I'm yellow to be afraid of the blood and not to want to shoot. What am I afraid of? The brightness of the blood, or the hotness of it, steaming on the snow? Or his dead eyes and the sound he would make when I put the knife in his throat? I'm not afraid. I've done it all before. Why not today?

The buck looked up and saw Colin, but could not recognize his stillness. He raised his nostrils, tested the wind, bit at the cedar again, but was still uneasy. He moved away, along the little cedar, as though he still meant to feed, but not feeding. He disappeared behind a big fir and Colin saw him only once again, far up the hill, turning to look back.

Colin's mood was built, not broken. I am alone, no one has seen me, no one but me can ever know the buck was there. No one can ever know anything I do back here in the woods. He turned up the hill again and began climbing steadily into deepening snow. He climbed far beyond the last sign of deer, then turned along the hill and hunted the barrenness of the deep snow. The wind grew steadily in the trees and the rain had turned long ago to heavy snowflakes. It was late in the afternoon when fear and shame caught up with him again and turned him, strained and sweating, down the hill. He had to hunt now and find his deer and kill. He did not want to face Martha with the knowledge that he could have killed and had not. He did not want Earl to be able to tell him that it was better to hunt in the open logging works.

8

MARTHA Ensley worked at her garden in the cold rain of a day early in March. She was happy because she loved gardening and it was good to be getting such an early start. The last of the snow had disappeared soon after the end of January; February had been cold and sunny; now March brought rain, a cold rain still, not a growing rain, but there were many things to be done in the two or three weeks before it would be time to plant seeds.

The camps had opened up again and Will had been working at his old job for nearly three weeks. Wages were very low and the men were organizing and there was strike talk. Even Will, who had little use for unions, had shown some interest. "It's no better than starvation wages," he had told Martha. "Maybe they can't pay any more and keep running—that's for us to find out. But if there's something to spare the men should have it. The laborer is worthy of his hire."

Martha broke a clod of wet earth with her fork. There'll be fighting of some sort before it's all over, she thought; men always come to that. But if they work for a little while it'll be a help.

Will's got to get his pride back and he'll never find it in the way this last year has been. There's a lot to be thankful for, though. There's been plenty to eat and a good roof over our heads and the children are still in school. Perhaps it was wrong to make Colin start hunting; sometimes Will hates him when he brings in a deer. No one could have guessed he'd be so good at it; Earl says he's a natural hunter, the best he has ever seen. In some ways he's a lot like brother Jim was, the quiet kind; they always make good hunters. But Jim was a much neater man than Colin, he was never all feet and hands and loose joints like Colin is, not even when he was a boy. It must be in the way they think more than what they do, and in how good their eyes are. Colin has good eyes, like Jim's; he is always seeing something before anyone else —a hawk over the chickens or a deer in the pasture or the first robin that comes.

She lifted a forkload of the heavy, clinging earth, drew in her breath sharply, set the fork down and leaned against its handle. It's too wet, she told herself, too wet and heavy. She breathed carefully, to keep the pain away while she rested. In a little while her breathing was calm again and she went back to her digging.

She forced her thought straight on, as though there had been no interruption. It has been bad for Will to feel that Colin was the man of the family when he came in with a deer. He wouldn't ever have felt that in ordinary times, and he wouldn't have allowed Colin to go hunting in ordinary times. But there wasn't meat without that and the boy was doing it on his Saturdays, so there wasn't anything he could say. And it isn't as though Will could have taken to going out himself after all these years. He's not the kind to change easily, over anything, and that's a good thing most of the time; it makes for a steady man, a good worker and a good family man. But it's hardest of all on that kind when things go wrong.

Will is a good family man. He's always been good to the children; he believes in God in his old-fashioned way, really believes in God, and he's tried to pass that on to them. He never swears in front of them, they've never seen him drunk or careless with himself, the way so many men are. He earns good wages, comes home when his work's done and brings his money with him. He's a good husband and a good father. It's a lot to be thankful for.

I am thankful, truly thankful. I only wish . . . I only wish he could be closer to us, more part of us. I love Will. I would have liked to hold him close to me sometimes and to be held sometimes. I would like to sit with my hand in his sometimes, just for no reason except that we are close. But it doesn't happen, it can't happen now. I suppose I'm still afraid of him in a way, the same way I was before we were married. I used to think then that it would change. He's never done anything to make me afraid, but it hasn't really changed. Perhaps I should have tried harder—I know I should. Perhaps it can still happen, we can still come close. I'm an old woman to be thinking such thoughts; it's hardly respectable to think them at my age. But we poor weak humans need some other human close to us and I don't think any God would call that sin.

Martha knew she was crying, but there was no acuteness of grief or misery in her tears, only regret for what might have been and hope for what might still be. Her thoughts were prayer now, prayer offered silently in the spring rain and as naturally as thought, without even a lifting of her face to pray. Not for me, O God, not for me, but for Colin. Let him come closer to his father and his father closer to him. Give him cause to look up to his father and respect him and feel strength from him, as a boy should. He needs that help more even than most boys do. Colin's a strange boy, too strange and moody for the world to be easy on him. He needs some strength of his own, just as Will needs it and finds it in his work. Only Colin needs more than just strength in his body and skill in his hands. If he could be more like Margaret, sure of himself as she is, less of a dreamer; he will grow out of all that, I know, and find his place, but he needs help, the kind of help a boy gets from being close to his father. In some ways Will is more of a child than Colin ever will be again, but Will has his place in the world; he knows his work and his work gives him his place and lets him earn all that money he has been bringing home for so many years—just the work of his hands and his big muscles, and a way of thinking about caps and stringers and donkey-sleds.

Will is a good man and I should be content for Colin to grow into a man like him, except that Colin is not a man like Will; he is less like Will even than Margaret is and he has to find something more if he is ever to be a full man and a happy man. I don't believe it is wrong to ask that for my child. I ask it for his need, not just in a mother's pride and in the hope we all have that our children will grow up to be finer people than we are.

Martha stood quite still for a moment, her hands folded on the handle of her digging fork and her body bent forward over them. Her face was strained, but she was no longer crying. Her prayer worried her a little, as her prayers often did. She wondered if it might not be too direct and practical and personal. She knew she had to stop her gardening and go back to the house and sit down for a little while, and she knew that she had to make another prayer: Give me strength, Jesus, to go on doing all that I have to do. It happens so quickly now, I get tired so long before anything is finished and my heart beats so fast over little things even, that I'm afraid. They need me, especially in this time when things are so hard for Will and while Colin and Margaret are still growing up. Give me strength to go on until everything is right and safe again.

She walked slowly and carefully up towards the house, still stooping forward a little because that seemed to ease the pain in her chest, and with her hands thrust into the opposite sleeves of her coat, to shield them from the cold rain. If I make a cup of tea, she told herself, and sit down quietly with it for ten or fifteen minutes, I shall be strong and ready again when the children get home from school.

NEITHER the children nor Will Ensley suspected that Martha was sick. She had always worked hard, from the first thing in the morning until after supper, and she had always stopped several times during the day to sit down with a cup of tea. She allowed herself to move only a little less briskly now and she brewed an extra cup of tea and sat down with it only when the pain of her heart forced her to. After the first recognition of her trouble Martha herself was able to forget about it, almost to deny it. She told herself that it was natural to slow down a little at her age and she convinced herself that she could remember for

66

years back the straining at her chest and the dizziness that came on her when she did too much.

The camps worked steadily through the spring and into the summer. Will Ensley's pay-checks were the smallest he had ever brought home, but he was working at his own job in the way that he knew and trusted and he found once again a sense of security and peace of mind in the routine of his working days and the clear headship of his family.

For Colin and Margaret the summer passed quietly and was little different from the previous summer except in the regularity of their father's comings and going. He was easier with them, less moody than in the previous year; but he had become active in the union and while he found a certain satisfaction in the authority and responsibility that this gave him, his conscience was never entirely calm under it; at one moment he gloried in the sense that he was serving his fellow workers, in the next he remembered the wordy violence of leaders like Mike Varchuk and the paid organizer, Miller, and felt that association with them was a betrayal of his whole life.

Martha made no concession at all to the fact that Will was working for regular wages again. She forced every part of the farm and garden exactly as she had the previous year and kept Colin and Margaret working as steadily at it.

Neither Colin nor Margaret was deeply conscious of any fundamental change in the way the family lived. Martha herself had anticipated the change, accepted it when it came and put her counter measures to work; but to her it was less a change than a part of life, a personal and family problem that could be solved within the family. She was aware that other families were facing similar problems and she helped when she could the Mayhews, the Meldrums, the Sorettos and others of her neighbors; and, just as naturally, she expected and accepted the occasional help they could offer. It was all done without organization, without sense of effort or obligation; it was a simple projection of the pioneer's reaction to adversity, no more than a phase of normality.

Margaret accepted a responsibility for the family that was only a little less than Martha's because it grew from her own wish to test and prove the strength and ability she felt within herself. At

6 7

times she wished she had Martha's responsibility to the full—a family of her own and the need to plan and work for it. It seemed to her she would do it differently, with everything planned and organized instead of growing out of a mixture of experience and tradition. It irritated and worried her to see Martha doing so much herself; she seemed to go on and on through the days, always finding things to do and doing them because she found them rather than reminding someone else to do them. Like clearing out the chicken-house when Colin left it too long; and picking and canning all the cherries when Margaret herself should have done it over the previous week end.

Then, just for a moment, she saw her Mother's problem more clearly. It isn't so easy to organize a family like this, she thought. Dad's always so deep in his own affairs he doesn't notice what's going on; he never works around the place, the way Mr. Mayhew does at his place. And Colin's so absent-minded; nothing could change that. I'm just as bad, always going out somewhere or studying at home, studying with Mr. Siddons, studying with Mildred.

I think Mildred's sort of crazy about Colin; that sounds silly, but it's not; she looks quite different when she's talking about him, her voice goes very soft and you can see in her eyes that she's looking at him even though he isn't there. Colin won't talk about her. He doesn't blush every time he sees her, the way he used to, and he's not as awkward with her as he is with lots of people; but there's something tight and straining inside of him and sometimes, when he thinks no one is watching, he sits and looks at her as though he thought he would never see her again.

Perhaps I imagine some of that. Perhaps I'm jealous of Colin with Mildred because she talks about him so often and seems to bring him between us. I must be or I wouldn't feel this way when I know she wants to help him. Yet it makes me afraid for him, as though she was going to hurt him instead of help him.

COLIN lay on his back under a maple tree beside the creek in the alder flat. It was a very hot day in July and he had just come down from the mountain, after climbing to where he and Margaret had turned back the previous summer. Traveling by himself had been easy, much easier than with Margaret or Johnny Harris. He could have gone on farther, perhaps right to the top. But he had promised Margaret they would do it together and had turned back faithfully just beyond the place she had failed to cross.

He tried to understand the sudden fear that had broken her confidence on the narrow ledge, and could not. But tomorrow would be different. They would have the rope and she would know she was safe and cross easily. Tomorrow, his mind said, tomorrow, tomorrow. Before this time tomorrow. It's hard to believe that. It will be clear of timber up there, and we shall see over into Wind River and the big lake and all the way to the mountains at the head of the valley. And the little trees will be flat and twisted and there will be snow in the shady places and flowers where it's sunny. There will be wind and clear air and high clouds. And no one else near.

He felt his heart pounding at his chest and his breath short and his body hot, hotter than it had been when he was climbing. He moved restlessly, trying to break the strain of excitement and expectation. It seemed weakness to him, dangerously close to fear, and he remembered it had touched him just as fiercely when he had left Earl to hunt alone for the first time.

He lay back, feeling the moist earth against his shoulder blades, and gradually his heart slowed and his body relaxed. He could feel the strain of his climb now, pleasantly, in the muscles of his thighs and belly and buttocks. He was conscious of the day's achievement, of having earned this rest, this distant, pleasant awareness of his body. Looking up through the green of the maple leaves over him, he saw blue sky and white clouds. As he had half-known they would, these made him think of Mildred Hanson. He let himself think of her, with his body as well as his mind. His body had earned this right by its struggle with the hill, just as one of Arthur's knights might have earned a similar right in triumph over some darker, stronger opponent. Momentarily Colin tried to deny that the right was his, but his body told him plainly that it was and he yielded to it, remembering other such yieldings when he had lain in bed on winter nights. The strain was across his shoulders then, as well as in legs and thighs, from carrying his deer

69

out of the woods, and his face was hot and stretched with burn of wind and cold rain. But the right was the same, irresistible and safer with each use, the body's reward for successful endeavor, the mind's delight in the setting of soft, imagined things against the fresh memory of harsh and challenging things.

9

THE day that Colin and Margaret started to climb the mountain was hot and dry and still. They milked very early, laughing at the surprise of the cows and their unaccustomed hesitation about coming into the barn.

"We shan't get as much milk," Margaret said. "But we'll make it up tonight so long as we get home on time."

"We won't. Not unless we quit again."

"We've got to be back for supper. Mr. Grant's coming in and he told Mother he wants to see you."

"There's always something to wreck it," Colin said. "I should have gone on yesterday, when I had the chance."

"I won't quit on you," she said. "I promise I won't."

The shadows were still very long and there were tiny pockets of mist here and there along the creek as they crossed the alder flat. The intense stillness of a hot day's dawn was everywhere about them and small birds flickered among the trees and brush near the creek, feeding actively ahead of the day's heat. Colin walked his own swift, awkward pace across the flat and Margaret followed in silence; she knew he was still irritated by the thought that they had to be back by supper time, not so much because it reduced their chances of reaching the top of the mountain as because it set a limit to the day's freedom; but she knew also that he would forget this in time, as they climbed away from the flat and he began to let his eyes and mind work upon the things of the hillside.

Colin in the woods and Colin at school are two quite different people, Margaret thought as she watched his angular back and shoulders under the faded blue shirt. Generally I think of him as a baby, weak and shy and almost helpless. You never know what he's going to do—stumble over something, break something, spill something; he is sure to stand wordless when he ought to say something, or blurt something out when he ought to keep quiet; his clothes and his hair are always untidy and he is afraid of people and things that couldn't possibly hurt him. In the woods you don't notice any of that. He isn't afraid of anything; he always knows what he is going to do. Walking behind him like this I feel as though he would do anything he could possibly have to do, solve any difficulty or danger that could come up. He still looks awkward, his clothes are still a mess, his hair is still untidy, but none of that seems to matter. When I see him like this I think Mildred's right about him; I believe he could *be* something. But he can't be something by running away from everything and that's what he's doing here, today, climbing the mountain, even though he is good at it.

They had crossed a bench and were climbing round the first easy bluffs when Colin turned round and asked: "Want a rest?"

"No," she said. "Not unless you do."

"We'll take one anyway. There's lots of time."

They sat side by side on moss-covered rock and Colin said: "There's a mink around, quite close."

She looked at him in mild surprise. "Did you see it?"

"No," he said. "Can't you smell anything?"

"That musty smell, you mean? Is that what it is?"

Colin nodded. "Sure. He's quite close, just a little way up the bluff from us. I heard him as we came up. That's why I stopped."

Margaret was silent for a moment, then she said: "Why did you stop? We might have seen him if we had gone on."

"I don't know," Colin said slowly. "Because he was scared, I suppose. He must have been or he wouldn't have made the noise and let out his scent. It isn't very nice to scare things. Anyway, you see things best when they don't know you're there, not by chasing them."

Margaret picked up a little stick and probed at the dry moss between her feet. "I don't see how you know all those things. I mean about the noise a mink makes and the way it smells and what it's doing just from hearing it."

"I've seen them."

"Where? I never have."

"Along the creek sometimes. And down near the beach. It's quite easy to see things when you're alone and quiet, and when there's plenty of time." He stood up and looked ahead, up the bluffs. "Only there never is plenty of time," he said. "Let's get going again. Once we've passed this bluff we can work back to the creek. It'll be cool along the creek."

When they found the creek it was an easy, slanting funnel in damp rock, steadily noisy in little cascades that fell into basins of clearest water. "It goes a long way like this," Colin said. "I didn't try it before yesterday because I thought it might run into a straight bluff somewhere. But it doesn't."

He turned away again and climbed on, making little sound even on the bare rock, his feet always sure, never slipping. Behind him Margaret climbed her best, stretching her legs to find the footholds he had found easily, using her hands and arms to help her. She was breathing hard and she felt very hot, in spite of the cool dampness around her and the cool sound of the water, but she said nothing and climbed on. There was wind in the trees now, summer wind, fresh and strong but without violence. Fire wind, she thought. That's why they are going to shut the camps down again. Dry weather and the steady westerlies, Dad said last night. They've got to do it, he said; even a cable running over a stump could set a fire and the wind would drive it out of control in no time. They had been working for two weeks now on the early shift, starting out at two in the morning to catch the night's humidity, but even that was not safe any more and this morning they had not gone out.

Margaret stopped thinking and gave her whole effort to climbing. Climb and climb and climb, her mind said, won't he ever stop and rest? I can't ask him to, after what I said in the barn

7 2

this morning and after what happened last time. But in a little while Colin looked back and saw how far below him she was. He waited for her and as she came up to him she said: "Couldn't we stop for a minute?"

He pointed up. "Just a little farther. There's a flat place before the next climb."

So they went on and came out of the funnel of the creek to a broad sunny bench. Colin lay down and she lay beside him in the bright sunshine, watching the branches of the firs and hemlocks move in the wind against the blue sky while her lungs strained to fill themselves and calm her body.

After a little while, Colin said: "We're almost up to where we turned back last time. Do you want to try it again?"

Margaret lay quite still, her eyes closed, remembering the steep place that had stopped her, the six-inch ledge, and the straight face above it that had seemed to push her outwards until she dared not move along it either way. "We've got to, haven't we?" she asked quietly.

"There's a way round it," Colin said. "It'll take much longer."

"We've got lots of time, haven't we? It isn't noon yet and we're quite high."

"We don't know," Colin said patiently. "We don't know what we may run into."

He's going to make me decide, Margaret thought, and I wish he wouldn't. It's an awful feeling when you're afraid of falling and you can't move. It doesn't happen to him. I remember climbing trees with him and climbing on the roof of the barn and he never got scared or seemed to think anything of it at all. It's nice lying here, resting and feeling the wind and knowing I can see the blue water away down below there through the trees if I want to sit up and look. It's far enough really. Yet I want to go on, just as much as he does. No, not as much. I want to go on and see something I haven't seen before; it's much more than that with him, much more. I don't know exactly how or why, except that it's in him and part of him. But I can tell how important it is simply because he keeps so calm about it now we've started.

"Let's go the hard way," she said at last. "We've got the rope this time and I won't be stupid about it again."

7 3

"It won't be so hard," Colin said. "It never is the second time."

Margaret sat up. "Not for you maybe. I'm not so sure about me."

An experienced rock-climber would have found no difficulty at all in the bad place. It started easily, a long, steep rock-slide cutting into the face of a gray cliff. They climbed it cheerfully, stopping to look back over the treetops to the islands and water far below them and the high mountains of Vancouver Island beyond the smaller islands. Blenkinstown was tiny and far away under the smoke of its two sawmills; the slope of the hill below them still hid the farm, but Colin said: "We'll see it from a little higher up. I'll show you."

Margaret thought: I wish we could go on right to the top like this, just climbing over boulders, with nothing to worry about except getting out of breath. But they were at the source of the slide already and Colin had stopped. There was a rock face in front of them now, and on the left a wall of rock and on the right another face of rock with a slanting, narrow ledge across it. By crossing on the ledge, Colin had said, they could come to another funnel that made easy climbing to the top of the cliff. Margaret looked at the place and remembered. Last year she had stopped twenty feet out along the ledge, frozen by fear of falling, and Colin had come back to stand beside her, touching her, speaking gently and calmly until she was able to move back to safety, his voice guiding her at least as strongly as the grip of his hand on her arm.

He said now: "This is where we use the rope."

He lifted the loose coils over his head, freed an end and passed it to her. "Round your waist," he said. "I'll go across with the other end and take a couple of wraps around something solid." He bent down to fasten one of his shoes, then looked up at her, smiling. "You won't need it, you know. It's just to make you feel good."

"I know," Margaret said. "I'm going to be all right. I was just silly last time." She thought: I've never seen him smile like that before. He hardly ever smiles and when he does he sort of hesitates and looks down. But now I feel as if his smile had touched me and gone on inside me and made me better than I really am.

Colin stood up and turned away towards the ledge along the rock face. She noticed that the end of the rope was in his hand, not tied around him. "When you come," he said, "don't hurry. And don't think any more of it than when you walk those cross-braces in the barn. It's easier, really."

Margaret watched him step out on to the ledge. The first few feet were wide enough for him to walk easily, then he had to turn in towards the face and move sideways for fifteen or twenty feet until the rock footing widened again. He went without hesitation, keeping his body very straight, balanced on the balls of his feet, his hands easily at his sides. Margaret watched him, half-expecting him to trip or stumble, knowing that he would not. I should have made him tie the rope to himself, she thought. He can't be so sure as he seems up here when he's so different everywhere else. Yet he is, and I know he is. Everywhere else he is my little brother and I have to watch for him and worry for him; now he's suddenly like an older brother, much older, much surer, much stronger. He doesn't know anything about mountains; he can't know because he has hardly been in them any more than I have. Yet I believe in everything he says and does—he doesn't even give me a chance not to.

Colin had crossed the narrow part of the ledge and was walking easily where it widened again. She saw him lean forward for a moment with the rope in both hands, then he straightened and looked back to her. "All set," he said. "Take lots of time and don't think about anything except getting across."

Margaret stepped hesitantly on to the ledge, then forced herself into firm movement over the easy part. She turned to face into the bluff much sooner than Colin had and began to edge her way along, her arms stretched out and the palms of her hands against the rock face. She felt her legs quivering and the muscles of her thighs seemed soft and useless in spite of the effort she was forcing upon them. The rock seemed to lean towards her and force her outwards and she felt terror growing in her. It's because I'm a girl, she thought; he shouldn't expect me to do it; my breasts make all the difference, I can't get close to the rock like he can. But it's my head that's touching the rock, not my breasts. It's just that my legs aren't strong like his. I'm not going to quit

7 5

again, I'm not going to, I'd rather fall all that awful way down and break to pieces than quit.

Colin's voice reached her, calm and easy and soft. "Stand straight, Marge, don't lean in so much. Stand straight and balance. It's easy that way."

She stood quite still, listening to him, feeling the panic draw away from her. She forced herself to straighten back, slowly, outwards, away from the rock, until her weight was squarely on her feet again. Then, quite suddenly, it was easy. The balance of her body told her she was secure; secure, upright, relaxed as Colin had been when he crossed. She let her hands fall away almost to her sides, holding them out only a little, the palms turned inwards. Her eyes looked straight at the rock from a few inches away. She moved her feet, moved them again and confidence grew in her. The ledge widened and she was across.

She found Colin standing at the base of a deep cleft in the rock that climbed away between narrowing walls to a distant slit of light. They stood side by side for a moment, then Margaret pointed up the cleft and asked: "Is that the way we go?"

Colin nodded. "It's the only way there is from here. And it's easy, at least for the first part."

"Shall I take the rope off?"

"Yes," he said. "We'll put it on again if we need to."

For several hundred feet they were able to climb side by side. The floor of the cleft was a sloping mass of raw boulders, varying from a few inches up to twenty feet or more in diameter, angularly shaped, solidly wedged together. It was damp in the cleft and the sunlight seemed very far away; a few ferns grew palely here and there and there were mosses and lichens in the drier places, but otherwise there was nothing to shield the rawness of the rocks. Margaret felt awed by the place, by its silence and by the hugeness of everything in it—its boulders, its walls, its height, the gigantic forces implicit in the chaotic litter of thousands upon thousands of apparently immovable tons. She asked at last, as they climbed: "What made it? An earthquake?"

"I wouldn't know," Colin said. "I hadn't really thought about it. Must have been the rock was weak and broke away or washed away. It's just part of the mountain. It's the way mountains are."

7 6

Their voices seemed muffled, yet there was a hollow quality of echo in them. "It wasn't water or ice that did it," Margaret said. "Or the boulders wouldn't be sharp and square." She searched through the simple fragments of geology she had learned at school. "Maybe it happened when the mountains were first pushed up. Maybe it split here and the rocks broke away as they cooled."

Colin shook his head. "I don't think so. The rock is all too new. I think maybe there was a softer rock underneath and it washed away, then all the hard rock broke up and caved in. I guess a person'd have to be an expert to say."

The climbing was more difficult now and slowed them and kept them silent. The summit of the cleft was less than two hundred feet above them and the way to it was very steep. Looking up at it, Colin thought: it might stop us, just the last twenty or thirty feet might stop us. It can't do that, it wouldn't be fair after all this going so well. We wouldn't have time to come back down and go round the other way now, either. We've got to get up today, I've got to see how it is up there, how it feels to be at the top and see all around.

He heard Margaret stumble and slip behind him, heard the clatter of rocks rolling away from under her feet and on down the slope of the cleft. She was safe, he saw at once, her arms around a big boulder, but the slip had scared her. He moved back down and stood beside her. "We'd better put the rope on now," he said.

From there they climbed slowly and carefully. They had about sixty feet of rope and Colin would climb to the full length of it, then turn and take up the slack in his hands as Margaret began to climb towards him. After her slip, he had warned her: "Try out any place you are going to step before you put your full weight on it. Don't trust anything that doesn't feel solid. Keep trying until you know it's O.K." He had had to search his mind to find this to say; for him the climbing was still easy and natural and only Margaret's slip had made him realize that it was less easy for her. He had anticipated her difficulty on the ledge and had solved it a hundred times in his thoughts during the year since their previous failure; but in the tumbled slope of the cleft, with its infinity of crevices and footholds, he had supposed that she would be as

7 7

secure as himself. Now, standing with his feet apart, firmly planted, holding the rope so that it did not pull on her, yet could instantly check the least slip, he felt a power in himself that was unlike anything he had ever known before. He knew it instantly for a good feeling, strongly based, rightly earned; but he put it away from him in concern for what he knew was still above them, the narrow precipitous way out of the cleft.

They came to it at last and stood side by side on the pile of small, loose rocks that sloped from the sheer face. It was a true rock chimney, less than three feet wide, twisting only a little through some thirty feet of climb; there was no apparent slope to the three walls that formed it and from where they stood it was difficult to imagine a crevice for foot- or hand-hold anywhere in the smooth rock.

Margaret looked at Colin. Her face was flushed with the exertion of climbing and her body felt weary with disappointment, but she knew that he would feel it far more than she would. "That's the end," she said gently. "Isn't it? We can't go any farther."

Colin was still looking up and she knew as she spoke that there was no disappointment in his face. He shook his head slowly. "No," he said. "I've been thinking about it for a long time. It's just the way I was hoping it might be. We're going to make it."

"Don't be silly," she said. "You'd have to have wings."

He looked down at her and again he was smiling, with the same easy confidence that was so unlike him. "Sit down," he said. "I'll tell you about it. I'm sure we can make it—if you're game to try."

"I've got to be. I promised not to quit on you. But I still don't think there's any way except wings."

"Remember the hay chute in the barn?" Colin asked her. "You bet me I couldn't climb that once."

"Sure. And you put your feet against one side and pushed your back against the other and got slivers in your back. What's that got to do with it?"

"I got up into the loft didn't I? It's the same here, only no slivers."

Margaret glanced quickly over her shoulder at the cold, dim

light of the chimney. "You're not going to do that here," she said. "I won't let you."

"It's the same," he said. "Only easier. A little longer, but easier."

"It's not. There was hay underneath you in the barn. You'd be killed if anything went wrong here."

"It'll be easier," he repeated. "Rock is never smooth like boards. Nothing will go wrong."

His calm insistence was as strange to Margaret as his smile. She felt trapped and afraid and she resisted. "Maybe you can do it. I know I can't. You're not going to leave me here, are you?"

"You won't have to do it. We've got the rope. I'll make a sling you can sit in. I know how to."

"You can't pull me up there. I won't let you try, even."

"Yes I can, if you help a little the way I show you. Look, Marge," he said earnestly. "Do you want to know something?" He paused, but she said nothing and he went on: "All we've got to do is get through here and we're at the top. I'm sure of that."

In spite of herself Margaret felt an echo of his eagerness. I've got to stop him, she thought. I know so much better than he does, I've got more sense than he has—I always have had. But if we could get through there and find the sunlight and the wind again, suddenly; if we really were at the top and could see all around us, how good it would be. Nothing would seem silly then. I should know what it's like up there, really and truly know, and it would be part of me forever. He wants all that, too, and something even more than that. I can't be the one to keep him from it again, after he has waited for me all this time.

She stood up. "We can try it," she said. "But please, Colin, be careful. Come back if it's too difficult. Promise you will."

"Sure," he said. "I just want to try. I know I can make it."

79

IT was difficult getting into the chimney. Colin found a way up the left wall at last, using every smallest roughness or break in the rock to get him to the point where the two walls came close enough together to let him wedge his body between them. Once there he settled himself securely and rested. He looked down at Margaret. "It's going to be O.K.," he told her. "You'll be able to rest like this whenever you want. And there's quite a slope on the inside face a little way up. With the rope you'll almost be able to walk up it."

He began to climb then, forcing his body upward until his legs were almost straight, finding new footing on the opposite wall, forcing again. It was hard work and his body strained to it, but his mind worked freely and intensely ahead of him. His throat was dry and his heart was beating fast with excitement and he thought: what will it be like? Will there be grass or moss or heather or flowers or just rock? Will it be easy from there to the top? I think that's grass at the edge of the hole above me. Will the little twisted trees be there? Shall we see over into Wind Valley? All those things can go wrong so often; nothing is ever how you expect it to be, but this must be. Let it be, God, please God. Let it be real mountain, different from anything else, different to look at, different to feel, different to know. This isn't an ordinary day, this isn't an ordinary thing we are doing today. Something is going to happen from it, something big and important. Let it happen, God, and let it be big.

He reached the twist in the chimney and saw that from there on he could climb the inside wall without difficulty. He worked his body over, found footing and settled himself solidly. Looking down, he could still see Margaret. He called to her to start her climb and took a gentle strain on the rope as she moved in towards the base of the chimney.

Margaret trusted the rope and climbed boldly. Once or twice Colin lifted her almost bodily over a difficult place, but she found the roughnesses of the rock as he had found them and wedged her body as he had wedged his, and in a little while she was beside him. Ten or fifteen minutes later they were out in the sunlight again, standing on short dry grass, looking over the gleaming water and the tiny islands to the ranged peaks beyond and a distant haze beyond those that might have been the Pacific Ocean.

"We're above timber, anyway," Colin said at last. He turned and looked behind him. "But we still don't know how far we've got to go. It looks from here as though that next little hump might be the top, but I know darn well it isn't."

Margaret stood very straight, facing into the wind, letting it blow her hair back and flatten her skirt against her body. "It's nice here. Couldn't we stay for a few minutes?"

"Sure," Colin said, and sat down in the grass. He reached into his pockets and brought out some hardtack and a couple of battered candy bars. "Do you want to eat? I brought these for you."

Margaret laughed. "I didn't trust you," she said. "I brought some of my own."

Colin was thinking: it hasn't happened. We've made it, we've beaten all the bad places and come out above the timber, but it's not really so very different. Sure, you can see out for miles and miles and it feels good to be here, but it isn't so much really. He asked Margaret: "Are you tired?"

She shook her head. "Not now." Her eyes were bright and the wind had flushed her cheeks and her teeth showed strong and white between parted lips. "It's exciting. I love it. Why don't people live in places like this?"

"There's fifteen feet of snow here in the winter," Colin said.

Margaret laughed. "I shouldn't care. It'd be fun, living in a house almost buried in snow and looking out of the front door and seeing all the rest of the world 'way down below you."

"How'd you get to school? How'd you get grub and mail and all that stuff?"

"Don't be so practical," she told him. "I'm supposed to be the practical one. They could have a town up here if they wanted to. They do build towns on mountains. And they make tunnels under the snow to get from one house to another."

"That'd be just swell," Colin said. "To come all the way up here and bring the same old mess right along with you."

Margaret turned to look at him. "Isn't it what you wanted?" she asked. "You were so happy on the way up, but now you're sour. You ought to be proud. You planned it all and made it happen."

Colin rolled over on to his stomach and pulled impatiently at the grass. "It's O.K.," he said. "It's swell. Let's go on the rest of the way now we've seen it all from here."

IT took them over an hour to find the top of the mountain, though it was easy walking all the way, over gentle slopes, around great outcrops of rock, along dry creek beds. Colin's mood changed slowly as they traveled. There was sparse timber all over the face of the mountain, wind-torn and rock-hard in the exposed places, tall and slender where there was shelter. They found a tiny lakelet in a hollow and followed the creek that fed it through soft meadows. The creek bed climbed away from the meadows into the rocks again, and little flowers that were strange to them both bloomed everywhere. Once or twice they saw deer on the open slopes and Colin recognized a wolf track at the edge of the swamp that drained into the little lake. Once, in deep shade between two walls of rock, they came upon a stretch of deep snow; but through most of the journey the sunlight was brilliant all about them and the wind was fresh and strong against their bodies. Always, as they climbed, the earth widened below them, opening up new valleys, raising distant peaks above the nearer ones, uncovering lakes and river beds, the long white spray of falls on the mountainsides, the smooth, graceful sweep of distant glaciers.

The mountain top was bold rock, terraced by wind and driven snow, supporting a few dwarfed and twisted trees in the clefts of its sheltered side, but essentially a hump rather than a peak. A little pile of broken rock, built by some forgotten surveyor, marked its highest point. Colin saw it from a distance and pointed to it. Margaret uttered a little cry of pleasure and relief.

"Now we can really say we've been at the top, we can really know. I was so afraid there would be no way to be sure."

"I think we'd have known anyway," Colin said. "There doesn't seem to be anything else nearly so high. But it's good to be sure."

They went on to the cairn and stood in silence, one on either side of it, looking out over the tremendous stretch of country that opened away to the north and east, on the far side of the mountain. The whole world seemed blue and green and white before them—blue of water, green of timber, in infinity of shades, white of the glaciers and snow peaks, blue again in the sky and white again in the sailing summer clouds. Colin drew a deep breath of satisfaction. It had been better every minute since they had started away from the chimney, strangeness piled on strangeness, half-expected yet always unexpected and beyond expectation. He thought: this is of me and I am of it. Nothing here is evil, nothing is touched, nothing dirty or destroyed. The wind is strong and clean, the rock is strong, the little trees are strong; this is how I knew it would be, how I wanted it to be, why I came.

Margaret said at last: "We could have come here long ago. Why didn't we?" She sat down on the rock beside the cairn. "You always did want to come so badly. Why? Did you know it was going to be like this?" She swept her arm in a half-circle over the sweep of the valley, from the river's mouth to the high peaks. "Was that what you wanted to see?"

"Partly," Colin said. "But I wanted this, too." He moved his foot on the rock. "And this," he said, pointing to the slope in front of them. "All the things we've seen since we got up above the timber, the close things as well as the far things."

Margaret leaned forward and hugged her knees, half-closing her eyes to look up at him against the bright sky. "Don't you ever get tired?" she asked him. "Don't you ever want to sit down?"

"Sure I do," Colin said. "I was tired after we climbed that last bad place with the rope. But it's been easy since then. And right now I want to look at it all."

Margaret pointed down at the wide river mouth to the north of them. "Is that Wind River?"

"Sure it is. You know that. You can tell it from the map on the wall in the kitchen, easy." His finger traced the tiny gleam of the river back through the standing timber of the valley until it widened into a long, narrow lake. "That's Wind Lake," he said. "See that valley halfway up on the far side? That ought to be Carlson's

Valley. And the next big valley, just up beyond the head of the lake would be Amabilis Creek. And the other big lake in the main valley is Christina Lake."

He was completely absorbed in his own unfolding of the valley's secrets and Margaret watched him in surprise. "Well," she said at last, "you certainly have studied it. How much more do you know? What about the names of all the little lakes down there?"

"It's harder to figure those," Colin said. "See those three up the south fork of the main valley? I think those are Wolf and Loon and Beaver. Gem Lake is a little farther up, just out of sight." He sat down on the rock, still gazing out across the valley. "Something else I know. Everything beyond the divide on the far side of the lake is Menzies National Park. All those tallest, jagged mountains with the snow on them. They drain down into Menzies Lake, and that's in the park too."

He lay back with his hands behind his head, stretching his long body comfortably. "Boy," he said, "that's quite some valley. Earl Mayhew says it's the last big untouched valley on the coast."

Margaret still sat with her arms around her knees, but her eyes had turned to identify each thing as Colin named it. Now she turned her body a little so that she could watch him. "Why was Mr. Mayhew talking about it? Did you ask him?"

"No," Colin said without moving. "I don't think so. We often talk about places like that—places we'd like to go someday. Why? Is there something wrong with it?"

"Is that why you wanted to come here? To see the valley?"

"Only partly. I told you that before." He rolled over a little, on to his side, so that he could look at her. "Heck, what is this anyway? You ask a person more questions than a schoolteacher."

Margaret did not smile. "You're crazy about the woods, aren't you, Colin? That's all you think of, woods and mountains."

"What's the matter with that? Can't a guy think about things he likes? Woods and mountains never did anybody any harm."

Margaret moved awkwardly but her face had a determined look that Colin knew, both in her and in his mother. "No," she said. "But a person can be too single-track about anything. There's lots of other things that should be just as important for you."

"What for instance?"

"Oh, going to college. And knowing more people. And reading more. Those sort of things."

"What brought all that up?" he asked her. "Did Mother tell you to say it?"

"No."

"Mildred Hanson, then?"

Margaret flushed. "Sort of," she admitted. "But I think the same. Look, Colin, if you go to the woods for all your life you'll be running away. It isn't right for you to do it. You know it isn't."

"The woods is the only place I'm good for anything. They're the only place a guy's free to act like himself, without everybody watching and yammering at him."

"Nobody's bothered you at school since Tod Phalling went away. The kids all like you."

"That's what you think. It's O.K. for you. You're good-looking and the same size as everybody else. Nobody thinks you're queer or nags at you all the time to act different from what you really are."

"You're not queer," Margaret said. "You make yourself seem queer just because you're shy and you give in to it. That's what I mean about running away. Lots of people are shy, but they make themselves get over it and soon nobody knows the difference."

Colin lay flat on his back and watched the high white clouds across the wheeling sky. Let her talk, he thought, she doesn't know what it's like. Everything always did go right for her. She's better than me around home or in school or pretty near any place else you can think of, except maybe here on the mountain. Sure, she's going to college, but that's no reason she should expect everybody else to go too. She's neat and tidy and all pulled together. Anyone can tell right away, just from looking at her, that she's smart and things go right for her. I wish she wouldn't drag all that stuff up today, though, when we're away from it. She doesn't generally get on to it when we're out on a trip together—that's one reason why she's so good to go with. It's funny about people, you never can tell what they're thinking, not even when they're your sister or your mother or your old man. You don't even know what they're seeing. It could be something you see

85

looks quite different to them. Take Margaret up here, for instance. She's so much smarter than me, so much quicker about things, it could be none of this looks the same to her. And even if it looks the same, that's no reason I should think she feels the same way about it.

Colin raised himself on one elbow and looked past the cairn at his sister. "Marge," he said. "What do you like best about all this?"

She was sitting with her clenched fists together under her chin, her elbows on her knees. "I like it all," she said slowly. "The whole thing. Just looking at it makes my heart beat fast and I feel as if I wanted to be every place at once and make it all mine. The high mountains are most exciting, I guess—those and the way the river is, all quicksilver where you can see it between the trees." She paused, then went on: "If it had to be just one thing, I think I'd say the lakes and most of all the little ones sitting up at all different levels on the sides of the mountains. They look so friendly."

Colin lay back again, satisfied, and for a little while neither of them spoke. Then she asked him: "Colin, don't we have to start back soon?"

He sat up again and looked at her with suspicion. "Why? Do you want to go? Are you sick of it already?"

"No, of course not. I'd like to stay here for days. But we have got to be back for supper. You haven't forgotten about Mr. Grant, have you?"

Colin turned and looked at the sun. "We've got a little while longer," he said. "Going down will be easy, but we'll go the long way, round all the bad places, so it'll take time."

"What are you going to say to Mr. Grant?"

He looked at her again, quickly, and again suspiciously. "How do I know? I don't even know what he's going to say to me."

"Yes, you do. You know what he said this spring—that maybe you could go in the woods with him and run compass next year. He'll ask if you still want to go."

"You could be right," Colin said. "But I guess I have to wait till he asks."

"You aren't going, are you? Not in March like he said and lose all that school-time?"

"Sure, I am if he wants me to. Why wouldn't I? He's the best timber cruiser on the coast. A guy'd learn more from him than he ever would in school."

"You could go later, just for the summer, and not miss any school."

"He didn't say so. He said he was going up Wind River in March and work there right through till fall. I wouldn't miss any more than three or four months of school."

"Mother doesn't want you to go."

"When did she say that? Father said it'd be O.K. to go. He wants me to go. Mother said it wouldn't be so bad if I was just out of school for the summer."

"You won't be. If you go you'll stay out. All the kids that go off early to a summer job say they'll come back in the fall, but they never do. Mildred Hanson says they get used to earning wages and can't give it up. Or their families can't."

"Might be something to that," Colin said. "If a man's got a chance to earn steady wages these days he's got to be crazy to give it up."

"It's not going to be like that any more. Things are getting started again and we won't have to worry so much."

"Oh yeah?" Colin looked at her almost angrily. "A person'd think you didn't know Dad stayed home today."

"That's just for fire season. They'll open up again as soon as the weather breaks, Dad said."

"That isn't what Earl Mayhew says. Earl says they'll stay closed just as long as it suits them, and that means till it's time to cut wages again."

"Dad says Earl shouldn't talk like that. He says the companies need to keep working just as much as the men do. More, because they've got all that machinery going to waste."

"I know," Colin's voice was calm again. "One says one thing and another says something else. And they change, and get sore at each other about it. Dad is always sore at Mike Varchuk, but when the camp's been closed for a while he gets to saying almost the same things as Mike."

8 7

"That's the union," Margaret said. "It's supposed to get them all together, but it never seems to. Mildred says it will one day, but they have to learn the hard way."

Colin stood up. "Well," he said, "if it's going to be as tough on Dad as it was last time I'd just as soon have a job waiting. At least it'll mean there's something Mother can count on."

"There's plenty to do around home," Margaret said. "And Dad always finds something that brings in a little money." But he doesn't, she thought. When the camp's shut down he's not God in Genesis any more. He's just a man, and even his strength seems to go away from him gradually until he looks lost and shrunken and untidy instead of upright and huge and powerful. Colin's right: it would mean a lot to Mother to have something she could depend on in times like that.

"I guess we can't really tell what's going to happen," Margaret said. "But if you do go with Mr. Grant, don't give up school altogether, will you?"

"It's almost a year before it happens," Colin said. "But I don't suppose I will."

"Promise?" she asked him. "On your heart?"

Colin looked at her in surprise. "That's kid stuff," he said. "A person can't do that for something like this. It's too serious."

"Of course you can. The more serious a thing is, the more reason there is to make a true promise. Please, Colin."

He looked down at her, half-smiling. "Oh, O.K., if you want, Marge. On my heart. But it won't ever come up. The job'll be over by fall and I'll just naturally go back to school." He glanced up at the sun again. "No more sitting around. We've got to be on our way if we're going to make it on time."

Margaret stood up and Colin said: "Give you a start to that little flat tree and race you to the first swamp."

"Following," she said. "No fair short-cutting behind a guy."

"Following," he said.

MARTHA Ensley did not go away from her home very
often. She recognized certain occasions: every Sunday, without
fail, she and Will and the children went to the church in Blenkinstown; she went to the town's small whist drives and dances, usually spending the greater part of the evening in the kitchen,
preparing food or washing dishes; occasionally she went into the
town during the daytime, to attend a meeting, visit at the hospital
or do some shopping that seemed to call for her personal attention—though she infinitely preferred, from long habit, to do her
important shopping through the mail-order catalogs. When she
went to visit her friends it was either in full Sunday ceremony
with Will and Colin and Margaret, or else to help out because of
sickness or impending childbirth.

Essentially she continued the social habits of her mother's house
and her childhood, when neighbors had been few and distant.
Like her mother, she was a sociable and deeply affectionate
woman, and like most pioneer women she was extravagantly and
sincerely hospitable to any person, friend or stranger, who came
to her house. But the daily work of looking after her house, her
garden and her family amply filled her time and she would have
considered casual daytime visiting little less than a sin. When she
decided to go and talk to Joan Mayhew one afternoon in March
she was uneasily conscious of the break in a lifetime routine and
had to remind herself that her going was of importance to the
family.

Before she left she piled wood in the stove, filled the kettle,
closed all the drafts. That was routine. She wrote a note and
propped it on the table, where Margaret and Colin would see it
when they came home from school. That also was routine. Walking out to the gate, turning left along the road towards the village,
was still routine. But her thoughts were not routine. In spite of
her concern, she felt happy and excited. She liked Joan Mayhew
and the thought of talking with the tall, strong girl was reassur-

ing. She hasn't got a lazy bone in her body, Martha thought, nor a crooked one. She says what she thinks, straight out, and it's always good, sound common sense. I've heard them say she's too frank and it makes enemies for her, but I like it and I like the way her eyes look at you when she's talking; I like her broad white face and black hair, and the way she generally stands, so strongly, with her feet a little apart and her arms folded across her chest. Most of all, except her eyes, I like her voice. It's deep and natural, straight out like the things she says, yet simple and gentle; it's a voice that belongs to the women of this country, the real women who raise the families and keep them together.

Martha walked quickly, with short quick steps, her body bent forward a little, her head inclined against a fresh wind that she knew would soon bring rain. She turned in at the Mayhews' gate without looking up and hurried to the door of the house. It opened before she could knock and Joan was standing there.

"Why, Martha," she said. "How nice to see you." She felt the warmth of Martha's lake-blue eyes, met the dancing smile that was always near them. "Come in out of the cold," she said. "There's nobody in the whole wide world more welcome."

"I shouldn't be here in the middle of the day," Martha said, and turned to watch Joan close the door behind her. "But I thought it was time we talked."

Joan crossed to the stove and slid the kettle towards the holes immediately over the firebox. "We don't talk enough," she said. "The men do it all while we stay home."

Sliding her arms out of her old brown coat, Martha said: "I generally leave those things to Will, but it seems to mean more than usual this time." Joan moved a chair nearer the stove and Martha sat down in it. "Where is all your family?" she asked.

"Earl's up at the meeting," Joan said. "The kids are out in the yard—Earl made a sandpile for them last year and they never leave it alone."

"It's cold," Martha said.

"I bundled them up warm. They're both strong and healthy, praise be. It'll be different next year, I suppose, when little Earl starts school and the germs all follow him home. We haven't had a cold in the house all winter." She reached automatically under the table to touch the unpainted wood.

"It's always worst when they first start. That first year is too hard on them. But they get used to it after a while."

Joan poured boiling water from the kettle into the teapot. "How are you up your way? It's quite a while since Colin was around to see us."

"We keep well enough," Martha said. "We've got a lot to be thankful for in times like these. But it worries Will. He wants to take too much of the blame to himself. It's like an insult to his trade not to be working."

"It doesn't seem to matter any more whether they're good workers," Joan's voice was deliberately restrained, resisting any suggestion of special sympathy for Will Ensley. "It just goes on and on. There isn't work any more."

"Will still says it's going to pick up. He thinks the company may be bought out—that's why Mr. Grant was doing all that cruising up there last year."

"Earl talks the same old stuff," Joan said impatiently. "Shutdown for fire season, shutdown for snow. Open up soon as the rain comes. Or the snow melts. Or the sun shines. Or the heavens fall. Or hell freezes. What difference does it make what they say? It's always the same old story when it comes to buying groceries—no pay-check, no cash. It'll take two years of steady work to pay what we owe now."

"I know how you feel," Martha said. "This is the longest stretch of hard times I can remember. But it always does come out in the end—slowly, so you can't see it's happening, but it happens. Will's right about the signs. Little things, like Mr. Grant cruising timber, are what you notice first, and the rest comes later. He's going up Wind River next week—Colin's going with him."

"I'm glad," Joan said. "At least you'll have something you can count on. And I guess it must mean they plan on opening something up there, sooner or later. I'm glad for Colin too. It's just what he needs."

"I worry about it," Martha set her cup down gently in its saucer. "All my brothers were off in the woods long before they were his age and it seems natural to let him go. But Mr. Siddons and Miss Hanson think he ought to stay in school, and I guess young people nowadays need all the education they can get."

"Colin's made for the woods. He loves it and Earl says it all seems to come natural to him. Education may be all right for city folks, but there's a limit to it for people like us. Colin will make out all right."

"He'll go back to school in the fall. Mr. Siddons wants him to go right on through to the University, but it's early to talk about that yet. We can wait and see what happens to Margaret."

"You don't have to worry about Margaret. It'll be natural to her as breathing and talking. Colin's different. He's—he's like a wild thing. Pen him in and he's liable to go to pieces."

"I'm afraid you're right," Martha said. "That's why I worry about him. I can't help thinking that if he goes off in the woods with Andrew Grant he'll come back worse than ever."

Joan looked at her. "Why do you say 'worse'? There's good in being the way Colin is just the same as there's good in being the way Margaret is. People don't have to be good all the same way."

"I don't really know," Martha said slowly. "I don't know why I'm afraid for him, except that I feel it. I feel that there are things always waiting to hurt him. Things inside him and outside him, and it's very easy for Colin to be hurt." Watching her, Joan saw that her face was strained and lined and the smile had gone far back behind her eyes. "I haven't felt it so much lately. He's been happier this last year, more like a normal boy. But when there's a big change for him, like this going away on his own, I have to worry."

"Perhaps getting away into the woods has had something to do with making him happier. Perhaps he's finding what he really is when he's out there."

Martha's face brightened and the smile came to life in her eyes again. "Do you really think that? I've thought it sometimes, that perhaps he's going where he belongs instead of running away from it. If it's true he'd be certain to be happy, wouldn't he?"

"Yes," Joan said. "And I think it's true." She picked up the teapot and poured more tea. "Martha, do you ever stop worrying about Colin and worry about yourself?"

Martha looked at her in surprise. "Me? Why should I?"

"You're doing too much around that place of yours. You're working yourself to death. You should make them help you more."

Martha laughed. "Don't be silly. Work is nothing new to me —I've worked all my life. I'm not so quick as I used to be and I get a little tired sometimes, but it's easier now than when the children were small."

"No one can work the way you do without paying for it. I'm twice as big and twice as strong as you are, but I couldn't stand it, I know that. You ought to go to the doctor and have a good check-up."

"Nonsense," Martha said abruptly. "I'm spry as a cricket. And I didn't come here to talk about myself."

She stood up and held her hands towards the stove. "What are those men up to? Is it going to make things better or worse?"

Joan hesitated before answering. "I think they're right," she said. "I'm not sure they are. But it won't be easy. There hasn't been a loggers' union that amounted to anything for over ten years."

"There'll be trouble. Strikes when they need the work. Maybe fighting and violence. Do you think they're wise enough to understand all that?"

"They'll have to learn. Earl says the leaders know all about it and they expect to have a strong organization by the time they're ready to use it."

"Why are the leaders all foreigners?" Martha asked her. "Varchuk and Zobieski and this man Miller—he changed his name. Aren't there any Canadians who know what to do?"

"They aren't all foreigners—just up here. Earl says they're smart men. After all, half the men in the camps are foreigners; more than half."

"Then why do they need Will and Earl if they know so much?"

"Because the men trust them, Earl says. Johnny Meldrum and Mr. Sorretto and several others of the old timers are on the committee too. Earl says the company will have to pay attention to men like that and I think maybe he's right."

"Then you think it's a good thing?" Martha said.

"Yes," Joan told her. "I'm afraid sometimes, but I think it's good. It's got to be. Things can't go on the way they've been for so long. The men have got to have some say about what wages they'll work for and the only way they can have it is by getting together and all holding out for the same thing."

"That's all I wanted to know," Martha said. "I felt it was good, but I wanted to hear someone else say so. Will is so easily taken in."

Joan looked away from her. "He's a big influence. Earl says the men trust him." She looked back and met the smile in Martha's eyes.

"It'll take a lot more than Will to make this thing work out," Martha said. "I expect they know that as well as we do. It's not Will's kind of thing, nor mine either. But if he can help I'm not going to stop him."

Martha was standing with her small feet apart, her clenched fists on her hips. Her blue eyes shone with determination and her gentle mouth was firmly set. Suddenly they both laughed. "I think we'd be the ones," Joan said. "You and I. If only we could change places with them."

COLIN and Andrew Grant started for Wind River during the third week of March. It was a wet and windy day and the rain was cold, laced with snow streaks and fiercely driven. Grant had hired a small gas-boat to run their canoe and other equipment round from Blenkinstown to the mouth of the river. When he saw what the weather was he had said to Colin: "No use waiting for it. There's a cabin with a dry roof less than a mile above the salt water."

So now they were working the canoe up the easy tidal part of the river, with the flood following them. Colin was paddling at the bow, Grant at the stern and the gear was piled between them under the shelter of a tent fly. The wind was behind them, with the tide, but the river was appreciably strong against them, even at the mouth, and Grant used the river's bends and the eddies behind the little grassy islands to work against it. The river flowed to the sea across a treeless tidal flat fully half a mile wide, cut by a hundred deep channels and sloughs. Mallard and teal, pintail and mergansers flew from the water at their approach and passed and repassed overhead, sweeping down the wind or battering strongly against it. Colin heard the chatter of geese somewhere out on the flats and the lovely cry of the flocks in flight came down through the sound of the storm. He worked his paddle steadily, stroke after stroke without change or slackening, as Grant had told him to, and his heart was full of a hundred surging things that jumbled the endless flow of his thoughts in the wetness.

Mother was just the way she is when I go to school in the mornings, so busy and quick with everything; yet it wasn't quite the same and at the end she pulled my head down and kissed me and said: "Be good, Boy." That's the first time she's called me "Boy" since I was a little kid and it made me want to bawl. The old man didn't say much to me; he just kept talking to Mr. Grant about fir and hemlock and cedar and the prices of logs and how soon the camps'll open up. But he had sharpened my axe himself, the way he *can* sharp them, so the fine bit will cut a hair from just resting the hair on it. Gee, this sure is a great place for ducks and geese. I've heard them talk about it; but I never knew it would be like this. Mr. Grant doesn't talk much; he hasn't said a thing since we left the gas-boat. I wonder what he thinks about? He's such a little guy, but he's powerful; you can feel it right through the canoe every time his paddle goes into the water.

He's my boss now. But there can't be much bossing to a job like this, with just two of us in the bush, you wouldn't think. Just the same, he is the boss and Dad says to remember that and call him Mr. Grant and jump when he says anything. It sure feels good to be starting out like this. This canoe is a honey, so light and easy to paddle and we've got a real load in it too. The other kids are all in school right now. Algebra. I'm sure glad I'm missing that. Poor old Johnny, he'd sell his grandmother to be here doing this and he's sweating away at algebra.

Miss Hanson sure was nice when I said good-by to her yesterday. "Don't forget school," she said. "Come back in the fall. You'll learn a lot with Mr. Grant and maybe it will make you want to learn more in school." I wonder what she meant by that? She put her hand on my arm and her mouth was smiling and her face soft and her eyes the bluest I've ever seen them. I'm not going to let myself think about her any more the way I've been thinking. I know I'll want to, I want to now; I won't let myself, I'll stop it, I'll keep it down shut away inside me. I know I won't, it's too precious for that, too good and warm and rich when you're lonely, but I can worry about that when the time comes. Just for now I'll shut it out and keep it shut out, because it's good to be starting out like this, all clean and fresh; and I'll be strong and different and a man when I go back and see her again and she'll know that and treat me like a man.

They had come more than a mile from the salt water and the tall green timber was closing in to narrow the open meadow. A little ahead of them alder trees came right down to the banks of the river and Colin knew that they must be growing beyond reach of the tides. The river current was strong now but the wind was still helping and the canoe moved steadily under the paddles. There was a windowless farmhouse and a rotting barn on some higher ground near the alders and Colin thought: that would be where the guy lived that ran beef cattle here on the flats in the early days. He cut hay for them out of the slough and let them pick what they could off the flats, but he lost all his money at it in the end and had to pull out. Because he couldn't afford to get the beef to a market, they say it was. Seems a darn shame; it must have been a swell life in a place like this, with the cattle spread all over the flats and all the ducks and geese to see when you were looking for them and the mountains so close. He was married and had a whole lot of children. Mother remembers visiting there, by boat, when she was a little girl. And now they're all gone and the place has fallen apart.

Behind him he felt Grant slow the stroking of his paddle. "Ease up for a spell, laddie," Grant said. "The tide's away behind us."

Colin set his paddle across the gunwales and turned towards him. "We'll land at the old Underhill place," Grant said. "And have ourselves a bite to eat while she's coming up. The high tide is twenty-two feet and that'll save us near another mile of battling with the river."

ANDREW

ANDREW Duncan Grant was a short, spare gray little man. His eyes were a pale, hard blue, with bushy reddish eyebrows over them. His sandy hair was thin and graying, his nose was sharp, his mouth a thin line over a small but rocky chin. He was the son of a Hudson's Bay factor who had retired to Victoria from the prairies. Young Andrew grew up with sound mathematics, a hard integrity and a tireless body. At sixteen he was timekeeper in a logging camp. At eighteen he was camp foreman, at twenty a log-buyer. And then, being a bushman at heart, he turned to cruising and staking standing timber.

He was not a friendly man, nor a communicative one, and he rode Colin hard during the first two or three weeks they spent in the valley. They had made a base camp some miles up the river from tidal water and were working through the dark, heavy timber of the valley floor; the weather was consistently bad, cold and wet and windy, but Grant made no concessions to it and they lived in wet clothes and slept out in wet blankets night after night, returning to the comparative dryness of the base camp only when they had to. Colin was not unhappy. It did not occur to him that Grant was exacting and the cold wet gloom of the forest was what he had expected, almost what he had hoped for.

Grant made little effort to explain the work to Colin. He showed him how to mount the compass on the jacob staff, how to check it against the section line, how to sight it and how to pace off a tally of three hundred and thirty feet, allowing for broken ground and windfalls. Everything else he did himself, swiftly and easily, in a silence that seemed half-contemptuous, half-patient. But Colin was interested, and at home. He could not match the little man's quick, ferreting energy, but he had a power of endurance that let him handle his own work surely and easily and still left him free to watch everything about him. He found no monotony in the great trees of the flat valley because to his eye no two of them seemed alike; each had its own particular way of surging upward from its roots, each its own lean, its own color and texture of bark, its own climb to its lowest branches, its own marked position in relationship to its neighbors. Under the trees the ground, for all its riverbottom flatness, was as varied as the trees themselves; Colin's compass lines crossed swamps and creeks and larger streams, passed hummocks and hollows, led him over piled windfalls and rock outcrop; he walked on moss and on spruce needles, over gray gravel and red gravel, across sodden loam and on the spongy softness of rotted wood. From time to time they came upon the worn trail that was the valley's highway; lesser trails of deer and bear ran everywhere through the length and breadth of the flat and Colin's quick eyes always checked them to learn what had passed that way recently.

The original survey of the valley was so old that all the blazes were long grown over and the cedar corner posts were black and half-rotten, often covered with moss or lichen, blending almost perfectly into the forest. Colin gradually built himself a picture of that original survey and the men who had made it thirty or forty years earlier. Men much like himself and Grant, he supposed they were, probably more cheerful and more talkative, men who knew nothing of automobiles or airplanes, men who had known the Underhill farm in its prosperity and Blenkinstown when ox teams brought logs from the Ensley farm to the old booming ground in the corner of the bay. He learned to judge them by the shape and size of the blazes they had left, by the symmetry or roughness of the corner posts they had made, by the markings of their bearing trees, by the ancient score of a nicked axe blade, by the blackened stones of their fires, by the way one would hew bark from a leaning fir or another split dry kindling from a dead cedar.

By the end of his third week he could pace the sixteen tallies from section line to section line so accurately that he was rarely more than ten paces from the line when he finished. Grant gave up finding corner posts for himself because Colin was nearly always ahead of him; he slowed his impatience and he talked more often, but he worked as tirelessly as ever. They were up at dawn each day, breaking camp, cooking oatmeal and bacon and coffee. Through the day they traveled, stopping only to eat a quick lunch around noon. While Colin ran his compass lines and blazed his tally-marks Grant checked the timber and made his notes. Grant had a way of his own of covering ground in the bush. He moved quickly and actively and silently, ranging like a little gray dog, often far out of Colin's sight, seeming to care nothing for brush or windfall or hard going of any kind, if there were trees he wanted to see beyond it. He seemed to pay attention to nothing but the timber, yet he always knew where he was from the compass line and he could return from his wandering to one of Colin's tally-marks as surely as though it were a blazing light on a city street. And at the end of each day he knew of a good camping spot within easy reach of wherever they were. When they came to it he would slip his pack away from his shoulders and settle with his notebooks and figures until Colin had supper ready.

Early in the fourth week the weather changed sharply to sunshine and a warm wind that sprang everything to life. They were back at the base camp, near the main river, and Grant had worked all afternoon at his figures while Colin cut wood and straightened up the camp. Towards evening Grant came out of the tent and walked slowly to where Colin was sharpening his axe. He watched him for a moment, then said: "You work too hard, boy. Don't you ever want to go off fishing, or take a rest?"

Colin looked up in surprise and Grant smiled at him. "I know, I know, laddie. You think I'm a hard driver and you've got to keep up. So I am. So you have." He walked over and sat down on a stump. Colin started to say something, but Grant held up a forefinger and silenced him. "We're 'way ahead of ourselves," he said. "And in weather not fit for seals and sea-otters. You're as good as any compass-man I ever had and if you can keep to it there's no reason we shouldn't ease up a wee and act more like humans. Ye may not think it from what ye've seen, but there's a human streak in me."

"It's O.K. with me, Mr. Grant," Colin said. "I like it in the woods."

"Oh aye, it's easy to see that. And you're not a great talker either, which is a virtue on its own. But we've a whole summer of hard work and spare living in front of us. Except old Robbie, up at the lake, there's nobody in the valley but the two of us, so we may as well get to know each other a little."

Colin laughed. "I guess you know all there is to know about me," he said. "You've known Mother ever since she was a little girl and Dad pretty near as long."

Grant shook his head quite solemnly. "There's a lot more to a man than his mother and father. But suppose we cook us up a bite of supper now. Afterwards we'll take the canoe and catch us some trout for breakfast."

AS the summer drew on and they worked their way farther and farther up the valley, a slow, unspoken friendship grew between Colin and Grant. Grant changed little. He still drove relentlessly through his work, he still held to moody, day-long silences, broken only by a contemptuous word or two when Colin overran a line or slipped into some careless error with the compass. But his easier moods became more and more frequent and lasted longer. Grant's occasional scolding, sharply and bitterly expressed as it always was, bit into Colin, confused him and hurt him momentarily; but he quickly lost the hurt in the silence that followed and in the crowding of other thoughts that came to him through the quick and ceaseless searching of his eyes. Each day he saw and learned new things and he treasured them all, piecing them into his own steadily clearer picture of the complex world of the forest.

Because of the difference in their ages and because Grant was immensely secure in his professional skill and his woodcraft, Colin was slow to understand him. That Grant was a shy man he learned only on one of their rare trips to Blenkinstown to pick up supplies. They had taken the canoe into the wharf and were walking up towards the general store when they met Mildred Hanson. She came across to them at once and held out her hand to Colin.

"Why, Colin," she said. "You look so well. The woods must agree with you."

It was a sunny day and she was without a hat, so that her pale gold braids caught the sunlight. A short gray skirt swung from her hips and a clear blue blouse, open at the throat, reflected the blue of her eyes. Colin thought he had never seen her look so beautiful and he felt strong from his height above her. But he knew his hand was clammy in hers and his own voice sounded rough and awkward to his ears after the soft, easy song of her words. He grinned and looked down and said only: "It's swell up there, Miss Hanson." He saw her quick eyes turn to Grant, ready to smile, and knew somehow that Grant would not respond. He fumbled to introduce them, but before the words were out Grant had nodded shortly, muttered something and gone towards the store.

"Are you out for long?" Mildred asked Colin.

"Just for today," Colin said. "I guess—I guess I'd better go along with Mr. Grant."

Mildred laughed. "He's not very friendly, is he, the great Mr. Grant? You must be a silent pair, back there in the woods."

"Oh, we talk," Colin said. "But I better go now."

"Good-by, Colin," Mildred said. "Take care of yourself up there and come and see me before school starts."

Colin left her and hurried after Grant. As they turned into the store Grant asked: "Who was she?"

"One of the schoolteachers," Colin said.

"Acted more like a schoolgirl. Too young for me. Paint for lips." There was something defensive in the clipped sentences that Colin dimly recognized. He searched his mind and remembered Grant meeting Joan Mayhew at the Ensley house and how Martha had said later: "Andrew never did learn to be easy with the girls. He hasn't changed any."

That was their last trip out to Blenkinstown and they took the loaded canoe clear up the river to Wind Lake, lining and poling their way through the twelve miles of rough water in a single day.

"We'll go on to Robbie's," Grant said. "His cabin's about half-way up the lake, on Cameron Creek, and we can leave most of the stuff there. It'll be safer than in a cache."

They made Robinson's their base camp for nearly three weeks while they worked over the timber along Cameron Creek and along the lake shore on both sides of the creek-mouth. It was a pleasant time because Grant worked shorter days so that they were able to get back to the cabin nearly every night. He and Robinson were old and close friends, though they were very different types of men. Robbie was in his sixties, a tall thin man with bent knees and a sliding walk. He talked easily, laughed freely and treated Colin with the respectful admiration that age quite often has for the bright future of youth.

"Enjoy it all while you're young," he would say to Colin. "Don't let it slip away from you. Don't let old Andrew here work you to death just because he's a dour Scot. Andrew takes everything hard and look where it's got him. You take the canoe and the pole and go fishing. Or just go using your eyes to see God's good sights all up and down this lake."

And Colin would go, traveling the lake in the calm peace of the summer evenings, finding the creeks from Robbie's directions, learning the mountains for himself from Grant's maps. It was a partial fulfillment, but far more truly an extension of what he had done in climbing the mountain with Margaret the previous year. From parts of the lake he could see the mountain and even recognize the thrust of rock where they had sat by the cairn, but his strongest interest was in the high mountains to the north, in the fierce precipices of Carlson's Valley, two or three miles beyond Cameron Creek, in the deep mysterious fold of Amabilis Creek just above the head of the lake, and in the high white peaks that marked the boundary of Menzies National Park. On some evenings, with the lake glass-still, he took the canoe and paddled out to where he could see the tallest mountains in all their height. Then he would let the canoe drift while the sun sank and the colors changed, watching the coming of night to the valleys and the linger of light on the peaks and ridges, feeling rather than thinking, recognizing little of what he felt, knowing only that he was happier than he had ever been in his life.

At other times he stayed in the cabin and listened through the evening to the talk of the two older men. They were very different, the one simple and cheerful and talkative, the other taut and sparing of words, withdrawn, often harsh and bitter in judgment. Yet they had one thing in common: a contempt for the outside world and the people who lived there. Robbie would say, half-joking, half in earnest: "You're bad news, Andrew. There'll be others come after you and tear the woods apart and burn the hills. In a few years there'll be nothing left for me in all this country."

"Aye, they'll come," Grant would agree. "There'll be a railroad past your door and a spur line up the creek. But they'll come in their own good time, when it's ripe for money-making and some jumping jack with a hold on the purse strings pulls the whistle."

"You should know, Andrew. You walk with them and talk with them down in Vancouver and Victoria. It's you that tells them where the good timber is and how it can best come away and leave the cash in their pockets."

"If it weren't me it would be someone else. I give them an honest cruise for my fee and have done ever since I first put calipers on a tree."

"They have to make money or they couldn't have their cities with the electric light and automobiles and the painted whores on the corners. I've been out to Vancouver twice since we came back from overseas in 1919 and I don't mind if I never see the place again."

They both laughed, then Grant was solemn. "You want to watch it a wee, Robbie. A man shouldn't shut himself away too far."

"That's fine talk from a man that's been forty years sneaking through the bush like a panther. At least I've God's good daylight to shine down on me and a little free space to look out on." Robbie waved a hand towards the windows of his cabin that fronted on the lake.

"I'm out to the city three or four months of every year, with a collar and tie and all the trimmings," Grant said defensively.

"And I go out. Down to Blenkinstown to sell my furs in the spring and down there again to buy grub in the fall. If it was any more than that I'd be hanging around the beer parlors like the rest of them and turning into a half-man that couldn't walk an honest mile to save his life."

And the friendly argument would go on, back and forth between them, getting nowhere but establishing each man in his belief that the life he had chosen was right and good, while life in the cities was a pale, vicious half-life, dangerous and contaminating.

Often they talked more seriously, searching over things that were really important to them. Colin learned then that they were both lonely men, though Grant was by far the lonelier of the two. Robbie had run away from home in his teens and had learned years later that his mother had died soon after he left. He mentioned her often and it was clear that he blamed himself for her death. He had fought with the Canadian Mounted Rifles in the South African war and come back to work cattle ranches in Alberta until 1910. Then he had traveled west to the coast and somehow chosen his trapline on Cameron Creek. In 1914 he had volunteered again and gone overseas to fight in France. Between the wars and again after the second war he had been a heavy drinker and this, it seemed, was the source of his grievance against the outside world.

"Out there," he said, "you work a while and make a stake, then the job folds or you quit and there's nothing to do but hit town. So you hit town and all you can do there is drink to pass the time and blow your stake so it's decent to go back to work again. After a while it gets you and you don't even stay with a job long enough to make a stake. Up here there's always work to be done, trails to cut and cabins to build, and it's work you do for yourself without any boss to watch over you. I've got my trap-lines up the valley, I've got mining claims staked in the mountains—and good assays on them too, copper, and lead and silver and zinc." He paused to reach for his tobacco can and papers. "And when you don't want to work you can study." He waved his hand towards a shelf of books above his bunk. "Or you can just look around you and see what the millionaires pay thousands of dollars to see for a couple of weeks in the year."

"Nobody's arguing against ye," Grant said. "Not even Colin here. It might even be you'll wake up a rich man some day if that railroad comes and the claims are as good as you say."

"I've all I'll ever need right now, with the fur money to buy tea and coffee and beans and rifle shells. There's more deer and fish than I'll ever need right outside the door, more wood to burn, more berries to pick. There's ducks and geese in the winter, and bear fat for the rendering of it and grouse in the swamps."

"Aye, and huckleberries to make a brew of wine when you've a need for it. You're well provided for, Robbie, I'll grant ye all of that."

Robbie laughed and glanced towards the row of ten gallon crocks standing against the cabin wall. "Now, Andrew, you know I'm a moderate man. It's nothing more than a taste for friends like yourself that come visiting."

"You'll die of your moderation yet," Andrew told him.

Robbie nodded. "That day'll come," he said. "It has to."

1 3

WHEN the time came to leave Cameron Creek Grant had a full day's work to do on his maps, so Robbie and Colin took the canoe up to Amabilis Creek and set up the new camp there. It was an easy day and they had ample time to catch a mess of trout and cook an early supper on the beach before starting back down the lake.

While they were eating, Robbie said: "You're the first compassman Andrew ever had could get along with him. Mostly he runs his own compass. He's a hard man to work for."

"I like him O.K.," Colin said. "He never bawls you out unless you're wrong. And he sure knows his work."

"Andrew's the best there is. Timber's his whole life, always has been, and if things had gone right he'd be up there with the biggest lumbermen in the province today."

"He likes what he's doing," Colin said. "He likes the woods."

"He does and he doesn't. Andrew's an ambitious man. I can remember the time when he thought nothing mattered in the world except starting his own logging show and building himself up to a real lumber baron. He made his start too—did real well at it." Robbie poked at the fire. "He'd be on top today if he hadn't got himself married."

"I never knew he was married," Colin said.

"There's a lot you don't know. Likely there's a lot I don't know, but I know some of it. I guess Andrew never was what you'd call a ladies' man, but when I first knew him he was always aiming to marry some girl and never getting up the nerve to ask her. Your mother was one and Will Ensley took her off while Andrew was still trying to scare up nerve to say 'Howdo' without stammering over it. The oldest Underhill girl was another—real pretty girl, too, and sensible. She'd have made a good wife for any man."

Robbie speared another trout from the frying pan and looked down the lake. Colin waited and said nothing. "The woman he did marry, well I guess she must have married him. Never saw her, but I heard all about her. One of these girls with so much mother you never thought to look around and see if she had a father as well. Good-looking, they say, and proud and mean as a weasel—take everything, give nothing. Of course, that's all from Andrew's friends and it might be there's two sides to it." Robbie paused to finish his trout and pour a cup of coffee. "This was just the time Andrew was going good with his logging show, building her up steady and making deals that would put him up where he wanted to be. Seems like she was just as ambitious as he was, only her ambitions was for spending, not making. She had to have a big house in Victoria and servants and clothes and friends in to afternoon tea. And they'd gab and think up more ways to spend money faster than Andrew could make it, until in the end there wasn't anything he could do that was good enough for her any more, so she up and took the baby and went off some place with Ma."

Colin listened closely, trying to fit what he knew of Grant into Robbie's picture. "Where are they now?"

"California. Hollywood, I guess. Last Andrew told me the mother was trying to get the kid into the movies. I guess she's still ambitious."

"Why did all that stop him going ahead?"

"Well," Robbie said slowly, "that's mighty hard to say. There's not many of us do the things we do for the reasons we say we do. Andrew's still married to that woman, he still sends her and the kid money—darn near all he makes. He says if he made more he'd have to send her more, so he just don't make it. To my way of thinking, Andy's not that small. He's a hard man, but I can't

106

figure him doing anything just for spite. Seems to me more likely he was just disgusted when he saw what having money did to people—that, and he wanted to keep away from people who knew what had happened. A man's self-respect is pretty important to him, and a good woodsman's always got it when he's in the woods."

Colin stood up and stirred the fire. "Robbie," he asked, "is there anything wrong with a fellow wanting to get back in the woods—to put in his life there, I mean, the way you and Mr. Grant do?"

Robbie looked at him sharply "A young fellow, you mean? That ain't no way for a young fellow to start out. Why, a young fellow's got the whole world ahead of him. There's nothing he can't do if he sets his mind to it, so long as he's sound in wind and limb and got a good head on his shoulders. Don't you listen too much to us old fellows. Most of us is here because we got disappointed with ourselves—we couldn't make the grade on the outside and got scared and come away where there was nobody to laugh when we messed it all up."

"That wasn't the way it happened to you. You like it here."

"I'm not so sure it ain't," Robbie said. "I never was any hell for success outside, that I could see. Sure I like it, or I wouldn't have come. But that don't mean I didn't run away to get here."

"You aren't sorry. I don't think Mr. Grant is sorry."

"Andrew hasn't quit the outside—you'll see, he'll get in there yet and come out on top. Him and me's different, and it's more than just education. We believe in different things. You won't see Andrew out looking at a lake in the sunset like us here. When he looks at a tree he's figuring what she'll cut out down at the mill and when he looks at a mountain he's wondering how much timber will come off without a switchback in the railroad. Andy's hard and he's practical. It's all figures to him." They were washing the supper dishes at the edge of the lake and Colin watched the colors of the sky touch the cheap tin plate in his hands. "I don't mean to make him sound all hard," Robbie said. "That'd be all wrong. Andy's got a heart big as a mountain. He's an honest man and a good friend—none better." He scooped sand into the frying pan, then glanced at Colin. "You might not think it," he went on. "But I'm a religious man. Andy believes in a god —I've heard him talk—but the God he believes in ain't no stronger than a real good man; more strait-laced maybe, especially about liquor and women, but not much bigger and not much stronger. I don't see it that way. Never could see God with a beard on his face and a thundercloud behind his head. God's in everything— in this sand and in those mountains and in that sky. More'n anything else He's in the way a man feels." He straightened himself slowly. "You're a young fellow," he said. "It'd be hard for you to understand. But if it weren't for the feeling I get that God's in me I wouldn't be staying up here alone like this. It's never been so strong any other place I've been."

As Colin listened to the old man he knew that the words touched himself, touched things he had seen and known and felt. He reached behind the words and tried to make what he found there break through and fit his experience; for a moment he thought that he could, then it slipped away from him and was lost. But he nodded slowly: "I know what you mean, Robbie. I know how it must be. I don't think you're running away. You can't be running away if you've come towards something and found it."

"That's wise talk," Robbie said. "And you might be right. When a man gets to thinking out all the angles on why he's done a thing, he's sunk. Like as not he starts thinking up reasons with a little bit of truth in them and forgetting reasons with a whole lot more truth in them. I never was one to lie to myself if I could help it, so I go a whole lot by the way I feel. And I feel right in here. That don't mean it's good for a young fellow, though."

"Why not? If he feels the same way."

"A young fellow's got no business feeling that way. It ain't healthy. A young fellow's got the whole world in front of him and he ought to want to go out and rip her wide open. When he's seen what's inside maybe he's got some right to an old fellow's way of thinking. But not before."

Going down the lake Robbie was silent. Colin dipped his paddle in the silent water, dipped it again and watched the pale stars come out in the light sky. The smooth ripples of the canoe's passing moved like silver over the dark surface of the lake. I feel good, he thought, better than good. But feeling good isn't feeling God in you like Robbie says. Or is it?

THEY finished the cruise of Amabilis Valley in mid-August. "That's the purest stand of silver fir you're ever likely to see," Grant told Colin. "And it's the only one like it within hundreds of miles of here. Right now you couldn't give it away."

"Why did we cruise it, then?" Colin asked.

"Because it'll be worth good money long before they get the railroad in here."

"How long will that be?"

"Might be ten years," Grant said. "Might be twenty. It won't be five years before this valley's worth money."

"Why does it change like that?" Colin asked. "Seems as though a thing that's going to be worth money in five years ought to be worth money now."

Grant laughed. "Ye've got the makings of a business man," he said. "Sure it's worth money, if you've got the money to put up and the nerve to put it up. That silver fir is as fine a pulpwood as there is and pulp's the future of this whole coast—it's got to be, now the Douglas fir's running out. Log prices are down to nothing right now and money's tight, but that won't last."

"You mean you think the camps'll get working again like they used to? Steady, all the time?"

Grant nodded. "It's never failed yet and it never will. It's a bad one this time and the money's badly scared. But it'll be sticking its neck out again—the head's out of the hole right now, for anyone with eyes to see it."

"Then Dad'll get his job back and everything will be the way it used to be?"

Grant nodded again. "There'll be grief and trouble yet while it's all working out. But there'll be camps working this fall, lots of them, and Will Ensley will always get his job."

"That's what Dad used to say himself when the shutdowns started, but it hasn't seemed to work that way. He doesn't say it any more."

It was still early in the morning, but they had had breakfast and were breaking camp. They had used the camp for only a few days, but it was a good camp and Colin liked it. The timber around it was small and clean and scattered; Amabilis Creek was very clear and very cold, not more than twenty or thirty feet wide here, fast running and shallow. The elevation by Grant's aneroid was over two thousand feet; Amabilis Lake was three miles downstream and Wind Lake another five or six miles down from there. Even with their packs they would make it out to Wind Lake well before evening, and Colin knew suddenly that he was sorry, that he did not want to leave the valley so soon.

"What is there up farther?" he asked. "On up the creek, I mean."

Grant turned and looked upstream. "Well," he said, "I'll tell you. If you ever want some really rugged country, that's the place to find it. I was through there once, around twenty years ago, right over the divide and down the Milky River to Menzies Lake and it was the hardest trip I ever made. There were four of us and two died of it."

Grant's tone was grim and Colin sensed that he wanted to leave the subject alone, but he said: "What happened? Why was it so bad?"

"You ask too many questions," Grant said. "It's time we got started." He swung his pack on to his back, picked up his axe and turned down the stream.

Colin followed in silence. Every step had suddenly become a retreat from what he wanted and he thought: if he doesn't want to tell me about it, why don't I go on up there and see for myself? He couldn't stop me. The rate the valley climbs beyond that last camp I'd be out of the timber in two or three miles. I'd like to see that. We haven't been above timber all summer and I sure wish we could have been. I wonder what happened to the guys that died up there. He says not to ask questions, but he never tells you anything, never even where the next job's going to be or how long it will last or anything. I guess we'll go down to Robbie's tonight, but he hasn't said so and now I can't ask him.

It was a hot day and Grant stopped at the foot of Amabilis Lake, where they had camped a few days earlier. The creek ran deep and slow through meadows at the outlet and it had been a

110

pleasant camp. They slid their packs from their shoulders and sat down, and Grant began to fill his pipe.

"You still want to hear about that trip?" he asked. "I guess there's no reason you shouldn't. I don't know why I shut you off like that just now, except that it's something I haven't talked about for years." He lit his pipe, drawing at it almost impatiently. "The whole thing was a mistake, and partly my fault. It was too late in the year for the trip and Tom Hughes made it worse by stopping to shoot a big goat. It all looked pretty easy then. When you get up beyond the timber this valley opens into a great wide gully and you feel safe as in a church—we did, anyway." The pipe had gone out, but he held it in his hand and made no move to relight it. "There's high mountains all round the gully and no pass out except what they call Windstorm Gap—that's over six thousand feet. Tom got his goat and we made it into the Gap. Then the bad weather caught us. There was snow on the ground already, lots of it, and we'd had some tough traveling. But the wind came at us right out of the north, driving snow so thick you couldn't see thirty feet. We got a tent pitched somehow and holed up in it for three days. The worst of the storm let up then, but we were short of grub and there was snow to our waists every place we looked." Grant looked at Colin. "Still interested?"

Colin nodded, but said nothing. His throat was dry and his body tense. Grant's short, abruptly spoken sentences made a strong, clear picture in his mind and his imagination built on it.

Grant went on: "We kept going instead of turning back. That was my idea and I guess it was wrong. Another storm caught us the next night and we were on an open ledge that time and never did get ourselves any kind of shelter. Tom was killed almost as soon as we started the next day—stepped on an overhang of new snow and fell a thousand feet with a hundred tons of snow going down after him. We couldn't even get down there and we wouldn't have found him if we had made it. John Lynch was in bad shape and Al Hughes and I weren't much better, so we had to keep going. We were down into the timber and clear of snow that night, but John was a sick man and he died less than a week after we got out—pneumonia."

Grant sat forward and put the pipe back in his mouth. "Not a very nice story, is it?"

"It was tough," Colin said. "But you did the best you could have."

"It cost two lives," Grant said. "And there wasn't any sense to it." He slipped into the shoulder straps of his pack and stood up. Colin stood up with him.

"You couldn't tell about the storm," he said. "If it hadn't been for that you'd have been O.K."

"We didn't have to go through that way at all," Grant said slowly. "It came out of boasting and kidding, no more than that. I was the one that knew better and ought to have stopped them." He looked at Colin. "I'm kind of glad I told you now. If you stay with the woods you'll be in a spot like that, sooner or later. When you are, you make them go back. Never mind the talk and kidding. You make them go back."

They came out to Wind Lake late in the afternoon and Grant said, as Colin had expected he would: "We can load the stuff and make Robbie's tonight, easy."

While they were loading the canoe, Colin asked: "Where do we go next?"

"There's two days' work near the foot of the lake," Grant said. "Then we'd better get you back to Blenkinstown. You won't have more than a week before school starts."

"I don't have to be there," Colin said. "If there's more work to do I'd sure like to stay with it."

Grant shook his head. "The job's done except for some bits and pieces I can do on my own. I wouldn't hold you out anyway. You've got all summer to make up for and the sooner you get working on it, the better."

Colin felt all the strength of the summer slipping away from him. He looked down at the loaded canoe, at the sweat-stained packsacks, the bright blade of his axe, the steel-shod jacob staff, the roped bulk of the tent. They had none of the meaning they had had a few moments ago. "Let me stay with it," he said desperately. "I'll catch up in school. Honest I will. Easy."

"I promised your mother," Grant said. "But it'd be the same if I hadn't. Listen, son, you've got a life in front of you. You're smart enough to make something of it. Don't make it tough for yourself by quitting halfway through school. Too many fool kids do that." Grant stepped into the stern of the canoe, reached for his paddle and swung the bow back in for Colin. As they started down the lake, Grant said: "Don't let it get you down, son. You knew it had to end sometime."

Colin drove his paddle for half-a-dozen strokes without speaking. He was looking ahead at the light ripple where Carlson's Creek ran out into the quiet lake.

"It'll be O.K.," he said at last, his voice flat and gloomy. He was remembering Robbie's words as they had looked down the lake from the mouth of Amabilis Creek. 'In the way a man feels,' he thought, that's what he said; well, it's all gone now. I don't feel any more.

PART THREE

THE BIG LAKE

1 4

MILDRED Hanson had stayed at the school to correct some papers and she hurried the quarter of a mile up the hill to the cottage she shared with Carol Maxwell. It had been cold in the schoolroom and the rain was cold as she walked, but it would be warm in the cottage.

She pushed open the door into the small living room and stood for a moment while her eyes got used to the light. There was a bright fire in the little fireplace and the room was warm and full of cigarette smoke. Carol was lying on the couch, an open book face down on her stomach, a cigarette in one long-fingered hand.

On a low stool beside her there was an empty coffee cup, a piled ashtray and several more books, all open and face down. Carol had turned her head as the door opened and lay watching Mildred.

Mildred slipped her coat away from her shoulders. "Did you hear about it?" she asked. "They're going back to work."

Carol nodded. "Yes, I heard. And they haven't got as much as they would have had a couple of weeks ago. I told you that man Miller was pushing it too far. He's single-track, like all the professional organizers."

"I know you did. But they've gained an awful lot, haven't they?"

"If they hold the union together, sure. But if too many of them lose faith and drift away because of Miller it won't be much good. This strike should be just the start."

"I'm glad they're going back, though," Mildred said. "Glad for all of them."

Carol smiled at her affectionately. "We should have a mirror right by the door," she said. "So that you can see what the wind and the rain do for your cheeks. Wheat-gold, sea-blue, rose-red, snow-white, all the trite words for lovely things. And so conscientious too."

Mildred laughed. "I just wanted to get those papers out of the way. I hate bringing them home. Did you start supper? I'm hungry."

"I peeled potatoes," Carol said. "And they're probably boiling by now. I made a salad with my own little hands. There are lamb chops in the ice-box. And all for you, my pet. I'm eating out."

She stood up, stretching her arms above her head. She was a girl of about thirty, very tall and slender, black-haired and dark-skinned. Her face was strong and sharp and keen and her eyes were very dark; with a little effort she could have been remarkably handsome, but it was quite evident that she had not made the effort and didn't intend to. Her hair was stringy and untidy, her black dress hung shapelessly about her and cigarette ashes marked the front of it; she wore no make-up and there was no ornament of any kind to relieve the dullness of her dress.

Mildred hung her coat up and smoothed the front of her skirt. "Where are you going?" she asked.

"To the Vickers'. A new policeman has just arrived and old Dan's got some kind of a promotion. He's a captain or a corporal or something all of a sudden instead of just a constable. June Vickers asked me. She's all tickled about it."

Mildred sat down on the edge of a chair and stretched her fingers out to the fire. "I'm glad," she said. "They don't have much fun, and Mr. Vickers has been here a long time."

Carol glanced lazily around the room. "I suppose I'd better go and wash my face," she said. "I'm due there at six and I ought to be hiking right now. Will you miss me, darling? What will you do? Go to bed with a good book?"

"No," Mildred said, without looking away from the fire. "I'll be up when you get back and the coffeepot will be on the stove."

Carol turned to go out of the room, then stopped suddenly, looking at Mildred's back. "That boy's not coming tonight, is he?"

"Of course," Mildred said. "He always comes on Thursdays."

"I should have thought of that," Carol said. "Maybe I'd better stay home after all."

Mildred turned slowly to look at her. "What *are* you talking about, Carol? Hurry up and change your dress."

"Sixteen," Carol said slowly. "Six-foot-two and big, even if he is gawky still. People in small towns do talk, you know, darling. Especially about schoolteachers."

Mildred flushed. "I wish you wouldn't say things like that, Carol. Even in fun."

Carol came a little way back into the room. "I'm sorry, darling. I'm always teasing when I shouldn't. But there's some truth in it, you know. The old cats would love to get hold of something like that. It's only once and they won't know anything about it, but I think you ought to send him away, just the same. He can come tomorrow night instead."

Mildred laughed. "I thought I was the fussy one. Go and change that dress. You've given them more to talk about than I ever will."

"Could be," Carol said. "But they don't talk. They never do about plain girls."

Mildred went into the kitchen and began to cook her supper while Carol was changing. Carol came out, kissed her and disappeared with a bang of the outside door. Mildred ate supper, changed her own dress, then tidied the living room and sat down to read. Colin was due at seven and he usually stayed till eight-thirty or nine. He was taking two grades in one year, to make up for the time he had missed the previous summer. Actually he was handling the work very easily and required little help beyond mild supervision, but Mildred had encouraged him to come as often as possible because she knew he would do little on his own, especially now that Margaret was no longer at home.

Through supper she had shut the implication of Carol's half-serious warning away from her. But now, sitting with a book open in front of her and the firelight warm on her face, she could no longer do so. Of course Carol's right, she thought, much more right than she thinks she is. She doesn't think there's anything attractive about Colin. What was it she said about him the other day? 'The primitive type, with the smell of the woods on him while the smell of his mother's pap still lingers; he doesn't just know whether to be a shy fawn or a roaring bull-elk and he never will know.' Then: 'He's like that father of his, not enough drive to be anything at all; that kind just lets things happen to it.' But she isn't right, Mildred thought calmly; nearly always she is right about people and she's kind about people even though she says such hard things; but not about Colin. There is something more in Colin than most people can see very easily, and it is something positive, something that he is, not something that happens to him. Perhaps it's only gentleness and kindness, but those are positive things and they can be very powerful. In Colin they will be; I used to feel that years ago, when he was only small, and I felt it again when I saw him down from the woods last summer. The same thing is in Margaret, but she uses it and makes it different; Colin doesn't use it, it's what he is and stronger for that, though not so easy to see. Carol doesn't look for things like that; she sees so many things so quickly that she expects everything to be plain, where you can see it and explain it. But people will feel that from Colin and respond to it; I think they do already.

She heard Colin at the door and went over to let him in. He

came in shyly, as always, and a little awkwardly, knowing that his hands and feet and body were too big for the room. He glanced around, as though expecting to see Carol Maxwell, then put his books down on the table. Mildred thought he was relieved that Carol was not there, but his deep voice sounded almost disappointed when he asked: "Miss Maxwell go out?"

"Yes," Mildred said. "I don't think she'll be back till after you've gone." She went back to her chair and sat down. "That Geometry again tonight," she told him. "You know where to start."

He settled himself with his books, then looked up and said: "Miss Maxwell is a swell teacher."

"It's good you like her," Mildred said. "She's very clever. She could have her Ph.D. if she wanted—she's done all the studying for it."

"She makes everything so interesting," Colin said. "Seems like you don't ever come near the end of what she knows and it's all there waiting, any time. Much more than is in the books."

"You're lucky to have her," Mildred said. "She could be teaching in university or anywhere she wanted, but she says she likes country schools."

"Seems funny," Colin said. "They must pay more in the big places."

"They do. But Carol—Miss Maxwell says country schools need good teachers just as much as the big places and she likes to live in the country. I expect she'll move on one day, though."

Colin turned to his work and said no more. The relationship between them was easy now, but his shyness never quite left him and Mildred had done nothing to draw him away from it since the day he touched her in the schoolroom. Deep in her teacher's soul, she knew she was wrong, knew that she should have found ways to build strength and confidence in him; but for a long while she had deliberately held the image of her own fault sharp and clear in her mind, using it to strengthen still further her familiar, calm control. The thoughts that had shocked her that bright spring day while the children wrote of mountains had come back many times, but she had learned to explain them to herself and she thought she understood them, though they still shamed her. Colin's power of attraction for her still waited in him and at times reached strongly out to her, but that, too, she had explained and thought she understood.

Sitting in the room while he worked, remembering the sharp thrust of joy in her heart when she had found him suddenly on the village street with Grant, she was able to tell herself that it was natural to have felt that, that any woman whose care was for children must feel it. Some girl will love him terribly one day, she thought; he's so helpless and yet so strong, and there's so much gentleness in him. Carol's wrong about him every way; the strength he has is not what she means by bull-elk strength, and the gentleness is not a fawn's gentleness; he's simple, but he's not primitive simple nor stupid simple; it is something in him that will keep him from hating or hurting anybody or anything and it can be made more than that, into something that will make him help people and do things for them.

She got up from her chair and stood behind him, looking over his shoulder. He drew away from the page in front of him and looked up at her. "O.K.?" he asked.

"It's good," she said. "You hadn't asked any questions for so long I was getting worried about you."

"It's so quiet in here it's easy to work."

She went back to her chair and sat down. I've been silly about it all, she told herself, so worried about being wicked and evil, always afraid for myself. Yet I'm strong about most other things, and sure, not hesitating or doubtful or afraid. I'm six years older than he is, a woman while he's still a boy. I'm not afraid of other men; there's never been one I couldn't keep in his place. I'm not afraid of Colin, I never have been afraid of him, only of my thoughts of him. And because of that I've held him away from me, cheated him of things I should have done for him, left him lonely when I knew he needed help.

"Colin," she said. "You aren't going off with Mr. Grant again this summer, are you?"

He looked up from his work. "No, I don't think so. He hasn't said anything about it. I'm not sure he's going himself."

"Don't go. You would never make it up again if you did."

"I might have to go if the camps don't keep working. They're starting up again the first of the week, but that doesn't mean there won't be a shutdown or another strike or something."

"Is your father glad they're going back?"

"Dad? He sure is. He figured they should have gone the first time the company offered. They had the wages then and that was the big thing, he said. He's awful sore at Miller, the organizer."

"Why should they strike again so soon?" she asked.

"I don't think they will," Colin said. "There's only a few of them want to. It's been tough for a long time."

"You liked it with Mr. Grant last summer, didn't you? I was afraid you weren't going to come back in the fall."

Colin smiled. "He didn't give me any chance not to come back. I tried to talk him into letting me go on with him, but it seemed like his mind was made up before I started. Mr. Grant is a hard man to talk around."

"I'm glad there's someone you'll listen to. He seemed nice when I saw you that day, but he certainly wasn't very talkative."

Colin flushed. "He's no talker, except sometimes with Robbie Robinson. But he's sure a swell guy to be in the woods with. There isn't anything he doesn't know about timber."

"Come and sit by the fire," Mildred said. "You've done enough work for tonight and you can tell me what it was you liked back there so much. You can talk a composition instead of writing one, for a change. It's good practice for speaking out in school."

Colin got up from the table and came hesitantly towards the fire. She pushed the stool over for him and he sat awkwardly on it for a moment, then moved to the floor. His body was tense and suspicious from the strangeness of the thing she had asked of him and for nearly a minute he sat staring into the fire. Then he said: "What do you want me to tell you?"

"Whatever you like," she said. "Try to make me understand what it was you liked so much and about your Mr. Grant and this Robbie Robinson. Start anywhere you like and just talk."

Colin leaned back against the stool and stared into the fire. He thought of the great trees on the flat of the valley below the lake, of the wet darkness under them, of the clear water and clean gravel up the little creeks. It was good there because it was new, he told himself; I didn't know anything there. It was better later on when I knew the score and Grant got friendly. Why does she want me to talk anyway? Why couldn't I just be here like this, near her, and both of us quiet? But I'd like to tell her, I'd like her to know, except that in talk things always sound foolish; you always forget things and the things that matter won't really go into words. If I could just lie here and think it and she could see it at the same time it would be different. That is how people ought to be able to talk, so they could both mean the same things at the same time.

"There's an old ranch," he said. "Down near the mouth of the river, just above the tide flats. It's falling apart now and nobody lives there, but it's a swell place; and in the old days some people named Underhill raised a big family there and had a school and everything." His body relaxed and he talked on steadily, describing the Underhill family and its life as Grant had described it to him. The rotting farm buildings, the overgrown garden, the landing on the river, the wagon roads into the brush, all came to life for him as he spoke; he saw the cattle on the flats, heard the clatter of the mower, the noise of the children in the orchard, smelled the sweat of the horses and the sweetness of fresh hay.

"People used to stop in there a lot," he said. "Mr. Grant did and all my mother's family when she was a child, anyone who was going up or down the coast and put in near the river. And the Underhills always fed them and looked after them and often if there were enough of them they'd put on a dance and people would come up from the camp that was here, where Blenkinstown is."

He hesitated and looked up at her face to see if she was listening. Their eyes met for a moment and he felt a softness in hers that made his pulses throb and forced him to look away. He began to talk again, of the big timber along the river, of the lake and then of Amabilis Valley. He tried to tell of the faith he felt from Robbie, but could not find easy words and turned away from it to tell her how the lake had looked from the mouth of the creek that night, how the shadows had fallen across the timbered valleys, how the sun had touched the tall snow peaks and the great rock faces. He forgot himself in the telling, forgot Mildred, became only a voice, distant to himself, and eyes that distantly watched the red light of the fire. The stool slipped away from him and he moved slightly to set his back against the arm of her chair.

Listening to him, feeling the warmth of the room, and its remoteness from all the rest of life, she let cold control slip away from her body and her mind. This is what I want of him, she thought, this is what he sees and feels and is. His mind has met these things and made something of them; he can bring them back and give them meaning for me, meaning and under-meaning, because that is there in the things he chooses to tell me and in the way the words come from him. I know now that he is one of the live people and I can make him grow; I have to because there is no one else who will.

Colin had stopped talking, but neither of them stirred. I should say something, Mildred thought, but not yet, not for a little while. He must go quite soon, but this will not happen again so naturally and so easily unless I leave the whole memory of it secure in him. She moved her left hand a little on the arm of the chair, towards Colin, but otherwise she did not move until she heard Carol's footsteps outside the door.

Carol came in quickly and stopped sharply, her hand still on the door. "Well," she said emphatically, then seemed to check herself. "You folks certainly look cozy. Know what time it is?"

Colin scrambled awkwardly to his feet, went over to the table and began to pick up his books. "I'd better start home," he said. "It must be pretty late."

"Don't hurry," Mildred said easily. "I'm going to make some coffee and we've got a cake out there."

"It's after ten o'clock," Carol said pointedly.

Colin moved towards the door. "The folks'll be waiting up," he said. "I better step on it. Thanks for everything, Miss Hanson."

Carol watched the door close behind him. "Thanks for everything," she repeated. "It's nice to know he appreciates it." She turned to Mildred and saw that she was angry. "Suppose," she said, "Old Siddons had walked in. Or the preacher. Or Mrs. Davidson. Instead of me?"

"I knew it was you," Mildred said. "And suppose it hadn't been. Can't he even sit near the fire?"

Carol slipped her coat off and flung it over a chair. "Don't be cross with your old aunt, darling. She's only looking out for your own good."

"You've frightened him," Mildred said. "He'll shut himself away again and I never shall be able to help him."

Carol looked at her. "You mean you're really serious about it? You really think you've found the streak of pure gold that's going to make him the Father of his Country or the Singer of its Songs?"

"There's something in him that isn't in most of us. I'm not sure what it is, but I'm good and sure it's a teacher's business to find out if she can."

Carol crossed the room and stood beside her. "My conscientious darling," she said. "I'll have to look at him again." The tips of her long fingers touched Mildred's pale hair, drew gently across the gold sheen and returned again. "If there's anything there you shall have your chance to wake it." She sat down on the arm of the chair beside Mildred. "Don't build too many hopes for him to live up to. There's nothing harder on a child than that."

"I won't." Mildred looked up and smiled. "But I've always felt someone owed Colin a break."

"You'd much better spend your time on the new cop."

"Another primitive?" Mildred asked. "Fawn or elk?"

"A craggy lion, darling. Tall, broad and magnificent. Granite jaw, hawk nose, steel-gray eyes, everything a girl could ask. He doesn't talk much more than your friend, but I've got a feeling he could make his words count."

15

MARTHA worked in her kitchen on a June afternoon and counted her blessings. Will had been working steadily since the strike and there was no suggestion so far of a shutdown unless a spell of dry weather made it essential. The strike itself had been a bitter and worrying time, but Martha had accepted it with a grim and almost glad determination; from the first she had held Will to his part in it, strengthening his resolve again and again when he showed signs of wavering or of reluctance in forcing a point. For her the issues had been simple: higher wages and no Sunday work. Because the strike won both points she was satisfied and her conscience was clear—the companies had been holding back something that it was in their power to grant.

Margaret had come back from Vancouver after her second year at the University and she was doing fully as well as Mr. Siddons and Mildred Hanson had said she would. She's changed a lot, Martha thought, much more a city girl than she used to be, quicker and busier and she talks differently and has more ideas and dresses differently. Perhaps all that would have happened if she had stayed right here, but you notice it more when she's been away. She's the same Margaret at the bottom, of course; she hasn't grown away from her family the way some girls do when they go to the city and she settles right in as soon as she gets back here. I'm glad she wants to be a nurse now instead of a teacher; all that about going on to be a lady-doctor later might come to something and it might not, but it's good for a girl to have ideas like that when you know she's smart enough to be able to go through with them.

Martha opened the oven door and took out a batch of bread. She turned the loaves upside down in the pans and set a clean dish-towel over them to hold in the moisture while they cooled. I don't suppose it's been easy for Margaret, she thought; Sister Edith never was an easy one to get along with and I can tell from the way she writes she thinks she's doing a lot for Margaret. She is, too; if Edith and Arthur didn't board her, Margaret couldn't go to school down there at all. But I don't doubt they get their money's worth back and a little more besides. If there's anything Margaret doesn't do in that house, from making beds to cooking fancy suppers, I'd like to know what it is.

It makes me proud of Margaret that she has never complained; if it weren't for Edith's letters and if I didn't know her so well I don't suppose I'd be able to guess what goes on down there. But Margaret is the determined kind, and that Miss Hanson has taught her a lot of things besides school work. She's got a big influence with Colin, too, making him study night after night the way he does to finish up those two grades. I didn't think Colin would ever settle to anything like that. Will says he can probably go up on the bridge-crew for a while this summer and next year he'll finish high school.

Martha lifted the lid of the potato pot and saw that the water was boiling. She heard footsteps outside and knew that Colin and Margaret were back from the barn with the milk. Will's late, she thought, and remembered, as she always did when he was late, the time the speeder carrying the bridge-crew had jumped the track. Two men had been killed then and all the others more or less seriously injured; Will had been lucky, with only a broken leg. His work's as safe as most, though, she reminded herself; a whole lot safer than the rigging crews.

Margaret came in then and Martha told her to set the supper table. "Your father's late," she said. "But he'll be here any minute and supper's all ready."

"We got nearly seventy pounds of milk tonight," Margaret said. "Colin says the rain has brought the pasture right up again." She took a pile of plates from the cupboard and Martha heard her quick, efficient steps go back to the table again. "You don't know how a person misses that, Mother, living in town. You almost forget that rain makes things grow."

Martha laughed happily. "So that's what we send you to college for." She looked up from the stove, listening. "That's them now. One thing about Mr. Varchuk's car; you can never mistake it."

Will Ensley's evening routine was fully restored. They heard him pause outside the door to loosen his laces and kick off his caulked boots, heard him murmur something to Colin at the separator. Margaret opened the door and he handed her his lunch pail without a word. Then he crossed the kitchen silently and hurriedly in his stockinged feet, as though ashamed of his working clothes, muttered an embarrassed greeting to Martha as he passed the stove, and went on into the bedroom beyond. In a little while he came back into the room, his working clothes changed for the bulky tweed pants and a thick dark-gray shirt. He spoke easily now and moved in a more relaxed way, but Margaret thought: he doesn't seem as huge as he used to. His shirt looks almost loose on him, but I remember when the largest shirts he could buy were always tight across his chest, so it seemed that the buttons would break away. His beard is just as square as ever, but it doesn't seem as black as it used to and his eyes don't seem as brightly black behind it.

She bowed her head and listened to the familiar intonations of his grace. "Bless this house, O Lord, and this family gathered beneath its roof. Bless the food that is before us and by its nourishment grant us strength to do Thy will." In the bad times, she remembered, the grace had sometimes faltered, sometimes wavered towards disillusion, sometimes shrunk into despair, sometimes forced out in hope and courage. It's almost like a diary, she thought, a daily part of him, so strongly a part of him that he lets it tell what he is thinking as nothing else ever does. Perhaps he feels it is secret to himself, that no one else will notice how much of him it gives away. But we do notice, all of us, me and Colin and especially Mother. Sometimes Mother waits so hard for it that she puts her head a little on one side to listen before he even starts to speak.

Mother's tired tonight. She's happy, but she's tired. Those long lines that run down past the corners of her mouth, from her nose almost to her jaw, don't fade out the way they used to. They're deeper and more tired when she's sitting quietly like this than when she's working. She doesn't seem old enough to have lines like that; she does everything so quickly and well and her eyes are so bright and young and laughing that I never think of her as old at all. Anyone who does as much as she does, who moves about so fast all day, takes so many steps, lifts so many things, uses her hands so much, is bound to get tired. When you get tired there are lines in your face, little lines at first, then deeper lines. And if you go on getting tired every day the lines get so deep they are there all the time, even when you're not tired. I suppose that's what getting old is. But I don't want Mother to get old. I don't want anything to happen to her ever so that she can't move about quickly and seem young and full of life; if that happened she wouldn't be Mother any more, if her eyes changed she wouldn't be.

For a moment, and for the first time in her life, Margaret saw and recognized death. Sharply, death forced itself upon her; people grow old, their bodies wear out from living and doing, they die. But not Mother, her mind said, not for years and years and years. She will change slowly and gently, her eyes will always laugh and burn blue, her hands will always move swiftly and surely, her feet will always be quick and light. I shall grow older myself, and change with her, and because of that we shall always be the same to each other.

Will Ensley said: "We moved out to the new trestle on the spur line today. Seems like the turn has come."

"That does look more hopeful," Martha said. "Things seem a little better everywhere."

"Not in the cities," Margaret said. "There are thousands of unemployed in Vancouver."

Will Ensley looked at her and frowned. "That will be changing. It can't all happen overnight. They'll get their chance— some of them will be getting it right here in Blenkinstown now the mills are running again and they're starting a new side up at camp."

"Some of the boys I know in town don't think so," Margaret said. "They're talking about organizing a big march on the government in Victoria."

Her father looked at her in astonishment and irritation. "Foolish talk," he said, and Margaret caught her mother's anxious glance and knew that she must say no more. "Child's talk and wickedness. If they get out of the cities and look for it they will find work."

"It's a hard time for young people, Will," Martha said gently.

"You can't altogether blame them for thinking there must be something wrong."

"They'll gain nothing by setting themselves up against authority, and I'm sorry that a child of mine should have any dealings with such people. If they were older they would know there's nothing new in all this and nothing that can be changed by threats and violence."

"They just want a chance to work, Will. And perhaps the government will do something when they see how many of them there are. People do get things by going out after them."

"There's some truth in that," Will said. "We gained something by the strike. But I hope there'll be no more of them."

Margaret watched him turn back to his food again, as though the subject were entirely forgotten. He's changed a lot, she thought, and Mother has too. I'm sure he wouldn't have given in to her like that a few years ago, and he would have been much angrier with me. We've all changed, I suppose, even Colin, though I think he's still scared of Father. In a way I am, but it's different because I can see through the being scared; I know that he isn't God after all, that he's quite a simple man and not nearly so wise as he used to sound. I wish I knew what Colin thinks. I must ask him sometime, except that it's a hard thing to ask exactly the way I mean it, and he probably wouldn't tell me anyway.

The meal was finished and Margaret was washing the dishes when Dave Vickers and the new policeman came to the door. Dave said cheerfully: "Hope we're not disturbing supper, folks."

"No," Martha said. "Everyone's finished."

Will was standing up and came across the room. "Come on in and sit down," he said. "It isn't often we get to see you." Will liked Dave Vickers. "Glad to see you've got those stripes at last," he added.

Dave laughed. "They're like old age and false teeth—you always get 'em if you wait around long enough. But I want you to know Constable Munro. I've been telling him that's a policeman's first duty—to get to know all the old-timers in his district."

Margaret turned away from the dishes and watched. Both Vickers and Munro were tall men, so tall that they stood in the low-ceilinged kitchen with slightly stooped heads, and both were in uniform. Vickers was a man of fifty or fifty-five, red-faced and heavy featured. He was cheerful and sure of his welcome, an easy-going man, used to liking people and being liked. Munro was much younger, about twenty-five Margaret thought, with a pale, hard-cut face and quiet gray eyes. He was wearing breeches and high boots and carried a police stetson in his hand; everything about him, boots, breeches, tunic, belt and holster seemed fitted and polished and in place, in sharp contrast to Dave Vickers' slightly sagging appearance. Dave introduced the whole family, then dropped his flat uniform cap beside a chair, loosened his belt a little and sat down. Munro sat stiffly in another chair Will had brought up for him, Martha sat in her own chair talking easily to him and Will settled to talk with Dave Vickers. Margaret and Colin went back to the dishes.

Colin reached past Margaret for a dish, so that his head was close to hers. "Gee," he said. "That's a lot of man, that new cop."

"Beautiful, but dumb," Margaret whispered back.

"How do you know?"

"He hasn't said much, has he?"

"Girls," Colin said. "You're always critical. He probably knows a whole lot more than you ever will."

"I'll believe it when I see it."

When they had put away the dishes they started out of the room, but Dave Vickers stopped them.

"Don't run away," he said. "I want to hear about college and the big city. I see by the papers you came through with flying colors again, Margie."

Margaret smiled at him. "That's only the second year, Mr. Vickers. I've got a long way to go yet."

"And you'll come through at the top of them all, my dear. It's an honor to the town to see your name where it is on those lists." Vickers shifted in his chair and looked at Colin. "You going to follow in your sister's footsteps, young fellow?"

Colin looked over at his father, then back to Vickers. "I don't know, Mr. Vickers," he said. "I guess I wouldn't make much of college."

"Nonsense," Vickers said. "I hear you're every bit as smart as

Margie was at your age." He turned to Munro. "Smartest family in this town," he said. "You ought to be proud of them, Will."

"Colin's coming up on the bridge-crew with me as soon as school lets out," Will said.

"Think they'll keep running for a while?" Vickers asked. The question was one that Margaret had heard asked a thousand times, and Vickers asked it casually; but something in his tone made her glance quickly at him, and she knew that Martha had noticed too.

Will had not. "Nothing to stop them," he said. "Unless bad fire weather and there's certainly no sign of that yet."

"Wettest spring in years," Vickers agreed. "If I were new to the coast like Clyde Munro here I believe I'd be applying for a transfer to the Interior right now."

"No logger minds a wet shirt in June and July," Will said. "I'll take the coast climate ahead of anything I ever saw east of the mountains."

"I guess there's no fear of another strike coming along to break things up?" The question was almost elaborately casual this time and Margaret felt again that there was purpose in it. She watched Clyde Munro's face, but saw nothing there beyond a polite, un-smiling interest. He's a cold one, she thought, hard and cold and I don't think I like him. But she watched him closely as Will answered.

"We don't want any more of that for a while. There was good in the last one, up to a point. But what we need now is a spell of steady work."

Margaret saw that Martha was looking hard at Will, trying to catch his eye. He must have looked towards her, because Martha shook her head twice, very slightly, very cautiously. Margaret recognized the warning.

"I heard Miller was up around these parts again," Vickers said.

Will moved sharply in his chair. "An empty vessel," he said sharply. "Sounding brass and a tinkling cymbal. He's wasting his time if he hopes to stir up anything among sane men."

"Have you seen anything of him since he got back?" Again Martha was signaling, almost frantically this time. Will started to speak, saw her, hesitated and blundered into clumsy denial.

"No," he said. "No, Miller hasn't shown up around any place I know of. He could be around, mind you, and I wouldn't know about it. But I don't think that's so."

Watching Munro, Margaret saw the muscles at the corners of his mouth relax ever so slightly. There, she thought, you almost trapped him but not quite. You haven't got anything, it didn't do you any good, you can go away now. Poor Father, he's miserable, he doesn't know whether he has done right or wrong. He's truly fond of Dave Vickers, he always likes policemen and he's said a hundred times that it is the duty of a good citizen to help them uphold the law. Now he's had to betray that, to put himself on the other side, the wrong side, the side of the unrighteous and the ungodly, the men without dignity or worth.

Vickers said easily: "It's not important, Will. I was just curious for myself. I don't suppose he is around or we'd have heard of it. I think you're right anyway, he wouldn't get to first base with the boys this time." He turned to Colin. "So you're going to work with your dad this year, Colin? You couldn't learn from a better man."

"That's right," Colin said simply.

"Colin would sooner be back in the woods with Andrew Grant, like he was last summer," Will said. "But Andrew's not going out this year, so he'll be learning to use his arms instead of his legs."

"It's a fine trade, the broad-axe," Dave Vickers said. "But it's dying out, like a lot of other good things. They're using pretty near all sawn ties now and more bridge timbers from the sawmills all the time."

"A sawn stringer will never have the strength of a hewn stringer," Will said. "And sawmill ties may be good enough for a mainline, but on a spur line where you want to take them up and use them again, nothing will ever beat hewn hemlock."

"True enough," Dave said. "I guess it's not so much they don't want the goods as they can't get the men to make them."

"The sawmill stuff is cheaper, too," Munro said. "At least at the start."

"That's all you can say for it," Will told him. "A trestle built of sawn timbers is no better than a house built upon the sand."

The tension had dropped away and the four adults talked

comfortably. Colin whispered to Margaret and they both went quietly out of the room. "Let's go to the hayloft," Margaret said, and Colin knew she wanted to talk.

As they walked towards the barn Colin said: "Do you still figure the new cop is dumb?"

"No," Margaret said. "He's plenty smart, I guess. But he's a cold sort of fish; figures he's a hard guy, I suppose."

"You sure don't give him any breaks, do you? I like him. I like the way he looks at you and the way he sits listening to other people talk instead of gabbing away all the time himself."

They came to the barn and sat down on the ledge of the wide doorway instead of climbing to the hayloft.

"Sure he listens," Margaret said. "Sometimes you make me tired, Colin. Couldn't you see what they were trying to do, trying to trap Dad into telling them where Miller is? Dave Vickers was doing the talking, but that Munro is the smart one. I'll bet he's been sent up here specially for that kind of stuff." She thought: why did I say that? I hadn't thought it until just as I spoke and I'm not sure it's right anyway. I knew I didn't like him long before Mr. Vickers said anything about Miller; I don't like him because he's cold and stiff and conceited, that's all.

Colin said: "Mr. Vickers said it wasn't important about Miller. What could they do about it if they did know where he was? It's none of their business."

"They'd probably put him in jail. They do put labor leaders in jail."

"They couldn't," Colin said. "There's no law against having a union."

"They do though. They put them in jail for something else. Pretty nearly everybody's done something he could be put in jail for."

Colin shrugged his shoulders. "Sounds crazy to me. I think Mr. Vickers just wanted to know if there's another strike coming up."

They heard the screen door slam and looked towards the house. "It's Munro," Colin said. "I wonder where he's going?"

"Looks as though he's coming over here," Margaret said, and

1 3 2

they watched the tall policeman walking towards them across the pasture.

When he came near Colin stood up, but Munro smiled and said: "Don't move. I just wanted to look around a farm again. You've got a nice place here."

Margaret looked at him suspiciously. "Did you ever work on a farm?"

"I was raised on one, Miss Ensley," he said. "I used to think sometimes I wouldn't mind if I never saw a cow-barn again, but I guess it gets in your blood. I can't pass one up now."

Colin met Munro's slow smile and liked him in spite of what Margaret had said. "I know what you mean," he said. "It must be quite something when you have a big bunch of cows to milk every day, night and morning. The most we've ever had is four."

"With us it was anywhere from twenty-four to thirty and generally three of us to milk. Most of the time I liked it fine, but once in a while it'd seem to get you down."

"Would you like to see the cows?" Margaret asked Munro. "They're Jerseys."

"I sure would," Munro said. "We had Holsteins."

"Can you find them, Colin?"

Colin nodded. "They'll be in the edge of the alders, near the creek."

He started across the pasture and Margaret followed him closely without another word to Munro. Farm-boy, indeed, she thought; he likes cows and barns. He does like heck. Next thing we know he'll be asking us about Miller. I'll have to watch he doesn't get Colin alone. Colin wouldn't tell now I've talked to him, but he's like Dad; he can't tell a lie and make it sound like anything except a lie.

She held herself very straight as she walked, and moved gracefully, in spite of Colin's swift pace. She knew that she looked trim and well-made, knew that her skirt swung handsomely about her knees and hoped that Munro was watching. At least he can see that we aren't all simple country people who'll fall for any soft line he wants to put out. Chances are he'll trip over his big boots before we find the cows, anyway; I hope he does.

They were in the alders and there was a big log across the way

Colin had gone. Suddenly Margaret realized that Munro was ahead of her, over the log, offering her his hand. "Thanks," she said. "I can manage."

They found the cows and Colin showed them off proudly. They were very tame with him, swinging their heads to his voice, standing for his touch, their eyes brown and calm and incurious. But when Munro moved closer they stirred nervously, watching him awkwardly, ready to swing away and plow off through the breast-high brush. He went on toward Brownie, the nearest of them, speaking gently to her, passing smoothly and quietly through the brush. She'll fool him, Margaret thought, old Brownie'll never stand for him and he'll look silly turning away to try it out on another one. But Brownie stood and he laid a big quiet hand on her back, near the shoulders and slid it along to her rump and she only watched him curiously. He stooped and Margaret knew he was feeling the milk veins and the udder; and she knew at the same time that he was really interested in the cow, that he hadn't been simply trying to make them like him there at the barn.

Munro looked up at Colin. "She's a good one," he said. "A four-gallon cow anyway."

"Four and a half when she's fresh," Colin said. "Brownie's the best of the lot. But I've never seen her stand like that for a stranger."

"Those neat-built Jerseys are often nervous, especially when they've got little feet like she has. They seem more like a deer than a cow if you're used to Holsteins. But they're wise too, if they've been treated right. Seem to know who means well by them."

Margaret watched his face. The big dope's happy, she thought; I believe he really was homesick for his old farm. Now he's up with Colin looking at Fern and she's standing for him too. That's all black mud in where they're standing and I didn't think he'd ever take a chance on getting those shiny boots dirty.

The three of them walked abreast back towards the house. Munro was as tall as Colin but seemed taller because he carried himself so well, and Margaret felt very small beside them. Colin asked: "Will you be staying here, Mr. Munro?"

"That's something they never let us know for sure," Munro said.

"But I hope so. I've never been on the coast before and I like this part."

"Will Mr. Vickers be leaving, then?" Margaret asked him.

"No, Miss Ensley. They've made Blenkinstown a two-man station and we're going to have a boat here when they get around to it."

"Who is 'they'?" Margaret asked aggressively. She was still trying not to like him.

Munro laughed apologetically. "The Commissioner, I guess, when you come right down to it. He's the one who decides. But it goes through a lot of people on the way up to him—sergeants and inspectors and different departments. I guess that's why we always say 'they.' "

Something in the simple explanation conveyed to Margaret the respect and affection he had for his force. That's why he holds himself so proudly and carefully, she thought, and why his uniform is so clean and pressed and polished.

"You like being a policeman, don't you?" She asked.

"Yes," he said simply. "A good policeman can do a lot for people."

1 6

COLIN swung the scoring axe in an easy rhythm, stroke after stroke so that the bright blade drove always the same depth into the soft wood. As he scored the face of the stringer he moved along the log, feeling his caulks bite crisply into the sapwood. He had been working on the bridge-crew for nearly three weeks now, scoring for his father's broad-axe most of the time, and the muscles of his shoulders and wrists had learned a control that brought him a deep satisfaction. At first he had been inaccurate and slow, although the axe was a familiar tool, and his father had drawn his attention to every error. But now Will Ensley worked in satisfied silence, swinging his own huge axe with the full power of his great arms and body, flattening the faces of his caps and stringers to plane smoothness in which it was almost impossible to find even a hairline where one of Colin's strokes had gone too deep or the slightest break where the scoring had been too light.

The bridge-crew was building a trestle on the spur line and it was a good show. It was a fair-sized trestle for a spur line, sixteen bents, the highest about forty feet to the cut-off, but there was new rigging on the driver, the piles were good, the driving was good and things had gone smoothly. Old George Smith, the foreman, who rarely spoke above a whisper and never took his hands out of his pockets, even to bend down and sight a cut-off, was less in evidence even than usual. He spent a good part of every day roaming the side-hill above the trestle, marking down deer that he claimed he would shoot in the fall. The crew was happy about it; George hadn't treated life that way since the first long shutdown.

Will Ensley's work was well ahead. For once there had been plenty of logs for caps and stringers and they were good stuff—the right size and really clean. He had a perfectly flat landing to work on right at the approach to the trestle and it was already ankle-deep in chips and shavings and full of the clean cedar smell that he loved. He hadn't faced such an abundance of straightforward broad-axe work for years and he shut himself away into it with the intentness he always used on the job, speaking scarcely a word to Colin or the rest of the crew even when they gathered to brew coffee and eat their lunches each noon.

The noon break was two hours behind them now and it was a hot July afternoon. George Smith had just come back from a short trip up the hill and was moving quietly about near the pile driver, smiling absentmindedly and seeming to care nothing at all about how the work was going. He stopped and spoke to Sam Boulder, the oldest of the regular bridgemen and George's best friend, squinted ahead at the bent the driver was working on, then climbed on to the driver to stand by Johnny Meldrum at the levers.

Colin finished the face he was working on and stood back to

look along the evenly spaced marks of his scoring. He had seen George Smith come over the hill and down the slope, had watched him walk the slim poles that were spiked to the caps of the completed bents, stop to speak to Sam and go on to climb on to the pile driver and stand beside Johnny Meldrum, as he often did when he was not on the hill. Vaguely Colin envied George his freedom. He knew he would be talking lazily with Johnny, almost knew what they would be saying. "Four-pointer, in the velvet, down under the blackberry vines" or "A whole brood of blue grouse, must of been ten anyway, so that wet weather in June didn't drown 'em all." That was George's talk, always, or something much like it. Occasionally something had to be said about the trestle, but it was always said as off-handedly as possible, and the bridge-crew liked that and worked better for it because it recognized that they were all skilled men. Once George had overheard Will checking Colin on the accuracy of his chopping. "Kid's doing pretty good, Will," he had said. "You won't get many take to it like he does."

"A boy'll never learn without telling," Will had said. But, like the rest of the crew, he respected George Smith and he said less to Colin from then on.

Colin walked over to the next timber and sized it up against the line his father had already stretched along it. He thought: it's easy work, this swinging an axe all day, easier than school-work and you hardly have to worry about it at all after the first little while; you can just go along with it, thinking your own thoughts, not even thinking really, just letting pictures go on and on through your mind any way they want to go. You do that in school and it always catches up with you—some teacher asks a question and you don't even know what he has asked. I like working with Mr. Grant better than this job. You've got to pay attention to that, but you've got time to think and new things to think about all the time because you're moving all the time. Here you can find new things to think about because things move and you see them, people move and talk and do things, or the pile driver chunks out the bridge-site and turns up old logs that haven't been moved for a hundred years. You can think about those and the moss growing on them and the dirt underneath and the insects inside. But it still isn't as good as moving yourself. And this job isn't as good as the other. It's like Miss Hanson says, a man needs something that makes his brain work, not just something that stretches his shoulders. Dad has to think a bit, but he's so used to the job it's hardly thinking any more. George Smith uses his head; he has to, a whole lot more than he ever lets on; the boys say he can figure out anything, better than the best engineer, by just using a steel-square; they argue about that—some of the boys say he bluffs a lot and he's really no more than a darn good carpenter. But the older ones say he can figure out any kind of trestle there is; Sam Boulder says he built one once with a horizontal and a vertical curve and there wasn't an engineer came near it from the time they chunked out until they put the ties on. But even George Smith is doing the same thing over and over until it gets so easy for him he doesn't really have to worry.

He watched the bright arc of his axe and for a moment was conscious of the rhythm of his work—the lift of the blade and the slide of his right hand along the handle, the timed drive of shoulders and wrists, the clean soft shock as the blade swept into the wood, repeated and repeated. His body felt powerful and sure. He was still thinking of Mildred Hanson, but his mind called her Mildred now, instead of Miss Hanson, and he wished she could be there with him at the moment of his power and certainty. If they were alone he could touch her, perhaps even hold her and feel her, small and cool and beautiful against him. If I could go straight to her from work I might feel like this and say what I want to say. Only it wouldn't really happen that way; I wouldn't be able to say it and she would smile a little or perhaps be angry, and send me away. She'd have to.

Colin heard the rattle of the speeder along the tracks before anyone else noticed it. He was well started on the new log, but he drove his axe firmly into the cut and turned to watch the speeder come into sight round the curve. He saw that his father had stopped work and was watching too.

Colin recognized Gordon Holman, the woods superintendent, and Red Peterson, the speeder-man. The others were obviously city men, but he could not remember that he had seen any of them before.

138

"The little one is Mr. Blenkin," Will said. "Don't stand staring at them. Get on with the job." He spat on his hands, picked up the broad-axe and swung it down in a great smooth stroke on the face Colin had scored. Colin swung his own axe, but as it fell he saw George Smith walk out on to the rear of the pile driver and shade his eyes to look towards the speeder.

Five men came up from the speeder, Mr. Blenkin with Holman, a little in the lead, the other three trailing behind. Red Peterson waited beside his speeder.

Mr. Blenkin walked straight up to Will and held out his hand.

"Glad to see you again, Will," he said. They shook hands and Blenkin looked around at the hewn timbers on the landing. "It's easy enough to see you haven't lost your touch." He turned and introduced the other men who shook hands with Will in turn. "These gentlemen have never seen real broad-axe work, Will," he said. "I was telling them about you on the way up here on the boat and I don't think they believed half of it. Have you got anything fancy around here to show us?"

Will set the head of his axe down on a log and crossed his huge hands on the handle. "There isn't much around a pile-bent trestle, Mr. Blenkin," he said. "You know that. Just straight hewing—caps and stringers and a mud sill or two."

"You framed the first bent the way you always do," Gordon Holman said. "And that's one of your sleds, under the pile driver."

They moved away to look at Will's work and Colin watched them. He felt proud of his father, yet ashamed for him too. There had been something patronizing in the way Mr. Blenkin spoke to him, in spite of his friendliness; it had seemed as though he were showing off a good work-horse or a hunting dog. But Will had accepted the attention proudly, stretching his great chest and holding his bearded head high as he went off with them. There's none of them can do what the old man can, Colin thought; that little Mr. Blenkin couldn't even lift Dad's big axe, let alone hew with it all day. Let them watch him and look over what he can do. He may not be as smart as they are most ways, but this is one place he's the smartest man there is.

He saw that Gordon Holman and Will Ensley were walking

back towards the landing. Holman was talking but Will was saying nothing and his face was set. As they came closer Colin heard Holman say: "We know you old-timers don't want any more of it, but that guy's around this neck of the woods again and he's going to make more trouble—so's that other one, Zobieski."

They were standing close to Colin now, Will with his feet firmly planted and his thumbs hitched into the belt band of his pants, Holman small beside him, hands pushed down into the pockets of his light cruiser coat, his lean face intent.

"It's nothing to us who's around," Will said at last. "We aren't going out again."

"You maybe think you aren't, but if they pull the rest of the crew you'll be out too, whether you want it or not."

"They can't do much, hiding out in the bush."

"They're holding regular meetings—we know that too. Look, Will, I'm just telling you for your own good. A bunch of you could get together and run 'em out in jig-time—just rough 'em up enough so they won't come back in a hurry. Show 'em they're not welcome."

Will turned away sharply and picked up his axe. "It's bad, Gordon," he said. "Have you talked this way to anyone else?"

"A few. You could have a bunch together in no time."

"Earl Mayhew?"

"No, not yet."

"George Smith? Leo? Tony?"

"No."

Will stepped up on to the log he was hewing and looked down at Gordon Holman. "Those men helped us when we needed help," he said deliberately. "My hand will never be upon them." He picked up his axe and swung it and Holman turned away to meet Blenkin and the others coming up from the trestle.

When the speeder had clattered out of sight around the curve, Colin asked his father: "Was he talking about Miller?"

Will nodded slowly and Colin saw that strength had gone out of his face and the lift of his shoulders was proud no longer. "What's the man to me, that they should plague me about him?" Will asked, and he seemed not to be speaking to Colin at all. "Our ways are different. He had his part and it is done. I have

140

my part." He held his axe so that the handle rested across his short thick thighs and somehow his body indicated the bridge timbers and the trestle and the woods all about him. "Let them leave me to it."

IT was two or three days later that Colin heard Don Williams' voice as he came down towards the shelter where the bridge-crew was eating lunch. Will had stayed up on the landing to eat. "Him and his goddamned beard and his Bible-punching play-acting," Williams said. "All he is is a company stooge."

Sam Boulder's voice asked quietly: "What's Will ever done to you?"

"Nothing. Nor ever will. But I sure hate a company man. It made me sick to my stomach to see the act he put on for the big shots the other day. More like a performing dog than a man."

Colin felt his face hot and his breath short. He half turned away, thought better of it and went on into the awkward silence of the shelter. For a moment he stood there, his big hands hanging at his sides, his head down, his eyes on the ground. Sam said something, but Colin forced himself to look across at Williams and said: "I heard you."

Williams laughed. He was a sandy-haired, blue-eyed man, two or three years older than Colin, heavily and strongly built. "Ain't that just too bad," he said. "What are you going to do about it?"

"It isn't true," Colin said, and Williams laughed again.

"Aw, shut it off," Sam Boulder told him. "You'll spend years trying to be as good a man as Will Ensley and like as not you'll never make it." He looked at Colin and nodded towards the little stove. "There's your old man's coffee, kid," he said. "Take it up to him."

Colin took the blackened can without a word and went away with it.

THE camps shut down for fire weather early in August that year and Colin was glad. Although he had learned the work quickly and well, he had felt always that his father was ashamed of his awkward appearance and expecting him to make mistakes. His father was nearly always silent on the way to and from work and mixed little with the crew on the job or even during the noon hour; he seemed tightly shut within himself by his age and his dignity and his craftsmanship, both unable and unwilling to become a part of the good-natured friendship that George Smith stimulated so easily in the rest of the crew. Most of the men had known Will for years and had accepted his aloofness and granted him the right to it long ago. Because Colin worked with Will and talked little, they let Will's aloofness include him and made little effort to draw him into their fellowship.

Colin had felt this isolation of himself and his father and at first his shyness had welcomed it. But in time he had come to hate it. George Smith, Johnny Meldrum, Sam Boulder and the half-dozen younger bridgemen who made up the crew seemed like free men and heroes, playing mightily in the sunlight while he and his father toiled like slaves in the shadow. To work as he did and to be in silent shadow was part of his father's dim, bearded godhead; but Colin had no godhead; he was condemned to silence and shadow and isolation by his own frailties, by his awkward body, his uneasy mind, his fear.

For one positive reason Colin had been hoping that the shutdown would come. Johnny Harris wanted to go up to Wind Lake to see Robbie Robinson. "I want to ask him about getting a trapline up around there," Johnny had said. "The old man says it's O.K. and I can take his gas-boat to run around to the mouth of the river. Want to come along if we get a shutdown?" Johnny was working for Blenkin Logging too, blowing whistles over on Side one. So the shutdown meant they were both free to go.

Johnny's "gas-boat" was a fourteen-foot rowboat with a small single-cylinder motor in it, so they ran right up to the old Underhill farm and dragged it up on the beach above tide level. They were in no hurry so they left their packs by the boat and wandered up to the old buildings. "It sure was a big enough house," Johnny said. "You wouldn't think a man would go to all that trouble in a place like this."

Colin had thought so often about the Underhills that he felt an immediate need to defend them. "He raised a big family on the place," he said.

"And went broke at it. Wouldn't do for a guy like you or me that hasn't got two nickels to rub together. We've got to find some other way to raise a family."

"I've got a hunch a man could make it stick," Colin said. "If he went at it right."

As they walked back to get their packs, Johnny said: "You wouldn't be thinking of trying it, would you?"

Colin looked at him in surprise. "Who? Me? Of course not. That would be for an old married guy, like Underhill was. A guy that wanted to raise a family."

"You seem to have done a lot of thinking about it," Johnny told him. "A person'd almost think you'd seen the place when they lived here."

"It's just what I've heard from Mother and from old Robbie," Colin said. But even as they shouldered their packs he was looking at the rickety legs of an old landing. And he knew the Underhill children had once lain at full length on its deck in the summer sun, dangling fishing lines as the tide came up.

THE weather was good and they took their time in traveling up the valley. They camped the first night about six miles up the river, where the trail passed near the edge of a big pool. After supper they went fishing and caught big cutthroat trout on caddis grubs and surprised a bear that was looking for salmon. To Colin it was like a return to the life he had lived with Grant, only better because of their freedom and because he liked Johnny Harris so well. Johnny was an easy friend; you could tell him things because he was a friend and know that he would treat them gently and understandingly, that he would answer with things of his own that enriched your things and bound him to you, as you were bound to him. Johnny was not shy or awkward or afraid; he was of the world, the fullest possible world of school and the village and people. Yet he could stand away from all that world if you asked him to and be with you and for you; yet, being of the world, he knew its thoughts and its answers, and being with you and for you he could explain the thoughts and quote the answers without impatience or contempt. Without realizing it Colin had learned long ago to depend upon Johnny's simple and direct wisdom to answer many questions that he would never have dared ask anyone else except possibly Margaret or Mildred Hanson. He asked him now, as they knelt by the edge of the river to clean the trout they had caught: "Johnny, what's a 'company man'?"

Johnny carefully slit the belly of the trout he was holding. "Depends who says it, I guess," he said. "But mostly it means a guy who's for the company—who thinks the company's O.K. and doesn't mind putting in overtime or anything else they want him to do. Why?"

"Is my old man one?"

Johnny picked up another fish and slowly considered the point. "No," he said at last. "Your dad's an old-timer and I guess he figures the company's O.K. But he was on the strike committee and he hasn't got the kind of job that makes for a real company man. A company man mostly is a side-push or a bookkeeper or some guy that's going to get a better job with the company if he keeps his nose clean."

"Just the same," Colin said. "Some people say Dad's a company man."

"What do you care?"

"They hate him for it. They talk like he was a scab or something. Like he wasn't a man at all."

Colin tried to make himself repeat what he had heard Don Williams say, but could not. "It's not something a guy can just forget about once he's heard it."

"Likely it was people that didn't know your old man. There's a difference between an old-timer who works steady for the same company and a real company man. Some guys just talk to hear themselves, anyway—don't mean nothing by it."

"He meant it," Colin said. "He said it like he hated Dad, like he'd just as soon do him real dirt or even kill him. You couldn't hate a guy like that if you didn't know him."

Johnny washed his hands off in the river and picked up the string of trout. "My dad says you can't hate a person you really know. You just hate what you think you know about a guy; soon as you find out a little more about him you stop hating him. I've tried that out on kids at school and it sure works."

"Did you try it out on Tod Phalling?" Colin asked.

Johnny looked at him and grinned: "I hadn't heard about it when he was around," but he added seriously, "I kind of think it'd work even with Tod. At least you wouldn't hate him quite so bad."

They had walked up from the river and Colin stirred up the small camp-fire. Johnny sat on his blankets, rolling a cigarette. Colin said: "I can't see hating guys and fighting and all that stuff. It makes me sick at my stomach. Maybe I'm yellow or something."

"A man can't crawl," Johnny said. "There's times when he has to fight. But he don't have to like it. Not liking it isn't being yellow." He lay back and drew happily on his cigarette. "You going to school again next year?" he asked.

Colin nodded. "No sense to quitting now. I don't mind it."

"My old man wants me to go back and finish. But I couldn't take it. I guess it's not so bad if you've been going right along, but going back to it seems like going back to short pants."

"Mother wants me to go to a university, like Margaret. So does Hanson."

"You can't lose," Johnny said. "You always were smart in school."

"I don't see what it gets you, unless you want to be a doctor or a teacher or an engineer maybe."

"What's wrong with being an engineer? You're a darn good woodsman and that's a fair start on it."

"I'm no good at figures," Colin said. "Even Hanson admits that."

"You ought to go, anyway. A guy who's been to college has got a chance at a whole different set-up of jobs. It means something."

"You've got to get some kind of job to pay your way through, to start with. I couldn't even do that."

"Guys do it all the time."

"Not guys like me. I wouldn't know where to start in. I've only been in Vancouver once in my life."

Johnny was silent, looking into the fire. After a while he said, "It's no use a guy trying something he doesn't believe in. You've got to believe in a thing to make it work."

"I know," Colin said. "The only time I believe in it is when Mildred talks about it. Other times I can't even remember how she made me believe in it."

Johnny had glanced up sharply when Colin used Mildred Hanson's first name, but he only said: "I know how it is with her. Seems like a person could do anything she said to do."

Colin was lying back on his blankets, looking up at the night sky through the trees. "I believe I could make it if she was down there. That's the only time I feel good for anything, when I'm with her or when I'm in the woods."

Johnny moved uncomfortably. "Sounds like you're crazy about her or something," he said.

Colin didn't answer. The words as Johnny spoke them hardly reached him, but he thought: I could do anything she said to do, but she'd have to be there or it wouldn't make sense. She'd have to be there and wanting me to do it. I guess that's what being crazy about a person really is. That's the way people feel about each other when they want to get married. But I'm only a kid and she's a grown woman. Maybe if I went through college and came back it would be different. People don't have to be the same age to get married. You get married and you live together and you know each other all through, you're never alone, you don't hide from each other, you don't lose each other, you have all of each other, you sleep together, you lie in bed naked together, you are for each other, together in everything. But it's only me that needs all those things, not her, and I'm a kid. I've no business even thinking about it like that. Seems like all I'm good for is dreaming about things that can't happen; I've always done it, ever since I can remember, and I've got to cut it out and do something for a change. Maybe if I worked and worked, this would happen; then

146

it wouldn't be just a crazy dream and I'd be right to be thinking it and wanting it.

He sat up on his blankets and looked across at Johnny. Oh hell, he thought, now I'm back where I started. I don't want to think about it any more. "Johnny," he said. "Johnny. Wake up and get inside your blankets."

But Johnny was sleeping soundly and he had to go across and touch his shoulder to wake him.

THEY camped at the foot of the lake the next night and laughed at themselves for making such a slow trip. But it had been a good day. They had turned aside from the trail a hundred times, to go down and look at the river, to search for a giant spruce tree or a corner post that Colin remembered from the previous summer, to follow a bear track or trace out a creek to its fall from the hillside. Johnny said: "If Robbie was white enough to leave a canoe at the foot of the lake for his visitors we could go on to his place tonight. But I'm too darn tired to hike all that way around."

Colin asked: "Does he know you're coming?"

"Sure, but he doesn't know when. I was talking to him when he was out last spring and he said to come in any time I could make it."

"Does he want you to trap with him?"

"No," Johnny said. "He promised he'd show me how to go about it, but he wants me to make my own line—up one of the other valleys and maybe along the lake shore for a piece."

Colin went over to the fire and swung the boiling pot away from it, threw in some coffee and swung it back to boil up again. "Do you think you'll go through with it? I didn't know you liked being in the woods that much."

"I like it O.K., but it's not that so much. If you've got a trapline you've got a job and nobody can take it away from you. You may not make a hell of a lot out of it, but you'll eat."

"I hadn't thought of it that way," Colin said. "But I guess it makes sense, the way things are. Or the way they have been."

"The way they are," Johnny insisted, emphasizing the last word. "There's going to be more trouble of one kind and another for quite a while yet, lay-offs and strikes and so on. They've run Miller and Zobieski and those others out of town, but that's as likely to make trouble as get rid of it."

"You mean they found Miller? I didn't hear that."

"Couple of nights before we left," Johnny said. "Earl Mayhew was in and I heard him telling Dad about it."

"Earl wasn't there."

"No, but he knew about it. It wasn't the police—just a bunch of guys the company got together. Earl says they beat 'em up pretty bad and put 'em on the boat and told 'em never to show up around Blenkinstown again or they'd get more of the same. Earl said Miller never lifted a hand to fight back, just let them go ahead and beat him till he fell down. Some of the guys that were there were kind of sick about it."

Colin felt a physical shock from the words. He said: "I didn't think those kinds of things happened any more."

Johnny laughed. "They sure as hell do. In the cities it goes on all the time—you can tell that from the papers. We don't see much of it because we live out in the sticks."

"But what's the sense in it? Why couldn't they just tell 'em to get out of town if that's what they wanted?"

"Scared I guess. My dad says people are always scared when they act like that—scared for their jobs, scared of another strike, scared because they don't understand. It doesn't have to make sense."

"Miller wasn't scared."

"Miller knows what he's doing. Earl doesn't like him and Dad doesn't like him, but they both say he believes in what he's doing, whether it's right or wrong."

"My old man doesn't like him either," Colin said. "But I guess he must feel the same way. I heard Gord Holman try to talk him into going out after Miller, up at the trestle one day, but Dad turned him down cold."

Johnny laughed again and Colin looked at him in surprise. "That sure lets your dad out of being a company man," Johnny said. "He'll be lucky if he isn't looking for another job."

"You mean they could fire him for that?"

"They wouldn't have to say it was for that."

For a short while they sat without talking, looking out over the quiet surface of the lake. Colin's thoughts strained at him but he could not lead them anywhere. He wanted to talk more and to hear Johnny explain more, but he couldn't find what he wanted to say and for once he wasn't sure that Johnny would be able to explain. Why do people hate each other? he wanted to say. Because they're scared, Johnny says. Maybe he's right about the guys that chased Miller out; they were scared the company would fire them if they didn't go along or scared Miller would start another strike; all except Gord Holman—it's hard to think of him being scared of anything, yet I suppose it's his job too, perhaps he's even scaredest of them all because he's got the biggest job. Don Williams hates Dad—I could tell that from the way he spoke—but he isn't scared of him and I don't see what else he could be scared of to make him hate Dad like that. And he called him a company man, but Dad isn't that because he wouldn't go along when Gord Holman said to and now Johnny says maybe they'll fire him for not going. He wouldn't know about that though; they couldn't fire Dad when he's the only broad-axe man they've got around there, one of the only ones left in B. C.

It doesn't make sense, any of it, the hating and beating and fighting and firing people. It's supposed to be a free country. Why can't a man just go and do his job and be left alone without all this other stuff coming into it at all? Why do Johnny and I have to talk about it up here, why do I have to think about it? It doesn't belong up here. It wasn't here at the lake last summer, not when I used to go out in the canoe or when Robbie and I were up at the mouth of the creek that evening or with Mr. Grant or any time. Why can't a person stay up here forever and keep away from it? That's what Robbie does, but he says it isn't right for a young fellow and so does Margaret and so does Mildred. And I kind of know what they mean; there's a part of me that wants to see it all happening and try to understand like Johnny does, only more. Part of me wants that, yet when I do see it I hate it. Sometimes I just wish it would all end, very quickly and suddenly, like a bullet in the heart. That's because I'm yellow. I used to wish that when I was a little kid and got in some kind of trouble. Now I wish it about big things, things I ought to try to understand.

"Johnny," he said. "Suppose Robbie isn't home tomorrow?"

"We could look for him. You'd know where to look, wouldn't you?"

"Up at his claims, I guess, is where he'd be. Sure, I could find those—some of them anyway."

"I hope we don't have to, just the same. We can have a whole lot more fun just fooling around the lake in a canoe than climbing mountains looking for mining claims."

Colin leaned forward, then pointed up the lake. "He's home," he said. "There's his light just went on."

1 8

WILL Ensley didn't get fired. But when the camps opened up again with the first rains in September, he wasn't called. Earl Mayhew was working and John Meldrum and Tony Soretto. Mike Varchuk had gone away, leaving his shack padlocked, but he had sold his car to Tony, so they still went to work the same way. After a few days Will rode up to the beach camp with them and tried to see Gordon Holman, but Holman was up in the woods somewhere and there was only old McPherson in the office.

"They'll be sending for you soon as there's work," McPherson told him. "You finished hewing for the trestle on the spur line before the shutdown."

"There's the new sled for the unit on Side One," Will said. "And there's work to be done on the water tower at Camp 5."

McPherson shrugged his shoulders. "I've heard him say nothing about it. He did say there was ties to be cut ahead on the new spur line. Contract."

"Contract?" Will said. "Did he say for me to work contract?"

"It could be he had you in mind. He didna say. But if he wants you he'll let ye know."

Will kept away from the camp for the rest of September and all of October, but early in November he shook off his pride and went up there again. Holman offered him a contract to cut ties on the spur line. It was a bad show and the price was bad, but he took it and forced it to pay him a wretched wage. It was sometime in the new year that he learned the bridge-crew was working on a new trestle, using sawed timbers; and sometime later than that the company hired a man from town to work on the donkey-sleds. It was nearly a month before Will told Martha about those things.

"I'd take Colin out of school to help on the ties," he said. "But there'll be an end of that soon enough anyway. There's hardly any timber left along there that'll make ties."

"There's something behind it all," Martha said. "There must be. It seems they don't want you to work for them any more. Why don't you go and ask Mr. Holman right out?"

"Maybe I'll do that," Will said.

But there was at least a measure of self-respect in the work he was doing. He could go to it daily with a quiet mind and drive his strength in the familiar way, breathing security from the scent of sapwood and crushed branches all about him, feeling it in the smooth shock of his sharp axes, the bite of his caulks into wood, the wetness of rain and snow against his face and body. It'll work out, he told himself. They'll need me for something else when this job's done. In times like these we've been through a man gets to imagining things for no reason at all, listening to women's talk, getting himself all het up when he only has to wait his time.

In the end he had to say something, and he did. Gordon Holman wasn't an easy man to see, but Will found him at the beach camp one day when he came in from work. "I'm pretty near through up there, Gordon," he said. "There's no more than a week's tie timber left and I have to go a long ways from the grade to get that."

"Got enough ties?"

"No. You'll have to bring some in to finish it out."

"There was enough timber up there when we checked it. You'll just have to reach out a bit farther, that's all."

"It's not there," Will said. "A man can't go back any farther at that price even if it was there, not and make a living wage."

"Seems like you've slowed up a lot, Will," Holman said. "Time was when you'd have made good money up there. I figured we were giving you a pretty good thing when we handed out that contract."

Will looked at him for a moment without speaking. Then he said: "I'm not slowed up so I don't know what kind of show I'm working on."

"Nobody's holding you to the contract," Holman said. "But if you can't handle that kind of a show any more it's going to be tough to find anything else for you."

Will turned sharply away from him and walked to Tony's car without looking back. He held his body stiffly, feeling the heavy squareness of his shoulders and the tautness of anger in the heavy muscles of his arms.

At suppertime he told Martha: "I saw Holman today."

"What did he say?" Martha asked.

"They think I'm getting old. They think I can't work the way I used to."

"Nonsense, Will. They couldn't think that. You're just as strong as you were twenty years ago." She checked herself and looked at him anxiously. "You *are* all right, aren't you, Will? The work's not getting harder for you, is it?"

Will laughed shortly. "Ask Colin here. He's young and strong. Did it look like I was getting old last summer? Did Mr. Blenkin say anything about it when he was up? Was the bridge-crew ever held up for timbers?"

"No, Dad," Colin said. "It didn't look to me like there was anyone else there could work the way you can."

"Then what do they mean?" Martha asked. "Why did he say that?"

Will shrugged his shoulders. "They want to make out I can't handle the contract. Holman says there's enough tie timber to finish out the spur line. Maybe there is if a man goes five or six hundred feet back in the bush. Not otherwise."

"What are you going to do?" Martha asked him.

"Finish it out," Will said. He turned to Colin again. "You'll have to come up there with me for two or three weeks."

Martha caught her breath sharply. "Oh no, Will. The boy's got to stay in school and graduate now that he's this close."

"A couple of weeks won't stop him. Will it, son?"

There was a look in his father's face Colin had never seen there before. The urgency of fear was in it, and pleading; but there was affection too, and pride, the same pride Colin had seen when Will listened to George Smith praise Colin's work on the bridge-crew. "No," Colin said. "Two or three weeks is nothing."

So Will finished out the spur line and when the last tie was on the grade they told him, as he had known in his heart they would: "There's nothing else right now. We'll send for you as soon as anything comes up."

He told Martha as soon as he got home. "They're holding that strike committee against you," she said. "Can't the union help?"

Will shook his head. "Not without another strike. I wouldn't ask that."

"Earl's working. He was on the committee. Why should they pick on you?"

"I don't know," Will said. "Unless it's because I wouldn't go out and look for Miller."

"Earl didn't go."

"Holman never asked him." Will walked across the kitchen and looked out of the window. "They'll need me again. I can go to town and hire out some place else until they do. Work's not that scarce now."

"Did you hear where Mr. Varchuk's working?"

"No," Will said. "It might be kind of tough for him to get on any place. He's quite a trouble-maker and . . ." Will stopped suddenly and looked at Martha.

"It might be just as good to pick up what work you can around here for the next little while," she said. "They might call sooner than you expect."

COLIN went to Mildred Hanson's cottage to pick up some books the evening before school closed. Mildred opened the door to his knock.

"Come on in," she said. "Carol's out. I thought Margaret would be with you."

"She had a date," Colin said.

Mildred smiled. "Not with the police force again?"

Colin nodded.

"I made some coffee," Mildred said. "Sit down while I get it."

Colin picked up a magazine from a chair and sat down. The room was very familiar now and he was easy in it. He was glad Carol Maxwell was out. He tried to like Carol because she was Mildred's friend and he admired the breadth and depth of knowledge that seemed always so ready in her quick mind; but he could never be easy with her.

Mildred came back with the coffee. "I made a cake," she said. "It was supposed to be a celebration—for Margaret as well."

"Did Marge tell you she won't be going back this fall?" Colin asked. "She's going into a hospital."

"I know. It's a pity. But I think she'll get the other year in sooner or later. I suppose that means you won't go to University either."

"I'm going to look for a job down there. I might make it that way." For a moment Colin was very conscious that he was no longer a schoolboy.

"Lots of people go through that way," Mildred said. "But it's much harder to find jobs than it used to be. I wish that aunt and uncle would give you the same chance they gave Margaret."

Colin laughed. "Margaret could work for them to pay her board, and the family could send her enough to buy clothes and books."

"Is your father still not working?"

"He's cutting cordwood," Colin said. "But there's nothing to spare from that. There's no work up at camp. I tried for myself."

He glanced at Mildred and looked quickly away again. "Dad'll get work though," he said defensively. "There's not many men can do what he can."

Mildred said nothing. She knew the town's story that Will Ensley was on the company's blacklist and knew that Colin must know it too. She wondered if Colin or Will knew that the blacklist was supposed to cover all the big companies. They ought to understand about it, she thought; they could fight about it better if they did—unless understanding would kill the last of Will Ensley's pride.

"What will you do if you don't go to University?" she asked.

"I don't know. Try to get work, I guess."

"Promise me something," she said quickly.

He looked up, surprised by the sudden intensity of her quiet voice.

"What?"

"That you won't come straight back up here, whatever happens. Stay away for at least a while. Go out and see something of Canada."

"Johnny Harris's got a trap-line up on Wind Lake. I thought . . ."

"Don't do it. Please Colin. You've got to grow. You've go to see what the world is and what you could be in it before you shut yourself away. What's right for Johnny Harris isn't right for you."

"I don't see why not. Johnny's my best friend."

"I know he is. Johnny's a nice boy and I like him too, but he hasn't got as much to waste as you have. You can go on growing and learning even if you don't go to University. You can be something. You can learn to help people."

"What do you want me to do then? Get a job in the city?"

Mildred thought for a moment before answering. "I don't think it matters, so long as you don't come back here or go to some other little logging town just like this. I want you to give yourself a chance. Whatever you do will lead you on to something else."

"How long do I have to stay away?"

"You'll know. A year anyway, then you'll know. Will you try it?"

Colin laughed nervously. "Sure I will. I'll take any job I can get. But a year's a long time."

"Not too long," she said, and they were silent again.

Colin tried to think of the meaning of his promise, but everything ahead of him was confused and suddenly strange beyond his imagination. He remembered the muddled, crowded streets of Vancouver and tried to see himself a part of them, looking for a job, working in a job. What kind of a job? In a drug-store, driving a truck, in a bank, how do people work in town? They have sawmills there, but maybe she doesn't mean that, maybe that's too much like the woods. They work in offices and factories and run street cars and load ships. How do you get jobs like that? Who do you ask? How do you know they want anyone?

"I think I'd sooner work some place outside the city," he said.

"It doesn't matter," Mildred told him. "Go as far as you like. I want you to see something else, so that you'll know all Canada isn't just mountains and logging camps."

"I know that now," he said seriously.

"You mean you've been told about it. Wheat and mining, railroads and shipping, fishing and furs and manufacturing. You've been told that in every grade from one to twelve, but I want you to see some of it for yourself, make it your own." The late sun was flaming through the west window of the room and across to Colin's face. Mildred went to the window and pulled the shade part way down, then came back and sat down again. Her movement had drawn him out of his thoughts and he was suddenly and strongly aware of her. The chair he was sitting in was too low and he stood up. She looked up at him and smiled. "I'm always nagging at you, Colin. I'm sorry. We may not see each other again very soon."

The words hurt him sharply, left him lonely in what she had asked him to do. He stooped and picked up the magazine that had dropped to the floor from the arm of his chair. "I'm not going right away," he said.

"Colin," her voice was afraid, though she tried to keep it strong. "Do you remember when I talked to you like this one day years ago. After school?"

"Yes," he said.

"I scolded you and sent you away. I shouldn't have done that. I've been sorry ever since."

"It wasn't your fault. I scared you." He looked down at her from his great height and saw her small and frail and young, as he had never seen her before. Quickly, almost gracefully, he knelt beside her. "I wouldn't ever hurt you," his voice was strained, almost fierce with strain. "I love you so much, more than anyone in the world. I can do anything you tell me to."

One of her hands moved and touched his hair. "You mustn't say that, Colin. Not now."

"When I come back?"

"You won't want to say it then. I'm an old woman, darling, compared to you. I'm like your woods and mountains—you haven't seen anything else. But now you're going out to look."

"I won't change," he said.

"Of course you will. That's why you're going. You'll change and grow and learn to think bigger and stronger things. That's what men have to do. That's what it's all about, Colin. Don't you see? There are so few who can be more than just job-fillers and time-servers, so few who can take and feel and understand and use what they see, turn it into something with meaning and life and growth. You can do all that. It's in you. You must stop being afraid, stop being shy and humble and easily hurt." She stood up and Colin stood up with her. Her face was unsmiling, near tears, full of the effort of her pleading; she was so beautiful to him, so far beyond any other beautiful thing the world had shown him that everything he was seemed to leave his body and become part of her. He wanted only to answer her pleading and let her eyes and her lips smile again.

"I haven't spoken just words to you, Colin," she said. "I've spoken your life and your happiness and the happiness of many other people. You have to believe in it. You have to try."

He took her in his arms then. She struggled and she said: "Please, Colin, please not now." But her body yielded and she lifted her face and he kissed her lips with a hard searching strength. He felt her body quiet against his strength, but the softness of her mouth forced against his and he knew only that until she wrenched her head sharply away. "Please, Colin," she said again and he released her and stood uncertainly, with his arms at his sides.

They heard footsteps in the gravel of the roadway, then the click of the gate latch and knew that Carol Maxwell was coming in.

Mildred's eyes were shining and her face was flushed. Her lips smiled to him. "You've grown up, Colin," she said, and the urgency of her voice strained at him. "You weren't afraid then. You did what you wanted." She reached out her hand and gripped his arm. "Write to me, darling. You're terribly important to me." Then she turned quickly away as the door opened.

PART FOUR

THE NARROW VALLEY

19

COLIN had found the place in the park during his first summer in Vancouver. It was a few square feet of rough grass, sloping down to the edge of a low bluff that looked out over the sweep of salt water between the Mainland and Vancouver Island; behind it the tapering, fluted trunks of three or four half-dead cedars, backed by heavy brush, shut away all sign of the footpath that passed almost within sound. No one else seemed to use the place and Colin came there whenever he could, to hate or forget the city in security.

It was easy to hate the city. The used, anonymous houses, the blank, eventful, hostile buildings, the hurrying concentration of its people in which the outsider had no part, the staring faces that never smiled and never questioned, all were easy to hate. But only when not seen too closely. When one looked closely the faces had meaning, each its own. The drab, staring woman on the street car, enclosed in her own concerns, had things to be concerned with—a home, a family, the things she must buy for them and do for them; the gray-faced old man, shakily gripping a pipe between porcelain teeth as though he would never again release it to talk, had his tenuous life still and his deep concerns—grandchildren, some precious hobby, some bitter fight that warmed his days; the laughing people in the big cars had flooded, stirring lives beyond the imagination; the young man hurrying had something to hurry for, a life to build, a woman to love, a family to raise. But seeing their deep concerns beyond the blankness only made the blankness more hostile, as the unshared bustle of the great buildings was hostile, as the closed hospitality of the houses was hostile, as the self-absorption of the hurrying crowds was hostile. To know that the city had sympathy and kindness and a shared life for its own brought full meaning to loneliness.

In the year since he had first come to it, Colin had never felt himself a part of the city's life. He had searched hopefully at first for a job that would take him through University. In a little while he was looking for a job, any job, that would feed him. Within two months he had worked at half-a-dozen places, always filling in for someone who was away on vacation. Then vacations were over and there were no more jobs, only the blank, defensive refusals, the hopelessness of searching, the sharp, helpless fear of hunger. He had left the city then, to milk cows for his board in the Fraser Valley. When the spring work came along there was a small wage as well as board and lodging, then nothing at all, then day-work in the hay harvest. Now he was back in the city again.

Colin lay in the grass and watched the water. He could find no pleasure in the quiet place today; only a sense of empty repetition that he hated, a sense of urgency that he forced away from him, a sense of failure that he accepted without protest. A tug was taking its raft of saw-logs slowly towards the mouth of the

Fraser, a flight of black scoters took heavy wing at the coming of a small powerboat, two murrelets disappeared in flickering dives a little way out from shore, a blue jay scolded in the brush behind him. A year ago all these things would have been consolation and renewal; now they were bitter things because they reached at his heart and told him he had no place or part in the city. They told him to go home and find them there, where they belonged, part of life, not secrets of a stolen hiding place.

Margaret had place and part in the city, had it as naturally as she milked the cows or climbed the mountain or did well in school. Colin had seen her two days ago and had drawn strength from her because she was confident, calm, efficient as she had always been. But the strength had died in him as the warmth of alcohol dies, quickly and leaving him weaker than before. "There's nothing at home," she had said. "Father's still not working and they're having a hard time."

"I could help out."

But she had shaken her head. "It wouldn't do any good. You wouldn't get work up there, any more than Dad. Mother wants to see you, but she said to tell you not to come."

"It's no good here," he had said. But she had given him two more names, two more people to go and face, to beg from without hope. When she told him about them the hope had been there, clear in her own confidence, but the next day it was faded and he had not gone. She had brought the message from Mildred Hanson, too, a calm and friendly message that recognized no failure or shift in purpose and carried no reproach for half a year of unanswered letters. "Don't be afraid to try anything in the world; whatever you do will be important one day, however it seems now." Those were the words, as nearly as he could remember them, and they renewed what she had said the evening before the last day of school. She had said then "a year anyway" and a year was gone and there was nothing to show for it, but she had not said "come back." Because, as Margaret had said, there was nothing to come back to? Or because nothing had come from the long, drab, muddled year? How could a person tell? Whatever you do will be important one day. Do hateful things, like asking again and again for a job that no one will give you, like living in the city with no friend to talk to, no house to go to, nothing that belongs to you or means anything to you. Do drudging things, like delivering packages from a store and getting bawled out for being slow, like getting up at five all winter and milking cows for a grouch who never figured anything was right.

It's easy for her to talk, Colin thought. What does she know about it? Everything has gone right for her, all her life. She's had it easy, then she wishes all this on to me when I could just as well be up on the lake with Robbie and Johnny Harris, learning things and getting some place. But the thought shamed him and its denial of her made a surge of loneliness that left him defenseless and almost in tears. The words he had found and once read to her came back to him: "So that my vigor, wedded to thy blood, shall strike within thy pulses like a god's, to push thee forward through a life of shocks, dangers and deeds . . ." He had watched her as he read them and, though she made no sign, had known that she accepted them. Many times he had used them to give meaning to the year's dull, hopeless striving; now he accepted them again and made amends for the denial, but he was still ashamed.

Out on the water the tug with its tow was passing out of sight round a point, and a big freighter, flying a flag he did not know, was setting across the Gulf for the Straits of Juan da Fuca. Colin looked down at the worn boot on his left foot. It was still a good boot and he still had some money; only a few dollars, but more than he had had when he pulled out of town the previous fall. So far there had always been something in time to keep him off the relief rolls, but that didn't mean there always would be. Plenty of people did come right up against it, and not because they didn't want to work; people who could do more than just score for a broad-axe or run a compass line, people who had had jobs and were used to working in town. Yet thousands upon thousands more people were working and eating and sleeping regularly, sure of themselves, sure of their lives and their jobs. And other thousands wanted work done for them. Somewhere in the city was the thing he was looking for, the one exactly right thing; one could look for it through newspaper advertisements, through employment agencies, by going out and asking. But the chance of finding it was infinitely small compared to the certainty that it existed.

There should be some way, he thought, of climbing to a great height above the city and looking down upon it, so that everything and everyone in it would be open to understanding. Merely wanting the thing so strongly and being so completely sure that it existed should be power enough to reach through and summon the thing. Faith, they said, faith can move mountains. But could you claim to have faith in the existence of something you could not name? They said also: you've got to know what you want in this world. Mildred had never said that; she had said only to go and look, that anything would be important. But how can you look when you don't know what you are looking for? The simple truth is that you can't, so you start dreaming impossibilities, like looking down on the city from a mountain and knowing everything in it.

Someone had turned into the brush from the footpath. Colin listened as the movement came on towards him, and turned his head slowly as the policeman came out by one of the cedars at the edge of the clearing. The policeman stopped, put his hands on his hips and stood looking down at Colin. He was a young man, strongly built and good-looking, but his brown face held no expression that Colin could interpret.

"Come here pretty often, don't you?" the policeman said.

Colin climbed slowly to his feet, smiling nervously and feeling foolish. "I guess so," he said. "Quite often."

"Last year, too. Work in town?"

Colin shook his head. "Looking for it. I was up the Valley all winter."

"Got friends in town?"

"No. My sister works at a hospital. That's all. My folks live up the coast."

"If I were you, I'd go back to them," the policeman said. "Town's no place for a young fellow these days." His tone was friendly, almost fatherly, warning.

Colin shifted his feet and smiled. "I was thinking something close to that when you came."

"Well, I wouldn't be too long thinking about it. Outside the city a man that's got his health can always find something to keep him eating. In town when you're broke, you're broke."

163

He turned away and Colin watched until he disappeared into the undergrowth, then listened until the slow footsteps passed beyond hearing along the footpath.

It wasn't the first time Colin had been questioned by a policeman on duty, but he was not by any means hardened to it and he could not settle back into his thoughts. The hidden place was no longer hidden, no longer his own; it had become a part of the city, open as any part of it and no more friendly. After a little while he got up and went away. He went out of the park and, almost from habit, followed the long hot street to the little square near the offices of the big newspapers. As always, there were men in the square, young men like himself, wearing blue jeans and work shirts, sitting on the benches or lying sprawled out on the narrow plots of grass. Colin skirted the square and crossed the street to look at the newspaper pages pasted up in the windows.

There was a freedom in the square, half-suspicious, half-friendly, that extended over to the windows where the newspapers were posted. Men spoke to each other, listened to each other, believed or disbelieved each other, became friends or enemies of the moment, moved on and forgot they had ever spoken together. Colin was not surprised to feel an elbow in his ribs, drawing his attention to a thick, square thumb that jerked out towards a two-column headline. Colin read: "POLICE TO ROUND UP VAGRANTS. Closer check of undesirables from now on, says Police Chief."

"Hanging out the old 'git' sign," a voice said beside him. "Time to hit the ties again, I guess."

Colin turned towards the voice and looked down into a cheerful, sun-reddened face. The eyes were blue and small, but widely separated by a twisted nose above a thick, humorous mouth. The hair was very light brown, almost blond, and tightly curled in a short thick mat. "They'd have to have something on you," Colin asked. "Wouldn't they?"

"You never been vagged?" The small eyes measured Colin sharply, but the mouth was friendly.

"No."

"They don't need anything you'd notice. Pick you up for breathing good city air when there's a drive on."

Colin thought of the policeman in the park. He nodded to-

164

wards the newspaper in the window. "Do you think they really mean that?"

"Bet your life they do. It won't last, maybe, but while it does they sure as hell mean it."

"What can they do to you?" Colin asked.

"Likely a floater the first time. Maybe thirty days if the city's been twisting the beak's tail." The blue eyes looked sharply into Colin's. "Say, I wouldn't be talking to the wrong guy, would I?" The head cocked on one side and the mouth laughed. "No, I guess you just ain't been around much, have you? Name's Blake," he held out a hand and Colin took it. "James Warner Blake. Curly's more natural, though."

"Colin Ensley," Colin acknowledged in the words all the quick attraction he felt from Blake's easy good nature. "Just Colin."

"O.K., Colin. I'm hitting the road tonight." They had walked away from the newspaper building and crossed the street to the square. "I got around twenty bucks and a blanket roll. How's about throwing in together?" Blake found an empty space in a corner of one of the grass plots and flopped down in it. Colin sat down more slowly beside him.

"I'm short of that," Colin. "Five or six bucks is all I've got."

"Don't mean a thing. I hit her lucky. Done thirty days in the can and come right out and got me a job painting a boat for a guy. Just finished her up yesterday. He figured I done good, too, and give me ten bucks more'n I had coming."

"Where are we going?" Colin asked.

Curly lay back in the grass and looked at the sky. "Well," he said. "They'll be starting harvest work on the prairies. That's good as any place, I guess, unless we find something better on the way."

"You mean ride the rods?" Colin asked.

Curly laughed. "I never done that yet and I've had me free rides from here clear back to Quebec Province a couple of times. You don't want to listen to all the guff you hear. There's lots of places to ride freights besides the rods. And most of them brakies ain't near the tough guys you hear about, neither." He sat up and looked at Colin again. "Where you from anyway? Not right here in Vancouver?"

Colin shook his head. "Up the coast. Place called Blenkins-town."

"Jesus," Curly said. "You had me scared for a minute. I didn't figure you for no city kid and I kinda take a pride in how I can size a guy up first time I see him. You ain't as old as you look neither. You ain't twenty yet."

"Nineteen."

"Me, too. Shake on it." They shook hands again solemnly, in the bright sunlight of the open square. "Looks like we was meant to get together," Curly said. "You're kind of long and awkward, like you wasn't growed to size yet. But you're strong and you done some work some place or other. And you ain't one of these kids gabs his head off all the time. Only thing you're short on is you ain't been around much. You ain't seen Canada. Your uncle Curly'll soon fix that."

Colin laughed. He felt enthusiasm and excitement he had not felt since he had first left home. "When do we start?" he asked.

Curly leaned over and looked at a street clock. "I got to see a man," he said. "Meet me down around Hastings and Main about six o'clock. O.K.?"

"O.K.," Colin said, and wondered if they would shake on it again.

2 0

CURLY Blake knew the railroads and knew the prairies. He and Colin traveled eastward, through the mountains, across Alberta and into Saskatchewan with little less comfort than they would have found if they had paid their way. Colin's depression had left him as soon as they were well away from the city. Curly was unfailingly talkative and confident, full of plans and enthusiasms.

"Wait till you see them mountains," he told Colin. "There ain't nothing like them. The rich guys go and stay up there all summer long in fancy hotels with fancy women. I'd sure like to take time out and stick around there for a summer myself. I'll do it one day, too, and take a doll along with me."

They were put off a train and spent a night in the mountains, swimming in a rough, ice-cold river, making camp among poplars on a gravel bar. Colin's efficiency impressed Curly. "Makes it all easy," he said. "You do it like you been on the road all your life, only more neat and quick. And me figuring to myself I was going to have to look out for you. All I have to do is lie back and light me a seegar, except I ain't got one. I thought you was crazy when you said to drag our stuff all this way down from the track, but you sure as hell knew what you were at."

Colin listened and felt fully alive for the first time in many months. He let Curly's friendly talk merge with the friendly roar of the swift little river and turned on his side to watch the high mountains against the evening sky. After a long while he asked: "How do we make out from here on?"

"Easy," Curly said. "There's a water tank up the track a piece and they never look for nobody to get aboard there—too far out in the sticks. You don't need to worry about nothing, not when you travel with Curly Blake. We'll be dossing down in good prairie hay inside of three or four days."

He was right. Within four days they had joined the threshing crew on a farm where Curly had worked the previous summer. Curly was welcomed; it seemed that he had a way of his own with aging machinery. Colin fitted easily into the work of pitching the sheaves, using his height and his strength tirelessly through the long days. He saw little of Curly, who was always around the machines during working hours and pursued complicated affairs among the girls of the nearby village each evening; but the sense of partnership between them was never lost.

By mid-September the outfit had finished its work and they moved on. Curly had a new packsack, three good silk shirts and a pair of dress pants; otherwise he was broke. Colin had fifty dollars.

"We done good," Curly said. "But I wouldn't want to winter

167

around that dump. We better head back west again and see if we can get us a late season job on the way. Seen any place you think'd make good wintering?"

"I liked the look of it after we first got through the mountains," Colin said.

"O.K. by me. Any place so long as it's off the bald prairie. There's cow farms around there and they're good places to look for winter work."

They put in two or three weeks with another threshing outfit a little way east of Marwell City, still in Saskatchewan, and when that was over Curly said: "We better make time or we're liable to wake up froze to death some morning. Happened to an old partner of mine last winter. This here Marwell's got a reputation for tough cops, but we'll make it aboard something soon as she's good and dark. The big freight hauls always do a pile of bull-cooking around there."

They went down to the yards at dusk and Curly sized up the situation quickly. "That's ours," he said. "Two tracks over. We better duck under and load from the other side." They saw a brakeman's light coming along the train and Curly said: "Checking her over. We got lots of time." But Colin sensed his tension and felt a growing excitement in himself. It was always exciting, but Curly usually made it a joke. Tonight he was not joking about it and the coldness of the still air was a warning. The cinders were hard and slippery with frost underfoot and the lights of the town were very bright in the clear air.

The brakeman passed them and went on his way down the long train. Curly said: "Now," and they crossed quickly to the train, ducked between two box-cars and came out on the other side. There was a flat car with a load of machinery about ten cars back and Curly began to run silently towards it. Colin followed more slowly, a little way behind. Curly stopped suddenly and Colin came up to him.

"We got a break," Curly said and pointed at the open door of one of the box-cars. "Want to take a chance on it?"

"Sure. Why not?"

"One of us'll have to keep awake to make sure they don't close it up on us. That's how guys get froze to death."

1 6 8

"Fair enough," Colin said. "We can watch it. We could wedge the door anyway, so they'd have a time closing it." He saw the quick flash of approval on Curly's face in the dim light.

"Let's go then," Curly said and climbed aboard. Colin moved to follow and the voice stopped him.

"Just a minute," the voice said. "Hold it right where you are." Colin felt a hand on his arm and stood dead still. Another voice said from behind them: "Where's the other one? There was two of 'em." Curly came back to the open door of the car and dropped down to the track. "O.K., copper," he said. "You don't have to come after me."

Very little was said. The hand was still on Colin's arm as they went through the lighted station house and Colin saw that the other policeman was holding Curly. The station-agent looked up as they passed through and said: "Only two tonight?"

The policeman holding Curly grinned. "Most of them's wise to this place now. There's just a few still have to learn the hard way."

When they got outside and started up the street Curly said: "Where you taking us? We'll scram out of town quick enough if you let us go. We ain't done nothing."

"No?" asked the policeman. "Lodging in a freight car. Trespassing on railway property. No visible means of support. And we ain't even searched you yet."

The four of them had stopped, but Colin saw him tighten his grip on Curly's arm to force him forward. Curly moved, then suddenly dropped his head and butted it into the blue-coated stomach. The big policeman grunted sharply, but he brought his left hand forward and down and Curly sprawled on the sidewalk. The other policeman was still holding Colin, who had not moved. "O.K., Don?" he asked.

"Little bastard pretty near winded me," he kicked Curly in the ribs. "On your feet, tough guy. You ain't hurt."

Curly got slowly to his feet and they moved on again. Colin said: "You O.K., Curly?"

"Can the talk," said the policeman holding him.

The city police station was just off the main street. They were booked and searched. Curly gave his name as James Baker. Colin heard him, searched his mind frantically, found nothing and gave his own name. Curly's policeman unlocked a door and they all went into a small room with three or four cells made of metal bars. Curly's policeman slipped off his coat.

"Want to get fresh again, kid?" he asked and smashed the back of his open hand against Curly's mouth. Curly stood with his hands at his sides and a trickle of blood ran down his chin. Colin felt his whole body stiffen with fear and anger. The figures under the naked yellow light were dim and wavering before his eyes; his voice would not come and his body could not stir.

"Watch the big guy, Joe," Don said, and hit Curly again with his other hand. "Looks like the punk's yellow after all." He lifted his hand again.

Colin moved then. He said: "Leave him alone, can't you?" and stepped forward. He felt a blow from behind, hard on the back of his head, jarring him clear down to his knees. He swung round and suddenly was fighting Tod Phalling again, a bigger, silent Tod with a club in his hand. Jeff Burnside was behind, not waiting this time but beating heavy blows on his back and his arms and his shoulders, and he also had a club. Colin went to his knees, struggled to his feet again and was hauled forward into one of the cells. The door rang shut behind him. Another door slammed and he knew that Curly was in another cell beside his. The light snapped off and he knew the policemen had gone.

Colin tasted blood in his mouth, put a hand to the side of his head and felt more blood. "Curly," he whispered. "You O.K.?"

He heard Curly laugh, a nervous muffled laugh, but the voice was calmer than his own. "I bin worse. I bin lots worse."

"What made the bastards do that?"

Curly laughed again. "Lesson Number One, pal. Never talk back to a cop. Never, never take a sock at one. You can't win. Jesus Christ, you'd think I'd know that by now."

Colin could feel anger still strong in him. "They didn't have to do it. It was like they did it for sport. The dirty yellow bastards."

"Listen," Curly said. "Forget that stuff. Dry it off, throw it away, bury it. It never happened, see, none of it. Unless you want a winter in the can. If them guys want to crucify us tomorrow morning, they sure as hell can do it."

170

"They can't get by with that kind of racket," Colin said.

"Aw, get yourself a lawyer," Curly said. "Go to sleep. You've had worse bunks. All kinds of 'em."

COLIN slept little. Every time his mind quietened he saw Curly standing in front of the big policeman, his hands at his sides, the bright trickle of blood running down from his mouth. He felt again his own slowness, the utter failure of his strength until moments after he had called upon it, but he knew that this had lost them little; that was what made the other violence so strong and so evil. There had been no possibility of escape from it, no smallest possibility of effective resistance to it, in spite of his own move to resist. The thought made his stomach knot and his body sweat in the cell's coldness. Curly had been less than a man to them when they hit him, less than an animal even; he had been something to hurt, something to make bleed and cry and crawl, a helplessness to punish with strength, because the head had once lifted, the eyes once brightened. Colin fought with fear and hunted reason through the long night.

Soon after daylight another policeman brought them breakfast and unlocked the cell doors. He pointed to a basin and a bucket of water in one corner of the cell room. "Better clean up," he said. "You'll be up inside of an hour. You're the only ones this morning."

"What's the charge?" Curly asked him.

"Vagrancy. Going to make an argument about it?"

"Hell, no," Curly said.

"That's good. The boys wouldn't thank you for bringing them down after night duty."

Curly went over to the basin, washed his face and rinsed his swollen mouth. "Looks kinda good," he told Colin cheerfully. "Might get by with thirty days."

"Is that good?" Colin asked.

"Sure as hell is. They could throw the book at us. Resisting arrest, assaulting a peace officer. I didn't tell you, but I bin picked up once before in this lousy town—that's why I give a phony name. That big lug that had ahold of you was there, but

1 7 1

I guess he mustn't have remembered it. Christ, we're getting all the breaks."

The trial was very short. They entered their pleas of guilty and waited for sentence.

"These men been here before?" the magistrate asked.

"No record, Your Worship."

"They been working?"

"They claim to. Out at the Kronstadt place. Finished yesterday morning. They've got money."

The magistrate nodded. "They'll need it before the winter's over. We'll leave it with them. Six months hard labor." He paused, then added: "I'll hold the warrant for twenty-four hours." He looked hard at Colin. "Understand what that means?"

"We've got twenty-four hours to get out of town?"

"That's right. If the police can find you this time tomorrow you'll be arrested and serve your sentence."

"We'll be on our way, Your Honor," Curly said. "We sure appreciate the chance."

As they passed beyond the edge of the city and out into the prairie again, Curly said: "That's one time your uncle Curly pretty near balled it up for fair. Just goes to show you coppers can act white part of the time."

No part of Colin's depression had left him and he said nothing. Curly said: "You sure as hell scared 'em when you started in. You shoulda seen how quick that Don quit poking at me to go and help his side-kick. I believe you coulda took the bastard if he hadn't." He kicked at a rock in the road. "I reckon it helped too; they was set to give us a good working over, but you coming in made 'em forget it. Don't you never do that again though. You take it and don't do nothing, same as I did."

Colin still walked with his muddled thoughts. He felt stripped and ashamed, and Curly's cheerful acceptance of it all seemed more shameful than anything else. "Christ," Curly said at last. "What's eating you. Don't you know a break when you get one?"

Colin turned on him sharply. "Break," he said harshly. "What kind of a break is it when they beat you across the face and you're supposed to stand there and take it? What's white about it? It isn't even human."

"I had it coming," Curly said mildly. "That was a fool trick, butting that son of a bitch and trying to twist away from him. Cops is scared of that kind of stuff. They'll always beat you up for it."

"Scared! What have they got to be scared of, with you half the size of either of them and them with clubs and guns?"

"Oh sure," Curly said placatingly. "Them hick town cops is ignorant bastards. They scare easy and they ain't got no judgment. Just the same, they got to watch it. Size ain't everything and they don't know I'm scared they'll get wise they seen me before. Looks to them like I figure I'm tough or else I've done something worse than just try to beat a ride on a freight. You got to see it their way, too."

"My sister's going to marry a cop," Colin said. "I used to think he was quite a guy."

"Christ," Curly told him. "You don't have to change your mind because of how you seen a couple of small town harness bulls act. All cops is tough—they gotta be. But any of 'em I've seen has got a human side too, like those guys not coming down to crucify us this morning." Colin said nothing and Curly glanced at him anxiously. "Don't let it get you down, pal," he said. "I know how you feel, like you wasn't worth a pinch of cow-dirt. It's always like that the first time they pull you in. I was the same myself, but it don't mean nothing. One night in the can ain't going to change the way a guy looks to other people."

Colin smiled and felt some of the bitterness leave him.

"That's more like it," Curly said. "We'll hitch a ride and buy us a goddamn big steak dinner next town we come to. Ain't nothing like paying for a big meal in a real fancy eating joint to get a man to feeling good again."

CURLY said: "There was a guy I traveled with in Manitoba two summers back. Name of Fred Symes. Claimed his folks had a place up around Hedley, fifty or sixty miles west of Edmonton. Seems like he lit out from home to get a change of scenery more'n anything else and he said any time I was up against it to go see his folks. The way he told it there's all kinds of work up around the ranch and they can always use extra help."

"They wouldn't want to feed two," Colin said.

"There's farm folks all around there, Fred says. Cow-farmers mostly and that kind will always use help if it's cheap enough. They raise kids to do the work, but the kids gets soured on cleaning out barns and nurse-maiding cows. So they busts the old man one in the mush and pulls out for the bright lights. Happens regular as clockwork. I run into all kinds of 'em."

They found the Symes farm easily enough. Fred Symes was home and Curly was as welcome as he expected to be. Within a day or two the Symes family found work for Colin at another farm three or four miles away. The owner, Joe Pauluk, was a tiny, brown-faced Ukrainian, barely five feet tall and probably in his fifties. His wife was a dark handsome woman of forty-five, only an inch or two taller than her husband but generously built and as quiet and reasonable as he was excitable and enthusiastic. There were four daughters, one already married at eighteen, the others still at school.

Colin quickly learned to like and respect Joe Pauluk. The little man was simple, almost childish at times, but in less than twenty years he had made a soundly producing farm of a hundred and fifty acres from Alberta bush; if it was clear that Mrs. Pauluk had been the calm, reasoning power behind the achievement, it was equally clear that Joe had supplied the driving enthusiasm and the full wiry strength of his little body.

"The farm she's big," he told Colin a few days after he arrived. "She's not big enough. Six hundred and forty acres I got, only a hundred and fifty I clear. No sons to work. Is bad. But the country she's good."

"Better than the prairies?" Colin asked.

"All Canada is good country. Most Ukrainians like the prairies; to be same as old country—tall wheat, tall sky. Too much like old country is not the best. My girls, they marry good Canadian fellows, come back to finish clear the old man's place. Everybody Canadians then."

"You have wheat," Colin said. "Tall wheat and tall hills."

"Sure," Pauluk agreed. "Sure. Seventy acres of wheat. But rye and oats too, and cows and pigs and chickens and the old lady's geese. In the good years the prairies are rich. In the bad years they are nothing. Here there is always something. The hills lean over a man and make him small. But they hold the rain and the snow, and that is good."

From Hedley Colin wrote Mildred: "I think I have seen some of the things you told me to go out and look for. This Mr. Pauluk I am working for is a Ukrainian, but I think in some ways he is more Canadian than any of us. Both he and his wife were born in the Ukraine and raised there, but they haven't spoken a word of anything but English—Canadian he calls it—since the children were old enough to talk. He tells me so often why Canada is a good country (mostly, he keeps saying, because there is lots of land for everyone) and how his children will grow up to be good Canadians. Yet they don't have an easy life. They work terribly hard, much harder than most people do out on the coast."

He wrote a great deal more, about the Pauluk family and the farm and his work there, about Curly, about Saskatchewan and their journey from the coast. He wanted to tell her about the arrest and the night in Marwell City jail; it was important to him, he knew, but somehow it was a vicious, unclean thing, in which she must have no part. The other things belonged to her as he told them, brought her close to him, built upon the feeling that had been between them that last evening in her cottage.

She answered at once and as he read her letter he knew that she had written in memory as clear as his own. "I knew you would find the sort of things you wrote about, and recognize them for what they are. I've wondered so many times since you left just how you would find them and what exactly they would be when you did find them; it is wonderful to know. . . ." She wrote also of Blenkinstown and the Ensley family: "Things are still not good here. Quite a number of families are on relief and the mill is shut down a lot of the time. It makes me very happy to see Margaret again and know she will be living here. It seems funny to have to think of her as a married woman, but Clyde Munro is a wonderful man and I know you will like him a lot when you come home again and get to know him. It has been good for your mother to have Margaret back in Blenkinstown. She misses both of you a great deal and things haven't been easy for her, but now she can be sure of Margaret's happiness and see it with her own eyes."

Mildred's letters, and others from his mother and Margaret, seemed to restore substance to Colin's life and set a sanction on what he was doing. He was happy with the Pauluk family. The girls were wild, undisciplined little creatures, full of easy laughter, but they liked Colin and respected him for his size and quietness. Joe and his wife seemed never to stop working. Mrs. Pauluk reminded Colin of his mother in her determination to make use of every least thing on the farm and in the country around it. Before Colin had been in the house two or three days she discovered he was a hunter. "Now," she said. "We shall have plenty meat. Because the old man is afraid of the woods we have no meat unless it walks into the fields. That is not a way to live in a country where there are deers all around." Colin killed a deer for her and when she mentioned bear-fat he remembered he had crossed the track of a small bear near the edge of the bush; he went back next day and killed again, and from then on her faith in him was unlimited.

Joe Pauluk was not a patient man. He had persuaded himself long ago that only a driving quickness could make up for the smallness of his body, so he was always in a hurry, always anxious, always scolding. But, like his daughters, he respected Colin. "For you the cows are quiet," he told Colin in the barn one night. "For you they stand still and give more milk. With me they are crazy things, always to stamp and move and toss their heads.

Many of them I have raised since they were born, but you are a stranger. Why is that?"

Colin smiled slowly and said nothing. He thought of Joe Pauluk clattering milk cans, of Joe scolding and slapping, often shouting with anger as he milked.

"Why is that?" Joe insisted. "If I keep out of the barn altogether, you get more milk. Tell me why is that?"

"They like you to move slow," Colin said. "All animals are afraid. Cows are very slow and very quiet and very easily afraid."

Joe nodded. "I think that is truth. When I come the chickens fly away. When the old lady come she can catch them and pick them up. She is slow and quiet. I am quick and noisy. You must tell me to keep quiet in the barn. Perhaps I shall learn."

It was the same with the other work. Joe was adding to his barn, hoping to make room in it for twelve more cows, all his hay crop and all the farm machinery. Like the house and the other farm buildings the barn was built of logs. Every day Joe and Colin went in to the bush behind Joe's cleared fields to cut logs and haul them down across the snow with the team. Joe used his axe with a quick fierce strength that completed a cut almost as quickly as Colin's slow and easy rhythm; but the work often went badly for him—a notch would not fit or a tree would swing away from the line of fall he wanted.

"The logs, they are like cows too?" Joe asked. "They want I should go at them quietly? They are afraid of Joe?"

Colin laughed. He liked the bright day and the crisp snow and Joe's company. "The team works for you, Joe," he said. "You shout and they pull."

Joe looked towards his team and his face lighted. "They understand Joe. They know he is always in a hurry, always shout and scream and don't mean nothing by it. The team work good for me. But the axe, no. She is fool me all the time."

Colin tried to show him Will Ensley's powerful, accurate way with an axe, tried to describe the full-arm, overhead swing of the great broad-axe, the downward arc of the blade and its clean, smooth bite along the grain of the wood. Joe listened and watched and shook his head. "Not for Joe," he said. "Joe is too old to change. To be quiet with cows, yes, I learn that. But with the

177

axe, no; with the team, no; with the plow, no. Joe must shout and hurry."

Joe had gone well back to take up his land and the Pauluk farm still had no near neighbors. The school that the girls went to each day was three miles away in a tiny settlement around which the Symes' and other farms were grouped, and the town of Hedley was two or three miles beyond that again. But the Pauluks were friendly and sociable people and they visited and were visited by several local farm families; and Mrs. Pauluk was a tireless worker at every possible community affair. At first Colin stayed at home when the family went out and sat silently in the cheerful kitchen when other families came to visit. But both Joe and Mrs. Pauluk worked to draw him out and gradually, because he was comfortable with them, he responded. The Symes family were as active socially as the Pauluks and Colin began to see a good deal of them and Curly. Curly wore his handsome shirts and made the most of the local girls. He was having a good time and didn't hesitate to say so.

"Softest winter I ever put in," he told Colin one day when he had walked over to the Pauluks. "They treat me just like one of the family. Fred's old man is a swell guy and so is the old lady. Sure feels different when you come up against real people like that. How're you making out over there?"

"They're fine people too," Colin said. "Couldn't want better."

"The old lady looks like she'd be a swell cook. He's a queer little guy though—jumps around like a cricket. How're you making out with the girls? The oldest one looks just about ready for it."

"Cathie?" Colin leaned on the handle of his axe and looked at him in mild surprise. "She's just a kid in school."

"Don't mean she ain't ready for it," Curly said. "You're right though, at that. There's plenty dames in this neck of the woods without taking chances on jail-bait. You ought to snag yourself one. It ain't natural for a young guy to be the way you are."

Colin moved his feet in the snow and picked up his axe again. Curly had urged him this way many times before and it made him feel uneasy and deficient. He had never told him about Mildred and did not intend to. "It's all right for you," he said. "But girls don't go for a guy like me."

"You ain't all that bad," Curly said. "All you got to do is work up a good line. Act like you're deep, maybe, or lonely. There just ain't no telling what a girl's going to fall for. You want to figure it the way I do. They all want what you got, but there's some won't admit it right off."

Colin remembered Curly's occasional admissions of failure during the previous summer. "Seems to me I remember times when they just plain wouldn't admit it at all for you."

They were walking towards the house now. "Time," Curly said. "That's all it takes. Only a guy ain't always got time. And there's some would take more time than they're worth, if a guy was to waste it on them." He stopped to kick snow from one of his boots. "Like Fred's sister, for instance, that was here around Christmas. She's a looker and you'd think she'd be easy-going like Fred and the rest of the family. But I knew to lay off soon as I seen her."

COLIN met Jean Symes about a week later. Since Christmas he had been hunting back from the Symes farm quite regularly, following the Vale River into the hills and working the open places along it, where the sun had melted the snow away from the brown grass. He was used to the country now and knew how to hunt it, but it still held a strange excitement for him, quite different from anything he had known in the coast country. The birch and poplar and little spruce trees were all strange to him, the sweep of the rivers was different and strange, the game was strange—he had killed a moose once, and seen others; twice he had seen caribou and held his shot because they seemed too beautiful to kill; even the deer were different, larger and prouder creatures than the coast blacktails. From all this he had a sense of being a foreigner and hunted the more keenly for it, constantly watching for tracks or signs that were strange to him. Every part of him was keyed to a pitch beyond normal keenness, and the hunting became a purification that stripped normal values away from him.

On the day he met Jean Symes he had killed easily and dressed his buck only a little way back in the woods. He was coming out to the farm to get Fred or Curly to bring back a horse for the buck and he found her suddenly, at the upper edge of the long field that sloped down towards the house. She was on skis, standing across the slope, hatless and with her head thrown back so that her pale hair caught the early morning sun. He stopped sharply as he saw her and stood perfectly still against the trunk of a tree. After several seconds he moved, stepping so that she would hear him. She turned to the sound and he came up to her; she was smiling and he saw that her face was beautiful.

"You must be the great hunter the boys talk about," she glanced at his hands on the rifle. "And a successful hunter, too, I see. I'm glad. It's so dull when the great reputations fail."

Colin had forgotten the kill, but the exaltation of the woods was still in him. He appraised her calmly, almost insolently, her blue eyes and scarlet mouth, the smooth throat framed by the open collar of her white shirt, the swell of her breasts, the curve of her hips.

"Well," she said. "Am I presentable?"

"You're like someone I used to know."

"Oh," she said. "How very nice. I suppose I should be flattered." She moved her skis so that the snow creaked under them and her neat body was more open to him; her mouth still smiled but her eyes were not friendly. "Where are you going now?"

The question reached through his mood. He became conscious of himself again and looked away from her. "I was going down to get the horse," he said.

"I can go for you. And much faster." But she stood quite still, her eyes willing him to look back to her again. "Well," she said. "Do you want me to go?"

"Don't bother. I can go. It won't take very long."

She laughed then and he did look towards her, but she had turned her skis and was already on her swift way down the slope, her slim body light and easy, the full sleeves of her blouse fluttering against the smooth air. Colin watched for a moment, then followed her.

Later, walking the road back to the Pauluks, he could not free his mind of her. He knew she was not like Mildred, yet he had spoken exact truth in the moment he told her she was. Like her, yet unlike her; younger and closer to him, yet unapproachable as Mildred had never been. He tried, in his loyalty to Mildred, to deny the attraction he had felt from her; but he knew that this was a loyalty Mildred had not asked of him, did not want of him. She had sent him out to look for just this, had told him that he would find it. "I am like your woods and mountains," she had said. "You haven't seen anything else." Loyalty became turned upon itself. He could deny the sudden power of this new woman only by denying the mission that Mildred Hanson had set for him.

Through the rest of the day, in the routine of his work, she became more remote; the exaltation of the woods had left him and he felt himself Colin Ensley again, an awkward, clumsy man, unproved, concerned with barns and cattle and heavy tools. He tried to fit her into it all and could not; her way was the swift way, over the bright surface of the snow; his way was slower, heavier, the weight of footsteps breaking through the crust.

In the evening Joe Pauluk came into the barn while Colin was milking. He had been to Hedley and Colin knew he had had a few drinks, as he usually did when he went into town alone; but in spite of that he was quite quiet. For several minutes he stood at the back of the stall, watching. Then, when Colin moved to another cow, he said: "That Curly Blake. I see him in town. He say in a little time, when spring come good, you move out."

"I guess that's right," Colin said. "Curly likes to keep moving."

"You don't want to move," Joe said. "I pay for spring work, same as prairies. Mr. Symes pay."

"I hadn't thought of it that way. Curly always did say we'd move on in the spring, and I figured to go with him. But maybe he'd change his mind if there was work to do."

Joe shook his head. "Not that Curly. I see other boys like him, lots of boys like him. They must be all the time go, go, go. Never stay any place. You are not the same as them."

"I guess not," Colin said. "But I kind of like to travel with Curly, just the same. He's been pretty good to me."

"Look," Joe said quickly. "I got no boys. You can have Cathie. She's a good girl, Cathie. She's make a good wife for a man. Then we build a house for you and you stay here."

Colin finished stripping the cow and stood up with the pail. "How about Cathie?" he asked.

"She's like you fine. She's do what me and her Ma say."

Colin said, very gently. "I haven't ever thought of anything like that, Joe. It would take time to think about it, quite a lot of time."

"You think," Joe said. "This place good for you. You think and we talk about it some more, yes?"

Colin said slowly: "It'd take a lot of thinking, Joe. I guess I'll go along when Curly goes. But don't ever think I don't like it here. You folks have all been swell to me."

"But you think," Joe said eagerly. "You think. And maybe you change your mind and stay."

At supper Colin watched Cathie and Mrs. Pauluk and was sure that neither of them knew of Joe's plan. Cathie played and giggled with her sisters, as always; was scolded, kept quiet for a little while, then began her play again. She was child, not woman. The Pauluks were arguing, as they often did, over their memories of the old country. Mrs. Pauluk liked to remember the good things, Joe hated to admit that anything had been good. Mrs. Pauluk remembered singing and dancing, gay and handsome colors in the dresses of her girlhood, the sound of a bell across the fields.

"Those things we have brought with us. It is only the bad things we leave behind," Joe said. "The wars and the fighting and the hunger."

"The children forget," she told him. "They grow up lazy and laughing, like Cathie. They are better here, but they forget many things, and some things they have never seen."

"It is good they forget. This is another country, here there is peace and a full belly."

"Very often we were happy there. I would not go back, but there was happiness and it is not right to forget."

"There was the fighting," Joe insisted. "Poles and Russians and Germans, always the fighting and killing."

"We were safe in the woods, down under the ground, with the sods piled over the door. The fighting would pass and there would be peace again."

182

"They were over our heads," Joe told Colin. "Running and killing and screaming. And afterwards we find them in the blood. This country is not like that. There is land for all."

"It was not only for land they fought."

"For land," Joe said. "For Ukrainians' land. Killing and screaming and fighting. The Russians were the worst."

"The Germans were the worst."

"All were bad. It was a bad place."

She agreed with him at last. "It is better here," she said simply. "But it is good to remember a little."

In bed that night Colin let his mind attempt to sort the day's happenings, but Jean Symes' smiling face and sharp words were over them all. He tried to think of Cathie, to find from her some trace of the excitement Jean Symes had stirred in him, and could not. He knew how to measure the thing that Joe Pauluk had offered him and felt the urge of his powerful liking for the little man. He knew with a clear mind that the farm and the Pauluks had given him happiness, a rest from himself, a new conception of his own strength and value. But he knew as clearly that Cathie was not for him and, ultimately, that the farm was not for him, however Joe offered it. Because he had a true affection for Joe and this was a rejection of everything most precious in Joe's life, the clear knowledge hurt him. Because Jean Symes, standing on her skis, her hair bright in the sun, seemed a creature from a different world than round, happy, good-natured Cathie, he felt ashamed. But he was still thinking of Jean when he fell asleep.

He saw her again three or four days later. She stopped her car as he was mending a fence near the road, pushed open the door and swung her feet to the running board.

"Hullo," she said. "So that's what you do when you aren't hunting?"

Colin lifted his hat and walked slowly towards the car. "I don't hunt so very often," he said. "Only when we need meat."

She looked at him, a little amused smile on her lips. "You don't look much like a woodsman. Or maybe you do. Where did you learn so much about it?"

There was a patronizing directness in her look and her words that confused him, but in spite of this he felt the warming flattery

1 8 3

of her interest. "On the coast," he said. He was standing beside the car now and she was still sitting there, looking up at him, her feet on the running board beside the open door.

"The boys say you can do wonderful things with an axe, too. I should like to see that sometime."

"I'm not so hot," Colin said. "My dad is the man that can use an axe."

"I don't want to see your dad. I want to see you." Again her tone was impatient, yet flattering. She was commanding and expecting obedience.

"I put in a lot of time at it. I'll be cutting cordwood over at your place next week."

"And I suppose I may come and watch you then," she swung her legs back into the car and started the motor. "Well, I can wait."

Colin watched the car until it disappeared around a curve in the road, then went slowly back to his work. He knew she had been annoyed, almost angry, and he felt in himself a slow resistance to her impatience and arrogance; yet he had wanted to please her, had been planning ways to please her ever since he had first seen her.

It was the same when she came up to where he was cutting cordwood on the Symes farm; she seemed able to draw him and repulse him in a single sentence, to offer herself and withdraw herself in a floating movement of her body. She came up during each of the first three days he worked there, and on the third day she said, quite suddenly: "Who do I remind you of?"

Colin's mind fumbled with the question, vaguely sensed its danger, but he said: "A girl I know. Not a girl really, a woman."

"Out on the coast?"

"Yes."

"Were you fond of her?" Her voice was gentle now and Colin lost his sense of danger.

"I still am," he said. "Very fond of her."

"In love with her?"

Colin hesitated. "She's older than I am," he said.

She turned on him then and her body shook with anger. "You and your old women," she said. "Go back to your old women.

184

Why did you ever come away from them if you love them so much?"

Colin stood quite still. He felt his face flush as though she had struck him, but he looked straight into her anger and he asked quietly: "Why do you hate me?"

"Because you haven't got the guts of a louse," she told him fiercely. "Because you're big and strong and you're supposed to be good at things and there's nothing in you, nothing at all. You never have been anything and you never will be anything. I don't hate you. You just aren't that interesting."

She turned quickly then and ran away down the wood road. Colin picked up his axe and drove it with all his strength into the tree in front of him.

2 2

COLIN and Curly left the foothills in the spring, as Curly had planned, and traveled the prairies through the summer. One warm September evening they made camp at the top of a high, steep bank above a small river. Colin had wanted to camp in the bush right beside the river, but Curly had talked him out of it. Colin was sitting with his back against a mound of dirt and dry grass, watching one of the big prairie hawks as it circled high in the evening air. "I'm for the coast," he said. "It's time I went up home to see the folks again. I haven't even seen my sister since she got married."

"Suits me," Curly swung the coffee pot off the fire. "It's time I hunted up my old lady again, too."

Colin looked at him in quick surprise. Curly had been born in Winnipeg and his parents had gone their separate ways while he was still in school; until now, he had mentioned them only as belonging to the distant past. "Do you know where she is?"

"Somewhere around Vancouver," Curly said. "I'll find her. It was her I went to see just before we pulled out. She ain't much good, but I feel kind of sorry for the old bat and she's helped me out a time or two."

Colin knew Curly too well to be shocked by the hard assessment. "Have you heard from her lately?"

"Letters, you mean? Christ no. Give her a pencil and she might lick it, but that's as far as she could go. I wrote her when I was at Fred's place last winter, but the letter came back. She keeps moving, but she's O.K. Got the old man's pension. Drinks it mostly, but she picks up enough on the side to keep eating and sleeping. Seems like that's the way she wants it."

The prairie evening was still and the mosquito hawks hunted high. A mallard flapped its wings and called from the reeds in a marsh nearby and terns were busy in swift graceful flight over the marsh. Colin watched it all gratefully. There had been a dozen, perhaps two or three dozen such evenings in the past two years; evenings when they had been camped like this, alone and beyond sound or hearing of other human beings, knowing little or nothing of where they were going or what they would be doing in twenty-four hours' time. Always there had been the high arching sky over them and the distances of the flat land around them, usually a bird-filled marsh and something, a barn or machinery or a belt of trees, to break the endless roll of swaying wheat or dusty stubble. Tonight there was the river behind them in its deep cut; and the land in front of them, to the west, was pasture, broken by patches of rough bush; but it was still prairie.

"Must have been quite a country in the old days," Colin said at last. "With buffalos and Indians and everybody riding horses. I'd sure like to have seen it."

"I'd as soon have her the way she is. A guy can go further and quicker with the freights or hitch-hiking than he ever could with a horse. And it ain't so goddamn far between towns any more. I guess them buffalo was worth seeing though. What made you think of them all of a sudden?"

"I don't know," Colin said. He was rolling a cigarette, very slowly, looking down at the tobacco against the white paper. "Because it's more natural here than most places we go, I guess.

I get to feeling that way quite often—a man must have had a better chance in the old days, when things were more natural."

"There was bums them days, same as there is now. I guess there was work too maybe, but a guy could stay poor all his life doing it. Seems to me we got it easier all around than they had it then. Take these winter camps them kids was talking about the other day. I'll bet the government didn't have nothing like them in the old buffalo days."

"Those forestry camps, you mean?" Colin asked. "Sounded like relief camps to me."

"Sure, that's what they are if you want to call 'em that. But those kids figured they was O.K., just the same—good grub and a good place to stay and they don't work the arse off you. That ain't much maybe, but I've seen times it would sure as hell have looked like plenty to me. You have too. You'd have been better in a set-up like that than the winter you put in up the Fraser Valley."

"What kind of work do they do?"

"Most anything. Fixing up parks, mostly; building trails and roads and fancy entrances, clearing brush, planting trees. Nothing dirty. Straight eight hours, too."

"It'd be a hell of a lot better than stalling around town," Colin said. "You're right about that. And I guess it's the kind of a job a guy wouldn't have to worry in. Just do a day's work and let it go at that."

Curly laughed. "It's working for the government, ain't it? You never seen anybody kill himself working for the government yet, have you?" He looked over at Colin sprawled against the hummock, and affection momentarily softened his sharp little face. "You long-geared old son of a bitch," he said. "You'll never get fired from any place for the kind of day's work you put in."

Colin watched the mosquito hawks against the reddening sky and thought of getting back to the coast. Rain, he thought, and big trees, and the creeks down the sides of the mountains. The creek in the alders, the creek where I used to stop after Tod Phalling had cleaned up on me, all those creeks running into the Wind River below the lake. Cameron Creek, by Robbie's cabin, the creek out of Carlson's Valley, Amabilis Creek. Wonder how Johnny's making out up there on the lake with Robbie? And

187

Margaret married; that's hard to think about. No more prairies, he thought, no more wheat dust, no more evenings like this one, with Curly always knowing what to do next.

"Curly," he said suddenly. "How'll we get together again?"

Curly was lying flat on his back, looking up at the sky, but he rolled over on to his side. "What's that?" he asked. "When it's time to start out again, you mean?"

"Yes," Colin said slowly. "I guess that's what I was thinking."

"It'll work out somehow. Maybe we'll both get us good jobs and won't want to hit the road next year. A person can't tell what's liable to happen."

Colin felt loneliness again, cold, gray, empty. "We better keep in touch," he said

"Sure," Curly agreed. "Sure, we'll do that."

IT was early in November when Colin got home, and after the first few days he felt he had never been away. The prairies, Joe Pauluk, the whole time with Curly, were immeasurably far from him, removed by the long journey through the mountains, by the other journey up the coast, but most of all by the close familiarity of everything about him—the smell of winter apples in the storeroom, the piled woodshed, Martha's quiet, happy acceptance of his return, the sodden maple leaves under the big trees out by the gate, the drip of rain from the barn roof. He had left Curly in Vancouver and they had promised again to keep touch; Colin had written already, but he knew that with Curly only the near things counted, the things in sight, the things one tripped over or ran into, and he did not really expect an answer.

Colin was busy from the moment he got home. He looked at the farm with Joe Pauluk's eyes and saw at once many things to be done; the fences were in bad shape, the pastures were run down, the chicken-house leaked rain, the barn needed repair, even the house itself sagged at one corner where a support had rotted away. He accepted these things almost gladly at first, using them to fit himself easily back into the life; but as he worked at them he felt a growing impatience and with it a sense of loss and despair that he did not fully admit or account for. Will was away, building a donkey-sled for some small outfit a little farther up the coast, but Colin knew that he had worked only occasionally during the past two years and there had been little money. There was only one cow on the place now, which Martha milked and looked after. He thought of Joe Pauluk and what Joe's little strength and his driving energy would have made of the Ensley farm.

Will came back when Colin had been at home for nearly three weeks, and the change in him shocked and hurt Colin far more deeply than the broken fences and dilapidated buildings. The square black beard was heavily streaked with gray, the bold face was thin, the great shoulders stooped, no longer forcing his thick chest proudly forward against the beard. These things Colin noticed and accepted. But the eyes were no longer proud, nor the voice, nor the words that the voice used. Will Ensley was tired, not in his arms or his shoulders or his chest, but in his mind and his heart. He looked searchingly at Colin when he first saw him, as though hoping to find some of his lost strength in his son, and he asked many questions about the prairies and about Colin's time away, old man's questions that seemed to listen for echoes of his own vigor in the answers. Colin answered him and talked with him, and they both searched with a fumbling awkwardness for some bond of understanding that they felt should have been between them. They did not find it.

Margaret was confident and happy as she had always been. Back on the prairies Colin had found it difficult to imagine her married to Clyde Munro, away from the family and mistress of her own house; but once he had seen her it was almost equally difficult to remember that she had once gone daily to school with him. He tried to tell her what he thought about Will and she said: "It's almost as though he had given up. He found out there was a new broad-axe man up at camp, so he went to town and tried to hire out from the agency—anywhere. They told him there wasn't anything, to look in again later."

"Did he?" Colin asked.

"Yes, he went down again. And they told him the same thing. He understood then and it just seemed to stop everything that had kept him going."

Colin thought for a moment, "Being blacklisted isn't anything to be ashamed of," he said.

"It's much deeper than that," Margaret said. She looked across at her husband. "He tried to tell Clyde about it once. What was it he said, Clyde?"

"It's his pride that's gone," Clyde said. "He's not a sure man any more. The things he believes in haven't worked out for him. He was telling me he believes in law and order, telling me over and over again—that's because he doesn't feel right about being tied in with those organizers."

"But he knows he was right," Margaret said. "Mother says he's told her over and over again that he couldn't have done anything else. And he couldn't have. But it's left him grouped with something he really despises—with people he calls agitators and troublemakers."

"He could have broken right away from the whole set-up," Colin said. "He could have worked the farm and made some sort of living at it."

"You know he couldn't," Margaret said.

"He could keep the buildings in shape."

"He's discouraged," Clyde Munro said. "It's not easy for a man as old as Mr. Ensley to change his whole way of life. Especially when he's been one of the top men in his trade."

Because Clyde was so obviously strong and sure in himself, his words had full force for Colin; for the moment he understood his father, felt as he had felt, thought almost as he had thought. But it was still difficult to accept that there was weakness in the great square body and the blackbearded godhead. He thought again of Joe Pauluk.

"They've been through some tough times," he said. "What are they going to do now?"

"Go on the way they are," Margaret said. "You can't change them. We can help out a little, and you can too, if you get a job."

"They'll take him back sooner or later," Clyde said. "It's not as though he was active in the union. I don't know why they've held out this long, except Gordon Holman seems to have it in for him."

"I guess it's time for me to pull out again," Colin said. "I've fixed what I can around the place and I'm not earning my keep there."

He saw Margaret look quickly at Clyde. "You could get on up at the forestry camp," Clyde said. "They're looking for a straw-boss that could teach the kids up there something about axe-work. Has to be a single man."

"I guess I'll pull out," Colin said. "If they don't want Ensleys around this neck of the woods they don't have to have them."

Margaret stood up and crossed the room to the fireplace. "Don't go off again so soon, Colin. It isn't fair to Mother. She'll never tell you, but she's been worried sick all this time you've been away."

"I write her as often as I can."

"I know, but she can't help worrying. It'd be a whole lot easier for her if she knew where you were."

Colin looked at Clyde again. "What is it?" he asked. "Relief work?"

"The camp is. But you'd be more like on the staff. They might even give you a chance to stay on with the Forestry Department all year around. I think you'd like it."

"Sounds like it might be O.K.," Colin said slowly. He thought of Curly—still in Vancouver, probably, making out somehow, planning without anxiety, watching for the break that he was always sure would turn up.

"Think it over," Margaret said. "I know it would help Mother a lot if you were near home."

Later, as he was leaving, she came to the door with him. As he started down the steps she called him back. "Colin," she said. "You haven't been to see Mildred. She was asking about you."

Colin felt his face flush in the darkness and a hard pulse in his throat. "I know," he said. "I haven't been visiting around much."

"She thinks a lot of you. You ought to go and see her."

"I guess I will," he said. "Soon as I get a free evening."

But when he went up to the forestry camp on Strathmore River a week later, he still had not seen her.

COLIN liked the camp and the work. They were developing a small park near the low, slanting falls across the Strathmore River, building roads and trails, flights of steps down awkward places, bridges across the tributary creeks, signs to guide the summer visitors. He had charge of about a dozen men who were supposed to cut and peel poles and split or hew cedar slabs for steps and tables and benches. The work was easy and familiar to Colin and he went at it with a quiet concentration. The men on his crew did little at first except stand off and watch him, helping occasionally to lift a pole or roll a log or cut away some brush, showing rather more activity when one of the regular foremen was nearby, setting their tools down again as soon as he disappeared, talking among themselves and rolling cigarettes.

It did not occur to Colin to attempt to drive them to work; he had been told to show them how to use tools, so he showed them in the only way he knew, by doing the job himself. When he needed help he asked for it. Otherwise he left them alone, to watch and learn if they wanted. Within a day or two they were working almost enthusiastically. They were the "single unemployed" of the province, most of them young and city-bred. Something in Colin's competence attracted them; the smooth shearing of bark away from polished poles over the blade of his axe, the flaking of chips, the shredding of grain from grain into clear, heavy slabs of wood; all the facets of a craft completely new to them reached in and touched some unused impulse to craftsmanship. Above all there was Colin's unconcern with them and concern with the work of his hands. He was a straw-boss, a symbol of authority to be resisted or at least evaded. But the symbol was without substance; resistance passed through, evasion evaded nothing, idleness without challenge became boredom. There was challenge in the bright blade of the axe, in the weight of the sledges, in the way the wood yielded to blade and wedge and saw. They responded to this.

While he worked in the camp Colin's feeling for wood and his skill and ingenuity in working with it developed steadily. The foreman, Dan Settler, recognized his ability at once and used him fully, constantly setting him new problems and broader projects. Colin was absorbed and happy. He worked steadily through each week, often spending the evenings drawing plans or working out designs; but at week ends he went home, cutting over the easy divide between the Strathmore River and his own valley to the road that ran down past Mike Varchuk's empty shack.

During this time he was closer to his mother than he had ever been. Martha had known an intense loneliness after her children had left home, the more intense because their leaving had seemed to complete the disintegration of the world she had planned and worked to hold together. She had known that they must go sooner or later, but she had believed always that their going would be part of the plan, an extension of the world she had built and a renewal of it through grandchildren in houses nearby. For nearly two years it had seemed that the plan had failed her. But now Margaret was near, in a home of her own, and it seemed that Colin might stay within reach until he also settled down.

When he came at the week ends Colin simply dropped his small pack in the woodshed and turned to the work of the place as though he was living there all the time. Occasionally he went out to kill a buck, but more often he worked on the fences or the buildings or in the fields. For the most part Will was away—the small camps along the coast and out among the islands were calling on him more and more frequently—so the two of them were often alone when Colin came in from his work. Martha found Colin even more silent and withdrawn than he had seemed before he left home, but she worked steadily and gently to bring him back to her and she felt a measure of slow success as the winter drew on. She said once, when they were at supper on a Saturday evening: "You're fond of this place, aren't you, Colin? Of the farm, I mean?"

"Sure," he said simply. "It's home."

"It could be quite a good farm."

"There isn't much clear land," Colin said. "There's heavy soil back in the alder bottom, but a person'd have to drain it as well as clear it. And you'd need bigger buildings, and machinery. It'd take a lot of time and money. I'm not sure I like farming that well."

"You were telling me about your friend Joe Pauluk," Martha said. "It must have been even harder where he started."

"I'm not sure," Colin reached forward and cut himself a slice of bread. "That's farming country back there—this isn't. And he wanted land so much. I don't think I want anything so much as Joe wants his land."

He had spoken evenly and calmly, not at all intensely, but the words made Martha afraid for him again. "You do want things," she told him. "I remember how you wanted to climb the mountain. And you've always wanted to go in the woods. Of course you want things."

"I know," Colin said. "But they're the wrong kind of things." I want Mildred, he thought, the way she was when I went away; and things like that night with Robbie at the mouth of Amabilis Creek, and the night on the prairie when Curly and I made up our minds to come back to the coast. And the time on the mountain with Margaret. Those things don't come back. They are people and places, not things you can use like Joe's land. "Farming is a pretty good life," he said. "But it isn't so much on the coast. There's darn few make a go of it."

"It's hard work. They give up for something that looks easier and pays big wages. But a farmer ends up with something. The others don't."

"It might work out." Colin thought of a herd of Jerseys and a big barn, pasture land cleared from the alder flat. "But a man'd have to be able to sell to the Company. They wouldn't buy from us."

Martha stood up and began to clear the table. "That won't last forever," she said. "Things like that never do." Let it rest there for now, her wisdom told her. At least he's thinking of it, he's not planning to go away again just yet. With a good wife to help him someday he could make this place into what Will and I should have made it. I'm not even sure that's what I want for

194

him, except that I want something that will protect him and I can't think of anything else. "Do you have to get back to camp tomorrow night?" she asked. "Margaret and Clyde will be over for supper."

"I can walk through in the dark," Colin said. "I blazed a few trees when I came down this afternoon."

EARLY in January a fresh crew of men came into camp. Colin worked as he always had, hewing and shaping and splitting, asking for help when he had to, using a man who was willing, leaving the unwilling to their own devices. But the temper of the new men was different and several of them were a good deal older than Colin. His interest in what he was doing and his easy skill with his tools had no appeal for them and they were careful to do no more than the barest minimum of work.

Colin noticed the change at first simply as a vague surliness in the men, which depressed and sometimes embarrassed him. A small group of older men, Mel Ross, Olaf Knudson, Charlie Merck and three or four others, usually sat or leaned through most of the day, talking and smoking; the rest of the crew did enough work to make some showing, but only one or two had anything approaching the interest of his former crew. The first clear break came when he asked Ross to help him roll a log. Ross was talking at the time and paid no attention. Colin asked him again and he said: "What's the matter, kid? Scared the push'll be riding your tail?"

The full implication of the question and its tone did not reach Colin. He shook his head and smiled good-naturedly. "Just trying to earn my keep."

"Go ahead," Ross told him. "You're the one that's getting paid to work, not us."

Colin understood then and felt a sharp stir of irritation. "You got a break when they quit charging for standing room," he said, and turned back to the log. Olaf Knudson, another of the older men, came up and helped him with it. Ross laughed and turned away.

Two or three days later Dan Settler called Colin aside as he was starting out to work in the morning. He asked one or two simple questions about the work, then: "How's the new crew working out?"

"O.K., I guess," Colin said.

"They aren't putting out the work," Settler said. "You had any trouble?"

"No. They don't get interested the way the others did, but there's no trouble."

Settler moved his feet and looked past Colin at a group of men walking slowly out of camp with tools over their shoulders. "This bunch is different from the last lot," he said. "Every second one's a sorehead. They'll take different handling."

"They'll settle down," Colin said. "When they see there's nothing else to do."

Settler shook his head vigorously. "They're shaping up for trouble. We got warning they're going to pull a strike." He was a nervous man and moved constantly as he talked, kicking at stones, putting his hands in his pockets, taking them out again. "Look, Ensley," he said. "You're a good workman, but you got to handle that crew so you get some work out of them. So long as you do all the work they'll take advantage of it, just standing around watching and trying to look like they was learning something. You've got to do the standing around and make the other guys work. That's what a straw-boss is for."

"You got to show them," Colin said. "There's not more than one or two of them know the difference between an axe and a peavey."

"Never mind that," Settler said. "Get them working. Don't leave 'em stand around and talk."

Over the next week or so the thing progressed steadily. In spite of Settler's warning Colin made little effort to change his handling of his crew. He knew that Settler was right and that most of the men watched him work and did nothing themselves, but he could not feel concerned about it. He was interested in the work and liked doing it; from time to time he had to have help and would ask for it; apart from that it seemed to him foolish to try to persuade unwilling men to do work that he could do faster and better alone.

Actually, in that last week before the strike, the men on Colin's crew worked better and more willingly than they had before. When Colin came up to them the morning Settler had spoken to him, Mel Ross asked: "What did the big push want?"

Colin grinned. "He told me to make you guys work harder."

"You going to try it?"

"I haven't bothered you yet, have I?" Colin asked. "You can set on your fannies till your pants rot so long as you don't get in my way."

"We might do just that," Ross said.

The rest of the crew was standing around, listening to them. Olaf Knudson said: "Lay off the kid, Mel. He's treated us good enough."

"I ain't bothering him none, just so he don't bother us."

"Might be just as good to help out a little," Knudson said. "If we don't he's liable to get fired and some proper son of a bitch take his place."

Ross picked up an axe and put it down again. He was thinking. But Charlie Merck said: "What do we care? We're going out on strike, ain't we?" He was a thin, hungry-looking man, with a long nose, a long jaw and sunken blue eyes. Ross turned on him fiercely.

"Shut up, Merck," he said. "You're so goddamned ignorant you got no business being alive, never mind talking. I think Olaf's got something. We can just as easy pitch in and make the kid look good."

Colin had picked up his axe some moments before and was scoring a fresh log, but he heard Merck say in a hurt whine: "That ain't no way to talk to anyone."

"Shut up," Ross told him again. Then: "O.K., you guys. Pick up some tools and get to work."

Colin laughed. "Don't anybody bust a gut," he said.

The strike came off in due course. There was a union of a sort and a measure of leadership from men like Mel Ross, but in spite of talk and preparations they seemed to drift into it rather than anything else. Colin was never very sure of the issues. They wanted a higher rate of pay, without the planned hold-back that was supposed to help them out when they left, and a promise that the camps would be continued through the year instead of closing

197

down in early spring, when work became more plentiful. The plan seemed to be to carry on all the domestic routine of the camp, but to do no work beyond this.

During the first two days there was a good deal of activity. Committees were formed and met. There were speeches. Dan Settler addressed the strikers and asked them to go back to work. A more senior official arrived from outside and addressed them more firmly, threatening to close the camp. Colin watched and listened with a growing sense of hopelessness. He belonged fully to neither side and neither side had need of him. He liked the camp, liked Dan Settler, liked the work he had been doing and the men he had been working with. He wondered what Curly would say about it or Joe Pauluk or some of the prairie farmers he had worked for. Here was food and a comfortable place to sleep, easy work, short hours, some pay. They want more, he thought; most of all they want to be sure of something, not to go back to town at the end of a couple of months and start looking again with only a few dollars between them and hunger. That's what they are striking about really, not about this camp or this park they are working on or Dan Settler or me. They are one little part of hundreds and thousands and hundreds of thousands of people, all across North America, who aren't sure they can do enough and get enough to keep them alive. Curly and I always knew we'd get by somehow, Joe Pauluk knows, but these guys don't know and they want to know. That's what they are saying now. They hardly know they are saying it and they have to say other things instead, but that is what they feel. If I felt the same I guess I'd be in it with them.

On the third day of the strike some trucks came in and loaded all the food that was stored in the cookhouse. The strikers had been warned that this would happen, but it seemed to take them completely by surprise and they made no move to stop the loading. During the afternoon the permanent staff of the camp, including the cooks, moved out.

Colin had said he would walk home over the hill and he went into his tent to pack his stuff. Olaf Knudson came in and watched him. Colin liked Olaf. He was a quiet, sensible man of thirty-five or forty, a commercial fisherman who owned his own gill-net boat and used the camp to help him through the winter. He watched

Colin in silence for a minute or two, then shifted the big curved pipe in his mouth and coughed.

"Looks like she's finished," he said. "Where'll you go now?"

Colin rolled up a shirt and stowed it down into his packsack. "Have to look for some place, I guess. I was just hired for this camp. You think the strike can't win?"

Olaf shrugged. "No money, no grub. They called our bluff. Tomorrow the police come in and we walk out. That's all there is to it."

Colin had finished his packing. He sat down on his bunk and looked up at Olaf. "Why did it happen?" he asked.

Olaf shrugged again. "Trouble," he said. "Trouble every place. There's right in it, too. Most of these kids got no place to go but hang around town when they finish up their time in camp. But this won't help it any. They should wait and get a good plan."

"What about you?" Colin asked.

"I'll make out. I can live on the boat and pick up a few dollars for grub between now and the start of the season. But most of them got nothing."

"I'm going down home right away," Colin said. "Want to come along?"

Olaf shook his head. "I'll stay with the boys. Till they hit town, anyway."

It was almost dusk and raining a little when Colin started over the hill. He had talked more with Olaf before leaving, but he still felt confused and helpless in the face of what had happened. Only two or three weeks ago the camp had been a happy place. It had seemed to him useful, sensible, hopeful. There were things to be done, problems to be worked out; the results of the work showed plainly and they were good; the men he was working with liked the job, liked their food, and their own lively entertainments in the evenings and over week ends, even ran off a small newspaper of their own in the camp. Nothing had changed; it was the same park, the same camp, the same job and bosses, the same food, the same weather; yet now the camp no longer existed except as a street of tents that would be taken down within the next few days, and a few groups of men who stood around and talked. These men weren't essentially different from the men who had liked the camp, yet Olaf had said they were right to strike. Curly would have said the same thing, Colin thought; he'd have been mad about it, but that's what he would have said. And so would Joe Pauluk.

Near the summit of the divide Colin slipped his pack under a log and turned back. It was dark when he came in sight of the camp again, but three or four big fires were burning down the center of the roadway between the tents, throwing red light on the tents, on the straight clean trunks of the trees, against the bowed dark figures of the men. Colin thought of a picture he had once seen of Valley Forge. A ragged army huddled around its fires, but without the stacked rifles, with the soft, insidiously cold rain instead of snow.

He went down into the camp and stood near one of the fires. He did not know any of the men around it, but one of them turned and said to him: "You were one of the straw-bosses, weren't you? What are you doing here?"

Colin hesitated, started to say something, but the man had already turned away. There was strong heat from the fires and the woolen clothing of the men steamed. They were talking of what was going to happen, whether the police would come in, whether they should go out quietly or make a stand.

Colin went on to the next fire. Again he knew none of the men except by sight and again one of them turned and questioned him. "Christ, I thought you guys had all pulled out. You was one of the pushes, wasn't you?"

Colin wanted to say that he was only a broad-axe man, not a push, but again the man wasn't really interested and turned quickly back to the group about the fire.

At the third fire he recognized several men of his own crew. Mel Ross was there and Olaf and Charlie Merck. They seemed better organized than the other groups. Mel Ross was controlling the talk and they were planning almost carefully what they would do. Ross said: "We got to have a fund if we're going to get any place. Most everybody's got a few bucks. We ought to be able to collect enough so as we can at least hang together when we hit town."

He noticed Colin then. "Where in hell did you come from, Ensley? Thought you pulled out hours ago."

"I came back," Colin said simply.

"Better pull out again," Ross said. "A job's a job these days. If the higher-ups ever get wise to you being with us guys you won't last long."

Charlie Merck waved his arms foolishly. "The guy's a stool-pigeon," he said. "Throw him out."

Without looking at him or raising his voice Ross said: "Shut up, Charlie."

Colin felt a hand on his arm, looked round and saw Olaf. Olaf drew him quietly a little way away from the group. "Mel's right," he said. "You've got a job and you may as well hang on to it."

"I haven't got any job," Colin said. "Not that I know of, except in this camp."

"They'll put you on somewhere else if you keep your nose clean. Why did you come back?"

"I figured I might be able to help out."

"Forget it," Olaf said. "There ain't nothing to help. Never was much and she's balled up for fair now."

"Then why don't you pull out?"

"That's different. I been in on it from the start. There's nothing you could do but tag along and likely they wouldn't even let you do that."

Colin looked towards the fire again. "Doesn't make much sense," he said. "Not any of it. Seems like every time you get started on something it runs right out on you."

"You'll be O.K.," Olaf said. He held out his hand. "So long, kid. Be seeing you some place."

Colin climbed the hill very slowly. When he reached the last place from which he could see the fires below him he stopped and sat watching for a long while. It was still raining and he could feel wetness spreading through the worn place in the shoulder of his mackinaw, but he paid no attention to it. The little dark figures moved about below and kept the fires burning brightly. Alone on the hill, Colin knew that Olaf was right. He didn't belong there and there was nothing he could have done.

LATE in the afternoon of the day after he left camp Colin saw a man walking down the road past the farm. The man's walk was queer and awkward, almost staggering, and Colin walked out towards the road to meet him. As the hunched, shambling figure came closer he recognized Charlie Merck and called to him. Merck stopped, stared blankly for a moment, then started jerkily forward. Colin saw that his clothes were torn and wet; he had no hat and his wavy blond hair was dankly tangled and full of fir and hemlock needles. He began talking excitedly when he was still several yards away.

"Christ," he said. "I'm all in. Jesus, I've had a terrible trip. Been in the brush all night and all day. There's wild animals up there. Jesus, I might've been lost and never come out."

"You better come in and get something to eat," Colin said.

"Food? Christ I ain't eaten since noon yesterday." He peered behind him, back along the road, moving his head sharply from side to side. "They come down yet? They gone by here?"

"Who?" Colin asked him.

"The boys. The boys from camp. They gone by yet?" There was a look of terror in the blue eyes that shifted from the road to Colin's face and back to the road again. There was terror, violence, fear of violence in the hunched body and the jerking arms.

"They went down by the main road two or three hours ago. They'll be out to the wharf by now."

Merck's body relaxed instantly and the fear died away from his face. "Let me at that grub," he said. "Christ, what I been through." Following Colin along the roadway to the house, he still talked. "I got ten bucks. I'm O.K. Got it out of the collection we took up last night. They'll never miss it."

Colin turned on him sharply. "You what?"

"Grabbed off ten bucks from the collection. It won't do them no good. A guy's got to look after himself, ain't he?" Suddenly he stared hard at Colin. "Christ, you was up there, wasn't you?

Sure you was. I seen you. Don't you tell them guys nothing. Christ, they'd kill me." The terror was back on him, jerking his neck and his arms to violent movement again. "Christ, I'd better get out of here."

Colin felt a revulsion that turned him sick, but he said: "Come on, you eat fast, then get the hell out."

Martha was in the kitchen and Colin told her only that Merck had been lost on his way down from camp. She cooked bacon and eggs and coffee and Merck swallowed them hungrily and nervously. He got up from the table immediately he was finished and went quickly to the door. Colin followed him. Outside he stopped and suddenly thrust his face towards Colin, drawing his lips back from his teeth.

"Can you see I been eating? I got to get back with them guys. I wouldn't want them to know I been eating."

"You're O.K.," Colin said. "Nobody could tell anything. You'd do better to worry about the money you stole."

"That's why I got to get back. They'll never know the difference just so I keep with them till they hit town. I gotta be going."

Colin watched the hunched form stumble down the wagon road and finally disappear from sight in the direction of Blenkinstown. When he went back into the kitchen Martha looked anxiously at his face.

"What did he say to you? He was a horrible man. Was he threatening you about something?"

"No," Colin said. "Nothing like that. But he wasn't much good."

"Sit down," Martha said. "I'll make more coffee. You look as if you need it."

LATER the same evening Colin went to see Mildred Hanson. His mind was a confusion of thought and sensation so oppressive that he wanted the calmness of Mildred's voice and face and body as he had never wanted anything before. It seemed to him completely natural to go to her and he wondered only for a moment why he had not gone long before, when he first came back from the prairies.

There was a light in the cottage and she came to the door as

203

soon as he knocked. She was as beautiful as he remembered her, as cool and golden and clear as he had known she would be. She recognized him without surprise, but her face softened instantly in a smile that reached out to him as plainly as the little gesture of her hands. "Why, Colin," she said. "How nice."

He knew as he followed her in that she was alone. The room was little changed and for a moment he felt himself a schoolboy again. There was pleasure in the feeling, so intense that he felt sudden tears in his eyes. He sat down and Mildred said gently: "It's been a long time, Colin. It's terribly good to see you again."

"I didn't come before," he said. "I know I should have. I'm sorry."

"I wanted you to come," she was standing beside the chair, looking down at him. "I told Margaret."

Colin looked straight in front of him at the fire. "I was afraid you would have changed," he said. "I didn't think it could ever be the way it was before I left."

Her right hand moved quickly towards him, but did not touch him. "I know. It was my fault. But I couldn't tell you—I had to leave you free. And I was afraid, too." Her hand moved again and touched his shoulder. "But it is the same, darling. It is the same if you still want it to be."

Colin stood up and they looked at each other and smiled. He saw that she was almost crying and drew her to him and kissed her, very gently because he was still afraid and unbelieving. But she held her body hard against him and forced her lips against his. In a little while she said: "We aren't easy people, are we, darling?"

"I'm not," he said. "Not even for myself. I came to tell you I'm going away again."

He felt her fingers grip his arm, but she nodded calmly. "I think I knew that," she said and drew gently away from him.

For a while they talked easily. Colin felt the strained confusion of his mind yielding to her calmness, but all the while a new tension was growing in him, of blood and muscle and feeling. She went into the kitchen to make coffee and he got up to pile wood on the fire. When she came back he sat on the floor beside her chair as he had the last time he was there, and after a little while she reached up and switched out the single light.

"Go on talking," she said softly. "Tell me everything that has happened. More about the prairies and Curly and Joe Pauluk. Tell me what you thought, as well as what you did."

Colin told her. She prompted him occasionally with questions and whenever she did so he knew that her soft full-throated voice stirred his body even while it calmed his mind and freed his words.

She said at last: "You've seen so many of the things I hoped you would. Don't they all begin to mean something to you?"

"Yes," Colin said slowly. "Things mean something. Places mean something. It's people that are hard to understand. You can't ever be safe with them."

"You've been with some fine people," she said. But she thought: that's what he's been telling me over and over again, not in plain words but in the things he has told most intensely. People are afraid, people are violent, people hurt you, people mean to hurt you; they like hurting you and there is no shelter from them except in being alone or in finding just one person that you know and love. He has learned so much, yet he has learned almost nothing because he still doesn't know how to protect himself from the Tod Phallings, from stupid policemen, from the hard, mean things that happen to everyone.

"I don't belong anywhere," Colin said. "Most people have their own way of living and it fits them. Even Curly has his way and it works."

"You're still very young," Mildred said. "No one's life comes ready-made. You'll find yours and be happy in it." Why do I tell him that? Am I afraid of what I've done to him, afraid that I've taught him to want something big without showing him how to find it? I've tried to show him and a teacher can only do so much; the rest has to come in other ways.

"I'm not unhappy," Colin said. He turned round and took her hand in his. "When I'm with you I know what I have to do and how I have to do it. When I go away I sometimes forget, but if you've once known you can't really forget, can you? It's always there, just lost for a little while."

"Yes," she said. "It's always there, in you and through you and part of you. It can only die if you make it die."

She bent her head a little towards him as she spoke and the light of the fire shone on her pale hair. He reached up and touched the shine. "I love you," he said. "I can't make that die. I tried once and only made it more alive."

Mildred saw the words like sun on morning mist, moving and beautiful before her, veiling everything except themselves. You've tried. Oh, my darling, who was she and what did she do to you, what has she made you? Colin stood up and raised her to him. She kissed him with the straining desire that her calm mind had held back through the years. She felt the hardness of his body and the power of his arms and then, while she still sought him, her mind took charge again. He is full man now, she thought, and I am a woman, not a teacher. He needs me, not for always, but now, tonight. My body can give him a strength that my mind has never given him.

He held her away from him and looked down at her, as he had the night before he went away. "You're like a stream in the mountains," he said. "Everything about you is beautiful. You mustn't send me away again."

She moved towards him, her head thrown back, her wide eyes at once bold and afraid. Her heart longed to hold his head to her breast, to cry tears over him and whisper: "Poor Colin." But her body moved to him as to a lover, freely and boldly. It was her mind's decision and her body's choice: not to mother, not to teach, but to love.

IT was very dark and Colin knew he had not slept. Something like sleep had held his body still and rested it while his mind raced with thought and wonder. He could still feel the straining arch of his stomach muscles and the clean emptiness of his body. So much was washed away, so many days and nights of throttled desire and starved fantasy. The unexplained things seemed suddenly clear, so many of the hard things seemed small and unimportant.

Her quiet hand was in his and he could hear her even breathing beside him; he thought she was asleep. There was no hurt or confusion for him even in remembering that she had cried. She had said: "Will you believe in me now? Does this tell you how I love you?" and the urgency of her voice had made her tears not sorrow but triumph. Even while she was speaking she held him close to her, so that he could feel her love's rejection of every fear and restraint that had ever come between them.

Later, more calmly, she had said: "It's still true that I'm not right for you, darling. I mustn't ever try to hold you." And he had taken her to him again then, more boldly and surely than before, to bury the meaning of the words beyond reach or remembrance.

Colin freed his hand from hers and sat up very quietly in the darkness. She stirred beside him, instantly, and he sat without breathing, hoping she would not wake. But she said: "Are you going away now, Colin?"

"Yes," he said and the finality of the word kept them both very still in the darkness.

Mildred's head was turned towards him and her eyes strained to find some shadow of him against the blackness. I must let him go freely, she thought; I must not cling or cry or do anything to weaken what has happened. I must be generous with him and honest with myself. Whatever I have given him is no more than I have taken from him. I have no more right to hold him now than I had a few hours ago—or a few years ago, when he was still a schoolboy. But this time I must not turn him away. He told me that. He said: You mustn't send me away again.

"Colin," she said.

"Yes."

"You're going to the lake?"

"Yes," he said again.

"You'll have to come out quite often, won't you?"

"Every two or three months, maybe."

He heard her body move and felt her head on his arm. "You know now it can't change," she said. "I can't take myself away from you. So you must come, always, whenever it is."

He leaned back and kissed her and their bodies touched; but he did not hold her. He felt her draw away and he stood up.

She said quietly: "I can make breakfast for you. I can be very quick."

"No," he said. "I don't need anything." He wanted to hurry, to be away from her sharply and clearly, with only this quiet darkness coming after his memory of her.

She came to the door with him when he was ready to go and stopped him there and kissed him and said quietly: "Good-by, Colin." But still there was only darkness. Even the faint gray of the rainy dawn to come was not yet visible over the mountains in the east.

PART FIVE

THE GULLY

25

THE whole of July had been very hot, with strong north-westerly winds, and the sky had been full of the smoke of big fires though there was no fire in the green timber around the lake. Robbie had come down from his mineral claims in the hills and Johnny Harris, seeing smoke at Robbie's cabin, had come up the lake to fetch Colin. Now they were all three together at Robbie's and it was a quiet evening under the smoke haze, so they sat on Robbie's new front porch to watch the strange red sun burn its way out of sight in the west.

They were used to each other now, very sure of each other, and they did not talk much. It was over eighteen months since Colin had come into the lake and in that time he had been outside about half-a-dozen times, never for more than a day or two. He had built himself a good cabin at Amabilis Creek and two shelter cabins farther up the valley, along his lines; and he had added the long porch to the front of Robbie's cabin.

Robbie moved in his chair and reached behind him for his tobacco can. "We'd be fighting fire right now if we was outside," he said. "Pushing shovels and axes on some goddamned fire trail."

"No ranger will ever come back here to pick us up," Johnny said.

"No," Robbie agreed. Then his tone changed to the protective, fatherly reproof he liked to use towards the two younger men. "But we could have a fire of our own some day. We'd be out fighting then."

Colin listened idly. Under the smoke the lake was less beautiful than usual, but it was quiet; and smoke haze lay along the deep valleys and the red light of the sun came along the lake to where their three canoes were pulled up on Robbie's beach. The lake had been good to him, as he had known it would be, and now Amabilis Valley was his and he was making the high mountains along both sides of it and at the head his own also. He claimed to be prospecting when he went into the mountains, but the claim deceived no one and Robbie and Johnny often kidded him about it. He laughed and said little when they did so. He had never explained, even to himself, what it was that he looked for in the mountains. Not just Tom Hughes, though Tom Hughes was part of it and had been ever since Andrew Grant had described his death in Windstorm Gap. The absorbing effort of climbing, power of lungs, power of legs and back and arms, utter confidence in the whole working of his body; the clean, windy space of the high country. And sense of possession. Perhaps that above all.

Colin was conscious of the radio only when Robbie reached over and shut it off. A man talking. The news. Robbie always listened to the news.

"They're going to have another war," Robbie said. "It's a worse mess over there every time you listen to it."

"They'll work it out some way," Johnny said. "They learned enough last time not to try it again."

"Don't you think it," Robbie told him. "The only way they'll ever stop that Hitler guy is with guns."

"What does he want now?" Colin asked.

"Just one more country is all," Robbie said. "And then another after that."

"Only part of it," Johnny said. "And he's got some claim on that."

"Part now and the rest later," Robbie said. "Them Huns ain't changed a damn bit."

Colin had heard Robbie talk that way before and had discounted it as the bitterness of an old soldier. Tonight, for the first time, some urgency of conviction in Robbie's words impressed him.

"Will Canada be in it?" he asked.

Robbie got up and walked to the railing of the porch. Colin watched his sharp-boned body, dark against the light surface of the lake. "The whole world'll be in it," Robbie said. "It'll be like the last one only worse. You boys'll see it, that's sure. I don't know but what I'm pretty near young enough myself."

"I'll believe it when I do see it," Johnny said and they sat in silence again. Colin tried to think of war, of wearing a uniform, carrying a rifle to kill men, going overseas to fight. It was not easy; he realized he had never seen a soldier. They wouldn't want us guys from back in the sticks anyway, he thought. They wouldn't even know about us. Poor old Robbie, it's just that he can't ever forget about that last war.

Later in the evening, when Johnny had gone out of the cabin for a little while, Robbie told Colin casually: "I saw your sister when I was outside last week."

"How was she?" Colin asked. "O.K.?"

"Sure. She said to tell you to go see your mother next time you're out."

"Marge said that?" Colin's shoes rasped against the floor as he moved in his chair.

"You ain't been going," Robbie said calmly. "She said that too. I was to tell you from me, not her. Only I figured you'd know who was back of it anyways."

Colin felt anger hot in his face. They could mind their own

211

business, he thought, both of them. But his anger was weak, not strong; ashamed, not proud. "I guess I should have gone more often," he said. "But I don't stay out there long. You know that."

Robbie's voice was still casual. "There's nobody driving you back." Then his tone changed. "Listen, son. A man's only got one mother and he don't have her here as long as he figures he's going to. You'll be sorry all your life if you let some slip of a girl come between you and her."

Johnny came back into the cabin then and Robbie asked Colin: "You seen any big old billy goats up in the hills lately?"

Colin steadied his voice with an effort. "Sure," he said. "There's two or three dandies up in the Gully. Why?"

"I'd like to get me some cooking fat against the winter."

"What's the matter with bear fat?"

"I'd sooner have goat, for a change. Ain't had goat fat around for years."

"I heard you say that once before," Johnny said. "Thought you were kidding."

"You shoot yourself an old billy in September and you'll see what I mean," Robbie said. "Pick out a big one, Colin, and you'll have yourself a dandy rug for that cabin of yours."

"O.K.," Colin said. "I'll look around next time I get up to the Gully."

COLIN had been camped in the Gully for two days. It was September and he had come to hunt Robbie's goat, but he had done no hunting yet. On the first day he had climbed up to Windstorm Gap, sure of it now that he had searched and rejected half-a-dozen other high passes out of the Gully. He had been there before but had never been far enough through. This time he went on and found the exposed ledge on which Andrew Grant and the Hughes brothers had waited out the night all those years ago. There was a faint powdering of snow on the ledge already and a hard cold wind was blowing through the gap, in spite of the clear blue sky above and the warm fall sunshine that lay along the Gully behind him and against many of the bare rock faces around him.

The ledge was a dank place that the sun touched only for a short while each day. Rock towered above it on one side in almost sheer climb to a mountain peak; on the other side it sloped gently for fifty or a hundred feet to an overhanging edge that cut away for a thousand feet or more to the start of the Milk River. It wasn't hard to picture that night on the ledge, waist-deep in powdery snow with a fury of wind hurling more and more snow at them through the gap; or the cold, stiff start at the earliest glimmer of the next day's dawn. Colin remembered Grant's words: "Tom was killed almost as soon as we started next day." They would have spent the night close against the rock wall. And gone on from there, wading the soft snow against the driving wind. Colin followed the ledge and found that it tapered in to within ten or fifteen feet of the wall, then straightened out almost suddenly and ran narrowly along it. In the corner, he thought, would have been the overhang. Looking down he could see the drop, almost straight for several hundred feet, then flowing away towards the creek bed through a massive snow-slide.

Lying in his camp near the head of the Gully's two miles of flat green meadow, Colin remembered all this and looked at the rifle that lay near him. It had been a good rifle, the tool of a man who had taken pride in his gear. It was in extraordinarily good shape; the stock was bleached and the barrel was rusted, but it was little more than surface rust and the mechanism still worked. There was a small gold plate let into the butt and the initials T. H. were still clear on it. Colin thought it must have been buried until this year, then exposed by the hot weather of July and August. Falling away from the man, it would have driven deeper into the snow bank than his body. For there had been no sign of the body.

The climb down to the slide had been enormously difficult, so difficult that Colin had slept the previous night still a hundred feet or more above it and had not attempted the climb back after finding the rifle, but had worked down the valley and found an easier way. There had been no sign of the body, not even a bone to show that the animals had found it, nor a knife or a waterproof match box to show it had been there. Yet Colin had been quite sure and before starting back he had built a cairn of rocks in a sheltered place near the edge of the slide and had slipped his own metal match box into the heart of the cairn, with Tom Hughes name in it. He had tried to remember whether Grant or Robbie had ever told him the date, but could not so he wrote only: "In September, about 1920."

Sometime this month, around eighteen years ago. Until Tom Hughes fell there no one had ever reached that slide. And from the time he fell until today no one else had been there. Grant said that. Al Hughes wouldn't let them go back; he had said that Tom couldn't be in a better place and wouldn't want to be.

Colin looked about him at the Gully. The level green meadow flowed away from him to the narrow entrance between the high bluffs of the canyon. It was late afternoon and the deer had already come down to feed. The mountains rose sharply and steeply from the meadow, climbing five or six thousand feet to hard, broken peaks. The shoulders of the peaks held high along both sides of the Gully and across the head of it. He could pick out the pass through Windstorm Gap only because he knew where to look for it and even so it looked less like a pass than a high ridge between two peaks. The floor of the Gully was already in shadow, but the sunlight was strong and clear on the face of the mountains beyond the meadow, where the slopes were more gradual and multiplied the Gully's width. They were hard rock slopes, Colin knew, rising in bluffs and benches and ledges, end-lessly and massively broken, never easy for long; yet walking country rather than climbing country, with plenty of browse for goats and deer, and berry-grown slides for the bears. He could see the goats, far above him, tiny white dots that moved. There were two almost on the route he had followed down and he wondered what they would make of his scent.

He got up from his blankets and began to build a small fire to cook supper. Walking down to the creek for water he saw that a mist was starting up out in the meadow and he stood a moment to watch the brown shapes of the deer in it and against it. She would like this, he thought. I tell her about the mountains and about places I've seen and she listens and listens as though I were saying the most important things in the world. But I don't think she's even been into the mountains, not really into them like this is. I must bring her here and show it to her instead of talking about it.

214

HE began to hunt early the next morning, working far up towards the head of the Gully, then swinging back along the west side to look for the big goat he had seen there earlier in the year. There was no sun on this day and a sharp wind drew down from the head of the valley, steadily cold on the left side of his face now, and growing stronger.

After nearly two hours of walking and climbing he knew he was in the big goat's country and stopped. His camp at the head of the meadow was almost directly below him; perhaps a thousand, perhaps two thousand feet down. A long way, Colin thought, because these on this side are the high mountains, higher than the mountains at the head of the Gully. He felt the clear, sharp excitement that high places always brought to him, excitement without fear or blame or anxiety. It was living and strong in him today, not because he was hunting but because of Tom Hughes' rifle down there in the camp below him. Colin did not try to understand it or explain it to himself. It seemed to him that he had always known he must find where Tom Hughes had died and that now, having found the place and marked it, the Gully was his and the whole valley was his in a way it never had been before. It was as though some shadowy restraint had dropped away from his mind and he was free to think clearly for the first time in his life.

Possession of the valley had become intensely important to him. It was important that his trap-line was formally registered, with boundary lines that took in the whole watershed from the highest peaks to the edge of the lake. It was important that Robbie and Johnny called it his—"Colin's valley," they said or "Colin's country." But most important of all were the marks he himself had set upon the valley; the big log cabin on the shore of the lake near the mouth of the creek, the two shelter cabins, the occasional blazes along his trap-lines; and beyond even these, the claim he set upon it and constantly renewed, with his feet and the effort of his body as he followed out the creeks and climbed the mountains and hunted the ridges.

He stood up, still looking down at the meadow. He could find his camp-site by the little tongue of timber that ran down a draw and spread out a short way into the meadow, and he knew that he would build another cabin there. Next year, as soon as the melting snow drew back from the meadow.

As he turned away and started up the hill he noticed that the wind was stronger, and gusty. The mountain tops were in the clouds now and snow-squalls swirled here and there about the high slopes. He climbed easily, always across or into the wind, following dry creek beds and narrow rock draws, turning occasionally along the benches. He came into snow and wondered for the first time if he would be able to find the goat. He thought of Robbie's continual warnings about the mountains: "You'll die in them hills if you keep going out there alone. Die of a broken leg, maybe, and take weeks doing it. We won't be able to find you. No one'll know you're missing until it's too late to look, anyway." Even today, in the snow and wind and on the bad slopes the warning did not touch him. He could not feel that he would ever die in the mountains; in the water, perhaps; or among men, riding a freight train, crossing a city street, in Robbie's war. But in the mountains he felt no fear of death. Often one had to travel slowly and carefully and it was hard work. Sometimes one turned back, because a place was impossible, not because it was dangerous. Storms could close in swiftly, shutting out sight with snow and cloud, driving wind and ice against one's body, but they had never seemed unfriendly; one found shelter behind a rock or under an overhang and waited them out.

When he came to the edge of the rock-slide the storm had lessened. The clouds were higher and the snow seemed to drive in narrow belts across the face of the mountain, though the wind was stronger than ever and broken by sudden fierce gusts that tore at his body and lifted the fallen snow to lash it past him like spindrift. The goat would be in shelter, Colin thought, and there was no hope of finding him unless the storm broke up later in the day. But he still worked his way upwards, along the edge of the rock-slide, because it would be better to hunt from above than below if the storm did clear away.

Then he saw the goat. It was straight above him, standing broadside, head towards the wind. The head swung and the short black horns turned directly towards Colin. Colin threw a shell into the breech of his rifle, chose his spot behind the shoulder and fired in the moment the gust came. He saw the goat swing sharply to the shock of the bullet, then driving snow hid everything that was more than fifty feet away.

Colin started up the hill, traveled ten or fifteen feet, then stopped. He knew the goat had not gone down. The bullet had hit him too far back, well behind the heart. It would kill him in the end, but he could carry it, perhaps for many hours and many miles. Colin moved under the sheltered side of a great boulder and waited there. The sudden wind had spoiled the shot, he knew, either by carrying the bullet or by its unexpected pressure on the barrel of his rifle. He saw again the moment before the shot; the bold powerful shape of the goat's great body, long white hair swept by the wind; then the confident turn of the heavy head. He was calm and sure, Colin thought, not afraid. He was living his life and I didn't have to bother him. Now it's all changed because Robbie said half-a-dozen words down at his cabin over a month ago. He's weak and dying and hurt, probably afraid.

In fifteen or twenty minutes Colin went on. The storm had lifted again and the clouds were very high, shredding against the mountain peaks, leaving the lower gaps fully exposed. He found the place where the goat had been standing, saw where the turn of his strong feet had flurried the snow, saw blood there, powdered over with driven snow, but heavy and deep red when he scraped the snow away. He was sure now that the wound was a bad one. The hunt became an obligation, short of the impossibility of atonement, touched with the humility of penance, but touched also by his close share in the life of the valley.

The goat had traveled steadily and easily at first, along the face of the mountain, towards the big lake. There was no blood, but Colin followed the track easily in the light new snow. Then the track turned sharply up a square-sided funnel, a bold narrow crack in the breast of the mountain. It was vigorous flight still, with great leaps; there was no blood and no faltering. Colin moved cautiously and quietly, watching constantly above him, but he had seen no sign of the goat when he came up to the ledge where it had rested. There was blood on the ledge, a heavy clot in the snow, and white hairs on the blood. Colin put his hand down and felt warmth. The track led on up the funnel, but it was less sure now, less bold; and once Colin found the snow sharply stirred and recognized the print of broad knees where the goat had stumbled.

The funnel ended in a short, steep slide of rock little more than a thousand feet below the peak of the mountain. The wind had dropped and the clouds had broken. Colin saw the big lake, still under clouds, far ahead of him and far below him. The meadow was hidden from sight by the slope and jut of the rock he had climbed, but the mountains at the head of the Gully were clear against blue sky.

The track had turned along the face of the mountain again, angling a little down. Colin followed it past the gap, across a deep draw and out on to the slope of the next mountain. The sunlight was bright and warm about him now and the clouds over the lake were breaking up. The track was easy to follow; too easy, Colin thought. He's heading for some place where he knows he'll be safe, where he's been safe before, likely, and knows he can shake off anything that's following him.

He was past the second peak and the next gap was coming into sight around the slope of the mountain. He saw the goat at once and clearly, less than a mile away, close under the rim of the gap. It disappeared as he watched, reappeared almost on the sky-line, then disappeared again. Out of the valley, Colin thought, and into what? Johnny's valley isn't that close down here, it can't be. Into more mountains? He left the track and began to pick his own way to the rim of the gap. An hour later he was in the gap, close under the rim, climbing with his rifle slung over his back.

The climb ended suddenly and Colin found himself in a narrow pass formed between the shoulder of the mountain he had just passed and a long ridge that ran down from the next mountain. The pass angled northward and was so narrow and had such steep sides that it seemed at first almost a tunnel. The goat track led along the floor of the pass, following a clear trail worn into the rock by generations of passing game. Colin glanced upward at the strip of blue sky, then back to the twisting crevice ahead of him. It seemed to him that the floor was as nearly level as anything could be.

He came out suddenly, so suddenly that it seemed that the

world had dropped away from him. The pass ended, broke off altogether, and there was nothing between the few feet of rock in front of him and a great broken mountain peak two or three miles away. He moved forward cautiously and could see the lower slopes of the mountain. Then he was at the edge and could look straight down, thousands of feet to a blue-green lake. Colin forgot the goat, forgot that he was hunting. He was aware of nothing except the tremendous hollow below him and the details that made it. Straight across from him the great mountain stood proudly out from all the other peaks. Along its north shoulder lay a sweep of ice and snow and from this there fell away a heavy stream of water, through fall after fall until it disappeared in the narrow belt of timber around the lake, then reappeared in a clouded semi-circle that spread out from the lake's edge into the blue-green. The lake itself was nearly two miles long, roughly oval in shape, filling most of the length and breadth of the floor of the hollow. There were tall mountains again on either side of the main peak, and tall cliffs barred the foot of the lake except where a thin dark line showed a high-walled canyon outlet. The roar of the falls opposite came clearly across to Colin and he could hear behind it the roar of other falls still hidden from him. He thought: no one ever told me about this place. Then: how could they tell me? No one knows except me. It's a lost place, hidden between John-ny's valley and mine. Yet it's part of my valley. This is the creek that runs in just below Amabilis Lake, the one I followed out to the high falls in the smooth rock I couldn't climb.

He thought of the goat again and looked quickly down at the trail to make sure he had passed that way. The track was clear right out to the break-off. Colin went forward and saw at once a broad ledge trail angling steeply down into the hollow. It was clear and smooth for as far as he could see, evenly covered with fresh snow; but its start was still hidden by the sloping rock shoul-der to the left of him. He lay down at full length and slid his head and shoulders forward over the break-off, rifle ready in his left hand. There was a rock ledge four or five feet below him, then a gap of six or eight feet, then the start of the ledge trail. The goat's tracks were plain on the first little ledge, and the snow was torn and tossed on the other side of the gap, where the trail started. That was all. Colin looked down into the sheer drop under the gap in the ledge. Tiny and far down, a square of white against a gigantic wall of black rock, he could see the goat. How it was lodged he couldn't tell, but the wall of rock seemed to run on far past it, perpendicularly and smoothly, until it eased into a broken slope a few hundred feet back from the edge of the lake.

Colin stood up and dusted the snow from his clothing. He knew the goat was dead and knew almost certainly that he could never reach it. But the hollow in the mountains and the hidden lake were his, more surely his than any other part of Amabilis Valley. He stepped forward and dropped down to the little ledge under the break-off. There he turned, balanced a moment, and jumped where the goat had failed. By nightfall he was camped in the timber at the edge of the hidden lake.

2 6

COLIN lived very simply in his valley, buying only essentials like flour and oatmeal and salt, hunting all his meat, growing a garden in the summer time, constantly learning new ways of preserving and storing food. But fur prices were low in those years and he had to work steadily on his traps through the season to make the money he needed.

He usually spent at least five nights of each week up the valley, working out over his lines from the shelter cabins, but he tried always, as did Robbie and Johnny Harris, to get down to his main cabin on Saturday night and stay there until Monday morning. The three of them had agreed on this mainly as a safety precaution; it meant that they had a rough weekly check of each other's whereabouts and could leave messages with a fair certainty of when they would be found. Colin found that he liked the arrangement and seldom failed in it.

Although he was little conscious of his body's discomfort when he was in the shelters or out along the lines, he liked the warmth and space and solidity of the big cabin, and he liked also the company of his few possessions—some books, the canoe paddles and the fish-pole standing in the corner, the photograph of Mildred he kept hidden behind the books on their shelf, spare packboards and snowshoes that he had made at different times, Tom Hughes' rifle resting on a special shelf he had built for it under the books.

He came down to the cabin one Saturday night in January of the year after he had found the hidden lake. It was dark when he arrived and it was a bad night, with a gale of wind from the south and cold heavy rain down at the lake, though it had been snowing farther up the valley. He built a fire in the stove and lit his two lamps and the cabin seemed immediately warm and friendly. He set one of the lamps in the window that faced on the lake, more from habit than anything else, because there was no chance that it would be visible from Johnny's place through the storm, and there wasn't the least reason to suppose that either Johnny or Robbie would come up the lake until the next day—and only then if the storm had died down during the night.

After he had eaten supper Colin lay down on the bed to read, but in a little while he put the book aside and simply lay there, watching the red-gold light of his lamps on the ceiling and listening to the drive of the storm outside. He had built the cabin very solidly and very carefully, and he could feel the strength of his craftsmanship in the way it stood against the storm, without creak or tremor, without the slightest draught or any feeling of dampness inside it. The walls were of clear cedar logs, peeled and carefully matched, faced on the inside and with a lining of cedar panels split from fine-grained old-growth trees. The floor was a double thickness of two-inch planks, closely laid and perfectly smooth. The whole building was twenty feet square, divided into three rooms, but Colin used only the big main room that ran along the full length of the side towards the lake.

Colin had taken most of his first summer on the lake to build the cabin and it seemed to him now that he had always known exactly where and how he would build it. It was in the small curving bay just below the mouth of Amabilis Creek, where he and Robbie had eaten supper and looked down the lake that evening during his summer with Grant. But it was well inside the bay, set fifteen or twenty feet above the lake on an easy slope under the trees. It was within sound of the creek, yet in less than ten minutes from it he could climb to four or five hundred feet and find his way back into the mountains without ever touching the valley floor again.

All through the careful building of the cabin he had thought of Mildred. He planned and built not as though she were going to live in it but as though she were watching, approving or disapproving. Often it seemed to him that he lived his whole life on that basis; not as though she shared it or were ever likely to share it, but as though it were dedicated to her, and received in return her spiritual presence. There was satisfaction in the dedication, live, positive, almost physical satisfaction that gave a sense of purpose to everything he did.

Now, lying on the bed, isolated by the sound of the storm, he used her again, imagining her in the room, moving about in it, noticing things, changing things, talking to him, making him talk as she did at the cottage. The picture was clear and convincing, easy to accept until he turned his mind fully upon it. Then it became blocked and clouded by problems and difficulties.

He remembered how happily she had gone down to stay with Carol Maxwell in California during the summer. "I have to go," she had said. "I have to study down there." But he had known she wanted to go and had felt again his old dislike for the hold that Carol had on her. Yet he knew how weak was his own claim to her. It existed only in loving her and in what she would concede to his love. She still said sometimes: "I'm too old for you, Colin." And the last time he was with her she had said: "I'm not good for you, darling. Some of it is right and good, but it isn't really right—for either of us." After they had been together for a few hours she would nearly always say something of this sort, something that broke in upon their closeness and held him away from her.

For a moment he became conscious again of the lamplight on the ceiling and the sound of the storm outside the cabin. It had been more difficult, he thought, since Margaret had come into it all. First there had been the message through Robbie. Then Colin had seen her in Blenkinstown. She had asked at once: "Where have you been this time?"

"I saw Mother yesterday," he said defensively.

"For an hour or two. You wouldn't even stay for supper. I know—I was out there today."

"I had to see Earl Mayhew," he said. "And get my stuff down to the wharf."

"Of course," she said. "You have so many important things to do. But you might show Mother a little consideration. And the rest of the family, for that matter. You haven't been near Clyde and me since you first went up to the lake. And it isn't very nice for us to have the whole town talking about you."

"There isn't anything to talk about."

"There'll be plenty, if you keep on the way you are now. You ought to think of Mildred's side, too. No schoolteacher can stand that sort of thing."

He had known then that she was saying much more than she knew and had sensed a dishonesty in her purpose. But she was still the stronger and there was little he could find to say.

Later, she had gone to see Mildred and they had quarreled. Mildred would not talk freely about it, but Colin knew it had hurt her and made her miserable.

Lying on the bunk, Colin let himself feel the bitterness of the quarrel with Margaret and searched faithfully through all the thoughts that came to spoil and break the dream. Yet the dream persisted, warm, enfolding, comforting; more like religion, Colin thought, than like being in love; a light and a refuge that he could find again and again as he needed it, here in the cabin, out along the trap-lines, up in the mountains.

He reached a hand towards his book again, checked it as he heard the footsteps on the porch of the cabin. He swung his legs over the side of the bed and crossed the room, to open the outside door. Johnny Harris stood there a moment, shaking water from his clothes, blinking in the light.

"For God's sake, Johnny," Colin said. "I never thought you'd be up on a night like this."

Johnny came in without smiling. "I took a chance you'd be down tonight. It got so I just couldn't wait till tomorrow."

"You're crazy," Colin said. "You'll drown yourself if you take chances like that."

Johnny began stripping off his wet clothes. "It wasn't so bad as I thought it would be. Not so dark and not so rough, and the wind was mostly back of me."

Colin opened a cupboard and brought out a rum bottle. "This ought to help a little. I'll make some coffee to go with it."

Johnny stood holding his hands out over the stove. "I quarreled with Robbie," he said.

Colin checked a spoonful of coffee over the open pot. "With Robbie? What in hell over?"

"Over his goddamned war. He's gone bugs about it. Can't ever seem to talk about anything else."

Colin laughed. "That's not so new it ought to bring you up the lake in this weather. Robbie'll get over it. So'll you."

"It's not that," Johnny said. "I'm just not built for this kind of life. I've got to pull out. Go somewhere else, get a job where I see some people. I don't see how you stand it away up here on your own. At least Robbie and I are close enough to keep some track of each other. You never see anybody at all."

"It just means I've got no one to fight with," Colin said.

Johnny laughed, a little ashamed. "We didn't fight. Just got kind of sore at each other and said things we didn't mean."

"What does Robbie want you to do? Go off and join the army so you'll be all ready if his war comes?"

"You'd think so, to hear him talk. He'll say: 'Young fellows like you and Colin ain't got no business burying yourselves away up here. You should be out where things are happening.' On and on like that, generally because I don't pay attention to his goddamned radio."

"Why don't you stay out of his way for a while?" Colin filled two cups with coffee and poured a good shot of rum into each.

"I guess I could do that," Johnny said. "Trouble is I think old Robbie's got something. That's why I get sore at him, I guess. All that stuff that's going on over there, killing Jews and taking over countries that don't want to be taken over. Seems like a person ought to do something more than just sit back and listen to the radio."

"It's a long way away," Colin said. "They've always had troubles over there. It isn't right, but they always have. I don't see you can help any by going outside."

Johnny drained his cup and refilled it. "What do we do up here, anyway, except kill a few little animals and skin them? What sense does it make, any of it?"

"Buys our grub," Colin said. "And there's nobody riding us."

"You stay up all summer too. You cut trails and build cabins and go off in the mountains by yourself. What does it get you?"

"What does any job get you?" You find the hills, Colin thought, you find the hidden lake. You see things and think things and learn things. He knows all that as well as I do. And the things that happen outside and make you sick at your stomach don't happen in here. You don't even have to think about them. He said: "I guess it depends some on what you want. If you want something different from this you have to go out and get it."

"Sure I want something different. I want to get married some-time and raise a family, like ordinary people. You couldn't do that in here. Hell, you never even see a woman in here."

"No," Colin said slowly. "I guess it wouldn't be easy. I guess people have got married and raised families on trap-lines. But I never heard of any."

"I wouldn't try it. Nor would you. You don't give a damn about women though. Don't you ever figure you'll want a family some day?"

"Sure," Colin said. "I think about it." It seemed strange to realize that Johnny knew nothing of Mildred. "I'll get me a farm some day and raise a family. There's not all that much of a hurry." He filled a plate with food he had been cooking and set it in front of Johnny, then sat down opposite him. "What's the real trouble, Johnny? Something's got you all het up. You didn't come all this way up the lake on such a lousy night just to tell me you want to get married."

Johnny put down the fork he had just picked up. "No," he said. "That's right I didn't. I came up because I darn near killed poor old Robbie tonight. If I hadn't got out of there I would have."

Colin felt a shock that was like pain through his body. He stood up sharply. "Is he O.K.? What did you do? Hit him?"

"No. Nothing like that. I didn't touch him. I just wanted to kill him, wanted to so darn hard I had to get away so I wouldn't do it. That's how I know I'm no good for this kind of life."

Colin sat down again. Johnny wouldn't ever kill anybody, he thought; he wouldn't even hurt anybody. But I guess it's pretty near as bad for some people to think anything that hard. "Listen, Johnny," he said. "You wouldn't ever hurt him. You might think you would, but you wouldn't."

"Yes, I would, if I got to feeling the way I felt tonight. That's what happens to guys back in the bush like this. They go bugs and kill each other."

"Not guys like you and me and Robbie. We might think it just for a minute, but we'd never do it. All you need is a change. Stick around here for a couple of days, then go down and pick up your traps and get the hell outside for a while. You can take a look around and get to feeling better and likely as not you'll be all set to go again by next fall."

Johnny leaned back in his chair and looked down at the table. "I believe I'll do that. It might help a whole lot. I'd hate to quit the lake for keeps, but I could take a while out. I could even miss a season or two and still come back."

"If you don't get married," Colin said and laughed.

COLIN had finished his cabin in the Gully and was carving carefully on the smooth face of the log over the doorway: "Colin Ensley. 23rd September 1939."

Although it had been hard to find materials at the high elevation, this was the best finished of all his cabins, smaller than the one at the beach, but of yellow cedar logs instead of red, the logs flattened on three sides and so closely fitted that he had not needed to chink them anywhere. He had pitched the roof very steeply and built a vertical shaft down to the doorway so that it would be open to him in any depth of snow. Two windows looked down the length of the meadow, a third at the back opened towards the peaks above Windstorm Gap; floor and ceiling and the insides of the walls were patterned with different woods, pine and yew, yellow and red cedar, hemlock and maple, all hewn or adzed to smoothness.

Colin wondered what Will Ensley would think of it. He would scoff at the frills, Colin thought, quote a text on vanity, perhaps be really angry at the wasted effort; Colin remembered his contempt for some of the more intricate work they had done in the forestry camp. But he would recognize the craftsmanship, the planning and fitting and careful use of the different woods, and probably admit it, however grudgingly. He would be right to be grudging because nothing in his conception of things would justify the cabin. It did not fit in with the trap-lines or with essential hunting or any clearly practical activity. It could have been as warmly and solidly built of far simpler materials in a fraction of the time. There was not even the justification of craftsmanship, because that could have been as sure and finished with any plan and any materials.

Yet Colin knew he had found complete absorption in the work, as he found now a lively satisfaction in setting his signature upon it by the careful carving of the inscription. And he knew also that there was reason and logic in building it here and building it with the care he had used. Whether there was need to or not he expected to travel and hunt the slopes and peaks of the Gully, to the last slide, the last draw, the last creek bed, the smallest cleft in the rocks. From this cabin the Gully was his, in spring or summer or fall or winter, whenever he chose to come up to it. The cabin marked his possession, would be there to mark it beyond his lifetime; it extended the meaning of the cabin he had built at the lake through the whole length of the valley and with that it extended his dedication.

He left the cabin the day after he had completed the carving, turning at the foot of the meadows to look back and see it dwarfed by the great peaks, a tiny human sign at the point of the long tongue of dark timber that sloped down the draw and touched the head of the meadow. He looked up the broken slope above the timber, searched among the peaks and found the gap through which he had followed the goat into his hidden lake. He had climbed through the gap and down to the lake three times now and each time had learned a little more of the valley. Little stunted deer lived in its shelter, goats came down into it and the bear had found it. There were fish in the deep lake and berries on the slopes and it was very hot there in the summer when the sun climbed high over the peaks and blazed down into it. Even in winter, he judged, it would be windless and almost warm, though the snow would pile deeply over the meadows around the lake. So far he had never climbed to the Gap in winter and he knew that the way down the ledge trail would be hard and dangerous in deep snow. Standing now at the foot of the meadow in the Gully, looking back at his new cabin, he knew he would build again sooner or later by the hidden lake. And he would find a winter way into the lake, either by the Gap or over the smooth rock that had turned him back at the falls.

At the beach cabin Colin found Robbie's note. "The war's on," it read. "Better come down the lake soon as you get out. Johnny's gone down to enlist." Colin read the words and tried to place them in his life. The thought of war, of his own country in war, was not so strange and remote as it had seemed a year ago. He knew the broad issues and understood them; the war was still a long way away, but the shadow of it was a dark and menacing thing from which there was no safe withdrawal. Robbie had been right after all, Colin thought: they would want men, every man would have a place, even men like himself and Curly and Johnny Harris. Johnny had gone already.

He looked around at the cabin and thought of the valley behind it. They would never come here. He tried to think of war, of men being shot as deer are shot, of bombs and planes and great guns, of men dying and struggling and dying. That part seemed remote, so far beyond imagination that he could see no place in it for himself. One went with other men, in crowds and masses, and was little noticed. But he could not find himself in the crowds. Robbie will know, he thought; he's been through it once. He crumpled the note in his hand and went out of the cabin to launch his canoe.

COLIN stood in front of the desk and listened to the officer. Slowly he realized that he was being rejected, as Johnny Harris had been, thanked for offering his services, something about medical category, not your fault, just a tough break.

"You mean I'm not fit?" he asked.

"The medicals say you've got flat feet," the officer told him. "They won't take any chances on those things. It's too bad. I'm sorry."

"I can walk all day," Colin said.

The officer smiled and shrugged his shoulders, then stood up and held out his hand. Colin took it, turned away and went out.

It was September of 1940, nearly a year after he had come down the valley to find Robbie's note. He had not tried to enlist then. When he got to Robbie's cabin he found Johnny Harris already back there, rejected because the arm he had broken playing ball had been badly set. That had tempered Robbie's advice to Colin. "No hurry," he had said. "It must be they don't want men. But they will, you see. This thing won't be over in a few months. You'll get your chance and so will Johnny."

Johnny had been upset at being turned down. He wanted no more of the outside world and was glad to go back to his trap-line in Carlson's Valley. Colin went back to his own valley and stayed there as he had before. But through the summer of 1940 the valley seemed to lose its power over him and he found it more and more difficult to stay away from Robbie and the news that poured in over the old battery radio. In the end he had gone down to enlist. It had not occurred to him that he would be rejected and Robbie had never suggested the possibility. Now there was nothing to do but go back, as Johnny had.

He stayed a night at the farm on his way through Blenkinstown. When he told Martha what had happened, she said: "I'm sorry, if that was what you wanted. But I'm glad you don't have to go."

"It doesn't seem to make any sense," Colin said. "Getting turned down for bad feet when you can walk all day and all night." But he knew now that he hadn't wanted to go, that he was glad to be back, on his way to the lake, instead of being taken up into the life he had seen about him at the recruiting center.

"What are you going to do now?" Martha asked.

"Go back to the valley," he said. "It's pretty nearly time to get the lines ready again."

"You're happy there, aren't you?"

Colin noticed, as he had so many times, how warmly blue and intensely alive her eyes were. But it seemed to him that her voice was strained and tired, slower and softer than usual. He wondered if she knew about Mildred and thought she did not, in spite of what Margaret had said. And if she did know she would feel about it as she felt about the valley, would say in her heart almost the same thing.

He remembered her question. "Yes," he said. "I like it fine up there. There's room to fall all over myself and nobody knows the difference."

He went down to the village early next morning to buy supplies and load his canoe. As he came out of the store he noticed a man in uniform standing by the wharf. The man turned towards him and he recognized Tod Phalling. Tod held out a hand and smiled. Looking into the pale eyes Colin felt an echo of the old fear, but Tod was friendly.

"Sure is good to see an old-timer around," he said. "I was beginning to think there was none left."

"Johnny Harris is up at the lake with us," Colin said.

"There's a guy in the unit knows you—Curly Blake."

"Sure," Colin said eagerly. "I traveled with Curly pretty near two years. How's he making out?"

"Curly's a good soldier. He's doing O.K." Tod looked at Colin's clothes, the stagged raintest pants and the woods coat. "You coming in?" he asked.

"I just got back," Colin said. "They turned me down."

"The hell. What was the trouble?"

Colin looked away from the pale eyes. "Medical. They didn't say what." He was remembering Tod's endless taunting of his clumsiness at school.

"That's tough," Tod said. "But they'll ease up. A guy'll have a chance to make it if he really wants to."

Colin looked back to his face again, expecting to find the faintly contemptuous doubt he thought he had heard in his words.

It was not there. "I'd like to get in," Colin said, and in that moment he did want to get in.

"You'll make it, sooner or later. We're due for overseas any time now."

They were still talking when Clyde Munro drove up in the police car. "Your mother's sick," he told Colin. "I was afraid I wouldn't catch up to you. The doctor's there. You'd better let me drive you back."

Martha was in the big bed she had shared all her life with Will Ensley. She was unconscious and her eyes were closed.

"She's had a stroke," the doctor told Colin.

Colin nodded and watched his mother's face. It was peaceful and unmarked and she looked very young. He wanted desperately to see her eyes again, to feel the warmth he always felt from their deep blueness. "Will she be conscious again?" he asked.

The doctor picked up one of the thin wrists and held it in his hand. "We don't know," he said. "She might even get over it. It's hard to tell with these things."

With Margaret, Colin watched Martha through that night and through the next day until Will Ensley came back from his work farther up the coast. Will came silently and hesitantly into the room, stopped at the foot of the bed and stood there with his great head bent a little to look down at Martha's face. He said nothing. There was no text, no word, no prayer, only the sag of the heavy shoulders, the deep lines in the broad face above the graying beard, the tenseness of the huge hands on the rail at the foot of the bed.

Will looked up at last and saw Colin and Margaret. "Has she spoken at all?" His strong voice whispered in the small room and Colin shook his head. "Which is the bad side?" Will asked.

Colin pointed to Martha's left hand and arm. "There," he said. "She can move this arm."

Will came round and stood at the right side of the bed. Colin expected him to kneel or at least speak a prayer, but he only took Martha's hand in his own and bent towards her. She moved then and her eyes opened for a moment and Colin saw the blueness. He felt Margaret move beside him and put out an arm to hold her back.

"Is that you, Will?" Martha said. "I'm glad you're here."

"Yes," Will said. "It's me. Don't try to talk. We're all here with you." He knelt then, still holding her hand, his big body awkward in its grief and fear.

Martha moved her head as though to look for the others, but her eyes did not open again. "Stay with me, Will," she said. "Like this. For a little while."

Colin watched his mother's face and saw the tired lines relax still further until her lips were half-smiling. He knew then that Will's coming had brought the deep peace to her face, that the smile was for him and all the little of her that was left was for him. He turned to Margaret and saw that she too had seen and understood. Without speaking, they went out of the room together.

2 7

SHORTLY after Martha's death, while Colin was still down at the farm, Will got word that his old job was open up at camp.

"Well," he told Colin and Margaret. "They learned it at last."

"Learned what?" Margaret asked him.

"That a buzz-saw won't do the same work as a broad-axe."

"You'll go, won't you?"

Will hesitated, but Colin knew that the pull of the old, known work far outweighed any remnant of pride. Will saw himself again as he had been for so many years, silent, sure, respected in his craft, secure in the scent of cedar and the rustle of chips under his feet. "Well," he said at last. "They've gone to the trouble to send for me. I guess I'll go up there and help out."

Later, when they were alone, Colin asked Margaret: "What about the place?"

"He'll stay here. He told me he would because he knows Mother would want him to."

"He can't stay alone. He'd be better in camp."

"Clyde and I can look after him for a while. What will you do?"

"I'm going back to the lake. I'm late there now."

"Will you try to enlist again? If the war goes on, I mean?"

Colin felt a surge of irritation at the question. "Why should I?" he said. "They've told me once I'm not good enough for them."

WHEN he got back to Amabilis Valley again Colin felt, as he always did, a sense of freedom from everything that had happened outside. It was already late and he had a lot to do to get ready for the season. Through the season he was always busy, traveling his lines swiftly and regularly, running trial lines along ridges and draws in different parts of the valley, checking the movements of game against his experience in other seasons. But in spite of almost steady activity, he could not find the complete absorption and strong happiness he had found in other years.

He had seen Mildred only once since Martha's funeral and they had both been strained and withdrawn, realizing that Martha in death was more decisively between them than she had ever been in life. As he was leaving, Mildred asked: "How soon will you be out again, Colin?"

"I'm not sure," he said and knew instantly that this was what she wanted him to say. "I guess I'd better plan to stay back there for quite a stretch."

"I know." She had lowered her head a little and something in the movement and the flat calm of her voice made him draw her to him. "I'm sorry it had to be like this, darling."

"It wasn't your fault," he said. And then, with wisdom she had not dared to use: "It will change again."

But it had not changed. Always before it had seemed to Colin that Mildred was with him as he traveled or rested, ready to share what he was doing, what he saw, what he felt. Now it seemed often that Martha was with him, more distantly, more purely, a little reproachfully, but so strongly that thought of Mildred could not come alive for thought of Martha. At other times he thought of the officer in the recruiting center, denying and rejecting the

233

strength that his body seemed daily to prove against snow and hills and harsh weather. Or of Tod Phalling, in uniform, accepting the fact of Colin's rejection without question, as something normal and expected.

In the spring, when his traps were all up and the snow had begun to melt from the hills, he took to going down to Robbie's again, to talk and listen to the radio. Johnny Harris had gone out, to work at Blenkin Logging for the summer, and once or twice Robbie tried to persuade Colin to do the same.

"You do too much thinking," he said. "You want to get out and see some people for a change."

"Why don't you go yourself?" Colin asked him.

"I go out more than you do. I've been for grub and mail three times since spring. Besides, I'm an old man. I've learned to stand being alone."

Colin was sitting on the steps in front of the cabin, carving a little figure from a piece of driftwood. He said slowly: "Do you ever feel you're alone? Really alone, I mean, with no one else but yourself?"

Robbie glanced quickly at him. "Sure, why wouldn't I? I'm alone plenty. But that's different to feeling lonely. I don't often get to feeling that any more."

"I guess that's what I mean," Colin said. "I don't ever get to feeling lonely. Seems like most of the time I'm not even alone."

"That don't make any sense," Robbie said. "If a man's by himself, he's alone. Hell, you ain't even got a dog up there, like I've got old Bonnie here." He reached down and pulled the bitch's ear. "If that ain't being alone I wouldn't know what is."

Colin nodded. He decided to let it go at that. For a moment he had wanted to tell Robbie that people you know very well, like Mildred and now Martha, seem to be with you when you are alone. He had half-hoped that Robbie would admit something of the sort himself, but now he knew he wouldn't. "I'm not going out," he said. "I want to make the trip through Windstorm Gap and down Milk River to Menzies Lake. I've never been through there yet."

"Sure," Robbie said. "That's O.K. Just so you're doing something it's O.K. But don't forget that's a Park over there. You don't want to get caught killing any deer once you're over the divide."

COLIN did not get out to Robbie's cabin again until fall. Robbie and Johnny Harris were waiting on the beach when he ran the canoe in and it seemed to Colin that their life together on the lake was suddenly back where it had been in the first years after he came in. The three of them walked slowly up to the cabin through the warm September sunshine and Robbie asked eager, almost boyish questions about Colin's trip.

"It's good country," Colin said. "I like it over there."

"It's a beautiful lake," Johnny said. "But I don't think it's got anything on this one. How's the trip through the Gap?"

"Fine, so long as the weather's good. It sure can blow up there, though, and it's tough in the wrong kind of snow."

"You're crazy to go up there when there's any snow at all," Robbie said.

"No," Colin said seriously. "I believe a person could make it through there in the winter any time the snow was solid."

They went into the cabin and Robbie began to cut meat for the meal. Johnny said: "What made you want to go through there? It's all Park over the divide. You can't get a trap-line in there."

"I don't know," Colin said. "Seems like a person wants to know what's in back of him. And that Park'll open up sometime. It might pay to know something about it."

Robbie threw several pieces of meat into the frying pan. "There's sense to that. There'll be tourists in there and you might be right in on the ground-floor." He reached towards the pepper-pot on a shelf behind the stove and noticed the letters leaning beside it. He took them and tossed them over to Colin. "Hell," he said. "There's some mail for you. Looks like a couple of government letters."

Colin took the letters. He ripped the envelopes open and studied the two similarly confusing interminglings of printing and typescript, then handed them to Robbie. "What the hell?" he said. "Looks like a call-up notice."

"That's what it is," Robbie told him.

"Call-up?" Johnny said. "Why don't I get one if Colin does?"

"Likely you will," Robbie said. He handed the letters back to Colin. "Looks like you're kind of late, but if you go in right away and tell them how it was you'll be O.K."

"You don't think I'm going through that phony set-up again, do you?" Colin said.

"Sure you are," Robbie said. "They'll come and get you quick enough if you don't."

"Don't be a nut, Colin," Johnny said. "Go on down and get it over with. They'll just throw you out like they did the first time."

"They won't get a chance," Colin said. "Let them come in and find me if it's so all-fired important to them."

IT was a very cold winter. There was only a foot or so of light snow down near the lake, but most of it had been on the ground since before Christmas, and now it was mid-January. All the way up the valley Colin had found powder snow so light that the least wind disturbed it; the side creeks were slowed to narrow trickles, Amabilis Creek itself ran softly and darkly between banks of ice, and there was ice along the edge of the big lake. But it was good weather for traveling and good weather for traps. For the first time since fall he found he could afford to stay over for an extra day at the beach cabin.

It was a brilliantly sunny morning, with only a light breeze that fanned down from the head of the valley. On the front steps of the cabin, sheltered from the moving air, Colin found the sun almost hot and he sat there to stretch and flesh his skins. He saw the canoe when it was still only a little way beyond Johnny's valley and watched it from time to time as it grew larger against the quiet surface of the lake. He recognized Robbie's little red Peterborough and saw that there were two figures in it. Robbie had seen the lights of his cabin, he supposed, and stopped in at Carlson's Creek to pick up Johnny. In a sweat about something, Colin thought; driving her with all they've got. Likely something bad about the war or another call-up notice or something. What do they do if you don't answer a call-up? They couldn't ever hurt a man out in this country if he didn't want to get caught. If he

236

had some matches and a few shells and a blanket he could travel for months and never need to go hungry.

He looked at the canoe again and suddenly knew that the second figure was not Johnny. A moment later he recognized Clyde Munro. He made a sharp, instinctive movement towards the door of the cabin, checked it and looked back at the canoe again. "The old son of a bitch," he said aloud. "He didn't have to do that to me. He could of let Clyde find his own dirty way up here." He felt his heart beating strongly and a dryness in his throat. For a moment he thought of his rifle, standing against the wall inside the cabin. He wanted it in his hands, wanted to be up the valley with it, traveling hard towards the Gully, towards the snow slopes above the Gully. Then flight seemed suddenly pointless. From a friend, he thought, from my own brother-in-law. He walked slowly down the beach to meet the canoe as it headed in towards the narrow shelf of ice. Robbie was standing in the bow, a pole ready in his hands to break the ice. Colin saw that his face was set and serious.

"Thank God you're still out here," Robbie said.

Colin caught the bow of the canoe and eased it on to the ice. "Why?" he asked. "What's the trouble?"

"Johnny's lost somewhere up the valley. Been gone since day before yesterday." Robbie stepped out of the canoe and Clyde came stiffly forward from the stern.

"You looked for him yet?" Colin asked.

Robbie shook his head. "Just half a day. Then I went out and fetched Clyde. There was no light up here and I couldn't see smoke through the glasses."

"There's coffee on the stove," Colin said. "Go help yourselves and I'll throw some stuff together. Where did he go? What makes you think he's lost?"

"He went to hunt goat," Robbie told him. "Said he'd be out to my place night before last, but he never showed up."

"Robbie followed his track for a way up the east side of the valley," Clyde said, "then lost it where the snow had blown away from the rock."

Colin looked up from strapping blankets to his packboard. "Goats? What would he want with goats this time of year?"

"It was a notion he got." Robbie set down his empty coffee cup. "Said he wanted to get up in the hills in the clear weather. Said a change of meat ought to go good."

For the first time Colin felt real concern. He remembered now that Johnny said he was going to learn his way about the mountains of his valley, discover them as Colin had the mountains of Amabilis Valley. He remembered, too, how Johnny was in the mountains, hesitant and cautious, always a little afraid, clumsy in a way that he never was on flat ground. Johnny knew nothing of the treachery of snow on steep slopes, nothing of the deceptively easy ways that can lead a man to a blind end of climb or drop with only a hard way back to safety.

"No chance he's in one of his shelter cabins?" he asked Robbie.

"Hardly, unless he's hurt or sick. Even then he'd make it out to the beach easier."

"Robbie fired a bunch of shots up the valley," Clyde said. "And there wasn't any answer. But he might be down in some place where he couldn't hear."

"You set to spend a night out?" Colin asked him. "Likely we'll have to if we get up in those hills this afternoon."

"I've got everything," Clyde said.

2 8

COLIN sat up in his blankets. The stars were still bright in the west, but there was a faint light in the sky behind the tall peaks to the east of the valley. The mountain over the hidden lake was clear and huge against the light, a broken, formidable silhouette, closely joined to the peaks on either side.

They were camped on a little flat place under a slab of rock that leaned like the roof of a shelter and had made a good reflector for the heat of their fire the previous evening. Colin slipped the blankets away from him and began to rebuild the fire. He set water to boil and saw that the light behind the hills was stronger, though the whole valley was still in darkness.

Clyde was still asleep in the warmth of his sleeping bag, but it was bitterly cold even close beside the fire; it seemed to Colin that cold gleamed through the darkness against the ice-sheeted rock and that the stillness all around him creaked and strained with it. He tried to hope for Johnny. Robbie had gone up the valley to the shelter cabins. If he found him he would signal, with rifle shots and smoke. But Johnny's track had led them up from the valley, out of the sheltering timber on to these slopes and terraces of ice-sheeted rock. It was a safe time, Colin thought; too safe. The powder snow had blown away from the rock almost as it fell. The few inches that had somehow clung to the rough surface had long ago melted in the sun of cloudless afternoons and frozen into ice almost as hard as the rock itself. Yet Colin's boot-nails had gripped it well as he and Clyde climbed through the previous afternoon and Johnny's sharp caulks had gripped even more securely. Too securely, Colin thought again, too safely. Johnny would have thought it easy and gone on to learn his mountains; he had gone on, at least this far, because Colin had been able to find occasionally the scars of his passing on the ice, occasionally the clear imprint of the spiked boots on sheltered snow patches in the gullies he and Clyde had crossed.

He heard Clyde move and looked around. There was strong light behind the mountains now and all across the sky, paling the stars, reflecting faintly down into the valley. Clyde asked him: "Have you been up long?" and at once crawled out of his bag and began pulling on his boots.

"There's no hurry," Colin said. "We can't move until there's light enough to see what tracks he's left."

Clyde came up and crouched with Colin beside the fire. Colin made coffee while they watched the light grow slowly on the snow-covered peaks across the valley.

Clyde asked: "Was Johnny a good woodsman?"

"Yes, sure. But he was no good in the mountains. He hardly ever went above timber."

Clyde watched the pink flush of dawn as it spread down from

the peaks across the snow slopes. "I've never been around mountains much myself," he said. "Some of those places we crossed yesterday had me scared stiff. But it sure can be beautiful."

"You didn't act scared," Colin said. "I've seen Johnny scared, though. That's why I'm worried about him now."

"What made him come up hunting goats this time of year if he's scared of mountains?"

"He's been restless ever since they turned him down for the army. I don't figure he was really hunting goats at all or he wouldn't have come along this way."

"I've been thinking that all along," Clyde said. "Seems like he was just walking, not hunting."

Colin nodded. "That's right. I guess it felt kind of good in the sun with all this open rock to travel and the mountains to look at."

They were silent for a while. Colin turned the bannock he was baking and Clyde reached behind him for his sleeping bag, dragged it up and wrapped it round himself.

"It's goddamned cold," he said. "I don't see how you stand it."

Colin cut the bannock and poured more coffee. The light was quite strong all through the valley when they had finished eating, so they made up their small packs and started out again.

It was easy traveling at first, over almost level rock, but Colin could feel that the ice had hardened again during the night and knew that his boot-nails were not gripping as they had the previous afternoon. Carlson's Valley was a strange place. It had a wide, timbered floor, almost flat, ending abruptly in savage bluffs of gray rock that reared with scarcely a break for two thousand feet or more, then rounded into the bench along which they had followed Johnny. The bench was broken again and again by deep, snow-filled gullies cutting back to the steepness of the high mountains that rose everywhere above it. It sloped always outward, towards the sheer drop to the valley floor, sometimes gently as at the place where they had camped, sometimes steeply. Looking ahead, Colin could see that the pattern carried on out of sight ahead of them, gully and sloping bench, gully and sloping bench, clear to the long smooth line of the glacier that fed the creek above the lake.

They came to a gully whose face was a snow-slide so steep that it seemed to Colin the snow must have frozen as it fell to stay there at all. Johnny had crossed it, somehow kicking steps that had held him.

"He could have died right there," Colin said. "He must have done that in the afternoon, when the sun had softened it." He thought of Johnny as he had seen him in the mountains, hesitating to cross a bad place, always cautious and on guard. What changed you, Johnny? What made you go on like this? Why couldn't I have known? We could have been together then.

Clyde was looking down at the long white slide of snow below Johnny's steps.

"I thought you said he was scared."

"Not that time he wasn't," Colin said. "Not scared enough." He started across the slope, kicking at Johnny's steps to test them. They were deep and the night had frozen them rock-hard. Clyde followed behind him and they came on to the new slope. It was steeper than most of those they had crossed, but Colin felt his way for the first few steps, found himself secure and began to travel fast. He hesitated only when he had missed Johnny's track for several hundred yards. Clyde came up to him and Colin looked into his face and saw that it was strained and pale and sweating.

"Don't mind me," Clyde said. "I told you I got scared."

"I'm sorry," Colin said soberly. "There wasn't any sense to flying at it like that. I could have stopped to tell you it was safe."

"That's O.K. I figured it was, but I just couldn't convince my-self. You tell me next time and I'll believe you."

"I've missed his track somewhere," Colin said. "But I'd have seen if he slipped." He looked around him, first along the slope, then out to the gap that marked the valley; then he turned slowly and looked along the slope of the mountains above them. "It's bad," he said. "If a man could only know what he was thinking. He couldn't have come this far and figured to get back to the beach the same night."

"We ought to see his track where it crosses the next draw."

Colin nodded. "You want to wait here while I look?"

"Hell, no. It's my job, not yours."

241

Johnny had found an easy way across the draw and his track was plain. Colin found it again on the new slope, cut deeply into the ice and frozen there. He knew then that Johnny had not turned back, that he had meant to go on and find a way down by the glacier to his cabin at the lake.

The sun was high now, above the peaks, lighting the valley, giving them warmth. A drift of wind came up the valley so suddenly that Colin stopped and looked around. There were clouds over the lake, the nearest of them already reaching to the peaks at the foot of the valley.

"We've had the breaks," he said. "From here in she gets tough."

"Looks like a southeaster," Clyde said.

Colin nodded. "Means we've got a couple of hours. After that we can start to worry about us, not Johnny."

He glanced ahead again along the slope, his eyes searching the monotonous alternations of dark steps and white terraces for the way Johnny might have followed. Then, as his body balanced to step forward again, he saw the glint of sunlight sharply reflected from something a little way ahead along the slope. He looked towards the mountains and knew that the broken ice could not have fallen away from them. He began to travel again, almost at a run. He could feel the ice hard and solid on the rock, but his foot slipped once as the slope grew steeper and he forced himself back to caution. The slope was very steep now and he wondered how Johnny had dared to cross it, then remembered that the ice had been softer for Johnny's crossing and his spikes would have bitten deeply into it. He thought of Clyde and turned to see him coming slowly and steadily, kicking at the ice to roughen it under each step. He came up and Colin saw that his face was strained and wet with sweat again. But Clyde asked him steadily: "What did you see?"

Colin pointed silently to the broken ice a little way ahead and they went on until they came to it. A six or eight foot width of the sloping rock was stripped of ice and below that a jagged mass of ice had been torn away from the main sheet, leaving the rock bare and black right out to the edge of the sharp step that dropped to the next slope. Johnny's caulk marks were frozen solidly into the ice one short step from the break.

"You think he slipped there?" Clyde asked.

"The ice slipped with him. Broke away above him. He didn't have a chance." He crossed the narrow path of the little slide and examined the ice on the far side. There was no mark anywhere on it. Colin looked back and saw that clouds had already closed in the foot of the valley, though the sunlight was warm and strong where they stood.

"He's down there," Colin said and walked the hundred feet or so of open rock to the edge of the step. Clyde followed and they stood looking down at a steeper slope of ice and snow running clear out to the bluffs that dropped away to the valley floor. Broken ice was scattered over the slope. Clyde dropped over the step ahead of Colin and worked cautiously out on to the slope in the path of the slide.

"Looks like he was dragging his rifle butt to try and save himself."

Colin nodded. "An axe would likely have done it." He let himself down over the step, then stood looking back again at the clouds. They were across the sun now and across the peaks, thin swift clouds, and it was suddenly cold. A few hard, dry pellets of snow fell around them.

"What do we do now?" he asked Clyde.

Clyde was watching the clouds. "Could he be alive?"

Colin knew what he meant. "He could be," he said, and pointed to where the slope disappeared from sight. "Depends what's over there."

"Can we get down to look?"

"I think I could. I can use the axe to cut steps. I've done it before." He meant Clyde to understand that the place was not for him.

"It's my job," Clyde said again.

"We'll both go," Colin slipped the packboard from his shoulders and took the coil of light rope he had slung over the top of it.

By the time they had tied the rope to themselves the wind was blowing in strong gusts, and squalls of snow were sweeping along the valley towards them. It was not necessary to cut steps at first, but they moved only one at a time over the steep and slippery slope. Colin watched Clyde's awkward, cautious movements impatiently. Now that he knew what had happened to Johnny he felt a fierce anxiety. He tried to tell himself that Johnny was dead, that the cold of the past two nights would have killed him if the fall had not. But he couldn't believe Johnny dead. The warmth of his own blood, the strength of his own hands, seemed to deny it in some way he could not understand. He knew that he had to climb down to the edge of the slope and see whatever lay below. And he began to know that Clyde would go with him, without slipping or failing or yielding in any fraction to the strain just short of panic that showed so clearly in his face.

The clouds had closed in the head of the valley and the afternoon was dark gray everywhere. The edge of the slope was only a few feet away now, but it was hard to see through the driving snow. Colin felt the wind cold through his clothes and the snow like needles against his face; he was glad because it meant that the old snow and ice would remain solid. He came to the edge of the slope and saw not a break but only a further steepening of the old slope. The drop-off lay somewhere ahead, hidden in the snow. Clyde came down to him, slowly and painfully, in the cramped awkwardness of fear, but without fear's hesitation. From now on, Colin knew, there would have to be steps.

He told Clyde: "I don't know where in hell I'm taking you," and pointed into the gray scud of the snow.

"We can't go back till we find out," Clyde said; and Colin knew he understood that the going back might not be easy.

He lifted the clumsy wood axe and drove it into the icy snow below him. It bit deeply and the step split out to his second stroke. From then on he was conscious only of cutting, testing, stepping, cutting, testing, stepping until he saw the sharp break of the slope's end. He stopped there, signaled to Clyde and watched him come down. Once a sudden gust of wind tore at Clyde's body, twisting his balance so sharply that Colin threw himself forward against the haft of his axe, buried deep in the ice, and waited for the rush of his fall and the shock on the rope. But Clyde recovered and came on down until they could speak. Colin pointed to the break.

"I've got to go out there," he said. "Get a good hold with your axe and keep the rope short."

Clyde nodded and buried his axe. He seemed confident now and Colin trusted him. He went down four or five steps, then drove his own axe savagely against the snow, testing for an overhang. The snow was solid and he came out on it to the edge and looked down. There was only whirling snow below him. He cut away a piece of ice, saw it go down and disappear under the cliff before the snow hid it, and he knew he was not far enough. He cut two more steps, drove his axe above him and stood straight in the second one. From it he could see the ledge, a good broad ledge, deeply snow-drifted and supporting trees, not more than thirty feet below him. He signaled to Clyde again.

Fifteen or twenty minutes later they were standing on the ledge together. The afternoon light was almost gone.

"He should be up this way," Clyde said.

They found him almost at once. Johnny sleeping, Colin thought, not worrying, not afraid, wrapped in his blanket, asleep. Clyde was kneeling beside Johnny, one big hand on his wrist, the other fumbling at his chest.

"He's alive," Clyde said.

Colin looked at the blackened embers of a fire near Johnny's feet, pushed his hand into them, felt warmth. For the next hour they worked steadily, rubbing life back into his feet and legs and hands and arms, and at the end of it Johnny was conscious. The ledge was sheltered from the worst of the storm, but Colin had been able to cut enough boughs to make more shelter and build a big fire. They poured tea and rum into Johnny and wrapped him in Clyde's sleeping bag. Then they made their own meal.

Eating it, looking out into the darkness beyond the falling snow, Colin felt a tremendous elation. It was not merely that they had found Johnny, that he was alive and almost certainly would live. Those things were in it, but over them and beyond them was the strength he had felt in Clyde. He felt it again now, in Clyde's calmness, his matter-of-fact acceptance of the night and the storm and the position they were in. He is stronger than his body, Colin thought, stronger than his mind, stronger than any total of his strength. He was afraid back there on the ice-slopes, yet he never paid any attention to being afraid. He was played right out before we even started down here, yet he came and he hasn't stopped for one moment since we found Johnny. While we were traveling he followed me, yet he made most of the decisions. Here on the ledge I'm following him.

Clyde's quiet voice said beside him: "We've got to splint that leg before we start out with him."

Colin nodded. "Is it a bad break?"

"Bad enough. More than one place. I'm scared for the foot too. I'm going to rub it some more in a minute."

Colin threw wood on the fire, then reached for the pot and poured more tea into Clyde's cup. An eddying gust of wind tore at the jackpines on the ledge and drove snow against them. "I can cut some snow blocks and stop that," Colin said.

"Good. It's going to be a long night, and it'll take us all our time to get him up out of here tomorrow."

"Not up," Colin said. "Down. I think I know this place and if it's where I think it is we'll be able to get right down into the valley."

Clyde looked at him and smiled. "That's the best news I ever heard," he said. While they were talking he had opened the corner of the sleeping bag and was working on Johnny's frozen foot again. "I didn't want to say it, but I figured that getting him up on top might be just a little more than tough."

Because they had used both blankets and sleeping bag for Johnny neither of them slept longer than a few minutes at a time during the night. A little after midnight Colin noticed that the shriek and hum of the wind against the rocks above them had died away. Then the snow stopped. He watched the sky and after a long while saw a star high up across the valley, then another near it. He threw wood on the fire and Clyde woke and they made fresh tea. Colin showed him the stars.

"We've got her made now," he said. "That's the only break we needed and I figured it wasn't coming."

They rolled cigarettes and smoked. After a while, Clyde said: "I was supposed to come in and see you this month anyway."

"About those call-up notices?" Colin asked him.

246

"That's right. You'll be going down there pretty soon, won't you?"

"I don't see why I should. They threw me out once."

"The draft board doesn't know that. It's all routine with them."

Colin threw his cigarette butt into the fire. "Why can't they ever leave a man alone to do what's right?"

"There's too many," Clyde said quietly. "It's all routine and red tape, but they have to do it."

"Would you take me in if I didn't go?"

"I guess I'd have to."

"I suppose it's your job," Colin said bitterly.

"Let's not quarrel about it," Clyde said. "You're going down there. You know you are."

Colin rolled another cigarette and lit it. He saw that his hand was shaking. "I guess you cops are all the same," he said. "The job's everything. You don't care what dirty stuff it takes you into." When Clyde didn't answer, he said, "Did you ever beat up a prisoner?"

"Not once I had him locked up. Maybe I'll have to sometime but I never have yet."

"Why would you have to?"

Clyde shrugged. "Ever tried to sleep with a couple of drunks raising hell in the cells? Ever watched your wife listening to their filth and trying to sleep? It can be plenty hard to take."

At the other side of the fire Johnny moved and murmured in his sleep. Clyde went to him at once, felt his face, reached into the sleeping bag and felt his hands. He nodded to Colin. "O.K.," he said and came back. He stirred the fire and poured more tea, then looked at his watch.

"Five more hours," he said. "And it ought to be light enough to start out."

Colin felt his strength again as he had felt it after they found Johnny.

"I'm sorry I shot my face off like that," he said. "There wasn't any sense in it."

"That's O.K.," Clyde said. "How long is it going to take us to get out tomorrow?"

Colin thought for a moment. "We ought to make it down into

the valley before noon. Then we can fix up some kind of sled and take him right down the trail."

29

COLIN waited behind the ruined wall and tried to keep warm. The wall wasn't protection, but it felt like protection and at least it blocked the cold wind that was blowing from across the river. There were no stars tonight and he supposed there would be more snow. Terry Murphy said there would be and Terry was usually right about the weather; he was usually right about food and rest and leave and mortar fire and canals and rivers and most of the other things that the war seemed to be made of. Terry was a lot like Curly Blake that way, Colin thought, but Curly was dead, had been dead for over a year, somewhere down in Italy with the Seaforths.

There was some firing across the river, and half-a-dozen light explosions that sounded like hand grenades. Colin moved, but Murphy's voice said beside him: "Too far away to bother us."

"Think she'll stay quiet all night?" Colin asked.

"No," Murphy said. "This here's a lousy place, in between two creeks. We ain't got no business being here." He spat into the darkness. "This Holland," he said. "This Nijmegen. Seems like we been in wrong ever since we come near the place."

Colin laughed. "We've had it worse. Want to go back to Caen?"

"We was young then," Murphy said. "And the climate was good. Anyways, they kept the snow up where it belongs."

They were comfortable enough, except for the cold, and even that didn't seem as bad as it should have. They had waited in so many places, hurried through so many places, gone out together so often in the seven months since D-day, that nothing seemed really bad any more. They were the last of the unit's original stretcher-bearers and at that Terry had been out for over a month with a leg wound.

It was always a canal or a creek or a river that stopped them now, Colin thought. Broken bridges, twisted iron, shattered masonry; planks, doors, girders, anything and everything wedged and zigzagged so that they could walk across. This time there was the rubber boat. They used it to get the casualties across the stream behind, between them and the dressing station, weaving it in and out among the wreckage on the creek bed, continually worried that the current would drift it against something sharp and tear a hole through the canvas.

It was hard to think back beyond the army, harder to think that there would ever be anything but the army. In some ways it wasn't so bad here as it had been in England or back in Canada. It made more sense. You did something and it was done. Back there you were always getting ready to do something that would probably never be done. Training, training and more training, someone driving or nagging or checking, morning, noon and night. "You won't last long if you don't learn . . ." "You better smarten up or . . ." "That stuff won't go when you get overseas." And the other one: "Kill the enemy."

There was enemy mortar fire somewhere over on the right and Colin heard Terry move beside him in the darkness.

"If they start that on us we'll have to get out of here," Terry said.

Colin knew he was thinking of the wall. It was queer how they both preferred it to the slit-trench they had dug nearby. There was something very comforting about the wall, even when you knew it was probably more dangerous than open ground—at least it was standard human shelter. In the slitty you were safe as you could be anywhere, but safe like a rat in a sewer. Some kind of animal, anyway. Fox-holes the Yanks called them, so somebody else must have felt the same way.

"We could just as well be back the other side of that goddamned creek," Terry said. "Don't take but five minutes longer to get up from there. Better yet, they could rig some way to get the jeeps over and save all the packing."

"If this stall keeps up much longer they're liable to pull us out into rest," Colin said.

"Sure, sure," Terry said. "And the zombies are coming up for reinforcements and that'll be the end of the war and we can all go home."

"Well," Colin said. "It ought to make some difference." Canada's two armies, he thought, the quick and the dead. Why did they have to pull that one on us? Call us up and then tell us we didn't have to go overseas unless we volunteered for it. Because of Quebec, people say, but there's whole units over here from Quebec. They either needed us or they didn't need us. And they did need us, that's sure; the unit's never been up to strength since D-day and I guess all the others are the same.

He shifted his feet on the cold ground. "I was a zombie for a while," he said.

"Yeah?" Terry's voice was surprised. "Me too. For a couple of weeks. Until I got things doped out."

"I stayed that way right through basic and advanced," Colin said. "It made me sore the way they pushed us around trying to make us join active. Most of the guys had some reason for staying the way they were." Both of us zombies, he thought, and we never knew it. You'd think it would have come up before this, except for the way a person forgets almost everything that happens in the army.

Terry moved again and the stretcher he was lying on creaked under him. There was more rifle fire, closer to them now, and several bursts from a Bren gun with it. "Sure," Terry said. "They had reasons. I listened to reasons till I got dizzy and went active. Bastards. They hadn't got any more reasons than the guys that went. Just figured their skins was too precious to get holes in."

"I guess it depends more on how it hits a man than on what reasons he's got," Colin said. "The dirty part was the way they put the pressure on after you were in." But he remembered the everlasting barrack-room talk, complaint and defense and explanation, some of it sincere, some the pale echo of other men's sincerity, much of it simply words that covered nothing, not even fear. The sum was not cowardice, nor quite selfishness, nor quite ignorance, but something smaller and meaner and more depress-

250

ing than any of these, a failure rather than a fault. We weren't generous, Colin thought; we hadn't any generosity in us.

Colin heard the break of frozen snow under footsteps and sat up to listen. A voice said quietly and clearly: "Stretcher-bearers."

"I figured that last bit was too close," Terry said.

They stood up and Colin folded the stretcher and shouldered it. The runner had come up and Colin recognized his voice when he spoke again. "One platoon. Over in the farmhouse."

"Can we handle it?" Colin asked.

"Sure. There's only one hurt bad. Some silly son of a bitch fumbled a grenade in the kitchen."

They walked down towards the farmhouse. They were in dead ground behind the high bank of the river and there was no firing now, but their boots were noisy on the crisp snow and the light of the stars was a shadowy brightness. Colin had the feeling of nakedness that often came to him when he was going forward. He was not afraid. To his own surprise he had seldom been afraid since the landing. In training, fear had been with him often, fear of his own clumsiness and foolishness, fear of the blind, driving urgency and hostility that seemed to build in the men around him. Here it was different. Fear was remote and invisible; the men one could see were working together, in friendship. Death was a bullet in the heart, swift, painless, far less likely to come than when he had wished for it years ago in the alder flat. Looking on death and suffering in many forms, he had tried to warn himself, had even tried to find fear. But the burnt and shattered bodies he had tended so often would give no warning, only work that pushed fear yet farther away.

They were near the farmhouse now and Terry said: "I hate this son of a bitching place. It's a hoodoo. I wish we'd get the hell out, forward or back. Don't matter which."

The words were spoken violently, without the easy humor that was an essential part of almost everything Terry said.

"Christ," the runner said. "This ain't near as bad as some places we been at. Like that christly canal for instance."

"It's a hoodoo, I tell you," Terry said. "Two nights ago them poor bastards getting burned like that in the tank. And now they've gone to spilling live grenades all over the kitchen floor."

They were passing the shadowy bulk of the burned-out tank as Terry was speaking and Colin remembered how it had been; the burned rags of clothing on the living bodies, the smell of burning flesh, the men in pain, strange, terrifying pain that shock did not restrain as it restrained the pain of most wounds. And the shocked pity in Terry's voice, so unlike his usual cynical yet kindly acceptance of wounds and death as an unwarranted visitation of labor upon him. "The poor bastards," he repeated over and over again as he worked. "The poor bastards. This goddamned, dirty war."

The runner took them into the farmhouse. The kitchen was at the back, a practically undamaged room, and there was a light behind blacked-out windows. The platoon sergeant was the only man badly hurt and Colin went to him at once. From the moment he began to work on him he was absorbed, utterly unconscious of the room and the other men in it. His hands were sure and strong, the bandages and dressings were familiar tools, and he had the sense of understanding that always came when he was working with wounded men; it was as though the injured body were his own, yet he was detached from it, knowing the channels of pain and the intensity of shock, and knowing also the true degree of damage in the wound and its relationship to the body's life. The work had meaning for him because many times, as now, he had seen pain draw away under his hands. The same power was in his voice and gestures, even in the red Geneva cross he wore on his breast and back. Now he was old in the fighting and most of the men he tended were new; because of this his assurance was stronger, his absorption yet more complete.

"Ready?" Terry was standing beside him. Together they lifted the sergeant on to the stretcher.

"The knee's bad," Colin said quietly. "He'll have to go back right away. What about the others?"

"Walking," Terry said. "Band-aid scratches. Them mortars is starting again."

Colin listened. "It's light," he said. "Same as they started up the other night."

The sergeant was a big man, but they were a good team, used to each other's stride and pace, and they crossed the hard snow easily, past the tank, past the ruined wall and down to the rubber boat on the near bank of the creek. The nearest of the mortar fire was over a hundred yards to the left of them and they paid no attention to it.

Fifteen minutes later they were back at the wall, but Terry said: "We better get down in the dirt. We're due for a pasting before morning, sure as this ain't Portage and Main."

The slit-trench was more ambitious than most of the dozens they had scraped out since D-day. The ground was dry and digging had been easy once they were through the frost, so Terry had cleaned out the overhang until there was room for a man to lie down under it on the stretcher. He set the stretcher down there now, fumbled for a moment and came up with a lighted cigarette between his lips. "What time is it?" he asked.

"It was around three-thirty when we came back from the creek," Colin said.

"Christ, it's a long bloody night. So goddamned cold a man doesn't even feel like going to sleep. You want to try to take a spell?"

Usually they slept in turns on a quiet night. But Colin only said: "What's the trouble, Terry?"

"Hell, I don't know," the cigarette glowed and faded in the dark. "Must be getting me down, I guess. Used to be I didn't ever think ahead. But now I want us to get moving and finish the damn thing. I want to get the hell home before it's too late."

"Can't last much longer," Colin said. "Not with what's piling into them all the time."

"What's the hold-up then?" Terry wedged his back more firmly against the end of the slit-trench. "Look at that poor bastard there tonight. If they'd wound her up yesterday or last month he'd be O.K. right now instead of crippled up for the rest of his life."

Colin knew what he was thinking. "They haven't got you and me tagged," he said. "We'd have had it before this if they had." An old thought came back to him: if you die in a war everybody thinks you had guts. They talk about you and put your name on a memorial. I guess it's a good thing they don't know how some of us die.

"I never seen you stirred up yet," Murphy said. "There's times

I think you like this goddamned war. Don't you ever want to get the hell home?"

"Sure," Colin said. "I'm going to get me a nice quiet farm and raise dairy cattle."

Terry laughed. "What about them mountains and trap-lines you're always talking about?"

"No," Colin said seriously. "If a man wants to raise a family he's got to forget that stuff. My dad's got a place where I could make out farming." There or the Underhill place. Better Underhill's, maybe, now the old man's got himself married again. Except it'd be tough to start up at Underhill's and it would have to be beef, not milk up there.

"You going to marry the girl that writes the letters?" Terry asked. "I thought you said she was your schoolteacher."

Colin felt his face flush in the darkness. "That's right," he said. "She is. But she's only a couple of years older than me."

"You don't want to marry one older than you. They wear out too quick."

"Like as not she won't have me," Colin said.

"Then what? You got others?"

Colin laughed. "Maybe I could find one. Most guys get married in the end."

"I ain't seen the one I'd marry yet. But I'm sure going to look around once I get the store going good." Terry had worked in a hardware store before he was called up and he planned to have a store of his own after the war. "Hardware's good clean stuff," he had told Colin. "And real interesting. And there's a big spread. A guy can make a clean-up if he knows his way around."

They were silent for a little while and it was very silent everywhere about them. For a moment it seemed that the war had gone on and left them.

"Christ, it's quiet," Terry said. "Something's going to happen, surer than hell. Them tanks'll be moving again, weather like this." He kicked at the snow in the bottom of the trench. "Go on talking," he said. "How come you stayed a zombie so long?"

"I told you," Colin said. "I got sore." He remembered the impersonal routine of the recruiting center, the sudden realization that he was through the medical board, in the army. The shamed resentment, the sense of having been trapped into something he had once accepted willingly. "They turned me down back in '39," he said. "Then called me up and said I was O.K."

"I've heard of that happening. It happened to a lot of guys. But it don't make much sense. If a guy wanted to go one time, why wouldn't he want to go the next?"

"I guess I didn't want to go the first time."

"Jesus, you're a hard guy to figure out. I never did get it straight how you came to switch over from a sniper into a stretcher-bearer. It don't add up when a guy's supposed to be the best shot in the unit."

"I'm yellow," Colin said.

He had spoken without emphasis or emotion, in simple explanation. Terry started, shocked by the word, then laughed. "Sure," he said with heavy sarcasm. "I seen that all along."

"That's right," Colin said quietly. "I'm not kidding. I can't fight. I couldn't kill a man. I thought maybe I could for a while, if it was going on all around. Then I found out I couldn't."

"So you transferred over?"

"They got wise and kicked me out. I got so I couldn't do a damn thing right in training. That Major Allison was a good officer. He figured I'd maybe make out where I didn't have to fight."

"That ain't being yellow," Terry said. "I'm not yellow, but there's been plenty times on this job when I was scared and you wasn't. I never seen you scared yet."

"I guess I'm not scared of dying," Colin said slowly. "That happens to you and it's quick. I'm scared when I have to do something. That's why this job's O.K. We've just got work to do. We might get killed, sure, but nobody's aiming to kill us." He shifted his feet in the snow and sat forward a little. "I used to work on a bridge-crew. A man can fall off a trestle and get killed or something can drop on him and kill him. There's sense to that because a man has to take some chances to do anything at all. But there's no sense to men hating each other and trying to force each other to do things they don't want to." He hesitated a moment, then he said: "A man could die in the mountains, like my partner nearly did once and it would be peaceful, almost like a

255

part of living; nobody would have been hurt by it, not really hurt, because there was no hate in it."

Terry shook his head in the darkness. "That's too deep for me," he said. "If a man gets hurt or killed he suffers just the same whether some other guy means it or it's an accident."

"It's a hard thing to explain," Colin said. "Even to yourself. I guess I'm not scared of being hurt or killed so much as I am of people wanting to hurt each other. It used to scare me even to see my old man get mad."

"Christ Almighty, that ain't being yellow. You said you was yellow."

"Yes it is. When the world's made up of that kind of stuff a man ought to be able to stand up and take his part in it, not run away and hide every time."

"Most men feel safer packing a rifle than they do packing a stretcher."

Colin moved a hand impatiently. "I know that too. I'm not talking only about the war. It's the whole of life. A man's got to be able to go out into it and do the things he's afraid of doing just as though he wasn't afraid. I can't."

"Everybody's different from everybody else. You do too much deep thinking, that's all. Like me earlier on tonight when we went up to the farm. I couldn't seem to leave off thinking about them guys being burned in the tank, then that crazy son of a bitch had to go and drop a grenade in a kitchen of all goddamned places. Seemed to me like the set-up was hoodooed." He looked up at the sky. "Not more than an hour to daylight," he said. "I'm going to get me some sleep."

He was asleep almost at once, and Colin sat on in the trench listening to his calm, even breathing. Suddenly he felt very tired and very lonely. He had Terry's feeling that this thing would never end, that they would go on and on, from river to canal to river again, always seeing death and smelling death and hearing the fierce heavy sound of death all about them. And if it did end, what would be left? Robbie and Johnny and Wind Lake all seemed very small and far away.

Clyde and Margaret had their own children, their own joined life to live. Even Mildred was far away, though she wrote so regu-

256

larly and so fully; reasonable, wise, strengthening letters, cool and orderly, with only a reflected light of the powerful love that had grown between them before Martha's death. He still did not know what it was that Martha's death had done to them, only that it had brought a sense of shame to him that all Margaret's reproaches had never stirred. It was not shame for his love of Mildred, nor even for the way of it, but rather because it had come between himself and Martha; and it was made suddenly strong because there was no longer the possibility of giving back to Martha whatever had been taken from her. If she could have known all of it, Colin thought, she would have understood and would not have minded. Wherever she is now she must know and understand.

And that must change something with the other, he thought. Mildred will know, Mildred will know. So much time has passed now, so many things have happened that it can't be still between us, whatever it is. Surely nothing can be between us if I live through this and if she still loves me. Then he remembered the letters, cool and controlled, lovely as a glacier's blue-green ice, remote from what he wanted of her as the unclimbed peak of Amabilis Mountain. As the first faint gray light grew in the east and the mortars started up again, he knew he was still lonely and it seemed there was little to hope for.

The mortar fire was heavy, patterned, accurate and there was artillery fire with it and behind it, all along the river. Terry woke at once and moved closer to Colin in the narrow trench.

"Means business," he said. "They're going to try and shift us the hell out of here."

Very soon they were working. There were casualties in all three platoons on the island between the two rivers and they were the only stretcher party. There was no time to carry back to the rubber boat, but they moved two men in from the open ground to the shelter of the ruined wall. "It'll take a direct hit to knock it over," Terry said. "And at least it stops the bits and pieces." Terry was calm and happy, Colin knew, and his big hands were gentle with the wounded men.

An hour after dawn a new company came on to the island and passed through to the high bank along the river. There were more stretcher parties now and Colin recognized the figure of the M.O. wading towards them through the ground mist. He checked the two wounded men, then stood for a moment with Colin, looking forward from the shelter of the broken wall.

"The R.A.P.'s moving up to the farmhouse," he told Colin. "And we ought to have the jeeps across the river any time now. These men'll be O.K. here. Any others you get, bring 'em to the farmhouse." He looked back at the wounded men again. "And watch the bleeding, corporal. These goddamned mortar fragments are bad."

Colin nodded. The M.O. was new with the unit, but he was a calm man and Colin liked him. Terry said: "We going to get moving again?"

"You can bet your life on that," the M.O. said. "There's enough Canadian armor on both sides of us to shift everything between here and Berlin." He turned to Colin again. "Better get on up to the farmhouse," he said. "They'll be looking for you there from now on."

They moved up through a strange quiet and saw that more and more troops were coming on to the island. Swirls and wisps of mist shifted with unreal slowness everywhere over the low ground and Colin had a sudden sense that he was a part of something gigantic and powerful, something welded into greatness beyond itself and full of purpose. The feeling passed and left him only with the certainty that he was very hungry and very short of sleep, but he found an echo of it again in the elation of Terry's face when they came to the farmhouse.

"This is it," Terry said. "We're on our way. Look at those babies moving up." He pointed behind them and Colin turned and saw tanks riding the mist and more men behind them. Then the mortar fire started again, intense and deadly, all along the bank of the river. They were called forward into it, brought back a wounded man, went out again. As they started back the second time Colin saw that the mortar fire was bursting over the bank, all across the flat ground between them and the R.A.P.

"Give it five minutes," he told Terry. "They'll shift again, likely."

The man on the stretcher had been unconscious when they loaded him, but he moved his head and spoke to Colin.

"Where's the damage, chum?" he asked.

"Left leg and thigh," Colin said. "You'll make out."

"You ain't kidding no one. It's the back, ain't it? There ain't any part of me moves except my head."

"They'll fix it," Colin said. "They can fix anything."

"Throw me off and take another one. One they can do some good for."

"You'll make out," Colin said again.

The mortar fire had shifted, so they picked up the stretcher and started out again. The steep bank was awkward on the slippery snow, but the flat ground was easy and good and they moved swiftly over it. The wounded man spoke from the stretcher again.

"You'd better of taken somebody else," he said.

Colin looked ahead to the farmhouse, saw Terry stumble, felt the ground heave under his feet. His knees bent to the shock, the stretcher wrenched sideways out of his grasp, then the heaving ground seemed to hit him in the face. He heard no sound and saw no flash, but he knew that he was blinded, on his hands and knees in the snow. Then he could see again, not clearly but enough. He crawled to his right, searching for the stretcher and the wounded man. But there was no man and no stretcher. Blood dripped from his face, into the snow and on to his right hand. He shook it away angrily, crawled forward and found Terry. Terry was face down in the snow and quite still and Colin thought at first he was dead. Then he remembered Johnny Harris in the snow. He reached out the hand with the blood on it and pushed on Terry's shoulder, trying to roll him over. It was too hard for him, so he moved again and used both hands and made it. Terry was dead.

PART SIX

THE HIGHEST HILL

30

COLIN walked slowly along the road from Blenkinstown towards the Ensley farm. It was late August and very hot. He was still in uniform, carrying a kit-bag over his shoulder, but he knew he was finished with the army. He had to report back to the hospital in thirty days, but they had told him it would be for discharge.

He had thought at first, when he stepped off the boat, that the town was little changed. Mark Dufler, the wharfinger, had recognized him and spoken the proper welcoming words. As he walked off the wharf Jim Hurley had stepped out of the telegraph office and held out his hand. "Welcome back, Colin," he had said. "Clyde and Margaret are away right now, so I sent the message out to your dad. I guess he couldn't make it down to the boat, but he's home." Colin hadn't expected to be met, but he remembered now that they sent telegrams. Next of kin: Mrs. Margaret Munro, Blenkinstown, B. C. It had seemed more logical to put down Margaret's name than the old man's. He had wondered at the time if the army might not find out about the old man and tell him to change it. The thought made him smile a little now. After four years the army no longer seemed all-seeing and all-knowing.

As he walked through the village he had begun to realize that it was changed. There were new stores on the main street, stucco-fronted and with the colored tubes of neon signs flaunting out from them. There were many people on the street, few of whom he recognized. And as he went on, past the school and on to the gravel surface of the old road, he saw that there were many new houses in little clearings in the bush. They were unambitious houses, most of them only half-finished, with tar-paper tacked to the outside walls; but they were in places where it had never occurred to him that houses would be built. There was even one beside the creek where he had cleaned up after the fight with Tod Phalling.

The new houses and the people moving in them and near them stirred a vague resentment in him. It was hard to believe that these ordinary things had been going on during the years he had been away, that people had had time for them or heart for them. He remembered the warnings they had been given in England before the hospital ship had brought them over: "You fellows needn't expect to find the flags out and the hero's welcome. People haven't any time for that. Life has been going on over there while you've been away. You'll find changes, but mostly you'll find things going on just the way they always were, your friends having a good time, making good money, getting ahead. Remember, that's the way you wanted it. That's what you fought for . . ."

It had seemed that they were wrong, until now. All the way across the continent the flags had been out and often enough the welcome had been there, waiting for them at every station as the train pulled in. The tall Canadian trains with the high-wheeled locomotives. Talk of Canadian places: "Think Timmins is a pretty good place to live, Bob?" "I'll be through to Winnipeg by Saturday." "Down to Windsor." "Calgary—Edmonton I go to really." Montreal, Toronto, Saint John, Toronto. Vancouver, Ottawa, Saskatoon, Regina, Quebec, Victoria, Lethbridge, Toronto, Montreal. "They're in a hurry to get the Westerners back home so they won't be cluttering up Canada too long." And proudly, chalked on the coaches of a troop train around a colored drawing of the unit insignia: "N. Africa—Sicily—Italy—France—Belgium—Holland—Germany—VANCOUVER. No thanks to you, zombies." More gently, the English names: "Soho, Piccadilly, Tottenham Court Road, Aldershot, Borden, Witley, Farnham. Sold out. No more bitter." There had been a lift to coming back, a shared triumph of escape, survival, hope. Shattered in the moment that the trains stopped for the last time, its little pieces scattered with the men who turned to their families and the busses, trains, boats, taxis that took them on to the street numbers and whistle stops, the farm and logging and fishing hamlets, the places where life had gone on.

Of course life had gone on. People had had a good time, high wages, plenty of work, essential work that kept them safe from the call-up. It only seemed strange that they should have been expanding, building up, changing familiar things that had seemed unchangeable. But that also followed naturally. There had been a deepsea ship loading lumber from a big new dock at Blenkin's mill. And Phalling's mill was much bigger than it had been, with a new refuse burner carrying a bold lettered sign on the seaward side. The town had gone ahead. Colin remembered someone had told him that down in Vancouver, or was it in England, someone in the hospital? The town had gone ahead, so people had come in and had built houses for themselves where it had seemed there would never be houses.

He had turned in at the familiar gate by the familiar mail-box before he saw what had happened to the Ensley farm. There were half-a-dozen new houses along the roadway in the barn field—houses like the others he had seen, unambitious, half-finished. Farther back in the field were some piles of lumber, the foundations of another house, two or three automobile trailers. Close by the house was a cluster of small cabins. Colin stopped in amazement, then turned slowly around and looked for the big maples by the gate. They were there. He looked again at the house and knew it was the house, knew that the barn was the place where he had milked Martha's cows. For a moment he wanted more than anything to turn and go away, go anywhere but into the house where he would find his father and the woman his father had married.

Then he saw Mrs. Gibberd in the doorway, waiting for him. She had seen him and waved to him, and he went forward to meet her. Mrs. Gibberd, he thought, Mrs. Ensley now. She must have made him do this, he'd never have thought it up by himself.

But he went on and she smiled as he came near and said: "Welcome home, Colin. Mr. Ensley's right inside washing up. We didn't expect you this soon." He saw her eyes on his face, assessing the scar of his wound and he thought: there isn't so much to see there, the medicals did a good job. She touched his arm and tried to take the kit-bag from him. "You shouldn't have carried that all the way out here when you've just got out of hospital," she said. "We could have had them bring it up later. Come on in and sit down."

His father's bulk was behind her in the doorway then. Colin saw an old man, stoop-shouldered, gray-bearded, the head bowed forward a little between the stooped shoulders, the broad, bold face heavily lined, tired, shrunken away from its boldness. He slipped the bag from his shoulder and stepped forward into the kitchen. "Hello, Father," he said.

The old man looked up at him and held out a thick, still powerful hand. "You look tired, son," he said, and the gentleness of his voice touched Colin so that he felt tears close to his eyes. "Come in and sit down."

Colin passed into the kitchen and sat down. The room had been painted, he saw, and there was a new stove and a new sink and new chairs. Mrs. Gibberd had gone to the stove and was cooking a meal for him. Will Ensley sat opposite him, watching his face with the same gentleness that had been in his voice.

"You'll find the place changed a lot, Colin," he said at last, and there was anxiety in the voice that had once been so resonant and over-powering.

"Yes," Colin said. "It's changed." You've changed it, he thought, you've dirtied it and killed it for me. And why shouldn't you? It's yours, not mine. Not yours really, hers. But she's dead or she'd never have let you do it. Don't crawl to me and tell me why you did it. I'm no part of this any more, no part of this house, no part of this place.

"I made your father do it," Mrs. Gibberd said from the stove. "He's not strong enough to work any more the way he used to and we had to make something out of the place."

Colin looked out of the window at the houses along the road. "I know," he said. "I could see there were changes all the way along. A lot of new houses going up. It's the same everywhere, I guess."

"The Mayhews and the Hunts and the Meldrums wouldn't sell any land," she said. "So they came on out to us. We had put the cabins up before that." She came over with a great plate of food and set it in front of him, then went back to the stove for the coffee. "Go right ahead and eat, don't mind us. We had ours an hour ago."

Will was looking at Colin's uniform and the ribbons over his left breast. "Have you got to go back?" he asked. "I thought it was all finished."

"To the hospital," Colin said. "They check you pretty close."

"We heard you were wounded. They sent word to Margaret. Is it likely to trouble you?"

Colin touched the scar on his face lightly, then raised his arm to show the free movement of the shoulder that had been injured. "No," he said. "I'm O.K." He could see they were genuinely worried about him, afraid for him and afraid of him, and his resentment faded. "How's Margaret?" he asked. "And Clyde? And all my nieces and nephews?"

"You'll be proud of them when you see them," Mrs. Gibberd said. "Little Clyde's just like Margaret. And the girls are like Clyde. I'm not sure about the baby."

COLIN knew Mildred would not be back until school started in

September; she had written from California and the letter had been waiting for him in Vancouver, forwarded from the hospital in England. She had not known he was coming home and it was an anxious letter: "I do hope they will send you home soon. You say you weren't badly hurt, but it's worrying to think how long they have kept you in hospital. I want to see you and *know* you are all right. And I want to hear you talk. We've had only letters for so long. They're not enough." For so long, he thought, and now this much longer. And what shall we be to each other when she does come? I used to be so sure she would know, but will she? Perhaps I'm the one that should know.

He used the first few days of his leave in going to see the Meldrums and the Mayhews and in re-exploring the alder flat, finding the old cattle trails grown over and the drinking places along the creek unused except by deer. Once he tried to climb the mountain, following the route he and Margaret had used years before. At first it went well for him; his legs were strong and his lungs were good and he felt all the old happiness of being alone in country that he loved and understood. Then, as the climbing became more difficult, he found that his injured shoulder would not do the work he asked of it. He went on, hoping that the stiffness and weakness would wear away with use. But weakness became pain, mild at first, then fierce and persistent, and his whole arm was useless to him. So he turned back at last and went down to the valley again.

He stayed at home the next day, moving carefully to keep Will and Mrs. Gibberd from knowing what had happened. On the day after his shoulder was better and he went out along the road to find his old trail to the forestry camp at Strathmore Falls. As he came to Mike Varchuk's house he saw that someone was living in it; the window frames had been painted, there was a new roof and faint blue smoke rose from a new brick chimney. A small, stooped man was working in the garden and Colin saw as he came closer that it was Varchuk himself. He thought for a moment of turning off the road and cutting round through the brush to his trail, but something in the way the old man was working there, alone in the garden of his lonely little house, something remembered of Will Ensley's disapproval of Varchuk, made him hesitate.

At least he's an old-timer, Colin thought. And walked on along the road.

Varchuk did not hear him until he leaned his arms on the gate and said: "Hello." Then the little man straightened up and peered towards him, the wrinkles of his brown face strongly shadowed under the brim of his hat.

"Young Ensley," he said. "Will's boy." He came to the gate and held out his hand, still peering as though his eyes were weak. "It is a long time, but I know the tallness and the shoulders."

Colin laughed and opened the gate. "I've seen taller than me," he said.

"Come into the house," Mike said. "There is beer, good beer, just ready for drinking. You are finished with the army?"

They went into the house and Mike got out his beer; he filled two glasses and set them on the table, then put two more full bottles beside them. "Drink up," he said. "There's plenty more."

It was cool in the little room after the hot sun outside and the beer was good, dark and heavy-bodied like the dark brown ale they had occasionally found in England. It seemed strange to be there in Varchuk's house after all the things he had heard said of him, after the mystery of his disappearance and the house's long emptiness. And Varchuk's quick acceptance of him seemed strange too.

"You are tired, son," Varchuk said suddenly. "War is a hard thing on the people."

"I'm O.K.," Colin said and touched the thin scar on his cheek. "This makes a line that isn't really there."

Varchuk nodded. "I saw it at the gate. You were wounded. One shoulder moves stiff, too." He took an opener and pried the caps off the two bottles of beer on the table. "We needed to have more in Spain. Then your war would not have happened."

Colin remembered that one story of Varchuk's disappearance had been that he had gone to fight in Spain with the McKenzie-Papineau battalion. "Were you there?" he said.

Mike bent forward and pulled up one trouser leg, then turned to show the ugly, infolded scar that ran along his shrunken thigh, from the knee up out of sight towards the hip. "We were the first front," he said proudly.

Colin understood the little man's quick hospitality. That's why he looks old, he thought, and why he speaks clearer English than he did.

He drank from the full glass, remembering the Spanish veterans he had known in the army; Stavic, who had refused to go overseas and been a powerful influence among the zombies; and Kroez of the sniper platoon, wise, dangerous, savage, killed near Caen. Intense, bitter and difficult men both of them, yet each as different from the other as they were sharply different from Varchuk.

"What you do, now you've come back?" Mike asked suddenly. "Go to work in the woods like your dad?"

"I thought I'd go farming," Colin said. "I'm not sure now. Everything's changed so much. I guess a person has to get used to it, then look around."

"There is no farm where you live, even if Will did not sell the land. It is not producing land and there is not enough."

Colin nodded. "I had thought maybe a man could run beef cattle over on the flats at the mouth of Wind River, the way Underhill tried."

"And now there is the new logging company there at the mouth of the river, and they talk of the pulp mill also." Varchuk laughed. "They have been busy while you were away."

Colin smiled. "I guess there's always the trap-line," he said.

"Furs, for the backs of rich women. No. There is more for you than that."

Varchuk opened two more bottles and filled the glasses again. Colin watched him curiously, trying to guess what might be behind his interest. It seemed closer and stronger than anything that would develop simply from the shared experience of war.

Varchuk sat down again and lifted his glass. "They say you are clever with the axe, like Will. It is good work for a man."

Colin moved his arm to indicate the injured shoulder. "I'd have to get this straightened out first."

"You are young and strong. It will get better. The iron is still in there?"

"I guess so. They said in England they might have to operate again." There's sense in what the little guy says, he thought.

There are worse jobs, and a man would have a better chance to look around for likely farm land than he would back on a trapline.

"You are lucky," Varchuk said. "We fought too soon. We must be our own doctors."

Colin glanced at him in quick surprise. Nobody called you out on that one, he thought; it was all your own idea. Watching his face, Varchuk smiled. "It is not important," he said gently, touching his wound. "It is important that those who fought against fascism should not quarrel. The fight against fascism is everywhere and all the time."

Colin stood up and turned restlessly towards the window of the little room.

"Who wants to be fighting all the time?" he asked. "Why can't a man just live his life and work at his job?"

"He must fight too," Varchuk said. "The worker must always fight, even to keep what he has." He poured more beer into the glasses on the table. "The union is strong now," he said. "Not like when you went away. But it will need the strength of the men who come back from the war."

Colin turned back from the window. He did not like Varchuk's gentle intensity and still did not understand its purpose. "We'll join, I guess. Why shouldn't we?"

"There may be some who think that those who did not go to war have gained more than is right. It is a danger. And there are always those who try to divide the workers."

Colin nodded. "They had the best end of it. But I guess that's their business. I'm not griping."

"Some will. They must be guided."

Colin laughed. "Don't ask me to guide them," he said. "They've got a right to the way they think same as I have. You picked on the wrong guy, Mike."

Varchuk looked at him, smiling faintly. "Perhaps," he said. "Perhaps. But you will help. Even Will helped us."

MILDRED arrived home a few days before Colin's leave ended. He went to the cottage as soon as he knew she was home and she met him in the doorway; she held out both hands to him and drew him inside.

"Colin," she said. "Colin, Colin, Colin."

He followed her into the small living room and for a moment they stood looking at each other, as though by looking they could wear away the years of separation.

Colin said at last: "You haven't changed. Everything else has, but you haven't." He wanted to tell her she was more beautiful than ever, richer and more deeply appealing even than he remembered her. But the words would not come easily to him and for the moment this other, that she was unchanged while everything else was changed, seemed the more important.

She laughed quietly, happily, still open to him. "I'm older," she said. "We both are. Five long years older." She raised her hand and touched the scar on his face. "Is that it?"

Colin nodded. "Does it look awful?"

She shook her head vigorously. "No. It's almost hard to find, except it changes your face somehow." She moved away from him. "Sit down," she said. "Tell me everything there is. About that. And the shoulder. And are you home for good? Everything."

Colin laughed. "I think you're younger and I'm older. Everything, all at once?"

"The shoulder first."

"It's O.K.," he said. "I have to have more treatments. But it's going to be O.K."

"How soon?"

"I have to be back at the hospital next Monday."

They talked on, quietly and easily, feeling the gaps in their knowledge of each other, still searching for change; and in the ease of their talking the time they had been waiting for passed from them, unused.

Mildred sensed its passing long before Colin. It seemed to her she had known it almost from the first. He had come to her freely, for the first time in his life. That alone was enough and she had accepted it, had offered him everything in the enchanted repetition of his name. But the time had passed and now they were talking calmly, without impatience or tension, as close friends, friends of a long time, no more than that. Yet it is there, she thought, in him as well as in me, and the shadow of Martha holds it quiet.

After he had gone she turned back to the job of unpacking. In a little while she was crying. The years, she thought, and the letters. And now this. Yet this may be right. The other would be so difficult, so dangerous for both of us, unless we needed it beyond everything else. And we don't or Martha would not still be there between us. Perhaps we don't know yet, perhaps the years are between us as well as Martha; and the letters and all the times we have turned away from each other and everything that has happened since that first day when he wrote about mountains and touched my shoulder. Now he will go back to his mountains.

She gave up what she was doing, went into the living room and sat down as though to recapture the feeling of his being there. If he needed me, she thought, and not the mountains, would I be ready for him? I was today, but would I be again, would I know? What would a woman do, not a schoolteacher but a real woman? I've always been his schoolteacher, even when we were closest and I tried hardest not to be. He will come to me again, as surely as he will go back to the mountains again. Let me be ready then, let me be free of littleness, just for that once.

COLIN spent most of that fall and winter in hospital, but they operated on his shoulder for the last time before Christmas, and by January the wound was healed. The doctor told him: "It'll be weak at first, but there's no permanent damage there. Get it working, easy for a while, then pile it on."

"Is using an axe O.K.?" Colin asked.

"Nothing better. Just watch it till the muscles build back, then give her hell. You'll never know we did a thing to it."

He was back in Blenkinstown by the end of January, staying with Clyde and Margaret, but going out to his father's place each day to cut cordwood. Within a month much of the strength had built back into his arm and shoulder and he hired out with the Blenkin Lumber Company. Gordon Holman was still superintendent and welcomed him warmly.

"Glad to have you back, Ensley," he said. "You didn't leave us to join, but there's always a job here for a returned man. Where do you want to work?"

"I'd be best scoring for a while, I guess," Colin said. "But I'll be able to handle the big axe again soon enough."

Holman nodded. "We heard you'd had trouble with your arm. Just say the word when it's in shape again. There's plenty of work for another broad-axe man. I wish we had your dad back on the job."

Why did you kill the strength out of him, then, with your black-lists? Colin thought. Why did you take his pride and make him an old man? He looked Holman in the eyes, searching for some sign of regret or apology. There was none. Only smiling, good-natured assurance.

Holman's hand touched Colin's shoulder in an easy, friendly gesture. "Glad to have you around again," he repeated. "I'd like to see you grow into the company the way your dad did."

"I might not stay with it as long as he did," Colin said and turned away. Grow into the company, he thought. You don't even remember what you did to him, you self-satisfied son of a bitch. It wasn't any more important to you than rolling a cigarette or going to the can.

Colin stayed on with Clyde and Margaret when he went to work in the camp. He liked them and liked their three children, and it kept him within reach of Mildred. It was evident that Margaret had never renewed her friendship with Mildred and she spoke of her very seldom. But when she did so it was without bitterness; and she made no effort to influence Colin.

Colin went up to the cottage frequently, sometimes for a meal, sometimes for an hour or two in the evening. Occasionally he and Mildred walked along the beach road on a fine afternoon or visited a farm to buy fresh fruit. Once he took her back through the alder flat and showed her the start of the climb to the mountain, but generally he kept well away from the road that led out to the Ensley farm.

During this time they held to the relationship that had grown out of that first meeting after his return. They were friends, with a closer intimacy for having been lovers, yet with a rigid restraint of passion that would not have been necessary between friends. As time went on this tension of unfulfilled love strained at them both more and more powerfully. Mildred felt it and in her wisdom was afraid; but the very faith that held her back from Colin would not let her deny him friendship. Colin felt it and wanted to use it to break away what stood between them; but for a long while he believed it was in himself alone and he dared not use it. Mildred had become again all that she had been during his schooldays—cool and unattainable, infinitely desirable, yet set beyond any reach of desire by the qualities that made her so desirable.

Mildred still probed and searched to bring out the things that were shut deepest in him, but her searching was gentler than it had ever been and the more effective for that. Now war had given him experience far beyond her knowledge and she made him describe and explain it to her until it took on clearer values for himself.

"You didn't hate the army," she told him once.

"Why do you say that?"

"You say it. You were very happy sometimes—often when the fighting was going on and you were with your friend Terry Murphy or one of the others."

"I suppose that's true," Colin said slowly. "If being happy is being too busy to be miserable."

"No," she insisted. "It's more than that, much more. It's being able to forget yourself. And you only do that when there's something so big, so tremendously important to be done that it takes every part of you to do it."

"I didn't like it. I hated seeing men hurt and knowing they couldn't get right again. I didn't like thinking about them afterwards, or remembering how they were before they got hit or burned, strong and laughing and full of life."

"It isn't a question of liking something," she said. "But you did like it. You didn't wound them or burn them, you helped them. You knew they trusted you and depended on you, you could see the pain go quiet in their faces when you worked on them. You must have known lots of times that you had done something that kept a man from dying before he got back to the dressing station. You hadn't time to think about yourself then, you hadn't time to be afraid even. There were much more important things."

As he watched her speaking it seemed to Colin that she was more beautiful than she had ever been. All the beauty she had had ten years ago was still there, the glinting lights of her pale hair, the smooth stretch of the milky skin over her strong cheekbones, the clear blue of her eyes, the rich and gentle fullness of her mouth. She will never grow old, he thought, only more alive and more beautiful. He felt his love for her grow in him until his face was hot with it and his eyes could hardly see her face. His throat was dry with wanting her and he could feel the little quiver of stirred muscles all through his body. When he answered her it seemed to him that his voice came from somewhere outside himself.

"That was how it was," he said. "And it was like that because everybody was helping everybody else. Even in training nearly everybody tried to help the other guy, except a few that wanted to look extra good. And once we were on the continent it seemed like everyone was your friend except some guys you couldn't even see." He felt calmer now and pulled out his tobacco pouch and papers to steady his hands. "Back here you get to feeling that everybody's suspicious, everybody's trying to get ahead of the other guy, everybody's sore about something."

"You sound like one of the real old soldiers—the kind that spend their lives saying nothing will ever be so good as it was in the army."

He smiled at her. "You started it. You said I liked it in the army and made me admit it."

"Well," she said. "What's so bad about us all back here? This strike you're going to have?"

"No," Colin said. "We've got to have the strike—unless they give us what we want without it." He frowned and leaned forward in his chair with his elbows on his knees. "But the strike seems to bring it out more than anything else. Most of the boys think it's got to come, but they don't want it. They're scared of it and they're scared of each other. There's a lot of bulldozing going on and a lot of tough talk. Maybe I'm crazy, but it seems to me men ought to be able to get together without that sort of stuff if they really believe in something."

"There have to be leaders," Mildred said.

"I know, but not this way."

"You take it all too seriously," she said. "Come in the kitchen while I make coffee." He watched the firm, strong movement of her body as he followed her. He wanted to touch her, make her stop and turn to him, but he believed she had not restored his right to and he dared not. In the kitchen she did turn to him, abruptly, her face happy and young. "Are we going somewhere again next Sunday?"

"Yes," he said instantly.

"To see that Underhill place at Wind River?"

"If there's anything left of it," he said.

CLYDE also talked to Colin about the strike. He was a corporal now, in charge of the four-man detachment at Blenkinstown and several smaller detachments farther up the coast. He told Colin once: "I'd sooner face a Jap landing, the way we figured for a while it might come here during the war, than these labor troubles."

"I don't think there'll be trouble this time," Colin said. "Not the kind you'd come into."

"No strike has to mean trouble. But it's a time when trouble is very easily made. That's why it's always a policeman's headache."

Colin remembered the talk in the crummy on the way to work the previous day. John Halsborg's big voice saying: "Ask Ensley here. His brother-in-law's a cop."

"What about it?" Colin had asked in the expectant silence.

"They bringing extra cops in for the strike?"

"How would I know?"

Halsborg's laugh, bitter and hostile. "Here's a guy can't forget he was wearing a uniform himself a few months ago." Men near Halsborg trying to quiet him. Earl Mayhew's voice beside Colin: "Let it go, Colin. He's trying to get you sore. These goddamned power-saw fallers think they own the union since they started making big money."

Clyde crossed the room and stood looking out of the window. "Marge is late," he said. Then he turned back to Colin. "Maybe I shouldn't have said all that. I don't think there's going to be any trouble this time. But I hate strike duty or anything to do with labor troubles. Every policeman does. It's the only thing in this job that could ever make me want to take off my uniform for good—and I'd do it before I'd do some of the things that could come up."

"I don't see why a strike should be police business at all," Colin said.

"It isn't police business," Clyde said sharply. "Not unless things get out of control and there's property damage or people hurt. It's our business then and so it should be. The only trouble with that is we have to go against whoever's been doing the damage and that's always the strikers. The bosses may have pulled every lowdown trick in the book to make the boys step out of line, but that's not our business. All we're supposed to ask is who did the damage. Mind you," he added, "strike leaders can go out of their way to make trouble, too, if it suits them."

"Have you got extra men coming up?" Colin asked.

"Laid on ahead of time? Lord, no. They wouldn't send them if I asked for them and I sure as hell wouldn't ask. It's not that. I don't expect any trouble." He paced across to the window again. "I guess I'm beefing to you to get it off my chest, the way any man does when he's up against some part of his job he doesn't like."

Colin stood up. "I'll be glad when it's over," he said. "Seems like there's been nothing but strike talk and union talk ever since I got out of the army. If a strike will clear the air and put things back to normal, I'm all for it."

THE strike, when it came, was quiet and orderly except for an incident at the Phalling mill on the second or third day. Tod Phalling had inherited the mill on his father's death, shortly after he was discharged from the army. He made a half-hearted attempt to operate the mill with a few non-union men. But the picketing was effective and Clyde Munro warned that there would be no police support, so the men would not go through a second time.

Colin was picketing at the Blenkin mill for a few days, but there were no more incidents and the pickets were reduced to one or two men. It became quite evident that there would be no further attempts at strike-breaking and there was little to be done except wait; but there was still a great deal of activity around union head-quarters and the more aggressive leaders worked hard to keep the men together. After a few days Colin went up to his father's place to cut some cordwood, but Ray Kreutzer and Joe Davidson, two members of the strike committee, came up and told him to stop.

"Hell," Colin said. "It's just to give the old man a hand."

"He pays you, don't he?" Davidson asked.

"I never asked him to yet," Colin said.

"It might be O.K. then," Davidson said. "You could take it up with the committee."

"No," Kreutzer said. "If the old man don't pay him he'd have to pay someone else. Besides, he eats his meals free up at the house."

"Let it go," Colin said. "Skip the whole goddamned thing." He turned and flung his axe away from him so that it made half-a-dozen whirring circles in the air and buried itself solidly in the smooth gray trunk of an alder thirty or forty feet away. He looked at it with satisfaction, seeing the handle straight with the trunk of the tree, the unburied blade bright in the sunlight. "You guys make me tired," he said. "Let the son of a bitch stay there."

He stopped in at Earl Mayhew's on his way home and found

Johnny Meldrum there with him in the yard in front of the house. Joan Mayhew came to the door of the house. "If you boys want to come inside I'll make you a cup of tea," she said.

"It's more of a day for beer," Earl told her. "There's some in the ice-box. What do you say, Colin?"

"Sure," Colin said and they all sat on the steps and drank beer.

"Those guys make you quit?" Meldrum asked Colin. "We saw them going up the road."

Colin nodded.

"That's a lot of bull," Earl said. "You could go down and ask the committee and you'd be O.K."

"I wouldn't ask them for a damn thing," Colin said. "I'm going up to Wind Lake and work on my cabins till this mess is over. They can stand it."

"You still got that trap-line?" Meldrum asked.

"Sure have," Colin said. "I'll be using it again, too, the way things look to me right now."

"They're liable to stop you going up there if they know about it."

Earl shook his head. "I don't think they'd bother him. It's not like doing something where he'd be earning wages."

"There's some of the boys want to go fishing," Meldrum said. "They'd have been quitting to go anyway if the strike hadn't come along. They've been told they can't go."

"It makes some sense," Earl said. "They want everybody to be in it together. Makes it stronger that way than if some of them go off to other jobs."

"Doesn't make sense to me," his wife told him. "If you had a boat and went off fishing around this time every year I'd see you went, strike or no strike." She cupped her strong chin in her hand and looked affectionately at Earl. "I'm glad you haven't got one, though."

Colin said slowly: "Seems like the union's God Almighty all of a sudden. I guess it's a good thing—at least it's stopped blacklisting and that other phony stuff they used to pull when the company was God Almighty. But it's kind of hard to take sometimes."

Meldrum laughed. "Shake off one set of shackles and hook on another," he said. "Next thing you know there'll be closed shop around here and you'll be blacklisted if you don't join the union."

"That's a rough way to put it, John," Earl told him. "Closed shop would be our own business. We'd have some say in keeping it fair."

"Not with guys like Halsborg and Kreutzer and Davidson at the head of it. They're in the driver's seat, but good. There's not more than a dozen of them and a few stooges run the whole local. The ordinary plug is scared to get up and say a couple of words at a meeting—if he goes."

"We can change all that," Earl said quietly. "It's just a question of getting in there and working at it, the way they do."

Colin stood up impatiently. "Isn't there any way a man can be free to work at a job and mind his own business?" he asked.

"No," Earl told him gently. "Not any more there isn't. I guess maybe there never was."

Colin felt a sudden sense of desperation. He struggled to find some violent word or phrase that would express it, then shrugged his shoulders hopelessly. "I better get moving," he said.

"Stay to supper," Joan Mayhew asked him. "I can have it ready in a few minutes."

"Thanks a lot," Colin said. "But I better get moving if I want to start up the lake tomorrow. Thanks just the same." He looked at Earl. "And if anybody tries to stop me I believe I'll take a poke at him."

Earl smiled. "They won't," he said. "Don't let it get you down. We'll all be working again inside of a month."

COLIN stayed up at the lake for a little over a month. It was the second time he had been there since his discharge; but the big camp at the mouth of the river, the logging railroad and the heavy operation in the flat valley depressed him as it had the first time, even though the machines were all silent. He saw that the railroad was through to the foot of the lake now and they had been rigging a loading boom when the strike came up. There was a big raft near the dock with a donkey engine already on it.

He had stopped for a couple of days with Robbie and Johnny on the way up, then had gone on to Amabilis Creek. Robbie had seemed depressed and suddenly much older. "They're putting an

278

A-frame on the lake to log some of the good pockets while the market's high," he told Colin. "Andy Grant was right. They'll have a railroad up my valley first thing I know."

Johnny was more cheerful. "I kind of like to look down there and see the lights at night when the camp's working. And it feels good to have some place nearer than Blenkinstown where you can go to get grub and tobacco. They been real good about bringing freight through for us on the railroad."

Up in his own valley Colin forgot everything in the joys of rediscovery. All his cabins except one were in good shape. The exception was a shelter cabin that had collapsed under a heavy fall of snow. He rebuilt it into a far better cabin than it had been before, then went on to the cabin in the Gully. The snow had already gone from the meadow and the young grass was growing steadily. The deer had moved up from their winter haunts in the valley and the bears were working the swampy places for roots. There seemed to be game everywhere and Colin watched it and moved amongst it with a sense of possession, almost of fellowship.

There was still snow on the mountain slopes, but he climbed through it to Windstorm Gap, traveling warily and resting through the middle of the day while snow and ice, thawed by the hot sun, avalanched everywhere about him. He camped one night near the gap, then swung back over the known way to the narrow corridor that led through to the hidden lake. He made his way through to the break-off, where he could look down and see the little lake again. The snow was deep and wet and rotten under him, but he worked forward on it, trying to look down at the small broken ledge that made the platform for the jump to the start of the ledge trail. Somewhere just in front of him, almost under his feet, he heard a creak, then the sighing plunge of a great mass of snow down the face of the mountain. He threw himself sharply backwards into the corridor and did not try again.

Back at the beach cabin, Colin worked steadily on his traps and snowshoes and other gear for nearly two weeks. It was satisfying to feel the old, used things, rusted and rotten with disuse, come back to life under his hands. It was satisfying to know that the musty smell had gone from the cabin as the breezes from the lake poured through the long-closed doors and windows again, to feel the dampness draw out of the log walls, to see the arrest of decay and hear its creeping silence end. He thought again of Mildred, of her love of the mountains, of her deep pleasure in the short trips they had made during recent week ends. She could come here, he thought, she would be happy here. But only for a little while. It's no life for a woman. And if it's no life for a woman it can't be life for a man. Once the strike is over it will be easier and simpler outside. A man will be able to live his life there quietly and sensibly, work at his job, save money, find a farm somewhere. That doesn't seem so very much to ask.

When there was nothing more to be done at the beach cabin, he went up the valley again. But this time, instead of following Amabilis Creek up to the lake and on to the Gully, he swung aside to follow the little tributary stream that drained the hidden lake. It was bad country, a narrow little valley, steep-walled so that the sun scarcely found a way into it, damp and moss-grown. It had held good timber once, but a freak wind had swept it, piling wind-fall fifteen and twenty feet high; on the slopes the second-growth conifers were so thick that it was difficult to force a way between them; near the creek salmonberry and devils' club, alder and salal strove together in fantastic competition. Colin knew all this and was glad of it. For a while he worked along the creek, ducking and weaving and twisting a way through the brush. Then the valley drew in to a narrow, high-walled canyon and he climbed through windfall and second-growth almost to the ridge. He was on wet, moss-covered rock now, bare of brush and sparsely timbered. Occasionally he had to climb steep places, but he made good time and in a little while he was looking up at the first fall that drained the hidden lake. It was a handsome fall, wide and sharply white against the gleaming black rock on either side, dwarfed by the height of the sheer, bare walls that climbed straight above it for two or three hundred feet.

The place was very familiar to Colin. He had been to it only twice before, but he had thought of it a hundred times. Waiting for sleep or hewing bridge timbers, waiting for casualties, lying in hospital, through deadened miles of marching, he had forced it into his mind and held it there, searching always for some weak-ness, some easy way up. He saw now that he had remembered it well. The way was there, for fifty or sixty feet through the single flaw in the smooth face. Twice he had climbed that, to be stopped without further foothold or handhold ten feet below and twenty feet over from a flat lip that overhung the curve of the falls. From below it still seemed impossible. But from above it would be almost simple. A man could drive a stake into the rock, then work down and across from it on a rope, driving more stakes until he reached the head of the flaw. Once the stakes were driven and the rope fixed the way would be there, a way that would be open in any weather and at any season.

3 3

FOR more than a week after Colin came out from the lake the strike still dragged on. The men were restless in it, weary of the quibbling, technical nature of negotiations they no longer attempted to understand. When the settlement came they accepted it gladly and went gladly back to work; they had a good wage increase and better hours. These things were clear and concrete.

Colin slipped back into the painless routine almost without effort. He found it easy to sit near Earl Mayhew and John Meldrum through the long rides out to work, silently for the most part, shutting his mind in thought. It was a cool but pleasant summer, with rain somewhere in almost every week, and they were building a trestle across a long, swampy hollow in standing timber. He was using the broad-axe again now and his shoulder was strong enough to drive it steadily through the longest day without tiring.

He realized only slowly that the outcome of the strike had done little to ease the tension and anxiety among the men he worked with, and still more slowly that he himself was a part of the conflict. It was not by chance that he sat with Earl Mayhew and John Meldrum on the way to work. Halsborg and Davidson and several others of the more active union men rode the same crummy and there was a silent hostility between the two groups.

Earl Mayhew explained it when Colin asked him. "We wouldn't string along with some of the stuff we thought they were pulling," he said. "So they make it tough for us to have any say at all now."

"You mean it will go on then?"

"Sure it will. Until the rest of the boys see what the score is and throw them out. The way things are going now that's liable to be a long time. Most of them don't care who's doing the leading so long as nobody bothers them. And the ones that do care are scared to say much."

"What is there to be scared of?" Colin asked. But he remembered Halsborg's big voice challenging him about Clyde, remembered Kreutzer and Davidson during the strike.

Earl shrugged his shoulders. "Mostly the boys are scared of being made to look foolish. At a meeting especially—that's why they stay away. But there's more than that. Those guys can make it pretty uncomfortable out on the job for anybody who doesn't think their way."

"What do they want?" Colin said. "What's the matter with them?"

"Politics," Earl said shortly. "They like the little piece of power they've got now and they think they'll have a whole lot more when the big day comes."

"Mike Varchuk's a commie. Always has been. But he's not in there with them."

"Oh, Mike's pretty close. They're a little too crude, even for him, but he plays along with them."

"Mike's not looking for power," Colin said.

"No, Mike's sincere. Some of them are. Mark Swetzer gave away his share in a power-saw when someone told him he was owning the means of production. You've got to respect a man like that."

Colin nodded. "Mike'd do that, too," he said. He felt the old sense of helplessness and discouragement that had come to him so often. "But what's the use of it?" he asked Earl. "Where's it going to end?"

"It'll end the same way as it's ended before," Earl said. "In a split union. Then we'll have it all to do over."

After he had talked with Earl, Colin tried to settle back into the routine of the working days; but the thing seemed everywhere about him, threatening and insistent. It rode with John Halsborg and Joe Davidson in the crummy, rode again when they boarded the train to go out into the woods. It was in the beer parlors over the week ends, in the stores and restaurants and he knew that men took it with them into their homes. The men on the bridge-crew all belonged to the union and talked of what was happening almost daily, jokingly yet bitterly, during the lunch hours. Colin listened to them. They were easier, less afraid than most of the men he knew, less afraid than Earl Mayhew and far less intense, less afraid than Halsborg and Davidson and the other men who blustered, less afraid than the simple men who clustered near Halsborg and listened to him so often in strained silence. But it seemed to Colin that even these men, the quiet, warm men he had known so long, like Sam Boulder and John Meldrum and old John Smith were touched by fear, that fear and anxiety spoke through the bitterness of their jokes. He listened and he heard the stuff of violence all about him, fear, bitterness, hate and violence. A violence darker and more fearful, because it was between men who had the same lives, the same needs, the same dangers to face.

In the end he met the violence and made his answer to it. It was early in September, a few days after school had opened up and Mildred had come back from her summer holidays. Colin had been to see her at the cottage and had arranged to meet her on Sunday to go up to Strathmore Falls. As he walked back towards Clyde's house he met Earl Mayhew and Sam Boulder and John Meldrum and went with them into one of Blenkinstown's three beer parlors. Some men they knew were at a table near the door and they sat down with them.

It was a Friday evening and the place was crowded and noisy. John Meldrum said to Colin: "Don't see you in here very often."

"You can't blame him for that," Sam Boulder said. "These beer joints don't look much when you're used to English pubs."

"There's a difference, all right," Colin said.

"You're darn right there is," Sam said. "They let you act like a human being over there. Walk around if you want or play a game of darts or have a bite to eat. Here all you can do is sit and stare at a table full of beer glasses."

"They've been at it longer than we have," Colin said and for a while they all went over the old arguments about the province's liquor laws.

John Meldrum said suddenly: "Look over there, would you?" He jerked his thumb towards a table across the room. Colin followed the movement and saw Halsborg and Kreutzer sitting at a table with several other men. Halsborg was talking excitedly.

"The goon squad at work," Meldrum said.

Earl Mayhew sat around and picked up his beer glass. "Be fair, Johnny," he said. "Somebody's got to work up membership."

"That kind of a way?" Meldrum asked. "Ganging up on some poor dumb son of a bitch, calling him names, scaring the hell out of him? What kind of a union are you going to get that way?"

Colin looked at Halsborg's table again and saw that one of the men was sitting in sullen silence with his chair pushed back a little. Colin recognized him as a new man on the steel gang, a tense, dark man, part Negro. His hands were moving nervously at the edge of the table and his eyes watched Halsborg defensively.

Earl was answering Meldrum: "It'll work out, Johnny. They won't stand that forever. You can't bulldoze men in a free country and not have them turn around and throw you out sooner or later."

"Who is Halsborg, anyway?" Colin asked.

"There's lots like him," Earl said. "Started working in the woods during the war, to keep away from the draft. Found he was making big money with a power-saw, so he stayed with it." He glanced towards Halsborg's table again. Two men had moved away, but the steel-man was talking excitedly and angrily. "He wasn't a bad sort of guy until he got to be vice-president of the local a while back. Then they went to work on him. Now he's straight political. Thinks they'll make him a commissar or something when the revolution comes."

"He's big enough," Sam said. "Looks right for the strong-arm stuff."

John Meldrum snorted. "Beats his wife around some. That's as far as it goes. I seen him back down from a guy half his size in here one night."

Earl laughed. "He was alone that time. With the rest of the goons he can be quite a guy. Kick anybody's teeth in if somebody knocks the poor bastard down first."

About half an hour later Colin left them. He went out by the side door, into a narrow passageway that led to the street. Halsborg, Kreutzer and another man were in the passage. Halsborg had his hands at his sides, but he was pushing forward against the third man, forcing him against the wall. Colin heard him say: "Better think it over. Might be good for your health." Then he heard Colin and turned towards him. Colin walked on, came up to him, tried to get past. Halsborg blocked his way. Colin lowered his right shoulder a little, then drove it against Halsborg's chest. Halsborg staggered and crashed back against the wall. Behind him Colin heard Kreutzer say: "What was that for?" But he walked on out of the passageway without turning to look back.

On the street he stood for a moment under the bright lights in front of the beer parlor. Cars were moving and people were passing. His body was shaking and his heart was beating fast; his mind was dulled by a helpless anger that he hated. He knew that someone was standing beside him, not Halsborg because this was a small man. Then he heard Mike Varchuk's voice.

"They are fools," Varchuk said. "They cannot force the workers. They have not the strength. Later there will be no need."

Colin looked down at him. "Are you in this, too?"

"All men are in it, all men everywhere."

Colin felt the anger slowing in him a little and he wanted to laugh. "Bull," he said. "Men don't want all that stuff you guys preach. They want a chance to live and do things, build houses, sleep with wives, raise kids. They don't want to be afraid all the time and hate each other and beat each other up. Why can't you leave us alone?"

Mike smiled gently. "You will understand it better one day," he said.

"Like hell I will," Colin said.

COLIN watched the swing of Mildred's skirt as she went ahead of him down the long flight of steps towards the falls and thought he had never seen her so happy. The day was brilliant with sun that had the full warmth of summer, and the light westerly breeze was warm about them.

At the foot of the steps she stopped to lean against the railing and look up at the wide thin veil of water that poured over the slanting rock. Then, as Colin came up to her, she turned and faced him.

"I came here often while you were away," she said.

"You did? Why?"

She looked up at the long graceful flow of the steps behind him, weathered now and blending smoothly into the timbered hillside. "Because I knew you had worked here. And I could tell which work was yours."

He moved beside her and looked back at the steps. "We had fun building those," he said. "But it all broke up later on."

She nodded. "I remember." Then she said: "What is it that's broken up this time, Colin?"

He glanced at her quickly. "Nothing. Why?"

"Yes it has. You're going away again."

"Who told you?"

"No one. I just know. I know you so well, darling. You forget how well I know you."

"No I don't. It's the only thing I have—that and the valley. I'm going back there again." He knew suddenly that everything was changed for them, that the barrier was drawn away.

"What about that farm?" she asked.

He noticed that she was smiling, not concerned or angry as he had thought she might be. "I've got to think about it," he said. "Down here I haven't got any place looking for it. Up there there's time to think. I might think of something that would work for me."

They had begun walking along the wide foot-trail that led on past the falls. There was no one else in the Park in spite of the fine Sunday, and Colin was suddenly glad that the river was low and quiet in the summer heat.

"I'm not running away," he said. "That's my place up there, the only place I fit. A farm could be all right too, I guess. But it's not so easy to find one as I thought it would be."

"I've never been able to think of you as a farmer," she said seriously. "I've tried, but it doesn't work."

"A bush farm. Like the Underhills had."

"Perhaps," she said doubtfully. "Something would have to change in you first. I'm not sure I want it to change any more."

They had turned on to a side trail which led them up along a little creek that tumbled down the side-hill in an endless succession of tiny falls. They came to a bridge across the creek and she stopped again and asked him: "You built this too, didn't you?"

"Yes," he said. "It's outside the Park here, but I wanted to and they let me."

Beyond the bridge they left the trail and climbed through two or three hundred feet over the gray rock that bordered the creek. The climb brought them to a wide flat bench in which the creek was a deep narrow pool.

"I didn't know about this," she said. "It's beautiful."

"There are a hundred places like this in the mountains." Colin heard his voice suddenly harsh against the softness of hers. "I could take you to them if you'd come."

She turned away from the creek, towards him. "I'm going to come," she said. "That's why I'm so happy today. Couldn't you tell?"

He stood looking at her in unbelief, then she moved a little and he took her in his arms.

"When?" he asked. "How soon can you come?"

The smile went away from her eyes and he saw the beginnings of fear there, and pleading. "It's harder than you think, darling. It won't be right away. Can you wait a little?"

He laughed then and kissed her, kissed the serious mouth and the unsmiling eyes and felt her part of him as she had not been for years.

287

"Wait?" he said. "We should have learned by now to wait for each other."

She drew away from him at last, very gently, then led him over to the shade of the timber. She lay down on the soft, sloping ground under the trees and he saw that fear had gone away from her.

"It's not even ready for you up there," he said. "But I wish you could come right away. Just to see what it's like. You could, couldn't you?"

"Not and go on teaching school in Blenkinstown, darling. They're not sure about me now, but they'd be quite sure then. And it's worse than it ever was, with the camp there."

He knelt beside her and she put out her hands and he took them. "I know all that. I've thought about it often. You could come in the other way, by Menzies Lake, and I could meet you in there."

She shook her head. "Let me have a year, darling," she said. "One whole last year to finish it all out cleanly. I know it's awful to ask that, but I've planned it and arranged it and now it's the only way that seems right. You see, I hadn't meant to tell you so soon."

"Why does it have to be so long?"

She drew her hands away from his and lay back on the mossy bank. "Because I'm a schoolteacher, I suppose, with a little fussy mind that has to do everything a certain way." She looked up at him. "But we do have to think this time, darling. So far we've always let things happen and they haven't happened very well for us."

"I know," he said. "I'm the one that should be thinking and I haven't let myself. I should find the farm and have it ready for you before I ask you to come at all."

"No," she said. "We can find the farm together, later, if we want to. I'll come to you in the mountains, in the fall. You said that once—remember? Fall will come, you said."

Colin watched the brightness of the sunlight on her neck for a moment, then bent forward and kissed it. She raised her head and he kissed her mouth again, then held her away a little and she read the question in his eyes.

"Of course," she said. "My love." She moved towards him, hard against him, and she said: "Oh, darling Colin, why do I always wait until you are going away? Why can't I be generous, the way other women are when they love someone?"

"You are," he said. "You're the only generous person in the world."

She laughed, a little, deep-throated, satisfied laugh. "That isn't true," she said. She buried her face in his chest and he felt her strong body quiver against him. "You're the generous one, to let me come my own silly way. You've always been the one that gave and waited. That's why I love you so." She raised her face to his and he saw that the happiness was still in it, brilliant yet without strife, deeply calm yet with all the intensity of ultimate decision. "Love me, darling, please," she said.

Colin held her to him and felt the world draw away. Into the depths, his mind said, into the dark, enfolding depths. It is such a little way, yet one can go down and down into them forever. Even death is not so deep.

3 4

COLIN came down Amabilis Valley to his cabin at the lake through the storm of an early November day. It was a savage storm, violent with a gale of wind that broke limbs from trees and drove scattering sheets of ice-cold rain and snow through the protection of the timber. Long before he reached the cabin his thick woolen clothing was heavy with rain and his body was touched by a more exhausting cold than any he had known from snow and ice and the freezing winds of the high hills. He remembered this cold, this draining of all warmth, from low-altitude storms of other years. It made him think of death, a comfortless, strength-sapped, lonely death, unlike the swift mercy of a bullet or the peace of dry snow in the high places. The word "perish" was in this death, the word "exposure," the word "exhaustion." He felt his body powerful and resistant to them all, guarding its heat against the persistent, intense attack, secure in its reserve of strength. But he was glad when he came to the cabin and went into its close shelter.

Inside, his movements were habit. A twist of his shoulders freed the sodden packsack and dropped it to the floor; he set the rifle in its corner, took three steps from there and began to lay the fire in the stove—shavings, pitchwood, kindling; he lit the shavings and, with the same match, his first lamp. Then he was free to strip off his wet clothes.

The familiarity of the routine made it swift and automatic, almost unfelt. Yet this, like everything else in his valley, had new meaning for him now; over everything and through everything was the thought that she would come, not tomorrow, not even soon, but soon enough and surely. So surely that often in the hills he felt her with him already; so surely that thought must recognize the changes her coming would make in even this simple, changeless routine of return.

Through the evening, as the storm lessened, she was with him. She read beside him in the lamplight, stood beside him outside the door as he watched the few stars in the clearing sky and heard the dying wind still strong in the treetops, the dying swell still heavy on the beach, and she was beside him again as he slept.

He was up early the next morning, to a gray and windless day of gentle rain. As he cooked breakfast he decided to go down the lake to see Robbie; there would have been little movement of game during the hours of storm and it might be some while before he had another chance to go down on a calm lake.

He had cleaned up the cabin and was almost ready to start out when he heard the distant sound of the motor. Both Robbie and Johnny had outboards for their canoes now and he thought at first it might be one or other of them; but he saw as soon as he looked down the lake that it was a boat, not a canoe, that was coming. He turned sharply from the window and for a moment he felt something like panic. He glanced quickly at his mackinaw and empty packsack, gauging the time it would take him to get together the stuff he needed and start up the valley. Then he realized, with a sharp sense of astonishment, what he was doing. He said aloud, "What's the matter with me? Can't some guy come up the lake without me hitting for the bush?"

He went to the door, opened it and stood watching the boat. It was close enough now for him to see that there was only one man in it. From the logging outfit, likely, he thought; chances are he's going on to the head of the lake, won't even stop in here. But as he watched, the bow of the boat swung a little and he saw that it was heading directly for the cabin.

He stood in the doorway without moving while the little boat ran in to the beach and the man stepped out. He still did not move but watched while the man walked up towards the cabin— a big man, heavily built, with a round, cheerful face.

"Mr. Ensley?" the man asked as he came to the foot of the steps.

"That's right," Colin said and watched his eyes.

The man held out his hand. "Arnold's my name," he said. "Jeff Arnold. Mind if I come in for a few minutes?"

Colin took the offered hand and led the way into the cabin. He pushed a chair forward for Arnold, then looked into the kettle on the stove.

"I'll make coffee soon as she boils," he said.

"Thanks," Arnold said. He looked appraisingly around the cabin. "Pretty nice place you have here. Build it yourself?"

"Sure," Colin said.

Arnold nodded approvingly. "You certainly know how to go about it. Well, we won't disturb you much."

Colin turned sharply towards him. He knew this was what he had been afraid of. "You won't what?" he asked.

"We'll try not to bother you any more than we have to. When we start logging."

"You mean you're going to log the valley?"

"Sure," Arnold said. "It's a great stand of balsam and the price'll never be better. An easy truck show, too. We ought to be able to move the fallers in right after the new year unless there's a lot of snow."

Colin listened to the easy, casual words and felt anger and

291

despair grow in him until he could hardly speak. He said at last: "It's my valley. You can't log it."

Arnold laughed sympathetically. "I know how you feel. But you don't have to worry. We'll see your cabin doesn't get hurt. We'll take care of you—give you a job if you like. We could use you fine."

Colin watched him through narrowed, dangerous eyes. "*You'll* take care of me," he said. "*You'll* give me a job. Didn't you ever stop to think maybe there's people in the world don't want to be taken care of? People that don't want anything more than to be left alone?"

Arnold shrugged his big shoulders. He had dealt with difficult people before and had no intention of losing his temper. "We're just trying to make it as easy as we can for you. The timber's got to be logged."

"Why?"

"Because the market's right," Arnold said patiently. "Because the owners figure . . ."

"Owners!" Colin put a violence into the word that made Arnold stand up and face him. "What did they ever do to own it? They never even saw it. How can anybody own something he never saw?"

"Look," Arnold said. "I just work for them. Don't take it out on me. We're trying to make things as easy as we can for you. Hell, we'll be all through inside a couple of years." He turned and walked to the door. At the door he stopped and turned back: "Look," he said again, "trouble's the last thing we want. But don't ever think we can't handle it. We've run into your kind before."

"Get out," Colin said. He watched Arnold start down the beach, then suddenly crossed the cabin and picked up his rifle. He worked the lever swiftly, flicked the butt to his shoulder and held it with the sights lined steadily on the back of Arnold's neck. Then anger left him and he felt only helplessness. He lowered the rifle, walked to the bunk and threw it down on the blankets. He sat down on the edge of the bunk and a great weight pressing through his whole body made him rest his forearms on his knees and lower his head to his hands. He began to tremble uncontrollably. "The bastards," he said. "The bastards."

DURING the week after Arnold had come to the beach cabin Colin moved nearly everything he owned up to the cabin in the Gully. He worked intently and secretly. Several times he saw boats coming up the lake and always moved away before he could be seen. Once he watched from the bush while Arnold and another man came up to the cabin, knocked, opened the door and looked in, then went away. He knew a small tent camp had been pitched in the bay just over on the other side of the creek and that men were working on a line up the valley.

He took up the traps from the lower part of his lines and ran them out again within easier reach of the Gully. Once that was done he felt calmer, but he was not satisfied. He waited for a spell of fine, cold weather, then loaded a heavy pack and made the climb to Windstorm Gap. He had brought with him a small tent, which he pitched carefully in a level, sheltered place near the Gap. Then he went on over the divide into the Milk River valley, traveling steadily and swiftly until he was down to the timber line again. Just below timber he built a rough shelter and camped for the night.

During the next three days he prospected the valley for signs of fur and built another shelter within two or three miles of Menzies Lake. Then he climbed to the Gap again, spent a night in his tent and dropped down next day to the cabin in the Gully.

The intense, straining activity of these days occupied him fully and even gave him an exultant happiness. But as he traveled his trap-lines near Amabilis Lake and in the lower parts of the valley, anger and desperation returned to him. He traveled through to the beach and saw that a good-sized campsite was being cleared near the mouth of the creek. He followed the newly staked survey lines, trying to judge the scope and scale of the logging operation from them. Sometimes he spent hours watching the survey crew at work, himself unseen on a slope above them, behind a log or a root or a tree. At first he had played with his rifle, sighting it on the men as they worked, fingering the trigger. It seemed as though it should be within the power of a bullet to stop them at this early stage of things. A bullet fired high, to scare them out; perhaps several bullets, fired at unpredictable intervals over days of time, cutting into the ground near them or smashing in the transit as they worked, passing close overhead as they walked to and from work, crashing into the ridge-pole of a tent as they slept. But he knew in his heart that this would not turn them away. Perhaps a single shot, fired to wound or kill. But he could not find the strength of anger in himself, nor the cold desperation, to fire such a shot. These were not the men. And all too soon, watching them, he got to know them: Jake, the axeman and Slim, the head chainman, bold, cheerful men and close friends; quiet, frail, gray-haired Sandy, who ran the transit; Sam Carey, the plump and perpetually exasperated little man who always managed to fall over the least obstruction—log or root or brush or rock. Once they became individual men to him, Colin found himself watching them with tolerance, even with amusement. He left them and went back to his traps.

During the next spell of good weather he crossed Windstorm Gap again and ran out two short lines of traps from his shelter in the other valley. By the time he got back to the Gully again it was within a day or two of Christmas. He decided to go down and see Robbie and Johnny.

He found Johnny at his cabin and went on with him to Robbie's. Robbie welcomed them, as always, with a cheerful friendship that was almost fatherly. He poured them rum and made hot coffee and they began to talk. Robbie asked almost at once about the camp at Amabilis Creek.

"What are they doing up there? There's a pile of stuff gone up in the last month—everything from wash tubs to bulldozers."

"They're going to log," Colin said. "You know that."

Robbie nodded. "Arnold stopped by. Said you was kind of hard to do business with."

"That's too bloody bad," Colin said. "So will you be when they start to log your valley."

"I hope I don't live to see it," Robbie said. "But it's no use to fight it. A man may as well play along with them."

"It's hard to take," Johnny said. "I guess I'll feel about the same as Colin if they come to Carlson's Creek."

"Seems like there's no place left where a man can keep to himself and act like a man," Colin said. "Me least of all. Why in hell's name would they have to pick on Amabilis Valley first out of this whole goddamned lake?"

"Pulp," Robbie told him. "It's all pulp now. You and Grant helped them pick on that valley, first time you was ever in here."

The next day was Christmas and they made a big meal off two geese Johnny had killed, and drank a lot of rum. Afterwards Robbie went to sleep on his bunk. Johnny and Colin talked quietly with the rum bottle on the table between them.

"It's sure as hell good to have you back here," Johnny said. "I thought for a while you might be going to stay outside."

"No need of that," Colin said. "The way the outside is moving in with us."

"It won't be so bad as it seems now. They won't get up as high as your best marten country and Robbie says they'll likely be through in a couple of years."

Colin looked over at Robbie on the bunk and saw that he was sleeping soundly. "Look, Johnny," he said. "I wouldn't want Robbie to know this, but I'm moving over the divide. Into Milk River. I've got traps out there already and next spring I'm going to build me a cabin."

"Jesus," Johnny said. "You can't do that. That's park country. The whole goddamned works is game reserve."

"I'm doing it. They'll never know the difference so long as I go in from this side."

Johnny got up from the table, walked over to the window and stood looking out at the lake. "They'll catch up with you sooner or later," he said slowly. "Bound to. If the mountains don't make it first. You can't travel that Gap all the time and get by with it."

Colin laughed. "Look, Johnny. Remember the time we found you up the valley? You weren't suffering any, were you? There wasn't a damn thing hurt you till we began to bring you out of it."

"That's right. But I'm sure as hell glad you did bring me out."

"That's the difference," Colin said. "I don't believe I'd give a damn. That's why I won't ever die in the mountains."

Johnny came back to the table and poured himself another drink. "I still can't see it," he said. "Taking all those chances just because there's a few loggers come into the valley."

"I was figuring to work over that way before I knew they were coming."

"There's no more fur over there than there is on this side. Your line's been rested for years."

• "I know," Colin said. "It wasn't fur I was thinking of. I like that country. If it's park country they've got to leave it alone, the way it is, haven't they? They can't log in there or bitch it up any way."

"I guess not," Johnny said slowly. "But I still don't get it. If you want some place that's not disturbed you've still got the Gully and the mountains."

"You can't make a living up there, or find meat after the first big snow." He suddenly leaned forward across the table. "Can't you see, Johnny? A man's got to do something sooner or later. He can't let himself be pushed around and pushed around forever. Every place I've been so far, all my life, I've let them run me out. Now I've let them run me out of the valley. I hadn't even got the guts to stop and fight for that."

Johnny shook his head slowly. "It don't sound like you talking at all. You couldn't stop them any more than you could stop a rock-slide. It's their timber."

Colin reached for the bottle and poured himself another drink. "Don't pay any attention to me," he said. "I guess I'm tight." He looked across at Robbie and saw that the old man was still asleep. "You know, Johnny, sometimes I think I'm going crazy. Maybe I've always been crazy and that's the whole trouble."

Johnny laughed. "You've had enough sense to put me straight a few times," he said. "Seems to me I remember you were always pretty bright in school."

"You don't have to be dumb to go crazy," Colin said. "All you have to do is think hard enough about something that matters a hell of a lot to you. The harder you think, the worse it gets until you feel like you're backed into a corner and everybody's throwing things at you. You've got to either fight or get out some way. If you fight, you're crazy, like the rest of them. If you run away, you're yellow."

"That sort of a set-up only lasts for a spell. Sooner or later things work out right and you get a break."

Colin thought of Mildred. "I know," he said. "That's one reason I've got to work down in towards Menzies Lake."

"What's that got to do with it?"

"I'll tell you sometime," Colin said.

Robbie stirred on the bunk, opened his eyes and sat up. Johnny glanced anxiously at Colin, started to say something and checked himself. "Hell," Robbie said. "It's a good job I came to while there's still something in the bottle."

3 5

THROUGH the early spring months, whenever the wind drew up the valley, Colin could hear the sounds of the logging operation. The high walls of the valley seemed to echo and emphasize the irritating, intermittent rattle of the power-saws and he grew to hate them. The other sounds were familiar—the heavy roar of the donkey engine down at the beach, the rattle of the caterpillars on the slopes, the occasional rending crash of a great tree falling; but the power-saws were new and their nagging persistence strained at him in constant reminder that change and violence could reach back even into the hills.

About a week after the end of the season, when he had taken up his traps and stored them away, he tried to work through Windstorm Gap and go down the other valley. But it was an early season after a winter of heavy snowfall, and the tons of snow and ice that broke away from Amabilis Mountain during every hour of the day made the Gap impassable. He went back to the cabin in the Gully, made up a new pack and started out before daylight the next morning for the pass to the hidden lake. The slopes below the pass were dangerous with thaw and slides, but the danger fitted his mood and he traveled recklessly, finding pleasure in the thunder of avalanching snow and ice. He found his mind and body working smoothly together to calculate risk and evade death; often he crossed slopes while the glinting flecks of snow particles from the last slide still hung over them, knowing that another slide might follow at any time; once a great mass of snow broke away under him and he saved himself only by falling forward and driving the butt of his rifle deeply into a bank of snow that held; once he found himself trapped while fragments and boulders of ice rolled and bounced past on both sides of him, but he moved on amongst them and was not touched. He felt triumph in his safety and a restoration of his old faith in the hills that the sound of the power-saws had almost destroyed.

He had expected to find an overhang of snow where the corridor opened to the platform ledge and had made up his mind to try to break it away. But he found it had already fallen and he dropped to the platform and made the jump to the start of the ledge trail without serious difficulty. The trail itself was dangerous, but he traveled it late in the evening, when the air had begun to cool, and came safely through to the open water of the lake.

For a few days he was happy in the hidden valley. He built a rough shelter and hewed out the foundation logs for a cabin. No sound reached him from outside the valley. At nights he lay in his blankets, listening to the quiet murmur of falls not yet fully freed from ice, finding silence in the stars that filled the circle of dark sky overhead and outlined the peaks. Through the warm days the mountains shed snow and ice in an almost continuous roar of sound that held no jarring note for him. But he felt restlessness grow on him again and traveled to the foot of the lake, then climbed the lip above the falls to check the difficult route he had examined from below. The sounds of the logging reached him again there and he turned back from them. The valley seemed suddenly narrow and confining. Moisture was everywhere in it, pressing in on him from the wet and heavy snow piled on the lower slopes of the mountains, rising from the still surface of the lake, hanging in the motionless limbs of the trees. A man could live here, he thought, but it would press him down and destroy him in the end; not in summer or fall, perhaps, but in the hard winter silence and through the heaviness of spring. She could not come here and if she could come it is not a place for her. She is not here now, these are not her mountains, this is not her place. A man could live here but he would be a dying man, old and dying, without hope.

Colin stayed in the valley for almost a week longer, but made no further effort to test the way out by the falls and made little progress on the cabin. He built a raft and fished for trout and explored the lake more thoroughly than he ever had before. But the weather became cold and stormy and clouds blotted out the peaks and new snow fell. He broke his camp on a morning of storm and climbed the ledge trail gladly, into the snow and clouds of the pass.

He had intended to start out at once to attempt Windstorm Gap again, but the weather was still bad and his restlessness took him instead down the valley, towards the logging. He found that the road had been pushed right through to Amabilis Lake and split there to pass on either side, clear around the lake. No one was working there so he went down and walked along it for a mile or more to feel the strangeness of the clear and easy way through the country he knew. In the end it oppressed him and he turned back into the timber, following high along the east side of the valley until he was directly above where the fallers were working. From there he dropped down the hillside and moved unseen until he was within a few feet of two men who were working with a power-saw. He watched them drop a tree and slipped away, still unseen, to watch a caterpillar yarding out logs to the road.

The next day he traveled the other side of the valley clear down to the lake. They had left his cabin unharmed and there were a few wind-stunted trees still standing near the edge of the lake. The rest, the whole floor of the valley on both sides of the creek, was a tangle of limbs and stumps and broken tops and shattered saplings. The brutal destruction of logging was a familiar thing to Colin; he had grown up with it and long ago accepted it as a part of the life that men lived. But seeing it here, in the closely familiar place that had seemed unchanging, he felt rage pour like a red flood through his body and burst into his mind. He felt choked with it and half-blinded by it and his right hand gripped the stock of his rifle until the blood was held back from his fingers and they grew numb. "The bastards," he said. "They didn't have to do it like that."

He traveled swiftly back up the valley and angry thoughts surged like fire in his brain. He thought of how close he had been to the power-saw men and thought again how easy it would be to kill —to kill and slip away to the hills, then come down and kill again and again until they took the warning and went away. Better, he thought, a terror that did not kill. A crumbling of the mountains around the valley, a succession of rock- and snow-slides, always threatening, killing impersonally if at all, but making a certainty of danger that would turn them away.

He heard the power-saws on the opposite side of the valley and heard the deep-throated clatter of a diesel truck on the road and anger flared in him again. It held with him and drove his body until he was beyond Amabilis Lake, climbing through the scattered, slide-broken timber of the entrance to the Gully. Then the rhythm of climbing calmed him and he recognized the wildness of his thoughts. They were only men down there in the valley, tiny against the valley in spite of the noise and power of their machines. Men like Earl Mayhew and Sam Boulder, like John Halsborg and Ray Kreutzer; ordinary men who would pass on to work elsewhere and leave the valley to grow back to itself again. Anger against them could mean nothing and achieve nothing. The old sense of helplessness and failure came back on him until his body felt weighted under it and his step slowed.

He was coming into the meadow now. There were still great islands and peninsulas of snow on it, but he could walk near the stream without touching snow. The windows of his cabin shone clear pale gold in the westerly sun and he felt hope again. There is this, he thought; she can come here and see this. And there is the other valley, where she said she would come and from where she can come to this.

The next morning he loaded a heavy pack and started on the trip through Windstorm Gap to Milk River.

COLIN built the cabin in the Milk valley during the summer months. He had chosen a place about two miles up from Menzies Lake and five or six hundred feet above the level of the river, where a strong creek from the mountainside fed a small lake. There was good timber all around the lake, most of it small but clear and clean, with a few great cedars in the swampy places. Colin placed his cabin at the head of the lake, a few hundred feet along the lakeshore from the creek, just above a wide beach of gray gravel. Looking down the lake, a great snow mountain across the main valley was framed between the sloping walls of the draw. Behind the cabin the timber ended abruptly and the mountainside climbed steeply and roughly to the broad, sloping ledges that led to Windstorm Gap.

Colin built slowly and carefully, yet with a sense of purpose and urgency. Mildred was closely with him in everything he did now. He built for her as deliberately as he had avoided building his other cabins for her. Now he thought only of what would please her, of how to make her like the place, of how best to show the valley to her.

Very often, in spite of the urgency he felt, he left the work for days at a time to climb through the valley and learn it for her as closely as he knew Amabilis Valley. It became necessary now to find the safe and easy ways, yet still to reach the high places. Because of this it began to seem more and more often that she was actually with him, climbing beside him, standing beside him to look out over the sweep of the valley and the lake below from some high place, stopping to exclaim over the loveliness of a creeping, blossom-covered plant or the tortured beauty of a wind-stunted fir. Occasionally, yet more and more frequently as time went on, he talked aloud as though she were with him and even heard her voice in answer. He would wake abruptly from such moods, check himself in something approaching irritation and turn always to some exacting physical endeavor. Yet they held an intensity of pleasure and a depth of peace beyond anything he had known, and he returned to them.

Throughout the summer he saw no one in the valley except a party of climbers who passed through to climb the big mountain on the far side. But he often watched the boats of campers and fishermen passing on Menzies Lake and he knew that they sometimes came in and camped near the mouth of Milk River; one party of fishermen stayed there for over a week and one of them went up the river each day, wading deliberately and carefully, and working his fly skilfully over the swift water. Colin watched him with interest that grew almost to unspoken friendship, but he remained unseen and unheard.

Several times Colin crossed Windstorm Gap to his cabin in the Gully and twice he went down Wind Lake to pick up mail and supplies. Robbie was away in the hills each time and had left notes to say where he would be; but Colin felt no inclination to find him and simply scribbled a few words to say he had picked up his stuff, then went on his way. Each time he crossed northward through the Gap and came to the new valley again he felt a sense of freedom and relief.

Fall came early that year, with heavy frosts in September and a quick intensity of color through the valley. Colin was happy. It seemed to him his senses had never been so keen, nor the run of blood through his body so strong, nor hope so clear in his mind. Snow had already fallen on the high rock slopes, but the first October days were very warm and on one of them he followed the creek behind the cabin up to the first bench. There was a pool here, round and deep and very clear and a ten-foot fall entered at the head of it. A little belt of trees had found foothold on the rocky bench and grown strongly enough to make shade for moss and vine-maple and other small deciduous growth. Colin had found the pool when he was still searching the valley for the best place to build his cabin and it had reminded him of the pool on the creek above Strathmore Falls, so he had returned there often.

It was a windless day and the sun had warmed the rocks. Beside the pool heat and sunlight seemed trapped by the trees and intensified by the clear air. Colin stripped off his clothes and slipped into the pool, as he had many times before. He swam to the falls, dove under them and let the turbulent water roll his body and force it back down the pool. He came out then and lay on the warm rocks while the sun drew the water's chill from his body. For a while he watched a pair of bald eagles riding the air currents above the valley; then, as they drifted out of sight, his eyes and mind seemed filled and satisfied by the heavy green of the treetops against the pale, distant blue of the cloudless sky. He knew that he would bring Mildred here and that she would recognize it as he had. She would see it first in winter, with the falls half-frozen and ice at the edge of the pool and it would be strange to her. Then she would come to it again in summer and would know it. She had written from California, calmly, confidently, happily. "I have been so stupid, darling, but I don't think I need be any more. I understand myself now and I think I understand everything that has happened to us. I shall come in November. It will be a good time to start, with storms in your mountains and ordinary people everywhere close in their homes."

It would have been better now, he thought, better still in early summer. Yet she's wise to come in winter, then all the rest will be still ahead. I need so much of her, more than I can ever have of her, to be always with her, to be lost in her, cooled by her, borne up by her. She is strength and I am weakness; yet I am not all weakness and with her the strength that I have can find itself.

He began to dress, slowly, watching the light through the trees on the horizontal branches of the vine maples and their scarlet foliage. He hated to leave the pool, but there was work still to be done on the cabin and it was almost time to think of the traps again. As he climbed down the broken slope below the pool he heard a blue jay scolding somewhere along the lake. It scolded again, more fiercely and close by as he came to the cabin and he wondered idly what would be traveling the woods to disturb it now. Then he saw the man.

The man came forward through the trees quite slowly, looking about him as though surprised by what he saw. His eyes met Colin's and he nodded, but looked away again at the cabin and seemed to shake his head. He came up and stood beside Colin, still looking at the cabin.

"Comfortable little place you have here," he said. "Real pretty location."

"It's O.K.," Colin said. What is it to you, he thought. Then he realized the man's clothes were vaguely like a uniform and that he had a rifle in his hands.

"Your name would be Ensley, I guess?" the man asked. Colin nodded. "Thought so," the man said. "I'm Ches Burdick. In charge of the Park here."

"You better come in and eat," Colin said. "I was just going to cook up a meal."

"Thanks," Burdick said. "I guess I'd better take a look around first."

He walked to the front of the cabin and stood with his back to the lake, his feet apart, hands deep in his pockets. For nearly a minute he studied the front of the cabin and seemed to approve. He passed on, around to the other side, and stopped at the lean-to shed that Colin used to store wood. Colin knew he must have seen the hindquarters of the deer and the traps hanging there, but he said nothing and continued on his circuit of the cabin. When they came back to the beach again he stood looking at the lake for a moment. Then he said: "Mind if I take a look inside?"

"Go ahead," Colin said. "I asked you to come in and eat."

Burdick looked at him. "I'm afraid I'm going to have to take you out," he said. "I wouldn't want to eat without you knowing that."

Colin nodded. "I know," he said. "It's O.K."

Starting the fire, moving about the stove as the meal cooked, Colin was amazed at the calmness of his body and the steadiness of his voice. It was over now, he knew that; she could never come in here now. He watched Burdick, a quiet, slow man, sitting at the table looking out at the lake. Burdick's rifle was out on the porch, leaning against the wall just beside the door. Burdick waited quietly, asking only occasional questions until Colin set a plate in front of him. As Colin sat down, Burdick said: "Seems too bad. You picked yourself a swell place."

"What'll they do?" Colin asked.

Burdick shrugged his shoulders. "I wouldn't know. Never had it happen before. You've got a trap-line some place on Wind Lake, haven't you?"

"That's right," Colin said.

"You're liable to lose out on that for a spell. They'll likely cancel your license."

They ate in silence after that and cleaned up in silence. Then Burdick said: "You better throw your stuff together. We've got quite a piece to go." He walked out of the cabin and down on to the beach and stood looking at the lake again. Colin watched him, then turned back into the cabin, picked up his own rifle and came silently to the door. Standing there, beside Burdick's rifle, he worked the lever and threw a shell into the breach.

Burdick turned swiftly to the sound and saw Colin with the steady rifle at his hip. He raised his hands a little, holding the palms towards Colin, but stood where he was. "Don't try it, son," he said quietly. "It won't do you any good."

"I'm not coming out," Colin said.

"They'll send a bunch in to fetch you out," Burdick said. "You may as well come along now and get it over with. We can forget about this part."

"I'm not coming out," Colin repeated. "You get started back for the lake before something happens."

Burdick shrugged his shoulders again. "You're the doctor," he said. "But that don't make you anything except crazy."

"Get going," Colin said. "I'll be right behind you all the way down there."

Burdick started to walk along the edge of the lake, his shoulders square, his hands thrust into his pockets again. After a few steps he stopped and looked back over his shoulder. "What about the rifle?"

"You'll find it," Colin said. "When you come back."

3 6

COLIN watched Burdick's boat until it was a tiny speck far down towards the foot of Menzies Lake, then traveled swiftly back to his cabin.

The afternoon sun was still bright on the surface of the little lake, the air was calm, the cabin stood as squarely set in the timber as it ever had, light and pleasant, its door wide open and Burdick's rifle standing where he had left it. Colin picked up the rifle, ejected the shells and threw them one by one into the lake. Then he took the rifle inside the cabin and set it carefully on the table.

For a moment he stood quite still, looking at the pleasant room, at the sunlight streaming in through windows and door, at the strong, closely-fitted furniture, the matched and patterned wood of walls and ceiling and cupboards. It didn't work out, he thought, after all. It never does. Perhaps it was wrong, the way everything else has been wrong, ever since the beginning.

He went out to the lean-to, took down the remains of the deer meat, cut away a few pieces, then took the rest down to his raft at the edge of the lake. He pushed the raft out until it was over deep water, then dropped the meat overboard. He came back, took all his traps from the lean-to into the cabin and began to make up a pack.

By late evening he was in Windstorm Gap. The still air was very cold and there were clouds high in the sky, far above the mountain tops, for the first time in many days. Colin slept the night in his tent near the Gap and started out again in the dim gray light of the next morning, against the first whisper of the storm.

He had meant to get down to the cabin in the Gully before noon, spend only an hour or two there, then start for Hidden Valley. The fierce drive of the storm and the fresh snow everywhere held him back and there was little daylight left when he came on to the flat white surface of the meadow from the last slope of rock. He approached the cabin cautiously, checking it from every side before he went up to it. But there was no one there. Inside, he lit a fire, stripped off his wet clothes and made the first meal he had eaten since the one with Burdick the day before. The effort of climbing from the little lake to the Gap, the still greater effort of forcing his way down against the storm, had used him physically and mentally and he had had little time to think of his position. He had made his decision while Burdick was examining the cabin and thus far he had followed it through. For the moment, because it was utterly unlikely that anyone would attempt to travel through the storm at night, he felt himself safe; and he began to think again.

Sitting here, in the familiar cabin, he tried to find again the triumph he had felt in disarming Burdick and turning him away. He could not find it. He remembered only the bitter, hopeless calm that had come upon him when he first understood Burdick's mission and realized that everything he had planned and worked towards was lost, taken from him by this quiet, impersonal man who spoke for some vague and distant authority. It had seemed wrong that this authority could reach out so far, to this place where no one came in year after year, to set a sudden blight upon it, to limit freedom, deny possession.

So he had turned Burdick away, disarmed his authority. He had done it calmly and defiantly, secure in the thought of the hills, in the certainty that he could travel beyond reach of the authority that supported Burdick. It had seemed triumph then, and as triumph and elation had carried his swift, efficient journey through the Gap and down to the cabin in the Gully. It must carry him further, into Hidden Valley, and on through the difficult things he would have to do to live there without being found. But it was triumph and elation no longer, only a great burden of loss and destruction. She could never come now, there could be no place for her to come to, no part for her in what had to be done. Defiance of Burdick had been a trivial, ineffective defiance because his authority was remote and impervious. Burdick himself had not resisted, he had been quiet and impersonal, not an enemy. Even when he was facing the rifle he had been without hostility. There was no triumph, only loss.

Colin sat on at the table in the little cabin long after his meal was finished. He was unconscious of time or the storm outside or his body's fatigue, he was little conscious of his hurt mind's long and tortuous search for understanding of all the things that had happened. Hours later he slept, still at the table, his head on his outstretched arms, the oil lamp burning quietly beside him. He still had not made the choice between Hidden Valley and the journey out by Menzies Lake to find Burdick and give himself up.

THREE days after Colin had turned him away, Burdick came back up the lake with a policeman named Delker. They landed at the mouth of Milk River and Delker stood for a moment looking uneasily at the timbered slope of hillside above them. Then he reached to his belt and opened the flap of his holster. "I don't like it a darn bit," he said. "He could be watching us from up there right now."

Burdick shook his head. "He's lit out for the high mountains. Good as told me he was going to. They say he knows them like the back of his hand." He bent down to tighten a boot lace, then straightened and switched the rifle he was carrying over into the bend of his left arm. "Come on. I want to get it over with."

They walked for a mile or more in silence, then Delker asked: "Do you figure the guy's nuts?"

Burdick shrugged his shoulders without turning. "Could be," he said. "I wouldn't know. Seemed a nice enough kid."

"He's Clyde Munro's brother-in-law. Nothing wrong with the sister, but they say Ensley's always been kind of queer."

"He wasn't too queer for the army. He was three or four years overseas."

"That was enough to turn some of them queer," Delker said. "I never did go for this chasing after crazy guys."

"Didn't look to me like he was the dangerous kind."

Delker laughed. "You didn't stop to argue any."

"Nobody's paying me to argue with a gun," Burdick said.

They came to the foot of the lake and Burdick pointed out the cabin.

"Seems a goddamned shame to burn it down," Delker said. "What's the idea?"

Burdick shrugged his shoulders. "Once you call a place a Park you've got to keep it that way."

"A neat little place like that don't hurt it any."

"The boss says he's got no right to build there in the first place. If you let one get by he says they'll all be doing it."

COLIN watched the two men come up to the cabin and go inside. He had been on his way down the valley when he first heard them, to go out and find Burdick. Hearing them, he had swung back along the ridges to come out on the broken slope behind the cabin. It was a gray day, heavy with unfallen snow and very cold. But he lay in close hiding among a mass of broken boulders and did not feel the cold. Burdick had come to him, Burdick or someone who would do as well. He wished now he had gone closer to them, to make sure that one was Burdick. They were both dressed in ordinary woods clothes, both slow-moving men. Only one carried a rifle.

Colin saw them come out of the cabin. The man with the rifle was carrying Burdick's rifle as well as his own and he walked across and leaned both rifles against a tree a little way from the cabin. The other had gone into the lean-to behind the cabin, but he came back at once with an armload of wood. Colin watched as they both worked for several minutes over something at the back of the cabin. One man straightened and stepped back. The other still knelt. Then, so suddenly that it was a jar of intense pain through his mind, he knew what they were doing. He felt the soft, comforting jolt of the rifle against his cheek, saw the kneeling man sway and fall forward over the fire he had laid. The second man whirled and stood motionless for a moment, looking towards the sound of the shot. Then he turned again and disappeared behind a tree. Colin waited and watched without moving, the rifle still at his shoulder, another shell ready in the breech. The man he had shot did not move. But he saw the second man crawl to the rifles and take one, then crawl back to the cabin and along the edge to where his friend was lying. He moved the body, evidently searching for some sign of life. He stood up at last, shook his fist towards the slope where Colin was lying, then turned and went away along the edge of the lake. Colin watched him out of sight and still did not move.

Much later, when it was almost dark, Colin stood up and climbed stiffly down the slope to the cabin. Only when he stood over the body and saw that it was Burdick did he realize fully that he had killed a man. He knelt beside him, touched the quiet face and the great wound where the bullet had broken out of his chest. "I'm sorry," he said and knew that he was crying. He lifted the body carefully, carried it into the cabin and laid it on the big bunk.

COLIN spent two nights and a day in the cabin with Burdick's dead body. Much of the time he prayed, searching his mind for

309

prayers, remembering his father's texts and his own earliest beliefs. For a long time he would not be fully convinced that Burdick was dead. It seemed to him that the calm eyes would open and the slow voice would speak again, carelessly and easily, discounting the bullet's awful wound. He remembered the shot, the slight pressure of his finger, the slight, familiar jar against his cheek, the tiny, distant body falling forward and lying still. Death seemed nowhere in any of this. But it was here now, in Burdick's stiffened body, in the silence of the cabin that should have been burned, in the stillness of the lake's surface under the storm-filled, waiting clouds.

He accepted it at last, knew that Burdick would not speak or move again. Accepting it, he was lonely; and the cabin, like Burdick, was dead to him. Early on the second morning he made up a small pack, took his rifle and his axe and went outside. For a little while he stood looking at the cabin and the lake, watching the first slow, small flakes of snow come down as though squeezed from the clouds. Then he walked forward and knelt beside the wood and kindling Burdick had piled against the cabin. He lit a match and watched the cedar shavings sputter and catch in its flame. Then pitch caught somewhere, then larger pieces of kindling, then the wood. Flame reached out under the cabin. Colin took his axe and chopped with sure and powerful strokes at the lowest log until the flames could reach through to the inside of the cabin. Then he went to the lean-to and brought more wood and threw it on to the spreading fire.

"That was what you wanted," he said, and began to climb the rock slope towards the hills.

THE morning Colin left the cabin a party of ten men landed from three boats at the mouth of Milk River. Clyde Munro was in charge of it. Delker was there, two other policemen, and a game warden. The others were Blenkinstown civilians, and one of them was Tod Phalling. They all carried rifles and they were a tense group. Clyde knew this and tried to ease them as they stood around near the boats.

"The first thing we've got to do," he said, "is find Ches Burdick. When we've done that we start looking for Ensley."

"Suppose he's out looking for us?" someone asked.

"He won't be," Clyde said. "That doesn't mean we don't have to keep our eyes open all the way, but he won't be. Something else. If we do come up with him, don't shoot unless he does. I've got a strong hunch he won't."

"He shot Ches Burdick quick enough," Phalling said.

Clyde looked at him. "O.K.," he said. "And he can shoot quicker and straighter than any man of us here. So the best chance we've got is to take him without shooting. Understand?"

Phalling grinned. "You're the boss," he said. "If it was me I'd say shoot first."

Clyde turned away from him. "I'm going ahead with Jim Delker and the game warden," he said. "The rest of you come on in two groups, one minute apart, one minute behind us. A policeman with each group. O.K.?"

"O.K., Clyde," one of the policemen said. "We'll move up fast if we hear any shooting."

The group broke up and the men made new groups, talking among themselves. They were easier now that they felt a plan and pattern in what they had to do. Clyde slung his rifle and started out with Delker and the game warden.

AS Colin climbed away from the burning cabin he felt an immense loneliness. There was nothing now, there never could be anything again except himself. He passed the little pool in the rock below the falls and thought of Mildred. She would hear about it, somewhere down in California, and know that she was freed from her promise. His last claim on her was burning in the flames that would soon destroy the cabin, had been killed with the bullet that killed Burdick. Not lonely, Colin thought, but alone. And it was not oppressive, nor terrifying, nor even sad to be alone. There was regret in it, regret for Burdick and all the destroyed things. But there was also pride in it and a clean strength and a purpose. To find death alone, away from confusion and fear and contempt and hatred. Not to seek it, not to aid it in any way. But to find it.

He climbed out on to the last broad ledge before the valley began to narrow to the Gap and knew that he was looking into death. It crept slowly towards him across the face of the mountains, blotting out draws and ridges and pinnacles as it came, gray white and silent. He looked behind him then, back down the still unsheeted valley, and saw at once the dark figures of men climbing far below him against the snow. He turned and went on and the front of the blizzard swept past him, hiding the climbing figures, closing everything into silence that waited for the first fierce sound of the wind.

There was death in the blizzard, Colin knew, but still a chance of life. He believed he could still pass safely through the Gap. After that there would be the full force of the wind on the open slopes at the head of Amabilis Valley. Walking, a man might keep himself alive. In the dark, he would not be able to walk. So there was only the tent. If no one had found it from the other side, and if they did not follow from this side.

The thought stopped him. He remembered what Andrew Grant had said of Tom Hughes' death in Windstorm Gap: "If you're ever in a spot like that, make them go back. Never mind the talk and kidding. Make them go back."

He stood for a moment longer, feeling the storm against him, hearing the high hard sound of the strengthening wind. Then he turned back. He picked his place well, a narrow place where the ledge sharply turned a ridge of the mountain. There was a short steep drop from it down to the wide main ledge they must follow if they were still coming against the storm.

Colin waited. He waited without fear, without hope for himself, yet without reluctance. He knew that the storm had almost certainly turned them back already, knew that time was closing in on him, that in an hour or two at the most it would be too dark to travel through the Gap. But he knew also that he had drawn them there and that if there was to be death again it must be for himself, not them. So he waited.

He saw them easily, more easily than he had expected, when they were still two hundred yards away. Six men, climbing grimly against the storm, following the dim outline of his track under the newly fallen snow. He fired once, over their heads, and watched them scatter into cover. Even then he could have killed some of them, because there was little good cover on the ledge. He wondered if they knew it, if they were afraid, and he did not want to fire again though he knew he would have to if he hoped to hold them there.

He saw a man crawling towards better cover and fired near him. There was an answering shot and the bullet sang away from the ridge above him. There was a long wait. Then Colin saw another man crawling forward. He fired once more, but the man did not stop; instead he stood up and began to walk slowly forward across the open ledge. Colin felt panic touch him. He heard himself shout wildly: "Go back," and he brought the sights of his rifle squarely on the center of the man's chest. Then he knew it was Clyde and saw that there was no rifle in his hands.

For a moment Colin hesitated. Then he stood up, his rifle held down at full arm's length across his thighs. He saw Clyde wave, then felt the shock of the bullet solid and heavy against his left shoulder. It threw him back, half-turning his body, and he fell to his knees. He looked back over the ledge and saw that Clyde had dropped down into cover. He fired near a man who moved, waited a moment and fired a second shot towards the other side of the ledge. Then he slipped away behind the ridge and began to climb the next ledge at a run.

He turned two more ridges, still running, then dropped back to his smooth, effortless mountaineer's walk. He was afraid only of Clyde. Clyde had known he would not shoot to kill. And Clyde

313

would follow. It was Clyde who had brought those others up in the face of the storm and it was Clyde who would stand up and walk forward again, to find blood in the snow where Colin had made his stand and know that he was wounded.

Colin climbed on. He had wedged clothing between coat and the wound and it seemed to him the bleeding had stopped. There was little pain except when he tried to raise his left arm and he could detect no weakening of his body through shock or blood loss. He was still in shelter from the main drive of the storm, but the way turned out now, along the last jutting ridge that marked the entrance to the Gap. As he started towards the point of the ridge he knew he would be exposed to anyone traveling the ledges behind him, but he did not look round. If they're that close, he thought, let them shoot. But let them do it right this time, let them find the heart. At least I did that for Ches Burdick. It could have been the heart for me. A little lower, a little farther over; likely the guy shot for it, held high and pulled off a little. I always thought it would be the heart, I used to think it when I was a kid, used to think it overseas, a bullet in the heart, quickly.

Suddenly he knew he did not want to die. He was almost at the point of the ridge now and he stopped and looked back. He could see the ledge, white and empty around the long curve behind him, empty again through the next curve to where the falling snow shut it from sight. They were slow or they had turned back. It might be either. He climbed over the point of the ridge and met the full, howling violence of the storm. It tore at his face and hands, found openings in his clothing, held his body and battered it with the strength and weight of moving water. He put his head down and faced into it, not hurrying, not straining, yet using his body's strength to make speed from sure and measured movement. There was light still, a dim gray light that would not lessen much for an hour yet.

There were sloping ledges in the gap and rock that had to be climbed and slides that had to be crossed. He slipped once in climbing, because his left arm was not there to help him, but recovered. Once the new snow began to move under him, very slowly, but he crossed to safety and turned back to see the slide check itself and hold for lack of weight. He passed the narrow

314

place where Tom Hughes had slipped, and reached the broad ledge beyond. The snow was thigh deep now, dragging at his legs while the wind resisted his body. Once he stumbled and fell and lay for a moment feeling the warmth and shelter of the deep snow. He knew it would be easy and peaceful to die that way, but his mind turned from death and he got up and went on.

He came to the tiny draw that sheltered the tent and turned into it without caution. He had plowed a dozen paces through the deeper snow of the sheltered place before he saw that someone had gone in before him. He stopped then, but it was too late. The tent flaps opened and he saw a man there. The numbed fingers of his single good hand fumbled with his rifle, dropped it and he stood there, disarmed and helpless. Then he saw that the man was Johnny Harris.

"Colin," Johnny said. "Jesus, I thought you'd never come." He stumbled forward through the snow and touched Colin. "You're hurt," he said.

"How in hell did you get up here?" Colin asked him.

They went into the tent and Colin slid the light pack away from his right shoulder. "I haven't got much time," he said. "They're liable to be coming still."

Johnny looked out at the storm. "Through that? Nobody would come through against that tonight."

"Only Clyde. Clyde would and he's with them."

"They're down at your cabin too," Johnny said. He was heating a can of soup over a spirit stove. "That's what I came up here to tell you."

"Thanks," Colin said. His mind searched for something more, but he knew only that he was afraid for Johnny. "You got blankets?" he asked.

"Sleeping bag," Johnny said. "I'm O.K. Here, drink this." He handed Colin the soup.

While Colin was drinking Johnny came round to look at his wounded shoulder. "Leave it," Colin said. "You'll only start the bleeding again."

"You've got to take your coat off sometime."

Colin shook his head. "I'm pulling out soon as I've drunk this. Think you can get back down O.K.?"

"You can't go any place tonight," Johnny said. "You've got to stay here."

"And let them walk in on me when I'm asleep?" Colin shook his head again. "I've made it this far and I can make it to where they'll never find me."

"You didn't kill that guy, did you? Not like they say you did?"

"I killed him," Colin said slowly. "Jesus, Johnny, you don't know how easy a man dies until you've done it. You do a little thing, just moving your finger. And after that the biggest thing you can ever do won't change it."

"He must have done something to you first," Johnny said.

Colin shifted his body sharply and sat staring at the little flame of the spirit stove for a long while before he answered. "Yes," he said slowly. "He did something. He tried to burn the cabin. It wasn't my cabin, Johnny. It was hers." He looked at Johnny. "You and Robbie knew about her, didn't you? I know Robbie did."

Johnny moved his feet and looked down at them. "Sort of," he said slowly. "You wrote letters all the time."

"Burdick had no business doing that. She never did anything to him." Colin stared gloomily into the flame again. "Don't ever kill a man, Johnny," he said. "Nothing's big enough for that. They're so empty when they're dead." He reached forward and pushed back the tent flap. "I've got to get moving before I stiffen up." His voice was suddenly urgent. "They'll be coming close now."

"They'll never come tonight," Johnny said. "You could sleep. I'd wake you at first daylight."

Colin took his rifle and his pack and stood up outside the tent. "Help me on with it, Johnny," he said.

"You've got no place to go," Johnny pointed out at the storm. "You can't live a night out in that." But he held the pack while Colin slipped his right arm through and settled the tump line.

Colin held out his hand. "Don't worry, Johnny. I've got a place to go to. Tell Robbie I had a place to go to."

They shook hands and Colin went out of shelter into the storm again. It was almost dark now and his body had stiffened during the short rest; but he had taken the spare snowshoes he kept in the tent and traveling was less difficult. For a little way he followed the trail towards the Gully, squarely into the face of the storm. Then he turned off at right angles and began to climb the sharp ridge that led to the face of Amabilis Mountain. He felt fear then, a clear, penetrating, physical fear of death and loneliness, of the growing darkness and the storm and the dangerous way ahead of him. He wanted to turn back to Johnny in the tent, to go in and lie down and sleep until Clyde came to wake him. But his body loosened as he climbed and he felt its strength again and found strength in the sound of the storm about him. Fear died and he felt freedom.

The ridge grew suddenly steeper and there was little snow on it. He kicked his snowshoes off, slung them on his pack and went on again, climbing faster than before. It was almost dark and he could see only a few feet in front of him, but he knew where he was and he turned from the ridge across the steeply sloping face of the mountain. He stepped carefully now, counting his steps, and so found the tiny sheltered crevice he was looking for.

It was scarcely more than a crack, cut deeply into the face of the mountain, protected at the lower end by a sharp turn that killed the winds drawing up it, shut off abruptly thirty or forty feet from the turn by a straight bold face of rock. He had spent a night there once before, many years ago, an uncomfortable night with a single blanket and no fire. The next morning he had gone out and cut half-a-dozen little stunted trees and piled them at the lower end of the crevice. He found them now, dry and brittle under the fresh snow, and lit a small fire. Then he took the blankets from his pack, rolled into them and was quickly asleep.

He woke suddenly and thought he had slept until daylight. But he saw the embers of his fire still red and knew it could not be daylight. He looked up and found stars in the clear sky above the crevice. His wounded shoulder sent a wave of pain through his body as he sat up, but his mind felt intensely clear. He took more wood and stirred his fire to fresh life and felt the warmth of it against his face and body. He ate a meal from the food in his pack, then folded his blankets away, picked up his rifle and climbed out of the crevice.

The wind met his body like a singing sheet of ice. It poured in swift and sweeping steadiness across the open face of the mountain and drove against the peaks until they gave back a great body of deep sound in vibrations that quivered against the sky. Colin felt the snow strongly crusted underfoot, saw the full moon high and brilliant in the sky, looked down and saw an infinite swirling whiteness of wind-driven clouds over everything below him. He began to walk, boldly upright, striding like a giant, across the steep face of the mountain.

As he walked, pain left him and fear drew far beyond reach or recall. For a little while Burdick walked with him, a quiet calm Burdick who shrugged his shoulders and found death as small a thing as life. Then Martha was with him and Curly Blake and Terry Murphy and laughter was with them all, loud and free on the clean sweep of the storm under the mighty vibration of the peaks. Colin strode across the face of Amabilis Mountain until dawn showed light beyond the clouds in the east and the moon began to pale in the west.

He had used up the mountain then, had traversed the whole head of the valley. But he crossed to the mountains of the west side and followed them down towards the pass to Hidden Valley. New clouds came high on the wind and snow swept under them, blurring the sun as it rose, then burying it behind fold upon fold of sweeping whiteness. Colin came to the narrow corridor and turned along its level floor. All through the night he had sought for Mildred among the others who had come to be with him on the face of the mountain. She came to him now in the snow, in the quiet of the narrow place between the mountains. Her voice was with him and the feel of her and the strength of her. He came to the end of the corridor, looked down into the snow that whirled and drifted over Hidden Valley, and knew surely that she was there also.

He dropped from the corridor into the deep snow of the little platform above the ledge trail. For a minute or two he stood there, kicking the snow away, clearing space for his jump. Blocks of snow dropped away from the movements of his feet, broke, broke again and disappeared among the flakes of falling snow. He tested himself, feeling his arm for pain, and there was no pain. Cold was no longer cold and the sounds of the storm had become silence. There was brownness where whiteness should have been on the falling snow. Colin knew that he was tired, that he must jump to the ledge trail and follow it down to her while there was still a little strength left to him. He moved his feet again, to clear away a last lump of snow, then felt the platform heave under him. He jumped wildly and with all the strength of his body. For a moment he was crawling on his hands and knees, reaching blindly for the stretcher that had been torn away from him and the wounded man it had borne. Then he knew that his body was falling, that it would find the death his soul had neither sought nor feared.